GRIOT

EDITIONS

ANOTHER COUNTRY
James Baldwin

THE BLUEST EYE
Toni Morrison

ELBOW ROOM
James Alan McPherson

**THE HEALING/CORREGIDORA/
EVA'S MAN**
Gayl Jones

THE LIVING IS EASY
Dorothy West

MAMA
Terry McMillan

THE MAN WHO CRIED I AM
John A. Williams

SELECTED POEMS
Gwendolyn Brooks

SERAPH ON THE SUWANEE
Zora Neale Hurston

**THINGS FALL APART/NO LONGER AT
EASE/ANTHILLS OF THE SAVANNAH**
Chinua Achebe

THE WOMEN OF BREWSTER PLACE
Gloria Naylor

THE HEALING

CORREGIDORA

EVA'S MAN

GAYL JONES

•

THE HEALING
CORREGIDORA
EVA'S MAN

•

Featuring an Interview with the Author

by Michael S. Harper

GRIOT

EDITIONS

Quality Paperback Book Club • New York

CONTENTS

GAYL JONES: AN INTERVIEW

by Michael S. Harper

This interview with Gayl Jones first appeared in The Massachusetts Review *in early 1978. The interviewer, Michael Harper, is an accomplished poet and professor of English at Brown University, where he taught Jones (she received her M.A. from Brown in 1973). The extremely reclusive author grants very few interviews; here we find Jones relaxed and chatty about her own writing process and the influences on her work.*

Harper: Do you have any models for artistic conception, literary, historical, or autobiographical?

Jones: I used to say that I learned to write by listening to people talk. I still feel that the best of my writing comes from having *heard* rather than having read. This isn't to say that reading doesn't enrich or that reading isn't important, but I'm talking about foundations. I think my language/word foundations were oral rather than written. But I was also learning how to read and write at the same time I was listening to people talk. In the beginning, *all* of the richness came from people rather than books because in those days you were reading some really unfortunate kinds of books in school. I'm talking about the books children learned to read out of when I was coming up. But my first stories were heard stories from grown-up people talking. I think it's important that we—my brother and I—were never sent out of the room when grown-up people were talking. So we heard their stories. So I've always heard stories of people generations older than me. I think that's important. I think that's the important thing.

Also, my mother would write stories for us and read them to us. She would read other stories too, but my favorite ones were the ones she wrote herself and read to us. My favorite one of those was a story called "Esapher and the Wizard." So I first knew stories as things that were heard. That you listened to. That someone spoke. The stories we had to read in school—I didn't really make connections with them as stories. I just remember us sitting around in the circle and different people being called on to read a sentence. But my mother's reading the stories—I connected with that. And I connected with the stories people were telling about things that happened back before I was born.

When I was in the fifth grade, I had a teacher who would have us listen to music and then write stories. We had to write the stories that came to us while we were listening and then we would have to read the stories aloud to the whole class. I had started writing stories when I was in the second or third grade, when I was seven or eight, but didn't show them to anybody until her. Of course, my mother knew I was writing. Of course, I showed things to her. But my fifth-grade teacher was the first teacher I showed any work to. Her name was Mrs. Hodges. I remember I used to make stories and put the names of people in the class in them so that everybody would laugh. So then there was the music and the heard stories. It was an all-black school. I went to an all-black school until the tenth grade when there was integration. I say that because I think it's important. I think it's important about the music and the words, too.

A lot of connections I made with tradition—with historical and literary things—I started making later. I was writing stories in first person before I made connections with the slave narrative tradition or the tradition of black autobiography, before "oral storytelling" became something you talked about. At first, I just felt that the first-person narrative was the most authentic way of telling a story, and I felt that I was using my own voice—telling a story the way I would talk it. I liked the way the words came out better than the way they came out in third person. And I liked writing dialogue in stories, because I was "hearing" people talk. But I hadn't made any of the kinds of connections you make with your traditions other than the connections you make in living them and being a part of them. I didn't really begin to make the other kinds of connections till graduate school. I still don't like to stand away from the traditions, talking about them. You ought to be able to talk about them standing right inside of them.

In storytelling, you can do that—that's why I like storytelling. When you tell a story, you automatically talk about traditions, but they're never separate from the people, the human implications. You're talking about language, you're talking about politics and morality and economics and culture, and you never have to come out and say you're talking about these things—you don't have to isolate them and therefore freeze them—but you're still talking about them. You're talking about all your connections as a human being. You're talking about many dimensions instead of just one. You don't start with the answers. Someone asked me what answers did I have for such and such a thing. I said that I didn't have any answers. She said that when she read my book she could see answers. She could see I had answers. But you don't start with the answers, I don't start with the answers, I start with the telling, and sometimes the answers come out of the telling.

[H]: Can you distinguish between oral and literary or written influences?

[J]: Yes. When I'm working even. I know I can reconnect them if I read over something. There are a lot of sounds, though. A lot of times, literary (written) things also become oral influences for me, because of the way I read. I have to hear the words in my head—almost in my ears, too—all the sounds have to be there when I read—and when I'm writing too. I don't necessarily have to re-read things out loud because I hear the words while I'm writing them. In the process of writing them I have to hear them. My mouth isn't moving, but the vocal connections are being made, the sound connections—the same kind of speech energy is being used. When I write I can also hear other people talking. A lot of times if I'm having a person say something, other connections are being made with people I've already heard. Of course, sometimes I'll have people say things that I've heard said in another context. But other times, I'll just remember the patterns of the way things were said. The people will be saying entirely different things, but they'll be saying it with the patterns, the rhythms, that I've heard before. So a lot of times one's own speech rhythms and the speech rhythms of other people go into making a story. All the "heard" things go there.

I have a tendency to trust a lot of my oral influences more than my literary ones, with some exceptions. Those have to do with personal contacts and trusting the people's writing whose "voice" I can trust and who I feel can "hear." I usually trust writers who I feel I can hear. A lot of European and Euro-American writers—because of the way their traditions work—have lost the ability to hear. Now Joyce could hear and Chaucer could hear. A lot of Southern American writers can hear. Chaucer had to hear because he was writing in the "vernacular" at a time when "writers" wrote in Latin. The ballads were in the vernacular but they were oral. The "people" made them, not "writers." So Chaucer had to hear. Joyce had to hear because of the whole historical-linguistic situation in Ireland—the Irish spoke a different kind of "English," and of course they were forced to speak English by the invaders, and of course language has its obvious political implications. But *Finnegans Wake* is an oral book. You can't sight-read *Finnegans Wake* with any kind of truth. And they say only a Dubliner can really understand the book, can really "hear" it.

Of course, black writers—it goes without saying why we've always had to hear. And Native American writers, and Latin American writers. It's all tied in with linguistic relationships, and with the whole socio-psychological-political-historical manifestations of these linguistic relationships. I could keep giving reasons why different people have to hear and others don't. If you don't have to hear, if your humanity isn't somehow involved in hearing, you don't. Hearing has to be essential. You have to be able to hear other people's voices and you have to be able to hear your own voice. You say, in one of your poems, a man is another man's face. Maybe a man is another man's voice too. Most of my influences are essentially oral because even the written ones have to be "translated" into the oral before I can understand them. "Understand" really isn't the word, because "understand" is one-dimensional and it's a multi-dimensional thing. Maybe I should say: "I have to bring the written things into the oral *mode* before I can *deal with* them."

I guess language as heard fascinates me more than language as written— but I like to see words, too. I really do. I guess I wouldn't write if I didn't also like to see them. To hear them and to see them while I'm hearing them. But I don't always have to see them while I'm hearing them. But I always have to hear them while I'm seeing them. So many things in writing, though, are simultaneous. It's a simultaneous process. Many things occupy the same space and time.

[H]: Do you depend on any preconception of fiction or storytelling when you sit down to tell a story?

[J]: Well, for me fiction and storytelling are different. I say I'm a fiction writer if I'm asked, but I really think of myself as a storyteller. When I say "fiction," it evokes a lot of different kinds of abstractions, but when I say "storyteller," it always has its human connections. First, the connection to the listener, the hearer; but there's also the connection between the teller and the hearer. "Storytelling" is a dynamic word, a process word. "Fiction" sounds static. "Storytelling" for me suggests possibilities, many possibilities. I'm really talking now about feeling response to words. I have a feeling response to the two words, as well as to the fact that they mean two different things to me.

But I have no preconceptions of either one, really. When I sit down to tell a story I have to have the people there, and the voices, and they have to be in a relationship to each other. I don't think I've ever written a story with just one person. There are always at least two people, and there's always dialogue. I've never written a story without dialogue. I always have to have people talking. Speech has to be there. I guess you could say my method is improvisational. When I tell a story, the process of telling determines the way of telling.

I see myself as a storyteller also because of the connection between the spoken and the written. A lot of things are imposed upon the storyteller from the outside—other people's preconceptions—but I won't go into this. There are a lot of things you have to work in, through, and around. But the important thing for me is always to keep the human connections. The bad thing for me is when the writer loses the human—or humanistic—connection;

when the writer is irresponsible with language. Writing is a very responsible thing. It documents human experience, and when it documents it wrongly—that's the really bad thing. Black people and Native Americans in this country can attest to that. That's why it's necessary to make the connections between the oral traditions and written documentation, unless you're in an environment that maintains the integrity of the oral traditions. When you're not, it's necessary to document the traditions—to counteract the effects of the false documentations.

[H]: Is there a particular method you follow in writing a novel? You said recently that you began with situation. Could you develop this in terms of plot, or its absence, mode of speech, character quality, the building of climax, what is revealed and concealed in your treatment of situation?

[J]: I start with story—people—speech—relationships—situation. Story for me isn't "action" or "plot sequence" or theories about how things should be/are. It's people doing/being certain things *in relationship* to other people—mainly men and women. I'm mainly concerned about relationships between men and women. But it's also interesting to see how two men relate to each other, how two women relate. In *Corregidora*, I explore women-women relationships but not really men-men. The only men-men relationships are in the context of their response to women. But it's probably because I only know about men-men relationships in the context of their being with women—I don't know. But it's important for me to clarify relationships in the book—relationships in *situation*, rather than to have some theory of the way men are with women and vice-versa, or the way a daughter and mother are with each other.

The way Ursa is with her mother grew out of the situation of storytelling and my own living and seeing, and the same thing with the men and women. I didn't know how they would be with each other until they were being that way. When I was first writing the book, I really did think Ursa would stay with Tadpole. I really didn't expect him to do what he did. But after he did it, there wasn't anything else Ursa could do. Some things you start with. Other things are worked out in the process of creating and clarifying the relationships. It's like what Ursa said at the end of the book: "I didn't know yet what I would do." She didn't know what she was going to do until after she did it or right while she was doing it; she didn't know she was going to go back to Mutt until she was doing it. She didn't know until it happened in *situation* in *relationship*.

In a way, this is also a comment on how I write. Things have to happen *in process*. There's a question I ask—which one of the women asks—near the end of *Corregidora:* "What is it a woman can do to a man that makes him hate her so bad he wants to kill her one minute and can't get her out of his mind the next?" I didn't know the answer to that when I wrote the question. I didn't know the answer to that till the end of the book. I didn't know what the end of the book was going to be. I didn't know the answer till I had Mutt and Ursa being in relationship to each other at the end of the book. Then I made the connection between that and what it was that the Great Grandmother had done to Corregidora. Ursa only made the connection then. I only made the connection then. I only made the connection then, in the process of writing. Because, you see, I didn't know what it was that Great Gram had done to Corregidora, not in the beginning.

So I don't have any one method. For me, the idea of things happening *in process* is important because it strengthens my own feeling of connection with the oral storytelling and black music continuum. Modes of speech, character quality, all work themselves out in process. Maybe it's like what you mean when you talk about a musician creating an "environment." I don't know. But everything has to happen for me in the process of doing it. Sometimes I know how a story will end. And I know certain things that I want in a story, certain scenes, certain relationships, etc. But there are still all those "in process" things. I remember you said poetry is about process. Storytelling is about process, too. But I have no particular method. I always like everything to be different. I have always liked everything to work itself out differently. If I've done something, I don't like to do it again. Why do something again when you've already done it? Why say something the same way again? Why sing something the same way twice? I'm thinking about Billie Holiday here, of course. That's the tradition. I like to change a tune.

[H]: Did *Corregidora* go through any other conceptions than the novel? What forms were you experimenting with?

[J]: I never did type or show the first version of *Corregidora* to anyone. The whole thing was a sort of song. The narrative wasn't storytelling—it was a kind of ritual. And there was dialogue, but it wasn't the same kind of dialogue. The transitions were ritualistic. It was written in second person, the "you" narrative. Ursa was the one being addressed. No, actually it moves between the second and third and first—it starts off with "you." There are no real sequences of events. It doesn't have "scenes." I think I like Ursa telling the story better. I'd like to read over this very first version, though, to see what kinds of movements I make, or if I write a sequel to *Corregidora,* I could write it as a "song" rather than a "story." I could make it a ritualistic novel.

Some parts of *Corregidora* fit the description of this version. When I look over the first version I can see the "story" there, but it wouldn't have worked in the same way. The first version had everything in it except it didn't clarify enough relationships. My editor, Toni Morrison, felt that I should clarify the relationships between Ursa and her mother and between Ursa and Mutt. I added the scene where Ursa goes back and talks to her mother and also that one about Ursa and Mutt before the incident of the fall down the stairs. Now, that's very essential to the book. Both of these scenes are essential to the book. It became very important for me to clarify the relationship between Ursa and Mutt because I'd never done any really up-close scenes between a man and a woman before. I don't just mean sexual things—I mean the way they were "being" with each other. That became very important to me to be able to do that. The "scene" when Ursa first meets Mutt and the way they talk to each other is very important to me. So, the final version combines the "ritualistic" and "dream" sequences of the very first version with many layers of storytelling. The first version could not have been called a novel. It might have been called a prose poem or a song. In the final version, I was able to put everything together, the storytelling and the other. I like a mixture of forms and kinds of language. I like that kind of movement. The thing about "storytelling" is it's the kind of "form" that can bring in everything—that can make movements between kinds of language and kinds of reality—dreams and memory also being kinds of reality. I'm very much concerned with "forms" that can bring in everything. I found out that storytelling can bring in a lot more than just "story."

I was also experimenting with something other than language. I was also looking for a perspective that was "up-close," where there was no separation between the storyteller and the hearer. That was important to me too. I used to think that experimentation had to do with just language—but people can experiment with a lot of different kinds of elements of "story"—perspective, point of view, ways of presenting characters, kinds of characters—a lot of different things that involve language, but in a different way. Perspective, for instance. You could say I was experimenting with oral storytelling, using things you can learn from oral storytelling. In oral storytelling, the perspective is always up-close, because of the kind of relationship you have between the storyteller and the hearer. But not only that, there's also the direct identification of the storyteller with the story. Toni Morrison said she didn't feel there was an "author" getting in the way. That's what happens in the oral story—the storyteller identifies so closely with the story.

Actually, in oral storytelling there are three kinds of identification—the identification of the storyteller with the story, the identification of the storyteller with the hearer, and the identification of the hearer with the story. I was experimenting mainly with the "form" of oral storytelling. You don't have to beat around the bush to make a transition in oral storytelling. You just go on and make it. You can be talking about 1929 and then go right on ahead and talk about 1969, almost in the same breath, in the same space. Or like a preacher, he can be talking about something that happened last night in one kind of language and then start talking about Gabriel in another kind. The sermon, for me, also suggests that kind of "form" that can bring in all kinds of language, that can bring in just everything. So I experiment with a lot of oral traditional forms because of the things they can do.

And there's also a special relationship between narrative and dialogue in the oral story that helps to get the up-close perspective. The narrative in the oral story has the same essential speech tradition as the dialogue, and you don't have the sense of distancing. And so there is a freer movement, maybe a more natural movement between the two. I guess all experimenting involves language, but language with a lot of different connections, not just changing words and the syntax of sentencing in an obvious way. Many times it has to do with the relationship between the words and the people hearing the words, and not just the relationship between the words themselves.

I said some of the dialogue in *Corregidora* is ritualistic and some is naturalistic. I think most of the italicized dialogue between Ursa and Mutt is ritualistic. I should explain that. What I mean by "ritualistic dialogue" is that either the language isn't the same that we would use ordinarily, or the movement between the people talking isn't the same. No, there are really three things: the language, the rhythm of the people talking, and the rhythm *between* the people talking. In those technical books, they might call it "inaction rhythm." The forms I know just bring in everything. But there's a certain kind of rhythm that people create when they talk, when they start talking, a pattern of talk and response. So in ritualized dialogue, sometimes you create a rhythm that people wouldn't ordinarily use, that they probably wouldn't use in real talk, although they are saying the words they might ordinarily use. But you change the rhythm of the talk and response and you change the rhythm *between* the talk and the response. So in ritualized dialogue, you do something to the rhythm or you do something to the words. You change the kind of words they would use or the rhythm of those words. But both things take the dialogue out of the naturalistic realm—change its quality.

I want to go back and study that very first version, though, and see what I can learn from it. I like to make those kinds of connections, too.

[H]: Is there any connection between "Deep Song" and your general view of women singers—blues songs, the emblems of love and trouble between men and women?

[J]: The relationships between the men and women I'm dealing with are blues relationships. So they're out of a tradition of "love and trouble"—but I don't really have any general view of any of those things. I don't have any general view of women blues singers or of the relationships between men and women. But there is a relationship between "Deep Song," which is a blues poem, and *Corregidora,* which is a blues novel. Blues talks about the simultaneity of good and bad, as feeling, as something felt. In the poem, "Deep Song," how do people react to the words "good" and "bad"? I think people have just as much attraction to the line "Sometimes he is a bad dark man" as they do to the line "Sometimes he is a good dark man." It has to do with meanings and things having a lot of different meanings at once. The last line is "I love him." It isn't "But I love him." I think that's important because it has to do with being, and it doesn't set up any territories. It doesn't set some feelings off into a corner. "Sometimes he is a good dark man. Sometimes he is a bad dark man. I love him." It acknowledges both things. Blues acknowledges all different kinds of feelings at once. How do we know, for instance, "Sometimes he is a bad dark man" isn't really a repetition of "Sometimes he is a good dark man"? That's what interests me. Ambiguity.

Somebody said *Corregidora* was ambiguous. I think I wanted it to be. I always like it when there are a lot of different possibilities. Like, it's important to me that the man says something so softly that the woman can't even hear him. That's important to me, but I don't know why. I was listening to Billie Holiday when I wrote the poem—while I was writing it, I mean. I was writing it and listening at the same time. There was the record that had "Deep Song" on it and "Crazy He Calls Me." I think that's the title of the second one. It has that in it. The poem uses repetition, but I don't know why it came out the way it did. When I finished it, I knew it was different from my other poems.

[H]: Would you comment on your next novel, *Eva's Man,* in terms of situation, character, the elements of storytelling as the context changed for you, and the additions you made in the telling?

[J]: It's hard for me to talk about *Eva's Man* because of the way I wrote it—it went through so many forms, so many changes. It went from a novella to a short story to a novel, which is a strange sequence. If I try to describe the novella it will be much like describing the first version of *Corregidora*. It didn't progress by scenes. The woman was addressing the man, so the "you" narrative was used, and there were metaphors for a lot of things that had happened. Things were told as having happened, but they were metaphors for the things. And there was dialogue out of context of place and situation. It's really very different from the final version. The short story clarified "scenes"—the things that happened in the story—and it is told in the first person. The woman tells the story, and only a little bit of her past is seen. (Actually, there are two short story versions. One keeps the "you" narrative and it moves between scenes and the essential form of the novella, and the other uses first person and more scenes. Rather than saying "scenes," I should say it clarifies situations more.) The novel sort of reclaims the woman's whole past, and we see all the things that lead up to the later events—her relationship to the man at the end of the story—because we've seen other relationships that make a connection with that relationship.

Described that way, without saying what the events are, it sounds a lot like *Corregidora*, but it's not. The woman of the story isn't the same kind of woman either. There are stylistic differences in that I make a lot of different kinds of transitions between past and present and sometimes simultaneous showings of past and present events. Rather than have the woman thinking something, it becomes a scene without transition. It takes place at the same time in the narrative as the things that evoke the memory. Also, fantasy happens at the same narrative level as the "real" things. The movement is different. The way of telling is different. There aren't layers of storytelling, but there are many different dimensions to the woman's telling. I'm sort of dealing with memory and fantasy as well as storytelling but I want everything to be on the same plane of reality. I want one thing to move into the other without the feeling that they are essentially different. It's hard for me to put all the elements of storytelling together. But I did start with situation and character—the relationship between that particular man and that particular woman. In many ways, *Eva's Man* is a horror story. It really is. And I'm sure people will ask me if that's the way I see the essential relationship between men and women. But that man and woman don't stand for men and women—they stand for themselves, really. But I don't have any definition for the kind of man-woman relationship that *Eva's Man* describes. Their ritual isn't a blues ritual. I don't know what it is.

[H]: Would you comment on Zora Neale Hurston, her conception of fiction and how the study of anthropology might have affected her production and output as a writer and particularly as a black woman writer? Would you characterize her as a pre-feminist or feminist? What might her work teach upcoming women writers, and writers in general?

[J]: I think the problem of Zora Neale Hurston is a problem of perspective—and it has to do with the relationship between narrative and dialogue, and it has to do with where the storyteller is when he's telling the story. (They'll get on me about using "he.") I think storytelling and anthropology are two different poles in terms of perspective. In storytelling, you're inside the living experience; in anthropology, you have to step outside of it. I'm sure Zora Neale Hurston told stories differently before she had anthropological training than afterwards—I'm sure she did. When you're telling a story, you're looking at situations inside of them—in process. The anthropological perspective pulls you outside of the process, the situations. You have to make them static in order to talk about them. For me, *Their Eyes Were Watching God* is beautiful. It's one of my favorite stories. But there is a tension in the novel between the narrative and the dialogue; there is a problem of perspective—the world view in that narrative seems different than the world view in the dialogue. The narrative seems written out of a different tradition—one that separates the storyteller from the story and the people in the story, even though both Janie and Teacake come through for me as real and strong people. I feel as if the storyteller has been for some reason distanced from them, even though she knows them so well. But you know that she knows them. You know that she "lived" there.

And there is a separation between the hearer and the storyteller—something that comes between the storyteller and the story. In oral storytelling, the storyteller identifies not only with the story but also with the people in the story. The storyteller is standing in there with them—I don't mean that he has to be a character in the story, but he's in there. And there isn't a tension between the narrative and dialogue—both are out of the same linguistic and humanistic tradition. For me, Ernest Gaines solved the problem of perspective and narrative/dialogue relationship: the perspective being a part of the same speech community, the same essential world view, and telling the story to those people who also identify with that language and world view and with those human values.

In her anthropology books, I don't feel that Zora Neale Hurston stood outside of the community, talking about it; I feel that she addressed herself to people outside of that community of human values rather than that she herself was standing outside of it. All writers address themselves to their essential speech community, but when there have been historical breaks in the speech continuum, the writer has to mend those breaks—that is, if he is to write about the people in that speech community. I always feel it's important to write what you've heard rather than what you've read when you're dealing with how anybody talks. Certainly I feel the study of anthropology took Hurston away from the amount of "stories" she could tell. (The way anthropology looks at language should also be studied. The way it looks at language as well as people.) I would have liked to have seen her use what she'd learned in her "field trips" in stories that "coordinated" learning and living in a form that wouldn't have caused tensions between the two, because the form would have grown out of them. I mean here using a form and language that grows out of a certain community to express that community and at the same time that energy being directed back to that community, out of which the language came. It has to do with "energy relationships." The storyteller being energized and the people being energized. Storytelling is holistic—it brings in everything—and anthropology isn't. Anthropology is one-dimensional; it can't coordinate. It can't coordinate all the different kinds of forces that come at a person, that come at a storyteller. And the community Zora Neale Hurston came out of was about synthesis and coordinating all those different forces, all those different "energy relationships," and her storytelling would have stayed about that too, I think, if it hadn't been for anthropology. As I said, I have a lot of personal fears about those kinds of things—things that pull you outside of the synthesis, the coordination, how you handle in "story" all those forces, all those "energy relationships."

I don't want to characterize her as a pre-feminist or a feminist. I will say that she saw women as strong. And she has a sense of their wholeness. And this isn't necessarily at the expense of men. It doesn't diminish the men. In her autobiography, we have a sense of the kinds of tensions that can come from her feeling about herself as a woman, and what she could do and what she was as a woman. The Janie-Teacake relationship isn't one of authority-submission. The man and woman are both strong. And even though the woman in *Seraph on the Suwanee* feels the idea of "serving"—it doesn't diminish her strength. I kept thinking certain feminists might have got on Zora for that. But the man and woman are both strong in that book. Then, one also has to make a distinction between how a woman is in her own life and how she makes the characters in the book. Zipporah in *Moses, Man of the Mountain* isn't a whole woman. You have a sense that she could have been if it were her story. But the feminists would have probably gotten on Zora for that, too. But one can't really be consistent about a lot of different kinds of things in "story" because there are a lot of different possibilities, as in life. But I never like to categorize. I don't know what a pre-feminist is. I'm not really sure I know what a feminist is. I always write about independent women because that's important to me, and when you see *particular* women in certain ways, people have a tendency to say that's how you think. Right now, anyone who writes about independent women and/or from the point of view of a woman that shows the wholeness of that woman can easily be called a feminist. But the storyteller's vision as I see it shouldn't sacrifice the wholeness of anyone, man or woman. One might be able to call Zora Neale Hurston a feminist from her own living—or I should say feminists can identify with her, which is very different—and from the attitudes she expresses in her autobiography and her anthropological writings and the way you have the sense of her relating to men. She keeps her "wholeness."

I can't answer your question about what might her work teach upcoming black women writers and writers in general. Maybe her work might teach upcoming black women writers in terms of subjects and in terms of those things that it is necessary for the black woman writer to document—and I feel that there are things that only the black woman writer can document. (And there are things that a black man writer can document that a black woman writer couldn't, of course.) But I feel that *Their Eyes Were Watching God* is revolutionary because it does speak about the love relationship between a black man and woman—because it does speak about various relationships—and because Zora didn't have to go outside of the community. She could talk about the relationship of the man and woman to each other, and she could see that relationship as whole. She could see it in a whole way. I think about the Bigger-Bessie relationship here. You can't really see them because of those "other things" Bigger has to contend with. But in real life we see each other. And it's important that we see each other in fiction, in storytelling. I think that's an important contribution of Zora Neale Hurston— that she didn't have to see them before she could see us; or that she didn't have to see them and never fully see us. I mean our wholeness wasn't sacrificed because of them.

I think there are a lot of up-close man-woman relationship type things that the black woman as writer is able to document. June Jordan, in an article on Zora Neale Hurston and Richard Wright, was talking about that: how "love" as a subject is overlooked; how it's not considered important; and how this is a reason why *Their Eyes Were Watching God*, for instance, isn't considered as important as *Native Son*. But it is. She was saying that one thing doesn't cancel out the other, but black women writers are being influenced that way in terms of the things we have to deal with. But I also feel that we have to take the things we learned from Zora Neale Hurston further. Because it has to do with legacy. We have to solve the problems that she couldn't solve. We have to do something about the tensions that she had. And we have to keep her, you know. I feel good about Alice Walker that way. I feel that she is doing that. You know, keeping and taking things further. That's what legacy is.

You notice I haven't answered your question about writers in general, because I don't know. I think there's that idea of "humanization"—the relationship of language to human relationship, the human connections of language. All writers could learn about that. But I don't know. I don't know about writers in general. Depending upon how a person comes to Zora Neale and from where, they might overlook things that I would see, that Alice Walker would see, or that June Jordan would see, that would be important to us. And each of us would see different things too, you know.

But I don't know what people will see and not see in Zora Neale Hurston, or what they will refuse to see. I can only say what I feel should be seen, and a lot of it has to do with human relationship and language. What I mean is, Hurston is working out of a humanistic tradition of writing. And she got a lot of the subjects together that I think we will continue to deal with—the relationships between men and women, the role of women, the use of folklore, folk-saying—that kind of thing. She has a lot of insight in terms of the relationships between men and women and the roles of women. And you don't have the feeling that she had to go off somewhere to get subjects for writing. The important things can be right in front of you and very close to you: in the people and language that you know.

[H]: Have the Spanish novelists influenced your notions of fiction? And would you comment here on Chaucer also?

[J]: When you say Spanish novelists, I have to clarify and say Spanish American or Latin American novelists. (There's one Spanish novelist I like very much—that's Cervantes—but I haven't read many other Spanish novelists.) But the Latin American novelists—they're the ones. How have they influenced my notions of fiction? Well, the two that I think of right off are Carlos Fuentes and Gabriel García Márquez.

Influences: Images, myth, history, language, metaphor, movement between different kinds of language and levels of reality, different kinds of reality. Their influence has to do with the use of language, the kinds of imagery, the relationship between past and present with landscape. Because of the kinds of historical things that have gone down—that continue to go down—the "revolutions," the kinds of perpetual change—political things (Chile, Mexico, Brazil)—you don't come across many morally and socially irresponsible Latin American writers. They're technically innovative, but the technical innovation isn't devoid of its human implications. In this country and in Western Europe, you have writings where the humanity is lost, where the relationship of the word to the human being and the relationship between the word and the social/moral implications is either lost or ignored. But among Latin American writers as well as among Black writers and Native American writers—because of the historical and contemporary things that are going down—the "nightmares," the particular historical and contemporary nightmares—these writers are always responsible. The human implications, the moral/social implications are always there. So I feel a kinship with Latin American writers. I find them energizing.

And then there's also the language thing. For them, too, there's the linguistic thing. The *European* Spanish, the *European* Portuguese. There's the linguistic thing for them, too. There are all the things that the language that they have to use can't express for them either, not if you're taking in the Indian (Amerindian) and African—the *American* heritage. And so there's the *making* it express things. For me, that's why all the kinds of images are there—in García Márquez, the movement from one kind of reality to another—because it gives dimension to the language. The language is no longer flat and one-dimensional. You have the sense that they're trying to make the language do things. And it's not just to be playing with words, either; they have a stake in it; it has to do with their being; it has to do with what N. Scott Momaday calls "whole and consummate being"; it has to do with their sense of their humanity. I don't think I have to make the connections here. I think they go without saying. We have one-dimensional words to try to express multi-dimensional things. Some languages are multi-dimensional in that they can account for more things than this one can. There are a lot of things that this language won't account for, that are outside its perspective, you could say, that it doesn't have either the words or the forms for. That's what we're all looking for—the words and the forms to account for certain things that we feel need to be accounted for. Black people in this country have given the language more dimensions than it formerly had. American English has more dimensions than British English because of all the people who've gone into making it—Black people and Indian people and Chinese people, you know, have forced the language to see more than it would have on its own. It has to do with seeing. It has to do with seeing and hearing.

The Latin Americans have helped me in making movements between different kinds of language and different kinds of reality. They've helped to reinforce my own traditions. And I trust them. When I read them I feel I can read them with trust. The same way with Native American writers—I feel I can read them with trust. That's very important to me. To be able to read with trust. It's like listening to someone. There are people you can listen to with trust. Others you have to be careful about. I've probably done a bad thing the past two years—depending on the way you look at it—with the exception of Chaucer and Cervantes, I've read only Latin American, Native American, and Black writers.

Chaucer. I like Chaucer because he's a storyteller. Nowadays, when they teach Chaucer, it's not so important for the students to learn how to read him aloud—that's put in the background. What's important is criticizing the work—sight-recognition of the words, even if you can't say them—reading for meaning, for what's going on in the story. So nowadays you have a lot of people who criticize Chaucer but don't know how to read him, don't know very much about the language. But what a lot of people don't realize is that during Chaucer's time things were written to be read aloud or recited. When you write like that a lot of things happen structurally that wouldn't happen otherwise. I mean, you do a lot of things that you wouldn't do if people weren't going to "hear" this. That's why I studied and learned how to read Chaucer out loud. For me, he is one of the real storytellers of their tradition. A lot of real storytellers in English literature were back in the fifteenth century—the fourteenth—because they were good listeners. I mainly like to read Chaucer when I read him aloud. I can't really sit down and read Chaucer without starting to say things. He's also one of the few writers in the English literary tradition whose words can lift off the page. They're always talking about "winged." His words are "winged." The other storyteller of a later period that I like is Thomas Hardy. They—the critics, I mean—get on him, but that's because he's a storyteller. When you're a storyteller, you don't follow all the structural patterns they tell you to. When the critics talk about a lot of the writers back in the fourteenth and fifteenth centuries, they talk about how English prose wasn't really "developed" then. They say that's the reason why Sir Thomas Malory, for instance, wrote the way he did. That's the reason his sentences were "simple" sentences, and why he did a lot of connecting with "and" rather than other words and used a lot of repetition. But Thomas Malory could *hear,* and speech is always developed. What happened later was that writers (and critics) stopped listening. They stopped listening and how things "read" became more important than how they sounded. Even with dialogue, as long as dialogue read well, it was all right. It didn't really matter if it had any connection with how people really talked.

[H]: When you came to my class at Brown, before *Corregidora* came out, you read from the novel with specific reference to the read materials of the course. Would you comment on Afro-American tradition, as seen through Gaines, Toomer, Ellison, Hurston, Walker, Forrest, Wright, Hughes, Brown, Hayden, et al.?

[J]: I can't talk about it the way you've asked it. I can only talk about what I feel to be those writers' relationship to the Afro-American tradition. But I can't really do that. I can't deal with so many writers in the space of one answer and even begin to make all the connections. I'm not jiving my way out. I'm going on. I will try to point out *some* things.

You know, I say the names over in my mind, and I think about those people—who will speak of black writing as a "limited category," the implication being that it's something you have to transcend. And it surprised me, because I thought critics had outgrown that kind of posture. When I say the names over, every one of the people suggests and reflects all the possibility of human value. They're so very different, they do many different things stylistically—but in none of their writings are the human connections lost—the connections between words and human being.

In all the writers you mentioned, one can talk about the relationship between technique and social morality, conceptions of human value, the Afro-American world view. That's what I remember speaking about in your class. All of the writers are "saying" the Afro-American tradition. You know, I begin to say something and then I say, "But that doesn't say all of it. If you say this about Gaines, you have to say this and this and this. And if you say this about Toomer it's also true about Gaines and Walker." That kind of thing.

For me, Gaines maintains his connections through oral storytelling and his special relationship to the speech community he comes from. When I think of Gaines, I think of voice and story. I think of a perspective that's up-close and "inside." I think of ways of talking that I am unfamiliar with. I think of a form and language that can deal with horror as well as beauty—some forms and some language can't. I think of a person talking to me. I think of men and women talking to me. I think of voices that carry through time. I think of history and personal life memory.

Toomer—pain and beauty. A form that can take in pain and beauty. Poetry. Continual movement. The social reality of migration and displacement, human displacement. Language as magic and transcendent. Lyrical movement. Realistic view of reality. Women. Essences. Men and women.

Ellison—a long form. Prologue. Spaces. A long form that moves. Forms that move into other forms that move into many different conceptions and visions of reality. Jazz movement. Episode. Patterns. Identity. Shifts in identity in persons as well as the way of presenting situations. *Invisible Man* goes through many forms. For me, each chapter is a change of identity, of pattern, of ways of looking at self, reality. Picaresque. Slave narrative tradition. Storytelling. Other qualities of reality.

Hurston—close-up relationships between men and women. Concern with love, with folk-saying. Tension. A sense of separation in narrative and dialogue, between storyteller and speech community. Speech. Documentation of ways of talking. Folklore. Sense of community as integral.

Walker—concern with relationships. Tension in relationships. Men and women. Lyrical movement and moments. Relationships of tension. View of reality-experience—realistic. Caring. Pain and beauty. Like *Cane*, aesthetics and moral implications so interwoven that they cannot be separated. The word as magic, again. I also think of Jean Toomer and Zora Hurston. Acknowledgment.

Forrest—speech and music continuum. Jazz. Sermon. Incantation. Words as voice heard and music. Whole range of black speech and music. Ritual. A constant movement and flowing into. Magic song and sound and voice. Constant movement between different kinds of language. Social reality in whole form—history, language, sermon oratory and blues/jazz traditions, ceremonial, metaphorical legend, history and myth—the full range of verbal traditions.

Wright—blues storytelling, blues vision. Where is Bigger's history? Only a hint at his family life relationships and the way things are/were with Bessie. No sense of fullness. And maybe that's all part of the theme. Everything integrated into the forward movement of the book—the book never stops. Are there any flashbacks, even personal recollections? Is there any memory? Movement—how does the form reflect a social reality? a vision of reality?—continual movement. Does Bigger even know who he is? Who Bessie was?

Hughes—if a white writer had done the things he did to poetic structure he would have been called an innovator. Hughes takes the overall form from the folk tradition rather than incorporating folk material and folk-saying in the traditional Western poetic forms. So there isn't any tension between the forms, the overall structure of the poems, and the material, the subject matter of the poems. He, too, in many ways—in his poetry—solved the problem of Zora Neale Hurston, by taking the overall structure of his poems from the speech and music continuum and traditions. Jazz, blues, folk-telling, etc. Forms that can bring in personal recollection and history and things happening around him. Montage. Improvisational.

Brown—storyteller. The rhythms, metaphors of black folk speaking from the poems take over the whole form. Storytelling talking—the whole form. To hear his voice saying the poem—the whole rhythm of his voice telling the poem. The poem is his voice telling. And the whole poem is the rhythm of that telling. Poet-storyteller. And the humor from that tradition, the humor that is hard reality speaking, that makes one see what is real. The humor that does not camouflage the reality. What is real and hard. The human connections. The poem is the man's voice telling. The man's voice goes way back, the man's voice goes way back, broad and deep—the deep well of experience and being. Storytelling magic and the voices always there.

Hayden—ritual. History and experience as transcendent and human. The forms. Cosmic affirmation. The social and moral and historical realities cannot be separated from the aesthetic realities. You cannot refuse to see what is there. The poetry is "beautiful," but at the same time it "sees." Its aesthetics take in the human realities, the beauty and the cruelties. The human realities cannot be separated. The sense of permanence. The sense of magic. The sense that no human word in the poem is where it should not be. The sense of transcendence always. The spiritual and the human. Spiritual/human. The whole sphere. History, metaphor—spoken, told, written. Poetry is something cared for. Its human consequences.

[H]: Is any of your work autobiographical?

[J]: A lot of my earlier work—when I was in college—was autobiographical. I remember when I was in junior high school, that teacher, Mrs. Hodges, used to ask me to write plays for the elementary schoolchildren. I don't remember the plays, but I remember in them there were little rhymed things for the children to say. I remember they did two of them. I didn't keep copies of anything I wrote back then. And I remember even throwing things away that I'd written back in elementary school. So I don't have anything from way back then. Particularly now when I'd like to see the things.

I remember a couple of high school stories; one of them was a projection of the kind of life I thought I wanted. The woman character was a sort of anticipation of the kind of women I still write about—her independence, I mean. But in those days, when I was sixteen and seventeen, I had a romantic conception of what a writer was, and that story made use of that romantic conception. I used to write stories about writers, you know. Women who were writers. And the story would always take place somewhere far away. I remember a story called "The Guitar." The woman was a writer and all her friends were writers and they were someplace like Spain, sitting around at tables in one of those outdoor cafés and none of them ever had any money. That kind of thing. One of the things in the story was a real detail, though. Where the woman discovers a man sick in a hotel room and nobody will go take care of him, so she goes and takes care of him. I re-use this in a story called "The Roundhouse"—but the characters in "The Roundhouse" are more for real, in terms of me.

I didn't start writing about Kentucky until after I left Kentucky. Before, I would write about places far away that I didn't even know about. And I used to have an image of myself when I grew up—I didn't think it would really happen—but I was this independent woman, I never saw myself as being married or having children or anything like that, and I was always traveling, particularly to Spanish-speaking places, and I was a writer. It's funny to me about the traveling bit because I don't really have that desire now. I see myself back in Kentucky somewhere, still a single woman. A few friends, a few people I care about very much. But my whole conception is different. It wasn't until I was sixteen or seventeen though that I had all those romantic notions of what a writer was. Before that it was just something I was doing, and after that it became just something I was doing—but I think from about sixteen to nineteen was that very romantic time for me. Except at nineteen, I wrote my first Kentucky-oriented story, though it doesn't take place in Kentucky; it's about something in my grandmother's life, though not strictly biographical: it doesn't follow the events exactly. The working at the roundhouse during the First World War polishing engines, the taking care of the man—she hadn't met him at the roundhouse, he'd been staying at the same boarding-house—the marrying him, the details from her life I knew from my mother's telling me. Sometimes I'll use real life "details" and imagine so many things around them that they're not really the same thing anymore.

Most of my autobiographical writing is out of my system now. I can't say that any of my stories have ever been strictly autobiographical, though. "The Return" certainly isn't. "The Welfare Check" is only in terms of the woman's being like me. The only strictly autobiographical writing was in poetry—poetic journals.

When I was in undergraduate school, I used to write poetic journals about real things that had happened. So all my poems were journals—real happenings—with dialogue in them, because I remembered. Now, sometimes I write storytelling poems, using the things I learned from those journals, the style, the use of the first-person manner of telling. So whenever I write storytelling poems they sound like they really happened, and I have to tell people they didn't really happen. Now, I like to write things that sound like they really happened, when I tell a first-person story. It has to be like it really happened. I have to identify so closely with it—like in the oral storytelling tradition—that it really happened and the woman telling the story (or the man telling it—I have two short stories with a man narrator—but they are usually women) is really telling the story. I'm not telling the story—the person telling the story is telling it. And the same goes for when I'm reading a story—out loud to people, I mean—it's that person that's telling it. It's like what Toni Morrison saw when she read *Corregidora*—the author isn't there anywhere.

For that reason, a lot of people think the things I do are autobiographical; because when I'm telling the story or reading it out loud, I don't want to say "I" am those women, but those women are telling the story.

Then there was another stage after the poetic journals—where the woman narrator, even though the details of her life were different, was me in the sense that I needed her to explain myself. There was no way I could explain who I was to myself or anybody else except that way. Particularly my silence. I had to say something about it some way. In the short story "The Welfare Check," although I never worked in a welfare office or knew a man like the one in the story, the woman not knowing what to say and that kind of thing was a self-portrait, I guess. (About the man—I should say that, rather than not knowing a man like the one in the story, he wasn't a *particular* man.) And I felt that if people read the story or if I read it to them, they would feel less badly about my not talking and it usually worked that way. So I needed the women to be me at that time. And there were always these things about people who didn't talk and didn't know what to say.

Actually, that's still there. In *Corregidora,* it's still there in the character of the mother who doesn't know what to say to the man, Martin—"It was just like my mouth was there, but I just couldn't say nothing." That kind of thing. But in Ursa—she knows what to say. She talks to people, you know. So Ursa isn't at all a self-portrait. Maybe there are some things, some points. But I think that "talk thing" somewhere will always enter, you know—in one or another of the characters. So there are those kinds of autobiographical usings. Things that have been the causes of tension in my own life might be re-directed in the lives of certain characters. The man in "The Roundhouse" works but doesn't say anything and people think he can't talk—that kind of thing.

But for all the details of my own life, I'm not an autobiographical writer at all. I "re-contextualize" a lot of the things in my own life. There might be things people say in stories that I've heard said—certain "scenes" that really happened—but the whole thing could never be autobiographical or even strictly biographical—I mean, in terms of the details of another person's life. Sometimes I put a few things from the lives of people I've been told about, for instance. But the details of my writing now wouldn't correspond with any details in my own life. But I do make certain connections in terms of my own experience and relationships. Relationships that are important to me in real life become important in fiction. Someone asked me, for instance, if I had a theory about generations as matrilinear or something. I said no. But in terms of my own living—the women I've descended from have a special significance for me, have always had a special significance for me. So, although the women aren't the same kind of women and the details are different, that aspect is there and the generations of women are there because of something I needed to clarify in my own life, certain relationships between men and women, between mother and daughter, other relationships in the book.

You heard me mention how I always used to picture myself. Making generations. That can be "translated" into something in my own life. Ever since I was a kid I never really wanted or thought of myself as having children. At first, I thought, of course, that that was the natural thing that happened, that women naturally grew up and got married and had children. So I thought since that was what "naturally" happened, it would happen to me, too. I decided that I wouldn't get married till I was in my late twenties, though—which was unusual for the kind of community I grew up in. But then, when I was twelve, for some reason, I learned that you didn't just naturally grow up and get married and have children. So since I was twelve I decided that I wasn't going to ever get married or have children. And then something happened. I was going along—feeling that way—not feeling guilty about it or anything—not even thinking that other people might care about that kind of decision—that whatever I chose to do was okay. I didn't think about how parents might feel. In fact, I thought as long as it was something that I'd decided, it was okay. But then I realized that when you make that kind of a decision, you're not just making it for yourself, you're making it for your mother and your grandmother—I speak of the women here for another personal reason—and your great-grandmother; that it's not just you making that decision for yourself but you're making it for all the generations that came before you.

What made me realize this was talking to my mother. I really didn't think it mattered, you know. I'd never even thought about it—how she might feel. Because I didn't see it that way. And we were talking and I said I wasn't going to have any children or didn't want to have any children and then she asked me, "What about the generations?" And then I realized that it wasn't just me. And ever since then I've had this tremendous feeling of guilt, you know. I don't know if I should call it guilt, but . . . ambivalence. Right now, I'm not doing anything about generations. But when she said that it just went clear through me, because I'd never really thought about it. All the connections, you know. And I can't explain my feelings—maybe changes in feelings—about children, I mean. But that's the reason I think that there's the generations and the command to make generations in *Corregidora*. I mean the metaphor for something personal. The historical parallels are already there. The reason Ursa can't have children—that's another thing, that's another matter. It has to do with my life, but it has to do with another woman's life, too—so I can't talk about that. But what I'm trying to say is that Ursa's relationships could be "translated" into details in my own life, but *Corregidora* is really a metaphor for things in my own experience rather than being a direct statement.

[H]: What do you think can be taught—or not taught—in writing classes? What was most valuable to you as a student, in terms of examples, persons, how you acquired techniques as well as ideas about writing and what you wanted to write about? What was useful, and useless, in your experience in and out of writing classes and programs?

[J]: Well, I see writing classes mainly as guidelines, you know. You can point out things to people, make them aware of the possibilities and that kind of thing, but the responsibility of "doing" is always theirs, the responsibility is finally always theirs. I also feel that it's important that a writer, storyteller, has a hearer. Some people need the sanction of many hearers before they feel sustained, others need very few, some need only one—that kind of thing. For me, as I said, I need that contact with one trusted person. And I guess there also has to be that feeling that *they* trust, that they trust the voice in my stories. So I've said what's been most valuable to me as a student. But I feel all writers, all storytellers, need the example of persons, the presence of persons, as reinforcement. Otherwise I don't feel you can really maintain that human relationship and connection in what you're doing. I think a storyteller can go only so long talking to himself, you know, or to no one. But I keep getting back to what you say about a man is another man's face. Because there is always that kind of relationship between a storyteller and a hearer—the seeing of each other. The hearer has to see/hear the storyteller, but the storyteller also has to see/hear the hearer, which the written tradition doesn't usually acknowledge. But writing is finally a "doing." It isn't something that you talk about. I don't think the actual "doing" can be taught. I don't think writing "process" can be taught.

I don't know how I've acquired techniques. I think I've acquired them from reading and listening. But for me, technique has to be finally something that you don't think about—that's internalized—and that, for each work, the way of telling should grow out of that particular work in the process of telling. Even when I revise, I don't think of technique as technique. I think about how something can be told better. Ideas about writing have come to me, too, through personal contact, reading, listening. What I want to write about is something that grows as I grow. Right now, there are things there for me to write about. I have them. I have them because of the kind of "continuum" way I've been writing. So right now for me there isn't the trying to find the things to write about but the having the time to write about the things that are already in my mind. There are also things that I can't deal with now that I might be able to deal with years from now. I mean certain relationships that I might speak about with a different vision or that I might be able to handle more fully than I can right now. I also have a sense of place in my writing. A lot of my earlier stories—either they went far away, or, like "The Return," they never located the people in time or place. Sometimes that is good, but like I was saying, one should have a story-telling center in terms of voice—which doesn't mean one can't go off here and there in terms of voice and language—it just means there's that deep well that one can trust, that center. I think it's the same with place and time—the sense of a location so that the storyteller doesn't lose a certain moral and human perspective—which doesn't mean the storyteller can't go off anywhere in place and time that he pleases—but that there's always that deep part that he knows, that human center.

THE HEALING

BOOK

ONE

CHAPTER ONE

I open a tin of Spirit of Scandinavia sardines, floating in mustard sauce.
The woman on the bus beside me grunts and leans toward the aisle.
She's a smallish, youngish, short-haired woman, small Gypsy earrings
in her ears, looks kinda familiar. I offer her some of them sardines, but
she grunts and leans farther toward the aisle. I nibble the sardines with
one of those small plastic forks and stare out the window. The sun hitting the window makes a rainbow across a field of straw pyramids.
There's a few horses and cows grazing in the meadow, a whitewashed
barn and a farmhouse, one of them three-story farmhouses, and there's
one of them little tin-roofed sheds built onto the farmhouse. It looks like
one of them painted scenes, you know the sorta landscape paintings you
can buy at them flea markets. Or the sort of landscapes that you see on
television, where the different artists teach you how to paint pictures.
You can learn how to paint pictures in oil or watercolor, and they teach
you the secrets of painting and make it seem like almost anyone can
be an artist, at least be able to paint pictures in their style of painting.
A Bible's open in my lap. I'm holding it cater-cornered, trying to keep the
sardine oil off the pages, or the mustard sauce. When I finish the tin
of sardines, I drink the mustard sauce. The woman beside me grunts
again. I glance over at her, at them Gypsy earrings. She's got smallish,
almost perfect-shaped ears, and is a little but full-mouthed woman.
Most people likes sardines, or likes the taste of them sardines, but maybe
she thinks it's too countrified to be eating them sardines on the Grey-
hound bus, even Spirit of Scandinavia sardines. Ever since I seen that
movie about the middle passage, though, and they talked about them

Africans coming to the New World being packed in them slave ships like sardines in a can, and even showed a drawing of them Africans, that's supposed to be a famous drawing, so every time I eat sardines I think of that. Of course, I still likes the taste of that, and I don't think she refuse them sardines on account of that metaphor, though, 'cause I'm sure there's plenty of people eats sardines and don't think of that metaphor. I deposit the tin in a plastic bag that's already brimming with paper cups, Coke cans, and crumbled paper napkins, then I open a bag of corn tortillas, you know the ones usedta use the bandito to advertise themselves, till the Mexican-American people protested about that bandito, though I remember hearing a song once about a real bandito, not one of those commercialized banditos, but one of those social bandits that the people themselves sing about, like they're heroes.

You teach Sunday school? the woman asks, her head still tilted toward the aisle.

Naw, I'm a faith healer, I say. I give her one of my brochures. I start to ask her whether them sardines reminds her of the middle passage, but I don't, 'cause everybody, like I said, don't think of that metaphor. So I just give her one of my brochures. That brochure don't have no famous drawings in it, like the middle passage, though. It just got a few clippings talking about the people I've healed, some of them famous, but mostly ordinary-type peoples.

She don't say anything, and don't look at the brochure, though she's probably thinking a brochure commercializes the profession of faith healing, that is, if you can call faith healing a profession. I think she going to put that brochure in that trash bag with that sardine can and them paper cups, Coke cans, and crumbled paper napkins, but she don't, she put it in her pocketbook, one of them Moroccan leather pocketbooks, look like real Moroccan leather, not that imitation Moroccan leather. Course some people say that that real Moroccan leather don't look no different from the imitation Moroccan leather, 'cause the people that makes imitation Moroccan leather is more subtle and sophisticated than in the old days when you could tell imitation leather from real leather. You can buy you imitation purses these days, even Gucci, and think it's real. When she put that brochure in her pocketbook, though, I see one of them paperback books peeking out. I don't see the title of that book, though it seem like it the name of some kinda insect, a mosquito or something like that. Maybe it's a book about them African mosquitoes. I know about them African mosquitoes. And them Caribbean mosquitoes. I got me a friend nicknamed Mosquito, though she ain't named after none of them African or Caribbean mosquitoes. Her real name Nadine. I don't call her Mosquito myself, I call her Nadine. And she also got coupla them magazines, I mean the young woman I give my faith healing brochure. I'm thinking maybe she's reading *Essence* or one of them type magazines, you know, for the African-American woman, but it ain't, it's *Scientific American* and *Popular Culture*. It look kinda like *National Geographic* 'cept it say *Popular Culture*. I like that *National Geographic* myself. But them Americans on the cover of the *Popular Culture* magazine with they tattoos and nose rings and sculptured and painted hairdos kinda look like the kinda folks you usedta just see in the *National Geographic*–type magazines. But now people all over the world look like they could be in them *National Geographic*–type magazines, and not just the so-called primitive peoples.

She ain't say anything about that faith healing, though, that woman with the Gypsy earrings, but I know what she's thinking: that I'm some kinda charlatan and mercenary, or some kinda crazy woman. All that. If I ain't a faker, then I'm a crazy woman that just believes in her own fakery. There's people like that; they's innocent believers, or gullible believers, but it's they own fakery or somebody else's fakery they believe in. And it might not be fakery, it might just be other people believe it to be fakery. You don't always know fakery from fakery. 'Cause I can tell she's one of them skeptical types. One of them skeptics. Gotta be a skeptic to be reading that *Scientific American*, 'cause ain't that the magazine of the skeptical. The gullible reads the *National Enquirer*. Or maybe they ain't gullible, but just likes to be entertained. Fictional science and popular fantasy. And a lot of movie stars. You's got to have a lot of movie stars in a magazine to interest popular culture. Maybe I'm a crazy woman, though, 'cause there's been plenty to say I'm crazy, but in the small tank town I'm going to they'll welcome me. At least those who believe. The others, well, you know, when they witness the healings, then they'll come 'round. Most of them, anyway. In my head, I've already got pictures of my destination, as clear and vivid as if I was already there. And all them little southern and midwestern tank towns, they's all alike. I don't have to describe them little tank towns to you, 'cause they're all alike. I don't know why they call 'em tank towns, though. Them little towns. I think they call 'em tank towns on account of them water tanks, you know them water tanks, where the trains stop to take on water. And that water tank is always higher than all them little buildings in them towns.

I don't know if the modern trains still use water, but them old steam locomotives usedta stop in them little tank towns to take on water. They didn't have depots in a lot of them little towns, 'cause some of them was too small to even have depots, but they'd have them tanks. In some of them little western and southwestern towns where there's always droughts, probably them tanks collects water for the people themselves and not just for them trains. Sometimes the names of the towns themselves are printed on them tanks, you know, or the chief industry in the town sometimes uses them to advertise theyselves. The chief industry might be wine making or cigar making or coal mining or tractor manufacturing or maybe it's a cannery town, then the name of the town's leading employer is on that tank. Maybe that's free advertising for that employer, so's that employer'll stay in that little tank town and not take his business to Mexico or Korea. If it's one of them little tourist towns, though, the chief industry is the town itself. Then the name of the town itself is on that tank. Anyway, I think that's why they call 'em tank towns. If you ain't from a little tank town yourself, you've probably seen 'em on television or at the movies, one of them documentaries on television or one of them movies about ordinary working-class people. I remember there was a controversy when one of them movie stars bought herself a little tank town, bought herself her own little town, though I don't remember if that little town had a tank in it, though. I remember some of them townspeople was glad to have a movie star buy their town, and others were complaining that that movie star ain't done a thing for them but to buy their town. That movie star ain't done a thing for us since she bought our town, said one of the people in one of the newspaper articles where they talked about that movie star and her buying that town. Then the newspaper reporter asked them people whether they'd ever even seen that movie star in their town, and most of them said they'd never even seen her in their town. We seen her in the town when she first bought the town, one of them said. But after she bought the town they ain't seen her in the town. She didn't buy the town like in the movies, though, where this corrupt person is supposed to own the whole town and control the people in that town, and's got his hired gangsters to help him control the town, but her notion were the notion of a virtuous person buying a town so's to make it a better town. I guess they had visions of glory when she bought their town, her being a movie star, and their visions of glory wasn't satisfied, so they started complaining, or that newspaper reporter encouraged them to complain about that movie star so's he could get a story. Course there was others didn't want anybody to buy their town, movie star or not, or whether the movie star a virtuous movie star or a corrupt one. They wanted to own their own town. But whenever they talk about one of them little tank towns, they always show the town's tank that's usually got the name of the town on it or the chief industry. 'Cause them little tank towns don't have anything like the Golden Gate Bridge or the Empire State Building or Lady Liberty or even them Las Vegas casinos to give them distinction, so they show the town's tank. If somebody like Wayne Newton is from one of them little towns, they might put the name of Wayne Newton on that tank. This is Wayne Newton's town, it might say. It don't mean he owns the town, it means it's the town where's he's from, and the town's claim to fame. And it ain't just little southern towns that's tank towns, though, there's little towns up North that's tank towns too. Little towns in Maine and New Jersey and Connecticut and Pennsylvania, and somebody said that all the towns in Rhode Island is tank towns, though I don't remember seeing any tanks in any of them Rhode Island towns. But them that ain't got them water tanks, though, they still call 'em tank towns. So that tank town is just a metaphor for them little towns.

Anyway, in this little tank town, I'm supposed to stay with this woman name Martha Gaines, who right now's making ginger cakes, some of them egg salad sandwiches and probably some of that strawberry pie. This region's supposed to be known for its strawberry pie. And Martha Gaines supposed to make the best strawberry pie. If this region known for its strawberry pie, and Martha Gaines make the best strawberry pie in the region, then she must make the best strawberry pie in the nation and maybe even the best strawberry pie in the world. She ain't thought, though, to commercialize them strawberry pies and refer to them as Martha Gaines' strawberry pies. She could commercialize them strawberry pies, call them Martha Gaines' strawberry pies and sell them all over the world. I think she still work at one of them little factories in the area, though, one of them little doll-making factories. I think they make them Kewpie dolls, them little types of carnival dolls and them little dolls that's sold in gift shops. And she don't even get to put her name on them dolls that she makes; she's got to put the company name on them little dolls. And that's even the Kewpie dolls that is her own original design. I don't think she gets to make Kewpie dolls her own original design, though. I think them manufacturing companies like that have got they standard design. So's anyone who makes they Kewpie dolls makes the same design, though they's got several different designs for them Kewpie dolls. Course this region better known for its tobacco and its thoroughbreds, and there's a place in the area called Wigwam Village near Cave City, I think Cave City is somewhere near here, where you can spend the night sleeping in a wigwam, the motel is made up of these little wigwams or tepees, so that attracts a lot of tourists to the region, them people that's got a romance about them wigwams and tepees. 'Cause there's people that might not know one Native American or want to know 'em, but they romances their wigwams and tepees. I don't believe that it's in the ownership of true Native Americans, that Wigwam Village, though I think once that Wigwam Village or another Wigwam Village, they hired someone with a little Cherokee in 'em that poses as a full breed to tell the tourists Cherokee tales, or whatever the dominant Native American tribe in this area, I think Cherokees, but in the culinary arts, this region known for its strawberry pie. I told my friend Nadine about that Wigwam Village and she say she wouldn't stay in a wigwam or a tepee neither unless it were a real wigwam or tepee and in the ownership of a true Native American. I don't know what's the difference between a wigwam and a tepee myself, but I likes them strawberry pies, though. I asked Nadine, though, whether Native Americans has got they own cuisine, though, like other peoples, because I ain't never seen no Native American restaurants like other peoples' restaurants. She say that most American food has got Native American origins, and especially anything that's got corn in it, except she don't use the word corn for corn, she use another word for corn. I think she say maize. Like when I was in the Southwest I made sure I had me some of that fried cactus and some of them tacos that weren't Taco Bell tacos. Them tacos is made from corn, but you can also have wheat tacos. Any of y'all see that futuristic movie where all the restaurants supposed to be Taco Bell?

Maybe these tank towns is all alike, but in the culinary arts there's still some distinction. Even though McDonald's and Colonel Sanders and Taco Bell and McDonald's and Colonel Sanders and Taco Bell architecture is everywhere, you still find some distinction in certain of the culinary arts. In the evening we'll go to the basement of the Freewill Baptist Church and then I'll show 'em my miracles and wonders. Of course they's always three kinds of people there: them that believes without questioning, those that believe only when it's themselves being healed, and those who could suck a cactus dry—they ain't got cactus in this region, but the region I just come from, little town name Cuba, New Mexico—and'ud still tell you it ain't got no juice in it. I'll tell y'all the truth. If I wasn't the one doing the healing, I'd be among the tough nuts.

That's a big beautiful Bible you got there, the woman says.

Thank you.

It's one of those King James Editions put out by the Spiritual Harvest Bible Company. And Nicholas is on his way there to meet me, catching a plane from Kodiak Island, that's in Alaska, where he bought himself some land. He tell me he always have him them dreams of going to Alaska, though, ever since he were a youngster, during the days when

Alaska first joined the Union, and again when they was working on the pipeline, when there was a lot of mens going up there to Alaska to work on that pipeline, maybe even that Anchorage, and then he heard about that Kodiak Island. Kodiak Island, not Kodak. I think there's bears that inhabit that island. Ain't they got bear that they refers to as Kodiak bears. Then they's got the Eskimo people. I don't know if they inhabits that island, them Inuit and them Inupiaq peoples. I remember when one of them talk shows was doing a segment, though, maybe Sally Jessy Raphael or Geraldo, though probably Sally Jessy Raphael, on the men from Alaska and was trying to match them up with women, and them men from Alaska even had they own magazine advertising theyselves, and wasn't a Inuit or Inupiaq amongst them. I think there were one African American, though, that kinda remind me of one of them men in that singing group, the Village People, who somebody said is all supposed to be American masculine stereotypes or American stereotypes of the masculine hero—the "Indian," the cowboy, the soldier, the construction worker, the cop. Like them men that dances for them women in the nightclubs, you know, usually they costumes theyselves to resemble the masculine stereotypes of men. But Nicholas, even Nicholas kinda resemble them masculine stereotypes of men. Maybe this the last time he'll come along to bear witness to that first healing, that Nicholas, though, 'cause he's been hinting about retiring from the faith healing business, you know, saying that I can tell about my own first healing my own self better than any other witness. I thought about hiring me another "witness" but that would be duplicitous and Nicholas the true one witnessed the first true healing, and that ain't the same as a hired witness. He's thinking of maybe going into the private investigations business or maybe opening himself up a little shop, maybe selling sporting gear for the fishermen-tourists, up there on that island. Seem like he would be good at that private investigations business, for although he might resemble one of them masculine hero types, he still seem like he too much of a thinking man to be content with just selling sporting gear for the fishermen-tourists. Anyway, he's bought hisself some land up there in Alaska. I think he's originally from Denver, Colorado, somewhere out there in Colorado. To tell the truth, I ain't really sure where Nicholas from, though I think it's Colorado. It ain't Boley, though I remember once him telling me about that town of Boley, Colorado, supposed to be a town originally chartered by African Americans, one of they own towns. Least I think it's Nicholas told me about Boley. He ain't from Boley hisself, though.

Course there's probably a lot of fakers that hires theyselves witnesses, y'all know like them evangelist fakers—there's true evangelists and there's evangelist fakers—and some of them probably do better witnessing than the true witnesses. You know, maybe one of them evangelist fakers have a true witness to they healings, but the people don't believe the true witness so's they's got to hire theyselves a fake witness, 'cause the fake witness to the healings is more believable than the true witness. Now I'm wondering whether that would make the healer a faker, if the healings theyselves is real, but the healer got to hire a fake witness, 'cause even the true believers don't believe the true witness. 'Cause maybe the fake witness got more confabulatory imagination than the true witness that just got a knowledge of the healings. Ain't one of them scientists say something like that, about imagination being superior to knowledge in them scientific experiments and scientific theories. But Nicholas he say that I can tell about my own first healing my own self better, though, than any hired witness. Maybe that's the truth. All I know is that Nicholas himself usedta tell the tale with more fanfare, more flourish, more confabulatoriness. And when he tells about that healing, it sounds like a true tale; it don't sound like no confabulatory tale. Least the way he usedta tell the tale of that healing. Now he tends to be kinda dry. And those people that come to faith healing most of them want to hear confabulatory-sounding stories, which don't mean they's confabulatory stories they ownself. It's just that when people come to be healed, they just likes to hear them confabulatory-sounding stories. And there's other folks that comes to them faith healings not to be healed but to be entertained, like it's a circus or a carnival rather than a faith healing. Them sorts you don't know whether there's true believers amongst them or not. And then, of course, there's the scientific-minded people that comes to some of them healings, and you see them jotting down in their notebooks, and questioning the people that claims they's been healed, even questions Nicholas—I tell them they can watch me heal, but I don't answer they questions—and most of them decides it's the people's own gullibility that's healed them. There ain't many true believers amongst the scientific-minded, though there's them that says that science itself is a religion, just another form of the modern world's religion. So you can't categorize all the scientific-minded as a skeptical people. I think I read that in the *People's Almanac*, that that modern science just supposed to be another religion. When I first seen that *People's Almanac*, though, I thought it was like the Communist Manifesto, but it ain't. You know, talking about its being the *People's Almanac*, like the People's Republic of China.

Still the wonder's in what happened, the wonder's in the healing, ain't in how it's told. It's the healing itself ain't how it's told that draws the folks like bees to wild nectar. Or like flies to honey. But I think bees is fonder of wild nectar than even flies is to honey. Course the bees makes they own honey.

But that's always been the procedure, though. Nicholas stands up in front of the people and tells them all folksy-like about the first time I ever healed someone, and then, after they's caught up in the tale, whether they thinks it's confabulatory or not, I begin the healing. I tell them a little about the first healing my ownself, and sounding more folksy than I naturally am, 'cause when you's doing the healing you's got to talk about the healing yourself, 'cause amongst some that lends as much credibility as the healing itself, but like I tell the scientific-minded people or them media people that wants to write up they own confabulatory stories about faith healing in America, I'm mostly there to do the healing. You's got to heal people to prove to most people that you ain't just talk. Course there's some of them disbelievers, even amongst them that ain't scientific-minded and ain't the media types, that believes it's the talk itself that do the healing. That all you's got to do is talk that healing talk and there's some gullible folks that is healed. Or they thinks that you's some kinda hypnotist. After one of them healings, somebody ask me whether I'm some kinda hypnotist. I don't even know the laws of hypnotism. Ain't all the scientific-minded cynics, though, and ain't all the mystical idealists true believers.

But she don't look like no preacher woman. I wouldn't want her in no roodloft of my church and no pulpit neither.

She ain't a preacher woman, she's a healing woman. And us church don't allow women to preach anyhow. They allows a woman to teach but they don't allow her to preach. You know that preacher woman that come here and they told her she couldn't preach. They said she could teach, but they wouldn't let her preach. And what if a woman is called to preach the same as a man? she asked. But us church don't believe a woman is called to preach, even if she herself believe she is called to preach, and one of the women, you know the one from Memphis, say, Maybe she called to teach and thought she were called to preach. Maybe the Lord say teach and she thought he say preach. So she give that little lecture. She referred to it as a lecture, but it sounded like preaching to me.

Same difference.

I can already hear 'em talking about me, those flibbertigibbets. She ain't no preacher woman or a teacher woman neither, she a faith healer, one of them others be saying. What's the difference? She look like she belong on a submarine or on a motorcycle. They don't allow womens on no submarine. On the modern submarine they do, 'cause this is the age of feminism. Her and that bum's jacket. It's what they call a bomber jacket. Anyway, I seen her heal someone in D.C. I seen her when she healed in Memphis and then again in Kansas City. She even healed folks in Milan, that's over there in Italy. Dottoressa is what they calls her there in that Milan. I seen this picture of her healing over there in Italy and she were surrounded by all these Italians who looked just liked colored people to me. Say she's even healed folks in Brazil. I know they's got colored people in Brazil. Curandera's what they call her in Brazil. She sent us them article clippings about that. And them looking at her like they believes in that healing, and others like they's sure that she's a shyster. And she don't just include them clippings that quotes the true believers but also them that say they think she's a shyster and a subversive. Seems to me like if you's going to advertise your healing powers that you'd just include clippings of them people that says you's a true healer. 'Cept it just she wants us to make up us own mind whether she a true healer or not? I don't know if she's healed anybody over there in that India, though, but they's supposed to have a lot of they own healers over there, you know them yogis and such fabulous people, like them healing monks, and they probably wouldn't want to import no healer from over here when they's got they own true healers. They's got they own true healers everywhere, shamans the Native Peoples calls 'em, but that don't mean they might not want to import another one. I don't know whether she's ever healed any white peoples, though, I mean true white peoples, even there in Memphis, 'cause somebody say she especially likes to heal people over there in Memphis. What you mean the true white peoples? 'Cause in one of them articles she's with these peoples from West Virginia and they's looking like true white peoples, but then when you read the article it says they's colored people, or they white people claiming they's colored and's prouder to be colored than a lot of the true colored people. That's 'cause they's got the pride of being colored and ain't the prejudice. They's gullible when it comes to they own healers, the true whites, though, and them evangelists, but I don't believe they'd be true enough believers to believe she could heal 'em, I mean a woman of us persuasion, I mean true colored women. Seem like in all them clippings and them brochures they's colored-looking peoples in them photographs being healed, or white-looking peoples claiming to be colored. Not to say that they's true colored, even them looking colored. You know they's colored-looking people in the world that claims to be white the same as they's white-looking peoples claiming to be colored. What were her first healing? She healed herself. Aw, girl, you don't believe that! Yes, I believe it, 'cause that's the proof of a true healer. They's got to heal theyself first. You's got to work your own salvation first, even us preacher say you's got to work your own salvation first. He say when he preach it ain't to work us salvation for us, we's got to work us salvation usself. He say he can tell us how to work us salvation or how us religion say work us salvation, but we's got to work us salvation usselves. He say that almost every religion say that, ain't just us religion. He say he don't like to compare them religious books to them how-to books, 'cause he ain't a sacrilegious man, but most of them is how-to salvation books. But ain't none of them religious books works your salvation for you. There's people that hides from they own salvation, but even they's got to work they own salvation first.

I take off my bomber jacket in the heat, roll it up into a pillow and place it in the crevice near the window. The mustard and sardines still gives off its pungent odor.

She really do do some powerful healing, though. And she ain't a root doctor neither. She don't need no root to heal. Some people say that that is a superior form of healing when you don't need no root to heal. When you just healing people by knowing that they is healed. You know, that Christian Scientific woman that Martha know was talking about that. That they just heals people by knowing that they is healed. Other people, they trust them roots and herbs and potions, though. This woman just heals by healing. I don't know if she claims to be Christianly Scientific, though, or a Scientific Christian. I know she heals by healing and don't use no roots or herbs or potions. Wait till y'all hears about that first healing she done. I don't rightly recall the man's name that witnessed it, who was there at that first healing, I mean. He supposed to be here too, tonight, though. Wait till y'all hear. Wait till she sees, you mean. She healed me. You don't say. What was it you had? I don't rightly recall what it was called, or even if she named it, but when I walked I felt like I was walking in chains. I felt like I was in the old days of slavery and walking in chains. Or like them men we seen in them chain gangs that they's trying to renovate down South, down there in Mississippi or Alabama, I think. One of them states in the Deep South. Said they had brought back the chain gang in one of them southern states in the Deep South. Ain't that how they got the name gangster on account of them chain gangs? Naw, a gangster's a gangster. Somebody said that they made that against the law, ain't it? Them chain gangs, I mean. I think somebody said that they made that against the law, that they can make them prisoners work, that that ain't against the law, but that they can't tie them together on no chain gang, 'cause that chain gang is cruel and inhuman. How come you don't see no womens on them chain gangs, though? In all the history of the chain gang, I ain't never seen no womens on 'em. They usedta say there ain't as many criminally minded women as the mens, 'cause they say it's always easier for the womens to find work than the men, even that domestic work, but now they say they's almost as many criminally minded womens as mens. You've got freer women, but you've also got more criminally minded women. I felt like I was walking in chains. Doctors couldn't do nothing or didn't want to. I would go from doctor to doctor and couldn't none of them heal me, or didn't want to. The women doctors or the men. Then she just looked at me and know my trouble. She said the trouble would end, and touched me, and it did. That's what I mean by she heal by healing. Now I moves easy as wind through trees. Sometimes she speak a word and it's done. Other times she got to lay on hands. She don't prescribe none of them herbs and roots and potions, though. She ain't that sorta healing woman. Well, I heard other vile things and notions about her. Say she was a gambler. Say she was loose-virtued before she become a celibate. You don't always begin on the right road. Especially saints and prophets don't. They says that saints and prophets always begins as sinners, even them minor prophets. In fact, I don't know a prophet or a saint—I don't think they's any minor saints, a saint's a saint, ain't they? they talk about the minor prophets, but I ain't heard them talk about no minor saint— that ain't began as a sinner. When you reads tales about them saints and prophets, whether you reads about them in a book or sees it on the Learning Channel or TNT, or even learns about the modern-day saints and prophets that appears on the talk shows, though, seem like they all of them begins as sinners. Especially them male saints. Seem like they demands more of they female saints than they do of they male saints. Seems like they allows they male saints to sow they wild oats, but not they female saints. That's why you's got so many criminally minded modern women, 'cause they believes they oughta be able to sow they wild oats the same as the mens. Naw, there is female saints that also begins as sinners. You ever heard of that Saint Mary of Egypt? Is that the other Mary? Or is that the same Mary as that Magdalene? Was a rock 'n' roll singer they also says. Naw, but she did used to manage one, they says, that were her profession, a business manager. One of them rock 'n' roll and rap singers business managers. I don't know if she sing that rap or not, but I know she sing that rock 'n' roll. That Tina Turner–type rock 'n' roll. 'Cept she ain't no Tina Turner. Talk about them minor saints and prophets, one of them minor rock 'n' roll singers. And nothing to glorify the Lord in none of that music. Talk about people hiding from they own salvation. One of the beautiful people, though. And somebody even say she usedta be a beautician or one of them makeup artist out there in Hollywood. Seem like she'd know how to beautify herself.

Martha, tell us what stuff you know.

I got my sweet cakes and strawberry pie to make. All this gossip about gossip. Ain't gossipmongering a sin? Seem like gossipmongering oughta be a sin. Y'all is gossips' gossips. Y'all learn all there's to learn when she get here. And when that Mr. Nicholas get here too. She ain't gonna tell you no more about herself than's in them brochures, though, and what y'alls read about in them clippings, 'cause she believe that the important thing is the healing. Who Mr. Nicholas? He the one that witnessed that first healing. I like to hear him talk about that first healing almost as much as to witness the healings.

Saint Nicholas. Ha-ha-ha. Is he a saint too?

I want everything to be so fine. I'm honored that she chose to stay with me. And Mr. Nicholas too. I remember when I got healed, he witnessed for her, and a fine specimen of a man. She don't just pause with anybody y'all know and Mr. Nicholas neither. Course Mr. Nicholas usually stays at the hotels or the boardinghouses, 'cause he's the reclusive type. But she don't just pause with anybody, especially amongst the skeptical-type peoples that just wants to test her healing powers, you know. She knows I'm a true believer. And I'm one of the first people that she healed in them old early days when she first started with her faith healing. And I fancied myself to be one of the skeptics myself. I didn't believe she could heal a flea myself. And then I witnessed it when she healed her own grandmother. Straightened out her shoulders. Say she have a hump in her shoulders just like a turtle's. In fact, there's people usedta refer to her as a turtle woman on account of them shoulders. Other say it ain't on account of them shoulders, that she usedta be a real turtle, which is nonsense, ain't no real turtle turn into no human being, not in the natural world, but I know them shoulders kinda look like that turtle shell. They say she look like she have a turtle shell on her back and the healing woman healed that. But that's a whole nother story. Mr. Nicholas don't tell that one. He just tell the tale about her first healing herself. I could witness for her myself, but I ain't as good at witnessing as Mr. Nicholas. He one of them charismatic-type people. He more charismatic than the healing woman herself. What charismaticism she got come from them healing powers. When you heal, you creates your own charismaticism. But you needs somebody like that charismatic Mr. Nicholas to witness for you, though. If I was a healing woman, I'd sho want a man like Mr. Nicholas to witness for me.

I first seen her picture in the *Louisville Defender* before she started printing up them brochures. It talked about all the travels she'd done over there in Africa, and somebody asked her whether she had learned her healing powers from one of them Africans, whether she were a apprentice to one of them African healers, but she said she had never been a apprentice to none of them African healers, but did say that she knew of a African healing woman, but they didn't heal exactly the same way. And the woman who were interviewing her said that maybe that African healing woman had transferred some healing powers to her without her knowing it. I don't know, she said, maybe she put some healing powers in some zebra stew or something, but I do know that I never apprenticed myself to any of them healers over there. And then they did this little tabloid story about her, "I Healed Kong's Daughter," and made it so you'd think it's King Kong, you know with all that talk about Africa, at least that's what I thought when I read that blurb, 'cause there's only one Kong that I know about and that's King Kong, and then it turn out it this little Chinese girl named Kong, you know, that famous little musician prodigy she supposed to healed, so's she could continue playing her music, you know. Naw, she don't play the violin. I know who you thinking about, naw this little prodigy I think she play the flute. That's the healing that's supposed to made her world famous. I don't mean the little Chinese girl, I mean the healing woman. 'Cause that little Chinese girl she already famous. You know, that Chinese woman named Kong that's got all those Kong restaurants all over the world heard about her healing powers and hired her. That's her claim to healing fame. 'Cause if she was just healing ordinary colored people, I don't think anybody woulda heard about her at all or written about her in no tabloids. She mighta been written about in *Ebony*, but I don't think she'da appeared in no tabloid, and there's a lot of colored people that wouldn't want her to heal us usselves if she hadn't healed that famous Kong little girl, 'cause we's like that usselves. It's Kong that made her a star, at least in the world of faith healing. She don't look like she can heal a flea, though. Or them bees. You know, they's talking about them bees around here that needs to be healed, naw I'm not talking about them African bees, I'm talking about the native American bee, unless they's colonized bees, I mean originating in England, 'cause the farmers needs them to pollinate. Bees don't just produce honey, they pollinates. That's what they refer to as the ecological system. I wonder if she can heal them bees, if she can heal the human species. Do that Mr. Saint Nicholas heal? Is he a healer? A healer ain't necessarily no saint, is it, Martha? You can be healer and don't mean you's a saint. Bible say to be wary of folks of that sort. It warn you about them false prophets and them false saints. But the Bible also talk about them gifts of the spirit, and God don't give gifts of the spirit to looks. Tell her, Martha. Bible says Jesus was ugly, and He is the greatest spirit gift His ownself. Course the description they gives of him don't sound ugly to me. Sound like a man meant to be glorified. Supposed to have hair like lamb's wool and to be the complexion of brass. That sounds like a man meant to be glorified to me. If most of these people talking about Jesus see the real Jesus, though, they would probably run from him. These holy evangelists and religionists. I mean them that thinks he's supposed to have blue eyes and blond hair and

them Nordic peoples from Sweden or them Germanic looks, I mean
them Aryan-type Germans, not them dark-haired Germans, 'cause
them pictures you see of that Jesus even in us church that ain't the real
Jesus, that ain't the true Jesus that even the Bible describes. Like that little Buddha that Martha got that they make out there at that factory
where she work, now supposed that little Buddha was to have blond hair
and blue eyes? Suppose they made that little Buddha to look like them
little blond Kewpie dolls they make out there? Now I ain't amongst the
folks to say that Jesus is a African or even a North African, like that
schoolteacher telling us about, you know Little Sal, but that ain't even a
Mediterranean Jesus. Devil came as a angel of light. Ain't that what the
Bible say? Aw, girl, I know that. I usedta belong to the A.M.E., the African Methodist Episcopals, before I joined y'all's church. That's what it
says, don't it, Martha?

Yes, it does say that all right. It most certainly does. And Jesus is Jesus. I know there's folks who searches for the real, historical Jesus. But
Jesus is Jesus.

That smells so good, Martha. What is it? Ginger. Will she be here one
night or two?

Depend on how big the crowd is and how much healing need to be
done.

Do she heal crazy peoples?

Yes, I do believe she do. Seem like I heard she healed some crazy
woman in Memphis. Some crazy woman from over there in Memphis.
Seem like that one of her first healings, some crazy woman, or at least
amongst her first healings. I do know the crazy peoples do come to her
healings to be healed the same as the sane peoples, them that knows
they's crazy or has the suspicion of it. I know when she healed me, I think
there was several crazy peoples there that got healed, at least they didn't
seem to have no visible ailments. Yeah, that brochure do mention insanity as one of her cures. Yeah, that brochure do say something about insanity as one of her cures. I know that old brochure she usedta distribute
when she first started advertising her healings don't say nothing about
insanity, though, it just list the physical cures. I don't think a true healing

woman should advertise herself myself. I still know her to be a true healing woman, though. But that new brochure do mention insanity. She don't refer to it as insanity, though, she refer to it as a ailment of the spirit. She don't mention insanity at all in that brochure, or even eccentricity, she just mention ailment of the spirit, which she say encompass a lot of the metaphysical things.

Be here two days then, maybe three. Maybe stay the week. 'Cause they's plenty crazy people round here to heal, ain't it, Zulinda? Ailment of the spirit nothing. Metaphysical nothing. They's crazy. Big Sal is crazy. I know Big Sal is crazy. Y'all know Big Sal. Now I ain't talking about Little Sal, ain't that Little Sal, speak of the devil, I seen that bicycle she rides around on, I said that looks like Little Sal's bicycle chained up there, look like a little girl don't she, woman her age riding around on a girl's bicycle, now that's eccentric, a schoolteacher, you'd think she's one of her students, I'm talking about Big Sal. Everybody know that Big Sal is crazy. She look crazy her own self, if you ask me. Looking like she belong in a comic book. Though looking crazy don't mean you is. Do looking crazy mean you is? If that looking crazy mean you is, then them psychiatrists and psychologists would have more work than they's got now. Lotta people say us Wisdoms looks crazy us ownselves, but I know insanity don't run in us. Maybe some of the New York Wisdoms is crazy, 'cause that's New York, and seem like I heard some of them has been psychoanalyzed, but the Wisdoms from around here ain't crazy. I know that for a fact, though like the poet says sometimes the facts about a people obscures the truth about 'em. There might be some ailment of the spirit people amongst the people she heals in her world travels, or even amongst the New York Wisdoms, but around here the crazy peoples that's crazy is crazy. Ain't they, Zulinda? Martha, you acts like all crazy people is sane.

I get off the bus carrying a small overnight case made out of imitation crocodile. To meet me at the station's three middle-aged women in a Ford convertible. Martha's the driver and she's the slender one and the tallest, the others are the proverbial stereotypes of plump church womens. Cotton print dresses, pillbox hats, oversized vinyl purses that dangles from their wrists or elbows. Zulinda and Josephine don't hide their disappointment. I know they's expecting me to be more impressive, look less like some ordinary, common woman and more like a legend. More like some legendary healer. Even them pictures of me in them clippings and in that brochure looks more legendary. But people always say I don't look like my photographs. There's people look more impressive than they photographs, others look less impressive than they photographs. A lot of them models and movie stars, people say, looks more impressive in they photographs. Or if they do still look impressive in person, I know a lot of them movie stars people's always telling them that they looks taller on the screen. They might be the shortest man in Hollywood, but onscreen they look like the tallest. Now that rock star I usedta manage, she look more impressive in reality than in her publicity photographs and her album photographs. That's the same with them movie stars, like I said. That's why they always insists on giving them them screen tests, to test whether the camera loves them. The camera's gotta love them. They's gotta be photogenic. Now she's making herself them videos, that rock star, but them videos ain't half so interesting as the woman herself. It's Martha who comes forward to greet me first, bringing with her that odor of ripe strawberries and fresh ginger. We shakes hands. Hello, Martha.

The other women step forward to introduce themselves. They're staring at my blue jeans and bomber jacket, worrying that I'll appear in church dressed so outlandish. Josephine gives me a look, then holds out her hand. We shakes hands, then I shakes hands with Zulinda, but I know they're eager to test my healing powers. Josephine Wisdom's already telling me about her sinus problem and Zulinda Tage's already mumbling about her fear of cats. We walk together toward the car. I ride in the front with Martha, while Josephine's in the backseat taking Kleenex from her purse, hawking into it, and Zulinda's glancing up at the tattered ceiling and wishing they coulda borrowed the reverend's car, the Cadillac or the Mercedes, but though he's opened his church to me, he's one of them skeptical ones, and ain't about to lend them his Cadillac or the Mercedes either for some fool calling herself a faith healer. Still, she thinks that Martha oughta mend that tattered roof of that convertible. Gifts of the spirit ain't modern gifts anyhow but ancient ones, he believes, that skeptical preacher, though the Lord Himself supposed to be the same yesterday today and tomorrow.

Martha, why don't you ever convert your convertible? asks Zulinda.

I prefers the top up.

I wouldn't have me no convertible not to convert it, says Zulinda. I wouldn't have me none o' these old reckless tops if I didn't use it.

Martha got style, say Josephine through her Kleenex. Them fast womens rides around in them converted convertibles. You know them fast womens always got them converted convertibles. Martha got class.

Well, I likes me them converted convertibles and I ain't a fast woman, nor a slow one neither, and I got as much class as Martha. Everybody says I gots class.

When I'm scheduled to appear? I ask.

Aw, you got plenty of time to rest and freshen up, says Martha.

And *change,* adds Zulinda from the backseat.

Josephine hawks into the Kleenex. The *show* don't start till eight, she says, making sure I hear her call it show. Martha turns on the radio. This is an old Memphis song, the singer announces. Do y'all guys feel funky tonight? Martha turns off the radio, then turns it back on, twists the dial, only to find more funky music, then some of that gangsta-type rap, then little D'Angelo. She listen to a little of that D'Angelo music, some love's melody, sophisticated-type rap, which she say sounds more like real music, like intelligent music, than some of that other music, then she cuts the radio off.

I'm really looking forward to tonight, says Josephine. I wants you to cure my sinusitis. You going to, ain't you?

I don't say nothing. To tell the truth, I don't like to say what I'll heal until I heal it.

I guess for you it's easy to heal folks now after the long time you been doing it, says Zulinda.

The first time is easy when you got the gift of the spirit, says Martha. It ain't like them learned things, things you got to master. It were easy the first time, weren't it?

Yes, it were, I admit. I wasn't trying to be no healing woman. In fact after that first healing, I denied I was a healing woman, that that healing was just a fluke, then I healed a horse, I touched a horse's phalanges and I healed it, somebody was talking to me about one of their horses and I touched it and healed it. I guess I coulda just kept healing horses, worked for the racing industry healing their horses, you know, and then I went down to Memphis and healed a crazy woman. I don't just heal physical ailments, I heal ailments of the spirit, like my brochure says. Anyway, someone heard about my healing powers and someone else heard about my healing powers and then I just started healing, but in the beginning I denied I was a healing woman. I know a lot of people are skeptical of my healing powers. I was skeptical of them in the beginning myself, but I just kept healing people. Like you say, one of them gifts of the spirit.

Zulinda's thinking of a furry ball and gray radar eyes perched on her lawn. Martha even give her a book of cat poetry to help her get over her fear of cats. But that poem about that galloping cat, even galloping about doing good, made her more skeptical of cats. She's thinking that if I'm a real healing woman I'd know what she's thinking and heal her right then and there. How do you know who to cure first? she asks. I just know.

The car turns a corner and climbs a hill. The narrow road's lined with duplex houses, green and white and yellow. Beyond them the land slopes down to a railroad track. Zulinda's thinking that if I'm a real healing woman, I'd piece out the deeper fears, deeper than the fear of cats, and heal them too. She thinking she just test me first to see if I can cure her fear of cats. I reach down and scratch my ankle.

You ever got lost coming to these little out-of-the-way towns? Martha asks.

Naw, not really, but then I always got nice people to meet me like y'all. And it's mostly in these little towns that there's true believers. Ain't too many true believers in the big cities.

Martha smiles, but that cynical Josephine just blows her nose. Or true fools, she thinking. Them big city people ain't such fools, she thinking. They say she healed people in Rio, though. Ain't Rio a big city? And maybe them true believers in Rio is actually from them little towns, and they just comes to Rio to the big city. Zulinda hums a jaunty tune then changes it to a more holy one. The car sloping down bumps into the railroad track, crosses it, then climbs another hill.

Didn't know the train came through here, I say.

It don't anymore. Depot's closed down. A lot of these little train depots around here have closed down. Just the tracks left.

The women in the backseat are still thinking how common I am, how full of chitchat, and my vocabulary sounds elementary, it don't even sound like that preacher-teacher woman that give that lecture, ain't that wondrous and fantabulous vocabulary them healers uses, and if I could really heal, wouldn't I already just know about them trains too? And I don't talk that revelation talk, that prophet passion. Just some ordinary woman, could be one of them, or one of their daughters, one of their own girls. They're staring at my bomber jacket, its gray fur collar, imitation fox, 'cause I wouldn't have a collar with no real fox, like I wouldn't have no real crocodile, and my greased and braided hair. I'm one of their own girls, they're thinking. "Except maybe more streetwise and jazzy," thinks Josephine. "Full o' all that city flash." I know Martha's told them grand things about me, 'cause Martha's like that. It's Martha showed them all them clippings about me. "She a regular boogie-woogie," thinks Zulinda, clucking. Josephine blows her nose almost into the back of my head. Then Martha turns into the driveway. We climb out among honeysuckle bushes and them maple trees. Inside, Martha's house is spotless and smells like lemon oil. There's two of those comfortable flowered sofas, a long beige coffee table loaded with them whatnots—wooden elephants, a brass Buddha, state fair mugs, a little glass tiger. There's some of them little Kewpie dolls she makes, even a few multicultural Kewpie dolls. They usedta just make them white Kewpie dolls, but I guess now they makes them multicultural Kewpie dolls, or maybe they's Martha's own inspiration. There's an upright Steinway piano, mahogany and shining, standing beneath a gilded mirror. I watch the women reflected in that mirror. Martha's the gingerbread woman, Josephine's a chocolate eclair, and Zulinda's a lemon snap. I'm thinking of the names of horses I would've bet on if I was still a betting woman: Regal Fawn, Box o' Chocolates, and Banana's Kin.

I take you upstairs so's you can get refreshed up after all that long ride, says Martha. It's a real great pleasure, though, to have you here. Ever since you healed me, I've been wanting to invite you here to do a healing, but they says that your schedule has always been filled up with that healing in them other little towns. Well, when you first healed me, I wouldn't've known that you'da developed into a healer to be known worldwide. At least amongst the true believers.

At the top of them stairs, I can hear the women downstairs just chattering. She got on mascara. Teal blue. Did y'all see that? Teal blue. And dressed up like a soldier. But we's God's army, anyway. Aw, girl, I'll have to see to believe. I'm a true believer, but that don't mean I got to believe in that bogger. Harm a flea, but cure one?

You can rest up here, says Martha, reaching into one of them drawers and holding up a clean towel and washcloth. I'll call you. We can have a light meal here, but they want to have a real supper at the church, after your . . . presentation. I mean, the healing. Bathroom's down the hall. Where you headed after here, up North again?

Naw, Tennessee. Memphis.

There must be more true believers in Memphis than anywhere, 'cause seem like you's always healing folks in Memphis.

And there's a group in London, in Brixton, who've heard about my healing powers too, and want me to come over there to Brixton to do some healing.

I've heard about that Brixton. I know some folks name Brixton. They might be at your . . . healing.

Performance, she'd started to say at first. The healing? She hands me the rose and cinnamon towel and washcloth, then heads downstairs. I go in her bathroom and toss water onto my face and rearrange my braids. Listening to those voices downstairs. It ain't a auditory hearing, I should tell y'all. I mean, to y'all their voices would be inaudible or merely whispers, but to me they're as clear as Martha's glass tiger.

Is she gonna change? whispers Zulinda.

Why don't y'all come back and help me pack the cakes and my strawberry pie, says Martha. I thought we'd have us light ham and potato soup—for her—before we go on account of all that healing she be doing. Poor child looks weary . . .

If she were a true healing woman she wouldn't take no thought to light ham and potato soup.

We can put everything into this straw basket.

I'll have to see to believe. Don't look like she could cure a flea. If it's true, I don't see why God don't give such gifts of the spirit to good women like you, Martha, and a woman with class, instead of who . . . trollops.

Hush, girl. It ain't for us to judge. Zulinda, you hold my strawberry pie right. Hold it up like this . . . The last time you held my pie . . .

I come downstairs wearing a plain-cut beige dress, plain beige pumps, and a paisley scarf around my waist. Poised in front of the Steinway, Zulinda frowns at the paisley but grins approval at the beige dress and round-toed pumps. And Martha's palms are held up to demonstrate how to hold a imaginary pie.

Don't you tell me how to hold no pie, now Martha, says Zulinda. If I knows anything, I knows how to hold a pie.

CHAPTER TWO

Seeing him in the crowd. He look like he grown a little broader, even his facial features look broader, and there's more gray at his temples, and gray in his mustache, but other than that he look like the same handsome man, the same good-looking man. Seem like in all the men I know, there's something of the same man, or maybe it's just that women don't know men the same way that men know themselves; maybe we only know us idea of a man, and if we got us a certain idea of a man, then we see something of the same man in every man, 'cause it's us own idea of a man us own archetypal man that we think we see in every man, like maybe only all men know is their idea of a woman or they idea of the archetypal woman. Even that novelist that wrote that *Portrait of a Lady,* seem like that's just a man's idea of a woman or of a certain type of woman. 'Cept she a American lady in Britain and the American lady ain't the same type of lady as the British lady, 'cause in Britain you's got to be a true royal to be a lady. How I meet him? I met him one summer I spent up at the racetrack in Saratoga Springs, upstate New York. He was buying yearlings. After my show, he'll probably come up and whisper, A long time, and I'll say, Yeah. But for now I'm just watching him out of the corners of my eyes, pretending I don't know him, pretending I don't know him no more than the others come to the healing, pretending I don't even know his name, and listening to them flibbertigibbets.

She been celibate ever since the healing power came, leastwise they say that she celibate—aw, girl, you know what celibate is, you know I don't have to tell you what celibate is, what Big Sal say she is, but don't nobody believe her, that Big Sal, but Big Sal say she been to the moon too, ain't you heard Big Sal's tale of how she been to the moon?—but girl I could tell you stories, say one of them flibbertigibbets, and then she start telling stories about me I ain't heard my ownself.

Hush.

What she waiting for? Why don't she heal somebody? Heal.

Nicholas J. Love.

Who that?

Nicholas J. Love. I think that J. stand for Jess. They shoulda named him Jess Love, 'cause he look like it, don't he? He look just like Love, don't he? Well, he look like love ain't a jest with him. He supposed to testify. He the one witnessed that first healing. She don't heal till after he testify to the first healing. Anybody know anything about healing, you know you need somebody to testify. And can't just anybody testify, gotta be a true witness to the healing. Course them healings testifies to theyself, but you know healers, a lot of them they don't just heal, you's got to testify first.

Hush. That him now. That him. That big good-looking. . . . My, he's a mountain, ain't he, Josephine? Mountain of a man. What they call a man of impressive height. Nicholas J. Love. Who Mrs. Love? I wonder if he got a Mrs. Love. I know a man like him gotta have hisself a Mrs. Love. Look like he got plenty wanting to be Mrs. Love. I bet he got plenty womens wanting to be Mrs. Love. I know he got plenty womens wanting to be Mrs. Love. Martha, do you know if he got hisself a Mrs. Love? Look at Martha, looking like she wanna be his own Mrs. Love herself? I bet you could be his own Mrs. Love yourself, couldn't you Martha? Now, he look like he can heal somebody. Heal. I bet he can heal somebody. He remind me of a man I seen once at a carnival, though. They had him advertised as the tallest man in the natural world. The poster advertising him say he the tallest man in the natural world. Look like one of them Watusi. You know them Watusi. They's supposed to be naturally tall people. Men that is unnaturally tall to us is natural men to them. I didn't like the way they had him up there in that tent amongst them carnival freaks, though, like he were King Kong or the Mighty Joe Young or somebody—aw, you know the Mighty Joe Young, that's the other King

Kong—instead of a natural man. You's a free man, I told him. You's a free man, you ain't King Kong or the Mighty Joe Young and you don't need to be in nobody's carnival. Is you a Watusi from over there in Africa? I don't think he understood English, though, 'cause he musta spoken one of them Watusi-type languages. Then somebody, one of the carnival security guards, I think they call 'em security guards, come over and told me I wasn't supposed to be talking to their Tallest Man in the Natural World. He didn't say nothing to me, the tallest man himself, 'cause I don't think he speak us English language, but he seem like he appreciate the fact that I was talking to him even in my own language like he a natural man and not just the tallest man in the natural world. They musta gone over there to that Africa to get that man, though, 'cause even though they's got some tall men in America and they's supposed to have taller men in America than in Europe, they's supposed to have the tallest men in the world over there in Africa. They's supposed to have the tallest men in the world and the shortest men in the world. He ain't exactly the tallest man in the world, though, but he do look like he can heal somebody. Did they have the shortest man in the natural world? Naw, I don't believe they did. They mighta had the shortest man in the natural world, but when I seen the advertisement advertising the tallest man in the natural world, that's the man I wanted, so I didn't look around to see whether they was advertising the shortest man in the natural world. Heal. I've always liked average-sized men myself, though. Heal. The average-sized man is my ideal of a man. Not the tallest man in the natural world nor the shortest man in the natural world. Heal. He sho look like he can heal somebody, though, don't he? But her, I don't think she could heal a flea.

Nicholas comes down into the church basement, wearing khaki trousers and a white shirt open at the collar, and strides toward me, then we goes up to the front. I'm watching the other man while Nicholas is talking. Nicholas must notice him too, though he pretend he don't know him either. I've already heard and reheard Nicholas tale, so I don't listen to all of it, only the healing part. . . . I stabbed her, but the knife bent. Wouldn't go all the way in. Went in just enough to do some tiny damage but not what it coulda done. Then it bent. And I ain't talking about no rubber knife neither. I'm talking about a knife knife. Went in just enough to do some tiny damage but not what it coulda done. Then it bent. And you know I'm a powerful man.

Hush now, a woman shouts. Hush, hush now.

Can't explain it, Nicholas says. Some force beyond me. At first I thought it had struck a bone, that knife, and I'm a powerful man, and the bone bent it, that knife, and I'm a powerful man, y'all know I'm a powerful man, I know y'all know I'm a powerful man, but the anatomy ain't where a bone would be. She were as startled as I was, our healing woman. Hush. Hush now. The knife bent. And I'm a powerful man. Y'all know I'm a powerful man. A powerful man amongst powerful men. Hush. Then the knife just fell out. She put her hand to her chest, to the wound on her chest, took her hand away and the blood were gone. Right then and there it mended. I ain't seen it mend, I ain't witnessed it to mend, but I seen it mended. The first healing. I witnessed that first healing, but I can't explain it. She can't explain it neither. The healing woman can't explain it either. You ask her to explain how she heal that first healing, and she can't explain it. The healing woman can't explain it neither. Can't nobody explain it. I ain't met nobody that can explain that first healing. There's folks believe themselves to explain that first healing, even scientifically minded people, but they ain't explained that first healing to my satisfaction. Even the scientifically minded people ain't explained that first healing to my satisfaction. They even wrote about her healing powers in one of them scientifically minded magazines, but that didn't explain it to my satisfaction. They even wrote about her healing powers in one of them tabloid-type magazines, but that didn't explain it to my satisfaction. They even wrote about her healing powers in one of them slick magazines over there in Germany, translated it into English and resold it to one of these slick American magazines, but even that transcontinental explanation didn't explain it to my satisfaction. Maybe there's folks that can explain that first healing, maybe even ordinary folks that can explain that first healing and even explain that first healing to my satisfaction, maybe other healers themselves can explain that first healing, maybe other healing women themselves, or even other healing men, can explain that first healing, and even explain that first healing to my satisfaction, but I ain't met 'em. I ain't met anyone, scientifically minded, ordinary, or healers theyselves who can explain that first healing. It just healed. Y'all think only true believers try to explain that first healing? Ain't just true believers that tries to explain that first healing. Cynics and skeptics try to explain that first healing, and even they don't explain it to my satisfaction. That first healing. That first healing just healed. I wouldn'ta believed her healing powers myself if I ain't witnessed them. If somebody told me this a healing woman and I ain't witnessed her healings myself, I probably wouldn't believe 'em. I am not a gullible man. Nicholas J. Love ain't a gullible man. I am not a gullible man. I wouldn'ta believed her healing powers myself if I ain't witnessed them. And I'm the one witnessed the first healing. I told y'all I witnessed that first healing. Ain't I told y'all I witnessed that first healing? She were as surprised as I was, though. I seen that first healing, and that's why I'm here to testify. You can't falsify a healing like that. You can't falsify a true healing like that. I'm not the truest of the true believers, but I'm the one witnessed the first healing. I'm the one witnessed that true first healing. I'm the one witnessed that first true healing. You can't explain a healing like that, it's just pure wonder. A healing like that is just pure wonder.

Some look at me in pure wonder, others are looking at Nicholas in pure wonder, others are looking like they still gotta see to believe. Even if Nicholas a believable-sounding man, even if he a powerfully believable-sounding man. But a lot of them's looking at us like it one of them confabulatory tales of them UFOs, like it one of them confabulatory UFO tales that Nicholas telling. Like he telling them how he got hisself abducted in one of them confabulatory UFOs. And how one of them little confabulatory aliens that abducted him had them special and purely wonderful and powerful healing powers. You know they ain't gonna believe no tale like that. You know, they's too intelligent to believe a tale like that. And ain't none of them confabulatory aliens abducted them. If ain't none of them confabulatory little aliens abducted them, then there ain't no UFO and there ain't no confabulatory little aliens. But some others are in their own private world, looking like they themselves been abducted in one of them confabulatory UFOs, and would like to tell the people about them confabulatory little aliens themselves. Maybe some of them have heard the tale before about that first healing, or read about it in one of them tabloid-type magazines, but they've still got to see a healing for themselves. Nicholas is on a roll. He's on a roll. . . . And him? Perhaps he's merely looking like a man who knows the truth of it.

I thought she were a witch or something at first, says Nicholas. Even she didn't know what she were. And still she don't know. When she was healing some people up in the Dakotas, a few people started calling her the Healing Woman Healed Herself First. Maybe that's who she is. The Healing Woman Healed Herself First. And then when she's healing people in Memphis they just started calling her the Healing Woman. Maybe that's who she is. Well, I'm here to testify that she healed herself first. I'm here to testify that she healed herself first. I'm here to testify that this healing woman healed herself first. And now she trying to heal everybody that want to be healed. At least everybody that want her to heal them. I'm her witness. And that the truth. And I wouldn't trade truth like that for gold.

There's rumbles and hums and rustles, then Hush now!

Nicholas turns to me and smiles. He add that new thing about me "trying to heal everybody that want to be healed." And that new thing about "At least everybody that want her to heal them." He ain't had that in his witnessing before. Least he ain't said I'm trying to heal everybody. I come forward and take his hand again. I'm considered a tall woman, but beside Nicholas I just look average height. Yes! someone shout. Lord, today! exclaim another. A unbeliever mumbles, pirates, bandits, confidence people. A few snicker at a tale like that. Another starts singing.

I didn't even ask for the spirit gift, I begin softly. I weren't even prepared for the spirit gift. But it came, it came. I modulate my volume so's my voice grow gradually loud. It came. The Lord good. Yes. What can you do but claim what the Lord give. Hush. It's ain't me. It God who make you whole. A lot of y'all looking at me and just seeing just a ordinary woman, and asking y'allself how come a ordinary woman like me to be given a gift of the spirit, how come a ordinary woman like me to be given a spirit gift? Y'all thinks that just spirit gifts supposed to be given to extraordinary people, to extraordinary men and women, the kings and queens of the world, the princes and princesses. But that the point of them spirit gifts, the point of them spirit gifts, is that I am just a ordinary woman. I am just a ordinary woman, that is the point of the healing. The spirit gift extraordinary, but as for me, I'm just a ordinary woman. Come up. It God who make you whole. Praise the Lord, and accept his restoration.

And then I start calling names, like I've always known them:

Mr. Buster Gentry, Mizz Faustina Brixton, Mizz Gretel Loppie, Mizz Sheba Boss, Mr. Pete Menton, Mr. Bunyan Macheath, Mr. J. J. Ray, Mizz Sal Battle. . . . Come up and be healed.

Hush.

I lay my hands on a young woman suffering from a skin rash and immediately her skin become smooth and clear as a baby's. A elderly woman suffers from a bone ailment that make her lower back painful. I lay my hands on and she straightens, healthy, then bends forward and touches her toes. A baby's got chronic earache; I kiss both its little ears and they's made whole again. Gurgling and laughing, he don't wanna let go of my fingers. Then they's a young man who I'm unable to heal in public, 'cause it necrospermia he's suffering from, so before he comes forward I ask Nicholas to go inform him that we'll come privately to his home and heal him, and then he can expect that wife of his to have babies the very next year. Another woman's got psychic symptoms, restlessness, delirium, hallucinations, delusions: I hold her hands, stroke her forehead and kiss her.

I'm Mizz Sal Battle, she says. How you know my name? They calls me Big Sal. You said my name, so I figure you's a true healer. I got to believe in somebody know my true name. I figure anybody know my true name must be a true healer. Course you could just be going around asking folkses' true name, and just be a faker. But most folkses calls me Big Sal, they don't call me Mizz Sal Battle, and most don't even know my true name is Sal Battle, so if you'da asked them my true name, they'da told you Big Sal, so I figure if you says my true name, you's a true healer. Then, Hush, she whispers her joy. Hush. Hush. Hush. Hush.

And then there's that smallish woman from the bus. I ain't think she believed, but she come up. She ain't got no visible ailment either, but she got what them psychiatrists refer to as "incipient insanity."

I touch her forehead and she cure.

It's after midnight before the session over. After the healings, we give thanks, then gather around the table to feast.

A long time, he whispers.

Yeah, I say, turning.

But I know I ain't the woman he met up at Saratoga. I'm the one who touched the horse's phalanges and healed them. I'm the one who touched my own wound. I'm the one who healed my own self first.

He piles a plate high with fried chicken and potato salad and hands it to me.

Come out to the farm, he whispers, his hand on my shoulder. I haven't seen you in a long time, N'Orleans. You look regencrated. And Nicholas is beaming. Is it you and him?

But I shake my head. And N'Orleans, that ain't my true name, that just his sometimes name for me.

Then he whispers, He's free.

Who's free? Nicholas?

They freed Nicodemus.

Who's Nicodemus? Nicodemus? Oh, yeah, yeah. Nicodemus. That's good.

He stands watching me a moment, thinking maybe I'll ask him some more about Nicodemus, or how they freed him, or maybe—since he helped free Nicodemus? or since it ain't Nicholas and me?—agree to come back with him to his farm, then disappears up the basement stairs. I feel like I'm standing in the tropics. I wipe sweat from my forehead with the napkin. A tiny wind whips up.

I ain't breathed so freely in years, says Josephine, coming to me, touching her sinuses, marveling. He said we couldn't trade this for gold, and we ain't paid one cent over. Why, you must be a true healer, 'cause them other people they be demanding gold for this. Martha said we paid you little something, and for the transportation for you to come here, but ain't the gold that this is worth. Course somebody said you usedta manage one of them rock stars, and they is monied people, so you probably saved up a lot of money, mucho dinero, as the people say, and don't need to be greedy. Course monied people always wants mo' money. You don't look like you's monied to me, though. I don't know how you does it, though, being the ordinary woman that you says you is. How do you do it?

The Lord do it, corrects Zulinda, who's standing near the punch bowl, her phobia gone. It ain't no mystery. The Lord do it. It ain't no mystery at all. And if she were to demand gold for this, she might not keep them healing powers. That's probably the only reason she ain't demanded gold for this, so's she can keep these healing powers. I still don't think no gifts of the spirit to be given to ordinary womens, though.

Lord a mystery, says Josephine. His wonders do perform, and like Mr. Nicholas said we ain't paid one cent over.

When he say that? Where that Mr. Nicholas?

He just come to witness. He never stay to socialize. He one of them strange men.

That's 'cause he's amongst strangers.

I bite into a piece of fried chicken and smile at them both.

Mizz Battle think she dreaming. Look at Big Sal, she think she dreaming, and this ordinary woman, she got herself a mighty appetite to be so holy, ain't she? A mighty devilish appetite to be holy. They say you's supposed to hunger and thirst after righteousness.

Well, she the boss, if you ast me. Eat what she want. Us supposed to invite her here to heal us and then let her go hungry? And ain't asking no donations neither. Do that sound like a faker? Ain't even charged the people she done healed. She told them they could give Martha a little something for her strawberry pies. Something about Martha Gaines' strawberry pies. Martha say she likes making them Kewpie dolls. Heard her telling her she could start selling them strawberry pies they's so good. Ain't a healer supposed to be worth her hire? That make me a true believer even more than all this healing, though. Eat what she want is what I say. Ain't a healer supposed to be worth her hire? The gold that this is worth.

And that youngish woman from the bus, looking more familiar now. The one in the Gypsy earrings, riding that bicycle. I know her name now, but not who she is. Wondering how I knew what she had, didn't know what she had her ownself.

I thought I knew you, she's saying.

Know me? I don't say nothing, 'cause a lot of times when I'm healing, a lot of people claims they know me when they don't. Some of them knows me from the brochures, others from them clippings, but none of them don't know me. She do look kinda familiar, though.

I met you once in a beauty parlor up in Louisville. That's before you became a faith healer. I was reading in your brochure about you being raised in Louisville and originally being a beautician, and that's where I'm from, and then I realized that I know you. I was on my way up North to go to school, I mean when I first met you. I don't know if you remember me. It was my first time in a beauty parlor. It was my first time having my hair professionally straightened. Cornella and Jaboti's Beauty Shop.

Oh, yes. You that little girl. You don't look no older than you looked then, 'cept your hair's a little shorter. It's all those chemicals. Let me jot something down for you that you might start using, that is if you wanna keep straightening your hair. It ain't got no chemicals at all in it, no synthetic chemicals, just natural ones, made by a company in Brazil, and so harmless you can eat it, but it gets your hair just as straight. That is, if you want it straight.

Yeah, I heard them talking about that, that they was going to order something like that.

That's all they use in their beauty shop now, they don't use them synthetic chemicals.

I take out my notebook and jot the name of the product down for her and where it can be ordered. She can either order it from Cornella and Jaboti's Beauty Shop or from a wholesaler in Brazil.

I was looking at you and thought I knew you, I say. I was thinking that you look familiar.

I thought I knew you too, she's saying again, and then she cut herself a piece of that strawberry pie. She don't eat it, though, she just stand holding that pie and talking to me. I'm teaching school around here now, she say. I'm a schoolteacher. Harriet Tubman Junior High School, that's a new multicultural junior high school. I teach General Science but we emphasize multicultural contributions to science, as well as the sciences of different peoples of color. We even have a chart of the stars that has the different African names for the stars. A lot of people they don't know that Africans even named the stars, that different peoples, different so-called native peoples, have their own names for the stars, and have star charts just as accurate as the Chinese star charts, which are more ancient than the European star charts or even the Arabic ones or the star charts of the New World civilizations. Everybody's got their own cosmology. Everybody's got their own description of the universe. I helped them to form that school, though. Some people thought it should be a school just for African-American girls, "for colored girls only," you know, but I thought it should be a school for everybody and that we should teach about everybody, because to be a true citizen of the world, you've got to know about everybody. Of course, we've had people to be interested in the concept of Harriet Tubman Junior High but then to take their children out of that school, even though they're learning, and learning more in that school than some of the other schools, even some of the private schools, 'cause they just want them to know about themselves, you know, and telling us we're teaching too much about the minorities and women. But they just want you to learn about themselves. You might be teaching ninety-five percent about them anyway and they want that other five percent too. My name's Sally Canada. We're the other Canadas. I always tell people we're the other Canadas, you know, 'cause when people hear, especially people around here, 'cause you know she usedta work at one of the tobacco factories around here, the notorious Eva Canada, somebody said she tried to organize the first union in one of them tobacco factories around here, though that ain't the Eva Canada that everybody know about, but everybody that usedta work with her there likes to claim they know her, or claim they don't know her, but when they hear my name is Canada they think I'm kin to that other Canada, that notorious Eva Canada, you know, or they think that we're all criminally insane. I was a little girl when I first heard about that Eva Canada, when I first saw a picture of her in one of those *Police Gazette*–type magazines, and so a lot of the other little kids would tease me about that other Canada, and sometimes little boys would even be afraid of me on account of that other Canada, on account of what she done to that man, so I either don't tell people my name or I always make sure that people know that we're the other Canadas, that we're the other Canadas. Somebody say she out of prison now and a re-cluse somewhere. Maybe changed her name. You know when I told y'all that I didn't know I was supposed to make a appointment, I knew I was supposed to make a appointment, I mean for the beauty shop, when I come into y'all's beauty shop without a appointment, but I didn't want to tell y'all my name. I guess I coulda lied and give y'all a different name, like McCambridge or something—I've even heard that Eva herself is out of prison now and has renamed herself McCambridge, after that old movie star and uses that name—but I don't like to lie about my name. I didn't want y'all to hear my name Canada, even Sally Canada, and think I'm one of the other Canadas. That's one of those Canadas, I usedta hear people say. That's one of the reasons I wanted to go to school up there up North, up in Vermont, 'cause I didn't think Eva Canada's name as notorious up North, I mean in the Northeast. That's why when I got that scholarship to Bennington I went, because I was sure that no-body at Bennington woulda heard about Eva Canada. I was running from being identified with that other Canada. Even the Canadas that are the same Canadas don't want to admit it. I know Lulabelle Canada even changed her name and moved to Atlantic City. Or the Canadas that keeps their names they'll lie to you and tell you that they're the true other Canadas, when we're the true other Canadas. And there's another group of Canadas, too, that ain't any kin to Eva, and they claims they's the true other Canadas, and we just fictionalize ourselves pretending to be the true other Canadas. And there's even them that say that even Eva herself ain't a true Canada. Did I tell you I heard her name's McCambridge now? I usually don't talk this much, though, you know, even when I'm teaching, but you know, after you healed me, I feel so free. Anyway, people around here call me Little Sal on account of Big Sal, you know, to distinguish me from Big Sal. Of course, my students call me Mizz Canada. I know a lot of people around here because I teach their children. You know, I usually don't believe in faith healing myself. I'm usually kinda skeptical, being a science teacher, even though a lot of the early science, a lot of the alchemy is kinda mystical, but when I saw you heal Big Sal, who everybody knows is crazy, I thought you might be able to heal me. What craziness I have I've been trying to keep it to myself, to keep it a secret you know, to camouflage it. But when I saw you heal Big Sal, that's when I decided to come up and be healed.

She start to say something else, something about her healing, or Big Sal's healing, or some of them other healings, but then Martha join us near the banquet table. You must be tired, say Martha.

I am a bit.

Must tire you out so them healings, says Martha. Although she's made all that strawberry pie and all them sweet cakes, she's only got a little corn pudding on her plate. I healed her colitis years ago, but she still just nibbles.

I don't feel it while I'm healing. While I'm healing I feel energized. It's just afterwards that I do get sort of tired out.

While *He's* healing, corrects Zulinda.

Yeah, that's what I meant.

Martha stands in front of me like a shield, then leads me up them basement stairs. The teacher-woman looks like she wants to follow us, but she stays eating her strawberry pie. When I glance back, she's talking to Big Sal. Sane women again.

Then you shouldn't be tired, you, says Zulinda, from behind.

CHAPTER THREE

How did I first meet him? Not Nicholas, but the other one? The one come telling me Nicodemus free. Well, I'd come to the racetrack five o'clock in the morning 'cause they say you gotta come that early to watch them walk the horses and then most people have breakfast at the track restaurant. You can have breakfast at the outdoor part of the restaurant under one of them white and latticed canopies. The air smelled like lavender and fresh horse manure. Already a high-bred lady was sitting at one of them tiny breakfast tables. You know, one of them real wealthy-looking women, probably a racehorse owner. Somebody told me the way that you can tell wealthy people is they look well taken care of. Somebody told me that or I read it somewhere in a book. Mighta been a jockey's wife, that woman look well taken care of, 'cause a lot of them jockey's wives, especially them wives of them winning jockeys, them jockeys that's got they business managers and they talent agents just like they's movie stars or rock stars, them winning jockeys, looks well taken care of, but she look like a racehorse owner her own self, or the wife of a racehorse owner. 'Cause she look more well taken care of than even a winning jockey's wife. One of them wealthy husbands who bought her her own racehorse. I read about one of them wealthy husbands, maybe a racehorse owner himself, who bought his wife her own racehorse. She probably have all the diamonds and luxuries, and maybe even her own plantation-mansion 'cause she look like a woman of the South, or a southern belle wannabe, you know there's a lot of them northern womens that's got they ideas of the South before the Civil War from them romantic movies and storybooks and likes to vacation on them southern plantations, the ones that they convert into inns—I even heard of one woman that always insists on staying in the old slave quarters that they've converted into a guest house. Well, this southern belle wannabe, she got all the diamonds and luxuries and her own plantation-mansion and renovated slave quarters, but she still bored, so he buy her her own racehorse. She wearing a cucumber green dress and one of those green cloche. The dress look like it made out of layers of mosquito curtain. She just nibbling coffee cake and looking disinterested in them parade of thoroughbreds. Maybe that's how you can tell them wealthy people too.

But me and him was standing at the fence together. I wasn't sure what his nationality. He was wearing a business suit and I suppose he could be African American like me, but he had this other air about him, like a foreigner. You know, you seen them types of African Americans that got a kind of foreignness about them, some because they's spent years abroad amongst foreign peoples, like them diplomats and students and Army brats, others just has a natural foreignness, and people ask them what they are, 'cause you can't tell whether they's African Americans or one of them colored foreigners, and's always surprised when they say they's African Americans. And you know a lot of them colored-looking foreigners they don't want you to think they's African American, so I didn't know whether to ask him, Are you African American? 'cause he might be one of them colored foreigners that don't want you to think they's African American. Made me think of that Aladdin and his magical lamp. But he more dark-complexioned than that Aladdin, at least the Aladdin in the movies and the cartoons. I met me one of them Portuguese-type Africans once, though, that kinda remind me of him. One of them little Portuguese islands off the coast of Africa, where they's colored people, but they ain't as colored as the true Africans. What the name of that little island? I think it got a Portuguese-type name. Anyway, we was watching them thoroughbreds, and I don't want to ask, Are you African American? 'cause he might be one of them colored-looking foreigners. A handsome brown thoroughbred were led past. That's a fine horse, he commented. And there's some kinda accent. It ain't no

Portuguese accent, though, or none of them other romance languages. Ain't from Brazil or none of them Latin American countries. And that accent don't sound Mediterranean.

Yeah, I agreed, without turning, 'cause I didn't want him to think I was spying on him. He's a real challenger.

He looked at me when I spoke, though, on account of my own accent. People call it a Geechee accent. Don't sound like a accent to me, but other people call it a Geechee accent. Then some people tell me I got a blend of different types of accents.

Are you from here in Saratoga? he asked.

Naw, just visiting, and betting on the horses, you know.

We didn't say no more, just watched those horses. When they finished the parade, he asked me if I'd like to have breakfast with him. He himself he got some kinda foreign accent, like I said. It sounded kinda American and kinda foreign at the same time, though. Sound almost Eastern European, and I don't think they's many colored people in that Eastern Europe. But I know he ain't no Russian or nothing. Then his accent kinda remind me of that famous actor supposed to be from Austria. Maybe there's colored people in that Austria. Or maybe he one of them Dutch. I ain't as countrified as some Americans who think that the only colored people is in America, or that the only Africans is in Africa.

Where you from? I asked, when we'd found a table.

Germany.

Say what? But you's African-looking. You a real German? I was thinking you kinda sound like that famous actor from Austria. Austria, they speak German, don't they? Austria, ain't that the same as Germany? I mean, I know the only colored people ain't in America, I mean, I've seen Africans in Germany, but not any German Africans, I mean not any African Germans.

He just smiled and arched an eyebrow. Believe it or not, there are real Germans from Germany who look like me, he said. Real Germans in Germany who look like just about everybody in the world, like you Americans. Every time I meet an American, though, I have to explain who I am. Most think I'm African. Or from one of the former Dutch colonies. We've been in Germany for many generations, though, just like you Africans here in America. I'm an African German or a German African, to use your American way of defining who we are.

You speak good English, except there's a little accent.

Every American says that too. Of course, I speak good English. It's only you Americans who don't want to learn anybody's language but your own. You celebrate that in yourselves, but to us Europeans it's a flaw in the American character, one of the many flaws in the American character. You Americans are so good at pointing out the flaws in other "national character" but the flaws in your own "national character" you celebrate as virtues.

I glance at the high-bred woman, who bites into a rice cake, then holds it up like it's a tired moon. She looks toward us with curiosity, or rather at the African German with curiosity, then resumes her air of disinterest. It's a open-air restaurant, and we're sitting near a white railing. The railing's white to match the canopy. He's saying something about American culture. That American culture itself is a flaw, and even our own fascist tendencies, we celebrate as Americanism.

I'm real German, he says. But everyone asks that. Every American. I own a little farm in Kentucky now, though.

So how'd you get from Germany to Kentucky?

I kept being mistaken for an immigrant in my own country, you know, although we've been in Germany many generations, since the seventeenth century. Hottentot slaves, Ethiopian traders, you know. But to be mistaken for an immigrant in your own country? I came to your country once and we traveled through this area, I mean Kentucky, some German friends and I, we went to Keeneland and visited some of the horse farms, and I liked the country. So after being mistaken for an immigrant in my own country, I decided to come to a country where I really am an immigrant.

I was in New Mexico once and they mistook me for a immigrant, I mean a illegal immigrant. To tell the truth, I was kinda flattered myself. Course I had my passport to prove who I am. But if they'da tried to ship me back to Mexico I don't think I'da been that flattered. And I don't look like no Mexican to me, but there's Mexicans that look like me. I was in this little cantina, though, and they were raided by some immigration police, checking everybody's papers, you know. I know you need your passport when you're abroad, but that's the first time I had to use my passport in my own country. But they say whenever you're in those little border towns you gotta have your passport, like you's in a foreign country, especially if you don't look like their American idea.

During the war, the Second World War, being non-Aryans, we left Germany and settled in Zurich, in Switzerland. After the war, we returned to Berlin. I was born after the war and don't know all of that history, but I know we were exiles. But now we're treated like auslanders again, like foreigners, so that's why I decided to come to America. To be treated like a foreigner, I might as well be in a country where I am a true foreigner, where I am a true auslander. I spent some time in Alexandria, in Egypt. I thought I might settle there. But even there, everyone's dream is America, you know. The official governments won't tell you that. The ordinary people all over the world, they will tell you that their dream is America. Their politicians and intellectuals will complain about America, but the ordinary people themselves will tell you that America is their dream. They see the glamorous American movie stars, the glamorous American movies, and they think that's America. When I told some of my friends in Alexandria that I was coming to America, they all said that was their dream. My name is Josef Ehelich von Fremd.

That sounds like a German name. Alexandria, ain't that in Morocco? The only thing I know about Morocco is it's supposed to be a land without rivers. I remember that because that was one of our geography questions in high school. I don't know if it said Morocco's the only land without rivers, but Morocco's supposed to be a land without any rivers in it.

Alexandria's Egypt. Didn't I say Egypt? May I ask your name?

Harlan. Harlan Eagleton. Harlan Jane Eagleton. I usedta think I'd like to call myself just Jane, you know. But now I like Harlan.

Harlan? There's a Harlan, Kentucky. Are you from Harlan, Kentucky?

Naw, I was born in Louisiana, in New Orleans. My grandmother's from Louisville, Kentucky, though, and that's where I grew up. I don't know why they named me Harlan, though. Harlem, maybe. But Harlan. I guess Harlan Jane sounds better than Harlem Jane. You speak English very well. But I said that. And you said that was a flaw of the American character. One of the many flaws of the American character. But that ain't no different from most people, is it? Seem like most people turn they own flaws of character into virtues. They see other people's flaws, but they own flaws, they turn into virtues.

I grew up speaking English as well as German, you know. Most Europeans speak several languages. I speak English, French, German, Dutch, a little Portuguese. It's only you Americans who're stingy about language, who believe that your own language is the universal language. I guess it is the universal language. You've made it the universal language. You've made it so your language is identified with modernity, with internationalism. I even know some Americans, though, who've lived in Berlin for years, and in other European cities, and insist on speaking only English. Who insist on English only even when they're in other people's country. Most of you Americans. There are exceptions, of course. I have some American friends whose German is impeccable. Even some African-American friends who speak impeccable German.

I drink my coffee, nibble my coffee cake, and watch the high-bred woman. Josef's staring at me, though, then he's eating his cheese omelet.

Are you married? I ask. Your wife immigrate with you?

Yes, I've a wife, but she hasn't come over to the States yet. She's in Berlin. I don't know when she'll come. Right now, I've received threats, you see, and I'm trying to find out how seriously I should take them.

Threats? What kinda threats?

You know what kind of threats.

I'm wondering how seriously I should take him. All that business about being a Hottentot German or a German Hottentot. Like I said, I ain't so countrified that I don't know they's got Africans over there in Europe, even Hottentots, 'cause I've seen them on television, but maybe he's just jiving me, I'm thinking. But he's telling me again how he re-

ceived threats as soon as he bought him some of that prime land for his
thoroughbreds. They expected him to be one of them Aryan Germans,
and then when he appeared, buying up that prime land, that I guess
only Aryan Americans supposed to buy, he started receiving threats.
After he'd bought the land for his thoroughbreds, he went to some of
the local auctions, but some sort of consortium kept outbidding him,
even though his bidding prices were pretty high, but his bidding prices
weren't a match for a consortium, which he was certain had been formed
merely to outbid himself—it wasn't conceit—so he decided he'd come
to Saratoga, to the Fasig-Tipton sales.

When people think I'm German, an Aryan German, they don't have
a problem. . . . Of course Josef Ehelich von Fremd sounds like an Aryan
German, or what they believe to be a true German. I don't know our
original Hottentot name because the original Hottentots changed their
name to a pure German name or had their names changed to a pure German name, and there's nothing to distinguish my accent from that of
any other German, but then they discover I'm an African German and
not an Aryan. You know, in Germany I'm in arbitrage, but when I came
to America and saw your thoroughbreds. . . . I remember once when I
was in the city, at one of your restaurants, and I mentioned being German, the waiter thought I was "jiving" him, you know, as you Americans say, thought I was one of your locals only pretending to be German.
He'd probably seen one of those American movies, I suppose, with the
typical African-American jiver, the typical African-American Confidence Man, and he was certain I was playing some confidence game. My
credit cards were suspect, and then he got the bright idea, some friend of
his who spoke German said something to me. High school German, you
know. But my real German, which he didn't understand at all, still convinced him that I was some local pretender. He didn't understand my
real German, it didn't sound like the elementary German he'd learned in
high school German, so he was convinced it wasn't real German. Do you
think I'm a pretender?

No. I know they got splivs in Europe. I know they got splivs in Paris.
If they got splivs in Paris, I figure they must have them in Berlin.

But that's not telling me who you think I am.

I don't know who you are, but I know they got splivs in Europe, 'cause I seen them on television. Even got splivs in Russia. I know some of them Afro-Communists in the 1930s went over there to Russia and some of them stayed over there, and I know them Russians they've always had they own history with Africa, even before the 1930s. The most famous Russian writer he got African in him, you know, though they don't think of him as African they think of him as Russian, 'cause I remember this Russian writer, this Russian poet was being interviewed on television, and this interviewer points out that this famous Russian writer he's talking about is part African, and he kinda looks embarrassed, you know, because you know he's not thinking of him as part African, but Russian, not Russian African or African Russian 'cause he's supposed to be Russia's greatest writer sorta like the Russian Shakespeare, you know, and maybe also because he knows of the prejudice about Africans in America, the interviewer's American, you know, they had that on television, and I know you telling the truth about them Germans thinking you a immigrant, 'cause I read about them, and I even heard a African American over there in Germany talking about leaving Berlin on account of being mistaken for a immigrant of color himself and he ain't even a true German like you and talking about all them neo-Nazis over there in Germany, them neo-Fascists in Berlin, and them talking about Germany for the Germans, and say that even in Sweden they's got 'em, them neo-Fascists, and Sweden supposed to be the land of racial tolerance. So I know you telling the truth about them neo-Fascists over there in Europe, but it wouldn't be honest of me to say I know you telling the truth about who you yourself are, 'cause I don't know you. Deutschland für Deutschländer—one of them neo-Fascists on television were holding up a sign that said that.

Deutschland für Deutschländer, he corrects my pronunciation, though it sound like the same German to me.

I know all over Europe it's supposed to be the same thing. France for the French. England for the Englishmen. All them former colonialists and colonizers wants they own land for theyselves. Why I heard somebody say that if all them Englishmen and French and Germans in other people's country had to return to England or France or Germany, they wouldn't have enough England or France or Germany even for theyselves, and they would start recolonizing again. Of course the colored peoples of the world would say they wouldn't let them Europeans recolonize them again, but now they's recolonizing each other, them that ain't economically recolonized. So you send for your wife when you feel things is safe?

He nods, then he explains how he don't want any dirty tricks with his wife around, then he's explaining again why he's at Saratoga, to buy him some new bloodstock.

Maybe you should just send for her in spite of the dirty tricks, I say. She German like you? I mean is she the same kind of German as you? Is she a Hottentot German?

Not Hottentot. She's Afro-German, actually African American and German. She's fairer than I am and so is often mistaken for a true German. No one mistakes her for an immigrant. Sometimes they think she's Jewish or Italian. Her maiden name is Wandervogel, her African-American father, a jazz musician, changed his name to a German name when he settled in Berlin after the war, but she's not at all a migratory woman herself. But a man knows how to handle dirty tricks better than a woman.

It depends on what kind of dirty tricks. And what kinda woman.

He says something to me in that German, but I don't know that German, except Deutschland für Deutschländer, so I can't tell you what he say. But what he say sound kinda like the universal language to me.

CHAPTER FOUR

And you, are you married? he asks, stroking my jaw. I half-frown. You know, thinking that shoulda been his first question, whether I'm married or not. I'm wearing a wedding ring, but there's women who wears wedding rings that ain't married, just so's they don't have to deal with every joker. Least if you's a woman from the *Looking for Mr. Goodbar* generation. There's jokers that don't mind a woman being married, but at least the woman's got a wedding ring for a excuse. He ain't wearing no wedding ring hisself, but that's my first question: Are you married? Course a lot of you's probably thinking that this is the romance of a roguish woman on account of my being with him and he say he's married. Maybe this is the romance of a roguish woman, or maybe it's just him talking about protecting her from dangers, but me I'm supposed to be the other type of woman. She supposed to be the mystical type of woman and I'm supposed to be the common woman.

We're in the bedroom of his hotel suite, the furniture all gold and beige. One of them real expensive–type hotel suites, you know the kind you see in the movies, the kind I ain't seen except in the movies. I seen a hotel suite like that in one of them movies where the people win the lottery and then they go stay in this real expensive–type hotel. I think that Nicholas Cage in that movie. He play the role of the good man in that movie, and there's a good woman, and then there's the female rogue. Me I think it be more interesting if the woman play the female rogue play the good woman, and the woman play the good woman play the rogue. Course I guess them moviemakers got they own stereotypes of good womanhood. Ain't exactly the Plaza, though, but it's one of them expensive-type hotels. Gilded mirrors and that gilded-type furniture. Might not be real gold. Might be fool's gold. I don't think even them most expensive hotels got real gold. They's probably all got fool's gold. But that's the America a lot of foreigners see in the movies, and a lot of them think that's the true America. They think that's everybody's America. Or even if they know it ain't everybody's America, they think they come to America and it be their America. Or they read about people like Josef, who maybe the exception that prove the rule.

No, I ain't married now, I say.

Even got a tray with all kindsa fruits on it. Even kiwi and them Caribbean-type fruits. I don't know the names of all them Caribbean-type fruits. I'm eating one of them kiwi. You usedta think of them kiwi as exotic-type fruits, but now a lot of people think of them as ordinary fruits. In the tiny refrigerator there's all kindsa drinks—wines and beers and liquors.

What happened? he asks, lifting up a banana and then one of them Caribbean fruits.

Jealousy. You know.

Yours or his?

I rear my head back and try to whinny, like one of his prime stallions. I wipe kiwi juice from my chin. N'Orleans, he whisper, taking a bite from my kiwi. He eat that kiwi, though, like he still think it a exotic-type fruit. I wonder if he think of American women as exotic, even African women in America? He don't call me Harlan or Harlan Jane. He say N'Orleans like he think N'Orleans more my true name than Harlan or Harlan Jane. He pull my hair back from my forehead and kiss me. I weren't wearing braids then, just straightened hair, though I was using that special cream from Brazil that didn't have all them harsh chemicals in it, and made your hair seem naturally straight. You're a charmer. And say something else in German. Must be saying You're a charmer, again, but saying it in German. I don't know the German word for charmer, though. Then he say the German word for pretty. I know that word 'cause I heard it once in a German movie. *Schönheit.* Or something like that. Or maybe that *Schönheit* stand for Beauty Itself and not just being beautiful. Then he say something to me in French, and that sound like a more universal language than that German. Least that French sound like the universal language of love. Course if you's Algerian during that war, or a Algerian in France after the war, you wouldn't think of that French as a lover's language. I met me one of them Algerians telling me about them French. Some of them languages might sound like a lover's language, but they ain't a lover's language to everybody.

When I stand in front of his mirror, arranging my hair, he say, Stay longer. You're quite beautiful, you know. And then he say that word *Schönheit*, which mean Beauty Itself. I know I ain't so beautiful to be Beauty Itself. But I know how men is. You know, when they's speaking lover's language.

No, I got to go bet on my horses.

Are you ever lucky?

Always.

Why don't you come home with me? My farm's just outside Lexington. I've got some of the finest thoroughbreds in the state. I'd wanted to buy a larger farm, but they didn't want to sell so much prime land to a "foreigner."

What about the dangers?

You seem like you're the kind of woman who can handle it.

Well, I ain't.

I bet you are.

You don't know what kinda woman I am, I start to say, but I just look at him. Men is always like that with me. I ain't met a man that ain't like that with me. A few might tell me I'm beautiful, might even say I'm Beauty Itself, which I know I ain't, others might point out my flaws, but they's all sure they know what kinda woman I am. Now his wife, he ain't sent for her, 'cause of them dirty tricks. Probably one of them type of women he don't even wanna get her panties dirty. But me I'm supposed to be the sort of woman who can handle dangers? Course the neofeminists what that man call the feminazis would say that they don't want the mens to be protective towards them, or the chivalrous type. 'Cause chivalry is prefeministic or some shit. But me I be wondering how come he talking about protecting his wife from them dangers, but me I'm just supposed to be that other kinda woman. And then you be asking with Sojourner, Ain't I a woman too? Least that high ideal of a woman. That's why I've always been kinda ambivalent about that feminism. Them women that don't wanna be on no pedestal or say they don't want to be on no pedestal, 'cause seem like to me a lot of them wants to keep the perks of womanhood, is kinda different from the women that ain't never been on no pedestal. Course Sojourner ain't mean exactly that when she ask, Ain't I a woman too? I just look at him, then I laugh, like one of his stallions again.

Why don't you come with me to the track? I say. I'll pick you a winner.

I think I've already picked a winner.

The elevator doors slide open. In the lobby, a huge African American is sitting in a leather chair, watching us. Now I know he African American, though he the same complexion as Josef, kinda that gingerbread complexion, like they could both be in the Original Adventures of the Gingerbread Man, but he ain't got that air of foreignness about him. When we step out of the elevator, he get up and walk toward us. He the sort of tall man who when he stands up keeps standing until he's a height you'd hardly thought possible. He dressed in dark trousers and a beige shirt, and wearing a tie but no jacket. He as dark-skinned as Josef, like I said, but his eyes and eyebrows slant up kinda like an Asian's, at least the stereotype of them Asians, 'cause the real Asian eyes don't all slant up like that. He ain't Asian, though. He pure African American, if there such a thing as pure African American.

Harlan, I'd like you to meet Nicholas Love, he's coming with us to the racetrack, say Josef. I thought Josef a tallish man, but next to Nicholas, he look like a average-sized man. Course he look more well taken care of than Nicholas Love. But a lot of them Europeans always looks more stylish than Americans.

I say hello.

He nod.

You a German too? I ask, though I know he ain't. And I know the name Nicholas Love sho ain't no German name, 'cause them Germans got they own word for love. Course there could be Germans got English-sounding names, like they's Americans got German-sounding names and every other kind of language–sounding names. The Americans, like he said, might not want to learn other people's languages, but they's got to say other people's languages when they says they own names.

No, he say. And say it like it the only word in the English language he do know.

Don't you recognize a fellow American when you see one? ask Josef.

I smile, 'cause I know all along he a American.

Nicholas walk beside Josef, not me. Neither of them converse. Nicholas seem like he one of them quiet-type men, like I said, one of them taciturn-type men. I don't think he inarticulate, though. I just think he one of them taciturn-type men. Outside, the three of us climb into the back of a chauffeured Lincoln Town Car, Josef in the middle. The chauffeur, he a little Italian-looking man. Somebody you got to speak the Italian language to say they name. Like them Italian movie stars. When you say DeNiro or Pacino or Aiello, you gotta speak Italian to say them names. Kinda remind me of that Danny DeVito movie actor, though, 'cept it ain't Danny DeVito.

She's coming back with us to the farm, say Josef after a while.

Nicholas didn't reply. And I'm wondering who this Nicholas suppose to be. And then I'm wondering if these men thinks they's supposed to form some sort of ménage à trois with me, or some shit, 'cause you read about that ménage à trois shit in them confessional-type stories in them confessional magazines, and I'm about to explain to them that I ain't that sorta girl, that I ain't no freak, and no trollop neither, and that's when Josef explain who Nicholas.

Nicholas is my bodyguard, says Josef.

And I'm thinking that just like in the movies. Here I am thinking about the movies and about my favorite Italian movie stars, when he starts saying what sounds like a movie. I ain't never been in the company of nobody famous or rich enough for no bodyguard. He didn't guard your body this morning, I joke. I meant at the racetrack. And I ain't been trying for one of them blue joke, you know, but it come out sounding like one of them blue joke.

I mean at the racetrack, I explain. I didn't see him at the racetrack.

Yes, he was at the racetrack. He knows how to be invisible.

Now that's a virtue for a bodyguard, but I can't imagine that Nicholas Love who one of the tallest men I ever seen outside of the *National Geographic* or maybe on a basketball court no invisible man, though. I remember when I was in high school we had to read that book about the invisible man. I couldn't even imagine the invisible man himself being the invisible man, though that was the name of the book. I told the teacher that I always felt too visible myself, but someone else, one of them little shy-type girls, said she felt invisible, but it were invisibility because of her shyness not because of the ethos of race. And then after everybody laughed at the word ethos even though most people didn't know its meaning and thought it was a made-up word and thought she meant ethics then people was talking about the virtues and the vices of invisibility, and one of the boys said that the point of the book was the paradox, that the invisible man was supposed to be a paradox, 'cause he's supposed to be visible and invisible at the same time, that he the visible invisible man or the invisible visible man. Then we started talking about whether invisibility was pertinent to modern African Americans, especially in modern America where there wasn't as much overt Jim Crowism, at least there wasn't as much overt Jim Crowism as covert Jim Crowism. Still, I ain't seen him, that Nicholas Love, whether he the visible invisible man or the invisible visible man.

I wanted you to meet him, though, say Josef. So there'd be no surprises.

I glance across Josef at that Nicholas Love, who sit impassive, but it a alert impassivity. And like I said, I don't think he inarticulate, I just think he taciturn. He gotta be taciturn 'cause he don't have the disposition of a shy man. And that probably in his job description, that he supposed to be taciturn.

Will he disappear again? I ask.

When we want him to, says Josef.

Nicholas frown, though it almost imperceptible. At the entrance to the track, we wait for a man crossing the road with a wheelbarrow, then roll into the racetrack parking lot. Nicholas and the chauffeur, who a little man, kinda look like maybe he a former jockey, though he middle-aged now, get out, while Josef extend his hand to help me out. As I step out, my dress climb up to my thighs. A peculiar look from Nicholas, but one I know. I ain't no whore, I ain't no trollop, if that what he thinking. Mens they's always thinking shit like that about a woman, and especially us womens of color. Don't care what woman of color, Asian, African, Native American, African American or one of them islanders, the first thing they think is you's a trollop. Even mens of color thinks that about they own women. And it don't matter what sorta woman you are. I might be a scavenger maybe and a gambler, but I ain't no whore. I ain't no trollop. I just pull my dress down and climb out.

Nicholas comes with us as far as the betting windows. I place a bet and when I turn he ain't there. Finally, I puzzle him out, like a chameleon at the edge of the crowd. It's strange. At his height he should be the most visible person at that racetrack, but that's probably why Josef had hired him, 'cause he's a big man but know how to be invisible when he need to be. Like them detective books say about being able to hide in plain sight. That the first thing them detectives is supposed to learn is how to hide in plain sight. They's the original invisible men. The best bodyguards like the best detectives is probably them that know how to hide in plain sight.

Josef lead me to one of them boxes. I ain't never watched a race from one of them boxes, you know with the wealthy people, them VIPs. I always sat with the anybodies in the stands.

This is really something, I say.

What? ask Josef.

I explain that I ain't never been in one of the boxes with the celebrities and the rich and famous.

You mean you haven't charmed your way in?

I say nothing. I ain't like the way he ask that question, you know, but I ain't say nothing. We watch the post parade of thoroughbreds to the gate.

Who'd you bet on? he ask.

Creole Beauty. Got to bet on my own people.

I look around, looking for my own people. A high-browed man, serving what looks like mint juleps. Must think this is Churchill Downs, Kentucky, not Saratoga, New York.

He don't say who he bet on. After the race, though, I go to collect my winnings. Creole Beauty had ridden unhurried from the beginning, like the man say, while them other horse outran early, then in a flash of speed Creole Beauty edged up and ran hard in a good position near the rail; Creole Beauty! I stuff my winnings in my purse, take out my sunglasses and autograph book, then shove through the crowds to the fence to get the winning jockey's signature. Thanks. Around back, under the trees, you can observe the horses up close. A groom's leading one of them horses around a copper beechwood tree. Which is number six and which is number seven? I can't tell six from seven, a woman complain. One of them wealthy socialite-type women. Then she pencil something onto a folded newspaper, onto the racing form. Look like one of them types who addicted to gambling. One of them prime candidates for Gamblers Anonymous.

Which one did you bet on this time? Josef ask when I come from the window.

Previous Condition. Not to win, just to show.

Josef ain't say who he bet on, 'cause he ain't bet on them horses. He owns thoroughbreds, but he don't usually bet on none of them horses. He just mostly likes to watch them run. And he likes to watch them horses to test his skills at judging good horses. Seem like he'd better test his skills at judging them horses if he bet on one of them horses. And I know people that don't bet on them horses, they bet on the jockey. They don't bet on them horses, they just bet on the jockey. They don't bet on the winning horses, they bet on the winning jockeys. When my horse—runs with a steady speed, but always follows the winners—show, Josef held my waist and laugh.

Do you always win? he ask.

On horses, I answer.

I bet you always win, he say. I bet you bet to win. You should've been with me at the Fasig-Tipton sales. Help me buy a winner.

Oh, yeah, I say. I coulda done you proud.

Guarantee me a Triple Crown?

At least one. At least a contender, I say. I like a winning horse, but I also like them that's good contenders.

Now you know I ain't never been to them Fasig-Tipton sales neither. Ain't even know what the Fasig-Tipton sales was when I first come to Saratoga. Then heard people talking about the Fasig-Tipton sales, where they sell them prime thoroughbreds.

Aged and aging jockeys sit on the leather sofas and oak chairs reading newspapers and racing forms. Upstairs in my hotel room I turn on my tape of Miles' "Bitches Brew" while I pack—a few clothes, my tapes, hiking boots, raincape, one of them poncho-type raincoats, souvenirs of Tropical Park, El Camino Real, Santa Catalina, San Vicente, Mountain Valley, Fountain of Youth, San Rafael, Swift, Florida, Remington, Louisiana, San Felipe, Tampa Bay, Bay Shore, Jim Beam, Rebel, Cherry Hill Mile, Santa Anita, Gotham, Garden City, Blue Grass. Mostly jockeys' autographs and pictures. I ain't been to all of them races myself, but jockeys and friends of jockeys and just other gambling people who met me in Saratoga would send me things for my scrapbook. Then I shower and put on blue jeans and a banana yellow sweatshirt. I struggle downstairs with the heavy bag, riding the boogey, as Michael Jackson sings. In the lobby, I turn in my key, pay the exorbitant bill. It a second-rate hotel, but in August, when the horses run, even them second-rate hotels take advantage. But I got my exorbitant winnings. I head toward the door.

You try your luck at the track? one of them old jockeys ask.

I pushed it.

Are you leaving town?

Yeah. I blow him a kiss. See you next year.

You're on the ball, he say, as I go out the door. He one of the few colored jockeys. African-American jockeys. But if you think of yourself as colored, ain't you colored? And tell me about how in the old days all the colored jockeys they usedta have. They's still got colored jockeys, he say, except nowadays they imports them from Latin America, from places like Colombia and Panama, and they don't call theyselves colored. Now you know they have got as much boogie in 'em as me and you have. But he said he knew a certain colored man from East St. Louis who went around the jockey circuit pretending to be Latino, 'cause he thought that would help him get more work. He's rode in a coupla races, nothing spectacular. He wouldn't tell me the name of the jockey, though.

Josef's car is waiting. The driver puts the bag in the trunk and opens the door for me. Josef, out of his business suit, sits in the back in blue jeans just like me. Except mine is them flea market blue jeans and his is Bill Blass. Nicholas in the front with the driver. But Nicholas look like he more the owner of thoroughbreds than Josef. When I get in, the wheels start rolling.

The bed king-sized and as luxurious as the Mediterranean. Ain't that Alexandria in the Mediterranean? I enter a land of the most ancient of rivers, and then I'm now lying toward the window. The shadow of a guard stand on the railing and beyond rows of black fences where them thoroughbreds graze at night and exercise in the mornings. Beyond that them fabulous black stables, and Kentucky bluegrass everywhere. Grass that was so green, the saying is, that it look blue. But I seen greener grass in Africa and wonder what color they could call grass beyond green and blue. I heard somebody say once that you could tell people that been to Africa and people who ain't. 'Cept all the time I told folks I been to Africa, they don't believe me. They say I don't look like somebody who been to Africa. He ain't got no expensive paintings on his wall, except he got a color printout of what he say is one of them holopoems by a avant-garde artist name Eduardo Kac. I think he a Brazilian, 'cause that name got a Brazilian-type pronunciation.

The shadow of a guard parade near the window. I give a short laugh. I kiss Josef's chin. He tell me that window of his is bulletproof, then he kiss the edges of my hair. I turn back toward the window and watch the moving shadow. Josef kiss the back of my neck.

I ain't never been in the company of anyone who needed bodyguards before and no bulletproof windows, or even thought he needed them. But I been with others, ordinary people, who played games of who do you trust. Perhaps in they own way, everyone does. I even know people who put other people on probation till they prove theyself. People you's got to prove yourself to. Maybe even I'm that sorta person. Why do I keep going to Saratoga? I told Josef that I always won. But I merely win enough to keep me hooked, to keep me in the game.

He kiss the back of my neck again and I wonder what tune I'm stepping to. I remember the first time I come to Saratoga I went to this dance hall, this little restaurant that had itself a dance floor, and some man asked me to dance, and I'm dancing, and he say, What tune you stepping to? 'Cause don't seem like I'm stepping to the music. I always like that modern music, but seem like I can't dance to it. Or when I dance to one modern music, they got them a new modern music. Were they ever playing my tune? When I was married, though, sometimes, sometimes it felt like they playing ours.

I win enough to keep me hooked, I say.

What?

You asked me whether I always win and I said yes. I lied. The truth is, I only win enough to keep me hooked.

I sit with my legs folded yogi-like, you know them yogis. Through his mirror I see myself. I look like one of them bottled genie. I spring up off the bed and stand in the center of the room. I watch the shadow outside the window watching me. That paranoid fool even got the guard watching me, I'm thinking. I ain't mean to call him a paranoid fool, 'cause I'm a paranoid fool myself, and they say a lot of people in the modern day and age is more paranoid, but that guard watching me. Josef too watching me. With that cold-type curiosity. Somebody say that the curiosity of a rational man. Then he hold out his hand and I enter the river again.

Do you want to go horseback riding? he ask when he come out the bathroom. One towel draped about his shoulders and the other worn around his waist and knotted. Remember the Mae West line when she asks Cary Grant, Is that a pistol you're packing or are you glad to see me? He seem still glad to see me. Look like he saluting.

I don't ride.

Come on, I'll teach you. I'll start you with the gentlest mare.

I reach onto the night table and turn on my tape player. I still used a tape player, not a CD. Rod Stewart sing about hearts on fire. Do you think I'm sexy? I sing along with Rod.

Is that how you make your living? Josef ask matter-of-fact.

What, sex? I ask. My feathers ruffle up like a pouter bird's. I look at him sideways.

No, he explain. The horses. Gambling?

Naw, I'm a business manager.

What kind of business? he ask. Maybe now he think I'm a madam?

I manage a rock star. Joan Savage. Her name usedta be Joan Sage, then Joan Savage. You know, one of them rock stars keeps changing her name. Her real name's Joan Scribner, or some shit like that, but she say that don't sound like a rock star. Her ex-husband is name Savage, so she uses the name Savage. He ain't in show business hisself, though. Don't believe in show business. Have you heard of her? Joan Savage, I mean? She says a lot of people think she's named after Joan Crawford, 'cause she kinda reminds people of the early Joan Crawford, her type of features, except she's African American of course. But she's kinda that type, you know. Maybe she's named after Joan Crawford and don't know it. I know she likes to watch them early Joan Crawford movies, says she's one of her favorite movie stars. Says she usedta be her ideal of the female persona when she was a little girl, says she even usedta pretend to be her when she was playacting. That's what she says in her promotional literature. I think it's all hype myself, though. I'm her business manager and even I think it's all hype. She sings rock mostly. Sorta like Tina Turner, except she ain't even a legend in her own mind. Sometimes she tries to sing that new music, that rap, you know, but she's mostly rock. She ain't really a rap singer, thinks the younger women are better at singing rap, though sometimes she mixes a little rap with her rock. But she mostly likes that classical-type rock.

He say he ain't heard of her. I slip out the Stewart tape and put on Joan singing "Kiss Me Till It's Good." Or some shit like that. She'll grow on you, I say. Some of her tunes are more witty, more obscure, then she's got more commercial-sounding tunes. They liked her in Europe when we toured there. Especially in Paris. And in Japan. Joan's good, you know. She don't think she's as good as she is, though, 'cause she ain't one of the top moneymakers, you know, and that's how she judges good, or that's how she thinks other people judge good, but she's really good. Sort of a singer's singer, you know. Like an artist's artist. To tell the truth, she's better known abroad than in the States.

I turn up Joan, let her do her brand of magic. Listening to "Lola," one of her new songs, free verse lyrics, kinda combining rock and rap. I don't know if Joan the first singer to use free verse lyrics. Listening to "Lola." Lola some new singer she heard on a talent show and wants to encourage by writing a song for her. He don't think she's that good himself. I mean Josef. But then he says he's never been that much for popular American music. He doesn't like pop music. He prefers Wagner, Beethoven, Mozart, the classical-type music, mostly the Germans, some of the French composers, some of the Russians, some of the more classical-sounding jazz, not the decadent raunchy-sounding jazz. He's heard the work of a few African-American classical composers that he likes, who remind him something of the Germans, but who sometimes mix jazz with classical. And he says he heard some Native American music that he likes, that he heard on the radio, and that sounds sorta like New Wave classical music, or rather New Wave classical music sounds something like it. He says he likes that. He says if he were a music promoter, he'd promote that kind of music. "But they don't allow some of it off the reservations, though. They don't want it to be heard by anyone but themselves. What I've heard of it, though, it sounds like superior music. I don't know if it can compete commercially, but it sounds like superior music. Some of it's traditional Native American music, but you also have Native American composers writing new music based on the traditional tunes." We listen to Joan sing "Rebel Years," then a song she discovered in Port-au-Prince when we were roaming about the Iron Market.

We tour most of the year and then she goes off to her farm in Minnesota, and I go up to Saratoga and bet on my horses. I did spend one of my vacations at her farm, but it turned out to be a bitch, you know. . . .

In fact, when Joan made this rap-rock-type album, Joan was calling herself Joan "the Bitch" Savage, but we decided that that wasn't really the idea of herself that she wanted to promote.

I dig into a bowl of pomegranates on the night table, lean back on the pillow and listen to more Joan. The lampshades looks like they's stain-glassed windows. At one moment her voice is a porcupine, then it's butter.

I don't like modern music, he says. I don't like American music, and most modern music is American music. I like some of the African-American classical composers, some of the African-American avant-garde. You have a few British composers who are looking back to the pre-American pop influences of their own medieval ballads and folk songs. . . .

They like her in London too. The Londoners are really a wild bunch, not like I used to imagine them as being, you know. Well, I guess now with all them tabloid tales of the royalty you got a different idea of them British. Joan was reading this article about where they used to always depict the British in books and movies as kind of the moral center, you know, something like that, but now they just depict them as fools like everybody else. Or villains, or just ordinary boggers, you know. I usedta think all Europeans were pompous types, but they ain't. Joan made her first record in London, and there's folks who thinks she's British. She's big in Japan, as the song goes. She's got a sort of cult following here in the States. You know, them that don't judge their music whether or not it's on the pop charts. She ain't well known here at all, like I said, 'cause she don't make the pop charts, you know. And that's what American music is all about, whether or not you make the pop charts. Of course you can be on the pop charts and not be making any royalties. You can be heard on the radio and still be poor as shit. Lotta people think 'cause you're on the pop charts or they hear you on the radio or that you have a record deal, that you've signed a contract for a record deal, and even made a record, that means you got money. I usedta think that myself till I met Joan. You can be heard on the radio, but that don't mean you's making royalties. But a lot of them they're still paying back their record company. And people thinks they're millionaires. Or they'll see them singing on TV and think they're millionaires. Joan said when she made her first record, and lot of people thought she was a millionaire, 'cause those the only people they knows about that makes records, you know. They hear about Michael Jackson's millions or some of them others and they think anybody makes a record must got millions. Joan's real sensitive about that. You know a lot of them starlettes they wants you to think that they's got millions when they ain't. Course a lot of their logic is that if people think they got millions, it attracts millions. They might be on unemployment or some shit. I usedta think that myself, about them millions, till I started managing Joan. This little record company in London, one of them little independent labels, you know, is the one that recorded her first album. Joan says you don't make it till you make it in your own country, though. That's her logic. Then she's the sort that sabotages herself, or lets other people sabotage her. She's got more good gigs since I've been her manager, though, than when she called herself managing herself. Now she's got a few more recording contracts, a little more lucrative, and she don't just sign for any record deal the record company wants to give her. I got her out of one of her early contracts. But the fool is still trying to make it in her own country, though. I don't agree, about you got to make it in your own country, I mean, but we never agree. She says that every entertainer wants to make it in America, so why shouldn't she? I get her booked in a nice club in Paris, where they like her music, or I get her on a London television show, and the fool's asking me how come it ain't New York? Course if Joan was making it in New York, she'd probably get herself a new manager. That's when they get themselves new managers. Joan says she ain't like that. But most people don't know what they're like.

I sit on the edge of the bed, shuffle a pack of Turkish cigarettes, take one out and light up. My back hunched like a cat's, I swivel to stare at him, one knee up on the bed. I look at them lampshades. Tiffany glass?

Should I pack up and go? I ask.

What do you mean?

Since I ain't what you thought I am.

You don't know what I think you are, he says. Then he say again how he don't like American music, but he likes American women. He thinks American women are racier than European women. Then he ask me if

I knew what he meant by racy. I say yes. I ain't say that I ain't never thought of myself as racy. That I ain't never had the word racy applied to myself. Or maybe I am racy. Maybe I've grown into racy without noticing it. Maybe since I've been managing Joan I've grown into racy without noticing it. I puff my cigarette, watch the rolling smoke, tilt my head back and listen to Joan. Sometimes when I listen to her I don't know what she is either. Her music don't explain her altogether, but I feel that it's good. I wouldn't manage her if I didn't think her good. She must be good. She ain't at the top of the charts, but at least she got the music. And me when I ain't managing her, all I do is gamble. Racing in Saratoga, blackjack in Vegas. I don't gamble a lot, 'cause I ain't got a lot to gamble.

But when she played Vegas that other time, I didn't go near the tables. I sat in the hotel room with a former showgirl, an old woman who used to be a showgirl, a dancer in a chorus line. She said, I stopped dancing before they made me stop. I stopped dancing before they made me. When I started feeling like a fool I stopped, before I started to look like one. Her earlobes were stretched from wearing gold and brass earrings, kinda like them African women that wear them heavy earrings. The skin on her hands looked like a newborn baby's.

We watched the soaps, then a news story about these townspeople collecting all their rock 'n' roll albums and destroying them. I thought of that time in Africa, them Sonjo tribesmen. That Sonjo tribesman who used to test people for crimes. They'd form a circle around this one man, all them accused, and then he'd gyrate in the circle, and he'd pick out the one who'd committed the crime because he smelled wrong. Because when one is guilty one has the smell of guilt, the crime solver explained. It sounds silly, but maybe the body would emit odors. Sweat and nerves. Maybe no different from the lie detector principle, except the technology.

There was one woman, though, who gathered everything that her neighbors might destroy and hid it. She said she didn't like some of them albums herself, but she wasn't going to destroy them. Her neighbors in the background taunted her while she hugged a tattered album to her. For all I know, it mighta been a Joan Savage album. She hugged it to her, stared into the camera, and dared the world. "I don't like this album myself," she said, "and it ain't one that I would buy, but I ain't going to destroy it."

Josef, getting dressed, puts on olive green corduroy trousers and a light blue shirt. I'm thinking of how sometimes it takes someone else, a stranger, to point out what you've become.

Should I get up too? I ask.

If you want me to teach you to ride.

I get up, pull on my panties and jeans. Put on my bra and sweatshirt. What's that attached to your phone? I ask, pausing in front of it. One of them answering devices? I peer close. Why does it say Silent Conversation?

Actually, it's a telephone scrambler. It scrambles conversations. So the wrong ears won't hear. I always like to know about the new technology. That's a rather primitive device, though. They have even smaller scramblers now.

Paranoid bastard, I'm thinking, but, That's fantastic, I say. That's really fantastic. I love stuff like this. Technological stuff. I love the new technology myself. I've always liked stuff like that. But what's really spooking you? I push my sweatshirt down into my waistband and stand waiting for his explanation. What's really spooking you? What wrong ears?

He stands with his back to me, facing the window. I've seen only his guards, but none of the dangers he's been talking about. Maybe he's just a paranoid bastard, some rich lunatic from Germany. Maybe not even from Germany. Maybe he's from Germany, Kentucky. There's a Germany, Kentucky, you know. He keeps his back to me.

I put on the tape player again, softly. This is my scrambler, I say. It don't scramble conversation, though. Scrambles thoughts.

What sort of thoughts? he ask, turning. He scratches his jaw.

What sort of conversations? I ask.

Outside, the stable boy leads out his stallion and my mare.

So is this the monster mare? I ask. So what do I do first?

First you get on, he replies.

CHAPTER FIVE

I peek over his shoulder to see Joan standing in the doorway. She has a handful of yellow hair sticking up, looking like Don King's. She's wearing faded green gaucho trousers and a bright purple tank top and a purple bandanna, worn like the cowgirls wear. Chewing a pear, she watches us with an air of nonchalance and tepid curiosity like you'd watch reruns on an old TV. Make me wonder whether she's watched him with other women. She'd told me about his other infatuations, but said she didn't know any of his other women. She ain't exactly looking at me like she think I'm one of his new infatuations, though. She looking at me like one of us is a fool. Then she chew a little more of that pear. Which one of us is the fool? I whisper, There's Joan, at the same time that she close the door and he come.

What? he ask, rising up. Say what?

Joan was standing in the doorway watching us. Your ex-wife was watching us.

I don't know why I call her his ex-wife, 'cause he know that. Unless I'm telling myself she his ex-wife. Reminding myself that she his ex-wife and he her ex-husband. And thinking about that movie about that ex-husband and ex-wife, and him saying something about that being the first time he felt like a cx-husband when he heard about her being with some other man. I didn't feel like an ex-husband until now, said the man in the movie.

He look freak, like she ain't his ex-wife caught him with another woman, turn, look like he doing one of them yoga postures, look just like one of them yogi, you know one of them posture them yogi do, then dig his elbow into my shoulder. Not now. Before. I'm telling you about them old days, when I first started being Joan's business manager. Joan, the rock star. You know, like them flashback scenes. Lotta readers say they don't understand them flashback scenes. You got to always explain them flashback scenes. They just understand that chronological order. Seem like to me anybody seen a modern movie, even them old-time modern movies would understand a flashback scene. Or if you listen to jazz, seem like you'd understand them flashback scene. In them modern movies, though, they even got them parallel scenes, and seem like anybody can understand a movie can understand the flashback scene, and not just them modern movies. In them early movies they got them parallel and flashback scenes. Even them comic movies.

Anyway, he get up, dress hurriedly, and go downstairs. Seem like I hear him say Joan Darling. Just like he her now husband. Or maybe it just my imagination hear him say Joan Darling, like it her true name. I'm still laying in the bed, looking like a fool and rubbing my shoulder, then I get up and get dressed. Unhurriedly. When I go downstairs, Joan in the living room, sitting with her long legs thrown over the arm of the sofa and still looking nonchalant. Still got her hair sticking up looking like Don King's. Or looking like a character in one of them comic movies. You know that Laurel of the comedy team. And she even scratch the top of her head, looking like that Laurel of the comedy team. Except James play the Hardy to her Laurel. She looking at me, though, like I'm one of the Stooges. I look around for James, but he musta gone outside. Or maybe she told him to leave, I don't know. Maybe he'd made promises to her to be with other women only when she was on her tours. And ain't just with any other woman, but her own manager. Still that sounds more like a now husband than a ex-husband. Then she finish her pear and toss it into a ashtray. Then she scratch the top of her head, looking like that Laurel again. Then she open up one of them paperback novels she likes to read and pretend like she reading it. A Amanda Wordlaw novel. *Don't Let Cowgirls Fool Ya*. Not one of them Great Novels. She likes reading them Great Novels, 'specially the Russians, but she also likes them popular novels, and for nonfiction she reads both the popular nonfiction and them obscure, intellectual-type nonfiction. Maybe she signifying. *Don't Let Cowgirls Fool Ya.* That novel supposed to be about a colored cowgirl. 'Cept she say that novel ain't true popular fiction, it just satirizes the popular fiction. She say it uses the techniques of the popular novel to satirize the popular novel, but she also say this Amanda Wordlaw thinks that African-American writers oughta be able to write "the popular novel" and not just the Great African-American Novels. You know, like some book reviewers think that African-American writers are only supposed to write the Great African-American Novel. So this Amanda Wordlaw thinks why shouldn't they write a whole range of different types of novels, from trash novels and popular fiction to the Great African-American Novel. But this Amanda Wordlaw supposed to even satirize the Great African-American Novel. I think that Amanda Wordlaw a confabulatory woman myself, though, 'cause I ain't never heard of her. She must be a confabulatory woman or maybe that a pseudonym for one of them other literary womens, but one who want to maintain her anonymity. Maybe she write the Great African-American Woman's Novel under her true name, but them trash and popular novels under the name of Amanda Wordlaw. When I come in, she look up from that novel, still looking nonchalant. Then she look kinda sullen, then she look curious. That same curious I told you Josef look. But that before I met Josef. 'Cept I don't really think of that Joan as a rational woman, though. I look at her, then my eyes take a running turn about the living room, looking for James again, then I look at her again. She pretends like she reading that paperback novel again. On her coffee table are some other books: *The Dictionary of Clichés, World Treasury of Love Stories, Alchemy: The Medievalist's Royal Art, The Women Savantes, Modern African-American Sculpture,* a biography of Jim Thorpe, and a novel by Ishmael Reed. Now I know that Ishmael Reed ain't a confabulatory author 'cause I've read some of his books myself. She always include them Ishmael Reed novels on her shelves with the Great Novels, though in the bookstores where we buy her paperback books, when she's got a gig in different part of the world, they ain't on the shelves with the Great Novels. And them mail-order bookstores where she order some of her books, they don't list them with the Great Novels, neither, though we seen *The Autobiography of an Ex-Coloured Man* listed with the Classic American Novels. Joan think they would list *Invisible Man*, but they list *The Autobiography of an Ex-Coloured Man*. Joan say that's on account of them Ishmael Reed novels don't use the techniques of the traditional Western novel, she say that because they use the techniques of they own tradition, but when I ask her what they own tradition, she just look at me like I'm a fool. *Hermione?* Ain't that the name of one of them novels. Seem like one of them novels got the name Hermione in it?

I guess this means you're going to fire me, I say. I don't know why I ask that. Make her think that's all I'm thinking about, whether she fire me or not. I know when I'm negotiating one of her contracts, she tells me I'm crude haggling about the dollar bills. "Maybe I just want to make the record," she'll say. "Maybe I don't care how much they'll pay me up front. I'll just have to pay 'em back anyway. The important thing is getting the record made." And then I tell her about the history of them record companies screwing them Negro entertainers, and not giving them all they royalties and them recording companies making all the money on they recordings, you know, them race recordings before Motown, when they usedta call Negro music Race Music, and she still tell me I'm crude haggling about the dollar bills, and using that history of them record companies screwing them Negro entertainers as a excuse to be crude. Or maybe she thinking I should apologize for letting her catch me with her ex?

Why should I? she's saying. It ain't like we're still married or nothing, Jamey and I. She look at me, trying to look nonchalant again, or disinterested like that wealthy woman I seen at the racetrack, but it look like lightning sleeping in her eyes. She put the paperback novel on the coffee table on top of *The Dictionary of Clichés*. I start to say something, but can't find a way to say it, though I could mention the fact that it her exhusband she just caught me with, and that ain't the same as sneaking around with somebody now husband, even if he still do call her Joan Darling like it her true name.

I . . .

Darling, I don't care who you screw, or who he screws either, as long as it ain't me. James can screw you all he wants, or any other of his little infatuations, or get him a harem of girlies as long as it ain't me. He knows not to screw me. He knows better than to screw me. Jamey and his little group of serious thinkers. I shouldn't say that. When we were in grad school I usedta be one of his little group of serious thinkers. Or at least I thought so. He knows better than to screw me, though.

I know she ain't just meaning screw screw. I don't know the tale of they divorce, and I ain't ask the full tale. And don't know who precipitated the divorce, and don't ask. I sit down on the opposite arm of the sofa. She continue with her back to me for a while, then she turn to face me. My eyes take the same running turn about the living room, looking for James again, then I meet her look.

Of course I'm going to keep you on, darling, she say. You're my manager. You're the best. You're the best manager I've had. Trying to manage myself is a bitch, bitch. I like that. Trying to manage myself is a bitch, bitch. Then she narrow her eyes; the lightning in them ain't sleeping. You just ain't welcome to come here no more, that's all. You can manage me, but you ain't welcome here.

Then that lightning sleeping again. She ain't curious or even nonchalant. She stare away from me. No expression I can name. Then she thumbing through that book, *Don't Let Cowgirls Fool Ya.* Ain't she said something about that Amanda Wordlaw? Seem like once when she reading one of them confabulatory novels, she say, She my alter ego. I think she my alter ego. I think she my other self. I don't know why she say that, though. Seem like you wouldn't want a author of trashy novels to be your other self. Seem like she would pick one of them Great Novelists to be her other self.

What about him? I ask.

She shrug. The lightning still sleeping, but she wave her hands in the air. Then she looking at me like I'm one of her Stooges again. Don't be stupid, she say. And then she wave her hand in the air again like she brushing away my stupidity. And then she scratch the top of her head like Laurel. I guess she mean to say how can she tell him he ain't welcome. But that's what they always talking about on them talk shows. How when them women catch they man with the other woman them women go after the other woman and treat the man like he innocent. Not that he her now husband. But I guess they's even them like that about they ex-husband. Some women is probably possessive like that about even they ex-husband. Seem like on some of them talk shows, they's even women possessive about they own ex-husband, that stalks they ex-husbands and they ex-husbands other women, and more possessive about they ex-husband than when he their now husband. And then I'm imagining Joan on one of them talk shows:

So I went upstairs and opened the door and there they was screwing each other, my husband and my business manager, Harlan Jane Eagleton. I don't know if I can say screw on TV. Can I say screw on TV?

Yeah, sure. I don't think you can say Jane on TV, though. I'm just kidding ya. Four-letter word, you know, Jane. But you say he's your ex-husband he ain't your now husband, says the talk show host.

Yes, he's my ex-husband. He always felt like my ex-husband until I caught him with her, I mean I've known about him with his other little infatuations, but then I caught him with her and suddenly he felt like my now husband. You know, I always thought of him as my ex-husband, 'cause he is my ex-husband, you know, but when I caught him with her, I felt like he's my now husband.

Girl, you know you a fool, don't you? says the talk show host. The women that write to me, millions of women from all over the world that watch this show, always tell me the same thing, that my talk show helps them to realize that they ain't the only fool. They might be the fool that they know themselves to be, but at least they realize they ain't the only fool. Girl, you know you a fool, don't you, Hermione?

My name ain't Hermione, it's Jane, I mean Joan.

I thought you told me your name Hermione?

Naw, it's Joan.

It says here that your middle name is Hermione.

Naw, it's Joan. And what about the other girl? she ask. I ain't the only fool.

That's what I said, but girl, you ain't got to worry about the other girl being no fool, you just got to worry about you yourself being a fool. The other girl might be a fool too, even the very archetype of a fool, maybe even a fool's fool, maybe even a photogenic fool that I'll have my production assistant invite to be on the show, maybe Business Managers Who—Can I Say That on TV?—Their Client's Ex-Husbands but it's your own foolery that you got to recognize and ameliorate. If there's one purpose to my talk show, though personally I believe my talk show is a multidimensional talk show and not just one-dimensional–pop psychology–tabloid journalism like some of them other talk shows, but if there's one definable purpose to my talk show, it's for you fools to recognize you's fools and to stop being fools. Especially the female fool. Especially y'all Hermiones. And I'm talking about the female fools of every race and creed, Hermiones of every race and creed, not just the colored female fools, not just the colored Hermiones. Geraldo or Montel gotta deal with male fools. All the Hermans, Geraldo or Montel gotta deal with them fools.

How come you call them Hermans and us ain't Hiswoman's? ask Joan.

'Cause Hiswoman ain't nobody's true name, and Hermione is.

Anyway I come to Saratoga to bet on some horses. I went upstairs, packed my bags, and went to Saratoga. Then when I was staying in one of them little hotels in Saratoga, one of them little hotels with a Dutch name, I telephoned Joan from my hotel room.

Joan?

Yeah, what? What's it?

This is Harlan.

I know who you are. What is it?

About New York?

Yeah, so what? What about New York?

Do you still want me there?

I reminded her that she supposed to go into the recording studio in a month, then on tour. We're supposed to go on tour.

So, what's changed? she ask, and hang up.

As for now, mostly, we get along, except sometimes I'll catch that look of sleeping lightning, or maybe that lightning ain't sleeping. Maybe it just playing possum. Are you sure you want me to hang around? I'll say. You're the best, she'll say and grin, you know, the joker's grin that don't reveal nothing, or maybe just the entertainer's grin, the one that masks it all. Anyway, she keeps me on as her manager, and I ain't been to that farm of hers, and I ain't seen that James of hers. Tell me he's her ex-husband, and then acting like he's her now husband.

Like once after one of her gigs, I reach onto her dressing table and take out one of her cigarettes. I lit a match and then the cigarette. She don't smoke, but keeps them cigarettes in the dressing room for different folks. Joan's putting on mascara and peering at me out of raccoon's eyes.

Girl, you're a bold bitch, she say.

I say nothing. I ain't sure if she say bold or not, but I don't want her to repeat it. I don't know a woman like to be called a bitch, less they call theyself one. I've heard women brag on theyself as a bitch. Like when Joan were calling herself Joan "the Bitch" Savage. But me I ain't think that the right idea even for her to have of herself. Enough men to call women bitches than them start calling theyselves bitch. 'Cept Joan say the difference between the men and the women is that the women know how to call each other bitch without exactly say the word bitch. Like she could say, Girl, you bold, and still be calling me a bitch.

What would you have done if he was still mine? she ask, putting the mascara down. Then her hands fly into the pockets of her robe like they's nests. What'd you have done then?

I woulda sure stayed clear of him, I answer. I don't fool with other people's husband. Them that I know is married. I've fooled with husbands that I didn't know was husbands. I ain't a husband diviner like some women are. Course the age I am now ain't too many that's free. And them that say they's free ain't free. But you're the one told me he was your ex-husband and that. . . .

One of her hands fly out its nest pocket and fly backwards. She scratch her cheek and then put on her little orange cap. To tell the truth when she wear that little orange cap, she kinda remind me of one of them organ grinder's monkey. She a attractive woman, but in that little orange cap, she still remind me of a organ grinder's monkey. Especially when she got her hair straightened. When she wearing it natural, she don't remind me of no organ grinder's monkey. That little orange cap, you know, it's one of them deerhunter's cap, though, but she always wears it turned backward. It for her antihunting song. She wears the bib backwards, so you don't see the bib—I mean bill—and from the front it round and remind me of one of the organ grinder's monkey and his little round cap. But she's watching me. Like she the hunter. And I'm the deer.

CHAPTER SIX

There's one of your people looking out for us, I say as we ride along the fence. A man on a roan stallion hang back, away from us. It ain't Nicholas, but one of the other guards. I don't know how many security people he got besides Nicholas. I know Nicholas his chief security person, but he got men he claims is former policemen and former soldiers and former members of different countries' CIA, or different countries' equivalent of the CIA. I know one of them security people is Vietnamese, said he usedta fight in the tunnels of Cu Chi, or maybe that his own way of bragging about hisself, but I don't know the nationality of them others. And I don't know if he's truly employed former members of different countries' CIA or not, or if he just saying all that to be bragging. And one of them men look kinda like a Gypsy that Joan and I seen when she was singing in a nightclub over there in Paris. I think he a Gypsy but Joan say he a Turk. Or maybe he a Turkish Gypsy. We pause under a oak tree. The guard, a muscular, dark-haired man with disheveled eyebrows, pause under another oak. Some of his other guards are sitting on the veranda eating lunch. Brown bag lunches, lunchboxes, thermoses, like ordinary workingmen. They's all rugged-looking men, some with that rugged intelligence that you might associate with different countries' CIA, others look just like ordinary men, but maybe they know all that kung fu and karate, that martial arts, and don't need to but look like ordinary men.

Are you a spy? Josef ask.

I pull back on the reins of my horse. Horse want to lead herself.

Spy? What do you mean spy? Maybe he ask that 'cause he notice me spying on his security men. You know, maybe he just jealous seeing me spying at his security men and especially that Turkish-looking Gypsy or that Gypsy-looking Turk, and thinking maybe I'm more interested in his security men than in him, so he just ask me whether I'm a spy. I think he's joking, you know. Naw, I ain't no spy, I says. Then I realize he ain't joking about me being no spy, and it ain't even jealousy at me spying at his security men, and to tell the truth that Turkish-looking Gypsy or Gypsy-looking Turk also kinda look like that Steven Seagal, ain't it Steven Seagal the one supposed to study them martial arts in Japan? that spiritual kung fu—but who am I a spy for?—and I'm about to call him some paranoid fool. If he's got men that's truly former members of some countries' CIA maybe they's the true spy. Maybe one of them's spying on him for his government or us government or the Thoroughbred Breeders Association or maybe that arbitrage if he the sorta man to be spied on. But if he just a paranoid fool, then a lot of people is paranoid fools, 'cause them pop psychologists and even them ordinary psychologists say a lot of modern people is paranoid.

I steady them reins again. Horse still want to lead herself. I try to make that sound the jockeys make, but just sound like I'm clucking.

I think you're a spy, he says. And then he says something about how we met, as if I was deliberately watching to encounter him when he was standing up there watching them walk and exercise the horses. And that maybe some of them people wanting to play dirty tricks on him mighta hired me. They didn't want him acquiring the best Thoroughbreds in the state. They had a consortium to outbid him locally and then when they seen he was going out-of-state to acquire some Thoroughbred they sent me up there to spy on him. Especially since I'm telling him I'm from Kentucky just like himself, or rather that's the same state that he's immigrated to. Don't that sound like a paranoid fool? If I was a spy I wouldn't be telling him I'm from Kentucky just like himself. I'd be from Kansas City or someplace like that, or maybe even from New York. And seem like if they consortium could outbid him in the state, they just send they consortium up to the Fasig-Tipton to outbid him. I don't think that Fasig-Tipton got laws against consortiums of Thoroughbred owners bidding for they horses. Seem like them Fasig-Tipton people just wants to sell they horses to the highest bidder. Course ain't many splivs bidding on them horses unless they's sports stars or entertainment personalities. Seem like somebody say though that there's a wealthy colored woman that's in the Thoroughbred business who ain't no sports star or entertainment personality and that she bids on horses at that Fasig-Tipton. Maybe I seen her at the Saratoga racetrack but just thought her a ordinary woman.

Naw, I ain't a spy. 'Cept a spy in the house of love, I say, remembering one of those song titles. Or it a book title? I think I seen Joan with a book with that title. Seem like on her shelves in the midst of either the Great Books or the popular novels, she got a little paperback book called *Spy in the House of Love*. Ain't that Anaïs Nin? Seem like that Anaïs Nin got a book called *Spy in the House of Love*. Seem like that one of them Anaïs Nin books. I think she mighta even published that book her ownself, 'cause seem like Joan say a lot of them books she collect the authors have to publish they ownself, you know. But it's also a song title. I am a spy in the house of love. Something about a spy in the house of love. I look at him. I'm about to call him some paranoid fool, again, but he reach over and touch my jaw, his horse trotting sideways. Mine nibble grass.

What are you? he ask. Who are you?

A spy in the house of love.

Who are you?

I'm just Harlan. Harlan Jane Eagleton. I manage a rock star. Joan Savage. Joan "the Bitch" Savage. I think her middle name is Hermione. She ain't told me that her middle name. Or maybe that her maiden name, but I think that her middle name. I know there's a Hermione in her favorite book—that's *Steppenwolf*. Her husband name Savage, so she use that for her stage name. Sorta like Tina Turner, you know, except she ain't no Tina Turner and her husband ain't Ike, I mean her husband ain't in show business, you know. He some kinda scientist. But Joan a rock star. Well, she ain't exactly a star. And ain't exactly a bitch. She just likes to call herself a bitch, you know. She likes being a woman, you know, but she doesn't like women being judged by different standards than men are judged, you know. I think she means even colored women, but you know when she talks womanhood, she just says womanhood, you know. Like we were watching this politician who was talking about this female politician and so he says, And she's a attractive young woman. And you know, like that was a compliment. And Joan says, Now what's that gotta do with anything, but like this male politician that's like his highest compliment for her, you know, not that she's a good politician but that she's a attractive young woman. Joan's a attractive woman herself. And I'm a charmer. You said so yourself. Why don't you hire yourself a detective and find out who I really am if you're so paranoid about everybody? They's even got electronic detectives now, that just works using computers. All them guards and shit. You don't need all them guards. Well, I guess you gotta have your security people. I guess you ain't no different from the rich and famous they have on TV. They're always talking about the different security people they have. Every one of them stars and starlets has got they security people. Even the rich but not so famous got they own security people, and the famous but not so rich that can afford they own security people got 'em. It's probably better to be rich and not so famous than famous and not so rich, 'cause if you famous and not so rich people think you's rich when you ain't, 'cause they don't know it's possible to be famous and ain't be rich, 'cause they think if you's famous you gotta be rich. I just ain't never been around nobody that needed themselves so many security people, though. I mean, I manage Joan but she's nobody. I mean she ain't nobody, but she ain't a diva or nothing. She's neither rich nor famous. I mean, she's famous amongst the people that know her, but she ain't famous famous. Course with me managing her career she's a little more famous than when I met her, and a little richer, but not rich rich. She tells me I'm preoccupied with wealth and fame. That's her idea of me, you know. You know how someone can have a idea of you and even convince you that that's the true you. She say she don't judge good management by how rich and famous I make her, though that don't make no kinda sense, do it? I mean, how else do you judge good management? Do you think I'd be a good manager if as soon as I started managing her she become less rich and less famous? Not that she's truly rich or famous. She don't even have herself a entourage. All the rock stars got entourages, and even the wannabes. I ask her who she know that we can hire for cheap to sorta be her entourage, you know, but she say she don't want no entourage, or tell me I'm enough entourage.

Josef eyes as black as pepper. My horse try to lead herself but I pull back on the reins. I try to steady her. I ain't no experienced rider, y'all know. Josef reach out and steady her, and make that clicking sound.

Naw, I ain't no spy, I say. Then I imagine lighting up a cigarette and blowing rings of smoke in the air above him. My horse leads herself. I start to ask Josef more about them dangers he talking about, and why he thinks I might be a spy. And maybe he mean some other German word that mean the same thing as spy, but ain't exactly mean spy. Maybe there's a German word that mean the same as spy but ain't spy. Since I've been at his farm, though, I ain't seen any of them dangers, or heard any of the locals threatening him. Or maybe that was before he got all the security people, and now all the locals have heard the rumors about him having former policemen and former soldiers and former CIA-type people working for him. Or maybe they think he's some kinda gangster, just camouflaging hisself as a Thoroughbred owner. I've seen all these guards but I ain't seen what they's guarding him from. Unless it's hisself. A lot of them paranoid fools the guards they need is to guard them from theyselves, and to guard other people from them, more than to guard them from other people. When I ask him to tell me some more about that Germany, he starts talking about Prague, which I know ain't Germany. I know that Prague ain't in Germany. He's from Berlin, he says, but he say that Prague have always been his favorite European city. Most Germans prefer Paris, that's why Paris was one of the few European cities the Germans didn't destroy during the war, even when they occupied Paris they didn't destroy Paris, but he prefers Prague. Maybe my imagination as good as a tale he could tell me, though, about that Germany and what made him to be a paranoid. I'm thinking about some scene in Germany where some of them neo-Nazis mistook him for one of them immigrants of color, maybe a African or a North African, and he running from them neo-Nazis, and maybe that when his paranoia began, where he got his first security guards.

He ain't tell me about when he first got mistook for a immigrant in his own country, and I ain't ask, but years later when I dream about it we're riding them horses again and I ask, Tell me about when them neo-Nazis mistook you for one of them immigrants of color. Did they look anything like those guys in the movie *The Wanderers*? Did you ever see that movie *The Wanderers*? Joan say the same guy wrote the screenplay for *Sea of Love*, you know with Al Pacino, wrote that movie that *The Wanderers* based on, I mean wrote that book that the movie *The Wanderers* based on, that's Joan's hobby reading works of literature, you know, 'cept they seemed kinda innocents compared to the neo-Nazis they talk about on television.

That's when I hired Nicholas. He was there. He rescued me. It was in Berlin. . . .

You first met Nicholas in Berlin?

In my dream he start talking kinda like me.

Berlin, yes, Berlin. He was roaming about Europe a musician I think a musician, you know, he couldn't get any "gigs," as you call them, in America I think a musician I know he plays the French horn so he comes to Europe to Berlin and I, well I suppose I was roaming about my own country, I'm in arbitrage, you know, deciding whether I should leave Berlin, on account of all this Deutschland für Deutschlanders, you know, perhaps go to Africa or Prague, perhaps come to America. . . . Nicholas thought it was a fellow African American he was saving, you know. . . . And I thought he was a fellow African German saving me. . . . There's something about him that makes him seem more like my culture than his own, though I've never thought that I've anything like your culture, though people say my way of speaking English has something of your accent, your easy colloquialisms, and something of the German. . . . Then I hired him. It's not like he's a hireling, though. I still allow him to be his own man. I mean, he's still his own man. I mean, he works for me but he's still his own man.

CHAPTER SEVEN

Joan grabs my arm as I enter the recording studio. I wink at the guitar player who's leaning against the wall. Name's Jimmy Cuervo. I first heard him play in a cantina in South Texas and introduced him to Joan. They even started talking Spanish to each other and I heard her call him Caballero. His name ain't Jimmy Caballero, though, it's Jimmy Cuervo. Or maybe Cuervo the way them Mexicans pronounce Caballero, 'cause them Mexicans ain't supposed to pronounce Spanish the same way them Spaniards from Spain pronounces Spanish. Theirs is American Spanish. And them Mexicans, they's got they own music, it ain't that flamenco in Mexico, it's that mariachi music. Or maybe that mariachi music a Americanization of that flamenco. But even in Spain you's got two kinds of flamenco. You got that flamenco they do for them tourists, and then you's got the true flamenco, the flamenco that them Spaniards do for each other. Sometimes just the men do that true flamenco, and sometimes you's got men and women do that true flamenco. But for the tourists you's always got to have them women to do that flamenco, or you's got to have the men and women to do that flamenco, and them tourists they see and hear that flamenco, and they think sexuality, but that ain't the same as that true flamenco.

Maybe in Spain his true name be Jimmy Caballero, though, that Jimmy Cuervo, but in American Mexico or in Mexican America his name Jimmy Cuervo. And that Jimmy ain't his true Spanish name. Maybe his true Spanish name is Guillermo. Naw, Guillermo ain't the Spanish for Jimmy. What the Spanish for Jimmy? Jaime? Ain't Jaime the Spanish for Jimmy? Ain't Jaime Mexican for Jimmy? Anyway, that

Jimmy Cuervo, I call him a guitar player's guitar player he's so good. He's the kind of musician Joan likes to call a "working musician" 'cause he ain't preoccupied with stardom. One of them African-looking Mexicans from South Texas. A friend of mine from New Mexico, who first told me about Jimmy Cuervo and his music, and who I first heard perform in her cantina-type restaurant in Cuba, New Mexico, calls them kinda Mexicans "chitlins con carne Mexicans." Anyway my ex-husband Norvelle and I were playing pool in her cantina restaurant when Jimmy Cuervo comes in. It a cantina-style restaurant but she got one of them pool tables in it, you know. He's got his guitar and he asks whether he can play for free, and then if the people like him, he might get him a gig there. So he plays for free and the people like him, so she hires him to play there. That's the first time I heard him play, and then when Joan hires me to be her manager I think of that Jimmy Cuervo and tell Joan that he one of the best guitar players I've heard since Hendrix. Ain't Hendrix, ain't no guitar player that's Hendrix, but still one of the best. Joan say if he one of the best guitar players since Hendrix, he be famous and she woulda already heard of him. I tell her that's 'cause he don't really know how to market hisself, just plays the clubs and cantinas around South Texas. I remember when that Joan had her a gig in some town, seem like Seattle, Washington, or one of them towns, and so she takes me to this pawn shop and tells me that the pawn shop where Hendrix's daddy bought him his first electric guitar. And there's this big painting of Hendrix over the pawn shop and I figure it's a true tale and ain't none of them confabulatory tales. So anyway he sends us some of his tapes, that Jimmy Cuervo or Jaime Caballero, and Joan likes him and wants to make a record with him. Anyway, he gives me a approving look. Ferocious red bangs hang across Joan's forehead. Every time I see her she's got a different hairdo, different-style makeup. And she's wearing her favorite sweatshirt, one by the African-American sculptor-designer Catherine Shuger but purchased in Amsterdam, called Monkey Puzzles. Putting her hands onto my shoulders, she hug me close. She the best of pretenders. So who'd you win this time? she ask.

She put her foot up on a straight chair and pull up her socks. Painted figures make the socks look like they been tattooed. She's wearing the same gaucho pants she'd worn when I'd peeked up from behind her husband's shoulders—her ex-husband's shoulders.

I don't answer.

You were in Saratoga?

Right.

Who'd you win? Her eyelids are purple. So what gigs we get? she ask.

I tell her.

So tell me who'd you win? she asks. Maybe you should get me a gig in Saratoga. I know they got clubs in Saratoga.

When I don't answer, she goes into the recording booth. Jimmy Cuervo follows, strumming his guitar. Well, if Josef can be German, Jimmy can be Mexican. 'Cept ain't the sorta Mexican you see in the movies. Look more African than Mexican, like I said. Chitlins con carne. My friend from Cuba, New Mexico, say she first seen a Mexican look like him in one of them French movies, said that surprised her 'cause she ain't never seen no African-looking people in Mexico, not in them American movies. You know, 'cause in them American movies they's always got white people playing the Mexicans at least in most of them early movies or they's got them Spanish or Native Americans or Italian-looking Mexicans, but not no African-looking Mexicans. This little Mexican boy in that movie, though, look just like a little African, she say. 'Cept my friend from New Mexico telling me about how they had slavery in that Mexico before they abolished it, so I guess there's as many Africans in Mexico as anywhere. And there's little towns in Mexico where all the people look like they's Africans, she say. Is that true, Nadine? I'm asking. She the one own that cantina-style restaurant, Nadine. She a African American herself, except her husband a Mexican. I think she say he from Chiapas or somewhere in southern Mexico. I think he one of them illegal aliens myself, or usedta be one of them illegals. He look more Native American than Mexican hisself, though. Nadine say he look like a Aztec prince. Sure, it's the truth, she say, about they being whole towns of Mexicans that look African. I ain't been to any of them little towns myself, but I've heard about 'em. Some of them

Africans when they escaped slavery settled in them little towns. When I was in Texas City, before I come to Cuba, New Mexico, with my Aztec Prince—sometimes she don't even say his name she just call him her Aztec Prince—and then she start telling me a lot of confabulatory stories about Texas City, Texas, and how she use to drive a truck in Texas City, Texas, then she met her Aztec Prince and they come and settled in Cuba, New Mexico. The way she tell the tale, she supposed to have smuggled her Aztec Prince across the border her ownself when he escaped from that little revolution they had down there in Chiapas. Somebody else mighta smuggled him across the border, but I don't think Nadine smuggled him across the border her ownself.

In the recording booth, Jimmy Cuervo's singing with Joan one of them Mexican *corridos*, one of them Mexican ballads. They're jazzing or bluesing or rocking it up, though, so that it don't sound exactly like a pure Mexican *corrido*. Something about a man and all his different women, or a woman and all her different men. And then they sing some of the new songs: "Big Dick from Boston," "Phoebe, Little Phoebe," "Captain Hicks, Captain Jimmy Hicks of the Marines," "Ada Ross." Then they sang some songs she'd previously recorded: "Remora," "Randy Dandy," "Xingu" and "Kedgeree," and then she sang songs whose titles I think were from literary works she'd read: "The Odyssey of a Nice Girl," "The Map of Love," "The Clown and His Daughter," "The Hermit and the Wild Woman," "Mina Purefoy in Puritan City," "Wolfe Tone and the Wandering Scholar," "Aldonza del Tobosa," "Younghy-Bonghy-Bo," "Le Roman Experimentale" and "The American Song."

When she come out of the recording booth, Joan stand watching me.

Jimmy's always excellent, he's like caviar, she says. How'd I do? How'd I sing? Did you like the new songs? Did you like the *corrido*? He's teaching me a *canto hondo*.

Yes. Very much. You sounded real good. You know you always sound good. And your songs are always intelligent.

You're just saying that. You know I like to hear you tell me that I'm good. Jimmy's always excellent, though. He's like caviar. You'd think he'd be better known. Jimmy, could you return Mr. Calandrino's keys. You're like caviar. She hands Jimmy the keys to the rented recording studio. Sure, he says. He bows to me gallantly, then bows to her, then heads toward Mr. Calandrino's office. Then Joan says, Let's go have Chinese. You can help me pick an album title. We can go to one of Isabel Kong's restaurants. The elusive Isabel Kong. They've got the best food, though. I went to school with her, you know. Isabel Kong. You know, when we were in Paris I took you to Isabel Kong's. She has an Isabel Kong's in Paris. She says everybody thinks she's a gangster. A woman like her ain't supposed to have so many fine restaurants all over the world if she ain't into something illegal.

I don't know if I can trust you, I say.

Trust me, she say.

When we get to the street, she's still holding my arm. I slide my arm out of hers as we walk down the windy street. Few people look at her, 'cause she's dressed like a fool, but they figure she must be some sorta theatrical person. She almost slender enough to be a fashion model, though. Sometimes you see them fashion models on the runways dressed up to look like fools. They say them ain't the sorta dresses that real women are supposed to wear. The designers just make them to give their shows a little flair and make them more entertaining. You know, something for the fashion journalists to write about. For a while them fashion models got more famous than the movie stars, on account of they had more of that glamour. Then them movie stars started getting glamorous again. 'Cause for a while you didn't see a lot of glamorous movie stars. Even at them awards shows, you didn't see the glamorous-type movie stars. A few of them rock stars turned movie stars would look kinda glamorous. Then they started bringing glamour back to Hollywood, which some people call Glamourtown anyway. Joan walks like she onstage, anyway, doing a little jig, then she touch my jaw. She move her hand up to my jaw, quickly, like she going to strike it, but she don't. She touch it gently instead.

Let's go somewhere where we can have some champagne, Ashley, I hear a woman say as we walk down the concrete stairs into the Chinese restaurant. As always, I feel awkward navigating through the tight spaces between tables, but Joan move like she own even the tightest space. And she ain't a small woman neither. Neither one of us is small women. She a slender woman, but she ain't a small woman. We're led to our table. The waiter, a tall man who look more Indonesian than Chinese, pull out her chair first, 'cause he can tell by her behavior I guess that she the VIP, or maybe because she the more attractive of the two of us, but when he turn to me I'm already seated and reaching for one of the fried noodles.

Joan say something to him in Chinese and then order shrimp and fried rice in Chinese. I know that *ni hao*, that the only Chinese I know. And what's that other Chinese I picked up from Joan? *Ni shi neiguo ren?* That mean, Where do you come from? Seem like people need to know that in everybody language. And to ask them what they name? *Ni jiao shenmo minzi?* In her gigs in different countries, she always like to sing at least one song in that different language, and to say a few words and phrases in them languages, so she know how to say a little in a lot of different languages. And she know how to order food in almost everybody language. I order sweet-and-sour pork in plain English, 'cause I ain't learned how to order food in nobody language but my own, or the language that supposed to be my own. Joan say that's why she like to learn different people's language, 'cause she ain't never felt like English her own language. She say the language that feel most like her own when she speak it is Italian, but she ain't got no Italian in her that she knows about. I thought she would say Swahili or one of them African languages, but she don't, she say Italian. We sit in silence until Joan kick my shin under the table.

What do you want me to do? I ask.

She don't answer. She slide off her pumps and rub my hurt shin with her toe. She move her foot up under the hem of my skirt, like she think she in a X-rated movie. She punch at the hem, but don't go no further.

So what do you want me to do? I ask.

Do you really think we're birds of the same feather? she ask. You said once we were birds of the same feather, that I only imagined I was different.

I ain't never said that.

I take a bit of that Chinese pork. Joan always coming out with things like that, things I'm supposed to have said. She either dreaming I'm saying a lot of that shit, or her memory playing tricks on her, or she overheard somebody else saying that shit and thought it was me, or maybe it's some lyrics to some song she's writing or heard, 'cause I ain't said half the shit that Joan ascribe to me as saying. I mean, if it Joan telling you this tale, or her version of this tale, she probably be telling you all kindsa shit that I ain't said. And I ain't never imagined that me and Joan anything alike. I don't even think of her as my alter ego. She ain't even the sorta woman I imagine myself to be anything like. You can like someone and it don't mean you want to be anything like 'em.

You said you wanted me to help you pick an album title.

The Floating World?

Sucks.

The Spear Maker?

Sucks.

Alter Ego.

Too elite.

Remora.

No.

Do you know what a remora is?

No.

It's a little sucker fish that attaches itself to a bigger fish. Fable has it that—

Sucks.

Our Nig Joan?

Stupid.

Queen Joan's Songbook?

No. What about Queen Kong?

Isabel's name is Kong, I can't use Kong. But that's good, I like that. I'd like to do an album and do something with Kong in it. But I know Isabel Kong, and she'd think I meant her.

Stupid.

La Femme Pensante? *"Je ne suis qu'une femme, mais je suis une femme pensante."*

Say what? Sucks anyway. Why don't you go with one of the song titles. I kinda like "The American Song."

Sucks. Anyway, I think there's already an album named *The American Song* or *The American Songbook*. What about the name of some of
those horses you bet on? What about Creole Beauty? When I played that
gig in New Orleans, somebody thought I was Creole.

Doesn't sound rich enough for an album, you want something that
sounds rich, you know. I don't mean rich rich, not elite, but rich. A mar-
ketable title. Not something obscure. Not something you'll have to explain in liner notes. A rich title, but not rich rich.

When you first met me did you think I was rich? she asks. I mean
rich rich.

I don't know.

When you first met me did you think I was rich? she repeats. Did you
think I was rich rich?

I don't know. I musta thought you musta had some kinda money. You
look well taken care of, so I figured you must have some kinda money.
Plus, you never like to talk about the amount of money that you getting
for this gig or that contract, and somebody said it's only rich people that
think money talk is crude. . . . Poor people talk about money all the
time.

You know, you have never even asked me where I'm from. You have
never even asked me anything about myself.

I never ask people about themselves. I figure people tell you as much
about themselves as they want you to know. You want me to ask you
where you from? So where you from? Detroit? Kansas City? St. Louis?
Atlanta? I know you got a farm in Minnesota. Are you from Minneapo
lis? Your bio says that you're from New York, but I know a lotta jokers
in the business say they're from New York when they ain't. They're from
some little tank town, but they tell people they're from New York. I
know your passport says New York. Maybe you're from some ghetto in
Kansas City? Maybe you're from East St. Louis? West Virginia?

She get up abruptly. I see her talking to the Chinese woman at the
desk and then she walks outside. I pay the bill and follow her out. The
woman I pay the bill to is a short, round woman that remind me kinda

of Thaka, that Masai woman, except she ain't Masai, she Chinese, say something to me in Chinese, 'cause maybe I speak Chinese too, but I tell her I don't speak Chinese, it's just the other one speaks Chinese. Then I ask her if she's the famous Isabel Kong. Isabel Kong? she ask. No, no I'm not Isabel Kong. Isabel Kong in Hong Kong. She's starting one of our new restaurants in Hong Kong. I just manage restaurant for Isabel Kong. I not Isabel Kong herself. You think I'm Isabel Kong? Everyone thinks I'm Isabel Kong. No, no I'm not Isabel Kong. Don't believe the stories you hear about her. She is a good woman. She is for the Chinese people. She is all the time helping the Chinese people. A good woman. I a good woman, but I not Isabel Kong herself. When I get outside, Joan's walking with her hands in her pockets. I catch up with her.

Look, I don't see him anymore. It was just that one time, I say. Look, it was stupid of me, but you were divorced. It was you making the big deal about how you was divorced, and how you didn't mind if he saw other women. Bragging about how y'all's divorced and how you don't mind if he sees other women, as if it's your business to mind.

What do you mean bragging?

I mean, I didn't even ask you. Did I ask you? Maybe I did ask you, but then you started bragging. You said that you and he were divorced, that was the first thing you told me. Certainly I didn't ask you about him and other women, about his other infatuations. The way I figured, the way you were sounding was, if I was interested, then it was okay, 'cause y'all was divorced. And if he was interested in me, then that was okay. And you said said y'all didn't have no claims on each other, and you were talking about some of his other women that you'd heard about, some of his other infatuations, but. . . . But you were divorced. You both said you had no claims on each other. You seemed like . . . You for really seemed like. . . . You seemed like you wanted us to like each other. And the way he was acting, he was acting like he wanted me to like him. You know how men act when they want a woman to like them, that's the way he was acting.

Your own conceit. I don't think we know the same Jamey.

Well, I thought it was wonderful, you know, I mean the two of you still being good friends, you know, being divorced and all and still being good friends. I thought it was the most wonderful thing. . . . Being able to be divorced and—

So you had to test us.

Test? No, I admired you, you and Jamey—

You haven't a right to call him Jamey. He's my Jamey.

—how you and your Jamey both keep track of each other, are on friendly terms. More than friendly terms. How you care about each other. . . . I admire that, and I was thinking that must be the most wonderful way to be divorced. To be divorced like you and James are divorced. I mean, if you gotta be divorced, then to be divorced like you and James are. I've heard men brag about their ex-wives like that, telling you how them and their ex-wives are still friends and how even their ex-wives is friends with each other, that's nice, but that's just to brag on themselves more than their women, but you're the first woman I met to brag about her ex-husband, to truly brag about him, as your ex-husband, not just bragging on yourself. . . .

I'm trying to explain what I mean. And should I tell her that I started not only thinking the way they divorced wonderful, but then started thinking him wonderful. That he must be the most wonderful man. Or maybe it was just my own conceit. Was I testing them or myself? But she wave for a cab. When it pull up to the curb, she climb in without inviting me. The driver shaking his head at her orange hair and purple eyelids. Looking at her like she some freak. A trollop? Bitch, she mumble, slamming the door.

CHAPTER EIGHT

He had tiptoed into the room, and now he digging into my shoulder like a wrench. At first I think it one of his security guards, even Nicholas. That maybe they don't recognize me and think I'm some secret agent hired by the local Thoroughbred Owners Association or whoever Josef think playing dirty tricks on him. But then how did I get through them security guards? Maybe they think I'm some kinda Ninja or something. Most of the Ninjas you see are men Ninjas, but I seen this television show that had women Ninja. Maybe they think I'm some kinda woman Ninja, hired by the local Thoroughbred Owners Association. He even got security people working for him who claim they former KGB, and former security people when Germany was still East and West Germany. One of them security guards say he was with the East German police, but then when East and West Germany united he come to America, because they was putting a lot of them East German police on trial for crimes against the state, or something like that, except when they was working for East Germany it weren't crimes against the state, 'cause they was obeying the laws of the state. He one of them dark-haired Germans, though, he ain't one of them Aryan-looking blond-haired Germans that that Hitler describing as the superior race. That always seem curious to me, Hitler and his ambivalent aesthetics, 'cause even he himself weren't that blond-haired aesthetic ideal that he say supposed to be the aesthetic ideal of that Germany. A lot of them little countries he invaded have them stories about him separating the blond-haired people from the dark-haired people, and saying the blond-haired people the superior people, and the people didn't even have to be Jewish or Gypsies, they just supposed to have dark hair. And even a lot of white people ambivalent about they aesthetics. The same people that celebrate the suntan celebrate Snow White. You'll hear women selling that suntan lotion and talking about being too white till they put on that suntan lotion, and then you hear the same women saying they ain't white enough and trying to sell you another lotion that give you a fairer complexion. Joan say that that the influence over there in Europe when them Moors invaded most of Europe. That that's why a lot of them Europeans is ambivalent about they aesthetics, 'cause when the Moors was the rulers over there in Europe, the aesthetic ideal was to look like the Moors, and then when the fair-haired Christians won back most of Europe from the Moors, the aesthetic ideal was to look like the fair-haired Christians. 'Cept them original Christians wasn't fair-haired, amongst the Mediterranean peoples. They mythologizes that Christianity. So them Europeans have always been kinda ambivalent about they aesthetics. I don't know whether she read that in one of them nonfiction books and if that the truth about why them Europeans is ambivalent about color and does all that suntanning or just one of them confabulatory truths. Like that psychologist that wrote that book on the psychology of color. Maybe it him, that former East German policeman, or that Nicholas. Anyway, I jerk my hand out of the desk drawer.

Spy, he say. It a German accent, but it Josef German accent. I'm barefoot, in a Chinese silk nightshirt. Couldn't find my Moroccan sandals. I'd climbed out of bed and wandered into the study.

I'm searching for scratch paper, I explain. Moonlight across his jaw. I can see his black pepper eyes.

What d'you want with scratch paper? he asks. To write up your report on me? Who hired you? Who do you work for? The Thoroughbred Owners Association? Your government? Mine?

I start to tell him I work for the Thoroughbred Breeders Association not the Thoroughbred Owners Association, or Our Nigs, International: Spies in the House of Love and that he our prime suspect in love arbitrage, 'cause he always talking about that arbitrage, that he in the arbitrage business before he become a Thoroughbred owner, but you can't joke like that with no paranoid fool. Especially a paranoid fool that's got former KGB and former CIA and former soldiers and former policemen and former policemen for the former East Germany and former Vietnamese soldiers who fought in the tunnels of Cu Chi—either that or they's all confabulatory storytellers. Or maybe they all just told Josef them confabulatory tales just so's they could get hired as his security people. Seem like I seen that former East German policeman on television, though, telling them about the reason he was interested in coming to America, 'cause in East Germany they considered him a hero, or at least a good East German, but in the reunited Germany they considered him a villain, and that he'd rather be a first-class citizen in America—'cause they didn't know one German from another in America—rather than a second-class citizen or even a criminal in the reunited Germany.

Naw, to write down a song, I explain. I got a idea for a song. Anyway, if I was a spy, I'd be using the new technology. I wouldn't need to write up a report on you. I'd have one of those miniaturized cameras or some shit. Those miniaturized recorders. And you wouldn't even think I's a spy 'cause they'da trained me so well. Therefore, you should know I ain't no spy, 'cause if I was a real spy you wouldn't be suspicious of me at all.

You write songs for your Joan? he ask, letting go of my shoulder. Do you write some of her stupid music?

No, for myself. I don't show her my lyrics. They ain't her type of music. The type of romantic music I write she ridicules. She likes satire, wit, what she calls intelligent music. Intelligent and satirical rock 'n' roll. I like romance. I even like country music if it's romantic. The only country singer Joan likes is John Prine. She thinks he's the only intelligent country singer. She likes intelligent music. She thinks all African-American music is intelligent whether it's intelligent or not. You know, musical intelligence.

He don't say nothing. He's looking like her music don't sound all that intelligent to him, or much African-American popular music. Then he starts kissing me, nibbling me. You want romance? he asks. He draws me down on the carpet, kissing me, nibbling me, pulling up my nightshirt. Then there, beneath a leather chair that face away from us toward the Dutch windows, I can see shoes and trouser legs. He drops the core of an apple on the carpet, then scoops it up. I push up to get up, but Josef thrust harder. I watch the shoes and trousers. Josef rise up and kisses me again, nibbles me, then he pad out of the study. I turn on the desklight. Nicholas don't stand up and reveal himself, but I know it's him. Hiding in plain sight. I watch Nicholas' shoes and trousers, and think he going to say something, but he don't. I can hear the apple core plop in a nearby ashtray. Then he rise and leave the room. I keep searching for scratch paper, but have forgotten whatever song I intended.

CHAPTER NINE

This how I first met Joan's ex-husband James Savage. She introduced me to him her ownself. Harlan, I want you to meet my ex, she'd said, as he opened the door of the farmhouse. Honey, this is our lady lodger. I told her I'd show her how I spend my summer vacation, she said, sounding like a little girl, but a little girl in a confessional. Except I don't think a little girl in a confessional would call a priest honey. We shook hands, James and I. He'd been eating breakfast and there was a crumb on his lip. Joan reached out and scraped at it, then licked her finger. Um, banana bread. You smell like banana bread. Yummy. She sniffed under his chin then kissed him. He gave me a steady look before he said, Pleased to meet you. He was dressed casually in a blue workshirt with rolled sleeves and gray cotton trousers. He was wearing tennis shoes. He a average-sized man. He got a high, broad forehead and high, broad cheekbones, but a narrow chin. It narrow, but it still kinda square and prominent. His lips is sorta full. And he got a mustache with little bits of gray in it, though the neatly trimmed hair on his head is dark brown. His big brown eyes look like curiosity is they leading characteristic. And he got little dimples at the wings of his nose. I think they's dimples. Maybe individually his features is kinda strange, but put them together they make up a handsome man. I ain't say he a Denzel Washington or nothing, though he kinda got his self-possession, but he still a handsome man.

Harlan's my new manager, Joan explained. He nodded as if he already knew me, but didn't say anything, then we went inside and put our bags down on the living room carpet. He was puffing on a cigarette which he put out in one of them crystal tray. He mumbled something about giving up the nasty habit, that he ought to know better than to smoke, then he carried our bags upstairs, but when he came back down he was puffing on another cigarette. Joan had settled on the couch, reclining, with her legs thrown over the worn arm, facing the mantel and the fireplace. I sat in an armchair with my legs folded under me. Some of the furniture was old-fashioned, the couch and the chair of unmatched fabrics, and other of the furniture in the modern style. Look like the kind of furniture you might get in a flea market, mixing styles and fabrics, not the kind of furniture you'd think a rock star would have, even a not-so-famous rock star. Or maybe the furniture remind me of Joan's music, 'cause her music do mix different musical styles and textures, though it supposed to be rock 'n' roll. The couch was upholstered in a sort of woolen fabric, a plaid mixture of browns, whites, oranges and beiges; the armchair had silky upholstery of blue, purple and wine-colored stripes, its arms frayed and worn.

The farmhouse, though, looked larger inside than it did from the exterior. The living room was rectangular and had a sprawling chaotic look, the furniture not just a mixture of styles and fabrics but arranged haphazardly, catty-cornered as my grandmother Jaboti would say, except for the couch and armchair that faced each other. There's several of them leather chairs, and there's a rough-hewn wooden coffee table in the center, decked with albums of Joan's favorite singers, not including her own, 'cause she always say she ain't her own favorite singer, which surprise me 'cause I'm thinking seem like most singers would have theyself as one of they own favorite singers, 'cause seem like if somebody a singer they'd have that conceit of being they own favorite singer, even if they favorite songs is songs that other singers sing, but she say she ain't her own favorite singer, and even the songs that she herself sing ain't always her favorite songs. Now that don't make no sense, though. That not being your own favorite singer make more sense than the songs you sing not being your favorite songs. Seem like you'd just sing your favorite songs, don't it? 'Cept she explains that sometimes a singer don't have the range to sing they favorite songs, that other singers might sing their favorite songs better than they can sing 'em, and that they favorite songs might not be they own style of singing. 'Cause can't all singers sing in everybody style. They's some singers that can sing in everybody's style and every type of singing, so you can have favorite songs that other singers sing, as well as having other singers be your favorite singers. Still seem kinda crazy, you have the conceit to be a singer and ain't have the conceit to be your own favorite singer singing your own favorite songs.

She ain't tell me who her own favorite singer or what her favorite songs, but them albums mix assorted styles of singing, and not just American music, but Continental music, popular and classical, Caribbean and African and Latin music. And in American music it ain't just African-American music, it everybody's American music, even including country music. I remember reading a short story called "Why I Like Country Music" and written by a African-American writer, and seeing Joan's country music albums make me think of that short story. I don't remember, though, why he say he like country music in that story, but I don't think his reason for liking country music the same as Joan's reason for liking country music, and Joan ain't even from the country. Well, her farmhouse is in the country, but that don't mean you's from the country.

Joan glanced at her ex-husband. He's always such a mystery to me, she said. But he's so sweet. Ain't he sweet?

No, I'm not sweet, said James.

I'm thinking I'm in some stupid movie, you know, them talking that silly talk like that, ain't that lovers' talk, talking about whether he sweet or ain't sweet—looking at him, though, I bet he is sweet maybe even Sweetness Itself—then he put out his new cigarette before he'd half-finished smoking it. He have a high, lined forehead; his dark complexion, though, make you hardly see the lines. In fact, except for that little gray in his mustache, he look kinda younger than Joan, though she say they the same age. I guess that's why some mens likes to get theyselves younger women, so's they don't look younger than they wives. I think it's just a power thing myself. Though they ain't gonna tell you it got nothing to do with power, they'll just tell you that younger women fascinating. Which might be the truth. Maybe them younger women is more fascinating to a man. That's why they's got laws, though. 'Cause you's gotta have laws to help some of them men to decide who's too young. Course when them womens gets power, they tries to play that same power game theyselves, 'cept with them older women, you's still gotta look like you's a younger woman. You might be a older woman, but you's still gotta look like you's a younger woman. You can't be no Sean Connery if you's a woman, you's gotta be Cher. I think it's just a power thing myself.

You were sweet to carry our bags up, but we'll be no further trouble, will we, Harlan?

I said nothing. James puffed on yet another cigarette and rolled his sleeves farther up. Joan apologized for something, but I didn't understand it—some private matter. I thought of the Ring Lardner story in which the man can't go to bed without apologizing for something; he apologizes even to his shaver before shaving.

Joan kept kicking her legs back and forth. He gave her a couple of irritated glances. He looked at me again. And looking at me like I'm somebody he think he already know. He flicked ash into the tray. Joan told me you're a good manager, he said, the cigarette in the corner of his mouth. There was still a bit of crumb of banana bread on his lip. To tell the truth I wanted to wipe that bit of banana bread from his lip myself, or lick it from his lip, or kiss it from his lip, and then, Say what? I asked. Joan told me you're a good manager, he said. He took the cigarette out of his mouth, licked at the crumb on his lip, then put the cigarette back in the corner of his mouth.

I try to be.

Are you or aren't you? he asked with impatience, the cigarette dangling.

I am, I said. Yes, I am. I don't think I could manage anyone but Joan, though. I don't understand how these managers can have more than one client and call themselves managing, you know.

Yeah, Joan is enough to manage, isn't she?

And then I'm thinking, he every man I know. He ain't just hisself, he

every man I know. But then men, they's supposed to talk like that. Is you
or ain't you a good manager? They's supposed to have the vocabulary of
command, it's women supposed to have the vocabulary of suggestion or
innuendo. They say even little boys at play are always commanding each
other, whereas little girls at play are always suggesting. Course there's
bossy control freak little girls, and you's gotta have little boys that takes
commands from other commanding boys. And then I feel like they got
me in their stupid movie, and he almost as handsome as one of them
movie stars. To tell the truth he a handsomer man than Joan a good-
looking woman. I bet he is sweet, I'm thinking. Then he ain't looking at
me. He staring at Joan's feet, which rotating clockwise, then counter-
clockwise. He put out the new cigarette.

I've stocked the refrigerator and the bar, he say swiftly to Joan, but
still looking at her feet. He pick up a brass tray from the mantelpiece,
look at its content of butts, put it down.

You're sweet, she said.

It was good to meet you, he muttered, staring at me finally. But then
he looking at me like he ain't so sure we know each other. I'll probably
see you before you leave, he says.

Stay for dinner, Joan say.

I would, Joan Darling, but I got to go over some lab reports.

Joan say you some kinda scientist.

Yes, I am.

Yes, he is some kinda scientist, say Joan. The language of innuendo.

Yes, I am, he repeat. But he don't tell me what kinda scientist, like a
scientist a scientist. He take a package of Camels from his breast pocket,
examine it like it a lab report, then put it back.

What are you working on now? Joan ask.

That new book I told you about: *Symmetry, Matrices, and Molecular Orbital Theory*, he say, and that Joan looking at him like she know
exactly what symmetry, matrices, and molecular orbital theory mean.
He start to say something else about that book he working on, but he
don't.

Have dinner with us tomorrow then? I ask.

Okay.

Joan purse her lips together and frown. Looking like I ain't supposed to say nothing to him, her ex-husband, and it her introduced us, and even telling me how sweet he is, and even telling me he more sweet than even he think he is his ownself. Anyway, he nod to me, walk by her, behind the couch, pause for a moment, glance at me, then hug her head and whisper, Be happy, and left. Joan ran her hands through her thick hair, and pouted. Then she picked up one of James' half-used cigarettes, lit it with one of them antique cameo-type lighter, one of them real expensive-looking lighter, and puffed.

So what's the story? I asked.

What do you mean? she asked, then she combed her hair back with her hands. She took a long draw, then put out the cigarette.

You're on friendly terms. Maybe even loving terms, I said. Do you think you'll work something out? How long have you been divorced? I mean, are you legally divorced? Do you think you'll get married again? I mean, you're divorced, but you don't really give me the impression of being divorced, and he still calls you Darling. I know people who get divorced and get married again, and I ain't even heard them call each other Darling. And I ain't never been called nobody's darling myself.

That's when she laughed and told me that he'd stay her ex. He'll stay my ex, darling, if that's what you mean. Anyway, he's got his little infatuations now. Younger, sweeter women.

But like I said they didn't behave with each other exactly like any ex-spouses that I knew about. So what's going on? I kept asking, and suggesting that maybe they'd get married again. I just kept suggesting that maybe they'd get married again. And Joan kept looking at me as if I was overstepping my bounds, asking and suggesting that maybe they'd get married again, but then she started telling me again that he had other women, other sweet young women. That's why I always find that Prince Charles so curious, you know, 'cause all them other men's other women is other sweet young women. I remember me and Joan seeing that Prince Charles on that television and Joan she say something about respecting his choice in women, and I ain't know what she mean by that, 'cause it ain't the opinion of them media people. I ain't ask her what she mean by that, and that Joan it seem like she's always liking the people that ain't the media darlings better than the people that is the media darlings, when most people likes the people that is the media darlings, or the people that is at least photogenic and charismatic. And then she have me sitting there watching that Prince Charles talking about architecture. And then she say that thing about respecting his choice in women. And then she say something about American culture being a immature culture, which didn't seem to have nothing to do with that Prince Charles. And what America being a immature culture have to do with Prince Charles? Then she say again about respecting his choice in women. And what that got to do with architecture? But maybe it just 'cause he the exception that prove the rule.

Why you so preoccupied with us? she asking, and I forgot about asking her about that divorce 'cause I'm thinking about immature American culture and Prince Charles. Girl, I ain't even as preoccupied with us as you are. Why we divorced or getting married again or staying divorced or ain't staying divorced or wanna be lovers again and people you know that's got divorced and got married again? You don't even know us. You don't know us. Well, you know me, or think you know me, or know me about as well as I know myself, or know me about as well as I think I know myself, but you don't know us. I know us, but sometimes I don't know him. Or I know him about as well as I know me. Girl, I ain't even as preoccupied with us as you are. Anyway, he's got his other women, his other little infatuations, his young sweet things. All that talk about a lab report. It might be a lab report, or his book on symmetry, matrices, and molecular orbital theory, or one of his little infatuations, one of his young sweet things, she said, picking up one of his cigarette butts and looking at it, as if she thought he was as addicted to his other women, his little infatuations, his young sweet things, as he was to his cigarettes.

I didn't keep asking questions, though. I studied the patterns in my armchair. And then she told me how they have joint ownership of the farm, how she bought it when she got her first money from her first real gig. Then it seem like after she had her first real gig, they got divorced and all.

At first I thought we'd work things out, you know. I guess I thought it. I don't even know why we got divorced. Well, I know why we got divorced. I guess I know why we got divorced. It wasn't catching him with some other woman, even a younger woman, or shit like that, or him catching me with some other man. Certainly no younger man. What's there of interest? You know, like that Pepsi commercial. No stupidity like that. One man's enough for me. Somebody once said I'm like the woman in that poem—I forgot what poem—where the poet asks, What does a woman want? Why, her own sweet way. Course a poet would say, Her own sweet way. Maybe the bitch who wants her own way ain't sweet.

Shakespeare? I ask. I mean, the poet.

Naw, not Shakespeare. He knows what a man wants, and what a man thinks a woman wants, even the best of women. He's good at portraying bitches, but even they're a man's idea of a bitch. You know, even Shakespeare's sweet bitches are still a man's idea of a sweet bitch. Chaucer's the only old bard who seemed to know what a woman really wants, at least the Wife of Bath—and she ain't really a bitch, she's just who she is—but I don't think that's Chaucer either. Then she start saying something that sound like it right out of that Chaucer, you know what that woman say about all them husband she have, but saying it like it right out of that Chaucer, and then she say, A woman wants to be her ownself, just like a man wants to be his ownself. Anyway, I guess you can't have a marriage where both people want their own sweet way, want to be too much of their ownselves, and won't negotiate. We're friends, still. We're both friends. Anyway, he looks after the place when I ain't here. He stays here when he wants, keeps a lot of his research papers and projects here, has what women he wants, his little infatuations, his little sweet bitches, I suppose, or bitches in training, and then I come here after my tours and recuperate. Do you remember *Carnal Knowledge*? I was just thinking of those women in *Carnal Knowledge*, and the way those men would talk about those women? You know, I was wondering if men really talk about women like that, you know. Jack Nicholson and that other guy? Garfunkel? You know of Simon and Garfunkel, I think he played that other guy. He had a few roles in movies then. I guess people thought he was more interesting than Simon in those days, I mean for roles in movies. I was a bitch in training myself I guess when I first saw that movie. I remember thinking that's sorta like the stereotyped idea that women have of men, that they talk about us like that, like we're things, you know, when they're talking to each other about us, but then there was this movie, and there were these men talking about women like that. White men, but men are men. I couldn't imagine Jamey talking to some man like that about me. Of course I hadn't met Jamey then. I don't think I'd met Jamey then. But the Jamey I imagined. So it's like that, you know. I don't bring any of my own infatuations here. In fact, I haven't had any infatuations since we divorced. You'd think I'd taken a vow of celibacy or some shit.

She nuzzled back against the pillow. Yes, I suppose he even brings other women here. I haven't asked him whether he's had other women up here. I just suppose. He hasn't said as much, but I know he does. He ain't celibate. Even if he ain't in love, he's got to have some infatuation. He's a passionate man. I suppose he doesn't seem so, but he is. And men's ideal is always the harem, ain't it. That's the ideal of every man I know, even the monogamous ones. Who do you think invented the harem? Woman's ideal is always the one great love. Most women.

Some men's ideal is the one great love.

Maybe. But he still wants his concubines. I always let him know when I'm coming up here, anyway.

That must bother you, I said.

No, we're divorced. Why shouldn't he have other women? Maybe I'd mind if it was more than a fling, more than a little infatuation. But we're divorced. Why shouldn't he have other women? Why shouldn't he have younger women even? I don't own him, but sometimes I think he still thinks he owns me, though. Did you hear him call me Darling? Yes? He still calls me Darling. He still thinks he owns me.

He doesn't act like he thinks he owns you.

What?

I was going to say he acts like he thinks you still own him. But he doesn't act like that either.

Yes he does. I mean, like he still owns me. He's not the sorta man you can own. I mean, himself. She massaged the tip of her nose, then swung her legs down. How about a drink? Bourbon? Scotch?

Scotch, with some soda.

She was up and at the oak bar. It was rough-hewn like the table, but well stocked. Rocks? She glanced over her shoulder.

Yeah.

He's handsome, I said.

She gulped her bourbon. Yeah.

I like your house too. It ain't like a rock star's house. You know, how you'd imagine a rock star's house. . . .

Thank you.

. . . . Except the high-ceilinged rooms. . . .

What about a rock star's husband? Or ex-husband, I should say.

He seems secure in himself. He seems to know who he is. He doesn't seem like a harem maker to me. I bet you're his great love. Anyway, I'm talking to the Schacter people—

Let's not talk shop. Or love. Or even great love. Why is it when I say it it doesn't sound like love? Anyway, you settle those questions. That's what I hired you for. Not the question of love, or great love, I mean my career.

She got up, danced over to the bar, carried the bottle of bourbon back and set it on the table. She gave me a sullen look. Then she reached for another of James' unfinished cigarettes, lit it and puffed.

Just let me know when the deal is made, okay? Though I do want to hear that new guitarist Jimmy Cuervo, the one you said's from South Texas. What's his name?

Jimmy Cuervo.

But no shop talk, let's agree, and certainly not when Jamey's here tomorrow. I don't know my own mind when Jamey's around.

I don't believe that. You call him Jamey. That's nice.

Does he look like a James to you?

What?

A James. Rather than a Jamey?

Yeah, I suppose.

Maybe that's my way of still calling him Darling. Actually he's a Jim. He was named after Jim Thorpe, you know the Indian. . . . the famous Native American athlete, the one they called the top athlete of the first half of the century. You know, that movie we saw about Jim Thorpe, in the days when they didn't get real Indians to play real Indians.

There's real Indians in that movie.

Extras. Minor roles. Not Jim Thorpe. But in America you don't know who's a real native. I don't know why he was named after him, though. Jamey, I mean. He ain't got no Native American in him that I know about. And he ain't never been too fond of sports or athletics. I think his daddy or granddaddy's just a great fan of Jim Thorpe's. He looks athletic, he works out, even does yoga, Jamey I mean, but he ain't fond of sports himself, though. Jim, that's his name. He don't like it, though. I think it reminds him of that Nigger Jim in Twain's book. You know, Nigger Jim. Ain't you read Twain? Girl, I know you read Twain. That's high school. Elementary school. You can't be a American and ain't read Twain, girl. Talk about un-American. Girl, you ain't a true American. That oughta be the test for Americanity: Have you read Twain? I'm just kidding, girlfriend. I wonder what that book'd sound like if Nigger Jim had told that tale? I bet Twain couldn'ta imagined Nigger Jim telling that tale, you know, or if he'da imagined it, I don't think they'da published a book with Nigger Jim telling that tale, even the Nigger Jim of Twain's imagination. People don't think of Jim Thorpe when they hear Jim, they think of Nigger Jim. Twain's Nigger Jim. So he calls himself James, and I call him Jamey. If they wanted to name him after Jim Thorpe, I think he'd've preferred Thorpe rather than Jim. Thorpe Savage. That sounds like a soap star. You know that guy on the soaps with all those braids, the fine-looking one, you know that fine-looking young man with all them braids, the one on that soap, naw I ain't talking about A Martinez you know A Martinez ain't got no braids and he ain't on the soaps now anyway, they oughta put him in the movies. . . .

He looks kinda like Nadine's husband.

Who Nadine? That Kim Basinger movie?

Naw, I mean my friend Nadine. This woman name Nadine from New Mexico. Well, she ain't originally from New Mexico, but she own her a little cantina-style restaurant in New Mexico. Ain't I told you about Nadine? Her husband from Mexico, though, I mean the real Mexico, look kinda like him. She think he better looking than even A Martinez, though.

. . . .did you see that made-for-TV movie with him in it, you know that good-looking, that African-American actor with all them braids what's his name, now he could be a Thorpe Savage, but not Jamey.

She poured more bourbon, spilled some on the coffee table, dabbed it with her sleeve.

I promise you'll be bored, she said.

No.

This ain't Vegas. Jamey ain't as flamboyant as the kinda guys I know you like. He's a passionate man, but he ain't a flamboyant passionate man.

You don't know what kinda guys I like. I only go to Vegas sometimes. It's mostly Saratoga, the races.

She poured more bourbon while I nursed my old glass of Scotch.

Well, I meant, Jamey ain't like your gambling buddies, he's into microbes. He's too sweet for you. But maybe you like 'em sweet. I bet you like yourself some sweet, don't you? Have you got a sweet tooth? I've never had much of a sweet tooth myself.

Yeah, you told me he's a scientist.

A microbiologist and a chemist, a researcher. Generates ideas for some sorta research company. He partly owns the company, so it's sorta his own company. Anyway, they generate ideas in biology and chemistry, mostly, for other companies, you know. Then the other companies do the more practical research, but then he has his own research, independent of the company. Both practical and theoretical. To tell the truth, I'm not really up on what his research is now. I used to always know what he was researching. Now he prefers a lot of theoretical stuff, you know, pure ideas. So that's sorta like the ideal company for him, you know, just generating ideas. A lot of his ideas are somewhere in the stratosphere. Whatever's the highest sphere. I think the highest sphere's the stratosphere. I don't understand a lot of his theories myself. So I was just telling you it ain't Vegas. Or Saratoga, or whatever. Jamey and I ain't as flamboyant as your gambling buddies and jockey friends. We'll bore you.

She puffed the cigarette down to its filter. I was silent.

Here I just rest up and take things easy, and Jamey's. . . . he's passionate about his work, his research, but otherwise. . . . Well, this ain't Vegas.

That's cool, I said. I like him.

Now you see how I spend my summer vacations. She picked up another unfinished cigarette and puffed.

He didn't seem to me like a unpassionate man. I wondered if they still made love, but that wasn't a question I'd ask.

I know we ain't supposed to talk about it, but do you mind if I give the Schacter people a call from here? I asked.

Why should I mind? You're looking out for me, right? Do you think I'm too old to be a rocker? Jamey thinks I'm too old to be a rocker.

You're too old to be a rapper, maybe, but there're rockers older than you.

Yeah, we're the true rockers, ain't we? Our generation. The best rockers are us.

CHAPTER TEN

One evening in the dressing room, after one of her shows, I'm rubbing Vitapoint into her orange hair and brushing it. This orange shit is shit, I say. You oughta cool it. Why don't you just look normal and let the music. . . . let the music. . . . like Aznavour says. . . . He ain't rock 'n' roll, but you remember when we were staying in that hotel in Paris and saw Aznavour on the television. . . . I don't think you oughta try to be Madonna or Rodman. . . .

I was doing this before Rodman or Madonna, changing the color of my hair. The fans that know me expect me to change the color of my hair all the time. I was changing the color of my hair when I was singing in the little clubs in Rhode Island. I told you when I was going to grad school in Rhode Island, that's when I first started singing professionally. . . . Well, I didn't want to be a singer, I just wanted to help pay my way through grad school. . . . You didn't even see colored people with blond hair in those days, I mean colored people my color with blond hair. . . . Anyway, what's normal? she asks. I mean, even though rock 'n' roll now is considered a mature music. . . .

What do you mean mature music?

I mean when you got classical rock and modern rock you got yourself a mature music. You know when Billy Joel usedta sing it's still rock 'n' roll to me. Well, in those days I couldn't even imagine a music beyond rock 'n' roll. But rap ain't rock. That's what I admire about the young singers is that they could imagine something beyond rock 'n' roll. . . . I don't really like all the rap I hear, and I think a lot of the music could use some maturity, but I admire the fact that they could imagine something beyond rock 'n' roll. I mean, now that rock 'n' roll is pretty music, Establishment music. Except my rock 'n' roll. I think music should be kinda controversial, I mean popular music. . . . I don't want my music to be the Establishment's Darling. I don't wanna be the Establishment's Darling. But I don't want it to be just decadence either. Though I think modern music has gotta be a little decadent, otherwise it isn't really reflecting the decadence of the modern world. You know, except my music kinda satirizes decadence. Like Madonna and the Artist Formerly Known as Prince, or some of the rappers. Sometimes you don't know whether they're satirizing decadence or decadence itself. I like the bubblegum rappers myself, you know the sweet rappers. Intellectually I know what Public Enemy and those other rappers, the gangsta women and the gangsta men are doing, but I like listening to the sweet rappers myself, the healing-type music. . . . I don't want my music to just be decadence itself.

I say nothing. I watch her through the mirror. I brush. I don't dig you, she say. On her dresser there's a paperback book of Freud's. I think it's got something to do with sex, but it ain't. It's got something to do with wit. I mean the title of that book says something about wit not sex. I didn't know that Freud wrote about wit. Seem like whenever people talk about Freud, they talking about sex. I thought the only thing he wrote about was sex. Sex and dreams and even dreams of sex. Maybe that book got to do with the wit of sex or the sexualization of wit.

I thought Freud only wrote about sex, I say. Sex and dreams. I didn't know Freud wrote about wit.

That's the Freud of the popular imagination, she says.

You mean of the sexual imagination, I say.

She don't say nothing, then I think she going to start saying something about catching me with her ex. Her sweet ex. I'm always thinking she's going to say something about that, even when there ain't any mention of sex. When I seen that Freud, I'm thinking she signifying about me and her ex. But it ain't a book about sex, it's a book about wit. I don't know what sort of degenerate game you were playing in my house. That's my house. That's what I imagine her saying. Or calling me a self-indulgent little bitch, or some shit. I keep thinking she's going to say something like that. 'Cause that sounds like Joan. She's even got a song about a self-indulgent little bitch, except she wrote it before she met me. Or maybe it's a song about herself. Maybe it's her idea of herself when she wrote that song. But she don't say nothing about that, about me and her ex. She just look at me through the mirror.

I apologize, I say.

What? For Christsakes, girl, you still thinking about that? You still chewing on that old chestnut. How the hell was I to know? I wouldn't have opened the fucking door if I'd known you two were bumping boody like a couple of bonobo monkies or some shit. . . .

What do you want? I ask. Do you want me to leave? What's a bonobo monkey?

It's you still chewing on that old chestnut, not me, she say, thumbing through that book of Freud's. When I want to fire you, I'll fire you. You're a good manager. In matters of love, you might be a fool. . . .

I pull at the tangles in her hair, knots and pieces that look like fishnet. I massage her hairline. This shit is really destroying your hair, I say.

She pull at a piece of fishnet.

What's a bonobo monkey?

You. Well, I suppose even you've got more morals than them. Do you think animals have codes of morality? I don't just mean sexual morality, I mean. . . . well, the higher codes of morality. Do you think animals have a higher moral nature?

CHAPTER ELEVEN

May I borrow your phone? I ask. We're on the veranda. Beers and pizza. My treat. He said he'd never had pizza. Unbelievable. I start to say something about them Germans and Italians during the war. Lotta Americans think of that pizza as American food as much as they do Italian. But he say he ain't never had none of that pizza. So I'd ordered us some. Eating his he said he knew why he'd never had pizza. And then I know he mean he ain't never had that American pizza. He say he had the true Italian pizza that got a taste that distinctive from American pizza or Italian-American pizza. He say he like the true Italian pizza better than American pizza. I'll reverse the charges, I say.

Go ahead, says Josef, sipping his Budweiser. And no need to reverse the charges.

I start to tell him that ain't the way you drink Budweiser. He drinking his Budweiser like he think it supposed to be champagne. Course maybe that's better than them people that drink champagne like they think it Budweiser. What's this new contraption? I ask, picking up the phone from the table just inside the glass doors.

The same odd honeycombed device attached to the receiver as at the hotel.

If the red light goes on it means our privacy's been invaded, he says.

On the table are some papers. Some look like contracts, but they's all in German. And there's a few handwritten letters, also in German. Maybe there're from that wife he's spoken about, but he ain't got no photographs of her, at least none that's visible.

Oh, yeah? I dial.

The red light does not go on, but Joan's voice says sleepily from the other end of the receiver, Hello?

This is Harlan. Are you set for tomorrow? We're supposed to meet the Schacter people.

Where the hell are you? Do you know anyone named Norvelle? Anyway, someone named Norvelle called you from Africa. Zanzibar, I think. Ain't that in Africa? Norvelle? At first he thought I was you. A message? No. Ain't that that new promoter you were telling me about? You were talking about some African promoter for my music. Zanzibar? Ain't rock 'n' roll against the law in Zanzibar? Oh, that Norvelle. Yeah, your ex-husband, you told me about him, but you didn't exactly tell me his name. Norvelle. Is that his name, Norvelle? I don't know how he got this number. Maybe he put a private detective on your ass. He told me where he was staying over there in Zanzibar. He thought I'd already written the name of the hotel and I asked him the name of the hotel again, but he already hung up. So I didn't get the name of the hotel. Naw, I didn't get his phone number. I thought it was that promoter you were talking about. I thought you already had his phone number. Girl, if he anything like his voice, you a fool.

B O O K

T W O

CHAPTER TWELVE

When my husband started following around that Masai medicine woman, I told him I was going back to the States. I'd followed him all over Africa while he recorded the medical lore of various tribal doctors. He said that there was a lot of traditional African medical lore that had never been recorded or collected. For him it was exciting, but I was exhausted. Let him follow the native doctors from Korogwe to Morogoro, from the Rufiji River to the Great Ruaha, from the Uluguru Mountains to Meru, in the Eastern Rift Valley. Actually, I found the African cities—Nairobi, Lumbumbachi, Kampala, and Douala—more interesting than the little villages or the African bush. On television and in the movies you always saw the little African villages and the African bush, or the people on safari, or the native African medicine men and women, but you never saw the cities with their modern buildings and the bustle and automobiles and rumble and bicycles and mixtures of type and dress. My husband referred to these city Africans as "detribalized." But I liked them, the African businessmen I saw in the hotels, the market women, the college students, and I liked the tastes and sights and sounds and smells of the cities, but especially the islands off the coast of Africa, the islands of Zanzibar and Pemba.

Although Norvelle, my husband, had books on modern, urban Africa and the detribalized African he still behaved himself as if Africa was all bush or highland village or damp river valley. And the minute we got to the tourist hotel, before I could rest up from the previous expedition to meet some new African medicine man or woman, he'd rent a jeep or a Land-Rover or a van and head toward the next wilderness. I used to wonder what women did when they got trapped in the wilds without their tampons or SNs. Did they use leaves? I didn't have to find out, though, because after the first expedition I developed amenorrhea.

Still, near Lake Eyasi when we watched one famous medicine woman perform, it was no magic hokum-pokum like I'd expected. It resembled some intricate surgical procedure, but a makeshift one. Like when she pushed the reed into the man's belly and sucked out gallstones.

Why ain't the man showing any pain? I whispered.

Because he trusts her, said Norvelle, standing beside me with his notebook in which he scribbled notes and drew sketches. It looked like those naturalist's notebook you see in the library, except he's what's called a medical anthropologist. To show pain would be a sign of disrespect, he explained.

But he feels it? I asked.

Yes, but she's given him. . . . he gave the name of some natural herb, though I don't remember the name of it. Anyway, when she finished making the man well, she spit on him behind the ears. Norvelle explained it was another sign of goodwill and respect. But while Norvelle stood talking with her in Masai, or whatever the language, some Bantu language, I contemplated her bald head, brass earrings, and bare hanging ashy breasts. She smiled at the man she'd just cured, then she spat behind his ears again. A lot of respect, I mumbled, wondering if she could cure my amenorrhea. But just as well. Ignoring me, Norvelle and the woman continued talking.

Ain't we going to what's its place? I asked, back at the hotel. Ain't we supposed to go to some Gamba village?

And he had also promised to take me to some volcanic crater, the Ngorongoro, and he had planned to meet a highlander medicine man near Tabora. And afterwards he'd promised we could return to Zanzibar or Pemba, not to collect any lore, but to have a real honeymoon, to eat coconuts and lie on a beach or go to the markets not to query where such and such a medicine man or woman could be found, but to buy ornaments of coral or ebony. Not ivory, Norvelle said, because of the elephants.

He wanted to stay with her, he said, the Masai medicine woman. He wanted to go to the next village she decided to go to. He'd learned more lore from her than any of the others, so he'd already arranged to meet her the next morning. So I told him he could follow her to Kingdom Come, but I was going back to the States. I was still hot and funky from the last expedition, and even my Extra Power deodorant stick hadn't been made with the African bush in mind. I went and took a shower.

In the morning I boarded my plane. I ain't the kind of woman who'd follow a man anywhere. I decided that a long time ago. I'll follow a man just so far and then. . . . Well, you ain't heard my grandmother Jaboti's story yet. She claimed that she followed a man so far that she turned into a human being. Me, if I wasn't a human being yet, I wouldn't follow a man so far, even if his intention was to turn me into one. Or if that was his conceit, that by following him I'd turn into a full human woman. But that's another story, and most people think that she's a crackpot anyhow. But like all little girls, you hear how the older women, mothers and grandmothers, handle their questions of romance and love, and you make your own resolutions, mostly what you won't do. Listening to their tales is as close to a initiation ritual as you get in the New World.

Anyway, so when I look back on it now, of course it was jealousy, plain and simple. Jealousy, I guess. That Masai medicine woman with all her charms hanging out, and all his looks of admiration for her knowledge. And me dragging along behind, carrying the Nikon camera, and fighting mosquitoes and dragonflies and tsetse flies and funkiness and the heat and not knowing which way was up. . . . I'd have preferred to have been in one of the nightclubs in the city drinking palm wine. And do you suppose, though, if I'd been the anthropologist and told him I'd planned to follow some medicine man that he'd have come along carrying the Nikon? I think not.

And it wasn't that I didn't like that Masai woman. Thaka, I think he called her. A small, round woman, round head, round body, beautiful by the standards of her tribe. I liked her, but following him following her? No thank you. But once she'd surprised me by speaking English. And I found out that she'd actually studied European medicine, that

she'd been a top student in one of the mission schools and had won a
scholarship to study in London, and when she returned to the Rift Valley, she'd worked as a sort of medical liaison and interpreter between
the Tanzanian villages and some international medical organization,
Doctors Without Walls or Sans Frontiers or one of those organizations.
She herself, though she knew the European medicines, used traditional
medicine because the people themselves whom she worked with re-
sponded more favorably to that. Sometimes the traditional medicine
worked where the modern, European drug didn't. And when there were
parallel medicines, where a certain herb or root for instance contained
the exact same chemical compounds one found in a synthetic European
pill, she'd use the traditional herb or root. In fact, Norvelle said many
European medicines had and have herbal beginnings, such as the ma-
laria cure. When she used European medicine, it was introduced within
the African context. Least that's what Norvelle said about her in a article he wrote on the subject. Actually, Norvelle published a series of papers on her in a medical anthropology journal, and then collected them
into a book on traditional Masai medicine.

Are you a medical anthropologist, too? she'd asked, her accent British. I tried to picture her out of her traditional Masai clothes and in European, but I couldn't. Norvelle was making a sketch of her, and she'd
glanced at me and asked that.

No, I said. I didn't even know what medical anthropology was until
I met Norvelle.

You're just with him? she asked, sounding like I was some sort of
groupie or hanger-on.

Yes, I said.

Norvelle kept sketching her and I took photographs.

So when I said I didn't want to follow him following her anymore, he
drove me to the airport in the van. He kept looking as if he thought I'd
change my mind, you know, but I didn't. And his own pride, I suppose,
kept him from asking me to stay. Or did he feel relief? Did he want to be
free to be with her? Not just to study her, but to be with her? But he said
he'd stay at the hotel until I arrived in London, before transferring

planes, in case I changed my mind and gave him a call. But when I arrived in London, I merely transferred planes. If I'd called him, would he have kept his promise to be at the hotel, or would he already be with her?

At first he sent me postcards on which he scribbled bits and pieces of new medical lore he'd picked up. He sent translations of songs and chants he'd collected, because he thought I'd like them, or just to fill in the empty spaces. He even sent me some love magic chants from a Kikuyu medicine man, and told me about a special tree they have called the Mote wa Ombani. Mothaiga wa rwenda, he said it was called. Love magic. Just to fill in the empty spaces. He didn't speak of Thaka, the Masai woman, in any of his postcards, but I knew he still followed her. Then the postcards came fewer, then stopped. I went about for a while feeling as if I'd made a mistake, that I shoulda stayed with him in Africa, but I'd thought and acted for myself. I don't know how much was fatigue and and how much jealousy. Or how much was simply wanting to be my own woman. Anyway, I kept saying to myself, if it was a mistake, then it was my own. And I acted like the woman I imagined I'd become, not like the woman that perhaps Norvelle or any other man imagined for me.

Still, there was times I thought of going back to Tanzania to hunt up that Masai woman, for I figured finding her would find where Norvelle was. If he kept writing articles about her, then she knew where he was. The journal he wrote articles for claimed not to know his whereabouts. So I went to Saratoga and bet on a horse, and to my own surprise, I won.

When I got back to Louisville, Grandmother Jaboti told me, He been here.

Who was here?

Norvelle.

Didn't you tell him where I was?

I tried to. But he jumped to his own conclusions. You know how mens is. Thought you was off with some lover. I give him your address, but he didn't want to catch you with some lover.

So, did he say where he was going?

Couldn't get no word outa him edgewise after he thought he had done got your story. He think he know you, don't he? He brought me some palm wine. I never had it before, but I likes the taste of it. And a can of zebra stew. Now you know I wouldn't eat stew made from no zebra. And dressed up looking just like a African. And braids in his hair. I wouldn'ta recognized him if I didn't already know him.

I said nothing. I climbed onto a wooden stool and started cleaning brushes.

Maybe he be back, Grandmother Jaboti said. If he know you as much as he think he do.

I just cleaned brushes.

CHAPTER THIRTEEN

And no, there weren't any lovers, not at first, not till Josef. The first time, though, I spent with someone else it was this old jockey. We just talked and talked. I didn't meet him at the racetrack, though, but on the porch of a little hotel I was staying at. We both had racing forms. I collected old racing forms, so the one I was reading was one I'd just purchased, an old Saratoga race. He made a joke of that old racing form, then I told him I was a collector of them. So first off we started talking about horses and racing, then we started talking about anything and everything. We spent the whole summer talking and talking and then when it was time for me to leave he got all strange-sounding, like it had been more than talk for him. Like he thought he'd been courting me or something. So I went to bed with him. It was stupid. I told him I didn't want it to happen again, though. Then it won't happen again, he said. Then I told him about Norvelle and the Masai woman, and showed him some of the articles that Norvelle had written about her. He said nothing. He just looked at me. I don't know what he was thinking. He had long eyelashes for a man and this made him look exotic, but he still looked very masculine, a little man, you know how jockeys are, but still very masculine, and them long eyelashes made me call him Bird of Paradise or simply Paradise. But his name's Nathaniel. From West Virginia. He'd grown a little pounchy around the middle, he said, but the rest of him was still as trim and solid as when he won his first race.

Bird of paradise. I used to think that they were mystical birds—mythical birds, I mean—but they're real, them birds of paradise. Norvelle had this book about this man who went on this trek to New Guinea to discover them, and it was full of their pictures. Dancing on the ground and in treetops in their courtship dance. Norvelle said that was the sort of book he'd like to write, a pure naturalist's book. The man who'd written this pure naturalist's book had also formed a foundation to protect these birds, these birds of paradise, because they got the most beautiful feathers, and so they's hunted, and it's becoming harder and harder to find them. I guess that's why a lot of people don't know that they's real birds. Norvelle, of course, sent in some bucks to this foundation to protect the birds of paradise. Then he sent in some bucks to another foundation to help protect the human species. He didn't think it was right protecting birds and not protecting humanity. But he'd wanted to be a naturalist before he'd decided to become a medical anthropologist. He was in college during the 1960s and becoming a naturalist didn't seem "relevant" and certainly he didn't know of any African Americans who were naturalists, not pure naturalists, so he decided to become a medical anthropologist instead. He could've been a naturalist in Africa, but in those days people wouldn't have considered it relevant, the young militant students who were his schoolmates and who once took over an administration building. He wasn't one of the spokesmen for the group or even a mediator; he went back and forth bringing them food and water and made sure that they had enough to sustain themselves while they kept the administration building. The situation he said was resolved peacefully, though, and they got certain of their demands: an African and African-American Studies Department, more "teachers of color"—not just African-American teachers, but other teachers of color, more students of color, and assorted other demands that seem trivial now. From Oklahoma City, Oklahoma, where all the African Americans he knew had always been self-reliant, he'd felt ambivalent about some of the demands himself. He'd wanted to be relevant, though, so he made sure they had enough food and water.

Pretty-eyed birds, them birds of paradise, though. And of course it was the males who did the courtship dance, and like most bird species, it was the males who were the brightly colored, attractive ones.

When I told Paradise about the birds of paradise and why I was calling him out of his name—Nathaniel Bower—to call him a better name, he told me about the bowerbird and its nest of shells and fruit and feathers. He'd been searching for the meaning of his name once, like we all sometimes do, and discovered the bowerbird. It built a nest of shells and fruit and feathers to attract female birds. But the female birds didn't even use the nest. They were attracted to the male birds that built the best nest. They'd allow themselves to be mated in that nest, but then they'd lay their eggs in their own nest somewhere else. But he liked Paradise better. Or that I called him that, though most people just called him Nat.

So you want to travel the road back to him, he said when I told him about Norvelle. We were sitting on the porch of the hotel where both of us was staying there in Saratoga. A hotel with a long porch.

The road back to him got twisted, I said.

Then untwist it. But I don't think his bower is better than mine.

I didn't answer. Paradise said he liked to see me at the racetrack. At the racetrack, I sprang to life, and I was fun. And when I talked of Keeneland or the Kentucky Derby or the Santa Anita Derby or the San Felipe Stakes, or some new Thoroughbred or even some new jockey, or who won what race by what length victory. . . . But when I talked about Norvelle I just sounded like a fool.

Let's have dinner, Paradise suggested.

Sure.

He seemed surprised.

Look, I don't want you to have any illusions about me, though, I said.

Old jockeys ain't got no illusions. Old black jockeys got fewer than none.

Pictures of celebrities decorated the walls, movie stars like Clark Gable and singers like Billy Eckstine. And there was the other Billie, the Holiday, in her gardenias. So young then. The woman who owned the place said it was from an advertisement of her for her first performance in New York. In the thirties, she'd taken a train from New Orleans, the woman who owned the place. She'd seen the movie starring Clark Gable and Carole Lombard—no, it was Jean Harlow. The one that had put Saratoga in the limelight, or on the map, and so she'd opened a restaurant specializing in southern cooking.

I always look forward to seeing you, he said after we'd ordered. He had a way of talking that surprised me. Sometimes it was what you call proper, I guess from being around West Virginia bluebloods—or did they have bluebloods in West Virginia or just Virginia? He was born, though, he said, in New York, in Harlem, but his family, unlike most families in those days, had migrated south to West Virginia. While other people were moving north to the promised land, they were traveling south. His father he said had an obsession with trees and wanted his children to grow up around trees and not concrete. When he'd thought of West Virginia, though, he'd always thought of the mountains, of the West Virginia coal mines. But his father worked on farms, mostly, in tobacco and racehorse country, the part of West Virginia near the Virginia border. He stayed small, and around horses it just had seemed natural that he'd become a jockey. But his father would talk and talk and talk and talk about trees and being able to ride for miles and see nothing but trees and green. He taught his children to appreciate the green. Not the green of the dollar bill, but the green of nature, of the countryside. But then he stopped talking, because he was making the South sound like a paradise, and it wasn't no paradise.

I bit into a spicy chicken wing. I thought he was going to tell me some southern nightmare that his father had encountered, some southern nightmare like in that Billie Holiday's song, but he didn't. So I ate my chicken and looked at Billy Eckstine, then at Nathaniel. Then at Billie Holiday.

She says that's the very first advertisement of Billie Holiday's very first concert, I said. I wonder how much a collector would pay for that. She didn't have it framed or anything. I'm the one told her to frame it. I wonder if Billie Holiday ever come to Saratoga to bet on the horses. Did you see that movie *Lady Sings the Blues*?

Yeah.

I seen it two or three times. Read the book too. It's based on her autobiography. The book moves back and forth in time, though, more than the movie. You think you're in one time and the next chapter you're in another. Joan says it's kinda like jazz. That that's what she's trying to do in that autobiography, kinda suggest the improvisations of jazz. Joan says she sing like her voice is a horn. You know, try to do with her voice the same thing them horn players do. Like what Satchmo would try to do with his horn, she would try to do with her voice. That's why her voice ain't like no other woman voice. On account of that horn. I don't know if she ever been to Saratoga, though.

Seem like once I was here, somebody said "the lady" here. And there only one lady so I know who they talking about. I didn't see her myself, though, but somebody said "the lady" here and that the only lady I know anybody to be talking about. I remember when there were black jockeys up and down, though, he said. Now I'm 'bout the only old spook around. Oh, plenty of us come up here to bet on the horses, but ain't none of us riding them. I heard a man to say that if we weren't riding 'em and owning 'em we shouldn't bet on 'em. But you know we'll bet on 'em anyhow, 'cause that's how we are. I don't ride the horses anymore, though. I don't bet on 'em much myself. Sometimes I escort folks to the track, show them around the city.

I tried to imagine him as a young jockey, but I couldn't. When he retired he stayed in Saratoga, I guess for the green. There was still some green here. I looked at Billy Eckstine again, and then at Billie Holiday, and then at Paradise. I thought of that story by Carson McCullers about the jockey. I wondered if anybody had written any tales about jockeys like him.

The waitress set a shot of whiskey on the table for him and a sloe gin fizz for me.

Were you ever married? I asked.

Naw. In those days I wasn't taking any chances with a woman. I was too intent on being the best jockey around, you know. I had a few girls. You attract girls. No one like you.

I said nothing. I grabbed an ashtray from another table and lit a cigarette.

Is this your first time in the States? someone at a table behind us asked. Yes. I was in San Francisco first. I thought all Americans were like that, without values. Oh yeah? Is that Jean Harlow? Jean Harlow or Carole Lombard one. Carole Lombard? I wouldn't be knowing that one. Clark Gable married her. Oh, that one. I'd be knowing that one for certain.

Bird of Paradise gave me a large, warm smile. I tried to picture him in the winner's circle.

You still wear his ring, he noticed.

Yeah.

I did have a woman I almost married, once. I'd just had me a good season, my best season in the world and I was making a whole lotta bread, you know, and it turned out to be the bread and not me the girl was after. She'd take me for sure as long as I was dressed like a king.

CHAPTER FOURTEEN

Statuettes of saints crowded the shelves in my mother's and grandmother's beauty shop. They were my mother's saints because my grandmother thought it was merely entertaining to have them. No one in the family was Catholic. But a customer and a Catholic, pleased with a new hairdo, had given them to my mother and she'd kept them. Though a Southern Baptist, she was convinced they were holy. There was a little Peruvian saint who was our complexion, but the other saints were white. At least the one who'd imagined them had painted them white. Every time they got dusty, she'd diligently take them down and clean and polish them. Grandmother called them whatnots.

My mother attended church regularly and believed in the Bible passage which said: Whatever you do to the least of my brethren, you do to me. Something like that. She interpreted it to mean that you should treat everybody as if they were Christ. Whenever you're about to do something mean or disrespectful to someone imagine they're Christ, she'd say, and then decide how to treat them. That was superior, she felt, even to the Golden Rule. So, among some, she got the reputation for being a good and wise woman. Among others, she was considered a fool and a pushover. Needy people crowded to her door. So, as a child, I grew up thinking the whole world was needy, except for blue-haired and blue-veined Mrs. Smoot, who somehow kept above need. When I discovered there were other kinds of people in the world, people who weren't needy, though, I found them more interesting because less familiar.

When I got a chance to leave Louisville, even to go to beauty school in Cincinnati, I took it. But I had aspirations beyond beauty school. I audited a few courses at the University of Cincinnati. I remember once I went to a lecture on Nietzsche. At the reception I was standing at a table eating cheese and one of the girls in one of the classes I was auditing spotted me and came over.

I didn't know you were interested in Nietzsche, she said. She said something about our reading assignment, Camus' *The Rebel*. She didn't think Camus' book was genuine philosophy—literature but not philosophy.

But you'll probably ace it, she said.

I explained that I was just auditing the course, that I wasn't a regular student but studying cosmetology at the local beauty school. She laughed, picked up a piece of cheese and an oyster cracker and moved toward others, glancing back at me, whispering, laughing. "She's a beautician," I thought I heard her say. "I thought she was a philosophy major." I stopped auditing the university courses and concentrated on beauty, though I wasn't too sure what beauty was.

When I returned home one summer vacation my mother was entertaining some visiting African Baptists. Sometimes she rented rooms above the beauty shop and several of them were staying in those rented room, for free, because she wouldn't take money from visiting African Baptists. I knew there were Catholics in Africa, because there were Catholics everywhere, but I didn't know that Africa had any Baptists. Anyway, my future husband was escorting them and acting as their guide and interpreter. But since they spoke impeccable English themselves, his duties were mainly to interpret for them our curious idioms, colloquialisms and peculiar southern turns of phrase. They'd just been on a trip to Mammoth Cave, Kentucky, and it was all their talk—not of religious things. They kept talking about the transparent fish that swim in the underground streams at Mammoth Cave, what the tour guide had called spirit fish.

Norvelle and I watched each other before we even said a word. But it was only when the group was about ready to leave—still talking of the cave fish—that Norvelle spoke to me.

I enjoyed our stay very much, he said, as we stood together in the supply room where rows and rows of cosmetics and hair care products were stored. He'd seen me come back there and followed.

I'm sorry I didn't really get a chance to talk to you.

Well, I'm shy as the devil too, I said.

I lifted a jar of Ultra Sheen hair dressing. He smiled, reached into his pocket and took out a pad.

I'm an anthropologist, he explained. It's my first year at Bloomington, I mean the university there. I teach during the year, but in the summer I escort various African groups.

Mom says you know a lot of African languages.

A few. He kept both eyes on me, but I kept peering from him to the jar of Ultra Sheen. Well, I've always been good with languages. I just seem to pick them up, especially African languages. I just seem to pick them up. Anyway, here's my address, if you're ever in Bloomington.

You a real professor? I asked, looking at the card.

Of course I'm real.

You don't act like no professor.

He laughed. How's a professor s'posed to act?

Not like you.

I prefer fieldwork to the classroom, though, he said. I've never much liked the classroom actually. So I'm in blue jeans most of the time. I collect folklore, medical lore from different African tribes, to help to preserve it. You know, I'm what they call a medical anthropologist. But I'm boring you. Well, if you're ever in Bloomington. . . .

One rainy day after I'd finished beauty school and had worked for a couple of months in the family business as a licensed beautician, I appeared on the porch of a little stucco house in Bloomington. When he opened the door, I said, Surprise.

When I got inside he hugged me. I kept looking around. There was nothing but books and papers piled to the ceiling and photographs and sketches of Africa and Africans and masks and sculptures and drawings. I recognized none of them then, of course, except that they were African. Only later under his tutelage could I distinguish an Igbo mask from a Bambara, an Ife sculpture from one from Benin. And I thought the painted calabashes were also sculptures. And I had no idea who Skunder Boghasian was, but I thought the name sounded Scandinavian, not African. Nor had I heard of Lamidi Fakeye or Yemi Bisiri. I didn't know a Ashanti sculpture from an Anyi.

What are you looking for? he asked.

Another woman. Maybe you married or something. Maybe you got yourself a wife I ain't know about. I just remembered, you might be married or something.

Naw, I'm not married. He was wearing blue jeans and a light green sweater over a polo shirt. Except for the blue jeans, he looked kinda like a professor.

Ain't you surprised I'm here? I asked.

I'm happy.

I bet you angry I didn't write and tell you I was coming.

No, I'm just glad you're here.

I wasn't sure I'd show up. Didn't want to tell you I was coming and then not show up. You know, chicken out, or something. And then I wasn't sure if you really wanted me to look you up if I ever came to Bloomington. You know, how some people tell you that, just to be polite. *Mi casa es su casa.* But they don't actually mean it. Then I was thinking you couldn't really be interested in me, because if you're a real college professor then you'd want yourself a professional-type woman.

I don't say what I don't mean, he said. Then he kissed my jaw, then my mouth, then he took off my coat. And I ain't always been a professional-type man myself.

CHAPTER FIFTEEN

I was a turtle before I became a human being, said my grandmother. She was taking a new order of beauty products out of the boxes and restocking the shelves. The beauty products were from a wholesaler in New York. She thought New York beauty products were superior to local and regional products, even when the beauty products were manufactured by the same company and only distributed by a local or regional company. Perhaps she believed that the beauty products which they allowed to be distributed by local or regional companies had inferior ingredients. She didn't seem to notice the contradiction: that if those products allowed to be distributed by local or regional companies contained inferior ingredients, then wouldn't they sell her products with inferior ingredients? She said, though, that she could get a discount when she ordered the products in bulk from New York, whereas she didn't get a discount when ordering them from a local distributor. She even had the ambition of manufacturing her own beauty products, but said she would only manufacture them if she could make a better beauty product than those already on the market. And the beauty products that she herself manufactured would all contain superior ingredients no matter to what region they were marketed. Her beauty products marketed out West would have the same superior ingredients as those marketed to the Northeast or the South. She was however negotiating with the wholesaler in New York so that Cornella and Jaboti's Beauty Shop, Inc., could become a local distributor of their products. But wouldn't they sell her inferior products? Again, she didn't seem to notice the contradiction. Cornella and Jaboti, though, would advertise their New York connection, which would make them the superior beauty shop. In fact, they would advertise their international connections, for she was always sending to different parts of the world, wherever there were colored people, for samples of their beauty products. She was certain, though, that other nations wouldn't ship beauty products with inferior ingredients to America.

Then I saw this handsomest young man and took a liking to him, she said, as she put the superior beauty products on the shelves. Do you want to know how far I followed him? She chuckled. I followed him until I turned into a human being. Is that far enough for you?

Mother, rinsing brushes in the sink, said nothing, like she always did when Grandmama told her turtle stories. As soon as Grandmother turned her story into fantasy, Mother always brought it back to reality again.

She was a Turtle Woman in a carnival, explained my mother. She played the Turtle Woman. You know how them carnivals got them the Bearded Lady. Well, they's got Turtle Women and Crocodile Women and every type of freakish womanhood. They had her in one of them carnival tents and people paid their money to come and see the Turtle Woman. In those days, I think it only cost them a nickel or a dime to see the Turtle Woman or them other freakish women. Mighta just cost them a penny to see those freakish women, but that was considered good money in those days. They put a nacre shell on her back. A fake shell to pretend like she was part turtle and part woman. I don't even know if they paid her good money to be their Turtle Woman, but I guess they paid her better money than they were paying domestics in those days, but not as good money as they paid them factory workers, you know. You go up North and get you a job in one of them factories, that's good money, or even around here working in them tobacco factories after the war, that's better money, you know, than being a domestic. Or you could be a schoolteacher, but a schoolteacher ain't no kinda independence, and in those days, you know, all the schools were segregated, but that still ain't no kinda independence, and even the colored schools had to be obliged to the white superintendents, you know. The colored schools could have their own principals, but only the white men could be the superintendents, and not even white women in them days, just the white men. I don't even think they have white women superintendents these days. They can be principals in the schools, but not superintendents. Daddy saw her and fell in love. He knew the shell wasn't real, and that's the truth, but he kept coming to that carnival till she up and left the carnival and followed him. She said that he were the first man enamored of her among all the men that would pay their good money to see the Turtle Woman, and that them other men just thought of her as freakish, as one of them freakish women, whether or not they believed in the reality of that turtle's shell. Now that's the truth. That the truth. You can tell all the turtle stories you want to tell, but that's the truth. She say Daddy say that a fake turtle shell don't make her a fake woman, and that he more interested in the woman than the fact that she played a fake Turtle Woman in that carnival. She say that he could see the genuine woman behind that fake turtle shell. She say he say that she a more genuine woman than any woman he know, a category which he say ain't just limited to colored women, which some mens do. You know, how some mens do. They'll compare you to other colored women, but not to Womanhood Itself, and prefers every other man's woman to they own. You know, like that television show we were watching, and they were asking them men about they women, and all the other men complimented they women on their beauty, but when they asked the colored men didn't none of them say nothing about beauty, they complimented they women on everything but beauty, exceptin' those that had them the other men's woman, or them of us that most resembles the other men's woman. Ain't that right? Well, I noticed what them colored men said. She got them hunched shoulders, though, from wearing that fake turtle shell. That the truth.

I was five and sitting on the counter. When Grandmother finished putting them new beauty products on the shelves, she braided my hair. In the long mirror, I could see her. I could see her hunched shoulders that looked as if they had really gotten hunched like that from wearing a fake turtle shell. I couldn't imagine her, though, as fitting the description of "freakish women," like the Bearded Lady, although others might've seen those hunched shoulders as a sign of freakishness. She smiled like she knew that her tale was the true one, or that a tale could be true and not be a true tale—that perhaps her Turtle Woman stories were truer than any carnival tale. I didn't say whose tale I believed, though. I only squirmed as she twisted my hair into braids.

And spose I wasn't really a real Turtle Woman? she asked. Spose I wasn't? Spose I'm just a rogue in disguise. They had some real ones, though. Had a fake Bearded Lady but they had them a real Unicorn Woman, I know that for the truth, a woman with a real horn just like a unicorn, I mean a real horn just like a unicorn's and not a fake one, though some people swore it was a goat's horn that they just glued on, and a colored woman too, I mean a real colored woman, and that's the truth. A lot of people when they would see that sign advertising the Unicorn Woman, they'd think she a white woman, you know, 'cause all the unicorns in the storybooks is white, 'cause that's supposed to be a sign of purity, you know, and even the colored people that come to see the Unicorn Woman, they's as surprised as the white people that she ain't a white Unicorn Woman, 'cause even colored people thinks that white's a sign of purity, and she is a genuine Unicorn Woman, but a colored one. 'Cause ain't none of them seen no colored unicorn in none of them mythology books or storybooks neither, so colored people usselves thinks they's only white unicorns. Of course I heard someone say that even if she a real Unicorn Woman, she still a fake one, just by virtue of being colored. But I know that horn real and I know she a real Unicorn woman. And her horn as real as this braid. She lifted a braid in the air and waved it. She pulled it out like a horn, she did a little dance, and shook the braid again. At least I think that horn was real. I can't testify to the reality of that horn, but I believe it to be real. I mean, I know that horn to be real although I can't testify to the reality of it being a real horn. I mean, there wasn't nothing that Unicorn Woman said or did to make me disbelieve the reality of that horn.

Hush, said Mother, running water in the sink. She'll grow up and won't be able to tell truth from truth. You can't know the reality of that

unicorn horn and not know it's reality at the same time. That ain't logical in nobody's book of logic. It ain't inductive reasoning and it ain't de-
ductive reasoning. I don't know what kinda fallacy that is, but it sounds
like the fallacy of contrary propositions. It ain't classical logic.

I don't know whether it a contrary fallacy or a logical proposition,
say Grandmother Jaboti. It might not be classical logic, but it's Jaboti's
logic. Ain't it, Possum?

Well, she'll grow up and won't be able to tell truth from truth. And
look like she don't know how to tell truth from truth even now.

I don't say nothing, 'cause I don't know nothing about that logic. I
know she ain't meant truth from truth, though, but she didn't correct
herself and Grandmother didn't correct her either. And maybe she did
mean truth from truth? And suppose she mean truth from truth? Then
how that any different from Jaboti's logic. But truth from truth can't be
the fallacy of contrary propositions, can it? Ain't truth and truth the
same thing? What the opposite of the fallacy of contrary propositions?
The fallacy of equivalent propositions?

Tell me some more about the Unicorn Woman, I said, 'cause I ain't
know nothing about that logic. Did she follow a man anywhere to turn
her human? And how come a woman got to follow a man to turn human? I start to ask, How come a woman can't follow her ownself to turn
human? I ain't know nothing about that logic, but I know enough to
know that that don't sound logical, and that maybe they's got a fallacy
of impossibilities. Later, when I'd be reading through one of them books
of Joan's, it would say something about logical truth, and seem to distinguish logical truth from true truth, that is that something could be logi-
cally true, that is, fulfill all the requirements of classical logic, you know,
them different syllogisms and still not be truly true. I ain't sure that's
what that book on logic mean, though.

Now she's already human as far as I know, say Grandmother Jaboti. Just having a horn don't mean you ain't human. The unicorn is
more mythical, though, than the turtle, which is more a ordinary type
and common animal, so she were more attractive to the people, especially the mens, white and colored, and especially them idealistic and

romantic-type men that likes to idealize and romanticize women, you know, like Mrs. Smoot, you know, the pharmacist's wife was saying about her husband, or that's just her conceit about herself or her conceit about him, than the Turtle Woman or them other confabulatory women that they had at that carnival, you know, 'cause the turtle is ordinary and a common animal, and people even makes soup out of turtle. I don't believe anyone would make soup out of a unicorn, even if it weren't a mythical beast. They might try to corrupt its purity, like in that movie we seen, you know, but ain't even a fool would try to make soup out of a unicorn. I wouldn't eat turtle soup myself, though. Or turtle pies neither. Although people who considers theyselves good people eats turtle soup and turtle pies too. But you don't make soup or pies outa unicorns. The Unicorn Woman. . . . more men would go to that Unicorn Woman's tent than to the Bearded Lady or the Turtle Woman, and there's even them that considered her the ideal of womanhood, like I said. And she told me that she received a note from one of them romantic gentlemen that came to see her and that kept following her from carnival to carnival and the note say that he think she the ideal of womanhood, and there ain't many colored women that they considered the ideal of womanhood in them days, just like Cornella said. Except the woman name Horne, that Lena Horne. They would consider her a beautiful woman by anybody's standards, I mean anybody that's got standards of what's beauty, and don't mean us all gots to look like other men's woman. Now ain't none of the mens told me that I'm the ideal of womanhood, though, or even that I'm especially beautiful. Being a beautician don't means you's got to be beautiful yourself, it just means you knows how to beautify. Now, the mens, though, they's told me I'm a genuine woman, that is since I've been transformed into a genuine human woman and ain't a turtle, genuine or ain't, but it takes a true mythical woman to be the ideal of true womanhood, colored or ain't. Why, even the proprietor of that first carnival she was at become obsessed with her, until he found him a woman that he thought the more ideal of womanhood than herself. Then he sold the Unicorn Woman to another carnival, 'cause he didn't want them competing ideals of womanhood.

Least I think that's why he sold her to another carnival. The Unicorn Woman, I mean. . . . He didn't sell me to no other carnival, on account of I ain't no everyman's ideal of womanhood, except my man's, but the Unicorn Woman. . . .

Unicorn Woman my hairbrush, said Mother. Unicorn Woman my straightening comb. Ideal of womanhood? Woman's gotta be her own ideal of womanhood. Can't depend on a man for it.

Grandmother did the little dance, and shook my braid in the air, and told me again the tale of the Unicorn Woman. There's plenty of mens crazy about her, like I said, crazy in love or in infatuation and even follow her from carnival to carnival, her being a mythical-type ideal woman, but she ain't follow none of them. And she is still a carnival woman, except she ain't with the same carnival, she's got her own troupe of confabulatory-type people. She's a free woman now, free and independent, and can't nobody sell her, or rather sell her contract, when they decide that another confabulatory woman is their new ideal of womanhood. Now she got her own carnival troupe. I know a few fools myself that usedta follow her from one carnival to another, even since the war years, and is still following her from carnival to carnival, though now it's her own carnival, 'cause some mens is like that, but she didn't follow none of them men. If it's possible for a woman to follow her own-self, it's her. Free and independent. And's still gots mens crazy about her. Course to be crazy about a woman don't mean you's in love. It can just mean you's in infatuation, like I said. I think she were in love herself with a man they advertised as the tallest man in the world. But they's always advertising men as the tallest man in the world, and there's always another tallest man. But a Bearded Lady's a Bearded Lady anywhere. And to my knowledge there's only one authentic Unicorn Woman. And got her own carnival now. If I could transform myself back into a turtle, I could join it. But once you's a human being, you hunger for being human. Them that don't hunger for being superior to humanity.

CHAPTER SIXTEEN

The groom held the reins of the mare, a blackish-brown beauty, graceful, delicate. A horse like that could only be a Thoroughbred. I wondered what sort of horse I'd be. I mean if people were classified like horses. Well, I guess some people do classify people like horses. When they talk about such things as breeding. Only certain kinds of people are said to have breeding. Usually rich. Usually not nonwhite. Still I often found it curious that in horses Thoroughbreds were mostly nonwhite. You didn't see white Thoroughbreds. In the movies, sometimes the good people rode the white horses, or the wannabe good people rode them. But in the real world, the world outside horse racing, the people with breeding were mostly not nonwhite. Except in Africa itself. But somebody said that the names they have for African people in the New World are actually names of different breeds of horses or donkeys. Mulatto, for example. Some type of mule. Or like that woman I heard lecture. Joan videotaped her and made me listen to her lecture. The University of Creation Spirituality. Her name? I just remember Joan said from the University of Creation Spirituality. And she said the word ass. Said she preferred the word ass to the word donkey, because ass was a good American word, a good Anglo-Saxon word. Did she say Anglo-Saxon or just American? And fool. Her other favorite word. And Joan said those were her own two favorite words. Except that woman said, or seemed to say, that the only acceptable fool was a fool for the Lord. I don't know if Joan considers any fool an acceptable fool. Something about native religions. Part Native American, but a Catholic nun. Mary Jose? Joan had to explain to me some of her vocabulary. "Your vocabulary's gotten better since you met me, you know," she says. Except ass and fool. I don't think there's anyone who knows the English language who don't know the meaning of ass and fool. Anyway, Josef and I stood behind the black fence scrutinizing her.

She looks like a winner, I said. I leaned across the fence. She gave me a fierce look, as if she were not yet broken in, but I knew she was. I'd seen her maiden race, and I had the autograph of the jockey who rode her.

She's top-class, said Josef. People at the Fasig-Tipton wanted me to sell her, but I won't. Said one of their clients saw her and wanted to buy her. For breeding purposes, though, not to run any races. At least I think they said for breeding purposes; the client who wanted to buy her was kinda ambiguous. She's a fine specimen. She's top-class. You don't sell a top-class horse.

The groom holding the reins glanced at me and Josef. When Josef didn't give the horse more praise, he praised her himself. Her maiden race she did six furloughs in one and ten. Now you know this is a good horse. Ain't nothing ambiguous about a good horse. Top-class like Mr. Fremd say. And you don't sell a horse like this just for breeding purposes or even ambiguous purposes. They think 'cause she's a filly she ain't meant to run races. They just wants her for breeding purposes or other ambiguous purposes. This horse is top-class, like Mr. Fremd say. Be a major challenger in the Derby is what I think. Did brilliant at Aqueduct and Seminole. Impressive in the Santa Anita. Anybody that anybody in the racing business say this a good horse. Ain't nothing ambiguous about a good horse. A good horse is a good horse. All the sportswriters say that. I mean, all the sportswriters say this a good horse. I ain't read a sportswriter that ain't say this a good horse. I read one sportswriter, though, to lie and say we had to put them green goggles on her to keep her from being skittish on the track, but this ain't a skittish horse. We ain't never had to put no green goggles on this horse. He was talking about some other horse and lied and said it was this one. I don't trust none of them media people. There was some media people going around talking to the grooms and the exercise boys, 'cause they wanted to get a view of horse racing that ain't just the muckamuck's view, the view of the racehorse owners and the trainers and the star jockeys, you know, the muckamuck's view, so they come to the grooms and the exercise boys to get our opinion of the horse racing industry, to hear the opinion of the ordinary workingman, and I wouldn't talk to them, 'cause I don't trust them media people. They ain't truthful, and especially now like the man say that they accepts hearsay and innuendo and gossip as the truth, they ain't to be trusted, them media people. I heard one of us poets on television—maybe you seen her on television talking about the arts? The same poet that reads to the people to say that facts about a people ain't always the same thing as the truth about them, so I guess you can say the same thing about horses. But when they say this a good horse, they's telling the truth. Ran a big race in the Santa Anita, ain't she, Mr. Fremd? A super race. And that was a gummy track. That was a muddy track. A good horse on a gummy track is a good horse anywhere. She got her early speed like it were her Independence Day and did near-record time. Ain't she, Mr. Fremd? That's when some of them Fasig-Tipton people seen her and wanted to buy her, or one of their clients wanted to buy her. Why, if I weren't an ordinary workingman and could afford a good horse like this, I'd buy her. And I wouldn't buy her for ambiguous purposes. But you don't sell a horse like this just for breeding purposes. This ain't just a top-class horse, this is a classy horse.

She looks like a winner, I said.

She's top-class, said Josef. Bred right here.

Well, she looks like a winner.

She is a winner, said the groom. He held out a sugar cube or some bit of sweet for the horse. A good horse on a gummy track is a good horse anywhere. And when it comes to a stretching duel, she's the best. When it's a fast track, the mature horses, though, have got more confidence than this one. She ain't a nervous filly, she just needs more confidence in herself when it's a fast track and she's amongst the mature horses. But when it comes to a stretching duel, she's the best. I ain't never put no green goggles on this filly. This filly knows who she is and knows who she wants to be. That's how you train a horse. If I was a trainer myself and ain't just a groom, that's how I'd train my horses. I wouldn't train them how I want 'em to be, I'd find out what they want to be, and that's how I'd train 'em. Course you gotta have a top-class horse for that. You gotta have a classy horse for that. Some horses the only way you can train 'em is how you want 'em to be. They make good horses, but the best horses is them that knows what they want to be. Then all you gotta do is find out what they wanna be and that's how you train 'em.

The Thoroughbred flicked her tail, turned a huge brown eye towards me. It wasn't a fierce eye now. It was more curious than fierce. She whinnied. I wondered if any of them horses ever thought of training and taming people.

I usually like them with more exotic background, though, I said.

This is exotic to me, said Josef, waving his hands at the rolling green of his four-hundred-acre farm. America is exotic to me. So you think she'll win?

Win easily, I said. She'll start good and slow, though, move gradually, then she'll rally. As long as the pressure's good.

Yeah, that's when she behaves her best, said the groom. Ain't nothing nervous about this filly. The media man that said that is a liar. And the sportswriting women is as good prevaricators as the men. Them sportswriting women thinks if they's as good prevaricators as the men then that's equality. Why, when Mr. Fremd bought this farm, there was someone come out here talking about urban development. Now, they weren't talking urban development until Mr. Fremd bought this farm. 'Cause they didn't want a man like Mr. Fremd to own a farm like this, so they started talking urban development. They's good prevaricators, ain't they, Mr. Fremd?

A light urging, I said.

A little light urging, not too much, said the groom.

The jockey should ride with her, let her pull, I said.

Yeah, the jockey should let her lead. Let her lead, said the groom. 'Cause she knows who she is and who she wants to be. You know your horses.

You sound like you know her, said Josef.

For sure. She's the best. I could be a sportswriting man myself, and

I know enough about horses not to prevaricate. I usedta wanna be a jockey myself, though, but then I started getting too tall for a jockey, you know, so I become a groom. But this filly, she's the best.

And those were the days when you never really expected a filly to win.

And that's exactly what the groom said. There's them that don't expect a filly to win, but I'll bet on a filly any day.

On the shelves are books for horsemen: *The Illustrated Veterinary Encyclopedia, Breeding Management and Foal Development, Treatments and Medications, Feeding to Win, Equine Genetics and Selection Procedures*. I read somewhere once that Lexington had been a breeder's town in slavery days. Lexington at Cheapside had been the principal marketplace: horses, cows, Negroes. *Negro Genetics and Selection Procedures*. I wondered if they'd had such books. *The Illustrated Negro Encyclopedia, Breeding Management* and *Pickaninny Development*. I wondered whether people who used to breed slaves, when slavery was abolished, started breeding horses, transferred their knowledge of breeding slaves to breeding horses. I thumbed through the volume on *Breeding Management* while waiting for Josef to come back from the yard. The book was a gift to Josef. It said To Josef with Love, from Stellina. Mrs. Fremd? Or another Stellina?

Here you are, he said coming in, holding two glasses of white wine. He wore a blue-and-white-striped silk robe and a white cloth wrapped around his head. He looked like a Moroccan nobleman. Maybe he'd got that robe when he was in Alexandria, which he said ain't in Morocco, but Egypt. Morocco a land without rivers, but that Egypt got the Nile. Ain't that Nile supposed to be the oldest river in the world? The river of civilization. He was wearing sandals. The straps on them were made of a rope-looking fiber, probably sisal.

I like her, I said, meaning the horse.

He handed me one of the glasses. Cheers, he said. And then he said the same thing in German. I said *kampai*, a Japanese word I'd learned from Joan. I tried to think of a drinking song I'd once heard. Seem like that drinking song had something about rivers in it.

He stood sipping his. I pushed my legs up in the leather chair and sat on my feet. The farmhouse was colonial, almost a mansion, built in the 1850s with high ceilings and long windows. The attic was shaped like a castle turret. I think they're turrets, though they look sorta like dunce caps. The base of them is stovepipe-shaped and then at the top they's what looks like a dunce cap. And he got one of his security people sitting inside that dunce cap. And I think Nicholas' room somewhere up in that turret. It was like the builder of the farmhouse was trying to suggest something of the Old World in the New, and since there weren't true castles in America, to claim something of royalty. This supposed to be a democracy, somebody said, but throughout its history you still have people wishing they's kings, or wishing for kings and other royalty, and if they ain't trying to transform theyselves into kings and other royalty, then they's trying to transform other people into kings and other royalty. That's why they always likes to refer to other Americans as the king and other names of royalty. The real kings in Europe and America's kings fiction. They's even got a few true castles in America, because they's always them that think that a nation ain't a true civilized nation unless it's got castles. Seem like one of them early American writers said something about that, that America weren't a cultured and civilized nation 'cause it didn't have no castles in it. But they's always looking at the people's architecture to decide whether they's civilized or not. If they architecture look different from they own architecture, or if they civilization ain't in they architecture, then they ain't civilized. This mansion ain't a true castle, it just got a little turret on it, like it a wannabe castle. There are former slave quarters, but they'd been converted into bunkhouses where some of the hired men stayed. His top security people, though, like Nicholas and the former Vietnamese soldier who'd fought in the tunnels of Cu Chi, had rooms in the farmhouse. I stared out the window at a man sitting in a walnut tree. I think he one of the former CIA people, or one of them men claim to be former CIA or other government security people. He wearing braids, though, and I don't think when he worked for the CIA they would have allowed him to wear braids unless they'd wanted him to infiltrate some group of Rastafarians in Jamaica or something, but I don't believe the U.S. considers them Rastafarians a threat to their national security, so he must've started wearing braids after he left the CIA and started working for Josef. Maybe even that groom might be a security person disguised as a groom. I thought of a book of Joan's called *The Tree of Culture*. It had a Rastafarian-looking man sitting in a tree like that. The first chapter was about the pygmies of the Ituri Forest. Different people sat in trees indigenous to their cultures. An African sat in a baobab tree. Them Japanese sat in them banyan trees. I think they's banyan trees. Then them Japanese have got them miniature trees; they cultivate them miniature trees. I remember when Joan was in Japan, the Japanese announcer had introduced her as a "musical giant" from America. She'd mumbled before going onstage, "Musical pygmy." I didn't understand Japanese, so I didn't know he'd introduced her as a musical giant, but when I'd asked her why she'd mumbled "musical pygmy," she explained that it was because he'd referred to her as a musical giant, and she herself didn't think she was worthy of that title. "At least in America I'm a musical pygmy," she'd said. "But I heard someone say even Americans like to make people superstars before they're deserving of that title." Josef, beside me, held his glass in one hand and stroked my shoulder with another.

Kampai, I said again.

I like you, he said.

There's a man in the tree, I said. How come you got so many security people?

Josef looked toward the window. When people wanna play dirty tricks on you, you gotta be a prudent man. Do you want me to close the curtains? he asked.

Unless you want him to take pictures, I said.

I noticed he was sounding more like me, and I was sounding more like him.

At the corner of the stable, I watched the young groom rub Absorbine Hooflex on the hooves of a yearling. The young man sniffed some as he worked. A lean young man with the physique of a young Kenyan I'd once seen win the marathon.

Is that a good high? I joked.

He handed the bottle over to me, I sniffed some, felt my forehead ready for takeoff, passed it back. Too strong for me, I said. What does it do for the horse?

It's supposed to keep the hooves flexible. You know your horses on a racetrack, but you don't know your horses, do you? Horses are intelligent. They know you if you don't know them.

I watched him clean and brush the yearling, using a tiny vacuum cleaner to clean the hair on the flanks and remove dirt from the hooves. I watched him brush the horse's head and mane, apply medication to the bottom of one of the hooves. He had a handsome, clean, dark oval face, a tiny mustache and intelligent but unsettled eyes.

I think she's got a little infection on the hoof here, he said. She had a splinter fracture in the cannon, but that's all healed.

Will it mean a problem? I asked. I mean the infection.

Should clear up in a day or two. Get her ready for her first set of shoes, ain't that right, darling?

He rubbed her silken mane. You want to get out there and graze, don't you girl? You know I can't let you out there till tonight. Sun's too hot now. Bleach your hair. You don't want the sun to bleach your hair, now do you girl? You won't be as pretty with your hair all bleached out. He patted her. She's a good girl.

Someone came up behind me. Thinking it was Josef and without turning around, I grabbed at his hands and caressed them. Then I turned to stare up into Nicholas' face. I felt like a fool.

Why didn't you tell me it was you? I asked.

You already had hold of me, he said.

I moved away from him and walked back to the house.

She's a good girl, I heard the groom say again. You can't fool a horse. A good horse knows you better than you know yourself.

Nicholas said something that I couldn't hear. I don't know whether he was talking about the horse, though, or me.

And now Ladies and Gentlemen, our star, the fabulous Joan Savage, or as she prefers to be called, Savage Joan the Darling Bitch! Ain't that a contradiction in terms? A Savage Darling? A Darling Bitch? I like a good bitch, even a darling bitch, who allows you to call her a bitch, though, 'cause some bitches even the nicest darling bitches, when you calls 'em bitches, even the bitches that they are, even the bitches that they know they are, even wonderful bitches, like this wonderful bitch, or my wife who's a sometimes bitch, 'cause she ain't a bitch with everybody, bitches at you for calling 'em a bitch, and you better not call certain bitches bitches, even the bitches that they are, even bitches who are bitches and knows that they's bitches, even knows that they's wonderful bitches, even bitches as wonderful as this wonderful bitch, or my wife, who's sometimes a wonderful bitch herself, and even knows she's a wonderful bitch and knows how to bitch wonderfully, 'cause if you call certain bitches a bitch even when they call themselves a bitch like my sometimes bitch of a wife sometimes calls herself a bitch even if you calls 'em a wonderful bitch even a nice bitch then you learn the true meaning of bitch. This routine comes to you with apologies to you know who, who should never apologize for calling a mean bitch a mean bitch even when he calls the wrong mean bitch even a nice mean bitch a mean bitch. I heard somebody refer to comedians like us as comedians to the niggerphobics, but as a young comedian to the niggerphobic myself, with apologies to the author of *Negrophobia*, I could tell you the truth about some of the meanest bitches, and I ain't just talking about bitches of color neither, 'cause everybody likes to call bitches of color bitches but that ain't every bitch, except you know who, who should never apologize for calling a mean bitch a mean bitch even when he calls the wrong mean bitch even a nice mean bitch a mean bitch. . . . Anybody who watches the politically incorrect Comedy Channel knows who I'm talking about, but you better not call 'em a bitch, even every bitch. . . . My wife ain't no mean bitch, though, she's a sweet bitch, I mean a nice bitch, when she's a bitch sometimes, but suppose every woman's a bitch, suppose every bitch's a bitch, the mean bitches and the sweet bitches, the nice bitches, the wonderful bitches, the darling bitches, and the good bitches, if bitch was as common as woman or lady or girl, then you'd have *A Portrait of a Bitch, Maggie: A Bitch of the Streets, Fanfare for a Common Bitch*—there's a fanfare for a common bitch the same as a fanfare for a common bastard—I better say bastard or some of you bitches'll, especially my wife, start bitching at me for not being a egalitarian, *Don't Let Cowbitches Fool Ya*, you gotta be literate to understand my allusions, *Fanfare for a Common Bitch* is a piece of music, though, but I usedta be a professor of English before I became a comedian, but being a professor of English was a bitch, so I became a comedian, 'cause as a comedian I get to call a bitch a bitch, but suppose every noun was a bitch, then you'd have *A Bitch of a Bitch*, suppose every verb and verbal was a bitch, then you'd have *The Bitch of a Bitching Bitch*, but *Bitch and Bitchibility.* . . . and ain't none of y'all better call my little daughter no bitch.

Joan marched onstage to applause. The announcer, a local entertainer-comedian, a round-faced dark-complexioned man, who called himself Mr. Show Biz Hisself Though Not the King of the Comedians to the Niggerphobics with Apologies to the Author of *Negrophobia*, kissed her hand, referred to her as "our darling bitch" again, made a few gallant flourishes like the knights of old, or like the court jesters, and marched offstage. She was dressed in golden leotards with her hair in golden strings. She was wearing a sweatshirt that said SAVAGE JOAN THE BITCH DARLING rather than Darling Bitch as the announcer had said. She was wearing deep red lipstick and her cheeks were the color of Delicious apples. She was grinning. She was glowing. Then she just stared at the audience. Even from backstage, I could see that little wrinkle above her nose. A wrinkle or scar I'd noticed the first time I'd seen her. She said she didn't know what it was. She'd been born with it. A sort of birthmark. Anyway, she just stood and looked at her audience. Then she asked, Have you read the *Kama Sutra* today? then she started singing.

I watched from backstage. She was always good to hear. Always. A golden peacock. Like her other fans, I watched as she pranced across the stage. I remember when she first asked me to manage her. Do you like my singing? she'd ask. Yes, of course, I'd answered. She said that she knew of a certain singer whose manager didn't like her singing, but he managed her anyway. That seems sorta duplicitous, don't it? she'd asked. To be somebody's manager and don't like their singing your own-self. Not duplicitous. Duplicitous ain't the word I mean for it. I mean, you don't know when they're managing you and when they're managing you. She was drunk on gin and tonic and kept talking about this singer she knew, managed by someone who didn't like her singing. So she had to be sure I liked her singing, at least liked most of her songs, before she let me manage her. She sang mostly in English, but when she spotted a Japanese woman in the audience, she said something in Japanese and then sang a snippet of a song she'd sung in Japan. Then she sang in English again.

Onstage she was wonderful, but after each performance she'd shake her head and wring her hands in the dressing room. She craved but never trusted the applause. Sometimes she rushed backstage almost before the applause had happened. She reminded me of a young French woman vi-olinist in a movie that we'd seen, a young woman who always needed as-surances that she was good.

That's me, that's how I am, she'd said after the movie. I can't under-stand artists who are so sure of their goodness.

Why would someone want to be an artist who didn't think them-selves good? I'd ask, for I thought that every artist had the conceit that they were good, or they wouldn't be artists, and then I wasn't sure what sort of goodness she meant.

When I sing, I can't hear how I sound to others, and when I listen to myself I'm too judgmental.

You were great, I'd say. She'd sit in her dressing room, silent. You were great, I'd say again. Don't toady me. I really fucked up tonight. I'd poured myself a glass of bourbon and her a glass of a weird favorite, a combination of tomato and pineapple juice. They love you out there, Joan. They love you. Don't you know it? And that bit of Japanese you sang, that sounded really good. It adds another dimension to you. You ain't just another girl singer, you know. She'd light a cigarette, gulp a bit of the tomato and pineapple juice, sip some of my bourbon, then jump up and hug her shoulders.

Do you know Jamey never saw me perform, she said. He doesn't approve of me being a singer, you know. I don't even keep any of my albums up at the farm, because I know he won't listen to them. I'd be embarrassed for him to listen to me anyway, I mean, knowing he doesn't approve. If someone doesn't approve of you anyway, how do they know if you're good? And if he came to one of my performances at one of the clubs or even a concert, how'd I know it's really me he's hearing singing, or if he's just hearing the kinda singer he thinks I am? I don't think the others' applause would change his opinion, like that guy in that movie. He heard the others applaud the person he didn't think any good, so that changed his opinion. He didn't think the person a good singer himself, but he figured that so many people were applauding this person at this rock concert, that they must be good. Jamey would hear the others applaud at my concerts and be even more convinced I ain't any good. He'd hear the applause at my concerts and it would even more convince him that his opinion that I'm not a good singer is right. Or maybe I'd start singing like the singer he thinks I am and not the singer I know I am, just knowing he's in the audience. Like that time you told me you thought you saw Jamey in the club, and then I started singing like crap, like the singer he thinks I am, and then I realized it wasn't Jamey in the club and then I sang pretty good, at least like the idea I have of myself. He thinks enough of us jigs are singers and dancers anyway. That I'm just another stereotype. Playing the Nigger Entertainer. Like that magazine I subscribe to, for African-American entertainers, he doesn't think we need a magazine like that. How does he know I ain't playing myself? Maybe that's who some of us are. Maybe I'm the Archetypal Nigger Entertainer and not the Stereotypical Nigger Entertainer. Should I run from who I am? I remember we were watching this show and they had these so-called high achievers and when they got to the colored girl, they asked her what were her high achievements in and she said proudly, Singing, Dancing, Acting. . . . I think Jamey was expecting her to say something like Mathematics, Chemistry, or some of the other sciences, you know. Or even the languages, being some sorta linguistic prodigy. Russian, Chinese, Japanese. But she says Singing, Dancing, Acting. . . . one of the high schools of the performing arts, you know. Jamey just changed the channel. Nonsense. To tell the truth, I was kinda embarrassed myself, her considering those high achievements. Talents, maybe, but should they have included her among the high achievers? I mean, maybe I coulda understood her naiveté, to think those high achievements, but I know the folks who included her among the true high achievers weren't that naive. I mean, when the whites and the Asian Americans were saying such things like Mathematics, Chemistry, Physics and then she says Singing, Dancing, Acting. They coulda brought a black girl or boy out there who said Mathematics, Chemistry, Physics, you know, or some of Jamey's students, like one of his former students's a oceanographer in South Florida, and a colored girl, they shoulda had someone on like that, the real achievements, but instead they get someone who says Singing, Dancing, Acting, the stereotypes. . . . I was kinda embarrassed myself. So he's never watched me perform. Never. Never listened to any of my recordings. Never wanted to encourage me in that shit. The only colored girls he'll listen to are the divas, the opera singers. And only the best of the best divas. Jessie, Leontyne, Kathleen—is it Kathleen? All their different classical training, and the different languages they've got to learn. They're like Renaissance women. They're like Rembrandts. But me? Another Nigger Girl Entertainer. I was good, though, wasn't I, girl?

Yeah, but how come you asked them about that *Kama Sutra*?

Ain't you read the *Kama Sutra*?

Naw.

I'll have to buy you a copy. James has a copy. When I was up at the farm I saw it. A present from one of his little infatuations. Maybe she's a great infatuation. I don't know. A woman who works with him at his think tank, I know that much. An Indian woman, I mean, an Indian from India. I'd forgotten all about the *Kama Sutra*. I'd read it once when I was in college. Well, I didn't read it. I saw it once when I was in college. You know, the translation by Sir Richard Burton. Well, you don't know, because you don't know what the *Kama Sutra* is.

Richard Burton, the actor?

Naw, Sir Richard Burton. Supposed to know twenty-some languages and even more dialects. An explorer of sorts, a translator, and a lord in Queen Victoria's England who usedta travel around Africa and India, you know, the old British Empire. Anyway, he usedta translate what the Victorians considered nasty little books, you know. *The Amorous Man and the Sensuous Woman*, you know. But not just men and women, even the gods can be amorous and sensuous. The West can't imagine gods who are sensual, you know. Because spirituality is supposed to transcend the sensuous, you know, because all the Western gods and holy men are supposed to be virgins. Or celibates. You can't be holy and sexual. Anyway, the Victorians could only see the sensuality, you know, not the spirituality, or they couldn't understand a spirituality where there's. . . . to tell the truth I don't understand it myself, spiritualized sensuality or sensualized spirituality. I'm too corrupted by Western thought, I suppose. Whenever I look at the *Kama Sutra* it just makes me horny. Did I tell you when we first met, Jamey thought I was an Indian from India? The way I wore my hair, and the sorta clothes I wore then, those madras blouses, you know, and long skirts, and when Cathy told him I was in the sciences, for some reason, he thought I was Indian. Then, of course, he found out I wasn't. The accent he thought he heard was in his own mind. I told Jamey he forgot his *Kama Sutra*, that I didn't want it at my farm or in my possession. How could someone have a book like that in their possession and not just stay horny. . . .

EIGHTEEN

Back in the hotel room she sat with her legs thrown over a crimson chair. She was looking through an order form of paperback books she'd been working on: *100 Best Songs of the 20's and 30's*, *Test Your Own IQ: How Smart Are You?* (she wanted me to take the test, but I refused), several Dorothy Sayers detective novels featuring Sir Peter Wimsey, *Caligula: Emperor of Rome*, another Jim Thorpe biography, *Mao Tse-tung and His China*, *Brontë Country*, *Jack's Life: A Biography of Jack Nicholson*, *The Adventures and Misadventures of Peter Beard in Africa*, *Lupe Velez and Her Lovers*, *D. H. Lawrence: The Story of Marriage*, *Il Duce's Other Woman*, *The History of "The Gingerbread Man."* She tossed me *The Jockey Club's Illustrated History of Thoroughbred Racing in America* and kept looking through the other books: *O'Keeffe*, *Iva Toguri*, *Dictionary of the American Indian*, *The Cherokee Nation*, *The Counterculture*, *Concise Encyclopedia of the American Indian*, *Vamps and Tramps*, *Kingdoms of Gold, Kingdoms of Jade: The Americas Before Columbus*, *Anansi the Spider*, *Frederick Douglass*, *Black Americans: The FBI Files*, *Malcolm X: The Speeches*, *Island Encounters: Black and White Memories of the Pacific War*, *Ultra Intelligence: How to Make Fake Identification Papers and Become Any Nationality You Want to Be*, *Resistance in Hitler's Germany*, *The New Superpowers: Germany, Japan, the U.S., and the New World Order*, *International Politics*, *The Amanda Wordlaw Reader*, *The Wish for Kings: Democracy at Bay*, an anthology of African-American literature edited by Clarence Major, *The Moby Dick Project*, *Private Security Systems*, *Smalltown Girl Big City Notions*.

You don't have the name of the anthology edited by Clarence Major, I said. I can't order books without the name.

I don't know what the name of it is. I just know it's edited by Clarence Major. Not *The New Black Poetry*. I got that one when I was in grad school. I mean, one of his recent anthologies. You know, I'd like to record one of his poems. Maybe I could get Jimmy Cuervo to do the music. You know, one of his early poems, or one of the jazz-type poems. Do you think any of his poems have been put to music? Can you imagine making a musical out of one of his novels? Avant-garde, you know.

Then she told me to call him.

Call who? I asked. Clarence Major? I don't think he'd want you singing one of his poems. Who's his agent?

Call him, she said. I don't mean Clarence Major, fool.

Call who? I asked. Norvelle?

I still can't believe that you've been to Africa. I can usually tell people who've been to Africa. I don't mean they get Africanized, I mean I can just usually tell people who've been to Africa. I almost been to Africa. My friend Cathy Shuger, the sculptor and her husband Ernest were going to the Sudan, and they invited me after I got my divorce from Jamey, you know. But they're weirdos. Ern's okay. He's the one wrote a nice article about Jamey for one of those popular science magazines. But Cathy's a real weirdo. But they been to Africa, though. Cathy heard about that so-called new slavery in the Sudan and wanted to go over there. I think there was some sort of advisory for American tourists not to go over there to the Sudan, though, so Cathy says, I ain't an American tourist, I'm an American artist. So I think they went to Canada first and then went to the Sudan from Canada. I think they got as far as the Ivory Coast, though. Is it still called the Ivory Coast? I'm sure Jamey's told you about Cathy and her husband? She sometimes tries to kill him. Now she's seeing this Chinese allergist, I think he's Chinese, who thinks she's got an allergy to wheat. And's put her on some kinda allergy medication. Jamey's interested in that himself. You know, if her so-called lunacy might just be biochemical. You know, Jamey's interested in shit like that. I hadn't seen Cathy for years and then she writes me telling me she heard about my divorce and wants me to go to the Sudan with her and Ern, and telling me about how they think that her insanity might be an allergy to wheat. Her and that Amanda Wordlaw are friends, you know. That novelist I read. I haven't met her myself, though. She usedta run around the globe with Cathy and Ern, you know. A lot of rumors that they were some kinda ménage à trois, you know. I don't believe that shit myself, 'cause I know Cathy and Ern. I think Amanda got fed up with their bullshit, I mean Cathy's bullshit, so Cathy hears about my divorce, you know, and wanted me to go to the Sudan on some expedition to find out whether it's true that there are still slaves in the Sudan, so Cathy's on the freedom trail thinking she can buy some of their freedom, you know. I mighta been interested in going with them to the Sudan, you know, but not with Cathy over there singing another one of her freedom songs, or her equivalent to freedom songs, you know. Another freedom song, you know. She don't like my music either. I mean, she likes my voice, unlike Jamey, but she thinks I oughta just be singing freedom songs, you know. Just music with meaning, you know, the music of ideas, the music of revolution, the music of revolutionary ideas. Then I saw her again in New York, that's where I met you, and she told me that this Chinese allergist they met in the Ivory Coast, I think, says he thinks she might have an allergy to wheat. They were sitting in this café and he noticed how she started behaving when she started eating this wheat loaf. You know, he's sort of an expert witness, you know, as well as an allergist, whenever allergies cause criminal behavior, you know, and so he saw the way she was behaving after eating this wheat loaf, and how when the waiter put knives and forks on the table, Ern returned them, and put out plastic knives for Cathy, you know, and then after she ate this wheat loaf Cathy reached toward Ern with one of those plastic knives. Every woman's fantasy.

Not mine.

I think it's a game with Cathy, though. People say she's a lunatic, but I just think it's a game myself. Of course, if they prove it's an allergy, then it ain't exactly a game. But I think it's still a game with Cathy, though, allergy or not. 'Cause I remember in New York, Cathy was telling me about this woman she went to art school with, some bitch, who said that she wouldn't let anyone kill her art, that she'd kill them first, some shit like that, so I think it got in Cathy's imagination, you know. Whether a lunatic's imagination or pure imagination, I don't know. They were talking about women and art, you know, this friend of hers and Cathy, and about the relationship between men and art, and how most women don't usually behave like Gauguin, you know, that women artists don't pull a Gauguin, you know, not most of them, like if Cathy had to choose between Ern and her art, her sculpture, you know, she'd choose Ern, you know, so maybe she imagines that Ern does things, you know, to kill her art, to sabotage it anyway. That he's always doing these things to make her choose between her art and him, and she's always choosing him, but then what this bitch told her kinda got into her imagination anyway. So she doesn't like the fact that she can't pull a Gauguin, you know, that she can't devote herself to Art the way that male artists do, and people still consider them good people, you know, or good artists, if they're good artists. That how they treat their women doesn't mean anything usually. They're still great artists. I mean, if they're great artists. But women can't be good women and good artists. Something like that. That's why she admires Amanda Wordlaw, sorta in a perverse way, 'cause she abandoned her husband Lantis and her daughter Panda—Panda usedta be one of Jamey's students when he taught at the university, so he knows all the dirt about Amanda Wordlaw, you know. I mean she abandoned her husband Lantis and her daughter Panda for Art and her Art ain't shit. I mean, if you're a woman and you're gonna pull a Gauguin seems like to me you gotta be pretty sure your Art is Art. Well, some of her stories in *The Amanda Wordlaw Reader* are pretty good, almost Art, but seems like to me if you're gonna be a fool for Art, you gotta be pretty sure your Art is Art. I read Amanda Wordlaw 'cause she's entertaining, but the shit is still shit. I don't know. Some women are fools. I've met Ern, and he seems like a nice guy to me. Sorta like Jamey. But Jamey ain't that nice. Maybe Ern ain't that nice. I think he just takes that shit from Cathy, though. He ain't the sorta man just to take anyone's shit, you know. Jamey neither. But Jamey don't even take shit from me, though.

Jamey don't take shit from nobody, least the Jamey I know. That's why I call him sweet. He knows what I mean. Why, if I behaved like Cathy, least as rumor has it, Jamey and I'd've been divorced even before we even got married. I mean, I didn't even pull a Cathy and we're divorced. Well, I can tell who's been to Africa, though. And you don't look like you been to Africa or even almost Africa. You don't even look like you been to Detroit. Call him.

Sometimes when I'm with Joan I gotta look around to remember where we are. The generic hotel room. Oriental carpet, though—plush, silky, flowered.

Norvelle? You said you didn't get the number or the name of his hotel. I can't call all the hotels in Zanzibar. Plus, he's probably not in Zanzibar now, knowing Norvelle. He could be in some little African village that don't even have a telephone. I think he's still with that Masai woman I told you about anyway. He's writing this big book about her healing. He wants it to be a big book as comparable to the books on Western medicine, you know. They ain't lovers or nothing, at least I don't think so, 'cause I think they got a tradition that the healing women are celibate or something, I think it's their tradition, I know it's one of the traditions among some of the healing women that he's written about among the shaman women and healing women, you know, but he wants to write this big book about her healing. I got a note from his editor who wanted permission to use some of my photographs. You know I been to Africa, 'cause how could I take photographs of Africa, but ain't been to Africa.

You ain't been to Africa.

I couldn't take photographs of Africa and ain't been to Africa. I got photographs I took in Africa. I mean, they're in Norvelle's possession, but the credits is still me. He can't use any of those photographs without crediting them to me and paying me for them. I tried to get his address from that editor, but he claim he don't know it, that Norvelle secretive about his address. Seem like if Norvelle really wanted me, he could just give that editor his address and telephone number. I don't know, he musta called you when he was drunk or something. Too much palm wine. 'Cause, if he wanted me, he knows where I am. It's me who don't

know where he is. Well, I know he's in Africa, but Africa's a bigger continent. You know, Africa's a bigger continent than's on the map. When
you see a map of the world, they got it so that Europe and America is the
center of the world and the biggest continent, but Africa's a bigger continent than it is on the maps. They just do the maps like that, 'cause they
want you to believe in Europe and America, and we's supposed to consider them more important, you know, in the history of the world. But
none of the maps you look at is the true maps of the world. Norvelle he
got him a true map of the world, that shows Africa as big as it is and it
dwarfs them other continents. That's the true Africa. And I been there.

Naw, you ain't. I look like I been to Africa and I ain't even been there.
Call him.

Call who?

Call Jamey, you fool, she said. Naughty Jamey. His real name's
Naughton James, you know. If I didn't call him Jamey, I could call him
Naughty. He just calls himself James, though. He prefers James to
Naughton. He prefers James to Jim. Sometimes I call him Naughton. I
ain't never call him Jim. Naughty Jim Savage. That sounds like one of
them gamblers, don't it? You know them gamblers on those riverboats.
You know those movies about the gamblers on the riverboats. Naughty
Jim Savage. Probably the sorta role Clark Gable might play, one of those
riverboat gamblers, you know. Who else could Jim Savage be? A riverboat gambler. Call him. We can tell him to give up smoking. We can tell
him that smoking ain't a habit worth having. Maybe we can convince
him to give up smoking.

Don't be an ass, I said.

Call him, she said.

What do you want for breakfast? I asked.

Let's fly to the farm, she said, and have breakfast with him. Surprise
him. See who he's with. What new little infatuation. How'd you like to
see our Jamey screwing some new little infatuation? Or maybe the
Kama Sutra woman, you know, the one who gave him that copy of
the *Kama Sutra*. I mean when I caught him with you that was nothing to
catch him with you. . . . And you're still chewing on that old chestnut. I

mean, you're a girl scout you're a schoolgirl compared to what's in that book, the *Kama Sutra*, I mean. You're still in grammar school, girlfriend. You're still in elementary school when it comes to sex. Maybe you're in junior high school when it comes to love. I bet the only position you know is the missionary position. Do you know how the missionary position got its name? You been to Africa. Or do you just think Jamey's up at the farm peering into his primitive little microscope or working on some new chemical formula? Do you know something? I think Jamey's too good for the both of us. I think Jamey's too good for the likes of us. Sweet Jamey. I'm glad he's got a great infatuation. A woman worthy of him. Maybe he's got a great infatuation now, do you think? A woman worthy of him. Maybe he's in love again. Do you think he's in love again? He's some man, ain't he?

You're an ass, I said.

Don't you care who he's with? You're at least in junior high school when it comes to love. Maybe it's not just some little infatuation now, maybe it's some great infatuation, a woman who shares his ideals. A woman worthy of him. Jamey's great love. A woman who shares his ideals. I don't mean just the *Kama Sutra*, I mean she works with him at the think tank, you know. He's admitted her into his little circle of serious thinkers. I can imagine them, his group, and her the only woman in it. Scientists from around the non-Western world and her the only woman. She's supposed to be this great intellect, you know. In India, she couldn't use her great intellect, so she came to America. She's supposed to be the woman he imagined me to be when we first met. Can you imagine your Norvelle meeting the woman he imagined you to be? she asked. If I'm an ass, you're an ass's ass. An ass's ass's ass. An ass's ass's ass's ass. Don't you care who he's with? What little infatuation. Maybe she's just a little infatuation and he imagines she's great. . . . I know one of the guys who works with Jamey at the think tank and asked about her. He looked at me like he thought I was some kinda subversive. You know, the think tank people aren't supposed to tell anyone their little think tank secrets. But then when he knew that I knew about the *Kama Sutra* he started telling me about her. Not the sort of woman who's a little infatuation for any man. He said all the guys at the think tank are a little in love with her, you know. Then she gave Jamey that book. I suppose it woulda been sexual harassment, you know, if he'd given a similar book to her, I mean, if he'd given her a copy of the *Kama Sutra*. But the *Kama Sutra* is a classic of Indian literature. . . . I mean, it's not like some crude flirtation. . . . It ain't like giving someone a copy of *Penthouse*. She coulda given him a collection of Kalidasa's plays, though, or *The Indian Art of Spiritual Harmony*. . . . Ain't like your crude flirtation. . . .

No. I mean, you're an ass.

That's bullshit, she said. You know, girl, I saw the way you were looking at him when I first introduced y'all. Aren't you at least jealous that he's met a woman who's sensual, spiritualized sensuality, or sensualized spirituality, not the vulgar sensuality of the West, or whatever. I'm too corrupted by the Western idea myself, all sensuality is erotic, a beauty anyway, and a great intellect. Jamey's ideal woman. I guess I can respect Jamey that his ideal woman is intelligent, but this male pursuit of beauty I've always been ambivalent about.

You're beautiful.

Yeah, when I wanna be. But that ain't the point. And I ain't all that.

Who is? All that, I mean.

She's supposed to be all that, you know, Jamey's ideal.

She probably ain't all that. You're beautiful.

But why women gotta be all that? Why we gotta be flawless? It's just control. It's just power. You know, Jamey pointed out the first line in my forehead. He has lines in his forehead plenty, from thinking, you know, but he points out the first line in my forehead. I'm just sitting there reading, maybe listening to Miles and he points out this line in my forehead. You know, you got a line in your forehead. I remember when I had my first date, this guy says, You know, your complexion isn't so flawless up close. So what did that have to do with anything? You know. And then Jamey. My first line in my forehead he notices. I guess he didn't mean anything by it. It's just the nature of a man, you know. Pointing out a woman's flaws. Or the nature of anybody in power. Pointing out the flaws of them that ain't. Not that some fools don't need their flaws pointed out. You know what's funny. I don't mind him pointing out my flaws of character—all virtues to me. That line in my forehead, though. I'm thinking, what's this, so he's supposed to be pointing out every line I get in my forehead? Every wrinkle I get he's supposed to be telling me about it. But I ain't no fool.

I hope that ain't why y'all divorced, 'cause he pointed out the first line in your forehead.

Naw, I'm just telling you about the beauty thing. You know.

I think the beauty thing's your hang-up. So some guy noticed your complexion ain't flawless, so what? Guys always telling me about my flaws. I remember the first man that called me outa my name called me Possum, on account of I usedta didn't say nothing to nobody about nothing, and especially men. You couldn't get me to say a word to especially a man. In fact, Norvelle the first man I said more than a few words to. The psychologists would probably say it's because my daddy stayed in Korea with some woman, you know, some Korean woman rather than returning to America, or if he thought Korea the promised land coulda sent for us to come to Korea with him. We couldn't compete with that promised land or that ideal of a woman. I don't know. But I think a man like Jamey could love a woman just the way she is. Or how it pleases herself to be. That's what my friend Nadine says, that most men wants you to love them like they's a tree, you know, like they are, but they ain't supposed to love you like no tree. I love Norvelle, and even love him like a tree, but I just don't want to stay in Africa and follow no man around, you know, not even Norvelle. 'Cause that ain't my idea of a woman. Maybe if that was my idea of a woman, I'd still be in Africa, whether you think I ever been there or not. I know Jamey don't like your music, but he loves you like a tree. And I don't think there's many women that can say that. Loving somebody like a tree don't mean you gotta take they shit, though. What do you want for breakfast?

Bullshit, she said.

On toast? I asked. I phoned in an order. Ham and cheese omelet for her, Western omelet for me. I imagined eating my Western omelet on one of those riverboats with the gambler known as Naughty Jim Savage.

Like Joan say, the sort of role a Clark Gable type might play, or some-body resemble the Clark Gable type. Except I couldn't imagine me as my real self. Probably some blonde. I always wonder, though, why the ideal for a man tall dark and handsome, while the ideal for a woman al-ways some blonde. 'Cept in them countries where everybody blond. Na-dine say in them countries where everybody blond, blond ain't the ideal. 'Cept amongst the nationalistic types and their ideal of Nordic woman-hood. If people is blond seem like it okay for blond to be they ideal, but not amongst people that ain't blond and try to imitate the blond ideal, or think they ain't beautiful cause they ain't blond. Joan say, though, when she put on her blond wig, it to satirize that ideal.

Did I do good? she asked.

You're an ass, but you're good, I said. You're a good ass.

I'd rather be a good ass than just a good piece of one, even a good piece of intelligent ass.

When I grew older, I didn't believe the Turtle Woman stories, not the magical ones. Not the tales of how when she was a turtle she'd had to play all kinds of tricks to keep from getting caught by humans and put into a pepper pot floating with wild onions and garlic. I believed the one about the carnival, and even the tale of the confabulatory Unicorn Woman, but not that one. Not the tale of metamorphosis, of how when human beings chased her, like every turtle, she ran so slowly that in order to avoid getting caught she had to transform. Once they chased her into grass and she became grass. Another time they chased her into a valley, and she became a running stream, but all the time afraid that one of them would stoop and cup his hands and drink, so that when she willed herself back into a turtle again she wouldn't be whole. She'd have to look for the part that was missing. Even when I went to Africa with Norvelle and heard African transformation tales which sounded very much like that one, I still didn't believe it, or I thought it was just folklore.

Once when my grandmother was telling me her turtle stories, my mother came up on the porch with a bag of groceries, stopped and listened, shaking her head at the nonsense. The celery stalks at the top of the bag shook their green heads at the nonsense too. As soon as my grandmother finished her tale, my mother explained, Maybe you was a magic turtle in th'old days and maybe you changed yourself into grass and a stream, maybe that tale is true and not the carnival one, but you borned an ordinary human woman now. And an ordinary daughter's daughter. The celery stalks raised their green heads and nodded.

CHAPTER TWENTY

I'm going up to the mansion now, said his sister. Norvelle and I had just married and were visiting his parents' home in Memphis, Tennessee. Their house usedta be a boardinghouse; they'd purchased it and renovated it. Norvelle's father who do some freelance contracting, has his own freelance contracting company, had renovated it hisself, and they rented a few of the upstairs apartments. Norvelle's father look like a older version of Norvelle, but a more rugged type man being a contractor, while his mother a petite little woman kinda remind me of that woman played Tina Turner in one of them movie and Malcolm X's wife in another of them movie and also played in one of them futuristic action movies, you know, them new feminist-type movies where they got the woman to play the action hero. Usually it a white woman to play the action hero, but in this movie they got the African-American woman to play the action hero. Angela Bassett. That her name. She look like a petite little woman onscreen and up beside Denzel who play Malcolm X in that movie, though I don't know if she truly a petite little woman. She might just look petite in the movies. His sister, I mean Norvelle's sister Cayenne, was dressed in an old man's blue felt hat and a white organdy dress, her cheeks thickly rouged. She'd have been a beautiful girl if she weren't "off." No one had told me she was "off" at first, not even Norvelle. He'd just waited until I saw her and discovered for myself. It amazed me that neither Norvelle nor his parents behaved as if the girl were in any way an embarrassment to them. Ain't like one of them stories I read by LeRoi Jones before he become Imamu Amiri Baraka— ain't that his new name?—about people hiding crazy peoples like that in they attic. I ain't remember the exact lines of that story, but it say something about certain middle-class African Americans or colored people keeping crazy peoples like that in they attic. And ain't just colored people, but peoples in general 'cause seem like in one of them Brontë novels that man hide his crazy wife in the attic. Anyway, they took her as she was, I mean Cayenne, and expected others to accept her, as if her madness had its own logic. Even them that rented them apartments upstairs didn't treat Cayenne like she a crazy woman, and it even Cayenne who would collect they rents from them, and keep them rent books.

What mansion? I asked.

The King's, said Norvelle's father.

We were sitting on the long porch of the boardinghouse, or the renovated boardinghouse. Norvelle's father and mother was sitting in one of the swings. Cayenne was sitting on the porch steps and I was sitting in one of them lounge chairs. Norvelle across the street talking to a man who reminded me kinda of a brown bear. The man pruning one of them trees look kinda like a monkey puzzle tree, and Norvelle standing talking to him. I think he say the man's name Mr. Melville, the man who originally sold them the boardinghouse. Mr. Melville said the boardinghouse originally belonged to a woman named Wooley Boatman, but Wooley Boatman moved up to Alaska, at least she said she was moving up to Alaska, boarded up the boardinghouse and went North. Then he got a letter from her saying that she was in Toronto not Alaska, and sending him the ownership papers to the boardinghouse. Since he didn't know nothing about running a boardinghouse he sold the house to Norvelle's daddy.

What king? I asked.

The only king of Memphis. Elvis Presley, said Norvelle's mother.

Whenever his name was mentioned, Cayenne's face lit up. She'd go to the Presley mansion and stand outside the gates with his other fans, even when there was no longer any King to get a glimpse of. After a while, one of her family would walk up there and get her. She could be trusted to go there by herself, but she couldn't be trusted to come back. If no one went and got her, she'd stand out there all night.

They'll tell you the lie that he said that the only thing black people can do for him is shine his shoes, but that's just a lie, said Cayenne. That's just a true lie. Even Mr. Melville knows that that's a lie, and he usedta work up there at the mansion before he bought hisself this board-inghouse, or claims he usedta work up there, if that's the truth, but he knows things about Elvis that ain't in none of the fan magazines so he musta worked up there and say he even knew Elvis before that when he were a little poor boy like any other poor boy here in Memphis. I seen all Mr. Presley's movies, every one of them, and he's a better actor than a lot of these actors that they says is actors even if he ain't got no colored people in his movies. I ain't read nobody to say what a good actor he is, and that they shoulda put him in better movies, why if they'da put him in better movies, or movies with colored people in them, but you know they wouldn't want him to be the king of acting and singing because that would be too much king, but he can sing any type of music, though, and not just colored people's music. I got all his music. They tells me I ain't supposed to like Elvis, not really like him, but I likes him anyway. They tells me I ain't supposed to like Elvis, not really like him, 'cause he ain't originate that style of music that his claim to fame, 'cause his claim to fame ain't nobody else's music, 'cause that country music ain't his claim to fame, but I likes him anyway. And I don't believe that lie that they say about him saying ain't nothing colored people can do for him but shine his shoes, 'cause the colored people's liked his music before even the Grand Ole Opry people, 'cause I seen that in a movie. Course even in that movie they just marginalized the colored people, like Norvelle says, and you'd think he invented the colored people's music hisself.

I'd heard the same tale myself, but a different version of it. Somebody said it was some African-American women in his audience, who were behaving just like the white women were behaving about him. The King, you know. So the King stops singing whatever song he's singing, looks at them colored women acting just like the white women in his audiences, and says, Ain't no use of y'all colored women behaving like that about me, 'cause cain't none of y'all do a thing for me but shine my shoes. But then in some of them documentaries you got the King saying that his style of singing was influenced by listening to black people's music. Of course they don't mention the colored people every time they mention Elvis.

That evening Norvelle and I walked up to get her. He couldn't understand why she was such a big fan of Elvis, cause Elvis ain't even her generation. She collected all of Elvis' albums, though, and Elvis posters and other Elvis novelty items and collectibles. Norvelle ain't say whether or not he hisself like Elvis. I know he likes the pure African music, the pure music of Africa itself, and even have that music from South Africa even before Paul Simon introduced it to the world. My favorite Paul Simon, though, is when he singing his own music, that song about meeting his woman again after all those years and still being crazy. Not Paul Simon himself, but the man singing in the song. When I first heard that song I think he mean crazy, then when I hear it again I think he mean crazy in love. 'Cept it a better song to say just still crazy. That's a first-rate songwriter when you just say still crazy. Another songwriter think he supposed to say everything he mean. If he mean crazy in love he think he supposed to say crazy in love. Or maybe he mean both kinds of crazy, maybe he mean crazy crazy and crazy in love crazy and them other type of crazy like when people say that crazy man or you crazy man.

I don't know what she thinks about when she stands out there, he said as we neared the mansion, and could see her peeking through the gate with a crowd of others. She's in her own world.

We came to her and Norvelle pulled her away from the crowd of tourists mostly and draped a sweater on her slender shoulders.

Did you hear him? He was singing, she said.

That was probably some tape being played, said Norvelle. Maybe one of his other fans was playing a tape of Elvis' music.

During my stay with them I was afraid to be left in a room alone with her. I didn't know what to expect. Once, though, I'd come into the kitchen to get a glass of water and she'd surprised me there. I'd put the glass in the sink and turned. Standing in the doorway, she looked at me like she was the normal woman and I was the one a bit "off."

Is you going to travel with him when he goes collecting his folklores in Africa?

168

Yes, I said. We plan to honeymoon there. In Kenya, then Tanzania. Norvelle has to go to Houston first, though. He's supposed to give a lecture at the university—there's a medical anthropology conference—and then there's some people there who run this refugee center, I think, who want him to do some interpreting. He's the only one who knows a certain African language. . . . Some sorta refugees, I think. I think there's some sorta refugee center there. Maybe they're some illegal refugees or some shit, the way Norvelle explains it.

I hope you's a nice girl. I hope you's a nicer girl than you looks like you is.

It depends on what you mean by a nice girl, I said.

I hope you's a nicer girl than you looks is what I mean. 'Cause you don't look like you's a wifeable woman at all to me.

BOOK

THREE

CHAPTER TWENTY-ONE

I told the gum-chewing secretary who look like a Scandinavian, you know, one of those Viking types, one of them blond types, kinda look like a movie star herself, seem like I seen her in one of them movies, that we were there to see Mr. Schacter. I gave her Joan Savage's name, then my name. She said, You're early and told us to be seated, that he hadn't arrived yet. I stood looking at his wall of stars—that is the people that his company had made stars. And then there was another wall of them that he referred to as "emerging talents" because they weren't yet stars, but the Schacter people were promoting them and had faith that they'd become stars. In fact, the Schacter people referred to themselves as star-makers, although their wall of stars in the larger world of show business superstars might still be referred to as "emerging talents"—there weren't any Madonnas or Michael Jacksons or the Artist Formerly Known as Princes or Queen Latifahs or Whitney Houstons among them—but if Joan were so insistent on wanting to make it in America, her own country, I figured the Schacter people were good people for an emerging "emerging talent."

Joan was dressed in a feathered headdress and a feathered boa, pink toreador trousers, banana yellow stockings, one high heeled boot and one high-heeled shoe, wearing some kind of makeup that looked like neon, and looking like the very stereotype of a fool. The secretary looked at her matter-of-factly, like it was normal dress for the sorta entertainers that Mr. Schacter was usedta seeing. Rock star wannabes. Mr. Schacter didn't represent many rap singers, except for the mainstream-type rap, the "bubblegum rap," but none of the gangsta-type rap singers. She turned back to her computer. She herself was wearing one of those pink linen or linen-look suits, a white sweatshirt—not blouse—with blue necktie scarf, and on her feet were white running shoes. Except for the chewing gum, she fit the stereotype of the high-class broad, the modern high-class broad who wears running shoes. A Joan Fontaine type, though.

Weren't you in *Chinatown*? Joan asked, signifying. I mean, the movie, with Jack Nicholson.

I know who she signifying about, 'cause she do look kinda like that woman in *Chinatown*. But look kinda like all them blond women in the movies, like she could be all them blond women in the movies.

Mr. Schacter came in in a rush, took one look at Joan and knew who we were. Over the telephone I'd imagined an older man, but he looked like a youngster. I first met him through reading some of his Rock Journalism, though, and shoulda figured him for a youngster, since some of his comments on classic rock seemed from the perspective of a younger generation, not the Woodstock Generation. A tall, thin man, dark-haired, shaggy aggressive eyebrows, maybe like a young Jack Nicholson's, though taller than Jack Nicholson, and what Joan calls Steppenwolf eyes. Reminds me, though, a little of that James Woods, that other movie star. A young James Woods. And maybe even a little of Robert DeNiro, though they ain't the same type. A mixture of Jack Nicholson the Steppenwolf James Woods Robert DeNiro and a Wall Street banker type, the stereotype of a Wall Street banker type, like in that movie *Wall Street*. Before even taking us into his office he started talking fast. It was only until someone else came into the outer office, a demure-looking young woman, that he rushed us into his.

Have a seat, gals, he said. He rushed out the terms of the contract. So what do you think, Harlie?

Now I don't like nobody to call me Harlie, or any diminutive of my name, especially nobody I don't know. I coulda told the fool a thing or two, but I didn't want to screw up things for Joan. I didn't wanna sabotage her career, you know. I wanted to separate my manager's ego or rather my Harlan ego from my manager's ego and Joan's entertainment

possibilities and entertainer's ego, so I just let him call me what he
wanted, Harlie me, though I wanted to say, That's Mizz Eagleton to you,
boy, sorta like that song Billie Holiday sing. Billie Holiday ain't her true
name, but she wouldn't let nobody call her outa her name. Course her
name already Billie so anybody calling her Billie would call her Billie,
but that song she sing ain't nobody call her Billie. That's Mizz Eagleton
to you, boy. Now, if he had called Joan Joanie I mighta said something.
Or she herself mighta said something to the fool.

You don't talk to her, you talk to me, said Joan.

Ain't Harlie your manager? You're Harlie, ain't ya?

I'm Harlan, yes. Mizz Eagleton.

Well? From what I hear you're a real hot shot of a business manager,
one of the best new managers in the business actually. Somebody called
here asking about you, Nance said, probably read somewhere in
some entertainment tabloid—what's that new magazine, the *African-
American Entertainer?*—about your negotiations with us, trying to get
you to manage them, I suspect, but we didn't give out your number, no I
think Nance did give 'em your number, then she realized it's your private
number ain't to be given out, I apologize for Nance she's got show business dreams herself, you know, and likes to be nice to these bums 'cause
don't know who'll be a big star, you know, so treats every show business
bum like they's a big star, you know, but told them as far as we knew
you only manage Joanie here. To tell the truth, before our Joan got
you for her manager, I hadn't even heard of this girl myself. I know Mizz
Cavada—that's Nance my secretary—hadn't heard of her and she
knows every bum in the business. She knows more bums in the business
than I do and I'm in the business. But when you got show business
dreams you think the more bums you know in the business, you know.
To tell the truth I only keep up with the stars I make myself. I'm the
power behind the stars, at least the stars I make myself, so I don't have
to know every bum in show business, and I sure don't treat every bum in
the business like a big star. I don't even treat big stars like big stars. The
bigger the star the more you treat 'em like ordinary people. They ain't
royalty. Course there's royalty that flirt with show business, but they

don't want you to treat 'em like royalty. That's true royalty. But even true royalty can't buy stardom. They might can buy fame, but they can't buy stardom. Of course, stars gotta make themselves, but I'm one of the men who gives them the opportunity to make themselves. And most people haven't even heard of me. They've heard of the stars I make, those who've done the best at making themselves, but not of the man who makes the stars. Some starmakers advertise themselves, but not the Schacter people. She'd heard of Harlie, Nance I mean, but she hadn't heard of you.

Toot her horn for her, said Joanie. Maybe you should hire Harlan to manage you the tales I hear about you, boy. I'm my own manager now, Schacter. She cain't do a thing for me but my makeup, and the way I tell her to. Me myself and I. That's who you talk to. Me myself and I, International. I'm my own manager now. I'm my own starmaker, but I hear you're pretty good, though. Harlan says you write pretty good Rock Journalism. *The Village Voice*, ain't it? I ain't read any of it myself.

I sat down in one of the vinyl chairs and looked at them. I'd been her manager on the way to the Schacter office. I'd been her manager when we first started negotiating with the Schacter people. I just figured she was trying to embarrass me in front of one of the top booking agents, so I refused to be embarrassed. I sat down in one of the vinyl chairs. It was real leather, but it had one of those modern looks, you know in the old days they made vinyl that tried to look like real leather, now the modern designers are trying to make leather to look like real vinyl. Mr. Schacter even had one of those little stereotyped miniature practice golf sets, so's he could practice his golf swing. Joan looked at the miniature golf set like she wanted to practice her golf swing, though she don't even play golf, then she looked at the posters on Mr. Schacter's wall. He collected the posters advertising his talent's first concerts, at least the first concerts they'd had after signing with his company. Most looked like carnival acts, but a multicultural carnival, even a Native American among them—I didn't know any Native American pop singers—who the poster said combined traditional Native American music with contemporary rock. The poster also said he was collaborating with several contemporary Native American poets on a Native American rock opera.

Then one of Mr. Schacter's coffee table books caught my attention: *Spite, Malice & Revenge: The Complete Guide to Getting Even: Three Diabolical Volumes in One*: An A–Z collection of every dirty trick in the book. Warning: This volume contains some techniques which may be illegal; therefore it is offered for entertainment purposes only. The original publisher's price was over fifty dollars but Mr. Schacter had paid only nine ninety-five for it. Or maybe someone had sent it to him as a complimentary copy. Schacter didn't look like the type to need a catalogue of dirty tricks. I went over to one of the shelves that had a collection of Rock Journalism, including his famous essay on Madonna.

Well, from what I know, she's done more for you than that, said Mr. Schacter. Your makeup I mean. And if she did that makeup you're wearing, I'd get me a new girl to do my makeup and keep her for my manager. Makes you look like you're advertising yourself. Why, you look like a Las Vegas casino, or maybe one of them cheap Atlantic City casinos where you figure all the roulette tables gotta be rigged. With our label and connections you won't have to try so hard to sell yourself. You can be yourself. I like my stars to be themselves. I know you're more intelligent than you look.

And less intelligent than I wanna be, said Joan, then she started mimicking and improvising off of something we heard on the Comedy Channel, something that one of the politicians said, or someone satirizing one of the politicians said. Ah got more intelligence than Ah need, and more intelligence than you think Ah got, but less intelligence than Ah want. I manage my own career now, boy, she added, strutting about the room. Peacocking. She picked up the revenge book, looked at it with amusement, and probably made a mental note to add it to her collection— though she mostly liked to collect the obscure sorts of paperback books, fiction and nonfiction, that didn't make the best-seller lists—but didn't open it. She put it down.

I like my makeup and I like who I am, said Joan. Every dirty trick in the book.

. . .

That's all right by me, said Schacter, handed her the contract, and winked at me.

I glanced back into the Rock Journalism book, at the various photographs of Madonna. Tina Turner the only rock star of color in the book, though someone had written an article about the Japanese and rock, this place in Japan where the Japanese youth imitate their favorite American rock stars.

And those freaks you got on your walls don't look like they're striving to be themselves or anybody else, added Joan, then she looked at the contract casually and signed. I shrugged my shoulders, put the Rock Journalism book back on the shelf, then sat back down. Joan paraded over to the desk and handed Mr. Schacter the contract. Mr. Schacter smiled, winked at me again, and looked like the proverbial catbird.

Coming? said Joan imperiously.

I stood.

Good day, ladies, said Mr. Schacter.

He got you for a song, I muttered outside. He screwed you royally. You didn't even read that contract. I faxed him my corrections but he gave you the contract I originally bitched about. He screwed you royally.

I expected her to come back with something witty, one of her own metaphors for a royal screwing, or to tell me who screwed her royally before she even met Mr. Schacter or the Mr. Schacters of the show business world, but she didn't. At least, not until we got into the lobby, then she whispered, Who screwed whom before who caught whom screwing whom before who screwed whom?

TWENTY-TWO

This is marvelous, Joan, I said, peering into the microscope. I hadn't peered into a microscope since high school. I'd audited a course in research cosmetology at beauty school—not research cosmology, as I once read in one of those entertainment tabloids that profiled new managers in the business; they'd interviewed me and I'd said something about an early interest in research cosmetology but the media woman had written it up as research cosmology—I don't know a beauty school that teaches research cosmology, but you know how that is. We didn't even peer into microscopes in the research cosmetology class. They just told you about the chemistry of different cosmetics. And we learned how to make cosmetics using different foods: cucumbers, avocado, mayonnaise. Anyway, so I turned and it wasn't Joan standing in the bedroom door but her ex-husband, James.

I thought you were Joan, I said. This is nice. Is this yours? Well, I guess it must be yours. Joan don't use no microscopes in her act.

Yes.

It's like a whole little world.

He came and stood next to me. He smelled of tobacco and lavender.

That's my first microscope, he explained. My father gave it to me when I was seven. I was hooked. They make more powerful microscopes than that nowadays, though. Computer imaging and all of that. That's really primitive compared to the new electronic microscopics nowadays. I'm designing one myself. Looking into a microscope is rather like discovering new worlds, new galaxies.

He pulled out the slide I'd been looking at and put in another one.

This is wonderful. This is a whole little world, though, ain't it, primitive or not? . . . That's how my husband got interested in what he does. My ex-husband, I mean. His father gave him a record of African folk songs when he was little. And that's when he first started learning different African languages. He taught himself most of those languages just listening to them singing, and then he went to the local library to try to get African-language books, but then the only language they had was Swahili. So he wrote to the Library of Congress and got some books from them on the different languages. They sent him some of those books that the military use to teach their people different languages. He learned a coupla those languages when he was a little boy and just kept learning different ones. They're African Methodists or something, you know, so he's always been more romantic about Africa than I am. He's always thought of Africa as his land of origins, whereas for me my land of origins is New Orleans, you know. America. I don't think I should call it romanticism about Africa, though, because he ain't a fool. He knows who he is and he knows what Africa could be. I don't think he ever saw himself as colored, though, like most of us. You remember when we usedta be colored? Like that movie. You know, that Tim Reid movie. I know I usedta be colored. I paused. He goes around collecting medical folklore, though. I mean, my ex-husband Norvelle. He's an anthropologist. He was interested in being a naturalist for a while, though. But he's always been interested in things African, you know. And it ain't like a fad like with a lot of people. When Africa's in vogue, they's African. You know how a lot of us colored people are. When Africa ain't in vogue or Africa's just a land of embarrassments, we's multiracial or some shit. Or we's just Americans and don't wanna be no hyphenated Americans. Or they don't want you to be no hyphenated American when you's proud of being African. When they can shame you about Africa, then they tell you you ain't no true American. Norvelle, though, he's got all these African sculptures by people I'd never even heard of, you know. The traditional African tribal sculptures, anonymous, you know, 'cause them traditional tribal sculptors didn't put they names to they sculptures, like them European sculptors, but also he probably owns the largest collection outside a museum or even inside a museum of sculptures by named Africans. He's really cultured, I mean in our culture, in African and neo-African culture.

You needn't qualify it, just say he's cultured.

I know, but when people talk about culture, you know, when they say people are cultured—well, you know what they mean. They always just mean European culture. They don't even mean Chinese culture and they say Chinese culture is a more ancient culture than European culture, that them Asian cultures is more ancient than them European cultures. I remember when I was in high school, though, we had this teacher who was talking about culture, and you know, she kept talking about culture how people gotta have culture and treating us like none of us had any culture, mostly African Americans and poor whites, you know. That was when the schools first got integrated or desegregated and all the rich whites and numerous middle-class whites went to private schools, so in the city public schools you had mostly the African Americans and the poor whites or the lower-middle-class whites. So I guess she'd applied to teach in one of them private schools, but maybe she wasn't cultured enough herself, so there she was teaching in the public schools where ain't nobody got no culture, so she was talking about culture, like I said, and I thought she was cultured, you know, 'cause I only thought culture meant their culture. But Norvelle, that's my ex-husband—I said that, did I say that?—he sorta reminds me of them African noblemen. Why, a lot of us men remind me of African noblemen when you look at them as African men and not as colored people. So when I met Norvelle and went to Africa I learned that you could be cultured and not be European, you know. Like those Masai we met, they all act like noblemen, like men of culture, though they ain't all noblemen. But they's all men of they own culture. And the womens all women of they own culture, though the Masai men seem more cultured to me than the women.

He removed that slide and placed in another one.

Where's Joan? I asked.

She's out riding.

You got horses?

Just two. Both named after herself—Joan and Savage.

Your name's Savage too, I said. Savage ain't Joan's original name. Them horses is named after you and her.

He said nothing. I finished looking at the slides and sat down on the edge of the bed. He leaned against the counter where the microscope and slides were kept. His forehead was shining. On the shelves were a few chemistry books.

Where did you and Joan meet? I asked.

Harlem. We have a mutual friend who's a sculptor. Catherine Shuger. Joan calls her the Renegade. Do you know her work?

Sounds familiar.

A real nutcase, actually. A real strange woman. You've probably heard tales about her. From Atlanta, originally. In and out of asylums, not just asylums in America, but asylums all over the world—I remember somebody said she probably needed a good witch doctor—but she's a fine artist, though, I think. In some ways, she reminds me of Joan. I don't mean that Joan's a nutcase, I mean something in the personality. Anyway, she was having a showing there in Harlem. Does that kinda scavenger-type collage sculpture and that puzzle sculpture. Sorta introduced us. She's a bit of a matchmaker. Catherine Shuger, I mean. Has a husband who just puts up with her. Writes articles on pop science. The husband, I mean. Did a profile on me for an article on African Americans in the sciences.

Yeah, Joan showed me that article. That photograph they got of you don't do you justice. I take better photographs than that. You a more handsome man than that photograph.

They refused to print it anywhere but the *African American Journal*, the article I mean. Writes science fiction under a pseudonym. Well, he doesn't see himself that way. I mean, as a fool. He's in love, you know. Name's Ernest. Fine name. They say she's even tried to kill him several times—not the artist Catherine, but the other self.

Joan told me about her. I think. Or I read about her somewhere, in one of Joan's books. You know, she's always reading books, when she ain't doing her music. Seems like I read about her in this book of Joan's on sculpture.

182

Now she only makes what she calls Sculpture You Can Eat. Catherine Shuger. I don't mean to say that Joan's anything like that, it's just in the essential personality. You know, like sometimes when you read novels by the same writer, and it's like they're always inventing and reinventing the same character, the same essential character. That's Joan and Catherine.

People say I'm kinda like this friend of mine Nadine. We ain't nothing alike to me, don't even look alike, but a lot of people say we kinda alike, you know. We kinda talk alike, but we ain't nothing alike. People say I'm a big woman, but Nadine's sorta a giant compared to me. She's sorta like some of them African women I met while I was in Africa. From Kenya or Tanzania. Or like some African Amazon you might read about, you know. I guess they's got African Amazons. We's both from Kentucky, though. I didn't meet her in Kentucky, though, I met her in Texas. Then when my ex-husband introduced us, I discovered we's both from Kentucky. Now she's in New Mexico, though.

She's working with an allergist now that has this theory that it's biochemical. I mean, Catherine Shuger's aggression. It just might be. Some people believe that personality itself is merely biochemical. I'm a scientist, but I don't believe that science explains who we are.

Are you from Harlem yourself? I heard you say something about meeting Joan in Harlem.

Naw, I'm from Maine.

Maine? You mean they's got nigs up in Maine? Excuse my French. I guess you do kinda sound like Maine. Kinda high-toned. I was thinking you got a high-toned kinda voice when Joan first introduced us. I was thinking you kinda sound Canadian, but I know if you's Canadian Joan woulda told me you's Canadian. I know there's nigs up there in Canada, so they must got nigs in Maine. I know some nigs from Virginia that sound kinda high-toned like that, though, almost like them nigs from England, you know. You don't exactly sound like you's from England, though, but you's got one of them high-toned accents. We was watching this thing on television about the Maine fishermen. It was after one of Joan's gigs, and I kept wondering why she so interested in them Maine fishermen, and must be 'cause they kinda sound like you, and I don't know no other reason she be interested in watching no Maine fishermen. I mean, I found it interesting them talking about the different fish they's catching and how mens farms the ocean, but that ain't the sorta thing that interest Joan. I mean, if it ain't politics or the Comedy Channel or politics on the Comedy Channel, it's romance. You kinda sound like them, though. Them Maine fishermen. Except more classy. Now that's the true North. Up there in Maine. I mean, beside Canada itself that's the true North. I guess the slaves that made it up there to Maine didn't escape all the way up there to Canada.

I'm descended from free blacks actually, not slaves.

Oh, yeah? I heard about them. You think it makes a difference?

What?

I mean, you think it makes a difference whether you's descended from free blacks or slaves? I mean, they's the same people, ain't they? Or you think they's got a different mentality? Somebody say a slave can have just as much respect for theyself as a free man. I don't know if that true, though, 'cause seem like they's always telling you that if a slave got any respect for theyself, then they try to escape, so I don't see how no slave can have as much respect for theyself as a free man, 'cause then they be a fugitive. But then every free man ain't no fugitive. I mean, the free men that blames the slaves for being slaves and not free men, a lot of them ain't no fugitive.

He lift a eyebrow but don't say nothing.

In the stories set in Maine, there's never any nigs in 'em, though, fugitives or free men. I remember when I was in high school, we was assigned to read these stories set in Maine, and wasn't a nig in them. Sorta like those dialect stories but the dialect Maine dialect, you know. I know in that television show they didn't show any nigs fishing. 'Scuse me. Joan says I shouldn't refer to us as nigs. But she's got a book where they refer to theyselves as nig, I mean the narrator of the book refer to herself as a nig, not only her own nig but other people's nig.

Our Nig?

Yeah, I think that the name of that book. *Our Nig.* Then when I say nig she tell me I ain't supposed to say nig, and she got a book that say nig.

So how did you and Joanie meet? he asked.

At a party in New York. Not Harlem. Manhattan. To tell the truth, I sorta sneaked in. I saw these African-American musicians, one of them carrying a French horn, and sorta followed them, you know. I guess somebody musta thought I was one of them musicians' girlfriend. It coulda been a party for that Catherine Shuger you're talking about, 'cause it seem like somebody kept saying Sugar, and I know it was a party for some artist or one of those artist types and some of that food they had for you to eat looked like sculpture, like sculpture you could eat, and I thought they was just calling somebody Honey, you know, or had a sweet tooth. Seem like Joan introduced me to a woman named Sugar or I thought she was just calling her Sugar, you know, though it surprised me to hear a northern woman call somebody Sugar, even though they say a lot of northern people's got they roots in the South on account of that Great Migration. Anyway, I met Joan and we started talking and she asked me what I did. I said I was a beautician. She laughed. I guess because I was the only beautician at the party. Not even a makeup artist. Anyway, so she asked me to make her up and I did, right there where they were all partying around us, and she liked it. After a while, some of the party stood and watched, and maybe even the woman named Sugar amongst them, and after I finished, they applauded. Seem like I heard her say, Sugar, you think you a artist, this is a true artist. Or maybe I'm just thinking I remember that 'cause you telling me there's a real woman name Sugar. Or Shuger. So she hired me on the spot for her makeup artist, Joan I mean. She said she'd have hired me, though, even if the others hadn't approved.

And the managing? How did that come about? From beautician to business manager, that's a big leap. I mean, someone who doesn't know anything about the music business, who doesn't have any degrees in business or anything. It's rather incredible, to tell the truth. You're rather incredible, to tell the truth. Joan said that I'd think you a rather incredible woman.

It just evolved. I started doing the books, you know, making calls and stuff. She noticed it and said I might as well be her business manager. She'd been handling all that herself, you know, but she was getting more known, and she wanted. . . . I don't have no business training or background or degrees in business like you said and no I didn't know anything about the music business, just beauty school. And she uses it too, you know.

How do you mean? He was still standing near the microscope, but I had moved to the bed. You know. How do you call it? For pointers, for scores. She likes telling people I usedta be her makeup artist, a beautician. That the only degree I've got is a degree from beauty school and she ain't even sure about that. You know how Joan is. Like when we're at a party with some other entertainers and entertainer's expensive-ass high-powered Hollywood-type business managers and entourage and shit, and there's just me and Joan, and like her career's blossomed since I started managing her. . . . at least in Europe and Japan. . . . But I'm good. You can ask anybody in the business.

I have.

Hire a detective?

No, just casual conversation, you know.

Joan says you don't care shit about her career.

Oh, yeah? I don't. I care about her, though.

I said nothing. I crossed my legs and leaned back. His shirt was open at the collar. Tufts of curly hair peeked out from his broad chest. His skin was a wine-colored brown and he wore a mustache, like I told you, and had the look of a man I can only describe as being of another generation, though he's Joan's and my generation. Looking at him made me feel as if a old photograph from the 1930s or 1940s was staring back. Some portrait photograph by James Van DerZee or some of those African-American actors in those old Oscar Michaux movies, only darker complexioned than his leads.

He looked at me with a intensity. They tell me you're smart and you're tough, and Joanie's in good hands. I didn't hire a detective, but I know a few music people. Mostly people in advertising, publicity people, though, not musicians.

I said nothing. I got up and looked back into the microscope. I could feel him peering at me. I imagined him and Joan together, not making love, but maybe rubbing noses like the Inuits. "Give me an Eskimo kiss," some woman said to her lover in a French movie, a video Joan had rented once after one of her gigs, when we were back at the hotel. She listened, so that she could keep up with her French, while I tried to read the captions. I hugged my arms and thought of one of Camille Billop's sculptures with a woman hugging her arms. A ceramic. And then I thought of another sculpture, one of Norvelle's. The one where one sculptured figure—of a man?—held another—of a woman?—aloft. And they both seemed as if they'd taken wing, as if they were flying. Was that a Catherine Shuger sculpture? Maybe that was where I first had heard her name. He said it was by some African-American woman sculptor, but I couldn't remember her name. Maybe Catherine Shuger?

You don't like her singing, though, do you? I asked.

No. I think it's trash. I really think it's trash. Everybody doesn't need to sing. Especially us. The Houston woman, now there's a voice. If you wanna think of pop modern music. You know, the Houston woman. I'd say she's got the best modern voice. Bobby Brown's wife.

He'd love that. Bobby Brown, I mean. She treats him like he her Majestic Prince. You know, I bet on that horse. I don't think I won anything. She's very talented, you know. Joan. I mean modern singing is modern singing. It's not all about the great voice, though I admire great voices. Like Joan, she hardly ever reads the great writers, the great books. I mean, she reads the Great Books, she's got shelves of the Great Books. She reads them, but she also reads the trash, not just the trash, but she likes to read a lot of that obscure nonfiction, but she says the trash, the tabloid journalism, the tabloid novels, have more to do with the modern world, the trashy nonfiction, the trashy novels, the tabloids. Like she says those people who think the modern writers should write like the Great Novels, that that's not modernity. That the techniques of the trashy novels and even the comic books, the new type of comic books, describe modernity better than the Great Novels. Some people say it's supposed to be trash. Modern music. Like the new photography, you

187

know. Like modern art. You can't have a renaissance unless you've got decadence, someone says.

He said nothing.

She's really better than you know. I don't think she's trash myself. I mean, I don't think her music is trash. It ain't trash trash. If anything, she kinda satirizes the modern, trashy culture.

That's not all of American culture. It's American pop culture. I've heard that description of American culture myself, but it's just the pop culture people are describing, the media culture. Some of the technological culture, perhaps, but mostly the media culture.

But Joan would say that the pop culture's the only true American culture, that the other so-called culture is just wannabe Europeans. Like in architecture, McDonald's and Taco Bell–type pop architecture, that's more true American culture than the cathedrals. I ain't a culture nut myself, but I think she's got the right idea about modernity. The Madonna culture. I like Madonna, though. Like somebody said, she's a tramp, but I like her. I don't think she's a tramp, though. Maybe she satirizes the tramp ideal or the ideal tramp. I think she just, you know, satirizes pop American culture, and people think that's her. Like maybe Joan satirizes pop African-American culture. Like a lot of people think pop African-American culture, media culture is us. But that's sorta what you're saying, ain't it? And I guess we got our African wannabes like they got their European wannabes. I ain't a culture nut myself, though. Unless it's New Orleans culture, which is everybody's culture. She's really better than you know, our Joan.

I want her to be better than she knows. You know, she was a chemistry major when I met her. Our sculptor friend was sort of a prodigy, you know. Having her first shows when she was still an undergraduate. I was in New York for the first time. When I met Joan, when Shuger introduced us, she just started talking to me like she'd always known me and not talking the typical woman talk, and I asked myself, Who's this brilliant young woman? She was the first truly brilliant woman I'd met. I don't wanna qualify it and say African-American woman, because I think her intelligence is world class, or could be. Our mutual sculptor friend's a prodigy, but that's art. Intelligence in art ain't the same. Who are the lights of our century? I mean, in the areas of science and art. At least that the world knows about. Picasso and Einstein. But Picasso's not Einstein. That's not the same sort of brilliance, you know. People don't think of intelligence as synonymous with Picasso, but Einstein, yes.

I left the microscope and returned to the bed.

When we were in New York, Joan took me to a play about Picasso meeting Einstein. Joan thought it was good, but it wasn't as good as *Cats*. But I guess you gotta know more about Picasso and Einstein to appreciate a play about 'em, but everybody knows about cats. I played with the geometries of their crazy quilt.

Though when you look at those Einstein formulas, the formulas in his notebooks, someone said that kind of looks like art. And when you look at some of those Picasso's most abstract paintings it's kind of like science. Like a scientist's journals. Anyway, Joan and I, we went back to our mutual colleges, her in Connecticut and I at Fisk, but we kept corresponding and even made plans to do research projects together. We went to the same graduate school in Rhode Island, though. She was pursuing her intellectual theories, then she needed money to help pay her way through school, you know. She was a scholarship student, but it was just enough to pay tuition. She could've gotten in the Work-Study Program as a research assistant, any of the professors would've hired her, but she didn't want that. I think someone harassed her, you know, but I'm not sure, because in those days, you know, it wasn't a big notion, sexual harassment, though I remember there was a big ballyhoo about an article one of the professors wrote. "Up the Down Coed," I think. Someone from the English Department. I spent most of my time in the chem and biology labs, though. Only a few African-American professors in the sciences. Our advisor was one of them, but he was a physicist not a chemist. I remember Joan used to spend a lot of time talking with him about some of her theories. He indulged her, but his own interests weren't in chemistry. And there was another professor, a German, a chemist. Joan was doing something with spectroscopy, and he was one

of the leading experts in that field. I think he was an old Nazi myself. I
had only one course with him. Or rather I started to take a course with
him, but the first day he wouldn't even acknowledge my presence in his
class, my African presence, so I walked out. Joan stayed in that class and
took courses with him, though. I guess she sort of forced him to acknowledge her African presence, or maybe just the fact that she's a female. Even our writers don't write tales of invisible women, at least
none I've read. Anyway, Joan started singing at a local nightclub rather
than be anyone's work-study assistant. I don't think it was harassment,
though. If anyone harassed, it was probably Joan. I remember she used
to develop these intense relationships with people. Not lovers, you
know what I mean. And she's not like the other girls in the sciences, most
other women who take up the sciences. Most people who take up sciences, for that matter. Not just the idea people have of them in the popular imagination. The nerds. Of course, we scientists have a range of personality types like anyone else. But Joan's more spontaneous and witty
than most of the so-called rational types. Maybe it's just her ego. Or I
guess she prefers the limelight. There's not much limelight in being a research chemist. Unless you're one of the celebrity-type scientists. A pop
scientist. When Ernie Shuger wrote that article on me and I got a couple
of fan letters, Joan kidded me about becoming a pop scientist, a celebrity scientist. I think not.

She's brilliant onstage, I said. Don't you think? She's spontaneous
and witty there.

I've never watched her perform. I don't like her singing.

I took my shoes off and put my feet up on the bed. Maybe I was trying
to behave spontaneous and witty, if that was the sorta woman he liked.
The odor-eaters in them were worn. I shoved them under the bed.

I bet you like her singing, I said. I bet you're a closet fan. I bet it ain't
true that you don't listen to her, at least her recordings. I bet you're a
closet Joan Savage fan. I love your crazy quilt.

Let's go downstairs, he said.

I'd rather stay up here.

CHAPTER TWENTY-THREE

After her recording session Joan wanted to come back and have dinner in the room, so I ordered up. She sat on the corner of the bed, brooded and ate a ham and cheese croissant. I sat in a chair, a bowl of chef's salad on my lap, and turned on the television. The Comedy Club. Then on another channel they were talking about a bidding duel at a yearling sale, a bidding duel between a Saratoga breeder and another man, a foreigner. Then they referred to the other man as a German, but when they showed a closeup of the man's face, I almost dropped my salad.

That's the guy, I said, pointing.

What guy?

The guy I spent my summer vacation with. Up in Saratoga. Didn't I tell you about that guy? He's from Germany. You know I told you I met this colored guy from Germany. Did I tell you about this colored guy from Germany? African German.

I asked you who'd you win in Saratoga, but you didn't tell me. African German?

I don't know if that's what he calls himself, though. Like those Portuguese friends of yours from Rhode Island, they don't call themselves African Portuguese, they just call themselves Portuguese. You know, those Portuguese friends of yours, you said when you first met them in Rhode Island, you thought they were jigs, but they're Portuguese.

I didn't tell you that. Jamey musta told you that. They're his friends, not mine. I did sing in a club owned by one of them. I think Jamey got me a gig in that club. He didn't want me to sing in just anybody's club, you know. He won't admit it, and he never came to that club to hear me sing. 'Cause that friend of his said, How come Jaime never comes to my club anymore—I think he calls him Jaime. He had this club fixed up to look like a little fishing village in Portugal. Well, upstairs looked like a little fishing village in Portugal, but the downstairs part of the club looked like a regular Lisbon nightclub, which really looks like a nightclub anywhere. Anyway, so it was because I was singing there. I mean, that Jamey wouldn't come to the nightclub anymore. So this friend of Jamey's just thought it was because Jamey thought I'd be nervous, you know, with him being my lover in my audience, but I knew the true reason, that he didn't want me to be a singer anyway, he just got me the gig there so's he'd have some control, you know. I did think they were jigs, though, then found out they're Portuguese. A lot of them my own complexion, you know, but calling themselves Portuguese. Like the people from Cape Verde, you know. But you know, the Portuguese all over Africa and the New World, and the Portuguese the first colonists, and wanting to hold on to their colonies longer than anybody else, except maybe the English in Ireland. I learned to sing a few songs in Portuguese. That's when I first got interested in singing in other languages. . . . He's from Germany?

Yeah. They been in Germany since the seventeenth or eighteenth century or some shit. I thought maybe he was the son of one of those African or African-American soldiers that stayed in Germany after the war, you know, like you know after the war a lot of African-American soldiers, well some of them, stayed in Europe and the Pacific and married foreign women, you know, after the different foreign wars, rather than just be second-class citizens in America, you know, but he says they've been in Germany since the seventeenth or eighteenth century, not just since the war. That they're as German as the Germans. In fact, during the war they fled Germany, he says, and went to Switzerland, but then they returned to Germany after the war. But he says they're as German as the Germans.

I don't think anyone's as German as the Germans. I usedta have this German professor for chemistry. He's one of the leading chemists in the world. I think he's a former Nazi or some shit, Jamey thinks he's a former Nazi, but they still consider him one of the world-class chemists. He said he spent some time in Argentina after the war, but that don't mean he's a former Nazi. There were Germans who were in the Resistance, the Germans had a Resistance just like the French, but you just hear about the Nazis, and Jamey thinks every German of that generation was a Nazi. I don't think he's a Fascist son of a bitch or anything like that, though Jamey thinks he's a Fascist if not a Nazi and wouldn't take any classes with him. I think he started to take one class with him and then walked out. I remember he gave me this reading list. I thought it was going to be chemistry, but it wasn't chemistry, it was German philosophy. He said it would help me to develop my rational mind. And he usedta listen to Wagner all the time. You know what listening to Wagner means. That's probably why a lot of people rumored him to be a former Nazi, because the Nazis usedta love Wagner. But then when he'd listen to Wagner, he'd look all romantic, you know. I remember I saw him in the pub—the Graduate Center had a pub—in the pub listening to Wagner, earphones in his ears, but I knew he was listening to Wagner. He curved his little finger for me to come over, and when I came over he bought me a beer and asked me whether I thought in pictures, whether when I thought I thought in pictures, or whether I thought in words or in numbers or in abstractions. That was all he asked. I didn't answer, of course, because I thought everybody thought in pictures and words and numbers and abstractions, and that a scientist, even a true scientist didn't just have to think in abstractions. But I knew what he was trying to suggest, that if I thought only in pictures, that I must truly be a primitive. And I knew he was listening to Wagner because of that romantic look. . . . and he never called me by my first name, like the other professors. He called me Miss, well my name wasn't Savage then, but it might as well have been, the way he said it. But I liked the way he said it. And he asked me once why I hadn't chosen him for my advisor. Because I had this African-American professor for my advisor, you know, even though he wasn't a chemist, but a physicist, and he, the German professor, he was the most renowned of the professors in our department, more renowned than the advisor I'd chosen, and's got chemistry textbooks used in all the major universities and could've done more for me. I remember his study was some type of fish that was supposed to have healing powers or healing substances. I keep thinking the remora, but it was another fish, some type of tropical fish. I remember his colleagues thought he was a lunatic or something, thought he'd already made his reputation, so he could pretty much do any type of research he wanted. I remember I envied his freedom, though. A free man among free men. He worked with only a few graduate students, and only those he wanted to work with, and he was free to pursue his research. A free man among free men. He helped me decide what I wanted to be.

What do you mean? Free? A free woman among free women? I joked.

By helping me to decide what I didn't want to be. He said I could come and work with him and just pursue my own research. That was what I wanted. That was my ideal. I was developing this spectroscopic theory that I thought had real potential. I don't remember anything of it now. He knew I was having financial worries. He knew I didn't have enough financing for the sort of research I wanted to do. My scholarship barely paid my tuition. I could have gotten more money if I'd agreed to teach after college, but I didn't want to be a teacher, I wanted to do research. He said I wouldn't have any financial worries. He offered me money. He asked me whether I needed money. He asked me how much money I needed. He'd won prizes, he said, and so he didn't have any financial worries himself. And the university was quite generous, and he was always receiving grants to pursue his own research. He simply asked me how much money I needed for my research. He had a wife, he said, but he wasn't making any proposals to me that she wouldn't consent to. He had helped other students who needed money. And then he asked me whether I thought in pictures. . . . African German. I didn't know they had slaves in Germany. But I guess they've had slaves everywhere in Europe, made slaves out of Africans as well as each other.

I think they just came over to Germany, not as slaves. I don't know their history. I think he said he's part Hottentot or something. I found that interesting, that he actually knows his African tribe, that he could say, I'm part Hottentot. He said they weren't slaves when they came to

Germany, they came as free men. Hottentot, I think. I think he said Hottentot.

I read about that somewhere. That they usedta bring these Hottentots into Germany and put them on exhibit. One of those countries. I took an anthropology course once and they were talking about the relationship between the Hottentots and the Germans, but I don't remember exactly what they said about the relationship between the Hottentots and the Germans. I know they used to bring Africans into Europe and put them on exhibit, you know, when they weren't making slaves of them. Like the Hottentot Venus. I read somewhere about the Hottentot Venus. Somebody wrote a poem about her, but I read it somewhere else, in one of my nonfiction books, so I know it's real. But I think that was France. I know, they used to put Africans on exhibit in France. You know, in those intellectual saloons. I like to call them intellectual saloons. Zooing them, you know. That's what I call it, zooing people, when you don't treat them like human beings. I think that professor would've zooed me if I'd let him. If I must be zooed, then I'll zoo myself. There's a famous African man they put on exhibit like that too. I forgot the name of that man. A pygmy, I think. Somebody wrote a book about him, though.

Anyway, he's got all these bodyguards. I don't know if he's paranoid or what. Real wealthy, you wouldn't believe. That African German.

Yeah, I'd believe, she said. When I was playing that club in Paris, you remember that group of wealthy freaks we met. From New Orleans, I think. I read about them too. The free coloreds who used to go to school in Paris.

They weren't freaks.

You mean he didn't give you the bum's rush?

No. Maybe he thought I had money myself. At first anyway. He was treating me like he thought I had money. You know how people treat you when they think you've got money, and then how they treat you when they find out you ain't got shit. Or when they think you ain't got shit, and then they find out you got money, or they think you got money. Like this woman working in this company was talking about how her bosses were treating her like shit, but then when she moved up in the company, the people started treating her like sugar, and the same people used to treat her like shit, and then she became their boss. They were like bossing her around and then she became their boss. I read that in one of those books of yours on management styles and techniques. That's why, they say, you're supposed to treat everybody like sugar.

I treat everybody the same, she said. She straightened and watched the screen. The announcer was talking about the German buyer, how the German buyer had driven the bidding up to the largest it had ever been. The yearling he'd purchased had sold for five million dollars.

This is the largest that's ever been paid for a yearling, said the announcer.

Ain't he cute? I asked.

Naw, he ain't cute.

I mean Josef, not the yearling.

He ain't cute. He's beautiful. She sulked and bit into her croissant. How'd you meet him anyway?

I told you.

Tell me again.

I told her again.

Maybe he ain't paranoid. You know what they say about paranoia? How'd he get to be so rich anyway?

I don't know. I never asked him.

You wouldn't. Maybe he's a gangster.

I don't think so. He just breeds horses is all I know. Breeds and races horses. Gotta farm in Kentucky. Thought I was spying on him. I told him about you.

You told him about me?

Yeah. We listened to some of your music. He likes Wagner, though. You know, Mozart. That sorta music. I don't know what sorta business he was in over in Germany, though. He was telling me about some sort of business negotiations, but I wasn't sure what he was talking about. I didn't want him to explain what he was talking about because I didn't wanna sound ignorant, you know. I think he said something about arbitrage. That's when he thought I had money, and there ain't too many people who's rich and stupid, and least whilst people thinks they's rich they usually don't believe 'em to be stupid. But poor people can be as stupid as they wanna be, I mean even when they ain't stupid people thinks they's stupid, 'cause they's poor, you know. Like when people say, If you're so smart, how come you ain't rich? He says he's in arbitrage. What's that?

That's some kinda mediator. Arbitrage, you know. Maybe he's a mediator in different business disputes, you know, disputes between different businesses. Somebody Jamey went to school with does that shit. But he's a lawyer, though. I guess you don't have to be a lawyer, though, to do that. You can be a regular businessman and do arbitrage for other businesses. I know there are businesses that are just in the business of doing arbitrage for other businesses, contract negotiation and that kinda thing. Or maybe he's just a gangster and telling you that shit.

Just because somebody tell you a incredible story don't mean it ain't the truth. Like I remember when Norvelle and I went to this cocktail party at his university. He don't like to go to them university cocktail parties, but he went to this one, 'cause some famous African anthropologist or anthropologist of Africa supposed to be at the cocktail party. I thought it was gonna be a man, but turned out to be this woman feminist anthropologist. He thinks she has a lot of interesting things to say about Africa from the feminist perspective. There's another feminist anthropologist he thinks is bullshit, but this one he seems to sorta respect. She's sorta a Afrocentric feminist, though. I don't think that's the same as a feminist feminist. Or maybe she don't even call herself a feminist. She just look like a regular woman to me, though. So somebody asked me what did I do, 'cause people always wants to know what it is you do as if that tells 'em who you are, and I said I'm a beautician. And they thought I was lying or joking, you know, 'cause they didn't believe that Norvelle would marry a beautician, him being a university professor, that he would have hisself a professional woman, you know, maybe like that Afrocentric feminist anthropologist woman, you know, being a university professor and publishing in the scholarly journals puts him in the middle class, you know. Now you know you're not a beautician, this woman says. The provost's wife, I think. And somebody else told her, She's a photojournalist. Because Norvelle had used some of the photographs that I took when we were over there in Africa in some of the articles that he'd published about medical anthropology, you know, and got them published in a more popular magazine than his usual little articles that he publishes in the little professional journals 'cause most of them don't use photographs, you know. Norvelle says the more popular the magazine the more photographs they use, that's why the most scholarly magazines don't got no photographs in them, and that's even anthropology, 'cause the scholarly magazines don't want you to confuse them with *National Geographic*, though he uses some of my photographs in some of the books he writes, but they usually print all the photographs together in one section so that the books still look scholarly. So anyway they preferred to believe that I'm a photojournalist 'cause that's a more credible story, you know. Even though Norvelle's origins is supposed to be inner city in Memphis, you know, he's supposed to be middle class. They do own this renovated boardinghouse now, though, then that sorta makes them the landlord class, though he grew up in the inner city of Memphis, the Memphis ghetto, you know. But being a university professor that's the only type of woman that they could imagine that Norvelle could love, a photojournalist, you know. And I guess you prefer to believe that he's a gangster, that African German, 'cause I suppose for you that's a more credible story of how a African, even a German African or a African German, that ain't no gangster or entertainer could get to be a rich man. Like that friend of yours from Chinatown, that girl you said you went to school with in that private school in Connecticut, you know, when you were in undergraduate school, who you said everybody thinks is a gangster 'cause she owns all those restaurants and shit.

You mean Isabel Kong?

Yeah.

Isabel Kong and Little Lady Kong. That's her daughter. I think she is some kinda gangster, to tell the truth. Some kinda bandit, but very urbane, the urbane type of bandit. She was an art student when I knew her at school, and had all these ambitions of becoming a great artist, you know. I thought she was really good myself. They'd have these student exhibitions, you know, exhibitions of the student artist, her painting and sculpture. She thought I was an artist, when we first met, because it was at a student art exhibition, and she asked me which of the paintings and sculptures were mine, and couldn't believe it when I told her I was studying chemistry. We had only one African-American artist there, or who had aspirations for being an artist. And at first she thought I was her. And she comes over and says, Are you so-'n'-so? Because she was going to tell me she liked one of my sculptures, but I said that I'm not an artist, you know. Anyway, I saw her again when you got me that gig in Amsterdam. She said she was opening a new restaurant there, and she also wanted to open a new restaurant in Hong Kong. I think she makes false passports now, though, for illegal Chinese. I hear all sorts of stories about her, but it's not the Isabel Kong I knew at school. When I started singing, she thought I was being truer to myself, though, than when I wanted to become a research chemist. I remember when I started singing in the clubs around school, she'd always come to hear me. Then she had Little Lady—she's one of those little girls that you want to say your ladyship when you see her, not that she's conceited or anything; her real first name's Javana—out of wedlock and left school and opened her first restaurant. She still paints, but she just puts her paintings on the walls of her own restaurants, you know. Sometimes people'll see a painting of hers on the wall and want to buy it, but she says she doesn't know whether they want to buy it because they think it's good, or just because she's the notorious Isabel Kong.

Well, I never heard of Isabel Kong till I met you, but then I ain't into gangster lore. Anyway, all I know is he breeds racehorses now, and that's the truth, 'cause I seen his farm. And he ain't a gangster. And he's got all these security guards. He's a paranoid fool, but he's a likable man.

When the television camera panned the Fasig-Tipton sales arena, you know the tent where they have the sales, in the background, near a post, stood Nicholas. I started to point him out too, but I didn't. I finished the salad and put the bowl back on the tray.

When do you plan to see him again? she asked.

I don't.

She chewed.

CHAPTER TWENTY-FOUR

Who finished seventh in the 1971 Derby? he asked. Tribal Line, I answered, offering him some mixed nuts. You do know your horseflesh, he said smiling, taking some of the nuts and nibbling. I know I do, I said. I Ie counted out ten fives, handed them to me, all the while looking like he'd won. Make her go another round, said his buddy, frowning. He shook his head when I offered him some nuts. I've got to catch my train, fellows, I said, putting the bills in my purse. This is the second call. Fifth in 1969, he called as I hurried toward the doors. Top Knight, I called back. Fifth in 1972. Sensitive Music, I called back and waved. He was smiling. His buddy was shaking his head. I settled on the train and took out the new lead sheets Joan had sent. I glanced back out the window and the fellow I had won the fifty dollars from was waving and looking like he was in love, while his buddy stood nearby looking disgusted. I blew them both a kiss, shook some more mixed nuts into my palm, and settled down to go over the leads.

They were crowding outside the door, there for their daily handout, but Grandmother Jaboti wouldn't let them in. If they were mine, she said, I'd put them to work sweeping the floor or cleaning my brushes, and then I'd give the bums something to eat after they'd done worked for it.

She shushed them away from the door, telling them to wait till Cornella came.

You would think with all Cornella's saints that she'd tell these bums that they's only to eat by the sweat of they brow.

They ain't called bums nowadays, Grandmother Jaboti, I said.

A bum's a bum, she said. I ain't a politician, but I know a bum.

After a while, we heard footsteps upon the porch, then a jiggle in the latch of the door. Here's Cornella now. Watch 'em come running back.

Harlan, darling, what a surprise, she said as she entered. We hugged and stood smiling at each other and then Grandmother's bums and Mother's little Christs came marching in. Now, there weren't just men among the "bums," though, but a few women and children.

TWENTY-SIX

Cornella, you want to take her or you want me to? Grandmother Jaboti asked.

Now I should explain here that Jaboti ain't my grandmother's real name. She say it her carnival name. That once when the carnival she was working for went to Brazil, to Rio, that one of them Brazilians named her Jaboti instead of Turtle Woman, and so she just kept that name. Jaboti, she said, was a turtle trickster in Brazilian folklore. Me I don't know whether that's one of them true lies or not. I just know that everybody call her Grandmother Jaboti like it her true name.

You take her, said my mother. Mrs. Smoot, the pharmacist's wife, is due in here in ten minutes. Little girl didn't make no appointment, did she?

Naw, just popped her head in the door. Well, I've told her she's come to the right beauty shop because we only use New York and imported beauty products in our shop. We might be local, but our beauty products come from all over the world.

I didn't know I had to make an appointment, the girl explained. This my first time in a beauty parlor. She looked about seventeen and timid. She said again this was her first time in a beauty shop, that she'd never had her hair professionally done before. Her timidity reminded me of me at her age, when they used to call me Possum.

This your first time in a beauty parlor? Grandmother Jaboti repeated, as the girl climbed into the high chair.

Yes ma'am.

Lay your head back.

The girl lay her head back so that it was over the sink. Her hair was carelessly straightened and tied back with a rubber band; it looked dull and damaged, its edges uneven. You could tell she'd never had a professional conditioning or trim.

When you pull your hair back tight like this it breaks the edges off, said my grandmother. See how bad your edges is. Girl, what is you doing to your head? White gals can wear their hair like this. Colored hair is fragile. You wants a permanent?

Yes ma'am. I'm going away to college.

Well, I can't give you a permanent until I get your hair in some condition. It's too brittle now. Colored people's hair is fragile, so you gots to treat it delicate. I gots to get it strong or else it'll fall all out if I try to put this permanent in it. 'Less you wants to wear it natural. Them Afros is back in style. They ain't never gone out of style with me, but you know how some folks is.

No, ma'am, I want a permanent.

How long you got before you go off to school?

About two weeks.

What school is you going to? Kentucky State?

No ma'am. Bennington.

Been what? Don't believe I heard o' that one.

It's in Vermont. I got a scholarship to go there.

Grandmother took the rubber band off her hair, spread the girl's hair in her fingers and looked at it. Well, child, I do my best. I wash and condition it this week and straighten it regular, with the straightening comb, and then you put this cream conditioner on it every night and every morning and then you come back next week. Honey, how'd you get your hair in this mess?

The girl said nothing. I lit a cigarette and watched while Grandmother Jaboti washed her hair with castile soap. While the girl sat under the hair dryer, Grandmother asked, You want me to do you next, stranger?

No ma'am, I said. I might start braiding my hair.

She told me my hair looked like it had after the African sun had got hold of it years back, then she gave me a little jar of cream conditioner, and started telling me about some cream that she was importing from Brazil that was supposed to be better than them permanents 'cause it ain't supposed to damage your hair, it supposed to use some kinda natural relaxer made from some Brazilian plants and herbs. And they say you can even eat it, that it so natural that you can even eat it, that it's made of natural and edible ingredients. And then she said something again about colored people's fragile hair. I guess it take them Brazilians to discover something like that for us hair.

You come and help me wash out my brushes, she said, when I stayed seated at the counter. Acting like these bums that come in here.

She winked at my mother who was putting a bib around Mrs. Smoot's neck.

Got to put this bum to work, even if Cornella's bums don't work.

Where'd you say you going to school, honey? Mrs. Smoot asked the girl, as my mother greased her scalp with Vaseline, preparing it for a touch-up.

Vermont.

Mrs. Rampart's daughter went up there up North up there to all that cajolery up there. A lot of folks thinks the North is the promised land. I been North. Well, went in that direction anyhow, and ain't no more promise up there than any other land. My husband started him one of the first colored pharmacies around here. If you's a colored person in this country you's got to make your own promise. That's what other people's do when they come to this country, they makes they promise. Course, it's more difficult for the colored man to make his promise than them that can claim white.

Y'all keep calling us colored. We ain't colored, they don't say colored now, said my mother.

Well, when my husband started that pharmacy we was colored. And some of us is still colored, and we ain't all black, so how come they wants to call us all black. And white people ain't all white neither but they calls theyselves white. And I know I ain't African, I'm American. I've been to Africa, and when I was there, ain't none of them Africans thought I was African. When I first went over there to Africa, though, I thought they would consider me a African from the New World, but they consider me the American that I am. And I'm talking about the true African people themselves. We usedta call usselves race men and women, though. Anyway, that gal I'm talking about, that Mrs. Rampart's daughter went up there up North and went wild. A sweet girl before she went up there. Them northern gals I don't think they's as sweet as southern gals. When I'm up North up there when my husband goes to them pharmacy conventions in New York they refer to me as a southern belle, and me a colored woman, but that's just 'cause I'm naturally sweet. Well, I hope you stay sweet, little girl. Some little girls go up there up North and don't stay sweet.

I lit another cigarette and said nothing. I know she signifying about me.

When Grandmother Jaboti finished straightening the young woman's hair, she looked like a photograph out of the 1940s, the war years, rather than a modern young woman. She looked at herself in the mirror.

It looks nice, she said.

Well, you put this conditioner on it and get it conditioned and tamed before I can put that permanent on it. And talking about New York, this conditioner is from New York. It ain't none of this local conditioner, it's the best conditioner on the market. Course if they send me that Brazilian stuff, I can put that straight in your hair, without even this New York conditioner, 'cause that ain't supposed to damage it. Them colored people in Brazil supposed to have invented it from the herbs in they rain forest. Supposed to be so sweet that you can eat it. I been to Brazil, and if colored people anywhere can invent condiments for the hair, it's them Brazilians.

Ever been to Vermont? I asked the girl.

No ma'am.

It's nice country. The grass is so green. You wouldn't believe. They say Kentucky bluegrass is green, but that Vermont grass is greener. Only African grass is greener than that.

And the green in them Brazilian rain forest. At least they say the green in them Brazilian rain forest is green. I just been to Rio myself.

I bet you she gives a good show, said my grandmother. I don't understand what she singing about, though, but I bet she a real good entertainer. She sounds like she's a real good entertainer, I mean for that rock 'n' roll–type music. They's got this new music rap, you know, and I still don't understand what these rock-'n'-rollers is singing. They think I'm supposed to understand this rap music and I don't even understand rock 'n' roll yet. I bet she's a real good entertainer, though.

She is, I said.

I know what she's singing, said my mother. I don't know what all them rappers is singing, 'cept for Jazzy Jeff and the Fresh Prince, but I know what she's singing. That Jazzy Jeff and the Fresh Prince seem like nice boys. They're not gangsters.

We listened to another song. It was a ballad, but it had a wild and raunchy edge to it, almost like gangsta rap. I saw my mother in the corner looking disgusted. They make a song out of almost anything these days, don't they? And that language they use in that music, it ain't nothing but obscene. Except for Jazzy Jeff and the Fresh Prince. And a lot of the good and nice girls get in that show business and even they start singing that obscene-type music and glamorizing gangsterhood and themselves and getting freakish.

Now what you know about freakish? asked Grandmother Jaboti. What do you know about gangsterhood?

She sounds like a nice girl, though, what you tell me about her, but you would think she would sing more high-minded and intelligent-type music than that. Even them high-minded girls when they get into show

business. I guess intelligence don't sell. At least Jazzy Jeff and the Fresh
Prince seem like nice boys.

They make songs out of any nonsense, though, and somebody said
Jazzy Jeff and the Fresh Prince is just bubblegum music. I like them myself, but that's just bumblegum music, Grandmother Jaboti said. Public
Enemy is supposed to be the princes of rap, but I don't understand nothing of what they're singing about. I mean, I understand what they're
singing about, but I don't exactly understand their words. When finally
understanding some of Joan's words, though, she laughed and shook
her gray head.

Yes they do, I agreed. She's trying to experiment in that song, combining a rock ballad and rap. A lot of the male rappers refer to women
as bitches, excuse my French, so she's sorta signifying on a bitch's, excuse my French, version of that type of music. It's supposed to be a satire, you know. On account of so many of the gangsta rap singers refer-
ring to women as bitches, you know. So she refers to herself as a bitch,
you know, excuse my French. Except, she refers to herself as a darling
bitch.

I like it better when she sings plain, though. She got a voice as sweet
as candy when she wants to have one. She sounds like a darling. I don't
like all that embellished fanfare, though, said Grandmother, then she
looked at my mother. Reminds you of Jack, don't it?

Certain things don't belong in no song, my mother said. There's certain things that just don't belong in songs, whether it's rap or rock 'n'
roll. Where is all the intelligent music that people usedta sing?

Grandmother Jaboti popped her fingers. She started to dance. Do she
write her own songs? she asked, pausing in the midst of the tune.

Sometimes.

Them's obscure words all right. She continued dancing.

I hope you ain't cheating that girl, my mother said as I put on another
tape. I hope you's doing right by her. I hope you ain't cheating her like I
hear some of those stars' unethical managers do. They tell you all about
that in the *Enquirer*. You's got to learn how to manage yourself before
you can manage other people anyhow. And I ain't sure you should ever

try to manage other people. Don't manage other people and don't have them to manage you neither. Of course, when they gets to be a big star, peoples have got to have some kinda manager, but they should still know how to manage theirselves. Some people think freedom is managing other people, but it ain't. It's managing yourself. Learn to manage yourself. If you're a big enough star, you might have to have a manager, but when you've got these unethical managers, you've got to manage your manager. But you've always got to manage yourself even when you've got you a manager. So I hope you ain't cheating her, whether she's a darling or a bitch, excuse my French, and spending all her money on caviar and champagne. She probably needs one of them entertainment lawyers anyhow. And they say even they cheats people.

Mama, now you know I wouldn't cheat nobody. Since when have you started reading the *Enquirer*?

Well, I don't read it, but you can't help but to read it sometimes peeking out at you in the supermarket. Why, them managers and entertainment lawyers is always cheating people. And it ain't just the little stars, like the star you manage, but the big stars too. Some people think that freedom is to manage everybody but theyself. Learn to manage yourself. That is the key to freedom.

After the concert we went back to the hotel and ordered a late-night snack of Swiss cheese sandwiches and grape soda. Joan stood in the middle of the room grinning, purple stains on her front teeth. Then she grabbed her Swiss cheese sandwich and nibbled.

They forgot to put mustard on my Swiss cheese.

'Cause you're the only fool puts mustard on cheese. Most people put mayonnaise on it.

Jamey likes mustard on his cheese. I know a lot of people like mustard on cheese. I don't think we're all fools.

I said nothing. I ate a bit of my sandwich. It was the one with mustard. I handed it to Joan. She nibbled some of it, then put it back on the plate. Then she grabbed her liter of grape soda.

Do you remember that gig we did in Paris in the old days? she asked. When she talked about her performances she'd say we as if I were up on the stage cutting capers with her. You know like you see them stars giving interviews and they's always saying "we." You ask them about theyselves and they says "we." I don't think they mean it as the royal we, though. Most of them work with a lot of other musicians and stage managers and shit. And maybe they think that "I" sounds too egotistical, so they say "we." Joan, though, says it like she mean the royal we.

Yeah, sure.

We went to this Moroccan restaurant and I tricked you into eating camel sausage? she asked.

It tasted good till you told me what it was.

And you thought the couscous was grits.

She laughed and sat down, scooting to the edge of the chair. Sometimes she sat the way girls and women are admonished not to sit: with her knees apart, so you could see her panties. I bet you you wouldn't eat it after I told you what it was, but you ate some more, she said.

Yeah, I remember.

You've dragged me all over the fucking globe, she said. All over the fucking globe.

What do you mean I've dragged you all over the fucking globe? I've got you some good gigs, girl.

Why can't a recording artist just record music? How come we got to go all over the fucking globe entertaining people? That would be my ideal, just to record music. Why do I have to go all over the fucking globe entertaining people?

That makes you a star. And it allows you to be able to record music. Anyway, people who like your music don't just want to listen to a recording. They want to hear you sing in person. And you give a good performance. Some people sound better on their records. But you, you're good on your records. But I think people have to actually hear you to really appreciate you.

Show business. I've worked hard, and you've just enjoyed yourself.

I've worked hard to get you gigs. There's more people who know who Joan Savage is now than when I met you.

Just 'cause you'd never heard of me don't mean other people ain't. I've worked my butt off.

But you've had fun too. You've had fun.

Me, I've worked hard. I worked my butt off. I hardly knew what fucking country I was in most of the fucking time. It was all for you, not me. Places you never would have got to go in a million fucking years, if it wasn't for me. Your husband took you over there to Africa, but you got to travel all over the world because of me. That's the only reason you stay with me, 'cause you know on your own you—

You've enjoyed yourself too. You enjoyed yourself in Amsterdam. When I got you that gig in Amsterdam, you said Amsterdam? Amsterdam? You couldn't imagine going over there to Amsterdam to give a performance. But then when we got there, you enjoyed Amsterdam. I don't think you coulda gotten yourself a gig in Amsterdam. You couldn't even imagine Amsterdam. The fucking people didn't even fucking know you when you first sang in that little club in Amsterdam, but they know you now. Some of your best music was recorded in Amsterdam. And you've got your own promotion over there. That little promotion company.

Little promotion company is right. In somebody's basement. I thought it was a fan club. Promotion company? And I lost my fucking voice in Amsterdam. How could I have enjoyed myself in a place where I lost my fucking voice? I lost my fucking voice in Amsterdam.

That sounds like one of your songs. Well, you did record that album there, and you got yourself that little promotion company. Then you lost your voice. But then you got it back in Brazil.

Because you always wanted to go to Brazil. That's the only reason you got me a gig there. Then whenever we go anywhere you're always seeking out the lowlifes.

What lowlifes?

In Brazil, the slums. What do you call those slums? What did they have crab races there or some shit that you went to. Or is that St. Croix that has the crab races? I know somewhere in one of those countries they have crab races. I don't know whether they always had crab races or you started that shit so's you have something to bet on.

I didn't start it. It's an old tradition there. I don't know who started it. I was surprised myself when somebody asked me if I wanted to go to a crab race. So the crabs had little numbers on 'em, you know. So you picked out the crab that you thought would win. But they weren't all lowlifes. You had some European royalty staying at that hotel betting on those crabs. At least somebody said they was European royalty. Well, you had all kinds and classes of people staying there. That's what I like about a little island like that.

And in Port-au-Prince, for instance. Those lowlifes.

Oh, yeah. I'd wanted to bet on the cockfights, but they didn't allow women in. He wasn't a lowlife. He just helped me get into the cock-fights. He escorted me into the cockfights.

You were hanging all over him, a married man.

Just a gambling buddy.

I'd heard that women weren't allowed at the cockfights, but I'd gone anyway. No women, the man had said, when I'd got to the hut where someone said there were cockfights. I didn't understand Creole, so he told me in French and then English.

I stood outside the tin-roofed hut and waited for the proper fellow. When he came, I asked him to place the bet and promised that we'd divide the winnings. He rattled off the names of the cocks that were fighting, and I chose one.

You ain't seen the cocks.

I don't need to see 'em.

I handed him the money. He looked as if he'd never seen such a wad of bills before.

How do you know I won't run away with it?

I don't.

He shrugged and went inside.

I stood outside, listening to feathers fly. The man who guarded the hut gave me evil stares, like being a woman I wasn't only not allowed in the cockfight, but I shouldn't even be allowed near it. I lit a cigarette and moved away from the hut and waited near a palm tree.

Some time later the fellow came out waving money in his fists. He paraded in front of me like a bandy rooster himself, and then kissed my jaw, and would have lifted me skyward if he could have. We divided the winnings.

When Joan saw me "hanging on to him" in the Iron Market it was because we'd won. Joan and I'd been shopping in the Iron Market, and I'd spotted the man who'd bet on the cock for me.

Sandovar! I yelled.

We hugged and hugged. Now, he said, with his winnings, he could take his wife and children to another country. He said he didn't like his country and wanted to emigrate to another one. I asked him if he might come to the States. He said he didn't like the States much either. He said he might try to emigrate to the Bahamas. I hung on to him. He hugged me too, and tried to lift me skyward again, but like I said I'm a big woman. Joan, standing nearby, just looked at us. She wouldn't even come near enough to be introduced.

Am I embarrassing you in front of your friend? he asked.

No, of course not.

That's why I pretended not to know you, he said, glancing toward her.

You needn't pretend, I said.

Anyway, I don't give a good fuck what you do, Joan's saying. I don't know why I put up with you. I mean, a woman so starved to gamble on something that she'll bet on a fucking crab. A cock. I might bet on a cock myself. I work my fucking butt off, though, and you have a good time. Did you at least bet on the right cock? Did you win?

Sure.

I wouldn't set foot in Port-au-Prince today, even if you could get me a gig there. Talking about getting me gigs. I wanted that gig in New York, and you come talking about Port-au-Prince. Jamaica maybe, or some of them other little Caribbean islands. I liked St. Croix, though. Then when I did get that gig, I come in and the people don't even know who I am, giving me the bum's rush, and you're supposed to promote me.

Well, when they found out it was you, they treated you like royalty. You should be with me when I'm talking to some of the promoters and agents and club owners on your behalf. Talk about the bum's rush. Joan Savage, who's Joan Savage? If you were more famous, it might be easier to represent you. I think you're ambivalent about fame. You want to be a rock star.

A rock singer. Stardom is your game.

Well, whatever you want to be you always sabotage yourself.

When you and Jamey don't sabotage me.

How do I sabotage you? How has Jamey sabotaged you?

You only get me third-rate gigs, and Jamey. . . . he don't believe in me.

He don't owe you his belief. And I have gotten you some first-rate gigs, they just ain't in the States, and you think only the States is first-rate.

A first-rate gig in a fourth-rate little country is a third-rate gig.

She kicked the bottle of grape soda over, staining the thick beige carpet.

I got up and went into the bathroom and came back with paper towels. I dabbed up the grape soda, but there was still a stain. I mentioned the damage to the carpet and said her tantrums always made us have to pay extra.

What? Pay extra? You don't pay. You never pay. You play but you never pay. I'm the one who pays. Anyway, who's the man who's been following us? Another one of your lovers?

What man? What are you talking about?

The one who's been following us. One of your lovers?

I tissue makeup from Joan's round face, then rub in aloe cream. Let's go to a bar, I say.

I'm bushed, she says, slouching and hugging her robe. It's white with large, clownish dots. You think after a show I'm as gamely as you are.

No. I just want to catch a glimpse of that man. The one you said is supposed to be following us. Else you're as paranoid as Josef.

She perked up. Then she looked lazy, but she was game. Okay. Just put me on a little mascara and do something about these lines. She pointed to her forehead. You know that new cream you got that's supposed to erase wrinkles. Dr. Leonard's Facelift at your fingertips. And this stuff for my nails is great. You know, that hoof cream you said they use on horses but that's supposed to strengthen human nails?

Where is he? I asked, as we sat at a corner table.

I don't see him, she said, looking around. Don't you know your own lover?

She wore a dress that was the twin of the robe she'd been wearing. Oh, yeah, there he is. Over there at the bar now.

He's looking at you through the mirror. There's the bogger.

I stared at the mirror.

You mean you don't know your own lover? she repeated.

No, I don't know who he is.

Are you kidding?

I'd expected Nicholas, Josef's bodyguard, if anybody, though if he'd been following me I was sure he'd have been as visible as the lines in

Joan's forehead. The man at the bar was nondescript, ginger-colored, in a tweed jacket. He wore his hair longish, more the style of the 1960s or 1970s than the current style. I'd never seen him before. When he caught me looking at him, the man gave me one of those fish-eyed stares. I stood up.

Where're you going? Joan ask.

To find out who the bogger is.

Naw, girl, that man might be dangerous. I just thought y'all was play-acting, like some lovers do. I thought you knew him. He might be some crazy man. Look at that hairdo. He must think it's still disco. Speaking of disco, you were supposed to order that print of one of Donna Summer's paintings, the one I told you looks sorta like German expressionism. You know there are a lot of crazies these days.

There's always been crazies, I said.

Yeah, but not like these crazies.

Up at the bar, I didn't say anything to the man. I merely stood next to him.

I'd like a Josef, I said to the bartender.

What are you talking about, Lady? he asked, toweling off the counter with the end of his apron. What d'you want?

A drink. It's called a Josef.

I never heard of no Josef, ma'am. Must be a local drink. How d'you make it?

It's a German drink, actually. And you don't make it, it makes you.

Come on, Lady, gimme a break, will ya? What do you want?

I watched the man's expression through the mirror. It didn't change, still that fish-eyed look, but he swallowed his drink, set his money down, and left.

Well, give me a tequila then, I said. No, a sloe gin fizz. And a bowl of pretzels.

Lady. . . . He handed me my drink and a bowl of pretzels and I went back to the table.

So who was he? Joan asked when I sat down, saying nothing.

I don't know, I said, nibbling a pretzel. I think that fool I met in Saratoga, that Josef, the African German I told you about, hired somebody to follow me around. He thought I was some sorta spy or something. He kept asking me whether I was some kinda spy. I don't know what the fool thought. Maybe he is a gangster like you said. Or maybe he's just some wealthy fool who likes to have his women followed. Or thinks I'm his woman. I don't know. He thought I was a spy or some shit. He kept saying I was a spy. Then he caught me trying to find some scratch paper —I, er, you know, was having some ideas for some possible gigs and wanted to write 'em down—and he thought I was spying on him. He thought I was sneaking around spying on him. And he's the one invited me out to his farm. If the fool thought I was a spy, why'd he invite me out to his farm? Can you believe that? Now I think he's got some detective or some shit checking up on me. I remember joking with him about that. That he oughta hire some detective if he thought I was a spy or some shit. Maybe the fool did that. Seems like I'd've noticed him, though. You always notice them detectives in the movies. I think some of those neo-Fascists over there in Germany turned him into a paranoid or some shit. But why'd he think I'm a fucking spy?

Maybe he just wanted to know if you were telling him the truth about who you are. Or maybe Josef didn't hire him at all. Maybe your ex-husband hired that detective.

Naw, Norvelle wouldn't do some shit like that. I don't even think it would enter his imagination to hire a detective. Wealthy people hire detectives anyway. People who got something to protect.

Well, they have detectives now that you can hire to hunt up people, ex-husbands and shit, just dial an 800 number. If Norvelle is still in love with you, he could hire a detective.

Naw, Norvelle wouldn't do some shit like that. He wouldn't have to hire somebody to find out where I am. He knows where I am.

Maybe he hired somebody to find out how you are.

Naw, that ain't Norvelle. He wouldn't be hiring no detective. It wouldn't even enter his imagination to hire no detective. If he wanted to know how I am, he could just come and ask me. He knows where I am. I don't know where he is. I know he's in Africa, but Africa's a big continent. His editors don't even know where he is. I called one of his editors and asked how I could get in touch with him. I didn't want to actually get in touch with him, I just wanted to know where he was, and they said they didn't actually have an address for him, they just had a post office box, and they weren't even allowed to give out that information. Sometimes I'll read an article of his in one of the journals, you know. Sometimes I'll get a little money for some of the photographs I took while we were in Africa. Mostly photographs of that Masai woman and some Sonjo spearmaker. I took some photographs of the Moran and some baobab trees. Sometimes the journals and magazines like to use those photographs to accompany his articles, and I get a little money for those. I forgot to order for you. What do you want?

Nothing. She yawned.

I drank my sloe gin fizz, nibbled a pretzel and offered Joan one. She shook her head, then called over a waiter, who obediently brought her more pretzels and a beer.

Suppose he's dangerous? she asked, dipping a pretzel in her beer.

Who, Norvelle?

Naw, fool, the man following us. She sucked on her pretzel, and looked more nonchalant than she sounded.

Naw, it's just some fool. I had some fool like that following me when I was in beauty school. This guy came up to me and told me he was following me. They didn't have any stalking laws and shit in those days. And this some fool that I knew. He worked for this company that made these cosmetics that we used in our classes, this wholesale cosmetics company, and he used ta deliver the cosmetics and was always hanging around the beauty school, and he said he'd see me on the streets of Cincinnati sometimes and would follow me. He didn't pursue me or anything. He just told me that shit.

You don't know. Don't look like a fool to me. How do you know he ain't after me? Maybe I should hire a bodyguard.

You can't afford no bodyguard. And ain't enough people that know you around here for you to need none. Maybe it's Jamey. Maybe Jamey's checking on you.

219

Now I know Jamey ain't going to hire no detective for nobody. Jamey's the kind be his own detective if he need to do some detecting.

But then we'd know who he is.

We'd think we know who he is. She chewed at her bottom lip. Well, we can at least start packing those stunguns. Order me a stungun.

You with a stungun? Around me? Are you kidding? Yeah, I'll order you one. And maybe some of that pepper spray. And one of those little Swiss Army knives, if that'll make you feel safer. I don't think I'd trust you with anything else. It'd just be your motivation.

Back in the hotel room, she sat down on the couch breathing hard. She kept looking out the window to see if the man had followed us, but he hadn't. I turned on the TV. Mae West and Cary Grant. Maybe I ain't got no soul, Mae West was saying. Sure you have, said Cary, but you keep it hidden under a mask. Haven't you ever met a man who can make you happy? Sure, lots of times, said Mae.

THIRTY

You're like your wandering grandfather, my Grandmother Jaboti said, when I came back from one of the tours with Joan. Before going to Saratoga to bet on the horses, I came back to Louisville.

As for my grandfather, since there were no photographs of him, it made him seem a legend too, like her Turtle Woman tales.

I followed him, she said, until I turned into a human being.

The beauty shop wasn't open yet, and she sat on a high stool, stretching and yawning while I dusted and polished the hair dryers. She was always telling me about my grandfather, always telling me the same story, but I'd listen to it again, as if it was the first time I'd heard the story. But then she never exactly told the story the same way each time. Sometimes she'd add new details, other times she'd tell the same details, but in a different order, in a different syntax.

He was a traveling salesman, your grandpap was. Sold farm implements mostly to colored farmers, you know, 'cause wouldn't none of the white farmers buy from him, so he sold mostly to the colored farmers. Some of the farmers would pay him in money, but a lot of them would pay him with the produce from their farms, and the different foodstuffs like honey and molasses and butter and cornpone and then he'd sell some of the produce and foodstuffs and make his other money that way. And a few of them Quakers, now a few of them Quakers would buy from him, because they have always been the true men of God. A lot of them Quakers could make their own farm implements, but they would also buy from him. Them Quakers have always been true men of God. Back in the seventeenth century, though, when they first come to this country, they usedta own slaves theyselves, but then they decided to abolish slavery amongst theyselves, because they believed that they couldn't be true men of God and own slaves, and after that there wasn't a Quaker to own slaves, and they would help the slaves to escape from slavery. I seen me some Quakers at the supermarket. I wanted to say something to them, but I didn't know what to say to no Quakers. A Quaker man and his wife. Cornella said they wasn't Quakers, that they's probably them Pennsylvania Dutch. Did itinerant repair work, stuff like that, your grandpap. Farms all through the Midwest and along the coast, even traveled up North. And plenty more colored farms then than nowadays. The colored people started leaving the farms and traveling to the city, or the white people drove them off of they land, or tricked them out of they land. You have a whole history of them tricking the colored people out of they land, or the colored people fool enough to sell 'em they land or leave the land for the city. Even them bad ole days of segregation everywhere you had more colored people to own and work their own land, though. Anyway, your grandpap, he said he loved me and 'ud marry me but he wouldn't settle down with me. I run off from that carnival with him, but he wouldn't settle down with me.

She turned toward the long mirror and looked into it.

He wanted me to have some kind of security, though, because I ain't by nature no wandering woman. I wandered with that carnival, but that were the carnival's wandering nature, not mine. And I did my share of wandering. I wandered plenty in my young days. When I was with the carnival, we wandered all through all the States and up in Canada too and in Mexico and I told you about Brazil where they renamed me after that trickster turtle. I think that Montreal the most perfect place we went to, though. But, really, I was not a wandering woman by nature and then you get to the point where you don't want to wander. Well, so he married me, brought me to Kentucky, bought me this beauty parlor, but he wouldn't settle down with me. 'Cause there is some mens that is just like that. Don't make them no less ideal of a man. I usedta wonder how come Mrs. Smoot's husband stayed with her and mine ain't stayed with me and is just a itinerant man. But mine ain't no less ideal of a man. Bought me this beauty parlor, so's I could always take care of myself.

Do you know where he is now? I ask.

Might be a ghost like your daddy now.

Grandmother Jaboti like to call my daddy a ghost, but he ain't. He fought in the Korean War and he stayed over there in that Korea with some Korean woman. Somewhere. After the war. Said there's a lot of colored men that found themselves more freedom over there in that Korea and stayed over there after the war. Like in them other wars, them wars in Europe, a lot of them men after them other wars stayed in them countries, even the enemy countries, 'cause they thought they had more freedom there. I don't know the whole story myself, though it seem like there would be more honor in it, in staying in that country he found more freedom in, if he were a single man.

BOOK

FOUR

THIRTY-ONE

Who was Aristides' jockey? O. Lewis.   Vagrant? B. Swim.   Baden-Baden? W. Walker.   Day Star? J. Carter.   Lord Murphy? C. Shaver. Fonso? G. Lewis.   Hindoo? J. McLaughlin.   Apollo? B. Hurd. Then she began to skip through pages. Plaudit? W. Simms.   Manuel? F. Taral.   Chant? F. Goodale.   Exterminator? Knapp.   What, No first initial? Just Knapp.   Middleground? W. Boland.   Count Turf. I like that. C. McCreary.   Tom Tom? I. Valenzuela.   Lucky Debonair? W. Shoemaker.   Northern Dancer? W. Hortuck.

She tossed the racing book at me, then lay down on the couch and kicked her feet in the air.

Seattle Stew? Seattle Stew? Oh, I mean Seattle Slew. J. Cruquet. I'll take your word for it. I wish I had as good a memory as you, 'cept for Knapp. Tell me some more about that ex-husband of yours. Seem like you got a good memory for everything but that.

My husband, Norvelle, like I told you, is a medical anthropologist who collects medical folklore. After we married, I traveled with him to Kenya, to the Sudan, to Tanzania, to Zanzibar, to Pemba. We talked to blacksmiths, ironworkers, warriors. He'd have talked to lions, elephants, and gazelles if he'd known their language. He'd have talked to the mninga and camphor and mahogany trees. He'd have talked to the wild figs, if they'd spoken. He'd have talked to the oil palms. And surely the baobab if it talked back. He'd have spoken to the same dragonflies that I was trying to frighten away, if they'd spoken. He'd have spoken to all those mosquitoes.

It was only that Masai medicine woman who disoriented me because he wanted to stay with her, because he wanted to keep following her from Korogwe to Morogoro, from the Rufiji River to the Great Ruaha, from the Uluguru Mountains to Meru, in the Eastern Rift Valley. And I guess I also envied her independent nomadic life, traveling about, curing folks. I guess the only way she could express her wanderlust even though the Masai traditionally nomadic people was by being a medicine woman. Of course I thought the Masai men were more beautiful than the women with their bald heads and stretched earlobes. The men had long tresses and an elegance. I could understand the men's aesthetic of beauty, but not the women's. When I saw the warriors, the Moran, I was fascinated. When my husband talked to them in their own language I stayed back, admiring their headdresses of lion's manes and ostrich's feathers. Suppose I had followed one of them about?

Why did she spit in your ear? I asked my husband when he returned where I was standing, under one of those legendary baobab trees.

A sign of goodwill and respect.

We followed her to Sonjo territory. The Sonjo used to be the Masai's enemies, but now she's curing them. Now she's spitting in their ears.

We stayed in a hut that looked like it was made out of rock. A Sonjo blacksmith and his family. We sat in a circle and watched the Sonjo shape spearheads which he would sell to the tourists. Chants accompanied the shaping of the spearheads. Norvelle said that no work was done without chanting, which he called that space between speaking and song. I could tell by his expression that he was memorizing what the man sang, or rather chanted, and that he'd record it in his notebook. He said that a medical anthropologist had to have a good auditory memory. I asked him whether the Sonjo spearmaker would allow me to take his photograph. I didn't know if he, like they say when some of the Native Americans were first photographed, or when the Europeans first tried to photograph them, if would he think that a photo might capture his spirit. Norvelle asked the Sonjo spearmaker in his own language if I might take his photograph, and he said yes, and so I took his photograph.

And then the four of us were standing in the hut of that man who they said could detect criminals by their smell. It was not like the old days, Norvelle said. Now such men had to be licensed by the state, had to be official. Not everyone could be a criminal detector.

Then the criminal detector was looking at me. He said something to the medicine woman, and the medicine woman talked back to him. The man started staring at me more intensely, the medicine woman shook with laughter and I brushed flies. But the medicine woman let the flies sit on her face. It was their custom or religion.

Later Norvelle translated for me. He'd asked her what kind of criminal I was, and whether I was in exile from my own country.

What did she tell him?

She said to stop sniffing you, that you were already married, and that you don't like men who raise goats.

That made me like her. We followed her to a place where she helped a newborn baby into the world. She chanted as she worked. Norvelle said she referred to the woman as someone carrying two souls—her own and the baby's. She coaxed the new soul into the world. When the baby came, everyone gathered and spit on it for luck.

I brushed flies from my face and ate zebra meat with my fingers, a gift from the other women who had gathered to salute the new child into the world.

How long are we going to follow her? I asked Norvelle, as we lay on mats in a curtained-off corner of the hut.

She's a treasure chest of medical folklore, he said. She's a treasure. Why, I could write a whole book about her.

In the morning, outside, the woman was telling him something. She was shaking her broad shoulders ho-ho-ho-ho and Norvelle was laughing. Her face was painted like a zebra's.

What did she tell you? I asked when Norvelle spotted me, came and kissed my jaw.

Good morning.

What did she tell you? Why don't you speak English?

He looked at me, and then he said it was a joke.

What joke?

The Masai once had herds and herds of cattle, he said. The Sonjo once raided the Masai for their cattle. But the Masai proved themselves superior to the Sonjo in battle, so now the Sonjo raise goats.

I saw no joke in it. The criminal detector brought me a bowl of zebra stew, but the Masai woman took it from me. They stood fussing.

What's going on? I asked Norvelle.

She claims that he put love magic in it. That he put some sort of love magic in it so that you'd love him more than anyone else in the world.

Did he put love magic in it?

I don't know, he said. But don't eat it.

Now what's going on?

She's telling him to sniff himself and stop sniffing you.

That joke I understood.

Joan lets the snow from her fur boots drip onto the carpet. After the concert we'd trudged through the snow to the hotel. You know the scenes in the rock star movies or after the rock star concerts, the scenes where the fans are crowding around to get photographs, the rock singer surrounded by her or his entourage, the rock star's managers and bodyguards and handlers hustling them into a waiting limousine. Maybe the rock star'll sign a few autographs. That ain't Joan. When we finished her concert, she just trudged through the snow back to the hotel. I think there mighta been a coupla fans standing there to get autographs, and couple to have CDs signed. Nerdy-looking types.

He's not following us anymore, Joan said when we were upstairs. What did you say to him at the bar?

Not a thing. I ordered a Josef, so he must've told Josef we were on to him.

I turned the light on and she gathered into a leather armchair. I took off my rubber boots and put them on newspaper, but she let hers drip.

Or maybe Josef's sent someone else more clever. Take your boots off.

She took them off and placed them on the newspaper.

Doesn't it scare you? she asked. Having some man hire a detective to follow you around. Even if the man thinks he loves you. It's still some possessive bullshit. To think you got mixed up with some joker like that. You shouldn't pick up strange men, you know. Not in today's world. Admit.

Yeah, a little.

Not enough to make you stop your alley ways? Control yourself, girl.

Manage myself?

Say what?

I stare at her silver stockings, her braided hair smeared with red ocher. I turn my back to her. I light a Lucky Strike and inhale it into the pit of my stomach. I don't like people telling me who they think I am.

So what happened between you and Norvelle? she asked. I mean what really happened? I don't just think it's on account of that Masai woman. And I don't even know if I believe that story. Girl, I think you're just jiving me. I think you're just a con artist or some shit. A con woman. I think you just conned me. When we first met, I think you just conned me. Telling me you're a beautician. You knew I'd be intrigued. I bet you've just been conning my ass. Telling me all of your tales. You're probably a pathological prevaricator or some shit. I don't even know if there really is a Norvelle, or even a what's-his-name. Josef Ehelich von Fremd. Sounds like some name you made up or some shit. Girl, you got a credibility problem. And all that shit you told me about some tales sounding incredible but really being true, that's just better to con me with. Well, I saw him on TV that Josef. But he could still just be anybody. They didn't say his name. Probably somebody you read about. You're just a con woman. Shit. What's it they usedta call women like you? A adventuress? A colored-girl adventuress. A, what's that Spanish word, a *pícara*. They call the men *pícaros* and the women *pícaras*. Like the *pícara* Justina. Or the daughter of the Celestina. *Pícaras*. Rogues. Except true *pícaros* are always hungry; they're motivated by hunger, that's the motif in every picaresque novel, and you always seem well fed to me. Me I'm motivated by hunger. Maybe I'm the true *pícara*. But it's a hunger of the spirit.

I turn one hand on my hip, the other on the cigarette. I blow rings of smoke toward her.

Why don't I fix you up like a Masai woman, shave your head, put brass hoops in your ears? I ask.

So what happened between you and Norvelle, your imaginary ex-husband? she asked.

He took up with someone better, someone better than me, I said.

You're just conning me. Maybe we should tour West Africa? she asked. Or is it East? Maybe you could get me some gigs in Africa? We can hunt up your imaginary ex-husband and this imaginary Masai medicine woman.

I could get you some gigs in Africa, I said. Except I don't think they truly like your kind of music.

Sure they do. All over the world it's American music. In Africa, they love American music. American music is us. But those Africans, you can't fool them with fake music. It's got to be authentic American music. They know the real thing.

She went into the bathroom, and when she finally came back out, her head was shaved and she was wearing a crimson scarf around her loins. She gave an Oriental bow and showed her head a palette of colors, like photographs of aboriginal sand paintings she'd once shown me. Dreamings, they were called. This is art, she'd said. You make it and then you destroy it. Aboriginal. Dreamings. Then she sat on a stool and tissued off her head. Then she started singing one of her songs, too low for me to hear.

When she stood up, she plunged her fist into my stomach. I doubled over. I tried to straighten up, but there were spikes in the pit of my stomach. I started toward the bathroom and held on to the door.

You fucked him, she said.

Joan has purchased a videotape player, and in the hotel rooms after her performances, instead of watching the networks, even the Comedy Channel, we put in the videotapes. They ain't the sorta videotapes you'd expect. Not entertainments. Not video shows of her favorite rock singers. Not Tina Turner, or Rod Stewart, or Mick Jagger. Or the contemporary rappers: Queen Latifah, Public Enemy, Jazzy Jeff and the Fresh Prince. Or even the Artist Formerly Known as Prince. Or some of them other videos. I remember she once rented one of them videos on Australia told from the Australian aborigines' point of view, I think the man's name that narrated that video Ernie Dingo. The narrator a aborigine filmmaker. Then she bought a video by some singing group just because she like their name: Primitive Radio Gods. Or some of them old movies or old television series put on video. Instead of them types of videos, they're documentary films of international atrocities, in Latin America, Africa, Eastern Europe, the Middle East, and Asia. The titles of the videos are such as the following: *General Chun, Butcher of Kwangju, Pata Island Massacre—the Philippines, The Desaparecidos—the Disappearing Ones of Argentina, Eyewitness Reports of Repression and Terror.*

No one could survive after that, someone is saying on one of those films. I don't know how I survived. It was a miracle. Those people, they only look like human beings. They're devils. They're devils who only resemble human beings. They show nothing, no mercy. You tell them what goes on in there and they don't believe you. They put some kind of toxic substance on my tongue. That's why I speak the way I do. The doctors say there's nothing physically wrong, but it's memory. When they brought me out I had mold growing behind my ears. It was some kind of apparatus, something that looked like an iron gate. They stood me on my head for the whole day. They put this contraption on my hands. What it does is it stretches your fingers till they pop out of their sockets. They gave me a hundred lashes. They cut off my ear. They put it in and when they pulled it out it pulled out some of the rectal tissue. All I do is make candles, no politics, I'm a candlemaker, I'm not a politician. I do not make politics. I told them, but they were still shaking those rifles at me. I had a twelve-pound iron weight on my leg for two months. They put us in the cage with lizards and dragonflies. They made me put my fingers through some holes and something began eating my fingers. I kept hearing my woman through the door. He threw the rifle against my jaw. He pushed a fork in my groin. I kept dreaming of fruit, just fruit, and sometimes chocolate. Monsters. They put a hook in my shoulder and then they dragged me. They lay you down and put the iron on your abdomen so it will crush the abdomen wall. They made me sit with my penis in her face. They are animals, they are not human beings. They are devils. It was wasn't physical torture they were after, but forms of humiliation. They put my nose to the hole and made me smell vomit. Nothing but stench all the time. I was afraid because my wife was carrying a six-month-old fetus. At first they were going to torture her, and then they tossed her in the lunatic asylum. She says that there there was another pregnant woman. She will tell you her story. I'm ashamed to speak I'm ashamed to tell it.

First they used thick cables, then blocks of wood, then the ends of lighted cigarettes. I was raped first and then they used the end of a lighted cigarette. They didn't do anything else to me, they just kept whipping my feet.

They just kept pulling my testicles. They made me do sit-ups all day.

They just kept asking me questions. No physical torture. Nothing but questions and questions and questions and questions.

I sat as far back as possible from the screen, but Joan pulled her armchair up to the screen, as close as she could get while the eyewitnesses spoke of their terrors.

They crowded us into a room, and then tossed a canister of some contagion. Everyone's ears began to bleed.

This time, as she stared at the screen, I sat manicuring her fingernails. I soaked them and scraped them with the emery board. I removed the cuticles. I buffed.

How can you listen to that shit? I asked. I don't know about people like you, you know.

These are real people, said Joan. This is how the world really is. That Josef of yours he's a right to be paranoid. Those Fascists sons-of-bitches. This is the way the world really is.

I sighed and looked for more cuticles to remove.

While Joan showered and dressed, I went down into the lobby and played cards with the night watchman, who kept a flask of whiskey in his breast pocket, and talked about Lulabelle, the woman he'd been married to for forty years and whom he said I had ears like.

You got ears just like my Lulabelle. I tell her they look like seashells. Something precious.

How'd you stay married so long? I asked. Everybody I know is divorced.

'Cause they's fools, he said. You shouldn't leave somebody until you knows the logic of why you's together. I don't know why we's together, me and Lulabelle, but I know I loves my wife.

Jack of diamonds, two aces, and a queen of hearts, I said.

How are you in love? he asked.

I wasn't sure what he meant until I gathered my winnings.

Upstairs, Joan sat naked on the bed painted up to look like a zebra. Onstage she sang better than ever.

Do you remember Jean Claude Duvalier? she asked her audience. Do you remember Baby Doc?

They roared, Yes, and then they waited for her song.

Multa!

A Italian woman got up, least she looked Italian, climbed onstage and sang with her. And not one of those nerdy types. They were wild together. The Italian woman full of black hair and thunder. A windstorm.

You're good, Joan told her when the storm was over, and they were drenched, exhausted, sweat racing down their faces. They stood hugging. The audience cheered.

Are you a professional performer? Joan asked, backstage.

No, no, no, no, said the woman, delighted though that Joan would think her a professional, still shaking her narrow shoulders and broad hips.

Come to my dressing room, come with me, will you? asked Joan.

Is it okay if I bring my husband? asked the woman.

Sure.

She went to a tall, brown-skinned man standing near the edge of the stage, his arms folded, sullen. I'd noticed him when I'd been peeking through the curtain. He was sitting there watching Joan but looking like he felt himself superior to the music. How I imagined her husband Naughton James mighta been looking if he'd gone to one of her concerts. He wore beige corduroy pants and one of his eyebrows seemed a perpetual arch. The Italian woman bent to him; he shook his head and waved her away. She whirled around in a silk dress that looked like an Oriental tapestry. Returning to Joan, she mumbled something. I followed the two women into the dressing room. I went to the bathroom and came back as the Italian woman was telling her story.

. . . they each said they were protecting my how-do-you-say honor? and feuded with each other. Oh, I could tell you all sorts of terror stories about love feuds when these Sicilian men get their honor up, for it's their honor, their *onore*, not our. It's always a man's *onore*. I could tell you all kinds of terror stories. A game they enjoy to play, and we're the pawns. All women. *Onore*. You, though, you look like you're *fortunato* in *amore*. You look like you have a man who really loves you. But men, we're pawns to them. Only a few of us are queens. The rest of us are pawns in a man's game. I've been all over the world and it's like that. All women all over the world are just pawns in a man's game. Why, I was even in one of those little countries where the women have several husbands and even there they're pawns. It's not because the women are in control to have so many husbands. It's because the men are so poor that they have to pool their resources. One man can't afford to have one wife, so several men share a wife. When I first heard of polyandry, I thought it meant that women ruled, but it doesn't. The men share you. They'll sweet-talk you, but you're just a pawn to them.

Per amore o per forza, said Joan.

Oh, *parla italiano?*

Un poco. Molto poco. Non lo pronuncio molto bene.

Oh, yes you do, very well. You've got a very good Italian accent.

Che belleza! You're a great beauty, Joan commented. I can understand why the men fought over you. Why, you're a beautiful woman. Why, to tell you the truth, you're the most beautiful woman I've ever seen.

Ah, do you think so? In my own Sicilia, there are many like me. But you see it's only a game, only a *partita.* What are we?

Joan spotted me standing in the doorway.

Carolina Tola, this is my . . . *La presento alla mia* . . . business manager, Harlan. . . .

We nodded and smiled to each other. She turned back to Joan.

Abio—that's my husband—and I, we both love your music. We love it. Of course I love it more than he does, because. . . . Well, you know how men are. There are things that a woman sings, and only a woman knows the full meaning. You may sing for men as well as women, but only a woman knows your full meaning. I am not a *feminista.* I only think a woman should be true to who she believes herself to be. Or who she wants herself to be. Or who she imagines herself to be. I don't know what I mean, or whether I'm true myself to any of that. I don't think there are many of us who are true to our possibilities. I don't blame men for it, though. I am as much Sicilian as the men who fought love feuds for me. But we both love your music very much, Abio and I.

Thank you. You were good, you know. I thought you were a professional yourself. You should be onstage.

I'm very aggressive, no? But I've never had the desire for show business.

You stole the show.

Abio was embarrassed for me, you know. That's why he wouldn't come back. He said I embarrassed him getting up there acting like a fool. He likes your music as much as I do. Well, he doesn't like it as much as I do, but he likes it. But he wasn't expecting this. Eh, he's embarrassed for me. I didn't think you'd let me back to see you, so I thought well, I said I'd make you see me. And I like it that you don't have people keeping the audience away from you. . . .

That's because I don't have the audiences that try to get to you.

Well, you should. I think you're wonderful. This is not flattery.

Joan laughed and scratched her chin. She sat with her back to the mirror. I watched the zebra stripes.

Abio thinks that one should not let others see their—how does he say it?—that everyone should keep his little devils or his little gods inside. He thinks I'm always putting myself on too much display. Sometimes he thinks we were brought together so that I could wreak havoc on him. And he's had enough havoc. He thinks I display myself too much. I'm just being who I am. It's okay for you, he says, because it's your business, your profession, that rock singers are supposed to display themselves, but me, I'm the witch woman. I'm the *strega*.

And you're his *moglie*? asked Joan. She glanced at me. I love the Italian word for it. It sounds just like what we are. What they want us to be. It sounds more like that than the word wife, doesn't it? *Moglie*?

Ah, yes, yes, yes, said Carolina. I'm his wife, yes.

Where'd you meet him? I asked.

She snapped her eyes at me, but turned to tell Joan.

I was in London and disconnected. And he was there. His books had been proscribed by the South African government, you know, before Mandela, and he was in exile and he was getting them republished in London. Oh, we got along so. I'm not sure he knew what I was. My hair was short and then the sun had baked my skin almost as black as his. Oh, I was very dark, you know, and when those men had started playing those war games around me I had cut all my hair off. I told them to all bogger off and then I went globe-trotting. Abio didn't know what I was. He thought I was from some island. I was as dark as he was.

Oh, he had to know what you were, Joan said.

Carolina's eyes widened. She shook her shoulders. I'm not sure he did.

Oh, sure, he must have, Joan persisted.

You can't imagine how I looked! After I got away from that love terror. But I used to sit out in the sun all day. I was in the Kensington Gardens or the Kew Gardens. I was reading. I suppose that attracted him. I had a job working in a little foreign bookstore. A nice little man who owned the bookshop, well not so small a man but his shyness made him seem so. He let me dust the books, you know, because at first I didn't have the proper papers. And then I didn't need the papers, because new laws were being made, and so I got a full job there, because I knew the different languages, and they were mostly non-English titles. When the men would fight their love feuds over me, I'd study the different languages. I thought I might teach, but the only idea they had was to wife me. What did I need to know languages for? What did I need but to know how to please them in proper Sicilian? But in London I'd borrow some of the books sometimes and go reading in the gardens. The title impressed him, I think, and we got to talking of it. Something fashionable at the time. *Alla moda*. I don't remember what. Something German. A German modernist. I guess Abio was thinking what would a girl from the islands be doing reading something German. We found each other fascinating, from our different worlds. But we Italians, we are everyone's people.

She glanced at me, then spoke again to Joan, spoke almost in a whisper.

He thinks I fooled him into thinking I was a decent woman, though. And all the time he is discovering me. And now. And now what a savage I've become! Ha! When I first saw him, though, I thought he was the most beautiful man in the world. You wouldn't believe it to look at him what a political controversy he is, or used to be in the old South Africa. Why, you couldn't even quote from his books without its being a criminal act. I'd read him from smuggled books and those printed abroad. He says to be a controversy in his country all one has to do is tell honest stories . . . But we both managed to escape our terrors. I tell him it is not the old South Africa, and he should return there now, that many are returning there now. But he wants to stay in this country. I tell him that now he's a voluntary exile, because he could return to South Africa if he wanted to. I started to write Mr. Mandela a letter on his behalf, but he asked me not to. I tell him now he's a voluntary exile.

Good for him, said Joan. I've been to other countries and I'm not romantic about anywhere. Harlie still has illusions about Africa. I don't. I don't have any illusions about America either. I don't have any disillusions about it, because I've never had any illusions. Bastards everywhere.

He wanted to come here. *Mi sono uniformato ai suoi voleri. Ha un talento enorme.* He has an enormous talent, so I simply conformed to his will.

The heat in the dressing room made Joan's zebra stripes begin to look like zebra swirls. She played with them like fingerpaints, first her knee and then her elbow. Though she looked distracted, she was listening intently. I could always tell.

Il paese dell'abbondanza, Joan said wryly.

I don't know what she meant. Abandoned country?

We don't know how long we can stay here, though, said Carolina hastily. He's talking to the people at the university where he's teaching, you know, but we're both deportable, you see. Especially now, they don't think he has anything to fear if he returns to South Africa. We're both deportable. I thought we might go to Italy, but he doesn't want to go to Italy. He doesn't like Europeans, except for me. And London these days. Even the bookstore owner I worked for is a little Fascist. He made promises to me, and then when he saw me with Abio, I knew I'd made an enemy. He tried to win me for himself, he told me it was just calf love with Abio, but I knew I'd made an enemy. The little Fascist. But he had this idea of me, you know, the idea men have of we Italian women. And he too thought I'd befooled him. And then there's my love terror, and I don't want to return to Italy myself. We stayed in a little retreat with Carmelite nuns outside London, very noble women, the retreat full of

Florentine-style sculpture, imitation Cellini, one of the nuns a collector of medieval musical instruments, the celesta and glockenspiel, I think, and a maker of the best turtle soup—Abio wouldn't eat it though. We stayed in a cellar. Abio wrote and I read French literature. *Cent nouvelles nouvelles.* And some Boccaccio. What looked like the original manuscripts. Tales from the days when men spoke of true wifehood, as if there could be such a thing. There was a little Basque woman staying there, an exile too. She spoke only a little English, but said that outside of Spain she felt like a new creature. I don't know the basis of her exile, but she looked like the keeper of the conscience of her people, you know the type. Abio wrote a poem for her called "The Mythological Enchantress." I know it's for her, though he doesn't say so. It's more philosophical poetry and not like his political poems and satires. There was a spy for the Germans staying there, who'd been staying there since the war, but he never spoke to anyone. A slender man with small eyebrows. He must've taken a vow of silence. Sometimes I'd see him in the study. Once I saw him reading Capellanus, *De Arte Honeste Amandi. The Art of Loving Honestly.* He didn't say anything to me. When he saw me with Abio, I thought I'd made another enemy. When I saw him in the study again, he was reading *Trollope, the Autobiography.* He said nothing to me. I did not read in the study, but took the book I wanted into the courtyard among the monkey puzzle trees. When I returned the book to the study, the book he'd been reading was open on the table where he or someone had underlined the passage: "She is by no means a perfect lady: but if she be not all over a woman, then am I not able to describe a woman." A strange man. And then we came to America, Abio and I. Abio has a small teacher's salary and he's working on his magnum opus. I like his work, but I don't understand it. It's beyond the comprehension of an ordinary woman like me. I understand English, but I don't understand his. But he's like a weaver of perfect language. A British reviewer calls it Caliban style, Caliban language, but I think it's perfect language myself. I listen to cantatas while he writes, or my favorite Russian music, or Wagner, or the tenors. Sometimes your music. Abio hears it as pure rock, but for me it sounds like satire on the rock 'n' roll genre.

She was silent. Joan said nothing.

Abio is thought well of . . . internationally. The police in South Africa wouldn't be after him now, I don't think. . . . He wouldn't let me write to Mandela. . . . And we can't go to my country, like I said. The devil and the deep . . . So we said tonight we wouldn't think about it, we wouldn't decide what country we'd try to go to, we'd just come here and listen to you. I found I had to do more than listen. And he. He adores you. He doesn't adore you as much as I do, but he adores you.

She kissed Joan's fingers. He says that you're one of the best because you use terror and turn it into music. You do in your music what he tries to do in his writing. I don't think he'd know how to write about the new South Africa. He doesn't know why he's such a controversy, because he mostly writes about how the black South Africans treat each other, not so much about any regime. His books do not ignore the regime, but he's mostly interested in how the blacks are with each other. So he is ambivalent about the new South Africa. What if he returns there and the black powers themselves don't like his writings. Would they jail him too? Would they imprison him too?

Joan watched the woman.

But love terrors are such little terrors, aren't they? asked Carolina. We could return to Italy. What are love terrors?

But still they can kill you over love, Joan said. They can kill you over love as well as politics.

I slouched toward an empty chair and sat down.

But you made us happy. Even though Abio was embarrassed for me, you made us both very happy. We think that you're wonderful. He would have come back if I hadn't embarrassed him. He wanted to meet you himself, but I'd embarrassed him.

That's what you mean, said Joan. That's what you mean. That's what you mean. I thought you meant that.

What? I do not understand, said Carolina. What do I mean? Should I excuse myself?

What'll you do if your university can't help you? I asked.

She turned toward me, as if rescued. I don't know, she said, because you see, we are deportable. There is an immigration woman I spoke to who thinks I might be less deportable than Abio. Who wanted to play the color politics. But if Abio is deportable, then I am deportable. We have a great allegiance to each other.

Frowning, Joan tore a page out of a notebook, scribbled something, handing it to Carolina. Here's a place you can stay, she said. Deportable or not. We're all refugees anyway, aren't we? We're all from the same country anyway. I'll call my caretaker and tell him to expect you and to let you stay. Nobody'll bother you there. None of the bastards'll even know where you are. It's like a hidden world.

Quanto si paga?

Non ti dar pensiero.

Carolina looked at the piece of paper. Oh, thank you.

It's my farm, actually. They won't find you there. She wrote on another piece of paper. And this is my private number, if you. . . .

Oh, you are so kind.

No, I'm not, said Joan. Not at all. I'm a bitch.

No, you're wonderful. Who else would do this for us? Strangers.

I wish I was wonderful. I wish I was truly wonderful.

When Carolina left, I asked Joan why she'd called James her caretaker and not her ex-husband. She was silent, then she said, It's too much to explain. Anyway, he'll tell them who he is.

Are you going to tell him who they are? Are you going to tell him it might be a crime what you're doing? That you could get into trouble with the immigration people? Especially now, with this anti-immigration bullshit.

It ain't bullshit. You're bullshit, she said. I don't believe you should just open your borders to just anybody myself. I know I shouldn'ta let you in my house. If I took better care of my own border, I'd deport your ass. Naw, you can't just open your borders to anybody. You gotta discriminate. I don't like the color politics either, though. The Mexicans, the Cubans, the Haitians. Plenty of illegal Canadians over here.

I think it's legal for Canadians to be here, I said. I know I like going to Canada.

Well, I know there's some illegal Irish here and they ain't chasing them back to Ireland neither. I like the Irish, though. They usedta have signs that said no dogs or Irishmen allowed. I'm part Irish myself. Don't laugh. I am. I've got as much true Irish in me as I've got true African. I'm multiracial. I just don't play the multiracial game. It's all politics anyway. My culture is African American, so I'm African American. You look like you're multiracial too. You don't have to be light-skinned to be multiracial. You don't have to look like Vanessa Williams.

Which Vanessa Williams? I asked. I'm supposed to have Afro-Cuban in me. Us real name is supposed to be Aguila and not Eagleton, but some Afro-Cubans came to America and changed their names to Eagleton. I think *águila* in Spanish means eagle, don't it?

And I bet you got a little Indian in you too, ain't ya? You remember when colored people usedta always be telling people they got a little Indian in 'em? Ain't know which tribe, or even that Indians—Native Americans—got hundred of tribes, they just know they got a little Indian in 'em?

I know what tribes—Seminole and Cherokee. But I'm still an African in America.

Carolina and Abio suddenly appeared at the door of the dressing room. He smiled and thanked Joan for her generosity. He said he might not need to stay there at her farm, that his university might come to his assistance, or some of his fellow countrymen who were exiled in America, but he expressed his gratitude. He looked at me with curiosity, but said nothing. Then they excused themselves.

Joan sat shaking like she'd suddenly turned all nerves.

What is it? I asked. You afraid of the immigration police after all?

Naw, she said. She calmed herself, picked up the phone and called James. She told him to expect some guests at the farm. She told him their names, but not who they were, and that they were deportable. She put the phone down. She turned toward me.

Come and wipe this shit off my face, she said. Wipe this shit off me.

You are wonderful, I said. But I hope you don't get your fool self in trouble. I mean, legally, like I said, it might present a problem. I've got

some friends in South Texas who work with illegals, some friends of
Norvelle's actually, always getting their asses in trouble, working with
the illegals, refugees from different part of the world and people who
come here as illegal aliens, and especially now with all this anti-immigration bullshit. I forget what they call their organization. It ain't Am-
nesty International, but it's something like that. Norvelle calls it the
New Underground Railroad. He says it's sorta like in the old days of
slavery, when a fugitive slave was illegal. You know, the Fugitive Slave
Act, when escaped slaves had to be returned to their owners and that the
people really for human rights had to go against their government, you
know, like the Quakers, you know. Like in Hitler's Germany, when there
were these Germans who would give shelter to the Jews and even print
up fake identification papers for some of them and print up fake food
coupons. I read that in one of those books of yours, about some of the
Germans who would hide people hunted by the Nazis. Those people
have the idea that there's no such thing as an illegal human being, and
they consider the immigration police just thugs, but government thugs.
They ain't all thugs, though. I know this African-American guy who's
an immigration policeman. I met him when we were in South Texas.
Then I seen him on television when those Chinese illegal immigrants
were captured, and he was leading one of these Chinese women into the
detention camps. He wasn't treating her like an illegal, he was treating
her like a human being. I don't know about those white immigration police, though. I don't know if they see human beings or just see illegals,
you know. Somebody said that African-American guy married one of
those Chinese women, though, and stopped being a immigration policeman. Like that story I heard about this buffalo soldier who was
fighting the Indians and then he realized he shoulda been fighting with
the Indians, you know like in the Seminole wars, so he started fighting
with the Indians. They's always praising the buffalo soldiers for being
Indian fighters, you know. Anyway, Norvelle he contributes monetarily
to the cause, I mean those people who are helping the illegal aliens in
South Texas, because Norvelle's that sort, but he doesn't go run around
South Texas with those fools or fool with any of those illegals.

But I got me good hiding places, she said. Survivalists usedta own that farm before we bought it. You know what paranoids they are.

I seen you with one of those survivalist manuals in that collection of books you got. And you talking about them being clowns.

I didn't say clowns. I said fools. I didn't even say fools, you said fools. One of the survivalists had that book in the attic, so I just read it, you know. I got another list of books I want you to order for me though.

Encyclopedia of Saints   The Marathon Monks of Mount Hiei, or The Running Buddhas   All of the Women of the Bible   The Priestess Tradition of the Ancient World: Spritual Empowerment   The Ethiopian Jews   Beauty in History   The Politics of Beauty   Aristotle: On Man in the Universe   Prehistory and Protohistory   Archeology, Ideology, and Naturalism   L'Égypte   Images of Ireland   The Cambridge Encyclopedia of China   Ireland   Havana (for you since you claim to be Afro-Cuban) *The Unofficial Guide to Disneyland   Emerson's Essays   The Wisdom of Confucius   Natural History of the Intellect* (for Jamey because of his "quest for ideas") *The Rhetoric of Science: Inventing Scientific Discourse* (a copy for me and Jamey) *Who Stole Feminism?   The Third World and the Quest for Political Ideas   Japan   The Myth of the Explorer   A Social History of Ireland   China, Korea and Japan: The Rise of Civilization in East Africa Castles   India: Land of Dreams and Fantasy   The Complete Guide to Growing Nuts   Impressionist Cats   The Beauty of Horses* (for you) *The Turtle: A Natural History* (for you, on account of that confabulatory tale you told me about the turtle) *The Elephants* (you should send this to Norvelle c/o his editor) *Animal Minds   The Herb Garden   Cats, Cats, Cats   The Cats' History of Western Art   Japanese Gardens   Medicinal Plants   Chinese Cooking for Beginners* (for you, because you're getting fat, girl) *North African Cooking   Cats: Arts, Legend, History   Fake, Fraud, or Genuine?   Comic Book Artists* (they've got a profile of one of Jamey's favorite comic book scenarists, Martin Tage, you know the inventor of Guadalcanal, you know the first African-American woman comic book heroine) *How to Repair and Restore Dolls* (I need a hobby) *Politics or Culture?   Rumor Has It: A Curio of Lies,*

Hoaxes, and Hearsay (do you think you'd like this book?) *The Creation of Feminist Consciousness Sanctuaries of the Goddess Da New Album* (this is a tape not a book; a new rap group) *German Architecture* (the book which has the chapter on gables and metalwork) *African Architecture* (for Norvelle c/o his editor? or maybe you should read this, that shit you told me about preferring the tourist hotels to the primitive huts in the bush) *Slavery as Salvation: The Metaphor of Slavery in Pauline Christianity Disney Animation Art Mary Cassatt Leonardo da Vinci Start Sculpting: A Step-by-Step Beginner's Guide to Working in Three Dimensions* (I think this is the title of Catherine Shuger's book; if not make sure you order the one by Catherine Shuger) *The Painting of T'Ang Yin Drawing and Painting Animals Court Arts of Indonesia Mask Making* (remind me to tell you about Jamey's Korean maskmaker friend) *The Encyclopedia of Origami and Papercraft Yasuo Kuniyoshi's Women* (Jamey's Women?) *Actors as Artists African Art Joan Miró Music and Technology The Irish: A Treasury of Art and Literature Dalí Singer-Songwriters Elvis* (for Cayenne? She doesn't sound crazy to me) *Mozart Classical Music A Beginner's Guide to Opera* (for you) *Sculpture You Can Eat* (I know this is Catherine Shuger's book) *Frida Kahlo* And the book about that Cuban woman you know the one who was with Castro during the Revolution we saw her on television And the new Amanda Wordlaw novel, the one I showed you in that book review I don't remember the title but the book reviewer describes it as a "picaresque-jazz-impressionist-neo-slave narrative novel." I told you about the *pícara* didn't I?

Anyway the women in the book are supposedly not pleased with others' ideas of who they are and are constantly redefining themselves their own ideals or possibilities of womanhood. Not *Don't Let Cowgirls Fool Ya* or her early novels this one ain't just an American book but the heroine travels not just among different classes but among people of different nationalities and political persuasions it suggests more improvisational techniques and has sort of a modified frame and an open-ended resolution that's why she calls it picaresque, you know the techniques in those novels, like Lazarillo de Tormes, anyway all the men in it have the same name and the narrator sorta reminds me of you she calls it picaresque but it differs from the true picaresque because the true picaresque hero or heroine satirizes others while the heroine of this book satirizes herself more than others do you still think she's a confabulatory author even Jamey thinks so he saw me reading so many Amanda Wordlaw novels that he thought maybe I'm Amanda Wordlaw in disguise I think it's Catherine Shuger myself writing under a pseudonym. . . .

What did James say? I sponged her face with witch hazel, then rubbed in aloe cream. Then I put on some wrinkle cream. I just put the wrinkle cream on her forehead, though.

It's my farm and my notion, she said. What can he say but yes? What can Jamey say but yes? He's my Jamey and I'm his even though we're divorced. Like what Carolina said about having a great allegiance to each other. I thought she shoulda said love, but maybe what she says is good itself. I still have a great allegiance to my Jamey. But I ain't a pawn in no man's game. You others can be, but not this bogger.

CHAPTER THIRTY-FIVE

In the hotel room, while Joan is sleeping, I turn on the videotape. A Vietnamese woman is talking. She speaks with a deeper voice than most Asian women I've heard. Mostly the Asian women have high-pitched voices, while the men have low-pitched voices. But this woman has a low-pitched voice, almost like a man's.

I covered my mouth and my baby's mouth, she is saying, but those whose mouths weren't covered. . . .

I begin to think of another Asian woman, a Korean. My father, I told you, was in the Korean War and after the war he stayed in Korea and settled with a Korean woman. He wrote my mother a letter telling her simply what had happened. He did not give any philosophy behind what he did. He did not rationalize. He did say that Korea seemed a better world to him than America. I was just a small child, but I thought that if Korea was such a better world, he could have brought us all to Korea, that it seemed like a selfish thing for him to stay there with that other woman he spoke of. But still I loved him. And even though I was a small child, I thought I could understand what he meant when he said that for the first time he could feel some power and control over his life. He felt in charge. Perhaps I understand what he meant. Had she read the letter to me, because being a small child, she'd thought I wouldn't understand it?

And the Korean woman? She never spoke of her or of him after reading that first letter, but whenever she'd see an Asian woman on the street or on television, she'd stare like crazy, as if wondering if that was her. She wouldn't look at her with hatred, but fascination. Was she like this one? If he'd chosen her, could she be a bad woman?

. . . .but if our mouths hadn't been covered we would have suffered the same as the others.

CHAPTER THIRTY-SIX

I don't know if she spends her days waiting for him to come back like the women in the storybooks and songs do. I don't know, for it is never spoken of. He had fought in the Korean War and after the war was over, he stayed there. What else I know about him I guessed on my own, or learned somehow. By osmosis. Jack B. Eagleton his name, the B. standing for Booker. So my name's Harlan Eagleton. Harlan T. Eagleton, but I do not tell anyone what the T. stands for, because I don't think it's a name that anyone should be given. Well, I'll tell you. It's Harlan Truth Eagleton. Named for Sojourner Truth, not Truth itself. I know people named Sojourner but not Truth. I do not question. But when I dream, I dream of strangers coming to the door. I'd go to the door always expecting to be surprised by a stranger who'd turn out to be my father, returned from Korea. And when my mother started taking in those little Christs, whom my grandmother called bums, giving them soup and clothing and a warm gathering place, I used to stare at them all, thinking maybe one of them was actually Jack B. Eagleton in disguise.

Look at that little girl how she looks at everyone.

Can't take her eyes off you, man. She must think you her daddy.

Something must be wrong with that girl. Come here, Possum.

When my mother wasn't holding soup to them or goodwill clothing, she'd be silent, watching them as if they were the most interesting people in the world, or listening to their conversations. What they spoke of, their stories, I could never seem to remember, or didn't want to, stories about poor men, though one poor man always spoke of railroads.

My grandmother wouldn't listen to their stories at all. She'd put the bums to work. Here's a broom, John Henry, go out and sweep off the sidewalk. There ain't any trains around here.

Woman, you ain't got no fellow feeling. And my name ain't John Henry. I'm Mr. Hauberk. I might resemble John Henry, being a big robust man, but my name's Mr. Hauberk.

I'm a woman, but only one man can "woman" me, Mr. Hauberk, if that's your true name. I'll Mister you if you want to be a Mister. And a big robust man like you oughtn't to be no bum. And naw I don't got no fellow feeling if fellow feeling means that you's a fool.

She handed Mr. Hauberk the broom.

And who might that have been might I ask? The man to woman you. He held the broom like a staff and leaned toward her.

Say what?

The man to woman you. Who'd have the nerve to woman you? Who'd have the nerve to woman a woman like you?

She cracked a tiny smile at him, and then she shushed and shooed him.

CHAPTER THIRTY-SEVEN

When I return to the hotel, Joan's talking to Sandovar and two other Haitians. At least I figure they're Haitians, since they're with Sandovar. I halt in the door, then say hello to the men. Sandovar looks embarrassed, then he and the other two men stand up, their hats in their hands. They're wearing khaki pants and shirts and them sandals that look kinda like huaraches. You know them sandals that them Mexican peasants wear. Or them American tourists, a lot of them like to wear them huaraches in Mexico. Sandovar ain't in Haiti, but here in *il paese dell'abbondanza*. Nor had I remembered him as a small man. Here in America he looks like a smaller man. Or maybe here I just judge other men by Nicholas. One of the little saints?

What? I ask. What's going on?

Nothing, he mumbles. The other men shake hands with Joan, and say something in French to her, you know that Creole French, and nod toward me. They go out the door.

So what's this? I ask Joan. What's Sandovar doing here? What's all this? I didn't know you knew Sandovar. When we were in Haiti you wouldn't even come over and be introduced to him, when we won that cockfight in the Iron Market. When we saw you in the Iron Market, you were too hoity-toity even to be introduced to him. Some Haitian peasant. I ain't calling him a peasant, but that's how you's looking at him when we saw you in the Iron Market, like some Haitian peasant. So what's this?

Joan's silent. She reclines in her chair, looking imperial. Or impervious.

What are you up to now? I ask.

I'm just helping Sandovar, she said simply. I met him again. In fact, I didn't even know it was Sandovar until he showed up at the hotel. He knows Abio and Abio told me about him. They were at the farm and saw this group of Haitians being detained, and Abio said he knew one of them, that Sandovar is actually sorta a poet, you know, a poet of the people–type poet, you know, a peasant poet and told me about him, and this mutual friend went to the detention camps, and then managed to get Sandovar and the others released and when we met we realized we already knew each other. They're all exiles. I'm helping them.

You're sending them to your farm?

She nodded. The government wants to send them back to Haiti, but they don't want to return. Some American poets who know of Sandovar tried to get him out of detention, but some of his peasant poetry is considered anti-American, you know. I don't think they shoulda even told the people that he's a poet, you know, and that ain't his profession actually. We managed to get them out of detention, but. . . .

What are you doing? I mean, a university professor and his wife is one thing, Abio and Carolina, but they ain't going to let you get away with this. What are you trying to prove anyway? How are Carolina and Abio, by the way?

She picked up the phone and dialed. *Come l'hai trovato?* Tell him *meglio l'uovo oggi, che la gallina domani . . . Ti verro a trovare . . .* Ah, *non ha orecchio per la musica.*

Then she put the phone down and said, They're fine. The university is being a bastard with them, like I suspected. And they're still trying to sweet-talk Carolina, telling her that she shouldn't have any problem herself with immigration. But she won't abandon Abio. If he's deported, she'll be deported. Isn't that ideal? So they still need me.

You're crazy.

I'm in Memphis in a rented car parked across the street from the Presley mansion, Graceland, watching Norvelle's sister, Cayenne. I don't know if crazy women remember, but when I step out of the car and go to greet her she reaches out her hand to shake mine.

Harlan, she says. It's wonderful to see you. Harlan Truth.

I don't know how she know my middle name. I figure Norvelle musta told her, but I don't ever remember having told even Norvelle my middle name. I ain't told you Norvelle's own name, have I? Norvelle Goodling. Needless to say I don't use his name. Or rather, didn't use it when we were married. Harlan Truth Eagleton Goodling? Or even Harlan Goodling? Or even Mrs. Goodling? Even Norvelle, when he first started submitting his articles to journals, everyone thought his last name a typo.

Cayenne's hair's in spit curls; she wears a white sweater and a blue, flared skirt. On her feet are tennis shoes. Pink ones.

I can walk you home when you're ready, I say.

No, no, no, no. Not with you.

Why not?

Because he told us what you did. He told us how you left him. You stranded him in Africa, and they don't like you anymore. I like you. But I told you that you're not a wifeable woman, and I told him so, and he wanted to wife you anyway. I don't like you. I don't like what you did at all.

When was he here?

Yesterday.

Is he still here?

No, he left last night. Back to Africa, where you stranded him. They don't like you anymore. I like you. But I told you that you're not a wife-able woman. Neither am I.

I nod. I think of a witch doctor's wife I met when I was traveling with Norvelle in Kenya. She was afraid to leave her husband and she was afraid to stay with him, because of his magic. And she was afraid even to tell me of being afraid. Stupidly, I thought of her appearance on one of those talk shows, maybe the Oprah Winfrey show, with a string of modern women talking about their acts of marital defiance, and Oprah urging her on to independence. Imagine being a witch doctor's wife. Imagine the consequences of a simple no.

I don't know why I thought of that while talking to the crazy woman. But I remembered asking Norvelle about her. We were back in one of the tourist hotels, sipping palm wine and I told him about the witch doctor's wife.

Who?

The witch doctor's wife.

I don't call them witch doctors, I call them wizards. But their own name for themselves is. . . . He told me their own name for themselves, some African word I don't remember.

But what about his wife, she's afraid of him.

What about her? he asked, scratching in his notepad.

But one of her—Norvelle's sister's—curls dangles. She spits on it and rolls it back up. Still it dangles. She looks at me. He went back to Tanoa mania, she says. I don't correct her.

Have you stopped liking me too? I ask.

I like you. I don't like you. I always like you. I said I like you. But you'd better go. There's Daddy Pop.

I turn to see her father. When he gets to us, he treats me like I'm invisible.

Come to fetch you home, he says to Cayenne.

Maybe only witches should marry wizards, I said, as Norvelle kept writing in his notebook.

You mean wizards should marry witches? he asked. That way you think they'd be equal? Suppose a wizard has more power than a witch?

But they only want to marry harmless women, I said.

No woman is harmless, he said.

Then he started telling me about some feminist anthropologist, whose research was bent on proving, he supposed, that men and women were natural enemies. Man was like a tiger; you didn't hate a tiger, you just knew what it was, and you took precautions. You, being a woman, that is. He'd just read an article by her about the Lele of Zaire, of the Kasai region. Traditionally, there the women practiced polyandry. Say what? I asked. It meant they had more than one husband. In other parts of Africa polygamy was tradition, the men having more than one wife, but among the Lele of Zaire, of the Kasai region, the women had more than one husband.

I can't imagine polyandry.

You don't believe it?

I believe it, but I can't imagine polyandry. The witch doctor has one wife all right, and she has one husband, but she's terrorized.

Her research is shoddy, he said, talking about the feminist anthropologist again. But harmless women? None of you are harmless. And if there are any of you who are, or who think you are, well, I'd recommend a good shrink.

CHAPTER THIRTY-NINE

I can't remember my dreams anymore, says Joan, waking up, yawning and wiping sleep from her eyes. She'd been drowsing in a hotel room chair in downtown Atlanta while I watched television. A book was open in her lap, *The Dancing Wu-Li Masters*. I don't remember by whom. I'd glimpsed two of its chapters—one called General Nonsense, and other Special Nonsense. Joan likes to read shit like that. Me I'm watching the Comedy Channel. A show called *Politically Incorrect*.

Say what?

I said I can't remember my dreams anymore. When I was a little girl I used to remember my dreams all the time. They were always vivid and in color.

Mine are always in black-and-white. I can't imagine high-definition, color dreams.

Do you remember your dreams? she asks.

Yes. Always. Well, most of the time.

On television the *Politically Incorrect* audience applauds and guffaws.

CHAPTER FORTY

When I go into Joan's dressing room, there's James leaning against the wall. He's the last person I'd have expected to find there. He looks animated, in conversation, till he sees me; then his look is noncommittal.

Speak of the devil, says Joan, layers of teal blue mascara on her eyes.

How've you been? James asks, moving a bit away from the wall.

All right, how about you?

Pretty good.

Pretty good, Joan mimics. How about a hug, y'all?

We keep to our own spaces.

Did you come to see Joan's show? I ask.

Naw, he's here in Chicago for the ASS meeting—

AARS, says James.

AARS, that's what I said. . . . and just happened to see I was headlining this joint. Our paths just happened to intersect, so he stopped over to say hello. The polite thing to do, you know. But he didn't see the show, did you, darling?

No. I couldn't get tickets.

I say nothing. I think Joan'll say something about getting him tickets, but she don't.

Maybe the three of us could have lunch tomorrow? he asks. There's a nice little French restaurant I saw around the corner. I know you like French food, Joan.

I can't, says Joan. And I don't like French food. I like New Orleans food, that's a little different. But maybe you and the fat lady control freak can have lunch. See how fat she's gotten? That's all that camel sausage and couscous and shit. And those sloe gin fizzes. And that sweet tooth of hers. Course she probably just looks pleasantly plump to you. Or is that pleasingly plump? Like those girlies in those old Renaissance paintings when it was in vogue for women to be full-figured, you know. Well, in my business I gotta stay slim myself. Rock 'n' roll keeps a gal slim.

James clears his throat, glancing sideways. Would you like to? he asks.

Okay.

You can pick her up at the Hyatt Regency, says Joan. Our control freak. What's a manager but a freak who likes to control other people.

Say around one? he asks.

Okay.

Swingmeakiss, says Joan.

He bends and kisses Joan's cheek, nods to me, and leaves. There is an odor like lavender and brandy. Not a heavy odor, a light one. And a hint of tobacco.

He still presents a fine figure, doesn't he? asks Joan, eyeing me. Real classy. Classy 'n' bold. That's one thing you can say about Jamey is he's got class. Not everybody changes. Some of us stay the same. Some of us are concerned about our figures. Course they say men age better than women. I don't think so myself. I just think it's a power game.

She mighta said he hadn't changed. But he'd seemed a new sort of man to me. Or maybe I was a new sorta woman. Somehow I felt less bold in his presence. Either he'd changed or I'd changed. And not just fat. And it's Joan the control freak. I just manage her career, but it's her in control.

Why'd you do that? I ask. Invite us to have lunch with each other.

Because I know you want to. I know Jamey wants to. You, I can't always figure you, but I know Jamey wants to. And you like French food. I know you like French food. They're known for their pastries. Or you might take Jamey to the Montego Bay. They've got some good Caribbean food. And then there's Shy Harry's. I think they just have ordinary American cuisine. But I know you like French pastries. And anyway you're a bore. That's my act when I'm offstage, not yours.

You're no bore, onstage or off. That's what James said first attracted him to you. I mean, besides your intelligence—your spontaneity and wit.

Did Jamey say that?

Yes. You're no bore.

You want to fucking bet? If you don't have lunch with him, our Jamey, I'll bore the shit out of you.

In a French restaurant, we eat Chateaubriand, *pommes de terre, haricots verts*. I'm looking at the *haricots verts* but he's looking at me.

What's AARP? I ask, looking up from the plate at him, then I take a forkful of the *haricots verts*.

AARS, he corrects. American Association of Research Scientists. I also belong to AAARPS. African-American Association of Research Scientists. Of course, there aren't as many of us. And fewer women than men.

I lift another green bean. I think he's going to say something about Joan wasting her talents, her intelligence. Just another stereotype nigger entertainer, all those things Joan's told me he thinks about her, but he don't.

It's been a long time, he says.

Yes. I wasn't sure if you wanted to do this. But you know Joan.

Yeah, tell me. I feel like I've known her for centuries.

How's things at the farm? The immigration police been after you? I know a immigration lawyer if you need assistance. Or rather I know of one. I usedta meet all sorts of people when I, I mean when I when Norvelle and I, my ex-husband, you know.

No. Things are okay. Abio and Carolina went back to Italy, to Rome, not to Sicily. Several East Africans are staying there now, and several Haitians. Joan's even got a linguist staying up there, 'cause they don't all speak English. But you know Joan, she's always inviting strangers up there, so there's no problem there. A lot of people in the area just think they're her musicians. Show business people, you know. Anyway, it's Joan's farm.

What about the Haitians?

What Haitians?

You said there were several Haitians up there.

Yeah, I think they're Haitians. I think that's what Joan said. I don't really communicate with them that much, because I'm not as garrulous as Joan, and we decided it's best I don't know too much about them anyway. I don't know what Joan's ambitions are. I just do my research. . . .

What university do you teach at?

I don't work for a university, actually. I do my own private research. I use the labs of the institute, that's sort of like a think tank, you know, I'm a co-partner.

Oh, yeah, Joan told me something about that. That you generate ideas.

Yeah, we generate ideas and then research them, or other people research them, do the practical research, you know. It's really ideal. And then I have my own research. It's what both Joan and I wanted to do when we were young graduate students, form our own research company, not work for some corporation, you know, not work for the man, or even some university. Joan's always had these ideas about good, you know. I guess as a people, we African Americans have our own ideas about good, you know, the sorts of people we allow to be good, to consider themselves good. That only those who devote their intellect to the race problem can consider themselves good, that solve the race problem. Joan said she dreamt once that she came up with a chemical formula that solved the race problem, and it freed African-American intellectuals to devote their intellects to whatever other people, free people, devote their intellects to. But then after you devote your intellect to the race problem others come asking you, whites and blacks, why haven't you invented any rocket ships, sent men to the moon and the other planets, developed any new theories of the universe, built great cities. You know, the game. You're expected to solve the race problem, devote all your energies to the race problem, and at the same time you're held accountable for not creating anything, for not being an intellect in everything else, making grand contributions beyond race. That's why I went to Fisk rather than to one of the white schools, although I got several scholarships to them. The beginnings of affirmative action, you know. But I'd scored high on all the tests, felt I'd met the standards anywhere. I went to Fisk. I felt I could be myself. Not be out for myself, but just be myself. And to tell the truth there were more blacks at Fisk with my interests, interests in the sciences, than at the elite white schools. Joanie went to an elite white school, a private college in Connecticut, and said that she was the only African-American chemist there. The others were sociologists or anthropologists or some shit. I think one African-American botanist. I mean undergraduate school. Like I said, we went to the same graduate school. A lot of problems with self-esteem, you know, when she was in undergraduate school. Should she just do her chemistry research or play at revolution? And if she devoted all her time to the revolution, then what about chemistry? You know. Well, I shouldn't say play at revolution. Some of her classmates from those days are still waiting for the revolution. And one of them, a girl from Colombia, I think, the country Colombia, was in a real revolution. Or maybe from Chiapas. I usedta teach at a university, though. I taught at Fisk for a while, then I taught at a private college in the Northeast. Then I and a colleague I met at the AAARS decided to start this think tank, you know. It's more ideal for me, it suits my character more.

What is your character?

You know me. And I'll go up to the farm to make sure there're enough supplies. I know enough to help keep Joan out of trouble, though.

You'd keep her out of trouble, wouldn't you?

Yes.

No wonder Joan loves you.

He says nothing. I roll the sleeves of my cotton blouse up to my elbows, all my muscles tense. I breathe in the air of almond croissants and *escargots* cooked in garlic butter that infiltrates the tiny dining room. I look at the fluted crystal ashtray near his elbow and wait for him to light up a cigarette, but he don't. There is still, though, the slight smell of tobacco. There're tiny beads of sweat like dew on his upper lip and his forehead's shiny, but he ain't nervous. He don't seem so. He came in in a rush while I was already seated at the table. I notice that his upper lip is thin while his bottom lip is full. I try to remember kissing them. Norvelle told me once that Africans don't kiss. The traditional Africans. The detribalized ones kiss. But in Kenya, he said, among the Kikuyu, it had once been taboo to even make love in the daytime. If one did, one had to go through a rite of purification. One had to go to a wizard, a mogowhatever to be purified.

Why'd you just disappear? he asks. When I got back to the farm, you weren't there.

What did Joan tell you?

Not much of anything really.

She did admit seeing us, didn't she?

Yes, she said she saw us. Then she said all sorts of sinister things about you. That I shouldn't expect anything. That you're rather like an alley cat.

I make zigzags with my fork across my plate, plowing through mashed potatoes and green beans.

I started to write you a romantic letter, you know, but I never did. I started to call you, but I didn't do that either. Actually, I did write the letter, a rather passionate letter really, but I never sent it. Anyway, I wouldn't have known where to send it, except in care of Joan. And I wouldn't trust her to give it to you anyway.

So where are you staying? What hotel? I ask, cutting the Chateaubriand.

The Sheraton.

How long will you be in town?

Several more days. I'm glad you want to know.

Profiterolles au chocolat. Isles flottants. Tartes aux pommes.

I prefer Italian food, I comment. Joan says I like French food, but I prefer Italian food.

They say most Americans do.

I'd like to come and see you, I said. But Joan and I are flying to Amsterdam tonight.

He takes out a notepad and scribbles something.

Here's my permanent address, not Joan's farm. If you ever want to find me.

You know where I am, I said.

Yes.

Joan said your real name's Naughton. That it's Naughton James Savage.

Yeah. I've always sorta liked it. But Joan never has. The AARS has me as Naughton James Savage, though.

What about the AAARS? I ask, as the waiter brings our *isles flottants*.

Professor Doctor the Right Honorable Naughton James Savage, Esquire, he jokes. You know how we are about titles. Don't ask me about the ASS, though.

B O O K

F I V E

CHAPTER FORTY-ONE

What brings you here? She is sitting on a couch, her ankles crossed. Then she rests one ankle on the other knee and leans forward. Square yellow shoulders, square yellow eyebrows. Her eyebrows are shaped like the eyebrows of the Japanese courtesans—I think they're courtesans—in those imake paintings, those scroll-type paintings. I believe she's even wearing yellow contact lenses, but it's a long room and she's half in shadow, and I can't be sure.

Well, tell me what you're doing here? I've got all the help around here I can use, she says.

So you've finally decided to fire me?

Yeah, why not?

I stare at her yellow nails. Square. I turn and walk down the yellow-carpeted hall.

It is my first dream in color, not black-and-white.

I throw a section of the *Times* at Joan. We're standing in the entrance of the recording studio, in New York, where I've waited for her. Did you know what you were doing?

What are you talking about?

I motion for her to read. It is only a short paragraph. I probably wouldn't have even noticed it if Joan had gotten to the recording studio earlier. After I'd read the sports section, the horseracing page, I'd thumbed through the entertainment section, and then through items of world news. That's when I saw the little paragraph, hardly a paragraph. She reads it in clumsy haste, then gives me a blank look.

Did you know what you were financing? I ask. Did you know they were using the money you got from the Schacter contract—I suppose that's the money you used—to buy weapons? So they could try to take back their country?

Joan says nothing.

I thought you were financing them so that they could stay over here in this country, maybe hire themselves a good immigration lawyer, not to try to mount some kinda idiotic little coup. I mean, I thought that you were just helping them to stay here. You coulda hired them that good immigration lawyer I told you about. That woulda made more sense.

Joan says nothing.

They were all killed. Except Sandovar. But he's been detained. And you know what that means.

Joan says nothing.

I didn't know it was that. If I'd known that you were such a fool as that. Why didn't you tell me it was that? Did Jamey know what you were doing?

No. Jamey would've talked me out of it. He's like you.

I thought it was like with Abio and Carolina, helping them get political asylum or some shit. That you were just helping the refugees. That sorta fool, but not this other sorta fool.

Maybe we could hire someone—you know those mercenaries we saw on television—who can go into the country and get him out. You know, like the ones we saw on television who were training those people how to defend themselves. You know, Nicodemus—

Nicodemus?

That's his name, Nicodemus Sandovar. He's your lover and you don't know his name.

Oh. But he's not my lover.

Anyway, his family's still at my farm, his wife, his boy and girl. We could hire someone to go into the country, you know. . . . find out where they're detaining him and—

Stupid. Stupid. This ain't the movies, girlfriend. This ain't the movies. You're just stupid. Putting on your Quixote act.

When Castro returned to Cuba, he only had a few men in a boat. When he marched into Havana, he only had a few men.

Sandovar ain't Castro.

There must be mercenaries who do things like that that we could hire to free Sandovar.

Yeah, you could just hire you your own fucking private army, huh? Well, that takes more bucks than you got, darling. You ain't a big enough star for that.

What about that man you were telling me about, that Josef, if he's so rich. What about some of his security people?

Naw, that's bullshit. I don't even see Josef, and if I did, I wouldn't tell him about some bullshit like that. I told you I know some fools in South Texas who are into some illegal shit with illegal aliens, helping illegal aliens. I can give you their names, but even they don't get into bullshit like that.

It's not bullshit. I thought of asking Isabel Kong for help, you know, but if she's the gangster that they say she is, I might get myself into more trouble. Or she might think she'd get herself into more trouble, you know, than just the rumors about her. And Little Lady's a musical prodigy, I call her Kongapoo, a magical prodigy, you know, at one of those ritzy musicians' academies, and. . . . Anyway, these people you know, are they mercenaries?

Naw, they ain't mercenaries. They're just regular people who believe in freedom, free borders, you know. A few rumheads among them, but otherwise they're regular people. They're mostly working in the border towns, you know, and it's not shit like that. They're not mercenaries, they're just ordinary people.

How'd you meet them?

They're more friends of Norvelle's actually. I met them through Norvelle. He met them, well, he usedta be a guide for different African groups, you know, when they'd come to this country. I first met him when he was escorting some group of African Baptists. I told you he's a medical anthropologist. Well, he speaks different African languages, so some of these sanctuary movement types when they had this group of African refugees from some little country got in touch with him once to do some interpreting, 'cause he was supposed to be the only one in this country who knows how to speak this certain African language, so he took me with him when he went down there to South Texas. Anyway, I don't much keep in touch with them myself, 'cause they're originally friends of Norvelle's, you know, except this one woman's got a little cantina-style restaurant in Cuba, New Mexico, usedta help transport some of them illegal aliens. When I first met her I thought she was an illegal alien herself, and then Norvelle said she was helping to transport them. Things got too hot for her in South Texas, I think, so she moved to New Mexico. It ain't that commando-type bullshit, though.

We don't know how many there were. That's just how many they reported there were. Maybe the others can get Sandovar free.

Just stupidity. Crazy fool. This ain't TV.

But they did something. They did something. They did something.

They tried to change the world and make it better. They didn't just whine like all you. . . . They acted. That's why I admire Isabel Kong, if all the tales about her are true. They try to make her into a gangster, but she helps the Chinese. She didn't become the great artist she imagined she'd be, and maybe she doesn't have her idealisms like when we were in school and is more cynical, but she's a better woman. They say all idealists become cynics. Anyway, she's a better woman than she might have become if she'd just become that great artist.

Stupidly. I don't mean Isabel Kong, I mean you fools.

Well, they're real people, real everyday folks, not pretenders, like us. And the best you could imagine for your Sandovar is a cockfight.

A good cockfight. And at least we won.

CHAPTER FORTY-THREE

How we met. Joan and I. Birds glowing. On the wall, a tapestry of birds of paradise. I awoke, curled up on somebody's sofa. There were people in the room. Partying people, show business people, holding drinks and paper plates and some near the stereo dancing. A couple near the stereo dancing to Miles. Should you dance to Miles? Can you? Near me a couple was sitting. Man and woman talking. The man gets up to refresh the woman's drink. The woman says hi. Where am I? I ask. Where are you? But before she answers he's back with the refreshed drink and they're talking. I'm standing. Hangover.

Vaguely remember a bar. I'd just come back from Tanzania. On my way to Saratoga. Vaguely remember a bar. Where am I? Who brought me here?

Can I have a tequila, please?

Sure thing.

So whose party is this anyway?

Damn if I know. A party. I know a coupla the musicians. There's a famous fashion designer. A famous artist. But damn if I know. They just sent me over.

Who'd I come with?

I don't know. Scan the room. The man in the braids? Chinese? No, he's too dark for Chinese. But they have dark Chinese. In the mountains? Norvelle once showed me some.

Wait for someone to look at you with familiarity, like they know you. The stereo in the corner. All the other men could be my Norvelle. Shades and variations.

Who'd I come with?

Damn if I know.

How'd I find my way here?

Hello.

Did I come with you? Hi, I'm Joan Savage.

Savage or it was Eagleton. No, my own name Eagleton. I'm Harlan Eagleton. She has this full-lipped smile. I like her already. Scar near her nose, or a wrinkle.

Do you know whose party this is?

Some party, huh.

She hasn't the foggiest either. Her first New York party. Friends brought her. Friends of friends of friends of friends.

So you, are you an artist too? You look . . .

I told her.

Say what? Cosmetician? You mean makeup artist?

Naw, I work in a beauty parlor.

She laughed and then she cheered. It's about time I met somebody real for a change. Not these muckedymucks. A real gal.

But I. . . .

Come over here I want you to do my makeup. . . . I wanna see how good you are.

In Saratoga, in a hotel room, I sit with Nathaniel. The old jockey. Paradise. We're watching TV. We're sitting in his rocker/recliners, the kind that massage you. A Brazilian actress is talking about a new Brazilian film, called *Pixote*.

. . . because we have so many problems to solve before art, though art is my life . . . so many people living terrible lives . . . but art is my life . . . I wanted to go with them. It was a difficult choice. A difficult choice. But I come from an old artist family. I'm a dancer first and a singer and I make humor . . . *Ele esta louco por ela* . . . *Sim. Sim. Sim. Sim* . . . I don't want to make only one thing in my life . . . I want to know all the mystery, make all the mysteries that my art can do . . .

Suppose they'd allowed Joan to go with them? I ask. I think she'd've been that foolish. Playing revolutionary. Well, she could play revolutionary, but for Nicodemus Sandovar and the others it wasn't play.

So where's she now?

Back in the studio, recording her new CD. Something to do with refugees or some shit.

And what about you? Where are you?

I don't answer.

Paradise pours me another glass of champagne, bought with our winnings, then he pours himself a new glass. We all meet as strangers, and mostly stay strangers, even when we think we know each other. It's funny, I was thinking of you, though, and then you appeared.

Speak of the devil, huh?

Or think of her. But I know better than that. All I know is it's better to love, it's better to love. . . . What do you think?

Norvelle once told me that there were certain African folk tales that never gave you an answer; they only left you with a dilemma. Dilemma tales, he called them. What else had he said about them? They were a way of learning. They were another way of learning. What had I learned? I'd just grown fatter, as Joan had said. But Joan. What had she learned? She'd started singing more revolutionary songs. But I don't think she'd really learned anything. Maybe she thought if she got really good, got famous enough, she could hire her private army—free Sandovar or some others. I don't know what the fool imagined.

More champagne, please. Tell me your whole story.

No one ever tells their whole story. What's the name of Joan's new CD?

Siamo del medesimo paese. I told the fool don't everybody know Italian.

What does it mean?

Siamo del medesimo paese. We're all from the same country. *Siamo del medesimo paese.* We're all from the same country.

In the storage room, Mother and I open boxes of new supplies. Grandmother Jaboti has ordered a whole box of Royal Crown and Mother complains that only the old-time women still use Royal Crown, that modern women put on light conditioners and texturizing creams.

Did you ever believe her turtle stories? I ask. I mean when you were a little girl and she first told you.

She puts several jars of hair dressing on the shelf before she answers. Yeah, I suppose I did. I suppose when I was a little girl I did. Little girls like to believe fantasies like that. I even imagined that I was a Turtle Woman transforming myself to free myself from the tyranny of others.

She puts several more jars on the shelf. But I'm a grown woman now and not so foolish. I'm a grown woman now and got my own grown girl.

FORTY-SIX

Harlan, Harlan, exclaims Josef, giving me both his hands and ushering me into his house. I thought I'd see you in Saratoga, he's saying, still holding both my hands.

I tell him that I didn't go this year, that I don't gamble anymore, that there are no longer any horses that I want to bet on.

Not even mine? he asks.

No, not even yours.

Come on. I want you to see someone.

I expect to meet his wife, but when I walk into the living room, there's Joan curled up on the sofa.

Your Joanie, says Josef. You made me a fan of hers, and so I invited the two of you. I thought it would be a pleasure. Joan's not dressed in her stage clothes, but looks like any ordinary woman in ruffled blouse and straight skirt. Except the edges of her hair are lavender.

Well, what's it to be? Joan asks, rising. Champagne, Manhattan, Screwdriver?

I've got to go check on one of my Thoroughbreds, but you girls can catch up on old times. And to Joan, he said something about some proposal she'd made to him. I'll consider your proposal, he said. At least, I might know some other people you can submit it to. Had he invited her here or had she invited herself? Was she still on that old chestnut about trying to free Sandovar?

Did you know he was married? Joan asks, handing me a Screwdriver.

Yes, I knew. I told you I knew. I told you about his wife, and how he hadn't sent for her because of the dangers.

No, you didn't tell me.

Yes, I did. Why didn't you tell me he'd invited you here? When I spoke to you about that new contract. They sent it to me and I told you I'd be forwarding it to you. You could have told me he'd invited you here.

Then you'd not have come.

No, because I'd figure you'd got someone new to play games with. I used to admire you. I mean in the beginning. Poor girl makes good and all that. I admired you so much, your will, your determination to better yourself, and still keep some integrity, a little integrity. And I liked the way you ran things, the way you seemed to belong anywhere you decided. Like when I first met you at that party. If you'd told me you were an artist I'd have thought so. You could have told me you were anyone and I'd have believed you. I used to think you were real, not an imposter like everyone else. Not a pretender like those other jokers.

You've always thought me a rogue.

No, not in the beginning. And even if you are sort of a rogue, you never really pretended to be anything else. I forgave you my ex-husband. After all, he's my ex, and I believed you. I believed in you.

I sip the Screwdriver. And now I will tell you the truth of it. Josef has gone out to check on one of his Thoroughbreds, like I told you, and left us alone together with drinks. But it is not intoxication. It is not insanity. It is Joan holding the knife. She has come up to the chair, in the living room, looking as if she is bathed in light, and there is something sparkling. Suddenly the knife is here and casually she drives it in. This is the truth of the story. Not Nicholas' tale, but this one. The knife bends even before Nicholas gets to the chair to grab her arm, and save me. I think it has struck bone and bent. But it's struck not where any bone would be.

I thought you were a real person, she says. But you're not even a human woman, you're not even a real human woman.

This is the truth of it. The knife fell out. I put my hand to the wound and it healed. Nicholas came to save me, and Joan stood there raising her arms to the ceiling in disbelief.

And when you discover you can heal yourself, that you simply put your hand to a wound and it heals, you soon discover you can heal others. First a horse suffering from a fractured phalange, and then a Turtle Woman.

But Joan, though she witnessed the first healing, didn't believe it then and claims not to believe it now, no matter how many wounds I cure or bones I straighten.

I still listen to Joan's music, though. Joan's new music, the music of revolution, the music of refugees. And if I happen to be healing folks in a town she's playing in, I'll go sit in her audience and applaud. I still believe in her.

But me? She thinks I've set myself up as a healing woman just so that perhaps my husband Norvelle will leave the Masai woman and start following me around. But that's baloney. That's pure baloney. Let Norvelle follow that Masai woman to Kingdom Come for all I care.

Is it her? Yeah, that's her. She don't look like no healing woman to me.
You sure she can heal? She healed herself first, then a horse and then a
woman who looked like a turtle and I have read testimonies of peoples
that say she done healed them. Don't look to me like she could heal a
flea. What's that she wearing? Aw, girl, come on and let's go introduce
usself.

Mizz Eagleton, I'm Mizz LaPorte and this is Mizz Bryce. Church sent
us out to welcome you. That all you got? Travel light, don't you?

I let her carry the overnight case while I hold onto the CD player, its
earphone stuck in my ear. Listening to Joan.

Mr. Nicholas is already at the house, says Mizz LaPorte, glancing
back at me. He say he your witness to the healings.

Yes.

What's that you listening to?

The gospel.

That's real nice to carry it around with you. Plenty of the young folks
does that, but it ain't no gospel they listens to. It's that rap. Ain't that
nice? Music, our preacher says, cures the soul. But I know some of that
music don't cure nobody soul. This modern world-stuff.

Ain't it the poet that say it music the greatest good we have below,
and all of heaven that mortals know. The greatest good we know, and all
of heaven we have below. Music or love.

Della gives me a conspiratory look, then says, We done advertised
you all around, you know, so we're expecting a real capacity crowd. But
I bet you always do draw a capacity crowd, don't you? You know you's

the first healing woman that I met. Do you think he'll follow you till you become human?

Say what?

Them that follows you say that you really heal and it ain't just rumor.

To tell you the truth, I'm not the sort of woman I'd imagined I'd become. . . . .

Preacher say that some people secretly prefer their flaws to their virtues, because they mistakenly think that it's virtues that make people the same, but flaws that distinguish them, that give them character. Preacher say that them is the sorta people that is enamored of they flaws, and them is the hardest peoples to free from they sins. 'Cause what they love best about theyselves is they flaws. They cultivates them. But if you is a true healing woman, he say you can heal some of them peoples. To one whom much is given, much is required.

When I arrive, he stands. They told me he would be Nicholas. Surely, they hadn't asked him his name. They'd heard about the man who was my witness, heard his name was Nicholas, and simply assumed this was him. Surely, they'd said Nicholas because everyone knew Nicholas was the one I'd always traveled with. A man named Nicholas. But the man standing here is the last man in the world I expected to find. Or maybe the first man I'd hoped for.

CORREGIDORA

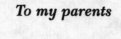
To my parents

I

It was 1947 when Mutt and I was married. I was singing in Happy's Café around on Delaware Street. He didn't like for me to sing after we were married because he said that's why he married me so he could support me. I said I didn't just sing to be supported. I said I sang because it was something I had to do, but he never would understand that. We were married in December 1947 and it was in April 1948 that Mutt came to Happy's drunk and said if I didn't get off the stage he was going to take me off. I didn't move, and some men put Mutt out. While I was singing the first few songs I could see Mutt peeking in, looking drunk and evil, then I didn't see him and thought he'd gone on home and gone to bed to sleep it off. I always left by the back way. You go down some narrow steps and through a short alley and then you be to the Drake Hotel, where Mutt and I was staying then. I said good night and went out back.

"I'm your husband. You listen to me, not to them."

I didn't see him at first because he was standing back in the shadows behind the door. I didn't see him till he'd grabbed me around my waist and I was struggling to get loose.

"I don't like those mens messing with you," he said.

"Don't nobody mess with me."

"Mess with they eyes."

That was when I fell.

The doctors in the hospital said my womb would have to come out. Mutt and me didn't stay together after that. I wouldn't even let him come in the hospital to see me when I knew what was happening. They said he'd come in when I didn't know what was happening. They said when I was delirious I was cursing him *and* the doctors and nurses out.

Tadpole McCormick was the man who owned Happy's Café. Square-jawed and high-cheekboned, he was one of them Hazard, Kentucky, niggers. I was singing in Happy's when Demosthenes Washington owned it, about two years before Tadpole took it over. I never did know how it got the name Happy's because I never did know anybody named Happy that owned it. Tadpole said he got his name because when he was a kid he was always messing around tadpole holes. He came to see me when I could have visitors.

"How you feeling, U.C.?" He didn't sit down in the chair by the bed but stayed standing.

"Awright."

"They tell me you been doing some hard cussing while you was sick."

"Yeah."

He didn't say anything. I could tell he felt awkward. I asked if he wanted to sit down. He said, "Naw thanks." Then he said, "Well, I just wont to tell you he's been barred from the place, so when you get back he won't be troubling you."

"He's been barred from my place too. What are you doing in the meantime?"

"Got a little combo. Eddy Pace's group."

"Aw."

He said nothing.

"Do you know what's happened?" I asked.

He nodded.

"Do you ever feel as if something was crawling under your skin?"

He nodded again.

"Taddy, will you take me home when it's time to go?"

He said yes.

When it was time to go home he didn't take me back to the Drake. He had three rooms over the café. I slept on a couch that let out as a bed. He slept on the couch that didn't let out. I was still weak and there were the stitches that wouldn't be out for a while. The first meal he fixed me was vegetable soup. He didn't have any. He sat by the bed.

"I'm glad you didn't think 'home' meant the Drake."

"He wasn't barred from the Drake," he said.

The soup was good but I only ate the broth. I kept feeling as if I would throw up.

"I thought you'd want more," he said.

"Naw, I'm not very hungry. My stomach still feels tender, all those liquids they had me on."

It was evening but I didn't hear even any faint music from below.

"Where's the combo?"

"I told them not to come in tonight."

"What about business?"

"You more important than business."

I said nothing. I could tell he felt awkward again. He took the bowl and went back to the kitchen. When he came back he said, "They still come to drink." Then he said, "I'm going downstairs. I'll be back up later to see if you want anything."

"Okay."

He left.

When he came back, I opened my eyes.

"I thought you were sleeping," he said.

"No."

"You should be. How do you feel?"

"Still weak. It's not so much how I feel in my body."

"What do you feel?"

"As if part of my life's already marked out for me—the barren part."

"You can't expect a woman to take something like that easy."

"What about the man?"

"You mean Mutt? You don't intend to go back to him, do you?"

"No, I mean any other man."

"If I were the man it wouldn't matter. I don't know about any other man."

I said nothing. I might have wanted him to say that, but I hadn't intended for him to.

"I feel like sleeping now," I said.

He turned my light out, and went into the next room where the couch was. He closed the door.

I lay on my back, feeling as if something more than the womb had been taken out. When he was downstairs, I'd looked at the stitches across my belly again. When they were gone, I'd get back to work again, that and . . . I couldn't help feeling I was forcing something with Tadpole. What our talk was leading to. Something I needed, but couldn't give back. There'd be plenty I couldn't give back now. Of course, I'd get the divorce from Mutt . . . I went to sleep.

The next morning Tadpole found me staring at the ceiling.

"Didn't you sleep?"

"Yes, I just woke up early that's all."

"They said you could have juice for breakfast. Nothing solid yet."

"You going by their menu?"

"Yeah."

He went into the kitchen and came back with some juice. While I drank, he emptied the bedpan. When he came back, he stood watching me. I was frowning, but I didn't tell him to stop. When I finished, I handed him the glass. He took it back and came back and watched me again.

"What is it, Taddy?"

"Nothing. I'm going down now."

"Okay. Is that what you wanted?"

"I'll be back to check you a little later."

"Okay, Taddy."

He watched me a moment more.

"What is it?"

"The doctor wants you to come back in a couple of weeks for a checkup. I'll take you."

"Okay."

He went downstairs.

When he came back, I'd been sleeping, but woke up as soon as he opened the door.

"Have a good sleep?"

"Yeah."

"Cat Lawson made you some chicken soup."

"Thank her."

"I did."

Catherine Lawson lived across the street from Happy's. She straightened people's hair. She wasn't a regular hairdresser, but people would go to her anyway, and give her a couple of dollars for doing it.

He pulled up the little table and brought me a spoon from the kitchen and took the foil from around the bowl.

"I better get your pill first."

He got the pills and I took one and a little water. I didn't eat the pieces of chicken. My stomach still felt queasy.

"They said you had gastritis too. You weren't eating right."

"I was eating all right."

"Or worrying too much."

"I can't talk to you about it."

"I know most about it already."

"Then I don't have to talk to you about it."

When I finished he moved the table away and took the bowl back in the kitchen.

"She said if you want anything to just send over for it."

"That's sweet of her."

"No, it's not sweet. She cares about you."

"That's good to know."

He touched my forehead.

"They said you had those nurses scared to death of you. Cussing them out like that. Saying words they ain't never heard before. They kept saying, 'What is she, a gypsy?'"

"What did you say?"

"Naw. I said if she's a gypsy I'm a Russian."

"How do you know you ain't? One a them might a got your great-grandmama down in a Volga boat or something."

"Those pills make you silly?"

"I'm already silly."

He said nothing. I said nothing else. He sat down on the edge of the bed.

"Ursa Corre. I know what the 'U' stands for but I keep getting the last one wrong. Corrente. Corredo."

"Corregidora. Old man Corregidora, the Portuguese slave

breeder and whoremonger. (Is that what they call them?) He fucked his own whores and fathered his own breed. They did the fucking and had to bring him the money they made. My grandmama was his daughter, but he was fucking her too. She said when they did away with slavery down there they burned all the slavery papers so it would be like they never had it."

"Who told you all 'at?"

"My great-grandmama told my grandmama the part she lived through that my grandmama didn't live through and my grandmama told my mama what they both lived through and my mama told me what they all lived through and we were suppose to pass it down like that from generation to generation so we'd never forget. Even though they'd burned everything to play like it didn't never happen. Yeah, and where's the next generation?"

He nodded but said nothing.

I asked, "How's Cat?"

"She said she didn't have no complaints. I was passing down the street and she said, 'You got U.C. up there, ain't you?' I said, 'Yeah.' I thought she was going to say something, you know. She said, 'Come on in here. I fixed her up some chicken soup I wont you to take over there. I didn't wont to take it up myself, cause she just got back and women get evil after something like that and I don't like to mess with no evil women. Tell her I be up to see her when she feeling all right.' "

"Yeah, I wondered why she didn't come herself. Tell her I stopped cussing."

"Yeah?"

"Uh hum."

"I went in there and it smell like she had somebody's head on fire . . . They ain't told me shit."

Gayl Jones

"What?"

"I mean like your grandmama told you. I guess some people just keep things in."

"Well, some things can't be kept in. What I didn't tell you is old man Corregidora fathered my grandmama and my mama too."

Taddy frowned, but he said nothing.

"What my mama always told me is Ursa, you got to make generations. Something I've always grown up with."

Tad said nothing. Then he said, "I guess you hate him then, don't you?"

"I don't even know the bastard."

He frowned and I knew he hadn't meant the old man, but I went on as if he had.

"I've got a photograph of him. One Great Gram smuggled out, I guess, so we'd know who to hate. Tall, white hair, white beard, white mustache, a old man with a cane and one of his feet turned outward, not inward, but outward. Neck bent forward like he was raging at something that wasn't there. Mad Portuguese. I take it out every now and then so I won't forget what he looked like."

"You didn't know who I meant?"

"I didn't know until after you'd said it."

He said nothing. He didn't make me answer. He left me and went downstairs again.

A Portuguese seaman turned plantation owner, he took her out of the field when she was still a child and put her to work in his whorehouse while she was a child. She was to go out or he would bring the men in and the money they gave her she was to turn over to him. There were other women he used like that. She was the pretty little one with the almond eyes and coffee-bean skin, his favorite. "A good little piece. My best. Dorita. Little gold piece."

Great Gram sat in the rocker. I was on her lap. She told the same story over and over again. She had her hands around my waist, and I had my back to her. While she talked, I'd stare down at her hands. She would fold them and then unfold them. She didn't need her hands around me to keep me in her lap, and sometimes I'd see the sweat in her palms. She was the darkest woman in the house, the coffee-bean woman. Her hands had lines all over them. It was as if the words were helping her, as if the words repeated again and again could be a substitute for memory, were somehow more than the memory. As if it were only the words that kept her anger. Once when she was talking, she started rubbing my thighs with her hands, and I could feel the sweat on my legs. Then she caught herself, and stopped, and held my waist again.

"*. . . He was a big strapping man then. His hair black and straight and greasy. He was big. He looked like one a them coal Creek Indians but if you said he looked like an Indian he'd get mad and beat you. Yeah, I remember the day he took me out of the field. They had coffee there. Some places they had cane and then others cotton and tobacco like up here. Other places they had your mens working down in mines. He would take me hisself first and said he was breaking me in. Then he started bringing other men and they would give me money and I had to give it over to him. Yeah, he had a stroke or something and that's what turned his foot outside. They say he was praying and calling in all his niggers and telling them he'd give them such and such a amount of money if they take it off him but they all said they didn't put it on him. He got well, though, and didn't die. It just turned his foot outside and he behave like he always did. It did something to his neck too, because he always go around like he was looking for something that wasn't there. I don't know how he finally went,*

*because by then I was up to Louisiana, but I bet he didn't
go easy. Yeah, he have that took afterward. I stole it
because I said whenever afterward when evil come I
wanted something to point to and say, 'That's what evil
look like.' You know what I mean? Yeah, he did more fucking than the other mens did. Naw, I don't know what he
did with the others."*

Sweat inside her hands. Her palms like sunburnt gold.

"Were you sleeping?"

"Naw, I was dreaming."

"About what?"

"I've already told it."

He said nothing. He had boxes with him.

"I brought your things."

"I was going to ask you to, but I didn't want to bother
you again."

"I should have thought about it. I didn't think about it
till you started talking about that picture."

"Aw. Was *he* there?"

"Naw. He moved out. They said he boxed up your stuff
and they put it in storage. They didn't know whether anybody was going to come and get it or not."

"They didn't say where he went?"

"Do you care?"

"Naw. I don't care. Let me see if you've got everything."

"There were only these two."

"I didn't have much."

He put the boxes down in front of me and moved things
around as I directed him. Everything was there.

"The photograph's in that brown envelope."

He took it out and looked at it, put it back. He said
nothing. He put the boxes at the foot of the bed.

"Tell me when there's anything you need out of them," he said.

"I thought you'd say something," I said.

"He looks like you described him."

"They say they all get crazy when they get old."

"How were you *really* taught to feel about him?" he asked, looking at me hard.

"How I told you," I said, angry.

"My grandmother was white," he said. "She was a orphan and they had her working out in the fields along with the blacks and treated her like she was one. She was a little girl about nine, ten, 'leven. My granddaddy took her in and raised her and then when she got old enough he married her. She called him Papa. And when they were married, she still called him Papa."

"Maybe I should ask you how you were taught to feel."

He said nothing. Then he said, "She never got crazy though. One of the children came out black and the other one came out white. But she never did get crazy though."

I said nothing. I told him when it was time for me to soak in the tub to help the stitches come out he'd have to help me. I told him they thought I was going home with a husband or a sister. He said he'd do whatever I needed done, then he frowned and said he had to go back downstairs again. I asked him what his mama was, but he was already out the door.

". . . His wife was a skinny stuck-up little woman he got from over in Lisbon and had her brought over here. He wouldn't sleep with her, so she made me sleep with her, so for five years I was sleeping with her and him. That was when I was from about thirteen to eighteen. Then she started looking real bad and then she died on account of the climate. But they had me sleeping with both of them."

"*You telling the truth, Great Gram?*"

She slapped me.

"*When I'm telling you something don't you ever ask if
I'm lying. Because they didn't want to leave no evidence of
what they done—so it couldn't be held against them. And
I'm leaving evidence. And you got to leave evidence too.
And your children got to leave evidence. And when it come
time to hold up the evidence, we got to have evidence to
hold up. That's why they burned all the papers, so there
wouldn't be no evidence to hold up against them.*"

I was five years old then.

There was a knock on the door.

"Come in."

She poked her head in first. A dark, dark woman with
straightened hair drawn back and tied with a rubber band.
A smooth-complexioned woman, she was close to sixty, but
looked forty-five. She came from a family that stayed
young-looking.

"Catty, I didn't think you was coming to see me."

"Did Tadpole tell you what I told him?"

"Yeah." I smiled.

"I thought he tell you. I don't like to come around when
women have their evil spells."

She was inside now, sitting on the edge of the bed.

"Why? Cause you get evil too?"

She laughed.

"I brought you some more broth," she said, getting up. "I
put it in here in the refrigerator, and tell Tadpole to heat it
up for you and don't feed it to you when it's cold." She
came back from the kitchen and sat back down. "You seen
your bastard?"

"Naw. Tadpole said he moved out of the hotel and they
don't know where he's gone."

"Well, I see him hanging out in front a the place every evening. He hang around there awhile, peeping in 'cause he can't come in. You know Tadpole barred him from the place?"

I nodded.

"Yeah, well, he peep in and then he go on down the street. He don't say nothing to Tadpole and Tadpole don't say nothing to him. Once I saw him I just come on over across the street and said, 'Mutt, you ain't got no business hanging around out here, she don't want to see you.' He looked at me evil—Christ, that man's got evil. He looked at me and didn't say nothing but 'Shit, Miss Lawson.' Now, when have he called me Miss Lawson? He call me Cat like everybody else do. He walked on. So I ain't bother the nigger no more. Just let him stand out there, and walk on when he get ready to walk on."

I was frowning.

"He ain't going to bother you no more. I didn't mean to scare you. I don't think he mean to bother you no more. Just stand out there and get a look. You know how mens are when they do something like that. After they get a look, they just go on away and leave you alone."

"Some of em."

"I didn't mean to scare you."

"I ain't scared."

She looked at me harder than she'd ever looked, then she softened.

"It wasn't just the fall, was it, baby?"

"What do you mean?"

"You was big, wasn't you?"

"He didn't know."

"Did you know?"

"They said I was about a month pregnant, little over a month."

"They tell him?"

"Naw, I don't think so."

"You know which him I'm talking about, don't you?"

I looked away from her.

She said nothing, then got up. "Well, you start to working again things be all right. You got two men evil over you. I passed Tadpole downstairs he act like he didn't want to speak. I ask was you up here. I knew you was. He said Yeah. I asked if you was sleeping. He said Naw, he didn't think you was. But trying to get him to say something was like pulling his teeth, so I just came on upstairs."

She patted my leg through the sheet.

"I got to get back down now, baby. You be all right. I promised Elvira I'd do her hair."

"Awright, thanks for the broth. They gave Tadpole a menu, but I don't think he knows what to do."

"I be checking up on you then. I just wanted to make sure you wasn't evil."

"Naw."

She patted my leg again, and left.

She hadn't been long gone when Tadpole came up.

"What did she want?" he asked.

"She just came to bring me some broth and see how I was feeling. She told me to make sure you heat it up before you fed it to me." I laughed but he didn't.

"Why she stay so long?"

"You know how it is when you get to talking."

"I seen her out there talking to Mutt Thomas the other night."

I frowned. "She was trying to tell him to go away."

"But he wouldn't listen, would he?"

"Naw. Why didn't you tell me he was hanging around out there?"

"I thought you'd find out soon enough. I just didn't want to bother you now."

"Well, I found out."

He started to leave.

"She wasn't saying nothing about you, Tadpole."

"I didn't say she was."

He went out. I turned over and tried to get some sleep.

I stayed there, and when it was time for the stitches to come out, he'd help me into the tub to soak, and then when a half-hour was up, he'd come with a towel and help me out. He'd never stay in the bathroom. Once, after I'd soaked for a half-hour, he knocked and came in with the towel. He helped me out by the arm. He had a way of looking without looking, only enough to help me in and out. It was a big thick green towel that covered me down to my knees. I held it around me under my breasts.

"The stitches are about gone," I said. He was still holding my arm. "You haven't seen the scar."

He said he hadn't looked.

"You can feel it," I said. "I can just reach down and feel it. It's going to leave a bad one."

"I reckon," he said, helping me back to the bed. I sat down on the edge of it, drying myself off. He went back to let the water out. He came back and put my feet up. I handed him the towel, and got under the cover.

"You ought to be able to get in and out by yourself."

"It's only so I won't slip," I said.

"The doctor wants to see you again in a couple of days."

"I hope that means real food when I get back."

"Maybe."

He was sitting near the bed and I took his hand and put it under the sheet.

"You can feel it, can't you?"

He said yes. I thought he was going to take his hand away, but he waited for me to.

"It's worse when you touch it than when you look at it."

"I suppose. Most scars are."

I said nothing, then asked, "Has he still been out there?"

"Yeah, he's still out there."

"You haven't said anything?"

"Naw, he's outside. I can't bar him from looking."

"Tell him that 'can't come in' means 'can't look in' either."

He laughed. "I can't tell him that."

"You could make him go away."

"*I* can't make him go away."

"What does that mean?"

"Nothing. He's waiting for you, that's all. See you come out and sing, and know you're all right."

"That's what Cat said. Is that what he said?"

"I ain't talked to him."

"I thought maybe you might have."

"Naw. He looks and I look. He knows I don't want him in here and he don't come."

"My butt."

"What?"

"He ain't come in cause he ain't seen what he wants to see yet."

"He ain't coming in then."

I nodded. "Okay."

He said nothing. He stood up.

"After I see the doctor, I want to see a lawyer," I said.

He nodded. He patted my belly through the cover, and went back to finish cleaning out the tub.

When he came back through, I had my eyes closed. I could feel him bending down, but he must have stopped midway because he didn't finish.

"I'm awake," I said. I didn't open my eyes.

He bent down and kissed me. Then I heard the door close.

"I am going to take you off the pills and see how you feel," the doctor said. He had finished examining me, and I was sitting in the chair near his desk. "If you start getting nauseated again, take them. I want to see you in two more weeks. Is Mr. Corregidora with you?"

"That's *my* name, not my husband's."

"Oh, I see. Is Mr. Thomas with you? When I looked out there I saw a man standing with you. I'd like to see him."

"Naw."

"Aw, okay."

"You can take Mutt's name off there anyway."

"What do you mean?"

"I'm filing suit for divorce."

"Well, when I looked out and saw that man standing there I thought you'd stopped blaming him."

I said nothing, and stood up. When I got outside, Tadpole came over and took my elbow.

"See you in two weeks," the nurse said.

"Okay."

"How'd it go?" Tad asked.

"Awright."

"What do you mean awright?"

"He took me off the pills, unless I get nauseated again."

"What's wrong?"

"Nothing."

We walked to the door.

"He thought you were Mutt," I said quietly. "I mean, my husband. He thought you were Mr. Corregidora."

"What?" He was frowning.

"He didn't know I kept my name and Mutt kept his."

"When do you come back?"

"Two weeks."

"I mean what time?"

"Same time."

"Did he say you could work?"

"I didn't ask. I forgot to. Should I go back and ask?"

"Naw."

"Yes, I'd better," I said. "I was planning to start whether he said so or not."

He took my arm slightly, but I went anyway. We were standing in the door. Tadpole stood aside to let somebody pass. I asked him to wait for me. "Where would I go?" he asked.

When I got back, Tadpole was still frowning.

"What did he say?"

"Anytime I feel like it."

"I'll go ask him myself."

"No. He said anytime I feel like it, after the next two weeks. He said it meant building up time. One hour one night. Maybe hour and a half the next. Like that. Till I build myself back up again."

"I would've asked him if you hadn't told me," he said. "I'll get you a stool."

"I don't work sitting down," I said.

He said nothing, and we got in the car. When I looked over at him, he was looking as if he was mad at me. When he saw me watching him, he looked ahead quickly, and turned on the ignition.

When we got back I said I was tired and wanted to lie down. It was around noon. I'd had a ten o'clock appointment.

"Same time, same position," I said.

"What?"

He was hanging up my sweater and his jacket.

"He had me up on the table so he could look at the scar. Every time you go to the doctor they say, 'Get up on the table' or 'Take your clothes off and get up on the table.' Somebody ought to say Naw."

"That's what Cat did once. She said the man told her, 'Get up on the table.' So she said, 'I told that bastard, Naw, I wasn't getting up on the table. And he didn't make me neither.' "

"How you know?"

"You know Cat talk the same way in front of men as she do women," he said.

"Yeah."

"You know when she was married to Joe Hunn he broke the window out of his car and come in and said, 'Honey, you got a piece of cardboard?' and she went in and got him a Kotex box. He just as silly as she is though. He used it. People said, 'Man, where you get that thing?' Making men laugh and embarrassing women. I don't see why they didn't stay together, cause they was just alike."

"You never can tell," I said.

He said nothing. Then he said, "You know what I mean. Both. Not silly. But bold. You know."

"Bold silly."

"Well . . . How did he say the scar looked?"

"He said it looked good. I said if this supposed to look good I hate to see one supposed to look bad."

He raised up my blouse. "It looks good," he said.

I put my blouse back in my skirt.

"Did you get a chance to talk to the lawyer for me?"

"Yeah. He said he'll take care of it."

"Well, when he gets ready for me to sign anything, tell him I'll be in there to sign it."

"I told him."

I patted his knee. He smiled a little, but said nothing.

"What do you want, Ursa?"
I looked at him with a slight smile that left quickly.
"What do you mean?"
"What I said. What do you want?"
I smiled again. "What all us Corregidora women want.
Have been taught to want. To make generations." I stopped
smiling.
He looked at me. "What do you want, Ursa?"
"More than yourself?"
He raised me and kissed me very hard.
"I'll let you sleep."
"I don't want to sleep."
"Then rest."
"Okay."
"I'll be back up later and fix us something to eat."
"No, I'll do it."
"No, I want to."
"Okay."
He started to go.
"When the doctor gave you that menu for me, who did
you say you were?"
"I didn't say."
"Who did he *think* you were?"
He didn't say. He went downstairs.

". . . *The important thing is making generations. They
can burn the papers but they can't burn conscious, Ursa.
And that what makes the evidence. And that's what makes
the verdict.*"
"Procreation. That could also be a slave-breeder's way of
thinking."
"But it's not."
"No. And you can't."
"Not anymore, no."

*Gram was standing in the doorway looking down at me.
She looked tall then, because I was little, but Mama said
she wasn't no more than five feet.*

"... *His hair was so dark and greasy straight you could a
swore he was pure Indian, but if you even dare say something, he stick a poker up your ass, a hot coal poker. Naw,
but he wasn't though. He was from over there somewhere
in Portugal. Naw, it wasn't Lisbon. That's the capital. Naw,
I don't know where. He probably didn't even know where.
He was a seaman. Naw, a sea captain. That's why the king
give him lands, and slaves and things, but he didn't hardly
use nothing but the womens. Naw, he wasn't the first that
did it. There was plenty that did it. Make the women fuck
and then take their money. And you know sometimes the
mistresses was doing it too so they could have little pocket
money that their husbands didn't know about. And getting
their brothers and their brother's friends and other mens
they know, you know, and then they make theyselves right
smart money for their purse. Naw, his wife didn't do that.
She sleep with you herself. I guess she didn't wont no
money. Or didn't need none. Or just figure it was all the
same. That hot climate. Nose like a baby hawk. Naw, she
couldn't do a damn thing. Naw, she didn't give him nothing
but a little sick rabbit that didn't live but to be a day old.
So then he just stopped doing it. Naw, she couldn't do a
damn thing."*

"No, because it depends on if it's for you or somebody
else. Your life or theirs."

*I wouldn't take my eyes off her. She kept looking down
at me.*

"What you doing?"
Cat had come in but I hadn't heard her.
"Tadpole said you might be sleeping, but I said I'd just

307

peep in and see and if you was, I wouldn't bother you. He's got right evil these days."

"Yeah. Naw, I wasn't sleeping."

"Just thinking?"

"Yeah."

"I seen you staring wide-eyed at the ceiling, and didn't know if I should disturb that either."

"Naw, come on in."

She came in.

"It's nothing," I said.

She came and sat down on the bed.

"You okay? How did it go with the doctor?"

"He took me off the pills. He wonts me to come back in a couple of weeks though, and then I think I can start working again after that."

"It be good to hear you sing again. Eddy Pace was trash and all they doing down there now is wining and dining. I should say whiskeying."

"I'm sorry. I wish I wasn't being so much trouble to him."

"I didn't mean nothing by you."

"If he didn't have me up here he'd be having a band in."

"Aw, that nigger don't care. He rather have you up here anyway."

I said nothing, then I said, "But seriously, if I don't start feeling better in another week can I come stay with you?"

"Sure. You could've come stayed with me anytime. I just figured things was settled here."

"No."

She said nothing, then patted my knee. "Well, you be awright."

"Mutt still out there?"

"Yeah."

"Yeah, Tad said he was."

"Why you ask me then?"

"No reason."

She looked at me hard.

"Tad's seeing a lawyer for me about the divorce and when he gets ready I have to sign the papers."

"You got Tad seeing him for you?"

"Yeah, why?"

"No reason."

I looked at her, then I said, "I think maybe we might get together, you know, after all this is over."

"Then you don't want to move in with me."

"Yeah, you know, till I'm feeling better. I don't want to be a burden to him."

"You want to be one to me," she said.

I didn't answer.

"Okay," I said finally.

"Okay, what?"

"Okay, I'll stay here."

"Naw, I think it be better if you was over to my place. Sooner the better. But seem like to me you already together. People think you already together."

"Naw, we not. He's been a good friend. I don't care what people think anyway. I never have."

"What Mutt think?"

"Naw, nor what Mutt think. I told you that story. From the day he throwed me down those stairs we not together, and we not coming back together."

"It was an accident."

"You sound like if he was sitting here what he be saying. 'Aw, honey, I was drunk. Aw, honey, it was a accident. I didn't mean to do it. You know I wouldn't've done it. You know I'm sorry. All I wanted to do was take care of you like a husband should.' Now, what good am I for a man?"

"Why don't you ask Tadpole that?"

I told her to go to hell.

She said she was, if I promised I was still coming back with her.

I said nothing.

"Listen, honey, I'ma tell you something seem like you don't know or play like you don't know. Right now's not the time for you to be grabbing at anything. Any woman to be grabbing at anything. Out of fear. I don't know what. Ask yourself how did you feel about Tadpole before all of this happened. I know he's being good to you, but this is a rush job. Just thinking about the two of y'all getting together is a rush job. You know what I mean? He's looked at you and seem like you scared somebody else won't. You a beautiful woman. They be many mens that . . ."

I told her to shut up.

She looked hurt, then she looked evil. "Just listen, will you?" She didn't give me time to say if I would or I wouldn't. "You be taking what you need, but do you think you be giving him what he need?"

I said nothing. She got up and went to the door. Then she said, "But even he can't give you everything you need." Without turning around, she went out the door.

When Tadpole came upstairs to fix us lunch, I said, "I'm going over to Cat's."

He didn't make any of the expressions I thought he would make.

"Do you want me to take you?" he asked.

"Naw, I can take myself," I said.

"I'll take you," he said. "You'll have something to eat first."

"I can get something to eat over there."

"Well, you not." He left me and went back in the kitchen.

"Did Cat Lawson say anything to you?" I asked.

"She said you be staying over there now till you get back up on your feet."

"That all?"

"Yeah."

He brought me some lunch.

"Ain't you eating?"

"Naw, I had something downstairs."

When I finished eating, and was ready to leave, he had one of the boxes and me by the arm and said he'd bring the other box over later.

"Do I get visiting privileges?" he asked as we were going out the door.

"As many as you want."

When we got there, Cat was straightening Jeffy's hair. Jeffy was the girl who stayed with her when her mother worked and sometimes when her mother wasn't working. She couldn't have been more than fourteen. Cat was telling her to hold back her ear when we came in and was straightening along the edge.

"I didn't expect y'all so soon," she said.

"I thought you did," I said.

"Which room she got?" Tadpole asked.

"That one in there," said Cat, nodding to the room to the right of the living room.

"You burned me," Jeffy said.

"Hush."

The house had three other rooms, a kitchen and another bedroom and a bathroom, off to the other side of the living room. That room was the only one on that side. I saw a slop jar over in the corner.

Tadpole took the box back in the bedroom. I followed him in.

"Tadpole, turn back the bed for her, will you? My hands greasy."

"I can do it," I said.

"Tadpole do it."

"Ow," Jeffy said.

"I said hush."

"You burned me."

"Hold your ear. If you'd hold your ear like I told you to I wouldn't a burned you."

"I'm going back and get the other box," Tadpole said.

"Okay."

"Now you can let go," Cat said to Jeffy.

I came back in the front room. Cat was doing the back.

"Ain't you better get undressed and get in bed," she told me.

"I thought I'd sit up for a while," I said, sitting down on the couch.

"What the doctor say?"

"He said whatever I feel like doing."

"I know he didn't say that."

"As long as I don't overdo it."

"Well, you overdone it. Go get in the bed."

"You not my . . ."

"What?"

"Nothing."

"I seen your Sweet Daddy," Jeffy said.

"Hush," Cat said.

"What?"

"I'm just telling her I seen her Sweet Daddy."

"I said to hush up."

"He look like he haven't shaved in about a week."

Cat hit her up side the head, and she jumped out of the chair, crying, and ran out.

"You better get your ass on back in here, girl," Cat said.

"Tha's awright," I said.

"She be back," Cat said.

"I'ma tell Mama," Jeffy sobbed.

"I'ma tell your mama," Cat said. "Now get your ass on back in here."

Jeffy came back in and sat down. There were tears in her eyes, but she wasn't making any noise.

"You don't get twenty-five and automatically be a woman neither," Cat said to me. "You better get *yours* in there too."

I got up and went in the bedroom. I didn't feel like getting evil.

"That how old she is?" Jeffy asked.

"Yeah."

"She don't look it."

Tadpole came back with the other box. He started out without saying anything.

"Make the first visiting day soon," I said softly.

He nodded, and went out.

Cat came to close the bedroom door.

"If these niggers start worrying you," she said, "I might have to move you in the back bedroom."

I said nothing. She closed the door.

About fifteen minutes later, she opened the door again.

"That baby's hard, ain't she? She gone down to her mama's now. She be back up here though, cause Lurene got to work tonight. They put her on the night shift down to the factory."

"Aw."

"They just shifting her every whicha way. I said if I was her I wouldn't stand for it."

"If she didn't stand for it she wouldn't have a job."

"Well, I'm glad I do what I do. I ain't got a license, but leastwise I keep my own hours. And your job, you know. Something like that."

"I don't keep my own hours," I said.

"But you doing something you like doing. You got a

talent. A talent or a craft, that's what I say, and don't have those sons of a bitches hanging on your neck all the time. And daughters of bitches. When I was young I worked in white women's kitchens, so I know how it is. Leastwise the factory ain't a kitchen, but ain't much different. Still got the devil on your back. Leastwise you like what you do."

"Yeah, I like it . . . There's always something you can do to keep your own hours."

"Now we ain't talking about that."

I laughed. "Well . . ."

"Hush."

She sat down in the chair next to the front-room door.

"I suppose I don't *mind* what I do. It ain't like when I was young though, you know."

"You don't seem old."

"I don't know too many people that *seem* old . . . Well, I better get up from here and leave you alone. Talking about niggers bothering you." She got up again. "Something I can get you?"

"Naw, thanks."

"Well, I let you rest. If you wont something, just holler." I said I would.

"He leave you alone, didn't he?"

"Who?"

"Tadpole."

"Yeah, he left me alone." I frowned at her. She frowned back, and closed the door again. Then she peeped back in the door.

"What the doctor say you can eat?"

"Anything."

"I fry you some chicken then for supper."

"Good."

She closed the door.

I settled back in the double bed, and pulled the covers

up to my neck. The bed was high and it was a large empty room, except for a cedar chest and a wardrobe. There was a window facing the street, with dingy white-lace curtains. I slept.

I woke up to the smell of scorched hair and fried chicken. There was a tap on the door. I said, "Come in." It was Jeffy.

"Miss Catherine wonts to know how much do you think you can eat?"

"A couple of pieces."

"That all?"

"I think so."

"What part do you wont?"

"It don't matter."

She closed the door, but not all the way.

"I wont you to take some across the road to Tadpole and down home to your mama, you hear? This bag's Tadpole's and this bag's your mama's. And don't eat none on the way."

"Yes'm."

The screen door banged.

Cat came in with a plate with two pieces of chicken, a wing and a breast, and mashed potatoes and peas and cornbread.

"I can't eat all that much," I said.

"Well, try."

"I thought you just meant a couple of pieces of chicken."

"Well, you got to have stuff to go with it."

I sat up in bed and she put a cloth across my legs and the plate on the cloth.

"Thank you."

She went and sat down on the cedar chest.

"You ate?" I asked.

"Yeah, we awready ate. I looked in before and you was sleeping so hard I didn't wont to wake you."

"This is good."

"Thank you."

I ate for a few moments in silence, grease on my fingers. It was good to get real food again. My stomach had started caving in.

"You know, every time I cook fried chicken I think of that time Joe Hunn and me was married. My brother-in-law invited us over to a after-wedding supper. He wasn't married hisself so he cooked it up hisself. He started cooking it when we got there and then said dinner was ready and seem like to me it couldn't a been more than fifteen minutes, but I didn't say nothing. And then we sat down to eat, and I bit down on a piece and it had blood coming out of it. And Gus, that's his brother, was just saying, 'Good, ain't it?' and Joe was saying, 'Yeah.' I didn't know if Joe was crazy too or just didn't wont to 'fend him. But I put mine back down on the plate and said, 'I don't know about y'all, but this going back in the skillet.' So they let me put theirs back in the skillet too. If they'd have started laughing, I would have sweared it was a joke, but they didn't even crack a smile. Up to the day we separated, I never would let Joe Hunn fry me no chicken."

I laughed.

She said, "Here I am talking about that chicken and you trying to eat. I wasn't thinking I might upset your stomach."

"Naw, you didn't upset it."

"Well, I be in the house if you wont anything. You wont another piece of chicken?"

"Naw thanks, this is fine."

"I don't wont to worry you out of my own house. Call me when you through."

I said I would.

Her chicken was crisp, not bloody. I was thinking how I

never did like to get chicken ready to fry. Somebody else get it ready, then I'd fry it. Down home in the country, Mama used to wring the chickens' necks on a tree stump. I never would look. But when she got it all cut up and washed I'd fry it if she wanted me to. And that time that man sold me that fish and I put it on the tree stump and it started wiggling and jumped in the grass wiggling. I never would fry any more fish after that. Cousin Jesse said she could hear me all the way down the road screaming. She came up to see what was wrong, and then she took it down to her house and fried it for me, but when she brought it back I swear half the fish was gone. That was all right though. I know she wanted to feed them children with it.

Cat came back and took my plate.

"You sure you don't wont no more?"

"Yeah, I'm sure. I'm not sure what this'll do. It was good though. Thank you."

"You got those pills in case you need them, ain't you?"

"Yeah."

She took the plate out.

"She sleep?" It was Tad.

"Naw, she just got through eating."

"Mind if I go in?"

"You just seen her this morning."

"So?"

"Well, knock."

He knocked. I said, "Come in."

"How you feeling?" he asked.

"Okay."

"She treating you all right?"

"Yeah."

He stayed near the door. I told him to come on in.

"Naw, I just came to thank Cat for the chicken she sent over and thought I peep in and see how you was doing."

"I'm okay."
"Eating solid?"
"Yeah."
He went back out. I smiled.
I heard the front door close, then Cat came in.
"That nigger both'ring you?"
"Naw."
"Well, if he bothers you, tell me, and I won't let him come in here."
"You know how I feel."
"I know how you think you feel. But I ain't going into that no more . . . He brought Eddy Pace's group back."
"Did he?"
"Yeah."
"That's good."
"Be bout time for you to go over there if you was on your feet."
"Yeah, the after-supper show. Then go back in the evening. You know that."
She said nothing.
"He across the street?" I asked.
"Yeah, he's over there."
"He don't know I'm here I guess."
"I guess he don't."
"Pull that shade down, will you? And keep it down."
She pulled down the shade.
"All he wont to do is see you start back to work again. Know you on your feet. So he won't feel guilty."
"He got a lifetime of feeling guilty. I don't know how many lifetimes."
"It ain't right you to feel that way. I know he did wrong and you got to suffer the consequences. But he got consequences too."

"He can go out and give other women babies. What kind of consequences he got?"

"Consequences of loving you."

"Shit."

She came away from the window.

"It took you a long enough time to pull that shade down. If you wont him to know where I'm at, why don't you go over and tell him where I'm at."

"I don't care if he know or not, cause it ain't none of my business. But I guess I don't wont him to know. 'Cause if he don't cause trouble, *you* will. All he wonts to do is *see* you. But I don't know what you wont."

"All I wont is not to see that nigger. He can go to Kocomo for all I care."

"Yeah," she said.

"Yeah."

"It bother you though, don't it?" She grinned. "Trying to make it with Tadpole McCormick."

"I ain't trying. I have made it, for your information. What's wrong with Tadpole?"

"It ain't what's wrong with *him*, it's what's wrong with *you*. And he's too blind to see it. That's what's wrong with him. Every since he got that place and seen you singing there he's been in love with you. I don't doubt he *got* the place cause you was there. But you ain't paid him half a mind till this. It was always Mutt Thomas, Mutt Thomas, Mutt Thomas. I ain't even going to say nothing about the men, cause that ain't my place. But if you didn't have eyes to see *then*, you ain't got eyes to see *now*."

"I see what I need to see."

"Yeah, that's probably your trouble."

She turned her ass to me and went out.

"Fuck you," I said.

"You can't."

"Y'all hush." It was Lurene's voice. The screen door banged. "You know that woman's sick in there. You ought to wait."

"Sick or not sick they's things she's got to be told."

"Shhh."

Cat didn't shhh, she talked louder. "I know womens that's had it out been up by now. I don't even believe *that* no more. Cause they kept her down to St. Joseph long enough before she even got out."

"Well, she be up soon, you get evil enough," Lurene said. "Jeff be up in a little while. I got her down there drying the dishes, and I told her to come on up here. Well, I see you tomorrow morning then. I ain't hardly got no sleep and they going to have me standing up all night. You know Philip Lorry, the one I said work out there?"

"Yeah."

"I think he's started to get sweet on me, honey."

"Well, you need something to make working out there worth it."

"Yeah, don't I though. Well, I see you."

"Awright."

"Here she is. You be good now."

"Yes ma'am. Here the key."

"You lock it awright?"

"Yes ma'am."

"Awright, see y'all. Ain't you going to kiss me? . . . See you, Cat."

"Awright."

"If that nigger love me he wouldn't've throwed me down the steps," I called.

"What?" She came to the door.

"I said if that nigger loved me he wouldn't've throwed me down the steps."

"I know niggers love you do worse than that," she said.

"Miss Catherine, can I have another piece of chicken?" Jeffy said.

"Yeah, go on in and get it. Then you go on in there and sleep on the floor. You got to sleep on the floor tonight."

"She don't have to sleep on the floor, she can sleep in here with me," I said.

Cat said nothing. "Yeah, I said yeah," she told Jeffy.

When it was time to go to bed, Jeffy came in with a blanket. She started putting her blanket down on the throw rug on the floor.

"Honey, I said you could sleep up here with me. You don't have to sleep down there on the floor."

"Miss Catherine said for me to sleep down here."

"Well, I said you can sleep up here."

I turned back the sheets for her to get in. She left the blanket on the floor and came and got in the bed. I could smell fried chicken.

"You wiped your hands, didn't you?"

"Yeah."

"You yes ma'am your mama and yes ma'am Miss Catherine, how come you don't yes ma'am me?"

"You ain't nothing but twenty-five. I got a sister up in Detroit that's twenty-five. If I yes ma'am her she slap the shit out of me."

I said nothing.

"You settled?" I asked.

"Yeah."

I turned the light out.

"I seen your nigger pacing up and down over there."

"He ain't my nigger."

"Well, he used to be."

"Used to ain't now."

"You just scared of him, that's all."

"I like to see the day I was scared of Mutt Philmore Thomas."

"That his middle name?" she laughed.

I said nothing.

"I bet you be scared if I said I was going over there and tell him you was over here."

"You better not. I might not be that much older than you, honey, but I know how to slap shit too."

She said nothing. I thought I had hushed her, but then she said, "See if I don't."

"See if I don't tell your mama I seen you over there in Hawkins alley with that Logan boy."

"Naw, that was Luella you seen with Wayne. I was just watching."

"Well, that means you twice as nasty."

"I bet you was fucking before I was born. How much fucking you think you goin do now?"

It was my turn to say nothing.

"It don't mean you *can't*," I explained. "It just means . . ."

"I heard Mama talking bout women like that. Mess up their minds and then fuck up their pussy."

"You too young to talk like that."

"You too young to have it took out of you too. Tha's what mama said. She said, 'Ain't that awful and young as she is too. Jeff, now don't you go over there both'ring that woman neither, cause she got enough trouble.' "

"Nigger, get out of here."

"You said I could sleep with you."

"Then shut up and sleep. I told you I know how to slap shit too."

"You supposed to be sick. You ain't sick."

"I will be if you don't shut up."

"See if I don't tell that nigger of yours."

I started to slap her. I was going to if she said another word. She must have felt it because she didn't say nothing else. She started breathing hard, and then she must have been sleeping. I turned away from her and slept.

I was drowsy, but I felt her hands on my breasts. She was feeling all on me up around my breasts. I shot awake and knocked her out on the floor. It wasn't even daylight yet. It couldn't have been more than three o'clock. There was a smell of vomit in the room, like when you suck your thumb.

"Naw, bitch, you get the hell out of here," I said. "You take that goddamn blanket and get the goddamn hell out of here."

She was crying, not from anything I said, but she must have skinned her ass when she hit the floor. I turned on the light and she was sucking her arm and getting the blanket and crying. I kept calling her a goddamn bull, but I didn't like what else I was wondering. I was wondering how Cat Lawson got her to mind. Because that wasn't the kind of kid that would respect anybody on account of age.

Jeffy stumbled out the door.

"What's going on in nere?" I heard Cat say. "What you do?"

Jeffy didn't say nothing. Catherine came into the room, rubbing her eyes.

"What happen? What she do?" She sat down on the cedar chest, as if she already suspected what she did.

"She started feeling on me all up around here and I knocked her off on the floor," I said.

"I knowed she was like that, tha's why I told her to sleep in here on the floor."

"Well, you should've told me she was like that before and

I wouldn't have said she could come in here and sleep with me. Why in the hell didn't you tell me she was like that before?"

"I told her to sleep on the floor. You should've let her sleep on the floor."

"Well, she seem like she too young to be like that. How the hell was I suppose to know? I didn't wont the child sleeping on the damn floor and catch pneumonia."

"It's a hot night."

"Well. She can catch pneumonia of the asshole for all I care."

"Don't worry, she catch it."

I couldn't restrain myself. "What, you goin give it to her?"

She looked at me, drowsy, and hurt and angry.

"I told her to sleep on the floor," she said.

I said nothing. She got up as if waiting for me to say something, but I still said nothing. Before she left, she cut me a hard look. I gave up wondering. I knew if Jeffy had got in the bed with her and started pulling that shit, she would have knocked her on the floor too. She would have knocked her past the floor.

It wasn't so much how much fucking I was going to do now, I was thinking, but the consequences of that fucking. Shit. Cat telling me about the consequences of him loving me. Shit. What the hell did that mean? And her story. What about her and Joe Hunn? If I hadn't stopped wondering when she gave me that hard-as-steel look I would've guessed that story. Maybe it's just a man can't stand to have a woman as hard as he is. If he couldn't support her in money, he'd be wanting to support her in spirit. And what if I'd thrown Mutt Thomas down those stairs instead, and done away with the source of his sex, or inspiration, or whatever the hell it is for a man, what would he feel now? At least a woman's still got the hole. Look, nigger, I still got my hole. Finger-pop it. Your mama's a bitch, she was laid in a ditch. Naw, dropped you in one. And what they had to do in those days. I always get back to that. The tobacco fields or coffee ones. Hard because you have to be, but still those tender-eyed women and hands tender behind tobacco calluses with their men. Hurt you into tenderness finally. Is it more his fault than mine? Naw, when you start thinking that way. Naw, that nigger's to blame. What's bothering me? Great Gram, because I can't make generations. I remember everything you told me, Great Gram and Gram too and.

Good night, Ursa, baby. Good night, Irene. *Honey, I remember when you was a warm seed inside me, but I tried not to bruise you. Don't bruise any of your seeds. I won't, Mama. I never told you how Great Gram had Gram. She thought she had to go to the toilet, and then something told her not to go outside to the outhouse like she was going to, and then she squat down on the chamber pot. And then that's how she had your Gram, coming out in the slop jar. That's how we all begin, remember that. That's how we all begin. A mud ditch or a slop jar or hit the floor or the ground. It's all the same. But you got to make generations, you go on making them anyway. And when the ground and the sky open up to ask them that question that's going to be ask. They think it ain't going to be ask, but it's going to be ask. They have the evidence and give the verdict too. They think they hid everything. But they have the evidence and give the verdict too.* You said that, Mama. *I know I said it, and I'm going to keep saying it.*
"Come in here."

I was out in the yard playing with the little boy from across the street. He'd bet me I didn't know how to play doctor. I bet him I did. We'd made a seesaw by putting a board across a tree stump. I lay across the board on my belly, and he raised up my dress. Mama saw us.

"Come in here. Go on home, Henry."

She jerked me in the back door by the arm, and slammed the door.

"Don't you know what that boy was doing? He was feeling up your asshole."

"I couldn't feel it."

"If I could see it, I know you could feel it."

"Mama, I couldn't feel it."

"Get on in here. Have people looking at you. What do you think, the neighbors ain't got eyes? What was he using?"

"I didn't feel nothing."

"Shut up. If I even think I see anything else, I'll beat you."

I bet you were fucking before I was born.

Before you was thought.

"Ursa, what makes your hair so long?"

"I got evil in me."

Corregidora's evil.

Ole man, he just kept rolling . . .

Cat knocked on the door. I said, "Come in." She came in, but stood near the door. It was the next day or, rather, later the same day. I was sitting up in bed.

Cat stood looking at me, then she said, "I'm sorry. I should have told you that was why I didn't want her in here."

"Tha's awright. It's all water under the bridge now."

"I still should have told you she was like that."

"I'd rather not talk about it."

"I just came in to see how many eggs you wont for breakfast."

"Two. As long as you don't send it by her."

"I won't. Anyway, her mama come and got her at seven."

"Does Lurene know?"

"I don't know what Lurene know. If she do, she haven't told me. They say Jeffy's daddy, something was wrong with him. But I didn't know him myself."

"You ask me, something must be wrong with all of 'em."

"Naw, don't get into that. Lurene's crazy about men as you are."

"Yeah, I heard her talking about some dude she got at work."

"Yeah, well, he help to make her day. Or I should say make her night."

I laughed. "Working night shift, he have to make her day."

"Well, I go fix breakfast."

"Cat, I don't think I can stay here."

"I make sure Jeffy don't even look at you while you here. I keep her outter here."

"It ain't that . . . I shouldn't stay here."

"You wont to be over there where that nigger is, don't you?"

"I expect to start back to work in a day or two," I said.

"Well, you stay here till you start back then."

"All right, a day or two," I said.

"Well, Tadpole be up in the air."

"What?"

"Hear you be singing again."

"I just hope I'm as good. It's been a long time."

"You be just as good."

"They didn't say anything about my throat. They didn't say it did anything to my throat."

"If it did they would've said something. You mean you ain't sing nothing since it happened?"

"Naw."

"Well, you sing for me tonight. Ain't use worrying for nothing."

I said nothing.

"I'll keep her out of here," she said, and went to fix the eggs.

"Trouble in mind, I'm blue, but I won't be won't be blue always," I sang and stopped.

"Go on."

I was sitting up in bed. She was on the cedar chest. I went on and finished the song.

She smiled and clapped.

"It didn't sound like it used to," I said.

"Your voice sounds a little strained, that's all. But if I hadn't heard you before, I wouldn't notice anything. I'd still be moved. Maybe even moved more, because it sounds like you been through something. Before it was beautiful too, but you sound like you been through more now. You know what I mean?"

"I know what you mean, but it's still changed."

"Not for the worse. Like Ma, for instance, after all the alcohol and men, the strain made it better, because you could tell what she'd been through. You could hear what she'd been through."

"Well, I don't have to worry about the men," I said.

"That'd make you go through more, not having a man," she said, and looked as if she'd wished she hadn't said it.

I went on as if I hadn't heard it. "Well, we'll see when I go on tomorrow."

"Tomorrow?"

"Well, okay, day after tomorrow."

"Okay. And first night make it just supper or evening, but not both. I'll speak to Tad if you don't."

"I don't think he'd let me sing both anyway."

"Naw, he wouldn't."

"You sure it's okay?"

"It's more than okay."

She left me. I lay back and tried to sleep, but couldn't. I started humming the part about taking my rocking chair down by the river and rocking my blues away. What she said about the voice being better because it tells what you've been through. Consequences. It seems as if you're not singing the past, you're humming it. Consequences of what? Shit, we're all consequences of something. Stained with another's past as well as our own. Their past in my blood. I'm a blood. *Are you mine, Ursa, or theirs?* What he would ask. What would I ask now? Do you want to see me? Naw, I don't want to see you, I want to screw you. When he wanted to make up with me he'd always ask if I remembered such and such a thing. Do you remember that time we . . . Hell, yes, I remember. Blues songs and stroking your neck and laughter and sighs inside knees that made us hold each other tighter. When he got back from work he'd ask me to rub his thighs. Do you feel how tight the muscles are? Yes. My hand on his belly then. The mark of his birth. I'd tell him, I have a birthmark between my legs. That would make him laugh. But it's your fault all my seeds are wounded forever. No warm ones, only bruised ones, not even bruised ones. No seeds. Let me in between your legs. It ain't a pussy down there, it's a whole world.

Talking about *his* pussy. Asking me to let him see his pussy. Let me feel my pussy. The center of a woman's being. Is it? No seeds. Is that what snaps away my music, a harp string broken, guitar string, string of my banjo belly. Strain in my voice. Yes, I remember your hands on my ass. Your damn hands on my ass. That vomity feeling when they squeezed my womb out. Is that the way you treat someone you love? Even my clenched fists couldn't stop the fall. That old man still howls inside me. You asked me how did I get to be so beautiful. It wasn't *him*. No, not Corregidora. And my spirit, you said, like knives dancing. My veins are centuries meeting. You scratched behind my ear and drew blood and then kissed where you scratched. You can't kiss where you scratched anymore. No, anyway, I don't believe what Cat said your reasons are. You don't treat love that way. When you came and heard my music you requested songs, and then when you had me alone, you requested more than my songs. I can still feel your fucking inside me. If it wasn't for your fucking I. When do you sing the blues? Every time I ever want to cry, I sing the blues. Or would there be glasses of tears? Yes, there would be spilled glasses. I came to you, open and wounded. And you said, Sing for me, goddamn it, sing. Your plate was stained with flies, and you kept requesting songs. I sang to you out of my whole body.

"Urs, do you remember?"

"Yes, I remember. Who told you I was here?"

"The girl did."

"I thought she would, the little bitch."

"If she hadn't, I wouldn't have found you."

"You never lost me."

The shit you can dream. I struggled out of sleep. My eyes felt as tight as fists, but they opened. Light came in through the yellow shade. The shit you can dream. They say it's what you really feel, but it ain't what you really feel.

I wondered if Cat was up. I got up and put on my robe. But I didn't want to see that Jeffy if she was out there, so I sat down on the cedar chest and waited. I still felt sleepy, but I knew I couldn't sleep. I held my arms around my belly. Then I got up and opened the door and went out in the living room. Jeffy wasn't there. I had expected to see her in there. The clock on the mantelpiece said it was close to five o'clock. I wrapped my robe around me and stood in the living room. Then I heard Cat talking.

"If you bother her again I'll give you a fist to fuck."

"I ain't going to bother her again."

"I said if you do you got my fist to fuck."

Then there was silence.

"I could've told you she wouldn't."

"What? You ask her?"

There was a loud slap, and then low crying.

"Laugh now."

"Please, Miss Catherine."

"I said, 'Laugh now.' "

Low crying.

"I didn't go in there to do it. I must've did it in my sleep."

"Shit if you did."

Silence.

"Shit."

"I grab the shit out of you, you little nigger."

"Shit."

"Hush."

I had eased back to the door and by the time the "hush" came, I'd stepped back into the bedroom.

"What is it?"

"Hush."

Silence.

I sat on the cedar chest with my robe open, then I got dressed. I think if Cat or Jeffy had come into the room then, I would've got evil. I would have got right evil. It wasn't until years later that I realized it might have been because of my own fears, the things I'd thought about in the hospital, my own worries about what being with a man would be like again, and whether I really had the nerve to try. But then I just felt evil.

I left the boxes at the foot of the bed. I put my bed-clothes and cosmetics in a sack and went out the door and across the street. I'd send Tadpole for the boxes later. The front door was locked and I went up the back-stairs and knocked on the door. It took him a long time to come.

"Ursa, baby, what you doing over here? You awright?"

"I want to come in," I said.

I must have been looking hateful. He asked me what was wrong.

"A lot of shit," I said. He'd been sleeping on the bed where I'd been sleeping when I was there. I went and sat down at the foot of the bed. He kept standing, looking at me.

"What do you mean?"

"Well, you know Jeffy stay over there."

"Yeah."

I didn't say what I was going to. "She just stay over there. I'm taking up Jeffy's space."

"That ain't why you here," he said.

I started to tell him, but didn't. I only told him about Jeffy in the bed, feeling all on my breasts. I didn't tell him what I'd overheard. I didn't tell him what Cat was. I didn't tell him why I'd really left.

"She should have told me Jeffy was like that before, and I wouldn't have said she could come in and sleep with me.

Cat knew she was like that, that's why she told her to sleep on the floor."

"She could have told her to sleep on the couch," Tadpole said.

"Cat don't allow nobody to sleep on the couch, because she says it's the only decent thing she got and she wonts to keep it decent."

"And you ain't going back over there?"

"Naw."

"I guess you wont me to go over there and get your stuff for you?"

"Little later. If you don't mind."

He said nothing.

"She seem like she too young to be like that," I said.

"Well, they start off young."

He came over to the bed and sat down.

"Sit closer to me," he said.

I sat closer.

He pulled me closer.

"Does it hurt?"

"Yes, a little."

"Did they say you could do it?"

"Yes, we can do it."

"How does it feel now?"

"Go on."

"How did you sleep?" Tad asked.

I said nothing. I put my cheek against his chest. He said it was time for him to go down and open up. I watched him rise.

After a while I got up.

"I thought you'd still sleep," he said, when he came back. I'd made the bed, but hadn't folded it back to be a couch.

"I'll just rest today," I said. "I want to start work this evening."

"Do you think you're ready? I don't think you're ready."

"I feel like it. The doctor said whenever I felt like it."

"After two weeks, he said."

"I feel like it now. I want to, Tad."

"No more than an hour, and only one show."

"The evening one."

"Okay. And I'll have them get a chair for you."

"I never sat down singing."

"Well, tonight you will."

"No, not tonight either."

"If you seem tired or anything I'll just tell them the show's over."

"I won't. I'll be okay."

"You rest a lot then." He unmade the bed.

I looked at him.

"I'll feel better if you rest a lot," he said, and went back downstairs.

I'd put on my robe but hadn't dressed. I sat back down on the bed. Then I started singing about trouble in mind. Still the new voice. The one Cat said you could hear what I'd been through in. I tried not to think about the rest of what I'd heard Cat say.

They call it the devil blues. It ride your back. It devil you. I bit my lip singing. I troubled my mind, took my rocker down by the river again. It was as if I wanted them to see what he'd done, hear it. All those blues feelings. That time I asked him to try to understand my feeling ways. That's what I called it. My feeling ways. My voice felt like it was screaming. What do they say about pleasure mixed in the pain? That's the way it always was with him. The pleasure somehow greater than the pain. My voice screaming for him to take me. And when he would, I'd draw him down into the bottom of my eyes. They watched me. I felt as if they could see my feelings somewhere in the bottom of my eyes.

I saw Mutt's cousin Jimmy come in while I was singing about trouble. He sat down at a table. I was singing my last two songs. Singing and trying not to see the face outside the window, troubling my eyes. When I finished, Jim came up to me. "Jimmy, how are you?" I asked. He asked me to come have a drink with him. I nodded and went over with him and sat down. I saw Tadpole watching us, but I didn't look back at Tadpole. I didn't look at the man outside the window.

"Do it trouble you me in here?" Jim asked.

"Why should it? You ain't him."

"You did fine. It's good to see you back."

I said nothing. Then I said, "Tell him to go away, Jim."

"He worries."

"Tell him I'm all right, and he can go away."

"He got the papers from your lawyer and signed them. He said if that's what you wont."

"Yes."

"It ain't what he wonts."

"I never did know what he wonted."

"He just wont you to come outside and say something to him."

"I already cussed him out. In the hospital I cussed him out. I thought everybody I seen was him and I cussed everybody I seen out. I kept looking up cussing everybody."

"He said he go away. He just wont you to come out and say something to him before he go away."

"I'm not going out there and say nothing to him, Jim."

He said nothing. He sipped his drink.

335

"I guess he be going away without it then."

"Don't do that, Jim. Don't try to draw my pity. It ain't there."

"It's there."

"What do you mean?"

"It's there. It's just turned all inside."

I wanted to slap him but didn't.

"I never have pitied myself and never will," I said.

"You pitied yourself when you left Bracktown and came to the city and you been pitying yourself ever since."

"Shit. Don't try to make it easy for him, Jim. I never thought of you that way."

"You never thought of me anyway," he said. He took another sip.

I watched him, but said nothing.

"What man was you singing to now?" he asked.

"What?"

"Once you told me that when you sang you always had to pick out a man to sing to. And when Mutt started coming in, you kept picking out him to sing to. And then when y'all was married, you had your man to sing to. You said that you felt that the others only listened, but that he heard you."

I said nothing. Then, "Don't worry about it."

"I ain't."

"Well, don't."

"I think there's your old man."

"What?"

"Tadpole Mac-I-want-my-woman-back giving me the evil eye. I think he wants you." He finished his drink and stood up.

I kept looking at him. I wouldn't look at the window, or at Tadpole, behind the bar.

"Thank you," he said.

"For what?"

"I enjoyed the music."

I rolled my eyes at him, but looked back at him.

"He told me to ask you something. He said you know what it meant."

"Ask me what?"

"What's a husband for?"

I took my eyes off him.

"It'll keep hurting, Urs."

I kept my eyes off him. He started towards the door.

"Him or me?" I called.

He went out. When I looked to see if Mutt was still there, he wasn't.

Tadpole came from behind the bar.

"You better get upstairs," he said.

He didn't ask what Jim wanted. I thought he would, but he didn't.

I got up, tired, but trying not to show it.

"You coming up?" I asked.

"I got to close up first. I be up. Do you want me to take you up?"

"Naw."

Tad went back to the bar. I saw men watching me as I walked across the room.

I went upstairs and undressed, put on my robe, but didn't get in bed.

"Songs are devils. It's your own destruction you're singing. The voice is a devil."

"Naw, Mama. You don't understand. Where did you get that?"

"Unless your voice is raised up to the glory of God."

"I don't know where you got that."

But still I'll sing as you talked it, your voice humming,

337

sing about the Portuguese who fingered your genitals. His pussy. "The Portuguese who bought slaves paid attention only to the genitals." Slapped you across the cunt till it was bluer than black. Concubine daughter.

"Where did you get those songs? That's devil's music."

"I got them from you."

"I didn't hear the words."

Then let me give witness the only way I can. I'll make a fetus out of grounds of coffee to rub inside my eyes. When it's time to give witness, I'll make a fetus out of grounds of coffee. I'll stain their hands.

Everything said in the beginning must be said better than in the beginning.

I didn't know what time it was when Tadpole came up.

"I thought you'd be in bed."

"Naw."

"Thank you for waiting for me."

I said nothing. He got undressed and came and sat beside me.

"You were beautiful, honey," he said. His hand went under my robe, stroking my shoulder.

"I know what they must have been saying about my voice," I said.

He shook his head. "It sounded like it had sweat in it. Like you were pulling everything out of yourself. You were beautiful, sweet."

"Did you see him?"

"Yeah, I saw him."

"I thought he might try to get in."

"Naw, he wasn't going to try to do that."

He still didn't ask me what Jim wanted. I was glad. His hands were gentle hard on my belly, then stroking my thighs.

"I love you," he said.

I said nothing. I was thinking I'd only wanted him to love me without saying anything about it. Cat had told me enough. I was grateful he didn't ask me the same question.

"What did you and Jim talk about?" he asked finally.

"He wanted me to come out and talk. Mutt did."

"And you didn't."

"He says Mutt's released me."

He was stroking my thigh.

"You heard what I said," he said.

"Yes."

"I want you to be my wife."

I nodded, but he wasn't looking.

"Did you hear what I said?"

"Yes. I mean, yes I'll marry you."

He drew me into bed.

"Are you relaxed now?" he asked.

I said yes I was relaxed now. I started to tell him Jim said Mutt wasn't coming back, but I didn't. Tadpole got between my legs.

"What's a husband for?"

"Somebody to give your piece of ass to."

"Mutt, just suppose something was in there when they took it out? What would you feel then?"

"Was something in there?"

"Just suppose."

"Don't make any promises you can't keep."

"... They would bend down with their fingers feeling up your pussy."

"You don't care if you ever see me again, do you?"

"Naw, I don't care."

"What do Mutt do?"

"He works in tobacco."

"What do you remember?"
"I could feel your thing. I could smell you in my nostrils."
What do blues do for you?
It helps me to explain what I can't explain.

I was already awake when he woke up. He looked over at me and rubbed under my eyes.
"You dark under your eyes," he said.
"That's mascara."
"Aw."
He touched my cheek.
"Do you know what your eyes do?"
"No."
"They make a man feel like he wants to climb inside them."
Fall to the bottom of my eyes. What will you do there?
"Can I do the supper show tonight?" I asked.
"Not unless you check with Dr. Stevens first."
"He said I should gradually increase time."
"Not your kind of gradual. You saw the chair I had sitting there for you."
"Yeah, I saw it."
"I think you ought to go tell Dr. Stevens you working awready."
"I feel like it."
"I still think you should go over there. I'll drive you over there as soon as I get things started and Sal gets here. Otherwise, I won't feel right."
I said okay I'd go.

"You pushed it, didn't you? Started to work now."
"I had to."
"How do you feel?"

"I'm all right."

"Well, the nurse'll take care of you. I'll be in in a minute."

I went into the examining room and undressed and got up on the table. The doctor came in. He started feeling my belly, feeling places and asking me if it hurt. I kept saying Naw.

"Did you get tired out last night?" he asked.

I said Naw.

"Well, there doesn't seem to be anything wrong. Any more nausea?"

"Naw."

"Well, get dressed. Stop back and see me before you leave."

I got dressed and went back into the doctor's office.

"I'm going to put you on some iron pills anyway."

He wrote out a prescription.

"Have you started back having sexual relations yet?"

"Yes, why? Is there something wrong with it?"

"No, there's nothing wrong with it," he said. "But just don't push it either."

He handed me the prescription.

"I don't think you need to come back for, say, three weeks. And we'll see how the work's going. Don't push your time too much. Like I said before. A little bit every night. I'd say don't push it more than a half an hour extra each time."

"I wanted to do the supper show."

"Forty-five minutes, then, each show. Then that'd give you time to rest in between."

I thanked him and started out.

"Make an appointment with the nurse, will you?"

"Okay."

I made an appointment, and then Tad and I went outside.

"What did he say?"

"He said there was nothing wrong with me. He wants me to get these iron pills."

Tad took the prescription and said he'd stop and get it filled on the way home.

I sang the supper show. There was no Mutt in the window. And in the evening, there was no Mutt. But when I got to the last couple of songs, Jim came in and sat down. When I finished I went over to the table.

"Mutt send you here to watch me?" I asked.

"I got just as much right to be here as anybody else," he said. He'd ordered a beer and was drinking.

"It's about closing time," I said.

"I just come in here to get me a little beer," he said. "I ain't studying you or Mutt."

"He left me when he throwed me down those steps. I didn't leave him." I hadn't sit down. I was standing, speaking low so I wouldn't draw attention.

"I don't know what's wrong with you, woman," he said loud. People turned and looked.

I was embarrassed.

"Okay, Jim," I said, again low. I could feel my eyebrows pulling together. "You got just as much right to be here as anybody, you hear."

"You trying to get dangerous?"

"Naw, I'm not trying to get dangerous," I said. I walked away.

When I got upstairs, Tadpole came in after me.

"What's that about?"

"He's just being a bastard."

"Wont me to bar *him* too?"

I didn't like the way he said it. I looked at him.

"Naw, he's got just as much right to be here as anybody," I said.

"He bothering you about Mutt?"

"Naw, he didn't say nothing about Mutt."

"I'll let you turn in," he said.

"What if I'd said yes?"

"I'd go ask him what right's he got to be here."

I didn't know if he were joking or not. He wasn't smiling. He went back downstairs.

I took one of my iron pills. I swallowed it and closed my eyes. I wanted a song that would touch me, touch my life *and* theirs. A Portuguese song, but not a Portuguese song. A new world song. A song branded with the new world. I thought of the girl who had to sleep with her master and mistress. Her father, the master. Her daughter's father. The father of her daughter's daughter. How many generations? Days that were pages of hysteria. Their survival depended on suppressed hysteria. She went and got her daughter, womb swollen with the child of her own father. How many generations had to bow to his genital fantasies? They were fishermen and planters. And you with the coffee-bean face, what were you? You were sacrificed. They knew you only by the signs of your sex. They touched you as if you were magic. They ate your genitals. And you, Grandmama, the first mulatto daughter, when did you begin to feel yourself in your nostrils? And, Mama, when did you smell your body with your hands?

"Was your mama mulatto?" Mutt asked once.

"I'm darker than her."

"Did that question make you mad?"

"No."

"You look mad."

"I'm not. It's a long story. Too long for now."

"Will you tell me sometime?"

"Yes."

I never really told him. I gave him only pieces. A few more pieces than I'd given Tadpole, but still pieces.

"Your pussy's a little gold piece, ain't it, Urs? My little gold piece."

"Yes."

"Ursa, I'm worried about you, you so dark under your eyes."

He tried to tell me I was working too hard, wasn't getting enough sleep, said that was another reason he wanted me to stop working at Happy's—besides the men. I told him my eyes weren't dark. I told him it was just the mascara. But then he tried to rub it off, and it wouldn't come off.

"Why did you lie, baby?"

And that time he had his cousin take a picture of me and him, and I kept staring at the picture.

He said, "We look good, don't we, honey?"

I got so embarrassed because it was me I was looking at, not *us*. I handed him back the picture and he put it on the mirror. But when he wasn't there I'd come by the bureau and just look at it. I'd never look when Mutt was home. But I knew why I was looking. Because I realized for the first time I had what all those women had. I'd always thought I was different. *Their* daughter, but somehow different. Maybe less Corregidora. I don't know. But when I saw that picture, I knew I had it. What my mother and my mother's mother before her had. The mulatto women. Great Gram was the coffee-bean woman, but the rest of us . . . But I *am* different now, I was thinking. I have everything they had, except the generations. I can't make generations. And even if I still had my womb, even if the first baby *had* come—what would I have done then? Would I have kept it up? Would I have been like *her*, or *them*?

"Did they have any other children?" I'd asked Mama once when they weren't there. I'd been afraid to ask when they were there, because I'd asked Great Gram once when I was real small if Grandmama had any brothers or sisters, and she'd given me this real hateful look.

Mama looked at me for a moment, at first like she wasn't going to answer, then she said, "I think there was some boys. I think they told me there was some boys, but Corregidora sold the boys off."

"Why?"

"Don't ask *them* that. The only reason I'm telling you is so you won't ask them."

"Ursa, wake up Ursa, baby."

He was stroking my hair.

"You must have been having a nightmare."

He got into bed with me, stroking my hair.

"Was it the old man again?"

"Yes."

He stroked my hair. "I'll stay with you," he said.

My voice was dancing, slow and blue, my voice was dancing, but I was saying nothing. I dreamed with my eyes open. All the Corregidora women with narrow waists and high cheekbones and wide hips. All the Corregidora women dancing. And he wanted me. He grabbed my waist.

"Ain't even took my name. You Corregidora's, ain't you? Ain't even took my name. You ain't my woman."

"You had a bad night, didn't you?"

"Yes."

"Get their devils off your back. Not yours, *theirs*."

I said nothing. I pretended I didn't know what he meant.

Tadpole arranged things with the justice of the peace and we were married. Tadpole wanted Cat Lawson to be the witness. I said Naw, then I finally conceded, because I couldn't tell him why not. I didn't know how it would be, because I was finding it difficult to even say anything to her. And I felt that she must have suspected why I left. I hadn't been over there since the morning I'd walked out, and she hadn't been to visit me. She scarcely said anything before the ceremony, and then when we were driving back, she didn't say a word.

"Cat got your tongue?" Tadpole asked.

"Yeah, I got my own tongue," she said. She was sitting on the side by the window. I was in the middle.

"You happy for us, ain't you?" he asked.

"You know I wish you all the happiness in the world," Cat said.

I didn't say anything.

When we got home, Cat said, "You can just drop me off here."

"You coming in and have a drink with us, ain't you?"

"Naw, Tadpole, it's too early in the day for me."

"Since when?"

Cat looked at me, but I said nothing.

"Come on," Tad said.

"Well, awright. I just have a nip though."

We got out of the car and went inside. Tadpole had Sal's husband, Thedo, take over at the bar while we were gone. His real name was Theodore, but everybody called him Thedo.

"Thedo, some champagne," said Tadpole.

"I just have some plain old Kentucky bourbon myself," said Cat.

"Naw, I got a bottle down there especially for the occasion," said Tadpole. "Thedo."

Thedo got out the champagne and poured.

"If I get a bellyache it's y'all's fault."

"This is delicate stuff," said Tadpole.

"Well, my stomach ain't been used to delicate."

Tadpole laughed. I drank. Then I said, "Honey, I think I'm going upstairs. I'm a little tired."

"Awright, baby," he said, frowning.

Cat was looking at me, but I didn't look at her.

"So long, Cat," I said, without looking at her, to make it sound right.

"Sure, see you around," Cat said.

I got up from the stool.

"All women just married act funny?" I heard Tad ask.

"Yeah," Cat answered.

It was a short time after I came up that there was a knock on the door. I knew who it was before she opened.

"Can I come in?" she asked.

"You already are," I said. I was sitting on the bed, getting out of my stockings. I laid them on the chair, then I took them off the chair, and put them on the bed beside me. Cat came in and sat down in the chair. I didn't look up at her at first. Then I looked up at her. She was looking at me calmly, but I could tell she was hurt. I was hurt too. She was sweaty from drinking.

"You look flushed," I said.

She said nothing. Then she said, "I heard you in there that morning." Her voice was steadier than I thought it might be, all the time I'd imagined such a talk.

"Did you?" I said. I had nothing else to say.

"It was easier not to let you know I heard you then," she said.

I said nothing this time.

"I want you to know I heard you now."

"What does it matter?" I asked.

"Don't make me feel clumsier than I already do," she said.

"I didn't know you felt that way," I said coolly now. She said nothing.

"Do you feel good treating me this way?" she asked.

"No, I don't feel good about any of it," I said.

There was silence. She sat looking at me. I'd stopped looking at her again. I could feel her flutter as if she wanted to say something, but she didn't. I wouldn't make it easy. I waited.

Then she said finally, "You don't know what it's like to feel foolish all day in a white woman's kitchen and then have to come home and feel foolish in the bed at night with your man. I wouldn't a mind the other so much if I didn't have to feel like a fool in the bed with my man. You don't know what that means, do you?"

I said nothing. She was crying but they were dry tears.

"I wanted to be able to come home to my own bed and not feel foolish. You don't know what it feels like."

She was looking at me, expecting something. She wanted me to tell her that I knew what it was like, but I wouldn't tell her. Yes, I know what it feels like. I remembered how his shoulders felt when he was going inside me and I had my hands on his shoulders, but I also remembered that night I was exhausted with wanting and I waited but he didn't turn toward me and I kept waiting and wanting him and I got close to him up against his back but he still wouldn't turn to me and then I lay on my back and tried hard to sleep and I finally slept and in the morning I waited and still he didn't and I thought in the morning he would but he didn't and I waited but the clock got him up and he went off to work and I lay there still waiting. I was no longer even angry with waiting. I just lay there saying don't make me use my fingers, and then I got up too. Yes, I could tell her what it feels like. *Do I have to wait until in the morning? Don't punish me this way. What's a husband for? Don't you feel like a man?* And wanting to cry and not wanting him to see me and turning over against the wall until sweat came out of my eyes but never wanting him to hear me cry.

"I didn't wont to be a fool in front of them and then have to come home and be a fool with him too. Couldn't even get in my own bed and not be a fool and have him making me feel like a fool too."

Two swollen plums for eyes. What are you doing to the girl? I wanted to ask. What about when it comes her time? Do you know what *I* mean? But she was telling me about Mr. and Mrs. Thomas Hirshorn and something that happened in the kitchen. She was a young woman, about my age. She lived in during the week and every morning at six o'clock she had to get up and get Mr. Hirshorn's breakfast because he was the supervisor in a plant, and his wife stayed in the bed sleeping. He always waited till she called him, but one morning he was sitting at the table while she was fixing coffee. "You pretty, Catherine, you know that? You pretty, Catherine. A lot of you nigger women is pretty." She kept thinking he was drunk, and wished he'd stayed in the room with his wife till she called him like she always did. But he kept sitting, thumping on the table, watching her, her bare arms in a housedress. "You ought to let me watch you straighten your hair sometime. Beatrice said you were in there straightening your hair." She was saying nothing and then when she'd got the can of coffee grounds down and was opening it to pour in the pot, he was behind her, touching her arm, and she dropped the can, and it banged and rolled across the kitchen floor spilling grains. He jumped back, and she was stooping trying to clean it up when his wife came in. "What happened, Tom?"

"That clumsy nigger. I won't have time to eat breakfast this morning, sweetheart."

While she was bending, she could see him bending to kiss his wife's mouth, then he went out the kitchen door, stepping over coffee grounds.

"You made a mess," his wife said, and went back to bed.

"I wanted to come back home to my own bed and not be made a fool of. You know what I mean?"

I said nothing. I waited for her to calm down. She kept watching me. I waited till the trembling stopped. I must have waited fifteen minutes.

"You over your hysteria now?" I asked.

"Don't judge me," she said.

"I won't judge you." I looked at her.

She was waiting for an embrace that I refused to give, then she stood up.

"Things pass over you like that," she said.

I didn't know what she meant, but didn't ask. She kept looking at me. I wouldn't look up at her.

"This means the end of it, I suppose."

"Whatever you feel it means," I said.

"I guess you didn't tell *him*."

"No."

"You won't, will you?"

I said nothing.

She waited a moment, then she said, "They never let you live it down." She went out.

"Yes, if you understood me, Mama, you'd see I was trying to explain it, in blues, without words, the explanation somewhere behind the words. To explain what will always be there. Soot crying out of my eyes." O Mister who come to

*my house You do not come to visit You do not come to see
me to visit You come to hear me sing with my thighs You
come to see me open my door and sing with my thighs
Perhaps you watch me when I am sleeping I don't know if
you watch me when I am sleeping. Who are you? I am the
daughter of the daughter of the daughter of Ursa of cur-
rents, steel wool and electric wire for hair.*

*While mama be sleeping, the ole man he crawl into bed
While mama be sleeping, the old man he crawl into bed
When mama have wake up, he shaking his nasty ole
head*

*Don't come here to my house, don't come here to my
house I said
Don't come here to my house, don't come here to my
house I said
Fore you get any this booty, you gon have to lay down
dead
Fore you get any this booty, you gon have to lay down
dead*

"*. . . There were two alternatives, you either took one or
you didn't. And if you didn't you had to suffer the consequences of not taking it. There was a woman over on the
next plantation. The master shipped her husband out of
bed and got in the bed with her and just as soon as he was
getting ready to go in her she cut off his thing with a razor
she had hid under the pillow and he bled to death, and
then the next day they came and got her and her husband.
They cut off her husband's penis and stuffed it in her
mouth, and then they hanged her. They let him bleed to
death. They made her watch and then they hanged her.*"

I got out of my wedding suit and was sitting on the
couch/bed in my slip when Tadpole came in.

"Y'all women sho act funny at wedding time," he said. He was excited with drink. He sat down and held me around the waist and kissed me. I'd been sitting stiffly but relaxed and returned the kiss. He squeezed my breasts.

"That hurt?"

"Naw."

"It hurts some women."

"It doesn't hurt me," I said.

I sat there, letting him hold me around the waist. I was saying nothing.

"I told Thedo to stay on the rest of the day. I thought maybe you might wont to drive down to Midway or over to Versailles or something."

"Naw."

"Aw, that's right, you said you was tired. You been taking those iron pills the doctor give you?"

"Yeah. I'm all right now though. I just felt a little tired. But I'm all right."

"You want to do anything? I'll take you somewhere else for dinner tonight. Maybe over to the Spider or something."

"I thought I'd be singing the supper show tonight."

"I won't have you working on your wedding day."

"You won't start that too, will you?"

"Start what?"

"Nothing. It's not the working. I'd like to sing for you."

"Sing for me here," he said. He unbuckled his pants and lay down on the bed. I sang for him, then we made love.

II

Sal Cooper and I had never been friends. She worked during the day and would leave during the supper show, so that we weren't there more than two hours together. But even during that time she'd always managed to avoid me. I tried to be friendly at first, but she didn't act friendly back, and I've always been the kind of person that when I see somebody don't want to be bothered with me, I don't be bothered with them. So it surprised me when she came over and said something to me. And when people started changing in their feelings toward me, I wasn't one to begrudge them. I didn't even suspect why she was being nice *then*, though now, when I think back on it and what she told me then, I think I know why. I'd married Tadpole, and Tadpole was dark like she was.

"How was the ceremony?" she asked, sitting down. She hadn't said anything when we came back from the wedding. She waited a couple of days before she said anything.

"It was nice," I said. I smiled.

She didn't return the smile but she had a pleasant look on her face. It was two o'clock in the afternoon, the time of day when there's not much business, and she was taking her break. I'd come downstairs because it was so hot upstairs, and I was tired of staying up there. We just sat there saying nothing. She was having a Coke. I had a beer.

"You know every since I first laid eyes on you I thought you was one of my long-lost relatives. I can't help it, I just kept feeling that you kin to me. You know, I'm a spiritualist. I believe in things like that."

I kept looking at her. I didn't know what she was talking about.

"I reckon you think I'm crazy, don't you?"

"No," I said, but I wasn't sure what I thought.

She sat silent a moment. I didn't say anything either.

Then she explained, "My mother came out the darkest, and so they wouldn't claim her. I don't know who they are. I don't even know what they look like. Mama probably wouldn't even know them now. She think they up in New York somewhere now though, passing. I don't know, but when I first saw you, I had that feeling."

"I couldn't pass," I said. I had to say something. I felt resentful, and a little angry because she was saying those things to me.

"I don't mean passing white. I mean passing for Spanish or something, you know. Like Cole Bean getting in the front door down at the Strand that time."

I started to say I didn't know, but I nodded.

"Come over here, baby."

I went over to the car. He was a black man but he had two white girls in the back seat. One of them was barefooted and had her legs up on the seat. Another black man was sitting in front, leaning across the seat looking at me. The other man was out of the car, smiling, showing his gold tooth.

"What's your name, baby?"

"Ursa."

"My name's Urban, Urban Jones. They both kind of sound alike, don't they. The Ur."

I nodded.

"What are you?" he asked.

"I'm an American."

"I know you a American," he said. "But what nationality. You Spanish?"

"Naw."

"You look like you Spanish. Where you from?"

"Kentucky."

"Maybe that's why you talk like that. What's your address? I want to come and see you."

I said nothing.

"What's wrong?"

"Nothing."

"Something's wrong, sweetheart. Your boyfriend wouldn't like it?"

I didn't have a boyfriend, but I said, "Naw."

"Well, he don't have to know."

"He'd have to know," I said.

"Well, I thought maybe I could take you out to dinner or something."

"No."

"Well, you pretty."

I smiled and said I had to go.

"Can I drop you somewhere?"

"Naw, I got to meet somebody."

"Your boyfriend?"

"Yeah," I lied.

He frowned, "Well, take it easy, honey." He got back in the car and drove off. I kept walking. That was the summer Mama had taken me up to Detroit. I was seventeen, but everybody said I looked older than I was.

"Do you know what you are?"

"What?"

"What all you got in you. I know you got something else in you that funny name you got."

I said I didn't know.

She kept looking at me. I could tell she wanted to confess something else, and to me. I took a sip of beer and waited.

"My mother married a light man so that her children could have light skin and good hair. But look what happened."

I frowned. We sat there saying nothing again.

". . . They burned all the documents, Ursa, but they didn't burn what they put in their minds. We got to burn out what they put in our minds, like you burn out a wound. Except we got to keep what we need to bear witness. That scar that's left to bear witness. We got to keep it as visible as our blood."

"I didn't bother you, did I?" Sal asked.

"Naw, you didn't bother me," I said. I didn't smile this time, but she was still looking at me as if she liked me for the first time. "No, I'm not bothered," I repeated.

"Cat thinks you're beautiful," she said, smiling, showing two gold teeth.

I said nothing.

"Cat ain't been around in a month of Sundays, have she?"

"Naw, she ain't been around," I said.

A man and a woman entered.

"I better go take care of these people," Sal said. She got up.

"You red-headed heifer." That's what that woman down in Bracktown called me. I wasn't even studying her man. He looked at me, I didn't look at him.

I sat there a moment, finishing my beer, then went back upstairs to take a nap before the supper show.

The last time I was in Bracktown, I went to the Baptist church with Mama.

"Who's that? Some new bitch from out of town going be trying to take everybody's husband away from them?" somebody asked.

"Naw, that's Ursa, that's my baby."

"Is that little Ursa? She growed up."

"Yeah, she have."

The church supper.

"Can I help you to some potato salad?" he asked me.

I let him help me to some. I didn't see she was with him but she kept watching. Then when he wasn't there, she eased over. "You red-headed heifer." Then when I was just walking down the street minding my own business, these two women in a car. "You red-headed heifer." I didn't stay long back in Bracktown. Just to see how folks was.

I'd slept for an hour when Tadpole came in. He was walking softly trying not to awake me, but I was already awake.

"Aw, I thought you was sleep," he said when he saw my eyes open.

"Naw."

"I was just over to Cat's," he said. "She said something crazy about going back to Versailles cause her roots was there. I told her her roots was wherever she take them. She said naw your roots are where you was born and you can't pull them up, the only thing you can do is cut yourself away from them but they still be there."

"Well, you can't sew yourself back onto them," I said. Then I thought that seemed a plea for her staying, but I didn't care.

"I finally told her to do whichever way she feel it," he said. "I had to tell her something. She act like she was looking for my approval or something. I just told her to do it the way she feel it. I told her she got all her customers here though."

"What did she say?"

"She said she try to get customers there too, and if she can't, then she do whatever she have to."

I said nothing.

"I told her to take care of herself. You going over there to see her before she leave, ain't you?"

"Yeah," I said, but I knew I wasn't going over there. I asked him when was she leaving. He said probably tomorrow morning.

"I said we be coming down to see her, but she said she didn't know where she was going to live yet. That's funny, ain't it?"

I said it was funny.

I went in to take a bath and get ready for the supper show.

Jim would still come in sometimes to have a beer, but now I didn't say nothing to him and he didn't say nothing to me. I'd got over my feeling that he was spying for Mutt. Maybe he was just spying for hisself. Mutt never stood outside the window anymore. I never even saw him by accident out on the street, or down in town anywhere, and nobody I knew had seen him. I was glad. It probably meant he really was gone.

"It don't hurt anymore?" he asked.

"Naw."

He was inside me now. I was holding his back. There was still a kind of tension in my belly.

"You fine, baby," he was saying. "There's nobody like you."

I was struggling against him, trying to feel what I wasn't feeling. Then he reached down and fingered my clitoris, which made me feel more. He stopped. "Please, honey." He fingered again. I wrapped my legs around his back, the feeling inside me. Tension in my belly, like a fist drawn up. "Please." He kept on.

"What am I doing to you, Ursa? What am I doing to you?"

I kept struggling with him. I made a sound in my throat. I didn't know what he wanted me to say. What I felt didn't have words.

"Am I fucking you?"

"You fucking me."

"What are we doing, Ursa?"

"We fucking."

He dug his finger up my asshole. I contracted against him. "You fucking me. Yes, you fucking me." He fingered my clit again, but it was painful now. "It hurts," I fretted. He took his hand away. I kept moving with him, not feeling it now. I waited till his convulsions were over. His sperm inside me. Then we lay back together, exhausted, ready to sleep.

"Urs, he's going to wont more."

"He knows what I ain't got. Don't talk to me. I don't know you."

"What do you mean you don't know me? I was in your hole before he even knew you had one."

"At least I still got one, ain't I? You didn't take that away from me."

"I couldn't if I tried."

"Did you?"

Sperm to bruise me. Wash it away. Vinegar and water. Barbed wire where a womb should be. Curdled milk.

"*Did I displease you so much?*"

"*Naw, you didn't displease me.*"

I came to you. Why didn't you want me? I lay on my belly waiting. That's what a woman waits for. To be fucked. A woman always waits to be fucked. Why didn't you? Now I'm without feeling.

"*Was I so bad?*"

"*Naw, you wasn't bad.*"

"*Did you forget so soon? I know you from way back, Ursa. That's what I said, didn't I? But you've forgotten.*"

"*Naw I haven't forgotten. I'm still thick with you. I can't get you out.*"

"*Does it feel good?*"

"*No.*"

"*Really, Urs? Really no good?*"

"*Yes. I mean, I'm lying. Yes.*"

"*What am I doing to you, Ursa?*"

"*You fucking me.*"

"*I thought you were still afraid of those words.*"

"*Didn't I tell you you taught me what Corregidora taught Great Gram. He taught her to use the kind of words she did. Don't you remember?*"

"*I got a terrible memory. I kept asking you, but you never would tell me . . . What am I doing?*"

"*You fucking me, bastard.*"

I dreamed that my belly was swollen and restless, and I lay without moving, gave birth without struggle, without feeling. But my eyes never turned to my feet. I never saw what squatted between my knees. But I felt the humming and beating of wings and claws in my thighs. And I felt a

stiff penis inside me. *"Those who have fucked their daughters would not hesitate to fuck their own mothers."* Who are
you? Who have I born? His hair was like white wings, and
we were united at birth.

"Who are you?"

"You don't even know your own father?"

"You not my father. I never was one of your women."

"Corregidora's women. Yes, you are."

"No!"

"What did Mutt do to you, baby?"

"I don't need your pity."

"It looks ugly in there."

"It's no worse than what you did."

"Are you sure?"

"Yes, you old bastard."

Great Gram, if she were back, what would she say?

"Be glad he didn't fuck you."

"Oh, but he did. What do you say to me now?"

"Where's the next generation?"

"Hush."

I am Ursa Corregidora. I have tears for eyes. I was made
to touch my past at an early age. I found it on my mother's
tiddies. In her milk. Let no one pollute my music. I will dig
out their temples. I will pluck out their eyes.

"What is it?"

"What? I'm all right."

"You weren't sleeping well again."

"I'm all right. Is it morning?"

"Almost."

"You said they never told you anything about your past.
I mean theirs. That's the same as yours."

"Naw. You know, they be some things that pass down.

But they didn't just sit me down and talk about it. But they be stories. Like, you know, about my grandmother. I took after Papa though, and the daughter that came out dark."

"Was she your mama?" I asked.

"Naw, my mama was the one that come out light."

"Aw. What else do you know?"

"Well, I know that they taught Papa how to be a blacksmith doing slavery, and when the slavery was over, he went on being a blacksmith, and then everytime he saved up some money, he'd buy a little taste of land, so the generations after him would always have land to live on. But it didn't turn out that way."

"What do you mean?"

"Well, they crooked up there. When Mama went into the courthouse to claim the land, somebody had tore one of the pages out the book. Tha's one reason I got away from up there. Aw, they let her keep the little piece of land where the house is, and I send her money every chance I get. But the rest of the land. Anyway, it's . . ."

"What?"

"Nothing. Anyway, they ain't nothing you can do when they tear the pages out of the book and they ain't no record of it. They probably burned the pages."

"*. . . Naw, I don't remember when slavery was abolished, cause I was just being born then. Mama do, and sometime it seem like I do too. They signed papers, and there wasn't all this warring like they had up here. You know, it was what they call pacific. A pacific abolition. And you know, people was celebrating and rejoicing and cheering in the street, white people and black people. And then they called Isabella, that was the princess, they started calling Isabella the Redempt'ress, you know, because she signed the paper* *with a jeweled pen. And then after that black people could go anywhere they wanted to go, and take up life anyway they wanted to take it up. And then that's when the officials burned all the papers cause they wanted to play like what had happened before never did happen. But I know it happened, I bear witness that it happened. Yeah, and Corregidora's whores was free too, but most of 'em Mama said he put down in the rut so deep, that that's bout all they could do now, though lot of 'em broke away from it too, but leastwise now they get to keep they own money and he wasn't getting hide nor hair of it. Mama stayed there with him even after it ended, until she did something that made him wont to kill her, and then she run off and had to leave me. Then he was raising me and doing you know I said what he did. But then sometime after that when she got settled here, she came back for me. That was in 1906. I was about eighteen by then. Naw, she didn't come near the place herself. She sent somebody to tell me where she was. Naw, she still think he was going to kill her. Whatever it was. By now I think he probly want to take her back, but I don't think she go back. Shortly after that I went off and met her and then we come back up to Louisiana where she was living then. Naw, I don't know what I would've done if she hadn't come. He wanted to keep me, the bastard. But it's hard to always remember what you were feeling when you ain't feeling it exactly that way no more. But when she come back for me, I was so happy I didn't know what to do, and was glad to get away from there. But by then I was big with your mama. Naw, she was born down in Louisiana. Then we come up here, you know, to get better work, and Mama was working for some Irish peoples, and I was staying home taking care of your mama and then little later on, Mama would stay at home and I was out working."*

"Didn't your daddy do anything?"

"What?"

"About the burned papers?"

"Naw, my daddy was in the war." He frowned.

"Died?"

"Naw. He went off to France during the war, and stayed in France."

I said nothing.

"You never talk about your daddy neither. It's always them women. What's your daddy like?"

"I don't know."

"What do you mean you don't know?"

"She met him when she was working down at the train depot. He just came in to get work, you know, help out and he ended up helping my mama out too, and then she had me and he went away again. He died up in New York somewhere. Some woman poisoned him. Mama never would talk about him. She said he had gypsy in him. Most of which I know my grandmama told me and told me not to tell my mama she told me. Mama never would have told me anything."

"You mixed up every which way, ain't you?"

"What do you mean?"

"You seem like you got a little bit of everything in you," he said.

"I didn't put it there," I said. I felt the resentment again, the kind I'd felt when Sal was talking to me. I didn't say anything else.

"I better get some sleep," Tadpole said. "It be 'bout time to wake up in a little while."

He turned away from me. I closed my eyes, but didn't go back to sleep. I wanted him again, but I said nothing. I waited for the alarm to go off. I stayed in bed while he got dressed to go downstairs and open up. Then I got up to get breakfast ready when he came back.

Tadpole watched me through the mirror. I was brushing my hair. We'd been married for several months now.

"Your hair's like rivers," he said.

"Is that why you married me?"

"Naw, that ain't why I married you." He laughed a little. "Naw, that's hardly why I married you."

I wanted to ask him why did he, but I was afraid to ask.

"I coulda sung with Cab Calloway," I said. "That time him and his band come out to Dixieland. He ask me to come up on stage with him, but I wouldn't do it."

"You lying."

"Naw, I ain't lying."

"Yes you are."

I grinned at him. "Yeah, I'm lying," I said. "There's a woman over on Deweese Street, though, every time she meets somebody she tells them that. I don't know if it's the truth or not. I don't even try to guess myself."

"Have you heard her sing?"

"Naw."

"Cab Calloway must've heard her do something, though?" he laughed.

I laughed, then I frowned. He saw me through the mirror. I hadn't meant for him to.

"What's wrong, Ursa?"

"Nothing."

"There's something wrong."

"Naw, they ain't."

"Come on over here, baby."

I came to him and he put his head against my belly. I had on my slip. Sometimes I went to bed in my nightgown. Sometimes I wore my slip.

"You feel all right, don't you, Ursa?"

"Yes."

"What's wrong? I know something's wrong, baby. I can tell something's been wrong."

I stroked his head, then I laughed a little. "I could've sung with Cab Calloway, that's all."

He didn't laugh.

"I love you, baby," he said.

It still got me somewhere inside when he said that, and I still couldn't bring myself to tell him the same. If he noticed it, he didn't let on. He squeezed me a little as if he were waiting for me to say something.

"If anything bothers you, Ursa, you know you can tell me. I've always been here for you to tell."

"I know, baby."

We said nothing for a long time.

"What was you doing up on that stage besides singing?" he asked, looking up at me, smiling.

"The same thing I can do here."

When we were together, he said, "I want to help you, Ursa. I want to help you as much as I can . . . Let me get up in your pussy . . . Let me get up in your pussy, baby . . . Damn, you still got a hole, ain't you? As long as a woman got a hole, she can fuck."

"I don't know if you can . . . you can't . . . I don't know if you . . ."

He was up inside me now.

"I don't want to do nothing till you ready, baby. I don't want to do it till you ready."

He was inside, and I felt nothing. I wanted to feel, but I couldn't.

"Is it good?"

"Yes."

"Is it good, baby?"

"Yes, yes."

"I just want it to feel sweet, baby. I just want it to be sweet."

"You don't have to . . ."

"I want it to be sweet for you."

I held him around his neck till I finally slept.

It was in the morning when he asked, "Did it hurt?"

"No."

He looked over at me. He had his head on the pillow, and I was looking toward him, my head almost on his chest.

"It was something. You can't tell me it wasn't," he said.

I said nothing. I kept leaning almost on his chest.

"You hurting somewhere, baby. I know you hurting somewhere."

I wished he wouldn't say that, because I wasn't sure what it meant to him.

"I'm waiting for you to tell me," he said. He seemed hard now. Before he had seemed gentle.

My chin was almost touching his chest when I said, "Let's stand."

We stood up but I couldn't get him inside me. I wanted to say, "I'm not relaxed enough," but I didn't.

He stroked me on the behind, pulling up on me, then he said, "You have to work too." He pulled up on me more, squatting down. He took me with him to the wall, squatting more. I still couldn't get him in.

"Work, Ursa."

"I *am* working," I said. It was almost a cry, but a cry I didn't want him to hear. I don't know how long it was between it and when I finally said, "Tadpole, I can't, I can't."

He stood watching me for a moment, and then he said, "Well, I'm not going to stand here all day."

He walked away from me and went in the bathroom.

I stood facing the wall, remembering that time I wanted it but Mutt was angry and wouldn't give it to me.

"Don't bring it here," he had said.

I bent down then to kiss him.

"I said, 'Don't bring it here, Urs.' "

"I just want to kiss you."

He turned away. "Shit, I know how it is. Mens just hanging in there trying to get some. It's the Happy Café awright. Mens just hanging around so they can get something."

"Mutt, you know it ain't that kind of a place. Tadpole don't run that kind of a place."

"I bet if I went over to one a those tables and I asked them what they have and they would tell me the truth about it, they'd say, 'Piece a tail, please,' and I asked them 'What tail' they say, 'That woman's standing up there. That good-lookin woman standin right up there.' Shit, I know how mens is. They just be laying in your ass if they could."

"You know I ain't give it to nobody else."

"How I know?" He turned on me, his eyes narrowed, then he turned his back to me. I tried to turn him back around, but gave up trying.

"Mutt, please," I said quietly.

"I said, 'Don't bring it here.' "

That was all he said. He made sounds like he was sleeping. I thought he was, until he asked me, quieter than I'd heard him ask anything, "Tell me if they ain't asked you."

I tried to touch him again.

"I said I don't want it," he said.

That time I'd gone in the bathroom.

When Tad came back, I was still facing the wall. I could feel him near me, but I didn't turn around.

"I knew about that other shit in the hospital," he said coldly.

"What shit?" I turned around.

"I mean that *other* shit," he said.

I was afraid to ask more. I knew by his look what he meant, and I was afraid that if I moved too far, he'd move farther. I held my stomach and turned back around to the wall. He walked on behind me and went downstairs to work.

One evening after I'd finished singing, a man came up to me and offered me a job singing Saturday nights at the Spider. I talked to Tadpole about it.

"Do whatever you want to," he said. "You your own woman."

I couldn't tell whether he wanted me to take it, or he was thinking too much about what caused the trouble between Mutt and me. I wanted to take it, because I wanted the change. It was different living there now, *and* working there. I felt different.

"I'd like to take it," I said. "You could probably get Eddy's combo to come back on Saturdays, don't you think?"

"You your own woman," he repeated.

I didn't say anything else. I telephoned the man and said I'd take the job. I had a two-hour show on Saturdays, playing piano and singing. Tadpole had Joe Williams playing piano for me there. Tadpole would come to pick me up after work. He came to pick me up the first night.

"Did you get Eddy's?"

"Naw, I got a girl," he said.

"Oh. Is she any good?"

"I think so."

Her show had ended when I got back, so I didn't see her, but Sal said she couldn't't've been more than fifteen.

Once when I was playing piano at the Spider, Jim came in. He was as surprised to see me as I was to see him. In fact, he looked like he couldn't believe I was there. And I hadn't reckoned with what his being there meant. If Jim could come in, I was thinking . . . I went on singing. There was a break between hours, and when I finished, Jim came up to say something to me.

"What is it?" I asked. I was sitting on the piano stool. He was standing with his drink.

"You stop working for your old man?" he asked.

"I still work there," I said.

"But you work here too?"

"Yeah."

"He got a pretty little thing working over there. I was over there last Saturday. I didn't ask about you. I just assumed you wasn't working." He looked at me. I knew what he was thinking.

"Naw, I'm working," I said.

"You get paid more over here?" he asked.

"Yes, but that's not my reason."

"You just wanted a little change of pace, that's all?"

"I guess so. Look, I better get back to work. That's what he pays me for."

He nodded, and went back and sat at his table. I could've taken a longer break but I just didn't want to talk to him. He left shortly afterwards. I didn't see him the next Saturday, but I finally saw the girl. She came in once during the supper show and went over and said something to Tadpole. She had long straightened hair and eyeliner around her eyes. She looked fifteen and older than fifteen. After she finished talking to Tadpole she went out. When I finished singing, I asked Sal if that was the one. "Yeah," she said. "Her name's Vivian. Fast little nigger." I didn't say anything to Tadpole about her. I kept going my Saturdays to the Spider, and Tadpole would come and pick me up afterwards.

But one night he didn't come and pick me up, and I took a cab home. When I got there Sal was still there, and Thedo was behind the bar.

"What's wrong?" I asked. "Where's Tad?"

"He had to go out somewhere," she said. She acted nervous. "Come over and have a drink with me."

"Where'd he go?"

"He didn't say where he was going. Come over and have a drink."

"He could've called me," I said. I went over to the bar with her, but then I turned and said I was going upstairs.

"She's up there with him," Thedo said in his low voice.

"Thedo," Sal said.

I went upstairs. I knew what I'd find. Tadpole drunk and that hussy in bed with him. I opened the door.

Tadpole looked up. They weren't doing anything now, but they'd been doing it. I came in the room.

"Get your ass out of my bed," I told the girl. She wasn't drunk or afraid of me, but she got up and started dressing. She seemed to be making fun of me without saying it, or even smiling. "If you want something to fuck, I'll give you my fist to fuck," I said, surprised at the words I'd echoed. I didn't touch her though. I just stood there watching her. She dressed as she would have dressed if I hadn't even been in there.

"Now, honey, you don't have to go on like that," Tadpole said. He was still in bed. "And Vive, honey, you don't have to leave."

Vivian dressed, told Tadpole she'd see him and went past me out the door.

"You see me," I said, but she'd already left. She hadn't closed the door. I closed the door.

"What right you got coming in here?" he asked.

"I'm your wife," I said.

"What do you do?" he asked.

I said nothing. I just looked at him. He was raising up, but then lay back down.

"Come on over here, baby."

I didn't move.

"You goddamn bastard," I said.

"You ain't got no right to go on like that," he said. "We wasn't doing nothing. I wasn't doing nothing but sucking on her tiddies."

"I don't give a damn what you was sucking on. Or what she was sucking on either."

"Do more for me than yours does."

"Shut up."

"Her tiddies do more for me than your goddamn pussy-hole do."

"Shut up, nigger."

"Nigger, yourself. You can't even *come* with me. You don't even know what to do with a *real* man. I bet you couldn't even come with him when you *had* something up in there. Don't give me that shit about he didn't wont you to work no more. A man wants a woman that can do something for him."

"You know what you can do for me."

"I know what you *can't* do."

"You knew what happened to me when you married me," I said.

"I know some women that can fuck your ass off you too after it happened to *them*."

"How do you know you a real man?" I said. "If you had to leave me for somebody that ain't even a real woman yet."

"She got more woman in her asshole than you got in your whole goddamn cunt."

I said nothing. I was holding back too much now. Then I said, "If you wanted to get rid of me, you didn't have to do it this way. It's not me, it's *you*."

I went out, leaving the door open. When I got downstairs I said nothing to either Sal or Thedo. I walked out. There was no Cat's to go to now. I checked in at the Drake Hotel. I'd kept from crying until I got in the room, and then I couldn't keep from crying.

Because I knew why he kept me waiting, Cat, that's why I knew what you felt, why I wouldn't tell you that I knew. A man always says I want to fuck, a woman always has to say I want to get fucked. Does it feel good? And all those dreams I had lying there in the hospital about being screwed and not feeling anything. Numb between my legs. Part of it was what I needed to make myself feel, what I had to know. Okay, I'll admit that now. But what changes? Mutt doesn't change. I couldn't go back to Tadpole, either. Not that he'd take me back, getting what he wants. What I feel crawling under my skin. That fifteen-year-old heifer. Even I didn't have eyes like that. What she needs is some of Cat's medicine. That would tame her. What am I thinking? Afraid only of what I'll become, because those times he didn't touch the clit, I couldn't feel anything, and then he . . . Why won't you, honey? But he turned away. Anyway, you knew what was wrong before you snatched after my ass. No, what's inside my head because those other women they could do it. Afraid of what I. No, I didn't push it, Cat. He wanted it too. He pushed it too. But with a man, it's easy to just push it away. The doctor said there wasn't anything wrong with me, Cat. I didn't go back, because there was nothing wrong, and he said it looked all right down there. I felt all right, and my strength is back. Why won't you turn back toward me? I'm so tired of waiting. Afraid of waiting. I gave you what I could. You didn't ask for that. You knew about the scar on my belly. You didn't ask for children that I couldn't give. What I wanted too. Afraid of what I'll come to. All that sweat in my hands. What can you do for me?

"What bothers you?"
"It bothers me because I can't make generations."
"What bothers you?"
"It bothers me because I can't."
"What bothers you, Ursa?"
"It bothers me because I can't fuck."
"What bothers you, Ursa?"
"It bothers me because I can't feel anything."
"I told you that nigger couldn't do nothing for you."
"You liar. You didn't tell me nothing. You left me when you threw me down those . . ."

It was a couple of days after I'd found them together, that there was a knock on the door. I hadn't left the room in those two days, mostly lay on the bed, sent down for some coffee. When I opened the door it was Tadpole. I didn't shut it. I didn't ask him to come in. I stood aside, and he came in. He stood there, looking at me. I still had on the dress I'd sung in, and I must've looked bad.

"This ain't good for you," he said.

I didn't answer him. I shut the door, though.

"I gave myself hell," he said. "That was the first time, Urs."

"First time is always a beginning," I said, still standing near the door. "It's what you wanted."

"Urs."

"Naw, Tad, cause when you got that girl there you was thinking it."

"We've got to work something out, Urs."

"Work what out? Little piece on the side? You be having me, but you gonna be having her, ain't you? When? Every time I go to the Spider, she be performing up in my bed."

"I was drunk, Ursa."

"I was sober, and I got a good memory."

"I gave myself hell."

"She still working for you, though, ain't she?"

"Yeah, she need the job, baby. She . . . she not well taken care of."

I laughed.

"Urs, you know you the only woman I want. I love you, Urs."

"What about your other need?" I looked at him hard. "Naw, Tad."

He'd started getting close to me, and put himself up against me, squeezing my ass.

"Baby."

"Tadpole, go away, please!"

"That was the first time, Ursa!"

"Won't be the last, will it?"

He just looked at me. I turned away from him. There was silence for a long time. I could feel him behind me. Then: "What are you going to do, fuck yourself?" he asked.

The door slammed.

I stayed in that room for two more days, and then I went to talk about getting on full time at the Spider.

I got on full time, and I guess Vivian was on full time
with Tadpole. The Spider was way on the other side of
town, and I hoped I wouldn't have to run into either of
them. I did see Vivian once, though, but played like I didn't
know who she was. We were standing on different sides of
the street. She was waiting on the bus going out East End
and I was waiting on the one going out West. She kept
looking at me, though, as if she expected me or wanted me
to come over and say something to her, but I just gave her
that "I'm not studying you, Vivian" look. She looked really
run-down and bad too, or maybe I was just imagining she
did. But I'm sure anybody who didn't know her would've
thought she was a woman in her twenties instead of fifteen
or sixteen or however old she was now.

"That's that woman that sing out to Happy's Café, ain't
it?"

"What?"

"That's that woman that sing out to Happy's, ain't it?" the
woman beside me asked.

"Yeah, I think so," I said.

"You got a hard kind of voice," Max said one day. Max
Monroe was the man that owned the place. He didn't try
to make me, because he knew how I felt about it. He had
once, though, but I'd set him straight. I was in the back
room having coffee when he came in. It was between
shows. Sometimes Max would be there for both shows.
Sometimes he would be there just for the last show, and
then close up. He was a square-shouldered man in his early
fifties. When he came in, he was laughing.

"What is it?" I asked.

He went over and got himself some coffee.

"Naw, it's just these people that live up top of me," he

was saying. "Get drunk and argue and then in the morning forget what they were arguing about. Still mad, but don't even know what it was for."

I said nothing. He sat down in one of the chairs, the one nearest me.

"Yeah, if you ever live in a rooming house, you got some crazy people, always keep you laughing."

"I bet," I said.

I didn't like him so close, and I didn't really know how to be friendly with him. When he talked to you, he liked to get right up in your face. I'd observed him with other people and he'd get up close to them too. Like if he was in a chair talking to somebody, he'd pull his chair up closer. He'd never made a pass at me or anything like that, but I still felt awkward. I remember once I was sitting outside just before opening, and he'd come over and talked to me, and instead of sitting in one of the chairs, he'd squatted down next to my lap and started talking. I'd wanted to move away, but I knew I couldn't, and there was nothing in his eyes to make me feel it was for any bad reason. Now he pulled his chair up close to mine.

"How was the first show?"

"It went pretty well."

"Lot of people out here tonight. We been doing good business since you been here."

"Thank you."

"Real good business. I knew when I seen you, get you here and we'd be doing good business. Something powerful about you."

I said nothing.

"Something real powerful."

I kept wondering if he were sober or drunk. I kept looking at him, and he kept looking sober.

"Yeah, that man and that woman's crazy." He was laughing again. "Just arguing up there all night long, and then in the morning don't even know what they arguing about."

"People's like that," I said.

"Yeah, they is, ain't they?" He was shaking his head. "I ain't never married myself. Cause I seen too many crazy womens . . . I don't mean nothing by you."

I laughed.

"I'm only kidding. It just ain't struck my fancy. Or I guess no woman ain't struck my fancy. I been a loner most of my life. Grew up as one and grew old as one."

"You not old."

He said nothing. He drank some more coffee and put his cup down. He reached over and touched me on the shoulder. I tried not to move. Sometimes I found myself not knowing how much men did meant friendly and how much meant something else. Or maybe I was just kidding myself. I wouldn't let myself tell whether it was a fatherly touch, or whether I should take my hand and remove his.

"You know you really helped this place. I ain't never heard nobody sang like you, and guess I never will. Naw, it wasn't nothing before you come. I hope you know this. I always feel awkward saying stuff like this, Ursa, but I just wont you to know how much I appreciate you being here. How much you doing for this place."

I said, "Thank you."

I kept waiting for him to remove his hand, but he didn't. When he tried to reach down between my breasts, I jumped up and almost spilled the coffee on him. It fell on the floor, some splattering against the hem of my dress.

"Naw," I kept saying, "naw."

"I didn't mean you no harm, baby. You know I wouldn't do nothing to hurt you. I didn't mean you no harm, honey."

He kept trying to pat me up but I kept moving away from him, till I got against the wall.

"Don't come over here no further, Max," I said.

He didn't. I kept looking at him. I knew he was sober.

"It ain't that way, Max. It ain't gon be that way."

"I didn't mean you no harm." He reached out his hand, but my look must have stopped him. He straightened his shoulders. "I really don't," he insisted.

"That looked like harm to me," I said quietly.

"It wasn't."

I tried to laugh. "A helping hand, I suppose?"

"If you want it to be that."

"I don't want it to be anything." I kept my eyes hard. "Always been that way, ain't it?"

"What way?"

"What you can get. Think you can get something. I mean some. When I was a little girl I used to go over with my mama to the beauty parlor. There was this man that just hang around there all the time. Mama asked me to wait outside for her, 'cause she wasn't going in there but for a minute. He come around me. You know, I was a friendly little girl then, I didn't know no better. He come over by me holding his hand out. 'Gimme what you got. What you gonna gimme? Gimme what you got.' He kept laughing. When Mama come out, she looked at that man real evil, and grabbed my hand and pulled me on away from there. When she got me home, she said didn't I see what that man was doing, he was reaching for me down between my legs. I just thought he was holding his hand out."

He looked hurt. "I ain't that man. I ain't like that. I didn't mean you no harm. You know a man gets . . ." He didn't finish.

"I know too well how a man gets," I said.

"I wasn't trying to make you or nothing like that. I just..."

"Don't lie, Max. I don't wont no lying," I said, and then I was thinking perhaps he *wasn't* lying, perhaps he didn't want to make me, just wanted to be hugged and touched. I said nothing else.

"You mad at me?"

He had straightened up even more now. Somehow I'd never really pictured him as being after women. If he had a woman, I'd never seen him with her, and I'd never been in the habit of asking around about people.

I didn't answer his question.

"You gon still work for me?" he asked.

"If we keep things the way they was. Otherwise, I'ma walk out. I don't know where I'm walking to, but I'ma go somewhere."

He stood there saying nothing. I almost thought he would let me leave.

"You know you too good to lose," he said finally.

"You won't touch me no more?" It was more of a plea than a question.

"Honey, I ain't gonna lay a hand on you."

"I'ma go home and change," I said.

He stood aside and let me pass.

Before I got to the door, he said, "I know how you feel about it now. There won't be no more."

I turned around and looked at him and smiled a little, then I went out the door.

"You got a hard kind of voice," he said now. "You know, like callused hands. Strong and hard but gentle underneath. Strong but gentle too. The kind of voice that can hurt you. I can't explain it. Hurt you and make you still want to listen."

"If you can't explain it, I can't explain it," I said, thinking about what Cat had said what seemed like a long time ago now. "But I think I know what you mean," I added.

He smiled. He was only friendly now. Nothing romantic. He knew I'd meant what I said.

"You a hard woman to get into," he said. Then he looked embarrassed, because he hadn't meant it the way I could have taken it to mean.

"You wouldn't want to try, would you?" I said.

"I guess not," he said, and got up.

I wouldn't have known what else to say if he'd stayed. I went back to the piano.

"*Ursa, have you lost the blues?*"
"*Naw, the blues is something you can't loose.*"
"*Gimme a feel. Just a little feel.*"
"*You had your feel.*"
"*Are you lonely?*"
"*Yes.*"
"*Do you still fight the night?*"
"*Yes.*"
"*Lonely blues. Don't you care if you see me again?*"
"*Naw, I don't care.*"
"*Don't you want your original man?*"
"*Naw, I . . .*"
"*I know what he did to your voice.*"
"*What you did.*"
"*Still, they can't take it away from you. But ain't nothing better for the blues than a good . . .*"
"*Don't, Mutt.*"
"*Come over here, honey.*"
"*Naw.*"
"*I need somebody.*"
"*Naw.*"

"*I said I need somebody.*"

"*Naw.*"

"*I won't treat you bad.*"

"*Naw.*"

"*I won't make you sad.*"

"*Naw.*"

"*Come over here, honey, and visit with me a little.*"

"*Naw.*"

"*Come over here, baby, and visit with me a little.*"

"*Naw.*"

"*You got to come back to your original man.*"

"*Naw. What you did.*"

"*Just give me a little feel. You lonely, ain't you?*"

"*I been there awready.*"

"*Then you know what I need. Put me in the alley, Urs.*"

"*Something wrong with me down there.*"

"*I still wont to get in your alley, baby.*"

"*Naw, Mutt.*"

"*What you looking for, anyway, woman?*"

"*What we stopped being to each other.*"

"*I never knew what we was.*"

"*Something you gave me once, but stopped giving me.*"

"*I want to fuck you.*"

"*That ain't what I mean.*"

"*I still want to fuck you.*"

"*What you stopped giving me.*"

"*I still want to fuck you.*"

"*Naw.*"

"*What he stopped giving you too?*"

"*Yes.*"

"*What you need?*"

"*Yes.*"

"*What you wanted from me?*"

"Yes."

"What you wanted from anybody?"

"Naw."

"I still want to fuck you."

"Yes, fuck me."

"Let me get behind you."

"Naw."

"Sit on my lap then."

"Naw, I don't want it that way."

"Then fuck you."

"So that's how the ole man made all his money."

"Yeah, that's how he made it."

"Forget what they went through."

"I can't forget."

"Forget what you been through."

"I can't forget. The space between my thighs. A well that never bleeds."

"And who are you fucking?"

"No one. Silence in my womb. My breasts quiver like old apples."

"Forget the past."

"I can't. Somebody called me over the telephone and said he was making a survey. He didn't sound right to me, but I asked him what he wanted anyway. He said, 'How do it feel?' I just hung up."

"That's too much mascara you're using, and those shadows."

"I made them, to cover up the ones that are really there."

"Tell me, Ursa, do insanity run in your family?"

"Corregidora, he went mad."

"They all do."

"Ursa, I want you again."

"We give each other too much hell."

"I never stopped loving you."

"Hush."

"Do it for me. I haven't forgotten."

"I have."

"Forget the past, except ours, the good feeling."

"What about ..."

"That was an accident. If I could, I'd give it back to you, but I can't. I'll let you take me inside you."

"It's good to feel your breath near me."

"Your original man."

"They told me what happened to you, baby."

"Who's they?"

"Yeah, they told me what happened. But you ain't got nothing to worry about, though. You still got a hole, ain't you? Long as a woman got a hole, she can fuck. Let me get up in your hole, baby."

"Leave me alone."

"Let me get up in your hole, I said. I wont to get up in your goddamn hole."

"I wanted to give you something, Mutt, but now I can't give you anything. I never told you how it was. Always their memories, but never my own. They slept in the bedroom and I slept on a trundle bed in the front room. An old slop jar behind their bed. I can remember how big the bed looked when I was sitting on the slop jar. Big enough to hide behind. The two women in that house. The three of them at first and then when I was older, just the two of them, one sitting in a rocker, the other in a straight-back chair, telling me things. I'd always listen. I never saw my mama with a man, never ever saw her with a man. But she

*wasn't a virgin because of me. And still she was heavy
with virginity. Her swollen belly with no child inside. And
still she never had a man. Or never let me see her with one.
No, I think she never had one. They kept to the house,
telling me things. My mother would work while my grandmother told me, then she'd come home and tell me. I'd go
to school and come back and be told. When I was real
little, Great Gram rocking me and talking. And still it was
as if my mother's whole body shook with that first birth
and memories and she wouldn't make others and she
wouldn't give those to me, though she passed the other
ones down, the monstrous ones, but she wouldn't give me
her own terrible ones. Loneliness. I could feel it, like she
was breathing it, like it was all in the air. Desire, too. I
couldn't recognize it then. But now when I look back,
that's all I see. Desire, and loneliness. A man that left her.
Still she carried their evidence, screaming, fury in her eyes,
but she wouldn't give me that, not that one. Not her private
memory. And then when Grandmama told me I hid my
face in the pillow and cried. I couldn't tell her I knew. I
could see her strong eyes full of fury, what she'd kept so
long. And I kept waiting for her to tell me, but she wouldn't
tell me. Sometimes I'd try to feel it out of her with my eyes,
but I couldn't get it. No. She was closed up like a fist. It was
her very own memory, not theirs, her very own real and
terrible and lonely and dark memory. And I never saw her
with a man because she wouldn't give them anything else.
Nothing. And still she told me what I should do, that I
should make generations. But it was almost as if she'd left
him too, as if she wanted only the memory to keep for her
own but not his fussy body, not the man himself. Almost as
if she'd gone out to get that man to have me and then
didn't need him, because they'd been telling her so often
what she should do. But he left before she could leave.*

Wasn't it that? Wasn't it you gave me something that I couldn't give back? And her body shook with the fury of my birth. She said I came into the world complaining, they didn't have to slap me. Into the world, her incomplete world, full of teeth and memories, repeating never her own to me. Never her own. And I remember now, I didn't feel it then, I never saw her with a man, never saw her with a man. I didn't feel it then, because they were all my world. And I never saw her with a man . . .

Something she kept not to be given. As if she'd already given. There was things left, yes. It wasn't the kind of giving where there's nothing left. It's where what's left is something you keep with you, something you don't give. I mean, the first giving made what's left. Created it. Do you understand? You nod your head, but do you really? And we'd have steaming cups of cocoa and remember. Corregidora, who gave orders to whores, the father of his daughter and his daughter's daughter. "How can it be?" Mama would ask. And when she talked, Mutt, it was like she had something else behind her eyes. Corregidora was easier than what she wouldn't tell me. They'd look at her. They'd tell theirs and then they'd look at her to bear them witness. But what could she say? She could only tell me what they'd told her. How can it be? She was the only one who asked that question, though. For the others it was just something that was, something they had, and something they told. But when she talked, it was like she was asking that question for them, and for herself too. Sometimes I wonder about their desire, you know. Grandmama's and Great Gram's. Corregidora was theirs more than hers. Mama could only know, but they could feel. They were with him. What did they feel? You know how they talk about hate and desire. Two humps on the same camel? Yes. Hate and desire both riding them, that's what I was going

*to say. "You carry more than his name, Ursa," Mama would
tell me. And I knew she had more than their memories.
Something behind her eyes. A knowing, a feeling of her
own. But she'd speak only their life. What was their life
then? Only a life spoken to the sounds of my breathing or a
low-playing Victrola. Mama's Christian songs, and Grandmama—wasn't it funny—it was Grandmama who liked the
blues. But still Mama would say listening to the blues and
singing them ain't the same. That's what she said when I
asked her how come she didn't mind Grandmama's old
blues records. What's a life always spoken, and only
spoken? Still there was what they never spoke, Mutt, what
even they wouldn't tell me. How all but one of them had
the same lover? Did they begrudge her that? Was that their
resentment? There was something, Mutt. They squeezed
Corregidora into me, and I sung back in return. I would
have rather sung her memory if I'd had to sing any. What
about my own? Don't ask me that now. But do you think
she knew? Do you think that's why she kept it from me?
Oh, I don't mean in the words, I wouldn't have done that.
I mean in the tune, in the whole way I drew out a song. In
the way my breath moved, in my whole voice. How could
she bear witness to what she'd never lived, and refuse me
what she had lived? That's what I mean.*

*But look at me, though, I am not Corregidora's daughter.
Look at me, I am not Corregidora's daughter."*

"Stop, Ursa, why do you go on making dreams?"

"Till I feel satisfied that I could have loved, that I could
have loved you, till I feel satisfied, alone, and satisfied that
I could have loved."

"Do you still hate me?"

"Yes. In the hospital, standing over me. You. I hated you.
I cussed you. And I've got more hurt now than then. How
do you think I feel? Why did you come back, anyway?"

"*I came to get you.*"

"*He made them make love to anyone, so they couldn't love anyone.*"

"*You'll come back.*"

"*If I do, I'll come with all my memories. I won't forget anything.*"

"*I'd rather have you with them, than not have you.*"

"*Mutt, don't.*"

I couldn't be satisfied until I had seen Mama, talked to her, until I had discovered her private memory. One Saturday morning I went down to the bus station.

I hadn't expected Bracktown to change, and it hadn't. When I stepped off the bus, there was Mr. Deak's store right where it had always been, with the tall porch, and those concrete steps leading up to it, except the steps used to be wooden and rickety, so I guess the concrete was a change. And it looked like he had painted the door. I didn't go in to say anything to him, because I knew he'd get to talking and asking me how things was, and telling me about everybody I didn't want to hear about. I hoped he hadn't seen me from the door, though, because then he mighta thought I'd got too uppity to stop in and say something to him. I went across the railroad track and started down the dirt road. I don't know how long they'd been talking about paving it, and still hadn't. It was all right when it wasn't raining, but when it rained there wasn't nothing out there but mud. A group of people were going to go into Versailles and have them come out and tar the road, but I don't know what came of that. Maybe the people in Versailles said that Bracktown wasn't a part of Versailles, even though they had their post office there, and went to school in Versailles. Bracktown was one of those little towns set back from the highway. All you could see

from the highway was Mr. Deak's store, and if you weren't
from the area, you wouldn't even know Bracktown was
there. It wasn't really big enough to be called a town, anyway. About twenty or thirty families lived there and so
they called it a town. All it had there really was Mr. Deak's
store, which did more business from the highway than from
the town, though that was the only place the town people
had to go, and there was a restaurant that was more somebody's house than a restaurant, and a church that must've
been one of the smallest churches in the country. The town
had a woman like Cat who straightened hair or, rather,
who straightened hair like Cat, except she was considered
the authorized beautician and had set up a beauty parlor
in the basement of her house, and instead of a barber shop,
there was a man who cut hair in his front room or sometimes
while they were congregated down at Mr. Deak's store.
Just a pair of scissors and a comb and his haircuts looked
better than the ones in the city. His name was Mr. Grundy.
I thought he would change, but he didn't. The last time I
was here, when Grandmama died, he still had that pair of
scissors and the comb. The older men still kept him, but the
younger ones, who had started wearing afros, were saying
they had their own scissors and comb. Mr. Grundy said,
then they never used the scissors and he wasn't too sure
they used the comb. In the summertime, he would sit his
barber's chair, which was really a kitchen chair, out on the
side of the road. I passed some women coming down the
road, probably on their way up to Deak's. I spoke but they
looked at me kind of evil. All I could think of was those
women in church that time, when I first came back, telling
Mama I must be some new woman in town who be trying
to take their husbands. I laughed, then I frowned. I couldn't
even take my own husband, I was thinking. When I had
come back for Grandmama's funeral, though, there had

been this one old woman, who had kept looking at me. She
had just kept looking at me. She'd looked at me when we
were in the church, and then when we were out at the
cemetery, she'd stood next to me. I kept feeling she was
going to say something to me, but she didn't until the burial
was over and we were going back. She didn't walk well,
and was carrying a cane.

"Ain't you Ursa?"

I said, "Yes."

"I thought you was. You look just like your grandmama
did when she was your age. You don't look like your mama,
you look more like your grandmama. Last time I seen you
you wasn't big as my stick. Now you a woman."

I had smiled at her, but didn't know what to say.

"I know you don't remember me, honey. You don't have
to say nothing."

I had felt bad, but then a man had come and taken her
arm. Then I recognized her because I recognized the man.
The man was Mr. Floyd. And she was Mr. Floyd's mother.

Mr. Floyd was the man who lived across the road from
our house, in a trailer. Everybody had a house out there,
except him, but the trailer had stayed put like a house. It
must have been before or during the time I was born that
he first come out there, because I always remembered seeing him. He was about Mama's age. Sometimes I would
wonder how much he knew, but I'd never had the nerve
to ask him. Ever since I was growing up he'd never come
over to visit us and we'd never gone to visit him. Mama
said he wasn't nothing but a hermit. But she didn't dislike
him the way Grandmama used to act like she did. I'd
only remembered seeing Mr. Floyd's mother once or twice,
and she'd only spoken to Grandmama when we'd all happened to be in Mr. Deak's store at the same time. She'd

asked my grandmother if she'd ever been to Midway, and my grandmother had told her no.

"You look like a woman that..."

My grandmother had looked at her hard, and then Mr. Floyd's mother had looked at me, and said nothing else.

Grandmama waited for Mr. Floyd and his mama to leave, and then we left.

I smiled now because I saw that chair sitting out on the side of the road. Mr. Grundy and three men, one sitting and the other two standing, either waiting for their turns, or just talking. Probably seen Mr. Grundy out there with this other man, and just stopped out there talking. They said, "How do?" I said, "How do?" back to them, and you know how men's eyes widen when some new and halfway-decent-looking woman passes. Sometimes she don't even have to be halfway-decent-looking, just new. I wondered what would have happened if I'd seen the women and the men at the same time, and the women had seen how the men were looking. They would've thought for sure I was after somebody's husband then.

"You Miss Corregidora's girl?" This was Grundy.

"Yes." I stopped.

"Well I be. You sho have growed. You was out here couple of years ago, though, wasn't you, when the old lady passed. I was scared to say anything to you then, scared you wouldn't know me. But seem like you changed again."

"Heavier."

"I wish my lady was heavy like that," said the man seated.

"Too young for you, Mose," said one of the other men.

"Mose think he still thirty," said the other man, laughing.

"Well, I know your mama gon be glad to see you, honey," Mr. Grundy said, trying to quiet the other men.

I smiled and went on down the road.

"Man, you spose to be cuttin my *hair*."

"Have some respect."

After I'd got on full time at the Spider, I'd asked Mama if she wanted to come live with me in the city, but she'd said Naw, said she felt peaceful where she was. I wasn't sure what she meant by "peaceful," but I thought, peaceful or not, she wouldn't have left that house. Too many memories. And I was almost beginning to be sure, more her own, than *theirs*. The lived life, not the spoken one. When I came up to the house it was the same one, the little wooden porch that looked too small for the swing that was on it, the honeysuckle bush, an old wicker rocker. And Mr. Floyd's trailer was still there, across the road, and a truck patch he must've just started. I knocked on the front, but Mama didn't hear me, so I walked around to the back. I left some avocados I'd brought her on the porch, telling myself it was so they'd get ripe, but the real reason I was thinking was Mama might feel I thought I couldn't come unless I brought something, but that was silly. I knocked on the back door. She heard me.

"Ursa," she said. "Hi you, honey."

"Hi, Mama." I went over and kissed her.

She was standing up at the stove, stirring some preserves. She canned things for people. They would provide the strawberries or whatever it was, and she would can them. The other thing she did, which I didn't like, especially now that I could send her more money, was work three days out of each week for some white woman who lived in Midway, who'd come and get her and drive her back. I kept hoping she would stop, but so far she hadn't.

"Whose preserves?" I asked.

"Mr. Floyd's," she said. "His or his mama's. I think he's gon give em to her."

She had gotten bigger around the waist, and looked like Grandmama and Great Gram used to look, the graying hair plaited on the sides and tied in a knot in the back, the way she had been beginning to look just before I left, the way I knew I would look when I got her age. I was in my late thirties and she was in her late fifties. She had stopped stirring to hug me. Now she turned the fire down.

"I missed you," she said.

I told her I missed her too. I always felt awkward saying things like that. I went over and sat down at the kitchen table. I was wondering if she would have said I missed you if she knew why I'd come. She stood with her back to me for a moment, and then she turned the fire off completely, put the cover on the pot, and came and sat down at the table opposite me.

"Do you want something? I've got some ham in there and I could scramble you up some eggs."

"No, I'm all right," I said.

"You sure?"

I said, "Yes."

She sat with her hands on the table.

"It's good to see you, baby," she said again.

I looked away. It was almost like I was realizing for the first time how lonely it must be for her with them gone, and that maybe she was even making a plea for me to come back and be a part of what wasn't any more.

"You look like a gypsy, them beads on."

I told her they were trade beads, what they used to use for money over in Europe somewhere. I didn't know where in Europe. She only nodded.

"You here for a long visit or a short one?" she asked finally.

"Naw, I didn't bring anything, Mama. I'm not staying. I'm getting back on the bus at three-thirty."

She looked away from me this time.

"I brought you some avocados," I said. "I left them out on the porch."

"They so expensive, Ursa. I was down to the store, and Mr. Deak was selling them for fifty cents a piece."

"I know how you like them."

She said, "Thank you." She looked away from me again. I could feel the strain and wondered if she could. I'd always loved her and knew she loved me, but still somehow we'd never "talked" things before, and I wanted to talk things now.

I put my hands up on the table. "Mama."

"What is it?" She looked at me quickly.

"Grandmama told me something."

She looked away. She was still beautiful, in *their* way of still being beautiful, and the way I knew I would still be beautiful when I got to be their age. I could see her mouth tighten. Her own hands had left the table and gone into her lap. She still had her apron on.

"She told me about the man you met at the train depot where you used to work. She told me how you met my father."

"What you want, Ursa?" she asked quietly.

"Nothing you don't want to give, but I hope you'll want to give it."

She was silent, then she said, "Suppose I told you I don't want to give it, I never wanted to give it."

"I'd ask you what you meant."

She laughed a little, the kind of laugh that's not really a laugh, as if one had to make more effort to get a laugh, and she hadn't made enough effort.

"It's not that I don't want to talk to my baby," she said. "I want to talk to you, Ursa."

"But you can't."

"No."

"You could try."

She said nothing. She still hadn't looked at me.

"*They* knew. If I came back to live with you, I'd have to know too." I hadn't intended to say that, and didn't like why I might have said it. I added quickly, "But I can't come back and live with you. I have to make my own kind of life. I have to make some kind of life for myself."

"I knew how situations was with you and Tadpole," she said.

I didn't ask her how she knew. There was always someone running to tell things like that. I looked away from her for a moment and then when I looked back at her she was looking at me. It was a quiet look. It was as if she were waiting for me to make her talk. I just kept looking at her, hoping that what was in my look would make her.

"Corregidora's never been enough for you, has it?" she asked.

"No."

"I thought it would be."

"What happened with you was always more important. What happened with you and him."

Her face tightened for a moment.

"Corregidora is responsible for that part of my life. If Corregidora hadn't happened that part of my life never would have happened."

"Wouldn't it?" My eyes narrowed a little, but not in a way, I hoped, that would make her stop.

She didn't answer. I wanted to ask her if *their* past could really have had so much to do with *her* own, but I just kept watching her. I wanted my eyes to say it. Some things I had to let my eyes say.

"He wasn't a man I met at no depot." She was shaking her head, looking away from me again. "Naw, I didn't meet

him at no depot. He worked at this place across the road
from the depot, where I used to go in to have lunch. I didn't
pay him no mind. He used to stand behind that counter
watching me, and I never did pay him no mind. He was a
good-lookin man, I guess. Yeah, your daddy was a good-
lookin man. Tall and straight as a arrow. Black man. You
know, kind of satin-black. Smooth satin-black. You come
out lookin more like me than you did like him, I mean about
the color. You got long legs like he had. Sometimes during
his breaks he'd sit down at one of the tables, and cross his
legs twice. You know how some people can do, cross their
legs and then bring his foot around, you know, like he was
winding his legs around each other. I used to try to do it.
I never could though. I bet you can. I wasn't studyin him,
though, cause you know then I wasn't lookin for a man.
They'd tell me, they'd be telling me about making generations, but I wasn't out looking for no man. I never was out
looking for no man. I kept thinking back on it, though, and
it was like I had to go there, had to go there and sit there
and have him watch me like that. Sometimes he'd be cleaning the counter and watching me, you know how mens
watch you when they wont something. It don't have to be
to open your legs up, though most times it is. Sometimes I
think he wonted something else, and then sometimes I
think that's all he wonted. I wasn't out looking for him, I
know that, and he never did say nothing to me neither,
except this one time. See, I'd always been coming to lunch,
and then this one time I come in there and had supper too.
Mama and your Great Gram was having something at
church, and said they wouldn't be home for dinner, and I
didn't wont to sit up in the house and eat by myself, so I
went over there. I was going to go over there, you know,
and then come on home, maybe listen to the radio or read
something, and then go on to bed. I went over there and ate

my supper. He looked like he was surprised to see me
when I come in. But this time instead of just taking my
plate away, he stopped there and said something to me.
He said it real soft. It was almost like I didn't hear him,
but I knew I heard him. I wasn't even looking at him. I
wouldn't even look up from the table. He was standing
there looking down at me. He said 'Hello' real soft. I
wouldn't even look up at him though. I talked back to him,
soft too, but I wouldn't look up at him.

" 'Hello.'

" 'Hello.'

" 'Your supper was okay, wasn't it?'

" 'Yes.'

" 'I'm glad. You ain't never been in here to have your
supper.'

" 'No.'

" 'I always like seeing you in here. They ain't nothing else
good about this place.'

"I said nothing.

" 'My name's Martin, what's yours?'

"I didn't answer.

" 'I always wanted to know who you was.'

"I still didn't answer.

" 'You always like to know who you talking to, or looking
at. I mean, if you like somebody.'

"No answer.

" 'You still there?'

" 'Yes, I'm still here,' I said so softly I almost didn't hear
myself, but he must've heard me.

" 'I'm glad you still there,' he said. 'I thought you'd got
up and gone.'

" 'No.'

" 'My name's Martin.'

"I still wouldn't tell him what my name was.

" 'I don't mean you no harm.'

"I wouldn't say anything. I just kept looking down at the table. I wouldn't even look at him. I felt as if tears were in my eyes, but I hoped he didn't see them. It was like I couldn't say nothing, Ursa, it was just like my mouth was there, but I just couldn't say nothing. I kept expecting him to be like the other mens was, and say real evil, 'You got a mouth, ain't you, bitch? I know you can talk,' but instead he was still soft. He said, 'I didn't come over here to mean you no harm, woman. I just wanted to talk to you.' That was the first time anybody called me woman. I didn't feel like a woman. I couldn't been more than your age when you left here. Naw, I didn't even feel like no woman and he called me one. I would've just stayed there, my eyes glued on that table. I know I would've just stayed there, till he left or something. I don't know. But all a sudden this ole woman come in selling these Jehovah Witness pamphlets and come over to him first. 'The Lord knows you guilty,' she said. I think that's what she said. He said, 'Yes, He does.' I don't know what else, because I put my money down on the table and got up and left. I could feel his eyes following me, like he wanted to push that ole woman away, but I could still hear her talking. Then I was out the door, and went on back home. I couldn't help feeling like I was saved from something, like Jesus had saved me from something. I went to bed real early that night. But still it was like something had got into me. Like my body or something knew what it wanted even if I didn't want no man. Cause I knew I wasn't lookin for none. But it was like it knew it wanted you. It was like my whole body knew it wanted you, and knew it would have you, and knew you'd be a girl. But something got into me after that night, though, Ursa. It was like my whole body knew. Just knew what it wanted, and I kept going back there. I told Mama and Grandmama that I had to work, you know, and I go there and eat my supper, and then I come home and eat supper again. My stomach got all stretched out too. I almost felt like I was getting a baby then. First two nights he wouldn't say nothing to me. Pretend like he wasn't even looking at me. I knew he was though. And I kept telling myself I wasn't looking for no man, I just wanted him to be my friend or something. You know, just somebody other than Mama and Gram I could go talk to sometime, you know what I mean. I wasn't lookin for no man, cause I didn't feel like no woman then. Sometimes even after I had you I still wouldn't feel like none. But then I just kept going there. It wasn't until bout the third or fourth night, he come and said something to me again, like he was getting up his nerve too.

" 'I wouldn't mean you no harm,' he said. Still that soft voice, almost like I really couldn't hear it now, or like I didn't want to hear it. 'I wouldn't mean you no harm, woman.'

"I think I mighta even been liking him calling me that, like men never did call women that before, or like that was just a special name for me, his special name for me.

" 'You ain't leavin again?' he asked.

" 'I haven't left,' I said. I didn't know whether he meant imaginary leavin or real leavin. But I was still sitting there.

" 'I want to walk you home. I'd like to walk you home tonight,' he said.

" 'I live kind of a distance. We live over in Bracktown.'

" 'You take the bus?'

" 'Yeah.'

" 'I ride you over there then.'

"I said nothing, but he took it to mean yes. Maybe it had meant yes.

" 'Who you live with?'

" 'My mama and my grandmama.'

" 'Maybe tha's why you seem like a old-fashioned girl.'

"I said nothing.

" 'I got to go over here and wait on these people. Don't leave now.'

"I said I wouldn't.

"I waited for him, and he stood waiting on the bus with me, and rode me home. He didn't even try to do nothing that first time. He didn't even ask me for a kiss. It was like we got along real well, like I wouldn't even believe you could get along that well with a man. But then I know it was something my body wanted, just something my body wanted. Naw. It just seem like I just keep telling myself that, and it's got to be something else. It's always something else, but it's easier if it's just that. It just always makes it easier. And then maybe he just wanted something else.

"He rode me home again, and then one night it had got kind of cold. You know, it was Indian summer and you never really could tell in the morning how it would be in the evening. I always took a sweater or jacket or something to work, but he didn't, cause he lived just right up the road, but, you know, riding me home all that way, he'd get cold, so he asked if he could go home and get his jacket first. He asked if I wanted to wait downstairs for him, but I said Naw, I said I'd go up. I guess I was thinking if I didn't it would be like saying that I didn't trust him. And then I was trusting him, and I was trusting myself too, because I really didn't think nothing would happen. But then he was getting his jacket, and then he all of a sudden touched my hand, and was talking about my hands, how I had nice long hands, and asked if I played piano, and asked if I minded if he touched me. Naw, I didn't mind, because I didn't mind it. Because I didn't think anything would happen, and I trusted myself, because I knew I wasn't looking for a man."

She stopped. I didn't ask her to go on. I knew she would go on when she was ready. She just kept sitting there for a long time. I just kept watching the side of her face, her mouth tightening again, the rows of plaits, the bun in the back, her profile. It was like I hadn't seen anyone so still as she'd suddenly gotten, more like when a movie freezes than in real life. Then the quivering started about her mouth again.

"It was like my whole body wanted you, Ursa. Can you understand that?"

"Yes, I can understand."

"I knew you was gonna come out a girl even while you was in me. Put my hand on my belly, and knew you was gonna be one of us. Little long-haired girl on my lap. You come out baldheaded though. They just kept looking at me, Mama and Gram. I knew they hated me then. Cause you come out all baldheaded. White skin before you got the little pigment you got now, and baldheaded. They hated me, but then your hair start to sprout, and got real long. I used to put a little ribbon on your head so people would know you was a girl. People didn't know whether you was a boy or a girl . . . I knew you'd be a girl. I knew my body would have a girl."

I said nothing.

She looked at me quickly, and then looked away again.

"He kept asking if he could touch me certain places, and I kept saying yes. And then all of a sudden it was like I felt the whole man in me, just felt the whole man in there. I pushed him out. It was like it was just that feeling of him in there. And nothing else. I hadn't even given myself time to feel anything else before I pushed him out. But he must have . . . I . . . still that memory, feeling of him in me. I wouldn't let myself feel anything. It was like a surprise. Like a surprise when he got inside. Just that one time. I didn't go see him anymore. I wouldn't even have my lunch there. Once he came to the depot and asked me why was I fighting him. I wouldn't say nothing to him. Then he just left me alone. He said he knew what I was now, and he could play that game too. I didn't know what he meant, but it made me feel bad. When I knew about you, Great Gram went and talked to him. I begged her not to, but he came and married me and then . . . he left me."

I wanted to ask if she would have left him, but I didn't. What I wanted to know now was if she had planned to leave him, but I couldn't bring myself to ask.

"Are you still there?"

I was silent.

"I went to see him only one time. He seen you. You was about two the last time he seen you, so I know you don't remember him."

"No."

"He was staying at some boarding house up in Cincinnati. I hadn't heard from him, and then he sent me this money. No letter, just this money and his address on the outside. I was mad at first, and then, Ursa, I didn't want him back or nothing. I even said my reason was to go give him his money back, cause I didn't need it, or wont it. When I got up there I just said I come to talk to him. Then I found out it was only just to get me up there. He knew when he sent that, I be up there. I was up there. He just stood in his door for a moment looking at me. He had on these khaki-colored pants, shirt on but chest all out anyway. I went in and he closed the door. He turned on me and first thing he said was, 'Bitch.' He said it again. 'Bitch.'

"I said, 'Don't hurt me.' I knew he was going to. I said, 'Help me, Martin, but don't hurt me. Just let me come here, and say hello, and ask you how you're doing. I just wonted to tell you things are all right with me and Ursa. I don't need the money.'

" 'Shit. Money's not how I helped you. I helped you that night, didn't I?' He held my arm. 'Didn't I?'

" 'You're hurting me.'

" 'I helped you that night.'

" 'No, you didn't, you hurt me.'

" 'I lived in that house long enough to know I helped you. How long was it? Almost two years, wasn't it? That's long enough for any man to know if he's helped. How could I have missed. I mean, the first time. The other times were all miss, weren't they, baby? They were all miss, weren't they?'

"He squeezed tighter. I kept trying to get away, but then he started slapping me, just slapping me all over the face. One time it was like he was going to go for some place else, like he was going to go straight for my cunt, or for my belly, or some place like that, but then he stopped himself, and just kept slapping me all over my face, twisting me, and slapping me all over my face. I didn't think I'd get out of there. I didn't think I would. I started to scream. And then I said, Naw, to myself. I said, Naw, I wasn't going to scream for no nigger, and having people coming up there and make me feel worse than I did already. I said, Naw, I wasn't going to scream for no nigger.

"But all of a sudden he just stopped. He just stopped and stood stone still. He hated me, Ursa. I know he did. I was holding myself all up on my face, and I know I was going to be black and blue all over, it hurt so bad. I was just hugging my face.

" 'Ain't I helped you, baby?' He was trying to grin, but it just made him look like the devil. 'Woman?'

"I didn't answer. I just kept hugging my face.

" 'Hurt, don't it?' he asked.

"I said nothing. I just wanted to get out of there. I didn't want him to do anything else, and it was like I was daring him not to touch me again, but I knew there wasn't nothing I could do if he did. I knew I wouldn't do nothing even if I could.

" 'What was you afraid of?' he asked.

"I said nothing.

" 'You could've let me. I know you could have let me. What were you afraid of, Correy?' He always called me Correy, you know.

"I still wouldn't say nothing. I never did tell him. I never would. I think he just thought I was just afraid of him being a man, or being too big, or too much for me or something. I never would tell him.

"He just let me go on to the door, then. Or I thought he was going to let me. He kept looking at me like he was hurt, and then when I tried to get around him to the door, he stood aside. But then all of a sudden he grabbed my pants. I had on these purple pants, the kind with the elastic waistband. He grabbed them by the waist, like when you're grabbing a child or something. He grabbed them and the elastic broke. I caught them before they fell down. He said he was sorry, but he didn't look like he was. I didn't bring anything with me, cause I was just going to see him, you know, and come on back home, so I didn't have anything. I was holding them up. I thought he would give me a pin or something but he didn't. He just stood looking at me, like he was real, real calm now, and then all at once the evil come back, and then he said, 'Get out.' He told me to get out. I ain't never seen a man look like that, Ursa. When you see a man look like that, you don't never forget it. It stay with you all your life. He told me to get on out of there and I did. He said, 'Go on down the street, lookin like a whore. I wont you to go on down the street, lookin like a whore.' I kind of looked at him, you know, and it was like I could see all that hurt there. He hadn't really softened, but I could still see all that hurt there. 'You took me bout as far as a woman can take a man without givin him nothing,' he said. 'Remember?' I went out. I didn't want to remember. I had to walk down the street, holding up my purple pants with one hand and holding my mouth with the other. My head was all hanging it hurt so bad, and I could feel it turning black and blue, and peoples was all watching. I know what they was thinking. The womens was looking at me all disgusted, and I was scared to borrow a pin offa somebody. Cause if I asked one of the mens for one, they would've thought I wonted something. This man leaning against this building kind of stood out and said, 'Baby, you know where Bud's Angel Bar is?' I just kept on walking. He said, 'Bitch, I ain't good enough for you, is I? I ain't good enough for you. Well, you ain't good enough for me neither.' I knew what he thought I was, but I just kept on walking."

I had leaned farther across the table, watching her. Just the side of her face was enough for me, she didn't even have to show me the rest, but she looked around and showed me the rest.

"I only went back to him once. He was staying at this boarding house, Ursa. All he did was start beating on me. He started beating on me."

I went over and put her head against my thighs.

"I carried him to the point where he ended up hating me, Ursa. And that's what I knew I'd keep doing. That's what I knew I'd do with any man."

. . .

"I'll walk you to the highway."

"You don't have to, Mama."

"I want to."

"Ursa."

"What, Mama?"

"I know about those other things you would never let me know."

I said nothing. She was telling me she knew about my own private memory.

"Do you want me to talk?"

"Sometime when you're back here and feel you have to."

"Awright."

She pulled her shawl around her tighter. I fingered my trade beads.

"You see all these colors in them, these formations?" I asked.

She looked at my neck, and touched them. We stopped walking for a moment.

"They form naturally," I said. "They just form naturally that way. No one paints them on."

"Those stripes too?"

"Yes."

She looked like she couldn't believe it, but I knew she did. She kept touching them for a time and then we started walking. We walked slowly.

"You didn't ask where your father is now, Ursa."

"Do you want to tell me?"

"No. I mean, I don't know."

We kept walking. We walked so slow it was almost like we weren't really walking. We had left early enough for me not to miss the bus, though, as if she had wanted to stand down there with me as long as possible before I had to get up on the bus, and she had to turn around and go back up to that house. The only thing that had changed in it was the kitchen, the old iron coal stove replaced with a gas one—the kind you used bottle gas from a tank outside the house, like people do in the country where there are no gas lines—and the old icebox replaced by a Frigidaire. She had moved the icebox into a corner and used it for storage space. And the old iron stove was still rusting in the backyard. The one they used to empty ashes from, lifting out those big iron rings in the top. That stove had always frighted me. When I was older, though, they'd make me take the tray out, and empty the ashes against the side of the road. The big bed was still in the middle room, except she had moved the trundle bed out of the front room, and put it in there too. I didn't know whether she slept in the big bed or the trundle one, and that wasn't something I felt I could ask her. It would have seemed ridiculous to an outsider, but to us I think it would have been a kind of prying she didn't want, or need. *They'd slept there before I did.* And in the front room that ageless china cabinet. The big one with all the good dishes and the silverware that was never taken out. I could never remember its ever having come out, even on holidays. The only time it was opened was to be dusted or polished. I'd never looked, but I think it had been imported from Brazil, or I used to think so. It was an expensive dark-mahogany thing, the best thing we had in the house. Great Gram used to be in charge of it at first, and then Grandmama, and now I guess Mama was. When I had gone through the house, it was still sparkling.

After a while, she began speaking again, hugging her shawl to her. It sounded almost as if she were speaking in pieces, instead of telling one long thing.

"After he come, they didn't talk to me about making generations anymore or about anything that happened with Corregidora, but Martin and me could hear them in there talking between theyselves. We'd be in the front room, and they'd be back in there in the bedroom, Great Gram telling Mama how Corregidora wouldn't let her see some man because he was too black." Mama kept talking until it wasn't her that was talking, but Great Gram. I stared at her because she wasn't Mama now, she was Great Gram talking: "He wouldn't let me see him, cause he said he was too black for me. He liked his womens black, but he didn't wont us with no black mens. It wasn't color cause he didn't even wont us with no light black mens, cause there was a man down there as light as he was, but he didn't even wont us with him, cause there was one girl he caught with him, and had her beat, and sold the man over to another planta-tion, cause I think he just wont to get rid of him anyway. Cause Corregidora himself was looking like a Indian—if I said that to him I have my ass off—so that this light black man looked more like a white man than he did, so I just think he wont any excuse to get rid of him. I don't even know how he got him. He didn't buy him himself, I think he just come in with a load of other mens they wont to work out in the fields, cause he had cane, you know. But anyway he wouldn't let me see him, cause he said a black man wasn't nothing but a waste of pussy, and wear me out when it came to the other mens. He didn't send nothing but the rich mens in there to me, cause he said I was his little gold pussy, his little gold piece, and it didn't take some of them old rich mens no time, and then I still be fresh for him. But he said he didn't wont no waste on nothing black. Some of them womens he had just laying naked, and just sent trash into them. But some of us he called hisself culti-vating us, and then didn't send nothing but cultivated mens to us, and we had these private rooms, you know. But some of these others, they had to been three or four or five whores fucking in the same room. But then if we did something he didn't like he might put us in there and send trash into us, and then we be catching everything then. So after that, first time he just talked to me real hard, said he didn't wont no black bastard fucking me, he didn't wont no black bastard fucking all in his piece. He was real mad. He grab hold of me down between my legs and said he didn't wont nothing black down there. He said if he just catch me fucking something black, they wouldn't have no pussy, and he wouldn't have none neither. And then he was squeezing me all up on my pussy and then digging his hands up in there. We was up in his room. That's where he always bring me when he wont to scold me about something, or fuck with me. Him and his wife was living in separated rooms then. Then he was just digging all up in me till he got me where he wonted me and then he just laid me down on that big bed of his and started fucking me . . .

"Any of them, even them he had out in the fields, if he wonted them, he just ship their own husbands out of bed, and get in there with them, but didn't nothing happen like what happened over on that other plantation, cause I guess that other plantation served as a warning, cause they might wont your pussy, but if you do anything to get back at them, it'll be your life they be wonting, and then they make even that some kind of a sex show, all them beatings and killings wasn't nothing but sex circuses, and all them white peoples, mens, womens, and childrens crowding around to see . . .

"Naw, he said he wouldn't've been nothing but a waste of my pussy, cause he said my pussy bring gold. But what was funny after that they kept claiming he did something. Not Corregidora, but this black man. I was only talking to him once, all Corregidora did was seen us talking, and I guess he figure the next step was we be down in the grass or something. I don't know, but they said he did something, and they were goin to beat him real bad. He was young too, young man, so he run away. When somebody run away, it almost mean you can do whatever you wont to with them. I think he woulda run away anyway, cause he had this dream, you know, of running away and joining up with them renegade slaves up in Palmares, you know. I kept telling him that was way back before his time, but he wouldn't believe me, he said he was going to join up with some black mens that had some dignity. You know, Palmares, where these black mens had started their own town, escaped and banded together. I said the white men had killed all of them off but he wouldn't believe me. He said that was what his big dream was, to go up there and join all these other black mens up there, and have him a woman, and then come back and get his woman and take her up there, but he had to find his way first, and know exactly where he was going. I said he couldn't know where he was going because Palmares was way back two hundred years ago, but he said Palmares was now. But they claimed he did something, and he had to leave before he planned to. Wasn't nothing but seventeen or eighteen. This ole man said he told him to rub garlic on his feet so the hounds wouldn't smell him, but he said the boy must've forgot to. We was all praying for him, though. They sent this whole mob of mens out after him. You know, they didn't need no mob for just one person. Mob and hounds. So they can have the hounds to smell out nigger blood, cause they trained them to do that. But it was only because Corregidora thought he'd been fooling with me when he hadn't, or that we'd been fooling with each other, cause all that was all uncalled-for. Sometimes I would be a little bold with him, little bolder than the others, cause I know I was the piece he wonted the most, so I said, 'He wasn't after my pussy. He ain't been after my pussy. He even too young to know

I got one.' 'Ain't no nigger on this place too young to know you got one, way I got them trained,' he said. He moved away from me, then he moved back toward me. He must've been fucking me while they was chasing after *him*. But maybe he did the right thing to run anyway, because maybe if he had stayed there, the way Corregidora was looking when he seen us talking he might've had him beat dead. I ain't never seen him look like that, cause when he send them white mens in there to me he didn't look like that, cause he be nodding and saying what a fine piece I was, said I was a fine speciment of a woman, finest speciment of a woman he ever seen in his life, said he had tested me out hisself, and then they would be laughing, you know, when they come in there to me. Cause tha's all they do to you, was feel up on you down between your legs see what kind of genitals you had, either so you could breed well, or make a good whore. Fuck each other or fuck them. Tha's the first thing they would think about, cause if you had somebody who was a good fucker you have plenty to send out in the field, and then you could also make you plenty money on the side, or inside. But he was up there fucking me while they was out chasing *him*. 'Don't let no black man fool with you, do you hear? I don't wont nothing black fucking with my pussy.' I kept saying I wouldn't. 'I don't wont nothing black trying to fuck you, do you hear that?' 'Yes, I hear.' Let his own color mess with me all they wont to. Sometimes I used to think he even wonted to be in there watching, but out of respect for them, not me, he wouldn't. Yes, tha's just how I was feeling, while he was up there jumping up and down between my legs they was out there with them hounds after that boy. Wasn't nothing but seventeen. Couldn't've been more than seventeen or eighteen. And he had this dream he told me about. That was all he wanted me for, was to tell me about this dream. He must've trusted me a lot, though, cause I could've been one of them to run back to Corregidora with it. But I wouldn't. It was because he seen us out there talking. I wouldn't even go tell him, cause I would've been seen telling him. And I kept feeling all that time he was running, he kept thinking I'd told something when I didn't. And then there I was kept crying out, and ole Corregidora thinking it was because he was fucking so good I was crying. 'Ain't nobody do it to you like this, is it?' I said, 'Naw.' I just kept saying Naw, and he just kept squeezing on my ass and fucking. And then somehow it got in my mind that each time he kept going down in me would be that boy's feets running. And then when he come, it meant they caught him . . .

"When they come back, they said they lost the boy at the river. They said they got to the river they didn't see him no more. We was all glad. We didn't show it, but the rest of us was all glad and rejoicing inside. But you know what happened? Three days after that somebody seen him floating on the water. What happened was they chased him as far as the river and he just jumped in and got drownded. Cause they didn't know nothing till three days after that when he rose . . .

"Corregidora must've done some rejoicing then. He didn't show it but he must've had it all inside. Ole man kept telling me if the boy had just remembered to rub garlic on his feet, the bloodhounds wouldn't've been able to follow. I asked him if he ever tried it. He said, Naw, but he heard of folks that did. I asked him where was they. He said they was gone. He didn't know where to, but they must've made it, cause didn't nobody bring them back."

She quit talking, and looked over at me suddenly, Mama again: "They just go on like that, and then get in to talking about the importance of passing things like that down. I've heard that so much it's like I've learned it off by heart. But then with him there they figured they didn't have to tell me no more, but then what they didn't realize was they was telling Martin too . . ."

It was as if she had *more* than learned it off by heart, though. It was as if their memory, the memory of all the Corregidora women, was her memory too, as strong with her as her own private memory, or almost as strong. But now she was Mama again.

"One day after we'd been married, I don't know, maybe six months. (He had come into the house to live, you know. Not on account of hisself but me. I kept saying I couldn't not help them out, and if we didn't live there, I couldn't help us and them too. He said he'd help us, all I had to do was worry about them. I said something about how little he was making. Naw, it was almost like he moved in that house out of anger, not for me, but for anger.) Well, he had gone fishing one day, but when he came back, though, instead of coming around to the front where I was, he went around the back to the kitchen and put them in a big pan of water, and then he was gonna come around to the front and have me cut them up and fry them. Well, what happened is he must've started through their room and there she was, sitting on that bed in there powdering up under her breasts. I don't know if she seen him or not—this was your grandmama—but she just kept powdering and humming, cause when I started through there, there she was powdering, and looking down at her breasts, and lifting them up and powdering under them, and there he was just standing in the door with his arms spread up over the door, and sweat showing through his shirt, just watching her. I don't know what kind of expression he had on his face. His lips was kind of smiling, but his eyes wasn't. He seen me and he just kept standing there. I was looking at Mama and then looking up at him, and after he seen me the first time

he just kept looking at her. She was acting like she didn't
know we was there, but I know she had to know. He was
just standing there like he was hypnotized or something. I
know she knew. She knew it, cause they both knew he
wasn't getting what he wanted from me. Cause you know
with them in there, I couldn't. I'd let him rub me down
there. I kept telling him it was because they were in there
that I wouldn't. But . . . even if they hadn't been. There she
was just sitting there lifting up her breasts. I don't know
when it was she decided she'd let him know she seen him,
but then all a sudden she set the box of powder down
and looked up. Her eyes got real hateful. First she looked at
me, then she looked at him. 'You black bastard, watching
me. What you doing watching me, you black bastard?'
She still had her breasts all showing and just cussing at him.
He started over there where she was, but I got between
them. 'Martin, don't.' He just kept looking at me, like it was
me he was hating, but it was her he was calling a half-white
heifer. Her powder and him sweating all up under his
arms, and me holding him. She kept calling him a nasty
black bastard, and he kept calling her a half-white heifer.
    " 'Messing with my girl, you ain't had no right messing
with my girl.'
    " 'I'ma come over there and mess with your ass the next
time you show it,' he said, but then I got him in the kitchen,
and there was them fish in that pan a water he had waiting
for me to clean. He pushed me away from him, and
grabbed them fish and started cutting them up hisself.
'What do we have to do, go up under the house?' he kept
asking me. 'What do we have to do, go up under the
house?'
    " 'Please, Martin.'
    "He just kept grabbing those fish and cutting them up.
    "When I came back through the house, Mama rolled her

eyes at me. 'Messing with my girl, he ain't had no bit of right.'

"After that, whenever Martin wanted to get from one part of the house to the next, he'd go around the house . . . But she just kept acting like she didn't even know he was there."

She was quiet again, and then she said, "They had us sleeping in the narrow old trundle bed in the front room, the one you was sleeping in afterwards. I kept telling him it was because they were in there I wouldn't, but then that time they weren't there he wanted to take me in *their* bed . . ."

I didn't ask her whether she had let him. That was something she didn't have to tell me.

When we got to the highway, Mama took my arm.

"I think what really made them dislike Martin was because he had the nerve to ask them what I never had the nerve to ask."

"What was that?"

"How much was hate for Corregidora and how much was love."

I said nothing. She squeezed my arm. "I'll try to pretend you're okay until you tell me different," she said.

"I'm okay, Mama."

She kept looking at me. I didn't like the way she was looking. I wanted to ask what about her now, how lonely was *she*. She'd told me about *then*, but what about *now*. Shortly after Grandmama died, she had written me a letter saying that Mr. Floyd had started to get sweet on her, talking about how he wanted to court her, but she said she hadn't let him. She said he could just stay across that road, cause all he really wanted to do was to move out of that trailer, and into *her* house, and probably bring his mama with him. I hadn't known whether to believe her or not,

415

because I knew too many of my own excuses when men came to the piano, and then Logan—the man Max hired to see to it that men don't bother me—was my best excuse. I could just give him that "he's bothering me" look, and he'd put the man out.

After a while, Mama squeezed my arm again. She kept hold of it until the bus came and she put me on. "Do you know me any better now?" she asked. I only smiled at her. She stayed standing there until the bus pulled off. She didn't let me see her walk back to the house.

I leaned back against the seat and closed my eyes. Then suddenly it was like I was remembering something out of a long past. I was a child, drowsy, thinking I was sleeping or dreaming. It was a woman and a man's voice, both whispering.

"No."

"Why don't you come?"

"No."

"What are you afraid of?"

"I'm not. I'm just not going with you."

"Why do you keep fighting me? Or is it yourself you keep fighting?"

I drifted back into sleep. I never heard that man's voice again.

I was thinking that now that Mama had gotten it all out, her own memory—at least to me anyway—maybe she and *some man* . . . But then, I was thinking, what had I done about my *own* life?

III

I couldn't have been more than ten the year the Melrose woman committed suicide. Mama had come into the house. Gram said something to her and then they started hushing each other because I was in the room. I saw the way they was looking, but Mama sent me back in the kitchen to light the oven because she was going to bake some rolls for dinner. I went back in the kitchen. They didn't think I could hear them, but I could. We had one of them three-room, straight-back shotgun houses. They was in the front room, and with just one room in between us, I could hear them. When I finished lighting the stove, I just sat down at the kitchen table and listened.

"Yeah, they found her over in Hawkins' alley," Mama was saying.

"Anybody know why yet?"

"They thought it must've been some man, you know, got her pregnant or something, but she wasn't pregnant."

"Had to been some man," Gram said. "I ain't never known a woman take her life less it was some man."

"I reckon," Mama said. She sounded weary. I didn't hear them say anything else, and finally Mama said she was going back in the kitchen and start supper. I put my head down on the table, so she wouldn't see my eyes.

It wasn't until later that I knew what they were talking

about. I was down at Mr. Deak's store, and him and these
men were talking. They weren't like Mama and Gram.
They didn't care if I was there or not. Mama had sent me
down for some corn meal. I thought it had happened in
Bracktown, but it wasn't Bracktown, it was up in Versailles that it happened, but the girl was from Bracktown
—one of Mr. Melrose's girls. She was in her twenties.

"Melrose is up there now," Mr. Deak was saying. "Her
mama is all to pieces. He told her to stay here, and he go
take care of it. They gon move her body down here. But
you know why he didn't wont Miz Melrose there, because
he gon try to find out what man's responsible, buddy, it's
gon be some fireworks in Versailles."

Mr. Deak was a little dark man who wore suspenders
all the time, and stood with his thumbs under his suspenders, not up near his chest, but down near his waist. He
must've been in his twenties, but I thought he was old then.

"You ain't forgot what your mama wanted, did you,
missy?" he said to me.

"Naw, sir." I went and got the corn meal. I didn't take it
over to the counter, I just stayed standing there.

The other man started talking. "How her daddy gonna
find out, and the whole police couldn't?"

"A daddy got ways the police ain't. Anway, she wasn't
nothing but a nigger woman to the police. You know they
ain't gon take they time to find out nothing about a nigger
woman. Somebody go down there and file a complaint, they
write it down, all right, while you standing there, but as
soon as you leave, they say, 'Here, put it in the nigger file.'
That mean they get to it if they can. And most times they
can't. Naw, they don't say put it in the nigger file, they say
put it in the nigger *woman* file, which mean they ain't gon
never get to it . . . You know, John Willie ain't gon do
nothing. But her daddy, now, that's something different.

You heard about the shot heard round the world. They gon be some rumbling over here in Bracktown when Mr. Melrose find that man."

"Maybe it wasn't no man, maybe it was just she went crazy."

"Naw, it was a man. I bet my eyeteeth it was a man."

Mr. Deak looked at me again, this time real hard, and I handed him the money for the meal, and ran out the door.

"Did you hear what happened to that Melrose woman?" I asked May Alice. She was my girl friend. She was a couple of years older than me, though, and had already started bleeding. She called it bleeding, so I had started calling it bleeding. Before then I had been taught to call it monthly or time of month. They told me about it when I was nine. They wouldn't have told me that early, but I'd found some of Mama's bloody sheets and had started screaming and crying, and they couldn't convince me that mama wasn't sick until they told me about it. When I told May Alice, she'd laughed, and every since that, she would start pointing out people and saying, "She bleeds." At first I had liked "monthly" but then I had started liking her word better. I hadn't started bleeding yet, but May Alice said I would start in a few years. She said she had started early, though, and sounded like she was bragging. She said it was a good thing I'd had that scare then, because if they hadn't told me, and I'd seen all that blood in my bloomers, I would have had a bigger scare. She said she knew this girl who hadn't been told and when she saw all that blood she thought something was wrong with her, but was even too scared to tell her mama, and went down in the basement and kept trying to wipe the blood off, but it just kept coming, and she thought she was dying or something. Then May Alice laughed at me again.

"She wasn't a woman. She wasn't any older than my sister," May Alice said now.

"Your sister's married, ain't she?"

"That don't make her a woman. Anyway, Mama keeps telling her it's time for her to start acting like a woman. She might've had it in her, but that don't make her no woman."

"Had what in her?"

"Dick, silly."

"What?"

"Her husband's thing. A man's got something different from a girl."

"I know that."

"You don't act like it."

"I ain't seen one, but I know what it looks like."

"How?"

"I don't know."

"Because we was watching Mr. Trumbo's dick get hard through his pants, and I told you. You don't remember nothing."

"I remember."

"Well, just because somebody had it in them, don't make them no woman. I had it in me, and I ain't no woman."

"How you have it in you?"

"I just did, that's all. I opened my legs, and Harold put it in me. He said, 'Open your legs up, May Alice,' and I did. I played like I didn't know what he was going to do, but I did. Then he put his thing in me, and my pussy got all bloody."

"You said you already bleed."

"I do, but that's not the only kind of bleeding a woman, I mean a girl, have to put up with. The first time a man sticks it in you, you bleed."

"Does it hurt?"

"It does for a little while, and then it feels good."

"Naw it don't."

"Yes, it does."

"How can it feel good if it hurts."

"I said it hurts for a little while, and then all the hurting goes, and then it feels good."

"I don't believe you."

"You will. Rate you going, you probly be my sister's age, but you'll say, May Alice told me it would feel good."

"Naw I won't. I'll say May Alice told me a story."

She just laughed.

When we were older—or maybe I should say when I was older—May Alice always seemed the same age to me; I was about twelve myself then, no, I was thirteen, because I'd just started getting my period—I was in the six grade and she was in the eighth, but we had recess at the same time, and I saw her and Harold leave the playground and go over in Mr. Jouett's wheat field. Harold came back first, and then she came back and came over where I was.

"May Alice, you going to have a baby if you don't quit."

"Did Miss Smoot see us?"

"I don't know. I don't think she was looking."

"You know what'll happen if you don't quit," I said again.

She looked angry at first, and then she kind of laughed a little. "I been trying to, but then it gets so you can't help it. You'll find out."

I kind of frowned. She was always mentioning the fact that she'd been having it and I hadn't, like when we were younger and she would keep saying, "I got a bigger hole than you got," and asking me if I wanted to see it. I said, "Naw."

"I'll show it to you if you show me yours," she said.

"Naw."

"Reason I got a bigger hole than you got is cause Harold been in me."

"Harold can't get in you. You ain't got no door."

"Yes, I do, cause I got one down between my legs."

Then when I first started bleeding, I tried to get back at her. I said, "You said it would be red. It looks like chocolate." "It'll get red," she told me, and it did.

"Anyway," she went on now, "once you had it in you, it seems like you have to keep having it in you. I heard Mama talking about this woman that didn't have it done to her and went crazy. You got to have it in you, or you go crazy."

"You lying."

"Naw I ain't. Mama said this girl, there was this man that used to come and visit her mama, and her mama never would let her do nothing, and then this man left her house, and went walking down the street, and this girl broke loose, and ran down the street after him, and tried to rape him, right there on the sidewalk. They put her in the asylum after that."

I kept saying she was lying, and she kept saying naw she wasn't neither. Then Harold came over by us, and he was grinning. I told May Alice I had to go inside.

I never did tell her about that time I was home by myself and Harold and some more boys came and was standing outside the kitchen door wanting to get in, and I wouldn't let them in.

"Let us in, Ursa," Harold had said. "Let us in so we can give you a baby. Don't you want a baby?"

They kept knocking on the door. I wouldn't let them in the kitchen, so they went around to the front, but that was locked too.

"Henry said when you was five you let him see your pussy," Harold said.

"I ain't five now."

"He said you let him feel all up in your ass."

"Naw I didn't."

"Open the door so we can get some. Don't you want a baby?"

I was in the bathroom when May Alice came in.

"Why'd you leave? Harold says you don't like him."

I said nothing. I was thinking of that time we had gone through the cut-off, May Alice and me, and Harold and those boys were there again. Harold had gone over to May Alice and the other boys were after me, but May Alice had thrown rocks at them. "Don't let them get Urs," she'd said. "Harold, make them leave." When the other boys were gone, she and Harold got over in the grass. They were rolling like they were playing at first, and then I knew what they were doing. They hadn't even told me to turn my head.

"What's wrong, Urs?"

"You know what'll happen if you don't stop."

"I can take care of myself," she said, then she stuck her tongue out at me, and left.

I didn't even know what she saw in him, except that day we had a dance at school and he asked me to slow-dance, and he kept getting real close to me, and he felt real hot down between his legs. I didn't know anybody could feel that hot. When he asked me to dance again, I wouldn't dance with him. He went over and said something to some boys, and these boys were standing over in the corner, looking at me, laughing. No one else asked me to dance that evening.

"We did it again last night," May Alice said.

We were on the stairs going up to class. She had a torn place in the hem of her skirt. „

"May Alice, you better quit."

She said nothing.

"He ought to quit if you won't," I said.

"You know a boy won't quit."

"Why not?"

She laughed. "Anyway," she said, "they be after it till you tell them to stop. But then after you start giving them some, you wouldn't feel right to tell them to stop. I mean, you wouldn't feel you had any right to tell them to stop."

"I would."

"Who you gave some to?"

I said nothing. She turned to go in her class. I kept on walking.

There was a boy at school who used to rub up against girls. Once when it was crowded and we were all going to the cafeteria he rubbed up against me. I wouldn't hardly eat for a whole week, thinking he'd given me a baby, even though I knew from May Alice that you couldn't get them unless you had it in you. I wouldn't eat because I thought starving myself would get rid of it. Mama had kept saying, don't you want such and such a thing, you better eat, Ursa, and I would keep saying I wasn't hungry. And then she had said, "You die if you don't eat." I don't know how long I could have kept it up, but then May Alice's own scare drove me back to eating again. Yes, she had had a scare before she got really pregnant. She thought she was pregnant and kept asking me whether she should take a coat hanger like she heard some people did. I'd told her it would probably ruin her more doing that than if she went on and had the baby. She wasn't even acting like she used to, like she would act when she was so sure of herself. She said she knew all about having babies but not how to get rid of them. I asked her didn't she know how to keep from having them. She said, Yeah, but Harold was getting so now he was getting careless, and I asked her wasn't she getting careless too. She said it was just that now she didn't like to ask him to use something, and didn't want to tell him to pull out.

But then her period had finally come that time. It was the next time that it didn't. At first she kept telling me it was only because she'd been eating too much. "I've just been eating too much, I've just been eating too much, that's all," she kept telling me. But that day when she couldn't tell me that anymore, I skipped class with her and we spent the whole afternoon sitting down in the wheat field, and she kept hugging me and crying, and hugging me, and saying why couldn't I have been Harold and then nothing would have happened. I didn't know what she was talking about then. She just kept hugging me.

She said her mama found out because she got suspicious when she'd stopped finding blood in her underwear when she did the wash. She'd tried to tell her that she'd washed it out herself, but her mama said she never did before, and took her down to Midway and had Dr. Roach examine her. May Alice said she wouldn't even look at the doctor, she just kept rolling her eyes at him. She said it wasn't like when you were making love or playing doctor, when a man opened your legs and looked at you down there. She said it was the most embarrassing thing a woman could go through. She said all she did was roll her eyes at him. Then she said the next week when her mama went to find out the results, she came back home and slapped her, and said the only reason she didn't keep slapping her was because she didn't want to be responsible for anything happening to the baby, and keep her from paying the consequences she deserved to pay.

May Alice kept asking me to go tell Harold she was sorry, but I wouldn't. I said she shouldn't be sorry, he should be. But she just kept telling me to go tell Harold she was sorry, like it was her fault.

"He won't come to see me," she would say. "Ursie, go tell him I'm sorry. He's mad at me. I know he is."

"He ain't got no right to be mad at you," I said. "You should be mad at him."

"Go tell him I'm sorry, please."

"I can't tell him that."

"Ursie, please."

I finally got up enough nerve to go tell Harold she said she was sorry.

"It ain't me, it's my mama," he said, and got away from me real quick.

The next time she asked me to tell him she was sorry, I wouldn't.

I was back in her room with her when Harold's mama came to talk to her mama. They had started to say something, but then May Alice's mama said why didn't they go out in the yard and talk, because she knew we could hear. May Alice and me went in the front room and watched them from the window, but couldn't hear anything.

"His mama just got out of the hospital having a baby herself," she said.

"How you know?"

She said nothing, then she said, "When we did it the last time, he was home by hisself. She was in the hospital then. His daddy hadn't come home from work yet."

I said nothing. I just kept looking out at the two mamas talking, and wondered what it would be like if one of them was mine, and the idea frightened me.

"What are they going to do?" I asked.

"His mama sho is ugly," she said, instead of answering. "She's the only one in the family that's ugly. I don't see what Harold's daddy see in her anyway, except but she's probably real good in the bed."

I said nothing. I just kept staring out at the two women. When I got back home, Mama had found out about May

Alice's pregnancy. I hadn't told her, but I guessed by now the word had started slipping out.

"I told you not to have nothing to do with that girl. I told your grandmama I used to see her back in that grass back there. Young as she is too. Girl like that, it ain't nothing but shaking hands. Let her see how hard he's gon be shaking her hand now. Nothing but shaking hands. I reckon you listen to me now, Ursa."

I said nothing.

"You hear me, don't you?"

"Yes, ma'am."

I didn't see May Alice again until she had had the baby. She was in the hospital, in a room with all these other women whose stomachs were swollen out. I almost hadn't gone in when I saw the rest of them, but May Alice had seen me, and I wouldn't have felt right if I'd turned around and left.

"I didn't think you liked me no more."

"I like you, May Alice."

"Harold don't."

I just stood there. She told me I could sit on the bed, but I wouldn't. I kept looking at her because I didn't want to have to look at the other women.

"You looking at me so funny," she said, and tried to laugh.

"Naw I'm not."

She said nothing, and then she started telling me how pretty the baby was.

"Did you go see him?"

"Naw, they wasn't showing the babies when I got here."

"Aw. Maybe you get to see him tomorrow."

I said, "Yes," but I knew I didn't want to come back.

May Alice started smiling.

"What you smiling at?"

"It's a hurt that feels good too. I mean afterwards. You remember what I told you and you wouldn't believe me."

I nodded.

She started telling me how the baby felt coming out from between her legs.

"Don't tell me about that." I stepped away from the bed.

"When it happens to you, you'll be wanting to talk about it too."

"Naw, I won't, cause it ain't gonna happen to me."

"Don't be such a baby," she said. "When you started bleeding you still acted like a baby. I bet when you have your first man in you, you'll still act like you do now. Like a baby."

I turned away and ran out. I didn't want to see May Alice anymore.

I remember when I got home I ran up to Mr. Deak's store.

"Mr. Deak, whatever happened to Mr. Melrose?"

"Honey, that ain't nothing for you to hear."

It wasn't until I was about fifteen that I learned from reading back papers in the school library that him and some man got in a fight at the Spider Web—not the Spider where I was to work later, but the old Spider Web that was long since torn down—and that he had either shot or knifed the man, the paper wasn't too sure which. But now Mr. Melrose was in jail, and the police had claimed they still didn't know whether the man he had shot or knifed had had anything to do with his daughter. They still didn't know why she'd killed herself. John Willie, of the police department, had said, "There's some things them people just won't let be our business no matter how hard we try. We still asking around though." I felt like going down to the county jail to ask Mr. Melrose, but I knew Mama wouldn't let me, and even if I had gotten in there, I figured Mr. Melrose would either think I was crazy, or resent me for meddling. I don't think anything ever worked me up so much as that woman, and I hadn't really known her, or paid that much attention to her, just seen her, because she was twenty-some years old, and a woman, and I was only a kid, but somehow I'd kept tying her and May Alice together. I don't know why I did. And it was always May Alice laying up there in that alley.

I never went to see May Alice no more, and then finally she and her mama moved to Georgetown, Kentucky. I'd seen her a few weeks after she got back with the baby, though. She'd stayed in for the first few weeks. I don't know if it was because her mama believed in those forty days or felt ashamed. But as soon as May Alice did come out, I saw her. It was hard not to see anybody in Bracktown. I was going across the railroad track to go to Mr. Deak's store, and she was coming back from there.

"Why you hate me?" she asked.

She still had on one of her maternity dresses even though her stomach wasn't big anymore.

"I don't hate you."

"Yes, you do. You ain't been to see me."

"I didn't know you'd be having company."

"You know you could come. You my best friend, ain't you?"

I said nothing.

"Did what I said in the hospital make you mad?"

I shook my head.

"Yes it did. That's why, ain't it?"

"Naw."

"Why then?"

I said nothing.

"All right. Hell," she said. "I ain't gonna stand here. Least

429

you could do for somebody is tell 'em why you don't like 'em. Shit. You ain't nothing *but* a baby. I was just talking, thought maybe I could help you. Even if a man stuck a dick as big as a tree up in you, you wouldn't get help. All you like to do is watch."

"I don't."

"You was, wasn't you?"

She started laughing. I wanted to say something real nasty to her, but instead I ran across the railroad track without looking. For a long time after that, I would just sit up trying to think of things that would have sent *her* running. Once Mama came by while I was whispering something and slapped me. "Who taught you that? I ain't taught you that." I just kept looking at her. But after that day, though, me and May Alice didn't speak to each other, and then finally her and her mama moved. I don't know if her father ever knew about her baby because she said he lived up in New Jersey, where he could get a job, and would send them home money. I just wondered why they moved to Georgetown and didn't go up to New Jersey somewhere.

When I first had people liking my singing, it was down at that place that was more somebody's house than a restaurant. When Mama found out she came and got me.

"I ain't gon have you singing no devil music. Me over there sitting up in church trying to praise God, and you over at Preston's singing to the devil."

"What about Grandmama's old blues records? You didn't say nothing to her."

She didn't answer, then she said, "That ain't the devil coming out of your own mouth."

I told her she didn't have to embarrass me, pulling me out of Preston's like that, with all them people watching. She coulda just told me. She said she ain't never known no

Corregidora to behave with just telling. That was when I told her I wasn't no Corregidora. She just kept looking at me, and then she told me she better not catch me down there at Preston's no more or else I have the devil coming out of my behind as well as my mouth.

We just kept having riffs like that until I just got on the bus and came to the city. I read in the paper where they needed somebody at Happy's. When I got there I just kept standing outside the place, afraid to go in. There was this man that come by, and just stood there and watched me. I was almost as afraid of him as I was to go in.

He said, "Whose woman is you?"

I wouldn't look at him.

" 'Whose woman is you' I asked."

I still wouldn't answer.

"You got your bitch on today, ain't you?"

I stood there.

"I said, 'Ain't you got your bitch on today?' "

I think I got up enough nerve to go inside just because I wanted to get rid of him. Tadpole liked me right off, and I got the job.

"I bet you some man's good woman, ain't you?"

Tadpole had put the man out.

When I first saw Mutt I was singing a song about a train tunnel. About this train going in the tunnel, but it didn't seem like they was no end to the tunnel, and nobody knew when the train would get out, and then all of a sudden the tunnel tightened around the train like a fist. Then I sang about this bird woman, whose eyes were deep wells. How she would take a man on a long journey, but never return him.

Mutt kept looking at me. Somehow I thought he would come up and say something to me like the other men did who'd looked at me like that. I hadn't wanted them or anything, but they'd come. His look was like theirs and somehow different too. He kept coming into the place, and somehow, even though he'd never come up to me, and I'd never said anything to him, he got to be the man I was singing to. I would look at him when I began a song, and somehow I would be looking at him when I ended it. He kept coming into the place, and then one night he got up and asked me to join him at his table.

"Where did you get those songs?"

I'd sung the ones about the tunnel and the bird woman again.

"I made them up."

"They real nice. I like the way you sing."

He asked me what I wanted to drink. I said beer.

He looked surprised. "Nothing harder? You give the impression of liking bourbon."

"No, that's all I drink."

He grinned. "You not such a hard woman. You try to sing hard, but you not hard. I bet you try to talk hard, too, don't you?"

I didn't answer.

"You don't have to say nothing," he said.

The waitress brought me my beer, and him his whiskey. We said nothing for a while and he kept looking at me. I didn't look at him, and then I looked at him. "What?" I asked.

"I feel I know you from way back," he said, and then he started telling me about some trouble he got in when he was back home. He didn't tell me where home was, and I didn't ask.

"I was wrong, though, but I got off."

"How could you get off if you was wrong?" I asked.

"Cause he wouldn't a did nothing to me, judge wouldn't."

"Why?"

"On account of him and my daddy. Yeah, cause he knew if it wasn't for my daddy he wouldn't even be the judge down there. You know, my daddy worked for him. It's a little town. You know how in these little towns they even make a farmer a judge. They made Judge Tackett a judge and he didn't have nothing but a ninth-grade education. 'You have to be a lawyer to be a judge,' that's what my daddy told him. Judge Brackman's a lawyer, you know. Well, he was running for election, and my daddy said, 'You a lawyer. Why don't you tell them you got to be a lawyer to be a judge.' So that's what Judge Brackman did, said you got to be a lawyer to be a judge. He used it in his campaign speech, and he got elected too. Tha's why now anything I do there, I can get off of it."

"Anything?"

"Wasn't nothing but a traffic charge," he said with a smile. "I ain't a bad man. I can be hard sometime, but I ain't bad." He looked at me carefully for a moment. "Naw, you ain't no hard woman."

"I know my way around," I said. I don't even know why I said it, it was just like it came out. I wasn't even sure it was true. It was just that I was singing in a place where a woman would know her way around.

"Do you?" he asked.

I drank my beer.

"My name's Mutt."

"Oh."

"I thought you might like to know who you talking to."

"Yes. I'm . . ."

"I know who you are."

I smiled, still holding my glass.

"You scared of me, ain't you?"

"Why do you say that?"

"The way you look at me."

433

"Naw, I'm not scared."

I drank some more beer and put the glass down. I was thinking of how the first night I saw him in there his hair hadn't been combed, and every night after that, he'd combed his hair. I smiled.

"What you smiling at?"

"Nothing," I said, still smiling.

He smiled. "You'll get over that," he said.

"What?"

"Being afraid of me."

He looked around him.

"This ain't really a good place for a woman."

I said I liked it.

He didn't say anything else about it, then. It wasn't until later that he started saying other things. He was a big man, not heavy, but tall big.

"I like you," he said. "I got some Della Reese records. She's my woman. I like you though. I mean, I don't just like your singing, I like you too."

I said nothing.

After a while, he said very quietly, "You got somebody?"

I said, "No."

He smiled a little. "Yeah, she's my woman. Her and Ella. The rest of em can't do nothing for me. Now the Lady Billie she ..."

When I told Mutt about Corregidora, it was before we got married. I hadn't gone to his apartment and he hadn't been to mine, but now we had gotten so he would come into my dressing room and we would talk there. He said he only knew one thing about when his people were slaves, but that it was enough for him. I asked him what was it. He said that his great-grandfather—he guessed great-grandfather—had worked as a blacksmith, hiring hisself out, and bought his freedom, and then he had bought his wife's freedom. But then he got in debt to these men, and he didn't have any money, so they come and took his wife. The courts judged that it was legal, because even if she was his wife, and fulfilled the duties of a wife, he had bought her, and so she was also his property, his slave. He said his great-grandfather had just gone crazy after that. "You can imagine how he must of felt."

I nodded, but said nothing.

"Don't look like that, Ursa," he had said and pulled me toward him. "Whichever way you look at it, we ain't them."

I didn't answer that, because the way I'd been brought up, it was almost as if I was.

"We're not, Ursa."

I had stepped back suddenly.

"What did you step back for, woman? I wasn't going to bite you. What in the hell did you step back for?"

He was looking at me with more hurt than anger. But when I came back toward him, he acted like he didn't want me then. Said he was going out and get himself a drink. He had come in before the show instead of after. When I got outside, he was sitting there drinking. I sang all his favorite songs to try to make up to him. The next time he said, "Ursa, baby," I let him do a little bit more of what he wanted, but this time he was the one who stopped himself.

"I'll wait till you ready," he had said, then he smiled a bit. "I started to say, I won't be ready till you are. But that would be a lie, Urs. I want you so much."

When he got up close to me, he was hot like a furnace. I backed away from him.

"If you won't have it this way, what about . . ."

I said no before he could finish.

"You didn't hear what I was going to say."

"I think I know."

"I'm going to ask you again."

I said nothing.

"All you act like you want from a man is a little peck on the cheek. Somebody ought to give you a little peck on the cheek, and I don't mean this one." He patted the side of my face.

I couldn't tell if he were angry or what. He pulled me back close to him.

I didn't let him inside me completely until the night we were married. I understood more than Mama knew about pushing a man out. He had never liked for me to sing that song "Open the Door, Richard" and I never would sing it after the first time because he'd said, "When are you going to let Richard in?" No, it wasn't so much he didn't like it as I felt uncomfortable singing it, or any song that had anything to do with opening up. I still sang the song about the tunnel closing tight around the train and the one about the bird woman who took this man on a long journey, but never returned him. "What's wrong, Ursa?" he'd keep asking, and even the night we were married, and he took me up to his room at the Drake Hotel, he'd kept asking, "What's wrong, baby? Ursa, honey, what's wrong?" He kept holding me and kissing me. We were both out of our clothes, but we'd done nothing yet.

"I can't, Mutt."

"Hell if you can't, you got a cunt, ain't you?"

I said nothing.

"What's wrong, baby? What do you call it?"

I still wouldn't answer.

The first time, a couple of months later, when I'd flared back at him with his own kind of words, he'd said, "You never used to talk like that. How'd you get to talk like that?"

I answered, "I guess you taught me. Corregidora taught Great Gram to talk the way she did."

"Don't give me hell, Ursa," he said now. "You know this is hell. Don't you feel anything? Don't you want me?"

"Yes," I said.

"I want to help you, but I can't help you unless you help me."

He had parted my legs, but I pushed him away.

"Any other man would say you was crazy. Any other man wouldn't put up with this shit."

"You don't have to." I hadn't meant to say it.

He'd started soothing me again, almost like one soothes a baby.

"I act like a child, don't I? Somebody told me even after I'd had a man, I'd still act like a child."

"You not a child. You something, but you not a child."

I let him get close to me again.

"Naw, Ursa, you ain't a child."

I let him get close till he was inside.

He kept asking me what he was doing to me, but I wouldn't tell him.

"What am I doing to you, Ursa . . . I'm fucking you, ain't I? What's wrong? Say it, Urs. I said I know you from way back. I'm fucking you, ain't I? Say it."

"Mutt, I . . ."

He laughed. "You ain't no hard woman, baby."

Stroking my hair, he came. "Are you still afraid of me?"

"Naw, Mutt."

"Are you sure, baby?"

"I'm sure."

He kissed my forehead.

May Alice had said that after you had a baby you felt like telling people. After I had had Mutt I felt like telling people, but at the same time it was something that you didn't tell, something that you kept inside. I think I was happy then. I would sing songs that had to do with holding things inside you. Secret happinesses, a tenderness. I think Mutt was embarrassed by the way I would look at him. Sometimes I would sing whole songs to him, and that's why I would think he had gotten out of the habit of sitting as close to the front as he did, but later I learned it was because he wanted to watch the other men, how they were reacting to me. I learned that it was because he'd got crazy somehow on account of me. Once I'd said playfully, when he brought the subject of the other men up, "You crazy, man." He'd answered me equally as playful, "You crazy, too, woman." But then it got so it wasn't playful anymore, and he'd meant everything he said about those men.

"When Corregidora had that stroke he didn't call in his men, he called in his women and said he'd give them any amount of money they wonted if they take it off him, but they said didn't none of them put it on him."

"Shit, I'm tired a hearing about Corregidora's women. Why do you have to remember that old bastard anyway?"

I said nothing.

"You one of them," he said.

"What?"

"If you wasn't one of them you wouldn't like them mens watching after you."

"They don't watch after me, Mutt."

"I wish you'd take that damned mascara off. It makes you look like a bitch."

"The thunder sounds like it's talking, don't it?" I asked.

"That's because you got music all in your head. The thunder ain't doing nothing but thundering."

"Naw, Mutt, it's talking. If you listen, you can hear it too."

"I seen the way Tyrone Davis was looking at you."

"He wasn't looking no way at me."

"A man don't like for other mens to look at they wives like that."

"Last night you didn't wont nobody to say nothing to me, and tonight they can't even look at me."

"Not the way mens look. A man know if a woman don't."

"Mutt, you crazy."

"You call me crazy again you gon see just how crazy I am."

I came home from work and he was laying across the bed in his shorts. He only went to my performances sometimes now, usually on Friday. We had been married about four months. It was near the end of March, and was just beginning to be warm in the day, but still cold at night. He hadn't turned the heat on, and didn't have a cover over him, and looked like he was freezing.

"Mutt, you'll catch your death."

I went over and lit the heater.

"What do you care? You got all them men."

"Mutt, you crazy."

He only looked at me this time. I hadn't meant to say it, and regretted it.

"Rub my thighs, baby."

"What's wrong with your thighs?"

"They tight. I been working all day. You know a man got to work. And working in tobacco ain't easy."

I felt he had some kind of trick, but I took my jacket off and went over to the bed and started massaging his thighs.

"Feel how tight they are."

"Yes." The muscles did feel tight.

"Get back behind there, you ain't rubbed behind there."
I rubbed behind his thighs.

"You ain't rubbed in between them."

I rubbed in between his thighs, and he kept telling me to move up just a little bit, and then he pulled me by the shoulders until I was up on top of him, and felt him through my skirt.

"You ain't had it this way, have you?"

"No."

He pushed me away real hard. "Well, you ain't getting it."

"Mutt."

That was when he first started to use that part of my feeling to try to pressure me into giving up the job. Whenever he wanted it and I didn't, he'd take me, because he knew that I wouldn't say, No, Mutt, or even if I had, sometimes I wonder about whether he would have taken me anyway. But those times that I wanted it, and he sensed that I wanted it, that's when he would turn away from me.

"Mutt."

"Take it someplace else."

"What if I do?"

He gave me a hard look. "Try me."

He made me think he was going to.

"My pussy, ain't it, Ursa?"

"Yes, Mutt, it's your pussy."

"My pussy, ain't it, baby?"

"Yes."

"Well, it's yours now."

He turned away.

Finally I got to the point where I tried to learn from him, play it his way. If he could be cold, I told myself, I could too. He'd been kind of funny about coming to the place lately. He'd come to the place, and kind of look around, like in those movies where those men come in and "case out a joint," one hand in his pocket, smoking a cigarette with the other hand, then he'd leave. But he never sat down at a table like he used to. He had moved from a front table while we were courting to a back table in the corner while he was watching who looked at me wrong, and then finally, just before he went and tried to grab me off the stage, he had begun to "case out the joint." If it had been anyone else, I mean, if I had been anyone else, and the consequences hadn't been like they were, seeing him standing there with his hand in his pocket, smoking that damned cigarette, would have made me laugh.

I was sitting on the edge of the bed. He had come in and cased out the joint, but then when I got home he wasn't even there. When he did come home he got undressed. I guess he must have thought I didn't want it, because he was going to give it to me. But this time I wasn't going to give it to him.

"What's the matter, Urs? Cat got your tongue? Cat or rat one. If the cat ain't got it, the rat have. What's the matter, woman!"

He was angry now, but he didn't try to force me in bed with him like I thought he would. And it was the first time I hadn't given it to him when *he* said yes. Maybe it was because I *did* want it.

"I'm just playing it your way," I said. "Something else I learned."

"My way or your own?" he asked.

No, he didn't force me down with him, and when I did want to give in he wouldn't take what I had to give.

"And that bastard you work for, he ain't no different from anybody else. He's all eyes too, and probably all dick."

Gayl Jones

It was after one of his joint casings. I said nothing.

"How many times you relieved his swelling? He ain't had you working there every night for nothing, have he?"

"Mutt, it ain't like that. He ain't tried nothing. He don't mean nothing to me."

"You got to mean something to him, though, way I see him looking."

"He ain't even really friendly. He's kind of shy, anyway."

"Them's the kind you got to watch out for. Play like he ain't friendly. But I bet he's got something friendly down there between his legs. Them's the kind womens come to anyway. The shy ones. I mean, since they don't come to the womens, the womens got to come to them."

"Like you?"

He said, "Shit."

The next night I heard some men laughing at Mutt. If he had ever heard it, he just didn't care. I was on my way up to the stage. It wasn't like a theater stage, but more like a reserved space in the floor, with a piano. I kind of stopped when I heard them. Mutt was standing near the back of the room, looking.

"What that nigger call hisself doing? Being Dick Tracy?"

The other man said softly, "That's his wife."

The man turned around. "Aw, scuse me."

I said nothing. I went on up to the stage.

Mutt must've spent several weeks acting that way. When I started singing, he would listen a little, look around again, and then leave. They have Shaft coats now. I guess he must've been wearing his Dick Tracy coat then. Yeah, if I was an outsider I probably would've laughed too. I just stood there trying not to let my embarrassment show in my voice. I sang "See See Rider." Somebody hollered, "Yeah, see what you have done, baby." "Tadpole gonna see see your behind out of here." "Let the woman sing," somebody else said. I sang "The Broken Soul Blues." People always got real quiet on that. Mutt left in the middle of "The Broken Soul Blues." Either he was getting disturbed in the mind, I was thinking, or he was just doing that to humiliate me. Naw, I didn't think he was crazy now, I just thought he was doing it all for spite.

When I came home he was turned over on his back. I asked him what was wrong. He said a man works hard all day and just gets tired sometime. I said nothing. Then he said something about a man working for a woman. He said, "A man works for a woman, a man don't work for hisself." I said, "A man's got to eat and have someplace to sleep too." He said, "A man sees to it that a woman eats and has some place to sleep, and *children*, if he got any, before he takes a bite or feels like he can lay his head down." I didn't say anything else to him. He asked me to come over and rub his back for him, to loosen up some of those tight muscles. I went over and rubbed his back. He fell asleep before I finished, or pretended he was asleep.

"That's what I'm gon do," he said. He was standing with his arms all up in the air. I was on my way to work. "One a y'all wont to bid for her? Piece a ass for sale. I got me a piece a ass for sale. That's what y'all wont, ain't it? Piece a ass. I said I got a piece a ass for sale, anybody wont to bid on it?"

"Mutt, you wouldn't."

"You think I won't. I'ma be down there tonight, and as soon as you get up on that stage, I'ma sell me a piece a ass."

I walked out the door.

Mutt was there. I'd started to tell Tadpole what he planned to do, but I didn't. I was afraid if I did, Mutt might not go through with it, and then there I'd be, looking like a fool anyway. I thought the best thing to do would be just to sing loud, and have Tadpole put him out when and if he started something. I was glad so far he hadn't started a fight with a man. I'd been expecting that, but instead he'd come in looking like damn Dick Tracy, making men rather laugh at him than fight him anyway.

Mutt wasn't there when the show started, but he came in the middle. I was singing one of Ella Fitzgerald's songs, and as soon as I saw him I kind of gradually increased the volume, hoping people wouldn't notice. The piano player, though, must've thought I was crazy, but he played a little louder too. A few men, I think, who had started waiting for Mutt to come in, looked around and saw him and kind of smiled. I was scared too, but I was still singing, and calling his bluff. I saw him raise his arm, and just keep it suspended in the air. Instead of saying anything, he just let it drop, and put his hand in his pocket and left. I ended the song loud anyway. And then I sang a very soft one.

When I got home he was sitting at the dresser. He didn't turn around to look at me because he could see me through the mirror. I closed the door and stood looking at him.

"I'm glad you didn't, Mutt."

"It wasn't on account of you, it was on account of my great-grandaddy. Seeing as how he went through all that for his woman, he wouldn't have appreciated me selling you off."

"Well, for whatever reason, I'm glad. I was hoping it was for me, though." I went to hang up my jacket.

"Don't act Missy," he said, angry.

"What are you talking about?"

"Don't act Miss Missy with me. I ain't *your* slave neither."

"I didn't say you was. I haven't treated you like you was."

He'd turned from the dresser and got up. He was standing looking at me real wild, like he would do something.

"I didn't say you was," I repeated.

I was looking hurt now, at least I felt hurt. And I was also afraid of him.

"I ain't looking for no argument," he said, and walked out, slamming the door.

I must've been asleep when he came back. I could only feel him getting up in the morning, getting ready to go to work. He had to be there at eight.

"They got a big-time band from Chicago coming out to Dixieland," Mutt said. "You think ole Crawdad'll let you off Friday night?"

He was acting more like himself, but lately I'd gotten into the habit of being cautious.

"His name ain't Crawdad, it's Tadpole."

"Crawdad or Tadpole, they both swim around in the same hole," he said, but not sarcastic. He was still in good spirits.

"I think I can get off," I said coolly.

"Come on, Ursa, baby, don't act that way. We need a little night out together, don't you think?"

I nodded.

"Come on over here, honey. Don't stand up there looking like that."

I went over to the bed, and sat down beside him. We made love and then slept. He was asleep before I was.

The big band from Chicago was probably the best group they'd had out there, but then I'd never really gone much, so I couldn't be a judge. Most of the time when they had something out there I was working myself. And then again my joy might have been just being with Mutt, acting the good way he was, and that got into the band's music. I couldn't jitterbug well and so Mutt and me mostly slow-danced. Mutt called it "two-stepping."

"You can't jitterbug?" Mutt asked.

"No, I never really got a chance to learn it."

"Well, you move good and easy this way though."

I didn't like what he was doing now. He was getting up really close to me, more like you see people doing in back alleys than on the dance floor, even though there were other people dancing pretty close. But what he was doing made me think of what people did in the bedroom. He kept making me feel him hard against me, and trying to fit himself in my crotch, and I kept moving a little to the side.

"Be still, woman."

"Mutt, please."

He was holding my shoulders tight, so that even if I hadn't been too embarrassed to move away from him, I couldn't have. Each time he would try to fit himself between my legs, I would move a little to the side. I know we must have looked bad to some people and funny to others.

"Mutt, we ain't in bed."

"You act the same way when we are."

He talked a little louder than I did.

"Mutt, I'm so embarrassed I don't know what to do."

When the song ended I was so embarrassed I wouldn't even look at people. We went over and sat down. I kept looking down at my beer glass. He was drinking rum cola.

"Mutt, I just don't understand you," I said, looking up at him.

"You mumbling, Ursa."

"I said I don't understand," I said a little louder, almost speaking through my teeth.

"You don't try," he said, and took a drink.

When the next slow song came on he wanted to dance again, but I wouldn't. He got up anyway and held out his hand to me, but I wouldn't take it. He kept looking at me real hard, like he was saying, "Take it, bitch. You better take my hand." He wasn't saying it, but it was all in his eyes. And after that was in his eyes, "Don't embarrass me, woman," was in his eyes, and then the hard hateful look was there again. I'd taken his hand when the "Don't embarrass me this way, woman" look had come into his eyes, and we were up on the dance floor when the hard hateful look was back again.

"Don't do that to me no more, Urs," he said.

I shook my head, and let him hold my shoulder hard, and try to grind himself into me. I swore, though, that if he asked me to dance again, I'd run in the bathroom before I'd get up on the floor with him. When the song ended, I could feel his hand move down to my behind. I saw some man look at me and smile. I didn't look at him again.

"How you doing, buddy?" somebody asked Mutt.

"I'm doing, man. How you doing?"

"I'm doing, too," the man answered.

I sat down, not looking at people. Then it was the part of the show where they asked somebody from the audience who could sing to come up to the stage. I'd forgotten about that part of the show. I'd never gone up the few times I was there, but I'd still forgotten. Tonight they asked if there was a female vocalist in the house.

"Go on up, Urs, don't be shy," Mutt said, pushing me a little on the shoulder.

I saw some people looking my way.

"No, Mutt," I said quiet, trying to give him the "Don't embarrass me this way, man" look, but it didn't come off.

"Go on up, Urs, you can sing."

I got up from the table and went in the ladies' room. I saw people's eyes following me like they thought I was going up to the stage at first, and when they discovered I wasn't they just kept watching me. When I came out of the ladies' room, that part of the show was over, and Mutt was standing outside with his arms folded, looking evil.

"Take you a age to pee?" he asked.

"No."

"Get your coat, we going home."

I got my coat, and we left. When we got home he slammed the door.

"You ain't got no right to be mad at me," I said.

He had that hard hateful look again.

"If you ever see me hold my hand out to you in a public place you better take it," he said. "I don't care what you do here, but if we ever in a public place, you better take my hand."

"You didn't have no right to act like you was in the bedroom."

"I wasn't dancing no different from the way other peoples was dancing."

"I didn't see no other people dancing like that. Close, but not like that."

"It look different than it feel, baby."

"You didn't have no right to put your hand on me, though, not where people could see."

"I didn't even touch nothing but your shoulders. Shit."

"Yes, you did. When that song was over you had your hand on my behind, right where people could see."

"Well, it's my ass, ain't it? When I screwed you last night and asked you whose ass it was, you said it was mine. Ain't no other man had it, or have they?"

"Mutt, that was different. You know it." I felt like I was going to cry, but I wouldn't, not in front of him.

"What made it different?"

"Cause people saw it. Cause we wasn't in here, that's why."

"Shit, you my wife, ain't you? We married, ain't we?"

I said nothing. He kept looking at me, almost like he was half grinning, half making fun of me. I turned away a little. I thought I was going to cry, but I didn't. I turned back. "You wont to show everybody when we out in public that you got your . . . piece—but when we here you act like you ain't got shit. I ain't no more than a piece a shit. Well, you got your piece a shit. I can play your game too, buddy. Tomorrow night you can just come on down to the place and sell your piece a shit, cause I don't give a damn."

I turned and went out the door. I went down to the hotel lobby and waited till I was in the toilet, and then I cried.

When I came back he was in bed. He didn't turn toward me, and I didn't tell him good night. He waited until I'd turned the light off before he hit back at me. "I was just pretend fucking, baby, like you used to do. Wasn't doing nothing but play fucking."

When he came to the place the next night, it wasn't to sell his piece a shit, it was to try to take it off the stage, and then when his piece a shit wouldn't get off the stage and Tadpole and some other men put him out, it was to knock that piece a shit down some stairs. I should have known something was wrong when he came home from work that night. He'd brought a bottle of bourbon with him. I was on my way out. It was a Saturday night in April.

"When you get there, Urs, just go over to one a they tables for me, and kinda lean down, you know how you can kinda lean down so you show a little bit of them titties, and then just ask one of em what he wont. If you don't know what he's gonna say, I do. 'Piece a ass, please.' 'Piece a whose ass?' 'Yours, good-lookin woman.'"

"Mutt, it ain't like that."

"Tell me if they ain't asked?"

Gayl Jones

He was all up in my face now, squeezing that bottle in that brown paper sack. I told him I'd be damned if I'd tell him a damn thing.

Mutt came in with his hands in his pockets, drunk this time. The other nights he had been a sober Dick Tracy, but tonight he looked like he couldn't hardly stand. When he started walking toward me I didn't think he would keep coming, but he did. He was within a few feet of me when I stopped singing, the look in his eyes somewhere between the mean and hateful and "Don't embarrass me this way" look. He didn't have his hand out, though. He had them both in his pockets.

"Come on, you going home," he said.

I didn't move.

"I said you going home."

I still didn't move. The place had got real quiet.

"What's wrong with that man?" somebody asked.

"He's crazy," somebody else answered.

"Already crazy, he don't need to be drunk, too," another said.

Mutt turned quickly and looked in the direction where the voices came from, and then turned back to me.

"Woman, you heard me."

I said nothing.

"You my woman, ain't you?"

I kept looking at him. I couldn't make out his look, and I was too embarrassed right now to look anywhere else. He still didn't hold his hand out, though. He seemed like he'd planted them more firmly in his pockets.

"You ain't they woman, is you?"

I stood looking at him. He almost had the "Don't embarrass me this way" look, but the mean and hateful one kept getting in the way. The hard look won.

"Bitch, you coming home," he said and grabbed for me. He almost stumbled and some men grabbed him. While they was taking him out he was saying, "You ain't they woman, is you? Is you they woman, or mines?" The men got him out the door. Tadpole came over to me and asked if I was okay, if I wanted to stop, but I said naw, I was all right. I finished out the show. Mutt kept peeking in, the mean and hateful look on his face, his collar pulled up. And then it was when I was on my way home, he knocked his piece a shit down those stairs.

"You was cussing everybody out," Tadpole said. "They said they didn't know *what* you was."

He was standing up over me in the hospital, the first person I didn't think was Mutt.

I don't remember what I said in the hospital, but Tadpole told me later that I kept saying something about a man treat a woman like a piece a shit.

"You got your piece a shit now, ain't you? You got your piece a shit now."

IV

It was June 1969. I was forty-seven, still working at the
Spider. I walked by one of the tables on my way to the
stage.

"I wont you to put me in the alley tonight, sister," one of
the men said. He was drunk.

"Will do."

"Next best thang to the blues is a good screw."

I sat down at the piano.

"Show business is funny, ain't it?"

I started singing a song, hoping that would make him
quiet. It did. I put him where he wanted to get. I sang a
low down blues. It surprised me he stayed quiet throughout
the whole show, otherwise Logan would have throwed him
out. When I finished, though, he came up to me. "Can I
bring you over to my table? Come on over to my table and
have a drink with me." I went over with him. I'd handled
drunks before, and he didn't seem like a dangerous drunk.
I sat down and he asked me what I drank. I said beer. He
ordered me a beer.

"Show business is funny, ain't it?" he repeated.

I said, "Yeah, it's funny."

"I'm sanging over at the Drake Hotel," he said. "I'm fifty-
eight years old and just got my first job sanging over at the

Drake Hotel, and I been sanging all my life. Show business is sho funny, ain't it?"

I nodded and drank.

"Before then I had to go around with a paper sack. They let you sang in their places, but I have to go around with a paper sack. Some people don't understand that. They say you looking for a handout. But I ain't looking for a handout. I been sanging all my life, and just got my first job yesterday sanging over at the Drake Hotel."

I said nothing.

"You come over there and see me, won't you?"

I nodded, but I knew I wouldn't.

"You won't forget where it's at, will you?"

"I know where it's at."

"Yeah, I been sanging all my life. You know how long Thelonius Monk was playing in that place all that long time before they discovered him. You know, I don't like to use that word 'discovered,' cause it's already there, ain't it?"

I nodded.

"Yes, indeedy, it's already there, but don't seem like they can see it. I don't know how many years daddy Monk was playing funk before they seen him. I call him daddy Monk because I wrote a song about it. I like to write my own songs, you know. I sing some of the others too, but I like to write my own. And I'm fifty-eight years old. You know, I don't like that word 'discovery.' Ray Charles is a genius, you know that? But let me tell you something and I don't have to spell it out for you cause you know what I'm talking about. Sinatra was the first one to call Ray Charles a genius, he spoke of 'the genius of Ray Charles.' And after that everybody called him a genius. They didn't call him a genius before that though. He *was* a genius but they didn't call him that. You know what I'm trying to tell you?

If a white man hadn't told them, they wouldn't've seen it. If I come and told them they wouldn't've seen it. Do you know what I'm talking about? I could've told 'em. You could've told 'em. Like, you know, they say Columbo discovered America, he didn't discover America. You hear that song where Aretha say she discovered Ray Charles. Now tha's awright." He laughed.

I laughed too.

"I could tell them about you, but they wouldn't listen. And you could come over there and tell them about me, but they wouldn't listen." He stopped, then he said, "You know you made me feel good sanging. You made me feel real good sanging."

He didn't give me time to say thank you. He went on: "You know the onliest other time I felt good was when I was in the Apollo Theater. That was a long time ago cause I ain't been back to New York in a long time. But the Lady was singing. Billie Holiday. She sang for two solid hours. And then when she finished, there was a full minute of silence, just silence. And then there was applauding and crying. She came out and was nervous for a full thirty-two seconds. And then she sang. And you see what they done to her, don't you?"

I said, "Yes."

"If you listen to those early records and then listen to that last one, you see what they done to her voice. They say she destroyed herself, but she didn't destroy herself. They destroyed her."

He was almost across the table at me, then he stopped, and sat back, as if he were exhausted. All the time he was talking, I could see Logan eyeing us, as if he were ready to come over any moment at my signal.

"It's a sin, ain't it? It's a sin and a shame. Naw it ain't a shame. It's shameful. That's what it is, it's shameful."

I didn't really see the difference then, but I nodded. He took another drink. He was drinking T-bird. Then he sat looking at me.

"I bet you got some good pussy."

I said nothing. I really hadn't expected that. I just looked back at him.

"Tell me if you ain't got some good pussy."

I didn't tell him anything. I just kept looking at him.

"I don't mean to get nasty," he said. "I just think you a good-looking woman." He leaned toward me. "Tell me if you ain't got some good pussy."

I wanted to go, but I just sat there, saying nothing. He sat back again.

"I know you got some good pussy," he said, as if he were giving a verdict.

A man we called Cat's-eye Marble because he had a popped eye, passed by the table. I said hi to him. He said, "You looking prosperous, baby, real prosperous." That was his favorite word. He went on by. I looked back at the man. He was frowning, still looking at me.

"You won't forget the name of it, will you?" he asked.

I said I wouldn't forget it.

"You be over to hear me, won't you?" he asked.

I nodded.

"I ain't going to be there but for two weeks. They only signed me on for two weeks."

I said nothing. He was silent. He drank some more wine.

"Did I make you mad?" he asked.

I said, Naw, he didn't make me mad.

"I didn't mean to get nasty with you. I ain't got nasty with a woman a day in my life, and I didn't mean to get nasty with you." He got up rocking. I started to ask him if he was all right, but didn't. "You stay sweet, you hear?"

I said I would. I told him to take it easy.

"You won't forget, will you?" he asked.

I said No I wouldn't forget. Then I nodded to Logan, who came and helped him outside. I went back to the piano.

"*. . . She liked me to fan her thighs when it was hot and then one day she had me fan her between her legs. Then after that she made me sleep with her, cause, you know, he wouldn't sleep with her, and then after that something went wrong with her. She had some hot prongs she come after me with, and she told me to raise up my dress and I know where she was going to put them, right between my legs. Cause she knew he was getting his from me too. But then that was when he came in. He grabbed her and knocked the prongs out of her hands and then he started beating her. That woman was black for days to come. After that he just kept her locked up in that bedroom and wouldn't even let me go near her. I guess she thought of it that way, the prongs I mean, from having me fan her between her legs. Thought of it that way in her mind. She just went crazy, that's all. Short time after that, she died up there. But there was a lots of thangs like that that was going on where the husband just let his wife do what she did, or he do it hisself if he was ready for some new pussy. But then lots of time too he just wont the one pussy and do like Corregidora did.*

"*. . . He fucked her and fucked me. He would've fucked you and your mama if y'all been there and he wasn't old and crooked up like he got. Mama ran off cause he would've killed her. I don't know what she did. She never would tell me what she did. Up till today she still won't tell me what it was she did. He would've killed her, though, if she hadn't gone. He raised me and then when I got big enough he started fucking me. Seem like he raised me fucking me.*

Yeah, Mama told me how in the old days he was just buying up women. They'd have to raise up their dress so he could see what they had down there, and he feel all around down there, and then he feel their bellies to see if they had solid bellies. And they had to be pretty. He wasn't buying up them fancy mulatta womens though. They had to be black and pretty. They had to be the color of his coffee beans. That's why he said he always liked my mama better than me. But he never said nothing about what it was she did to him. What is it a woman can do to a man that make him hate her so bad he wont to kill her one minute and keep thinking about her and can't get her out of his mind the next?"

I hadn't seen Sal Cooper much since I walked out. We'd see each other on the street sometimes downtown. We were polite, but we never stopped and talked. I usually kept to my end of town, going to work, then back to the apartment, except when I had groceries to get or some shopping to do downtown. But I rarely did shopping downtown. The drugstore on the corner had most of the things I needed and the grocery store down the road. I made most of the gowns I sang in and I wasn't one for changing costumes a lot. So that I'd only run into Tadpole maybe three or four times. We didn't speak or even acknowledge each other. I heard from somebody that he and Vivian got together, and then about five years ago he sold the place and moved to Chicago. Yeah, and the papers came for me to sign. I was a free woman again, whatever that meant. Sal Cooper I'd heard stayed on at the place when the new owner came. His name was Austin Bradley and he was from Columbus, Ohio. I heard that he was going to change the name of the place, but as far as I knew, it still had the same name. And people were still talking about going over to Happy's. He was going to call it some kind of club but I reckon he figured it was successful enough with its old name, so he just kept it. I think he imported some woman from Detroit to come in and do the singing. Some woman from one of them big cities up North. I think maybe it was Detroit or maybe it's just I keep Detroit on my mind, cause that's the only place I been out of Kentucky. Anyway, what's funny is when he first got there, he come over here and heard me sing and offered me a job singing over there. I told him, Naw thank you anyway but I had my job. I didn't tell him nothing else, but he musta found out about it when he went back over there and started talking to Sal. And then shortly after that he imported that woman from someplace up North. But I bet Sal must've been surprised when he said who it was he asked. Well, I was surprised myself him asking me, though some people say I don't look my age, I look younger than my age. I just tell them it's hereditary. I be forty-eight in June. Well, I never saw Cat no more. I didn't even hear anything about her till I saw Jeffrene that time. Yeah, Jeffrene's grown up now. They calling her Miss Jeffrene, except her mama, her mama still call her Jeffy or sometimes Jeff. I'd see her on the street, and she wouldn't speak and I wouldn't speak. Except one time I seen her she stop, like she was going to say something, but I started on by. She was standing out in front of the Freeze and Eli's dime store over on Third Street. I'd been down to the appliance store over there to pay a bill, and come out and there she was. She kind of jumped when she seen me, and stopped, but I was still going.

"Just walk on by," she said. "That's right. Just walk on by."

I started to, but then I didn't. I stopped to see what she had to say. I figured if I didn't like it, I could just go on.

I stood there looking at her. I must have been looking hostile because she said, "I ain't lookin for no argument."

"What is it?" I asked, still standing there. I think I had my hands on my hips or folded or something.

"I was sick with pneumonia. Didn't nobody come to see me but Mama. I got thinner. Did you notice?"

She did look thinner, but I didn't say I noticed. She had on blue jeans like she always wore, except when you seen her coming from work. She worked out at the narcotics hospital out there on Versailles Road. She was a nurses' aide, I think somebody told me. Now she had on blue jeans. They looked like they were a little too big for her.

I said nothing.

"Cat got your tongue?" She grinned. "She always used to wish she had it."

I looked away from her at the traffic light. She was standing close to the building and I was standing out on the sidewalk. Someone passed by and pushed me a little closer toward her. Then I stood next to the building, but away from her.

"You scared of me, ain't you?"

"Naw, I'm not afraid of you."

She said nothing, then she looked at me and smiled. "I don't think I'm taking too much for granted if I say you are."

"Jeffy, I've got to go."

"I seen Cat."

"How is she?"

"You care?"

I said nothing.

"I seen her down in Versailles."

"I thought she went to Midway."

"Well, when I seen her she was in Versailles. She don't

459

look too good. She start looking her age now, or letting herself look her age. I told her she better get her shit together. She was in a accident, you know."

I grimaced. "What kind of a accident?"

"She work over at the Wax Works, you know. One that makes Dixie Cups or something like that. She was reaching down to get something and got her hair caught in one of these machines and it pulled all her hair out. Well, it pulled all the top part out. Might as well say all of it. She was in the hospital about six months. What you looking like that for? You didn't care nothing about her."

"I do care."

"You could've fooled me."

"I don't mean that the way you want to take it."

"I don't want to take it any way. I wouldn't mind you giving me some."

My eyes hardened.

"Well, I'ma tell you about Cat," she continued. "She wearing that wig. She sued the company, and now they got to buy all her wigs for her. Shit, I told her I'd go down there and pick me one of them good wigs. I wouldn't be wearing one of them shitty wigs like she got. You can tell she got a wig on. I'd go down there and pick me out one of them wigs you couldn't tell was a wig."

"Is she all right?"

"Scalp healed all up. She said you can still see where it all come out though. I ast her to show it to me, but she wouldn't show it to me. I said I thought we meant more to each other than that, but she still wouldn't let me see it. I couldn't even touch her head. Now, you know that ain't right."

I said nothing. She kept looking at me.

"Bad thing to happen to a woman, ain't it?"

I looked at her, trying to keep my eyes hard.

"Things like that," she said. "That kind of thing makes you don't feel like a woman."

"When are you going to stop lying?" I asked. I had turned away from her and was looking in the store window.

"I didn't know I'd started," she said.

I said nothing.

"You didn't come to see me when I had pneumonia."

"I didn't even know you had pneumonia." I hadn't meant to say it. I don't know why I did. I stood very close to the window so she wouldn't see my eyes.

"I hope that woman gets her ass together," she said. "I kept telling her to get her ass together. Ain't no use a her bleeding over that shit, I said. I told her to get her ass together and keep it together."

"What did she say?"

"I think she was glad I told her."

She turned, looking with me into the window. She didn't get close to me as I thought she would, because I had kind of jumped. If she'd noticed it, she didn't let on. We were both silent for a long time.

"I used to come in here and buy those little dime banks they got in there," she said. "You know those little dime banks they sell?"

"Yeah."

"They got penny ones too. I didn't like the penny ones so much as the dime ones. They got some that you have to wait till you get ten dollars in them before they open up. Then they got some got a hole in the bottom, you can get your money out anytime. I used to like the ones you had to wait for."

I said nothing.

"I knew there wasn't nothing between y'all," she said. "I knew it even if you didn't."

I played like I didn't know who she meant. And then, I was thinking, maybe I didn't.

"I don't have to listen to you," I said quietly.

"Who do you listen to?"

I said nothing.

"Do you have anybody?"

I wouldn't answer.

"You know I got something for you when you ready for it."

"I don't want no shit from you, Jeffy."

"Woman like you got to get something, ain't she?"

I turned and walked away from her. She said it softly, but I still heard. "You *know* it felt good that time."

I looked back at her quickly, but walked on.

"Gonna be hard for you, baby," she said. "Ursa?"

"What?" I stopped, but didn't turn around.

"Maybe you can go see her? Maybe you can help her get her ass together."

She said it like she meant it, but still it strangled any impulse I'd had to go see Catherine. And after that day, whenever I saw Jeffrene, I'd cross the street.

I'd never seen Jeffrene with anybody myself, but somebody said she was going with one of the women patients down at the narcotics hospital. A couple of years back she had been being seen with a man from Versailles, but things hadn't worked out.

V

"You just showed that man your ass, didn't you? You could've tried to understand, tried to help him. But all you did was show him your ass. He wanted to help you."

I said nothing. Jim was standing up by the piano waving his hands at me.

"You show your ass to these mens and then when they try to get on it, you say Uh-uh, uh-uh." He kept waving his hands.

Logan came over and wanted to put him out. But I said No. When he went and talked to Max, Max came and said he wanted to put him out for good. But I said maybe they should just put him out for now.

"You don't care nothing, don't wont to know nothing," Jim said. Logan had him by the arm. "Just had your ass all up in his face."

Max waved for me to start playing so it would drown out what Jim was saying.

After that, whenever Jim came in, I wouldn't say nothing to him and he wouldn't say nothing to me. He stopped drinking so much where he got drunk. I guess he must've remembered what it was he said, but he didn't apologize. He just come in and drink just enough and then leave. Logan keep eyeing him though, and every now and then

Max'll come and ask me if Jim keeping his head. I just say Yeah. Seem like every time I look up, though, there's Jim. Least once a week. He be looking at me, but he don't bother me. He don't bother me and I don't bother him. Sometimes he be looking at me, though, like he's studying me or something, but then I give him a hard look and he look away. I don't ask him who he's studying, I just give him that hard look. I guess I could say something to him, but then I got in the habit of not, and just kept it. I guess he got in the habit of not too—just studying me every now and then.

I won't say I don't think of Mutt Thomas, because I do. But I ain't seen him in twenty-two years, and don't know if I know him if I did. I don't know if I know Jim if I didn't see him every time I turn around. But sometimes I find myself wonting to look at Jim to see if they's any Mutt in him, but I don't. Well, what this is all building up to, any-- way, is that Sal Cooper came in the other day. I just about peed on myself when I looked up and saw her, but I know it was me she wanted. Wouldn't be no other reason she be in here. I finished out the song I was singing and came over there where she was. Now Monroe let me play however way I wanted to, except the regular straight two hours Friday and Saturday show. I couldn't just stop in the middle of them. But I just stopped and came over where Sal was and sat down.

"I seen Mutt th'other day," she said.

"Why you telling me?"

"Cause I know how you still feel about him."

"Do you?"

"I knew how you feeled about him when you married Tadpole. I don't think Tadpole knew how you feeled at first, and I don't think you knew how you feeled."

"I knew exactly how I felt. I hated him."

She smiled but said nothing. Then she said, "At least you used the past tense."

"It's been a long time. I don't know how I'd feel. I don't know what I'd do. I still resent him."

"I know you ain't took no other man on."

"What right have you to . . ." I stopped. If it had been Cat I never would have started.

"I'm telling you because I seen him. He was over to the place. He can come in now, you know."

"I can imagine."

"I didn't even recognize him at first. He had this beard and look like a old man, look older than he is. I didn't know him till he come over and said 'Sal.' I said, 'That you, Mutt Thomas?' He said, 'Yeah.' Then I looked behind all that hair and seen it was Mutt. I told him you wasn't there. He said he know you wasn't. I didn't tell him where you was. But I figure he know, and be over here. I just wanted to tell you that he was coming."

"Thank you."

"You mad at me?"

"Naw I'm not mad."

"You something at me."

"I just said thank you, that's all. What do you want me to say?"

"You something at *him* then."

"I don't know what I am at him. I won't know till I see him. If he come."

"You don't think he's coming?"

"Yeah, I b'lieve he's coming. I don't know why I said that."

Sal stood up.

"Thank you," I said.

She didn't say anything, she just looked at me, then she went out.

Jim didn't come in that evening. If he had I would have talked to him. I don't know what I was feeling. A numbness. I knew I wanted to see Mutt, but I didn't know what it would be. I was excited, yes, that's what I was. I was excited about it. Mutt didn't come that evening nor the next evening. Jim didn't come either. It was a week before Mutt came. I knew him even with the beard. He wasn't heavier. He seemed solider. But I would have known him even if Sal hadn't prepared me. It was the Saturday-night show, so I couldn't stop. I sang on. I knew I was singing to him. I think he knew it too. But I knew I hadn't forgiven him. Even when I felt excited about seeing him, I knew I hadn't forgiven him too. I think he knew that as well, even when I finished and came over to the table. He said nothing. I said, "How are you, Mutt?" He nodded, and ordered me a beer, but he still didn't speak. When he did speak finally, he said, "Jim been writing me and telling me every now and nen how you getting along." I remembered that time when I thought Jim had been spying on me. But I wouldn't have used that word now. I just wondered who else Jim might have kept up on how things were going with me, because when I did feel I had to tell Mama my song, she listened, but it was the quiet kind of listening one has when they already know, or maybe just when it's a song they've sung themselves, but with different lyrics. As far as as I knew about her and Mr. Floyd, though, he was keeping to his side of the road, and she kept to hers. She said he was constantly asking her to make him some strawberry preserves, but that was all she'd done. And she never told me about any other man. She had written me something about having left a certain world behind her. I wasn't sure what she meant, but was sure that only one man could remake that world. My father.

"What does he tell you?" I asked.

"That you've still got your voice, that you're still Ursa."
I didn't tell him I'd known he was coming.
I drank my beer. I looked at the table, then at him.
"I want you to come back," he said.
I wanted to say I can't come back, but I couldn't say anything. I just looked at him. I didn't know yet what I would do. I knew what I still felt. I knew that I still hated him. Not as bad as then, not with that first feeling, but an after feeling, an aftertaste, or like an odor still in a room when you come back to it, and it's your own. I don't know what he saw in my eyes. His were different now. I can't explain how. I felt that now he wouldn't demand the same things. He'd demand different kinds of things. But there'd still be demands.
"Did you hear me?"
"I heard."
"What do you say?"
I didn't take my eyes from him. "Yes."
"I'm staying over at the old place," he said. I knew he meant the Drake. "I've got a job over at the Greenwood Cemetery. I know it's not the kind of job that . . . I was working in tobacco up in Connecticut. They got tobacco farms up there. Did you know that?"
I said I didn't know.
"Yeah. But then I just got tired of tobacco, I got tired of the smell, and I came back here. That's the first job I could get till I get something else. You know what I mean?"
I nodded.
"You remember my great-grandfather I told you about?" he asked. "The one with the wife?"
"Yeah."
"After they took her, when he went crazy he wouldn't eat nothing but onions and peppermint. Eat the onions so people wouldn't come around him, and then eat the pep-

permint so they would. I tried it but it didn't do nothing but make me sick."

I said nothing.

"You ready?" he asked.

I said I was. I told Max good night and went back with Mutt.

It wasn't the same room, but the same place. The same feel of the place. I knew what he wanted. I wanted it too. We didn't speak. We got out of our clothes. I got between his knees.

"You never would suck it," he was saying. "You never would suck it when I wanted you to. Oh, baby, you never would suck it. I didn't think you would do this for me."

It had to be sexual, I was thinking, it had to be something sexual that Great Gram did to Corregidora. I knew it had to be sexual: "What is it a woman can do to a man that make him hate her so bad he wont to kill her one minute and keep thinking about her and can't get her out of his mind the next?" In a split second I knew what it was, in a split second of hate and love I knew what it was, and I think he might have known too. A moment of pleasure and excruciating pain at the same time, a moment of broken skin but not sexlessness, a moment just before sexlessness, a moment that stops just before sexlessness, a moment that stops before it breaks the skin: "I could kill you."

I held his ankles. It was like I didn't know how much was me and Mutt and how much was Great Gram and Corregidora—like Mama when she had started talking like Great Gram. But was what Corregidora had done to *her*, to *them*, any worse than what Mutt had done to me, than what we had done to each other, than what Mama had done to Daddy, or what he had done to her in return, making her walk down the street looking like a whore?

"I could kill you."

He came and I swallowed. He leaned back, pulling me up by the shoulders.

"I don't want a kind of woman that hurt you," he said.

"Then you don't want me."

"I don't want a kind of woman that hurt you."

"Then you don't want me."

"I don't want a kind of woman that hurt you."

"Then you don't want me."

He shook me till I fell against him crying. "I don't want a kind of man that'll hurt me neither," I said.

He held me tight.

EVA'S MAN

for

MICHAEL S. HARPER

part
ONE

I

THE POLICE CAME and found arsenic in the glass, but I was gone by then. The landlady in the hotel found him. She went in bringing him the Sunday's paper, and wanting the bill paid. They say she screamed and screamed and woke up the whole house. It's got a bad name now, especially that room. They tell me a lot of people like to go and look at it, and see where the crime happened. They even wrote an article about it in one of these police magazines. That's the way they do, though. I never did see the article. It bothered me at first when I found out they'd used his picture in there, one showing what I did. It didn't bother me so much having mine in there. Elvira said they had my picture in there and my hair was all uncombed and they had me looking like a wild woman.

Elvira's the woman in the same cell with me down at the psychiatric prison. They let her go out more than they do me because they say she's got more control than I have. It ain't nothing I've done since I've been in here. It's what I did before I came, the nature of my crime that makes them keep me in here. The way they look at me. They don't let me out with the other women. When Elvira goes out, she reads the papers and comes back and tells me what's in them. She wanted to bring me that article but they wouldn't let her bring it to me. I wanted to see it at first, but then when she sneaked it in with her down in her underwear, I wouldn't look at it. I made her tear it up and flush it down the toilet.

"You know, they thought you was going to give that hotel a bad name," she said. "I mean, a bad name where wouldn't nobody wont to come and stay in it. But now it turns out that they's some queer people in this world."

"What do you mean?" I was frowning.

"I mean, they's people that go there just so they can sleep in the same place where it happened, bring their whores up there and all. Sleep in the same bed where you killed him at. Some peoples think that's what you was. A whore."

I kept frowning.

"It ain't me saying it."

I lay on my cot and stared up at the ceiling. There were also people saying I did it because I found out about his wife. That's what they tried to say at the trial because that was the easiest answer they could get. I've seen his wife, though. I didn't want to see her because I didn't know how I was going to feel. She came in to see me only one time during the trial. She was a skinny, run-down-looking woman in a black hat. For some reason, I had expected her to be a big, handsome-looking woman. She didn't say anything. She just stood there outside the cell and stared at me, and I stared back. The only thing I kept wondering is how did he treat *her*. Because it looked like he made her worse than he made me. I mean, if she was as bad-off on the inside as she looked on the outside. She must've stood there for close to fifteen minutes, and then left. She didn't have anything at all in her eyes—not hate not nothing. Or whatever she did have, I couldn't see it. When she left, I wondered what she saw in mine.

Even now people come in here and ask me how it happened. They want me to tell it over and over again. I don't mean just the psychiatrists, but people from newspapers and things. They read about it or hear about it someplace and just want to keep it living. At first I wouldn't talk to anybody. All during the trial I wouldn't talk to anybody. But then, after I came in here, I started talking. I tell them so much I don't even get it straight any more. I tell them things that don't even have to do with what I did, but they say they want to hear that too. They want to hear about what happened between my mother and father as well as what happened between me and that man. One of them came in here and even wanted to know about my grandmother and grandfather. I know when I'm not getting things straight, and I tell them I'm not getting this straight, but they say that's all right, to go ahead talking. Sometimes they think I'm lying to them, though. I tell them it ain't me lying, it's memory lying. I don't believe that, because the past is still as hard on me as the present, but I tell them that anyway. They say they're helping me. I'm forty-three years old, and I ain't seen none of their help yet.

I was thirty-eight when it happened. It don't seem like five years ago, but it was. It don't even seem like five months ago. I can still taste that cabbage I was eating. I was sitting in this place eating cabbage and sausage, drinking beer and listening to this woman onstage singing blues. I was in Upstate New York then. I've lived in Kentucky. I've lived in New York City. I been in West Virginia, New Orleans. I just came from out in New Mexico. I just up and went down to New Mexico after I got laid off in Wheeling. They've got tobacco farms in Connecticut. I been there too. I didn't travel so much until after I was married, and that went wrong, and then I said I would just stay alone. It's easier being a woman and alone in different places than it is in the same place. It had been a long time since I'd even said anything to a man . . . the cabbage was good, kind of greasy. They cooked it right with the sausage. I was sitting in the darkest corner. I saw him before he saw me. Tall, dark-skinned, good-looking man. Remind me a little bit of the way my husband might have looked when he was young. I didn't know him when he was young. He was old when I knew him. But it might've been why I wanted him over there—I mean, reminding me of a man I used to be married to. He just reminded me of him up to the point he came to the table, though, because after that he was just himself. He'd been looking for a place where to sit, and then when he saw me he came over where I was.

"You alone?" he asked.

I could tell he was from down South. I was from the South too. I'd sort of thought it before he opened his mouth.

"Not if you join me," I said.

He pulled back the chair and sat down. I was nervous, but I tried not to show it.

"What's your name?" he asked.

"Medina. Eva Medina."

"Medina your last name?"

"Naw. It's my middle name."

"You ain't scared of me, are you?"

"Naw."

"I'm Davis. Where you from?"

"Any place the train takes me."

"What do you do?"

"Nothing right now."

"You hard to get next to, you know that?"

"Not so hard."

I had sweat in my hands. I put one hand under the table and held the fork with the other. I wasn't eating.

"You on the road now?" he asked.

I said, "Naw, I'm here."

He laughed. The blues singer came out onstage again.

It was a little narrow stage close to the tables. He stopped talking and we listened. She sang "The Evil Mama Blues" and "Stingaree Man," "See See Rider" and "Wild Women Don't Get the Blues." While she was singing, he looked over at me and said, "She's fine, ain't she?" I nodded. She was still singing when he started talking again. He said he was from somewhere down in Kentucky. He worked with horses. He spent all his life working with horses. It was horses that brought him this way North.

I didn't tell him that I knew all about men that worked with horses, that I'd spent three years of my life in Kentucky. I let him go on talking.

"I seen this ad in the paper these people wanted you to bring some horses up to New Hampshire, so I did. And now I ain't been home in almost a year. Do you follow the races?"

"Naw."

"I don't bet on the horses myself," he went on. "The last time I bet on a horse, I didn't make nothing but a hundred and eighty dollars. Now that ain't no kind of money. You know what I wanted to do was send some money home, but then all I had to send was that paycheck and a hundred and eighty dollars, but you know that ain't no kind of money. When you send money home, you don't wont to send just a little taste, you know what I mean? You wont to wait till you get some real money."

"I know what you mean," I said.

"They call it the devil blues," the woman was singing, low now. Davis looked back. "She real fine," he said, then he looked at me. "I can tell you something about you," he said. "You ain't been getting it, have you?"

I didn't think he'd said that, but he had. I didn't know what to answer.

He looked at me. "I don't expect you to say nothing. I can read your eyes."

"Can you?"

"Yeah, that's why I came over."

"You couldn't see my eyes then."

He nodded. "Yes I could."

The waitress came over and asked him if he wanted something.

"I'll have the same," he said, pointing to my plate. "But don't put any mustard on the sausage."

When the waitress left, he told me mustard always looked like turd to him, baby's turd, and then he smiled and said he hoped he hadn't spoiled my stomach.

"No, my stomach's hard."

"I'll bet it is," he said. He looked at me carefully. "A woman like you. What do you do to yourself?" he asked.

I said nothing, then I said, "Nothing you wouldn't know about."

He laughed. "A mean, tight mama, ain't you? A old woman got me started. Old to me then. She was thirty-nine and I was fourteen and she lived next door and she got me started."

I was silent. "I'd've thought you got yourself started," I said finally.

"You a hard woman, too, ain't you? I *know* you got yourself started."

I didn't answer him. I was thinking of a boy with a dirty popsicle stick digging up in my pussy, and then he let me feel his dick, and it was like squeezing a soft milkweed.

"I got started like everyone else does," I told him. "I opened my legs. My mother said after you've done it the first time, you won't be satisfied till you've done it again."

"Have you ever been satisfied?"

"What do you think?"

"Let's get out of here."

"Where do we go?"

"Come home with me."

"I won't be good tonight. I'm bleeding."

"Then we'll wait."

His hand scraped my hair and he ate his food, then paid the bill and we left.

What Elvira said those people think I am, Davis probably thought so too. It's funny how somebody can remind you of somebody you didn't like, or ended up not liking and fearing—fearing is a better word—but . . . I hadn't said anything to any man in a long time. And I'd never said Join me before. He probably thought I was in the habit of sitting there in that dark corner just so men would . . . Yeah, they'd come where I was. "Shit, bitch. Why don't you stay in the house if you don't wont a man to say nothing to you." "Where you from, sweetheart?" "Shit, I know you got a tongue. I ain't never met a bitch that didn't have a tongue." And then when I was standing at the corner that time that man drove his car real close to the curb and opened the door. I just stood there looking at him, and then he slammed the door and went around the curb real quick. "Shit, you the coldest-ass bitch I ever seen in my life." "If you don't wont a man to talk to you you ought to . . ."

"Are you lonely?"

"Naw."

"You wont a ride?"

"Naw."

"You think I'm gon bother you. I ain't gon bother you. I was just askin if you wont a ride. Shit."

That was when the buses were on strike.

"Shit, you the coldest-ass bitch I ever seen in my life."
"Are you lonely?"
"Naw."
"Why you so cold?"
"You a evil ole bitch. Your name ain't Eva it's Evil. I wasn't doing nothing but trying to . . ."

Before Elvira went to flush the article down the toilet, she wanted to show me the picture they had of me. She folded it so that I could see the top of my wild head. Then she stuffed it in her bloomers and called them to let her be excused. He wouldn't let me comb my hair. I don't know why, but he kept me in that room and wouldn't let me comb my hair. Took my comb and kept it in his pocket.

"What the shit you wont to comb your hair for. Ain't nobody see you but me."

"I don't wont you to see me like this all the time."

"Shit."

I looked at him. I remember just looking at him. I said nothing.

I tell the psychiatrist what I remember. He tells me I do not know how to separate the imagined memories from the real ones.

"You know what I told you," Elvira says from her cot now.

I keep staring at the ceiling.

"The first man after you get out. The first man who does you wrong."

"Maybe I won't let no other man get close enough to do me wrong."

She laughed hard. I looked over at her ankles.

My mother and Miss Billie came in the apartment. That's when we was living in New York. Miss Billie worked with my mother at a restaurant. She and my mama worked in the morning, and got home around one. She would go get me from the woman who kept me. I was five and wasn't in school yet. Miss Billie would come over and visit for a while and then go on home. She was almost twice my mama's age. She didn't live in the same building we did, but one down the street. Every time she came and Mr. Logan was sitting out in the hall she would start talking about him, saying the same things she'd said before. Mama was listening like she'd heard it before. Mr. Logan was the old man who lived in the apartment next to ours. He didn't have a wife or anything and liked to sit out in the hall.

"I never could stand that man," she said when she got in the house. "He ain't nothing but a shit. He ain't nothing but a ole shit."

I know Mr. Logan could hear, the way the building was made. Mama took her back in the living room. The way the apartment was you came into a little anteroom Mama had fixed up like a sitting room. To the right was the kitchen, and to the left was the bedroom, and then the living room. So we'd always say "back in the living room." I slept in the living room on a couch that let out for a bed.

Miss Billie was talking all the way back to the living room. She wore a scarf sometimes that made her look like a gypsy. She had on the scarf now.

"Yeah," she was saying. "He used to be a carpenter. Every day I used to go over there to that building he worked on and watch him. And me no more than five or six then. No older than this little girl here. I don't even know if he remember me now, cause every time I pass him in the hall he nod but he don't look like he know me. Ain't nothing but a shit. You know, I used to watch him work on this building, and he would show me these

things he used, things for measuring, you know. He had
this stick with this little bubble in it, he showed me, said
it was so you could tell if things was level. Well, you
know, he showed this to me, and gave it to me in my
hand, so I could move it around and see how the bubble
in it moved. Then he said, 'I got another kind of stick
you can see.' He was the only one working on this
building, and we was standing where nobody couldn't see
us, and he got up real close to me and took his thing out.
I swear it was right up in my face. He told me I could
touch that one too. I backed away from him, but you
know, still stayed there looking, like I was hypnotized or
something. He had it in his own hand, and he was
rubbing on it. He kept rubbing on it till all this white
stuff—I didn't know what it was then—came out. That
was when I cut out and run. I still had his stick too. He
ain't never got it back . . . He retired, though, now ain't
he?"

Mama nodded. Miss Billie had told that so often and
I'd heard bits and pieces of it till Mama got so she didn't
even tell me to go in the other room, cause I could've
heard it from the other room. They were sitting in the
living room and I was standing up against Mama's knees,
looking at Miss Billie. She looked down at me, smiling
every now and then.

"Miss Billie, would you like a rum cola?" Mama asked.

Miss Billie said yes and Mama got up and went in the
kitchen. Miss Billie took me around the waist and sat me
up on the couch beside her. "Don't let that old man mess
with you, now, cause he ain't nothing but a shit."

"He ain't messed with me," I said.

The one in the building who had was a little boy with a
dirty popsicle stick. We were playing in this empty
apartment the landlady had left open. He said he wanted

to do me first and then I could do him. I couldn't feel
him doing anything, just moving the stick around, and
then he let me squeeze him like a milkweed.

"Do me now."

"What y'all childrens doin' in here? I'ma tell y'all's
mama," the landlady said.

She never did tell anybody, though. I got blood on the
toilet paper.

I was sitting up on the bed watching him. We were in
his hotel room now. I had my shoes off and my feet up
on the bed. I was hugging my legs.

"What's wrong?" he asked.

"I'll be okay after tonight. It's the first couple of days I
get the cramps, and then I'm okay."

"Ain't you got nothing to take?"

"Naw."

He reached in his pocket and threw me a little tin of
aspirins. He kept a jar of water on the night table. It had
little bubbles in it. I poured a little in a glass. I handed
him back the aspirin, but he said to put them on the
table, I might need them again.

He was looking at me and then he came and rubbed
his hand across my forehead. "Your forehead is like
butter," he said.

I said nothing. I'd never liked for anyone to touch me
around the head, but I let him. I reached up and touched
his wrist.

"How long?" he asked.

"Three days," I said.

The boy's name was Freddy Smoot. After he had that
popsicle up in me I wouldn't play with him any more.
Sometimes when I went down the steps and he saw me

he'd corner me, or he'd corner me downstairs inside the door. He was eight, but I was big for my age and almost as tall as he was.

"Leave me alone."

"You let me do it once."

"Naw."

He had another dirty popsicle stick he pulled out of his pants pocket. "Let me 'zamine you again."

"Naw."

Just then Mr. Logan was coming up the stairs.

"Mr. Logan, make him leave me alone."

Mr. Logan just looked at me, grinning, and walked on by.

He kept cornering me until he rubbed himself up against me and then he ran up the stairs laughing. I didn't even like to go outside unless I was with Mama and then he wouldn't bother me. Once we were with Miss Billie, and Freddy Smoot passed us.

"That boy's just like a little rooster, ain't he?" Miss Billie said. "Just like a little banny rooster."

"He *is* bad," Mama said.

"I caint even stand for him to look at me," Miss Billie said when we got in the house.

"Who, Freddy?"

"Naw, that shit out there. That ole shit out there."

"You let me do it once."

"She don't know how to act," Miss Billie said. She was talking about her daughter, who was fifteen. "All she do is think about that boy. That's why she got her hand caught in the door, cause she too busy thinking about that boy. Come crying to me. I told her she didn't have no business with that boy."

"How's her hand?"

"It's coming along all right. It hurt her like the devil, though. I told her to go and let the doctor cut it a little so he can release some of the blood. But she said Naw. That's why it hurt so bad, all that pressure on it. I told her to go and let him cut it a little right by the nail, and it would stop hurting. But naw, all she got her mind on is that boy. They get like that when they that age, though."

"Some of them like that before they that age," Mama said.

"Yeah, well, all I hope is she ain't let him had none, cause once she let him get some, she ain't gon rest till he get some more."

"Naw, once they done it, they ain't satisfied till they done it again."

"Yeah, that's what I'm worried about," Miss Billie said.

"*You let me do it once.*"

"*I ain't gon let you do it no more.*"

"*When you gon let me fuck you again, Eva?*"

"*You didn't fuck me before.*"

My mother said his mother wasn't no good. The men she had coming in there. White and black men.

"She ain't nothing but a whore," Elvira said about one of the women in the psychiatric ward.

"She don't look like one," I said.

"Don't none of them look like none," she said.

"I only knew one whore," I said. "Some woman that lived in the same building we did."

"Did she look like one?"

"Naw. Mama said she was."

Elvira laughed.

"Once you open your legs, Miss Billie said, it seem like you caint close them."

"What you say?" Elvira asked.

"I said what they used to say when I was a little girl." She asked me and I told her.

She looked at me hard. "What about once you close them?" she asked.

I sat squeezing my legs together, holding my knees. I had on a long skirt.

"You look like a lion," Davis said.

He was standing at the table peeling onions. He was going to make me his favorite salad, he said. Tomatoes, onions, cucumbers, lettuce, hard-boiled eggs. Sometimes bits of ham and cheese, if he had ham and cheese. Today he didn't have ham and cheese.

"You look like a lion, all that hair."

"It's the male lions that have a lot of hair."

"Then you look like a male lion," he said, laughing. "Eva Medusa's a lion."

"Medina," I said.

"Medina," he said. "How'd you get a name like that?"

"It was my grandmother's name."

"How'd she get that name?"

"I don't know. I think one time some gypsies came by their house, and one of them's name was Medina, and her mama thought it was a pretty name."

"Aw."

The onions made tears in the corners of his eyes. He wiped them on his sleeve.

"I don't know if it's true or not. That's what they told me."

"If they told you, then it's true."

"I can help," I said.

"Naw, you still got the cramps, ain't you?"

"Yes."

Elvira laughed. "Once you close them, do you keep them closed?" she asked.

I stared at the ceiling.

"I knew a man once," Elvira said. "He drove every woman he had crazy. I don't mean easy crazy, I mean hard crazy. Had some of em committing suicide and stuff, and even when these women knew how he'd done all these other women, they still wonted him. I guess they figured he wouldn't get them, figured they was different or something. He was good-looking too. But every one of em that went with him just got plain messed up. He messed up every woman he went with. That's the way I think of that nigger you had. That's why you killed him cause . . ."

"Shut up."

"Or maybe you that kind of a woman. Do you kill every man you go with?"

I stared at her.

"They call her the queen bee," Miss Billie said, "cause every man she had end up dying. I don't mean natural dying, I mean something happen to them. Other mens know it too, but they still come."

"Why do they still come?" I asked.

We were in the kitchen and Mama was making Miss Billie and herself and me some lunch. Miss Billie was sitting at the table. I was standing up beside Miss Billie, playing with her gold earrings, and she was hugging me around the waist. Mama was peeling some hard-boiled eggs.

"They come cause they think won't nothing touch them. They think they caint be hurt."

"Eva, why don't you go back in the living room and play. I call you when lunch is ready."

"Yes ma'am."

I made a circle inside Miss Billie's hoop earring.

"The queen bee," she said.

I went in the living room and got my jacks.

. . .

I had on a skirt with an elastic waistband. He put his hand inside my underwear until he touched the edge of the pad.

"Some women wear these so they won't have to do anything."

"I wouldn't be here if I didn't wont to do anything."

"Now all I got to put on this is vinegar," he said, going back to the salad. "When the vinegar touches the egg it smells like . . . a woman's smell."

"What were you going to say?"

He didn't answer. He had a sack full of paper plates. He got out two, and two plastic forks. He dished himself up a plateful and me a plateful. I stayed on the bed, but put my feet on the floor. He put my plate in my lap. He sat down beside me on the bed. He ate the lettuce and onions with his fingers and the bits of egg and tomato and cucumber with his fork.

"Egg's the same thing a woman's got up inside her," he said. "That's why it smells that way. It smells like fuck."

I frowned.

He said, "Excuse me." He took a bit of my egg on his fork, and gave me a bit of tomato from his plate.

"You don't wear earrings," he said.

"Naw."

"Most women who look like you do wear earrings."

"What's that suppose to mean?"

He didn't answer.

I put my finger inside Miss Billie's hoop and made a circle.

"I don't wont Eva to hear things like that," my mama said.

. . .

Davis saved most of his egg and ate it last, and then he folded my plate and his and put them in the sack he used for a trashcan.

"That was good," I said.

"It'll take a age for this room to air out," he said, then he put his arm around my waist and kissed me.

She wanted to take me and Freddy to the park, but Mama wouldn't let her take me to the park. She told Freddy's mama I was too bad to be taken to the park, but I knew it was only because she didn't want Freddy's mama to take me.

I saw Freddy's mama and a man kissing in the doorway. I was sitting out on the steps. Freddy was at school. I could see them up on the next floor, looking up between the stairs.

"You old enough to be in school, ain't you?"

It was Mr. Logan. He had put his chair outside his door and was sitting. I'd been too busy watching Freddy's mama.

"Naw sir," I said.

"Well, you look like you old enough to be in school," he said.

I looked back at him and got up from the stairs. "See you, Mr. Logan," I said and went inside my door. I was scared of him after what Miss Billie said. I kept expecting something white to come out of him.

That was our first year living in that building. My parents came from Columbus, Georgia, but I was five when Daddy moved us to New York, so I tell people I came from concrete. That same day I was sitting on the steps, Mama asked me to go to the store for her. I took a shortcut through this alley and that's when I saw Freddy and some more boys.

"There's Eva, we can get some."

I ran till my throat hurt . . .

Miss Billie had a bag of groceries.

"Y'all get on away from here," she said.

She waited for me until I got what Mama wanted, then she walked me home. She said they were a bunch of wild horses.

"We woulda got you if you didn't have that old woman to protect you."

He had me cornered on the stairs.

"Miss Billie ain't no old woman," I said.

"Well, she ain't no young woman. My mama's a young woman."

I started to tell him what my mama said about his mama, but I didn't. He was laughing.

His mama was standing in the door kissing a man.

The light was swelling from the ceiling. Davis said I was pretty. He put my chin in his palm. "You so pretty," he said. "Come lay on the bed with me, honey. I won't do nothing."

But his hands made rhythms in my belly. I could feel I wanted him already.

"Who are you? Where did you come from?" he asked playfully, stretched out beside me. He'd taken off his trousers. I was down to my panties, the sanitary kind, with the plastic strip in the crotch. I was still afraid I'd stain the bedspread, so he put a towel under me. He stroked my thighs.

"Sometimes I wonder myself," I said.

He said he could smell perfume and menstruation. He said he didn't like it. I kissed his mouth.

"I got all that egg smell out, and now you smelling up my room again." He laughed.

I laughed back at him.

"Now if it was another smell . . ." he said.

I sat up in bed and started singing, the song about staying until it was time for going. He said he liked the song. I lay down beside him again, scratching under my breasts. I could tell he wanted to suck them, but he didn't. I asked him to get closer because it helped the cramps.

"All that blood," he said. "I never could help feeling it was something nasty, even with . . ."

"What's wrong?"

He got up against my belly.

Freddy said him and his mama were moving to a house in Jamaica, New York, a house with a upstairs.

"So."

"You gon miss me, ain't you?"

"Naw, I ain't gon miss you."

He started laughing. "I'm gon miss you," he said.

He kissed me on the cheek and ran upstairs. I put spit on my hand and wiped my cheek off. He ran back downstairs.

"Here." He put it in my hand.

"What is it?"

"A knife."

It was a little pearl-handled pocketknife.

"I'm gon miss you," he said, and ran back upstairs.

Miss Billie had on wooden bracelets. She had on five wooden bracelets on one wrist.

"I wish I could get Charlotte away from that boy. She's just too restless. It ain't right for no little girl to be that restless. If she was a woman it would be something different. Even if she was eighteen. I told her I would send her down there to her daddy in North Carolina. She said if I did, she would run away. Ain't got nothing but that boy on her mind. I told her she gon get more than

493

her hand stuck in the door if she don't start thinking about something else. But they like that, though, ain't they? They just won't listen."

"Eva said Freddy and his mama are moving to Jamaica," Mama said.

"Well, I guess she musta found a better locality," Miss Billie said.

Elvira asked, "What about when you close them? Do they stay closed?"

I asked her if she had another cigarette. She was going to light it for me, but I said I'd light it myself. She'd wanted to light it in her mouth and then pass it to mine.

I usually didn't smoke, but every now and then I'd want one to give me something to do. At first they wouldn't let Elvira have any cigarettes, and then when she started improving, they'd let her have cigarettes.

"Yeah, they thought I was too crazy to even have my own cigarettes," she said, stuffing them back in the pocket of her dress.

She asked me again if once you closed your legs, did you keep them closed. I asked her what did she think.

Miss Billie gave me one of her wooden bracelets. That was when I started to school. She said they were ancestors bracelets. She put it on my wrist. She said something about being true to one's ancestors. She said there were two people you had to be true to—those people who came before you and those people who came after you.

"They heirlooms, ain't they? Ain't you suppose to give those to Charlotte?" Mama asked.

"I wanted Eva to have one," Miss Billie said.

Miss Billie said she was going to her husband in North Carolina. He was down there working in tobacco, and she said if she was going to have to work in a restaurant up

North, she might as well work in one down South, and be with her husband.

"I'm going on account of Charlotte too. You know how I was all worried about her and that boy, and that once it happened I wasn't going to be able to handle her."

"Did anything happen?"

Miss Billie said the first time he tried to do something, Charlotte came home crying and said she didn't even want to see him again.

He was up against my belly. "I ain't never got in no trouble over no woman," he said. "I know mens that kill on account of a woman. I ain't even fought over no woman."

"What would you do, just let her go?" I asked.

"Yeah, I'd just let her go. If she wanted to go, I'd let her go." He started laughing, and squeezed my waist. "Now, if she didn't want to go, that's another story. If some man was trying to take her somewhere and she didn't want to go, that would be different."

"I knew a man that killed another man on account of a woman."

"Was you the woman?"

"Naw. I didn't know her. I just knew the man . . . My cousin told me about how this man killed another man and they put him in jail for seven years. He killed him in the same restaurant we used to go in. He said they wouldn't even let him in that restaurant no more. He could come and peek in or he could send somebody in there and get him something, but he couldn't come in. Alfonso—that's my cousin—Alfonso said it was all on account of his temper. People were scared of him just on account of his temper. Alfonso said he wouldn't bother people he liked. Alfonso said he wouldn't bother me."

"He didn't kill nobody on account of you?" Davis asked.

I said nothing.

"Alfonso said he wasn't a bad man, he just had a bad temper," I said finally.

"Alfonso shit. I can feel you want me now, don't you? I can smell you want me."

"I can't now, Davis."

He got away from me.

"I'd like to, but I start getting pains afterward if I don't wait."

"Yeah, some women are like that," he said.

I played with Miss Billie's wooden bracelet until I lost it. I came home crying because I lost it. I went back looking for it, but I couldn't find it.

"You should've left it here," Mama said.

"Miss Billie told me to wear it all the time. She said I shouldn't take it off."

"Well, ain't nothing you can do about it now."

"I'ma keep looking for it."

"Somebody else probably got it now."

"If I see it on em, I'ma take it off."

"You won't know if it's yours."

"Yes I will. I'll know if it's mine."

"Eva, hush."

I was eight years old when I lost Miss Billie's bracelet.

II

WHAT I REMEMBER about the musician was that he was ten years younger than my mother. He was shorter than my father, and a half an inch shorter than my mother. When my mother and the musician started going together, my father said nothing. He knew what was going on, but he didn't say anything at all. My mother knew he knew, but she would bring the musician home when my father wasn't there. My father would know he'd been there, though, because the musician used to open his packets of cigarettes upside down. He wouldn't open them where the red string was, he'd always turn them over and open them. I asked him why once. He said he didn't know why, he'd just always been opening them like that. And so when my father came home, whenever he'd been there, there'd always be an empty packet of cigarettes in the house, opened upside down. After a while it got so every day there was that packet of cigarettes.

Once I saw my father pick up the packet and put it down again. I couldn't see the expression on his face. I was twelve. I'd just come back in the living room with my homework. When he turned around and told me hello, he didn't have any kind of a look on his face. He just looked like a man who was going about his business. He sat down and read the paper.

The musician's name was Tyrone. Mama met him

when she went out to this dance-hall with some girl-friends.

My father worked in a restaurant and didn't get home till real late in the evening. Around eight or nine some nights, and on Friday nights about eleven or twelve. He did different things. Sometimes he bartended, sometimes he'd work in the kitchen.

The first time I saw Tyrone I didn't know who he was. I came home from school and there was this strange man sitting there. Mama wasn't in there. He was sitting in the kitchen by himself. I just stood there. He looked like he was a little afraid of me too.

"Cat got your tongue?" Mama had come in. "Where's your manners?" she asked. "This is Tyrone."

I said hello and then took my books back in the living room. That was the first time I'd seen Mama with a man other than my father.

"I better leave," I heard Tyrone say.

"No, it's okay."

Then I heard her getting out pans.

I lay on the couch on my belly. I kept waiting for them to say something, but they didn't. I was thinking maybe they didn't want to say anything because I was there.

Finally he said, "When you came in there with your girlfriends, I didn't think you were married."

"I had my ring on."

"I never notice rings."

"Then it's your fault."

"That's all right, Marie. I'm going," he said.

"When am I going to see you again?"

"I don't know."

"What's wrong?"

"Nothing."

There was silence. He was going to the door and she was going with him.

"I didn't mean to find you either, you know," she said, and then he went out the door.

Mama came back there where I was. I looked around at her. She just looked at me. She didn't even have to tell me that she would be the one to say anything to Daddy if anything was to be said.

"Why don't you come peel the potatoes?" she asked.

I got up off my belly and followed her in the kitchen.

When we were in the kitchen and I was standing at the table peeling the potatoes on old newspapers and she was cutting up the chicken, I kept thinking that she would start explaining things, but she didn't. She just stood there cutting up the chicken. The only thing she said was "You can peel them closer than that. Look at all those potatoes you're wasting."

I said, "Yes ma'am."

And then she would just see him. The musician was in this band that would play different places around. They played at the dance-hall for about two weeks and then they would play somewhere else. After they'd been going together a little over a month, the man that owned the place where Daddy worked wanted them to play out there. It wasn't a big place, but they had a little dance floor. Daddy took me out there one Sunday when he was cleaning up, that's how I knew how it looked inside. And then I could come around to the back through the kitchen. By the time they wanted Tyrone and his group to come out there, Daddy already knew Mama was seeing somebody, and he already knew who it was she was seeing. I never did know how he found out. Sometimes I think Mr. Logan told him, sitting outside his door all the time the way he did, seeing everything. I wasn't afraid of him like I used to be when I was little, but I still hated to pass by him. He would always find something to say to me. Most of the time he would ask me how school was, and say, "Yeah, you got to get your education. You doing right to stay in school. If I'da stayed in school, I'd be a son of thunder right now. Couldn't nobody touch me." I used to think to myself, Wouldn't nobody wont to touch you. I didn't mind so much what he was saying as the way he was saying it, and the way he was looking at me. He never did try to show me anything, though. I thought Daddy might've been passing by one day, and Mr. Logan stopped him and said, "Your wife had a visitor this morning." That would sound just like him.

Tyrone's band went out to play where Daddy worked. They only played out there for one night, though. Tyrone played saxophone.

At first Tyrone was a little nervous about playing out there, because that afternoon I heard him tell Mama, "It ain't no way I can back out."

"You don't need to back out. Just go there and do your job. John's an intelligent man."

"That's what I'm afraid of. The way he acts. You can trust a man that gets angry. But you can't trust a man that takes things calm."

Mama said nothing.

"I don't even understand the situation I'm in," Tyrone said. "I'm in it, but I don't understand it. You and your husband's some strange people. Any other man . . ." He didn't finish. I was just hearing it, so I didn't know if Mama put her hand up or what.

Mama was thirty-two then, and Tyrone, he was twenty-two. I looked on him like he was a man, though, even though he was as close to my age as he was to hers.

When Tyrone got through playing out where Daddy worked, nothing happened. Maybe something did happen. Daddy came home and he said something about him for the first time. He didn't mention his name or anything. He said, "I seen your buddy tonight."

"What?"

"I seen your buddy."

Mama was silent. Then she said, "Oh."

What was really strange, though, was they still slept together. They'd close the door that separated their room from where I was sleeping, but like I said, the way the house was made, I could hear when they were making love. I'd always heard them making love, and it seemed strange to me when later I'd run across people who'd never heard their parents making love. But I suppose it seemed strange to them that I *had*. But they made love as if Tyrone wasn't happening. I used to wonder what was going through her mind. Not his, but hers. It wasn't until later I started wondering what would be going through his.

After that night, though, whenever Daddy saw Tyrone, he would say, "I seen your buddy today." That was all he would say. He would always see him outside the house somewhere, on the street or at the store or something, but never at home. The only thing he would see at home was that package of cigarettes opened upside down.

I don't know what I thought of Tyrone. He was just a man there. I never would say anything to him, and he never said anything to me. Whenever I came home from school and saw him sitting there, I'd say Hi, and then I'd go back in the living room. And then Mama would be in the kitchen fixing supper. Daddy had supper where he worked and then he'd come home in the late evening. So Tyrone would eat supper with us, and shortly after that he would leave.

When we sat at the table him and Mama would be talking but I never would say anything, I would be listening to them. He would mainly be talking about funny things that would happen when him and the band went different places to play. He was talking about this one woman who was drunk and dancing and then suddenly lost her bloomers. She was still dancing up a breeze and her bloomers were down around her ankles. I didn't think it was funny, but Mama laughed.

Sometimes Tyrone would wear this little round straw hat and dark glasses. He said that was his working outfit.

The first time Tyrone really said anything to me was one day I came in the house, and he was sitting there like he always was. We said Hi to each other, and Mama hollered at me from the kitchen. I went back in the living room. After a while he followed me in there.

"Do you play jacks?" he asked.

I nodded, but I thought I was too old for jacks, even though I was just twelve.

He took some jacks out of his pants pocket and sat down on the floor. I sat down on the floor.

"I haven't done this in a long time," he said, laughing.

"Most the boys I know don't play jacks," I said.

He said nothing and handed the jacks to me to flip first. I missed after the first two throws. When it got his turn he got up to his fours without missing.

He won the game. We just sat there.

"Do you want to play another game?" he asked.

"I don't care. If you do."

He said nothing. He was just sitting there with his legs folded, moving the jacks around. I don't know what made me look where I was looking. When I first started looking there, I didn't realize that's where I was looking, and then when I realized, I kept watching down between his legs. I don't know how long he saw me watching there, but all of a sudden he took my hand and put it on him. I was scared to look up at him. That was when Mama called and said supper was ready. He pushed my hand away and jumped up, and went in the kitchen. I kept sitting there until Mama said, "Eva, come on."

I didn't know what made him put my hand there because after that he acted like he was embarrassed. He wouldn't hardly look at me. He had the kind of look people get on their face when they're worried about something. I'd come home from school and say Hi. He'd say Hi but he wouldn't look at me.

Then after that he started bringing me things—things like popcorn and potato chips, doughnuts, cookies, candy, stuff like that. He never would give them to me himself. But Mama would say, "There's some candy in there on the table Tyrone left for you." I could still feel my hand down there. Sometimes when I would think about it, I would go and wash my hand. I don't know why I did that, though. Either I would do something to keep from being alone with him, or he would do something to keep himself from being alone with me. Like once Mama had to go to the store. He offered to go, but she said Naw, she would go. He sat in there for a while. I was back in the living room, but I knew he was sitting in there. And then he got up and went outside. I could hear him out there talking to Mr. Logan. I visualized him standing out there, smoking and nervous, talking to Mr. Logan, and Mr. Logan looking at him hard.

He didn't come back in the house till Mama came. She lowered her voice when they got inside, but Mr. Logan still ought've heard.

"What you doing out there talking to *him?*"

"He's all right."

"All he does is mind everybody's business but his own."

"He probably don't have his own business to mind. You can't blame him."

Mama said, "Well, he ain't nothing but a old shit."

Then he stayed in the house while Mama was getting supper ready.

She asked me to come and grease the pan for the biscuits. When I passed Tyrone, he was looking down at my feet.

"What's wrong with you?" Mama asked when I got in the kitchen.

"What?"

"You can grease ten pans with all that grease."

Mama always used to make fun of Tyrone's name. I remember close to when he first started coming, we were sitting at the table.

"Your mama name you after a movie star too?" Mama asked.

Tyrone looked embarrassed. He didn't say anything. He was kind of shy of her at first, even though they were going together. At least that's what I used to think, or maybe it's just he felt uncomfortable with me there, me being her daughter and all.

"When I was coming up," Mama said, sounding as if she was more than just ten years older than him, "people was naming their children Tyrone and Clark Gable. If they didn't name em Clark, they would name em Gable. Who else? Ronald Colman and names like that. You know what Mr. Logan's first name is? Valentino. He don't hardly use it, though, except when he has to sign something legal, cause he don't wont people to call him Val, you know. So most people just think his name is Logan and just call him Logan. That's funny, though."

"I was named after my grandfather, I wasn't named after no movie star," Tyrone said. He sounded like he was angry.

"I didn't mean to make you mad."

"I'm not mad." He still sounded mad.

"Well, it is easy to *think* you was named after him. My mother almost named me Claudette, but my father raised such hell, she didn't. He said she bed not name no daughter of his Claudette."

Tyrone laughed. "I'm sorry," he said. "It's just I hate for people to think I was named after him, when I wasn't."

Mama nodded, then she kind of laughed again. He looked hurt, like she was laughing at him, but she said, "I don't think Mr. Logan's granddaddy was named no Valentino, though."

Tyrone laughed. I laughed too. If Mr. Logan heard, I don't think he laughed.

"You remember how it feel, don't you?"

I said nothing. He said it real soft, almost in a whisper. Mama was in the kitchen and had the radio on.

"You remember how it feel your hand down there, don't you? I know you remember it, cause I remember it."

He'd gotten close to me. I was sitting on the couch, but he didn't sit down beside me. He just stood close to me, and if I looked across at him I'd have to look at the part of his pants where his private was. I looked up once, and it looked like it had that day, and I looked down at my book.

"I know you remember, cause I remember."

I sat real stiff. I remember thinking he was crazy. Then I kind of scooted over and then darted into the kitchen where Mama was. I didn't go into the kitchen right quick. I slowed down before I got there, and then when I got there I asked her if I could help with anything. She said, "Naw, honey." When I turned he was standing in the door. I would have had to squeeze by him if I wanted to get by, so I sat down at the kitchen table.

"You finished your homework?" Mama asked.

"Naw ma'am."

"Well, you go in there and finish it then."

"I just got a little bit more to do. I thought I'd do it after supper. My eyes are tired."

"Well, okay," she said. "Why don't you go and look at those beans and see if they need any more water."

"Yes ma'am."

I went and looked at the beans. I put half a cup of water in them and then came back and sat at the table. Mama looked at me and then went on slicing cheese for the macaroni. I could see Tyrone still standing in the door, but I wouldn't look at him directly. I didn't want to know what kind of expression he had on his face.

After that I would always sit in the room closer to the kitchen and do my homework. I'd always ask Mama if she wanted me to help her, and then I'd help her. Even though he was sitting in that room too, I was closer to her, and if he said anything, she would hear him. I guess she thought it was funny me sitting in there when I used to sit back in the living room. Maybe she thought I had a crush on Tyrone or something and was sitting in there where he was. I didn't even like his eyes on me. Like when I was writing my math problems or reading, I could feel his eyes on me. I didn't dare look up at him.

Tyrone was standing down below the stairs when I got home from school. I wasn't going to say nothing to him, I was just going on up the stairs.

"You see me, you can speak," he said.

I stopped at the bottom of the stairs, but still didn't say anything.

"You felt me and you can still feel me," he said. "You still know how it feel."

"I didn't feel nothing."

"Yes you did. I felt it, so I know you did."

"You crazy, man."

"Don't you call me crazy, you little evil devil bitch. Don't you call me crazy."

He reached his hand out like he was going to grab at me and pull me down there beside him. That was when the noise came. It came real soft at first, but it made Tyrone jump back. "Hoot." Then it came again louder, like somebody was calling. "Hoot." Like when somebody is out in the street calling. Tyrone stayed under the stairs. I stood there for a second and then I cut out and ran. When I got to the top of the stairs, Mr. Logan was looking at me. He was looking like he hadn't heard anything. I didn't know whether I should tell him thanks or not. I kind of smiled at him and then I darted inside.

When Tyrone was late coming back from the market, he told Mama he had stopped to talk to an old buddy.

It was as if Daddy was waiting till he saw them together. He knew about it but it was like it wasn't happening until he saw it. It was the same day he quit his job and came home. He said he wasn't going to work and take shit too. He said if he was going to work, he wouldn't take shit. And he said he wasn't going to take shit. He never did tell us what had happened at work. He didn't tell us that was the reason he came home early until about a week later. He'd go out every day, looking for another job, and we'd think he'd be working. He had come home early, and yet he knew what he'd find, knew they'd be there. And at the same time he was waiting to see it. He could have come home early at any time. Mama thought he had come home early just to see them. What I'm trying to say is he wouldn't come home until there was a real reason for him to, and yet he knew what he would find when he got there. He didn't find them doing anything, because if they ever did anything, it was before I got home from school. Because I was there. I was back in the living room. And anyway, when he came home they were sitting in the kitchen talking. I knew who it was when I heard that other door, and I knew they knew who it was. They'd stopped talking. I heard one chair moving. I kept waiting for Daddy to say something. They must've been looking and waiting. I don't know what kind of look Daddy must've had on his face, but I wouldn't have wanted to be Mama and seen it. That's what's still so strange to me, though. He knew it, and yet he had to see them sitting in there in his home, before he'd do anything, react, before he let his feelings out. I kept listening for him to say something.

"I left the door standin' open, buddy."

I remembered I had only heard the door open but not close. Tyrone didn't talk back to my father or nothing. He just got up and on his way out, Daddy said, "Close that door behind you, will you, buddy?" He closed the door. I was waiting to hear if he'd slam it or close it, but he closed it quietly like he was afraid of making any noise.

Then there was this other silence, waiting. I heard Mama's chair scoot a little like she was going to get up. Neither one of them was saying anything. I don't know how long it was. It seemed like ten minutes to me, but it couldn't have been that long. It must've seemed longer to her, having to see his eyes. Because she would've been looking right at him. She would've been looking right at him.

"Come on," he said.

The chair scooted and scraped, and he had hold of her arm. I didn't see them until they got to the bedroom. He had her arm and he was undoing her blouse. My eyes must've been all wide and scared. Daddy looked at me and kind of smiled. It was a love smile for me but a hurt smile for him. I don't know what kind of one it was for her. It must've been a love/hate one for her.

He said, "Close that door, will you, honey." He said it just like that. Real soft. Real gentle.

I got up and closed the door that separated the living room from their bedroom.

Then it was like I could hear her clothes ripping. I don't know if the gentleness had been for me, or if it had been the kind of hurt gentleness one gets before they let go. But now he was tearing that blouse off and those underthings. I didn't hear nothing from her the whole time. I didn't hear a thing from her.

"Act like a whore, I'm gonna fuck you like a whore. You act like a whore, I'm gonna fuck you like a whore."

He kept saying that over and over. I was so scared. I kept feeling that after he tore all her clothes off, and there wasn't any more to tear, he'd start tearing her flesh.

III

A NAKED HANGING light, a bed, a table, a yellow shade torn on the side. He made patterns with his fingers on my belly.

"Do you want me to use a rubber? I mean, when we do it?" he asked.

"Naw, not if you don't wont to."

I was seventeen when my cousin Alfonso and his wife came from Kansas City, Kansas. My mother said they were the cowboy part of the family. Some had stayed in Georgia, but some had gone West. She said she was the only one of the family who had come North, and she wouldn't have done that if Daddy hadn't wanted to make the move.

Now Alfonso and his wife, Jean, and Alfonso's brother Otis had come to live in New York. They couldn't get themselves a place to stay at first, so they stayed over at some hotel. Mama said she wished she could let them stay with us, but they saw what kind of space we had.

Jean and Otis came and visited us every now and then, but Alfonso was over there nearly every other day. He'd keep getting mad at something Jean did—we never did know what it was she did—and then he'd be over to our place. Mama said it must've been something she did back in Kansas City, and he just kept it in his memory. Otis never did know what it was either, but he said when they were in Kansas City, there was a certain hotel in Kansas

City, and every time Alfonso got mad at Jean—it was like a spell or something that come over him—every time he got mad at Jean, he would take her down to this hotel and start beating her out in front of it. He wouldn't take her inside, he'd beat her outside. Couldn't nobody do nothing with him, and they would send for Otis. Otis was the only one that could do anything with him, and he didn't even know how.

"All I would do is go down to the hotel," Otis said.

He was sitting on the couch in the living room. He was a big man but not fat. He had come by himself one day.

"Yeah, I would just go down to the hotel. I wouldn't do nothing, I would just kind of grab hold of his arm and say, 'All right, Alfonso. That's enough, Alfonso,' and he would stop. And there Jean would be bruised all up. I don't know why she ain't left him. It was my idea we come here. I told Alfonso he probably have more opportunity here, you know, but the real reason was I wanted to get them away from that hotel. I thought it might help."

"Has anything started up since they been here?" Mama asked.

"Yeah, that's what I came here to tell you, Marie. He got drunk last night and took her down in front of *that* hotel—the one we staying in—and started beating on her. But the woman stay with him, though. That's what I don't understand. She stay with him. If I was her I would've packed my bags a long time ago."

Mama said nothing.

"You know," Otis said quietly, as if somebody might overhear. "I almost suggested to him that maybe, you know, something was wrong with him, you know. But I ain't asked him since."

"What did he do?"

"It ain't what he did, it's the way he looked. If

anybody had a look that could kill, it was that one, and I ain't lying. The way I look at it now, it's her that's staying with him. If she can stand getting beat . . . You know what I'm trying to say?"

Mama nodded. She was staring down at her nails.

"I do what I can. Whenever he starts I go over there and touch his arm or take him by the shoulder and say, 'That's enough, Alfonso, all right, Alfonso,' and then he stops."

He had his arm thrown over the couch. Even though he didn't take up the whole couch, it looked like he did. Me and Mama were sitting in chairs.

It was late one night a few days later when I heard it: "Never know how you're going to love me."

"Open the cell, please. I want to go to the toilet."

"You must have bad kidneys," the guard said.

"What do you want?" Elvira asked, late one night.

I hadn't been sleeping, but thought she was asleep. I told her I didn't want anything from her.

"Well, you ain't getting nothing from that nigger of yours, neither, cause he's dead."

She started laughing. It was an almost noiseless laugh.

"It's like you sitting on a pot, sitting right on a pot, but afraid to shit," Elvira said.

I asked her if she was the pot or the shit.

She laughed hard this time. It was a short hard laugh, not a long one.

"I seen one of these men the queen bee got a hold of," Miss Billie had said. "He was laying in this restaurant on the floor. Some woman had shot him. Naw, it wasn't the queen bee that done it. What happened was that somebody told this woman this man of hers was down in such and such a restaurant with another woman. And what happened was he had his back to the door and he looked like this other man and she shot him . . . When you in those kinds of restaurants, though, you should never sit with your back to the door, cause no telling who might see you and think you somebody else. That's why when I go out I don't never sit with my back to the door. No telling who might come in . . . Yeah, she found out she had the wrong man, but he was dead then . . . I don't know how long they sent her up for. And that man was one of the queen bee's men too. And other men still after her. Sound like a lie, don't it? But it ain't, it's the truth. It's sho the God's truth."

Mama said she hadn't known anybody like that, like the queen bee. But she said she would be more scared to be the queen bee than to be any of the men.

"Suppose you really loved somebody," Mama said. "You'd be scared to love him."

Miss Billie said she hadn't never looked at it that way, but it must be hard on the queen bee too.

"Couldn't love who you wont to, have to love who you didn't wont to," Miss Billie said.

I sat in the living room with my hands on my knees.

"I know you ain't had to go to the toilet that much. What you in there doing, woman?" Elvira gave another hard laugh.

I sat back down on my cot.

"Scared to do it in here . . . Naw, you ain't crazy. When you first come you was crazy, but you ain't crazy now. They gon keep thinking it, though. Cause it's easier for them if they keep on thinking it. A woman done what you done to a man."

"You the pot or the shit?" I asked.

513

I lay down and turned my back to her. I watched two cockroaches on the wall.

"What's the matter, Eva? What you thinking?"

I watched the cockroaches and wondered how small cockroach turd was, how much liquid was cockroach piss.

"What do you want?"

Freddy Smoot's mother standing in the doorway kissing a man. She had on a tight-waist dress and purple lipstick. Got it on the man, he wiped his mouth off, kissed her again, wiped his mouth off. She had long thick hair and dark lines around her eyes. She got real close to the man and kissed him with her tongue out. Mr. Logan tried to show me his thing. I ran in the house and shut the door before I could see it. He had white stuff in the corners of his eyes. "Hoot. Hoot. Hoot. Hoot." His stick has a bubble in it.

I felt her breath on my neck, but when I turned around she was laying on her cot with her eyes closed.

"I know what's wrong," she said.

The cockroaches on the wall got close together.

"What does Miss Calley think about all of this?" Mama asked.

Miss Calley was Otis' mother. She was my mother's sister, but old enough to be her mother. Otis was older than my mother by two or three years, and Alfonso was almost as old as she was. So Mama had always called her sister Miss Calley, and when I saw Alfonso and Otis, I thought of them more as uncles than cousins.

"She don't know what to think. She always have thought Alfonso was crazy. You know, like she say our Uncle Nutey went off his rocker, she thought maybe Alfonso might've inherited some of it. I ain't even told her about the last two times Fonso beat up on Jean. You know, she told Jean that she could come stay with her, but Jean say she didn't wont to. Actually, what Mama thinks is that Jean just as crazy as Alfonso and that they need each other."

"Miss Calley still making those clothes and selling them to people?"

"Yeah, you go in there and she still got those clothes hanging up in there all over the house. Only thing is she still using a lot of them old patterns she got and people just ain't wearing them kind of clothes any more. You know, sequins all up over the top and everything. It's all right when people get her to make something specific for them, but some of them clothes just hang up in there."

"They'll come back in style. That's the way clothes do."

"Yeah, I reckon. Me and Alfonso send her money. That's the only reason I hated to come out here, leave her alone like that. I mean, Daddy's there, but he's down at the garage most of the time, and she got so she had all her family with her. But, you know, I feel like I'm the only one that can handle Alfonso. You know what I mean."

Mama nodded.

"You know the one question that's always been in my mind?" He took his arm off the back of the couch and leaned forward.

"What is it?"

"It's how long and hard he would beat on her if I hadn't come all them many times, because every time he's started beating on her, I've been there to stop it . . . Do you think he would've ended up beating her to death?"

Mama said nothing. She just looked at him. "Somebody would've stopped it," she said finally. "The cops would've come and stopped it."

"Naw, I be scared he'd turn on the cops, and then he be getting his self killed then."

Mama said maybe he was right.

"Yeah, I know I'm right," Otis said. He stood up stretching.

"I wish I could do something to help," Mama said.

"Naw, I didn't come here for you to help," Otis said. "I don't think there's nothing anybody can do. I think the onliest person could do anything is Jean, if she'd leave, but she won't leave . . . Except maybe she's right, though. Maybe he be worser off if she did leave and he didn't have nobody to beat on. You know, maybe that woman know more than any of us do."

Mama said, "Maybe."

Otis grinned at me, and told Mama goodbye, and left.

Miss Billie said, "Yeah, I guess I would be more scared if I was her than him."

I used to think the queen bee looked like a bee and went around stinging men, but once we were walking down the street and Miss Billie said, "There she is."

"Who?" Mama asked.

"The queen bee," she said under her breath.

She didn't look any different from Mama or Miss Billie or Freddy's mama.

"You just sitting right on a pot and scared to shit," Elvira said. "Sitting right on one."

"Naw, I ain't never got into nothing over no woman," Davis said. He was playing with my ankles.

I closed my eyes. He was laying with his feet toward my face, playing with my ankles.

"Why did you come here, Eve?"

"My name's Eva."

"Why'd you get so angry?"

"I don't know. I just never liked to be called Eve. I don't know why."

"All right, Eva, baby. You don't mind if I call you baby, do you?"

"Naw, I don't mind."

He squeezed both my ankles. "You a good-lookin woman," he said. "A real good-lookin woman."

"You looking at my feet," I said, laughing.

"Honey, baby, I know what your face look like. By the time I get through with you, I want to know you inside out."

He didn't see the lines in my forehead. I looked down at his shoulders, the back of his head.

"You know that song. I don't want to love you outside, I want to love you inside," he said, laughing. "Go something like that."

"Yeah," I said, and laughed some.

"Eva, Eva, sweet Eva," he said.

"You could be so sweet to me, if you wanted to," Elvira said.

"I'll help you stuff a candy bar up your ass," I said.

"You ain't so hard as you think you are. You just wait. You ain't near so hard as you think you are. You think cause you can bite off a man's dick, you can't feel nothing. But you just wait. You gon start feeling, honey. You gon start feeling."

She laughed her laugh.

"They told me hysteria was one of your problems," I said.

"Yeah, and I know what yours is. Got to go pee, my ass . . ."

"Y'all ain't the only people in the world. There's more people in the world than y'all," some woman from another cell hollered.

"Honey, we know you here too," Elvira said.

"Eva, sweet, sweet Eva."

He ran his hands between my thighs, and stopped when he hit my bloomers, the sanitary pad.

"I hope you got enough of these things," he said.

"Yeah, I brought enough."

"Cramps any better?"

I nodded. He kept his warm hand on the inside of my thighs.

"Shit or piss one," Elvira said.

The gypsy Medina, sitting in my great-grandmama's kitchen, said, "There's something in my eyes that looks at men and makes them think I want them."

"Why did you come over and say something to me in the first place?" I heard Mama ask Tyrone.

"There was something in your eyes that let me know I could talk to you."

"Didn't you see anything in the other women's eyes?"

"Naw."

Davis said, "There was something in your eyes."

"What?"

"I could tell by your eyes how you felt. I could smell you wanted me."

"I couldn't help looking."

I told Davis what the gypsy Medina and her husband did. They told Great-Grandmama they had a sick baby in the wagon, and said they didn't have any food, and asked her if she could give them some food for the sick baby.

Great-Grandmama was still living in Georgia, in the country, and kept chickens. She gave them two of the chickens, and some milk and ham. When they left, Great-Grandmama's cousin who lived down the road came up to the house and said, "I seen them gypsies' wagon stop up here. You didn't give em no food, did you?" Great-Grandmama said, "Yeah, I gave them something." Her cousin said, "I didn't give em nothing. I went out there and looked in the wagon and that baby was as big as I am."

Great-Grandmama said she liked Medina, though. She would have given them the food just for themselves. When my grandmother was born, she named her Medina.

Davis said, "Don't look at me that way. Don't look at me that way until you're through bleeding."

"You know where they keeping his penis," Elvira said. "They keeping it in the icebox, so it won't get all shriveled up, so they can use it for evidence. They took it out of that silk handkerchief you had it in and wrapped it in Glad Wrap. When you go to court, though, they gon put it back in that silk handkerchief. Which one of em had to show the penis around? Did they try to make you look at it?"

"Yes, but I wouldn't."

"Just like in that Bible story, ain't it? Except got his *dick* on a platter."

"Yes."

"You lied. They said you didn't bite it all off, like you told me."

"I did."

The gypsy Medina sat in my great-grandmother's kitchen. Her hair was thick gypsy hair. She said she had gone to those white people's house and these white people had sent them around to the kitchen where the negroes was.

My great-grandmother's cousin said, "They was up there to my place talking about these peckawoods. They peckawoods too. They don't even know they peckawood. You know, like that old man from Syria that keeps that store down at Frogs Crossing."

Great-Grandmama nodded.

"He come talking to me about what the peckawoods done to him. I told him he's a peckawood too."

Great-Grandmama said, "If he don't think he's one, he ain't one."

Her cousin said, "Shit."

The gypsy Medina, Great-Grandmama said, had time in the palm of her hand. She told Great-Grandfather, "She told me to look in the palm of her hand and she had time in it."

Great-Grandfather said, "What did she want you to do, put a little piece of silver over top of the time."

Great-Grandmother said, "No." Then she looked embarrassed. Then she said, "She wanted me to kiss her inside her hand."

Great-Grandfather started laughing. He worked in tobacco. He rolled his own cigarettes, but never rolled them tight enough. He had spit and tobacco juice on the tips of his fingers. Then he wanted to know where the ham was, and two of their chickens must've got lost. When she told him about the sick baby in the wagon that turned out not to be a baby after all, he roared.

"Don't you think that's funny?" I asked Davis.

He said, "People play tricks like that all the time. They don't have to be gypsies neither."

I asked him if that's where the word to gyp somebody came from.

They kept his penis in the icebox, wrapped up like a ham, and then in the courtroom, wrapped up in a silk handkerchief, like a jewel.

Davis squeezed my ankles. I squeezed the boy's dick. It was like squeezing a soft milkweed. I reached down and squeezed the back of his neck. The musician made me put my hands down between his legs.

"Do you think some things are meant to happen?" I asked Davis.

He said he didn't know what I meant.

My great-grandmother kissed the gypsy Medina in the center of her palm.

I reached down and squeezed Davis' hand.

When we made love he wiped me off between my legs with his silk handkerchief.

My great-grandmother looked inside the gypsy's palm and said she saw time there.

My great-grandfather said she was crazy.

I changed my position so I could kiss Davis inside his hand.

"Then do you think there are some things we can't help from letting happen?" I asked.

He laughed hard and put his whole hand on my belly.

"How did it feel in your mouth?" Elvira asked.

I didn't answer.

"Why didn't you chew it up and swallow?"

I told her not to fuck with me.

My great-grandfather's fingertips were stained brown.

"Shit, woman, what's a man got to do to make you love him?" my father asked my mother.

She said it didn't happen because she didn't love him.

She said she never knew how he was going to love her now. He said, "Act like a whore, I love you like a whore. Shit, woman," he said, "what's a man got to do?"

She said she never knew how he was going to love her now.

"How did it feel in your mouth?"

"Don't fuck with me," I said.

She asked me what did she have to do. I told her she didn't have to do nothing, because whatever she did, the answer would still be the same. She lay on her stomach. Her dress stuck to the crease in her ass. She wanted to know what she had to do.

"You ought to have them check your kidneys," the guard said.

When I walked past her she touched my behind.

Davis said I had a pretty behind. He was up against me. I could feel him hard.

"I thought you were asleep," I said.

"No," he said.

He put his lips against the back of my neck, his arm around my waist.

"It don't take you that long to pee," Elvira said.

"When you tensed up and nervous it does."

She started laughing, then she said, "I seen the guard get a feel."

Davis turned me around and put his tongue in my mouth.

"I bet he wasn't even that good. I bet you just hadn't had a man in a long time."

"How long has it been, Eva?"

"A long time. A long time . . . I thought you knew already."

He went in like he was tearing something besides her flesh.

"The trouble with you is you don't feel nothing," Elvira said.

"A real long time," I told him.

"Has the woman talked yet?"

"Naw, Captain, she ain't said a word," the detective said.

I was sitting in a chair in the Detective Bureau Office.

"She looks dangerous, too, doesn't she?" the detective asked.

"They all look dangerous."

My hair was uncombed. It was turning into snakes. Davis kissed the top of my head.

IV

MR. LOGAN HADN'T been seen in about three days. Floyd Coleman waited until my father came home before he knocked on our door. Mama went to the door, but he asked to speak to Daddy. She told him to come in. He came in a little bit, but he was standing in the door, nervous.

"What is it?" Daddy asked.

"You ain't seen Mr. Logan, have you?"

Daddy said, "Naw."

"Ain't nobody seen him," Floyd Coleman said.

"Maybe he decided to keep to hisself for a change and stop messing with other people's business," Mama said.

The way she said it made Daddy look at her. She moved away from them and sat down in a chair. I was standing near Daddy. I was fourteen then.

"We think maybe he's over there sick, or dead. We scared to go look."

"Did you knock on his door?"

"Yeah, Lawson kind of tapped on his door . . . We scared to go inside. We thought maybe you might go take a look. He might be over there sick or something."

Daddy said, "Shit," and went out the door. I started to go too, but Mama said, "Wait, Eva." I just stayed standing there. I could see Mr. Lawson.

In about ten minutes Daddy came back. "We gon take him to the hospital. He been over there sick for three days. Too proud to call anybody."

He went to get his coat. I asked if I could go too. Mama said Naw, I couldn't go.

"Let her go," Daddy said.

Mama said, "Naw, because that ain't no place for no girl."

"What, the hospital?" I asked.

"Naw, in that car with all of them men, and one of em dying."

"I didn't say he was dying," Daddy said.

"Well, she caint go," Mama said.

Daddy said he didn't have time to argue. He went out the door real quick.

"Grown men scared to go see about somebody that's sick," Mama said.

I looked at her. She turned her head away from me and went in the kitchen.

Mr. Logan was in the hospital a week, and then he died. Daddy never did tell us what it was he had.

The queen bee turned her head a bit and looked at me. We were crossing the street at the same time. She was dark around her eyes, but I couldn't tell if it was mascara or her eyes. She smiled a bit but didn't say anything. I was afraid to smile at her. It was summertime. She had on a short-sleeved dress and a silver bracelet on the upper part of her arm. She was as old as my mother.

"Does the queen bee have any children?" I asked Mama when I got home.

"I don't know. I don't even know her. Miss Billie was the one that knew her . . . Why do you ask a question like that?"

"I don't know. I saw her today. I was just wondering."

I wanted to ask how could they make love to her if they knew they were going to die.

Miss Billie said, "Because they don't think that anything can touch them."

I let the queen bee go across the street first. She smiled at me like people smile at you when they're afraid you won't smile back. She had a little waist and big hips.

"You got the kind of ass that a woman should show off," Davis said. "You ought to wear those tight skirts with the little ruffles around the hem."

I laughed. "I'd look crazy."

"Naw you wouldn't. If a woman got a beautiful behind, she ought to show it off."

"Davis, you crazy."

"Yeah, I could just sit back and watch you walk," he said.

I said he was crazy again. He slid his hand between my thighs.

"Yeah, we gon both be crazy in a couple more days," he said.

"Yeah, I was scared to go in there," Floyd Coleman said. He was sitting in the kitchen talking to Daddy. "Cause I had a bad experience once. I went into this man's house to see about him, you know, and he wasn't even no man no more. Decomposing, you know."

"Well, it's over now," Daddy said, wanting to change the subject.

"Yeah, well ever since then I just get scared like that."

"Well, it's over now," Daddy repeated.

Miss Billie put her wooden bracelet on my wrist. Then she said, "Let me see your hand."

I held my hand out.

"Naw, the other way."

I showed her my palm.

"Some people think you just got the future in your hand. You got history in it too," she said.

When Daddy found out that Miss Billie was going to North Carolina, he said he was glad, because she just wasn't "right" anyway.

I was sitting in the park when she came and sit down beside me. I didn't want her to sit beside me because I was afraid of her.

"Hi, again," she said.

I said "Hi," but I didn't say anything else.

She sat there not saying anything else. I could smell a little bit of perfume, not a lot of perfume like some women wear.

I didn't want to sit there with her, and I didn't want to get up, because I didn't want her to think I was getting up because she was there, so I stayed sitting there. I stayed sitting there until the man came.

"What do you want?" she asked. She sounded cold.

"You know how I feel about you," he said.

The woman looked over at me and then got up quickly. She was walking fast, but he was walking as fast. When they got to the sidewalk, they stood talking. I could see her face but not his. She looked sad. When the man turned, he was frowning. She started to take his arm, but didn't. She walked away from him quickly. He stood there for a moment, and then walked in the other direction.

"Why do you let him treat you like that?" Mama asked Jean.

Me and Mama went to see Jean one afternoon when Alfonso and Otis were at work.

"I told Otis not to talk to you," Jean said. "I knew he would, though."

"He's worried about you and Alfonso. He doesn't understand."

"Nobody understands. I don't understand."

They had moved out of the hotel finally and were living in a building a few blocks away from us.

"You stay with him," Mama said. "The way Otis talks about it, he's been beating on you for years."

Jean said nothing. She was a heavyset but delicate-looking woman who didn't straighten her hair. It was somewhere between being wavy and what they called nappy then. She had fixed me and Mama and herself some coffee.

"It's none of my business, is it?" Mama said after she'd waited for Jean to speak.

"Otis coming to you made you feel it was your business," Jean said. "I don't mind. It's just . . ."

"What?"

"I did go away once," she said. "He came and got me. He came and got me and brought me back."

Mama frowned. "Otis didn't tell me that."

"Otis didn't know that," Jean said.

"You haven't tried to go away again?" Mama asked.

"No," Jean said. Then, "You want to know something? When he came and got me, I was ready to go back."

"You a good woman," Mama said.

"Naw, I ain't good," Jean said. "I love him a lot."

Mama stood up, saying nothing.

"You know you can take as much beating away from a man like that as you can with him," Jean said.

When we got out in the street, Mama asked, "Did you see all up under her eyes?"

"Yes ma'am."

"It ain't no sense in a man treating a woman like that, is it?"

I said, "No ma'am."

Alfonso stayed with me in the kitchen. He'd come over one Saturday and ate with us, and then Mama and Daddy had gone in the living room. I said I'd do the dishes. We were sitting at the table and then I started to get up to clear away the dishes. He took my arm a little and I stayed sitting.

"Because I'm your cousin you'd tell me things you wouldn't tell other men?" he asked.

He said it real soft.

"I guess so," I said.

"Have you, you know, been getting it?"

I knew what he was talking about. I got up from the table.

"I thought you said you'd tell me."

"No," I said. "I mean no to your question."

I took a couple of dishes to the sink.

"You a virgin?"

"Yes."

"You don't mind me astin?"

"Naw."

He handed me a couple of dishes and I put them in the sink. I got some glasses.

"How old are you?" he asked.

"Seventeen."

"And ain't had the meat? Most girls your age had the meat *and* the gravy."

He dried a few of the dishes, and then went in where Mama and Daddy were. When he came back, I was finishing up the dishes. He took the dishtowel from me and dried the last plate.

"I came to talk to you again," he said.

I stayed standing up at the sink.

"You got a boyfriend?" he asked.

"Naw."

"Your mama said you stay stuck up in the house all the time."

I said nothing.

"I told her I'd take you around to some of the clubs and introduce you . . . if you want to go."

I said, "Okay."

"You don't sound too enthusiastic."

"Yeah, I want to go."

"Yeah, I'll take you around to some of the clubs. It ain't right for no grown woman to stay stuck up in the house all the time . . . Why don't you go in there and get fixed up and then I'll take you out."

He was still holding the dish. I took it and put it in the cabinet.

"You too old not to had the meat," he said.

"Yeah, you too old not to had the meat," Alfonso said again.

We were sitting in one of his "clubs." It was really a little restaurant called Bud's.

"Yeah, you way too old not to had the meat," he said.

I told him I'd get it when I was ready for it.

"You tougher than you let on, too, I bet," he said.

I said nothing.

"If you don't tell them how old you are, I won't," he said. "You look older than your age anyway."

The waitress came over and he ordered a bourbon for himself and a beer for me.

"You want to tell them we cousins? I mean, if anybody asks."

"Yeah," I said.

"You don't have to be so sure about it," he said, lifting his drink.

"I'm as sure about it as you are," I said.

He drank. I drank my beer.

The man came over and put his plate of pigfeet down. He didn't ask if he could join us, he just sat down. He went back up to the counter and got a bottle of beer and came back. Him and Alfonso didn't say anything to each other, but I could tell they knew each other. He looked like he was in his late fifties.

"Who's at you got with you?" the man asked after a while, pointing to me.

I didn't notice it at first, but I noticed it then. The thumb on his left hand was missing.

"My cousin."

"Shit. How did something pretty like that get to be your cousin? You his cousin?"

"Yeah."

"Shit."

Somebody passed by the table and asked how we were doing.

"I ain't doing, Alfonso's doing," the man answered.

"This is my cousin, man," Alfonso said.

"If she's your cousin, I'm your great-granddaddy and your uncle too."

"Man, I ain't lying."

"That Sweet Mama you had in here with you night before last, you said that was your cousin too."

"Naw, that wasn't me."

"Naw, it was Riley Mason and I know she wasn't none of his cousin."

Alfonso didn't say anything. He drank some more of his bourbon. The man sucked on a piece of pigfoot. I kept looking at his thumbless hand. He saw me watching him and I looked away. He put the meat down.

"Yeah, if you married me, I know I'd go somewhere. I know I'd go places, then."

"Shit, you old enough to be her great-granddaddy," Alfonso said.

"You ain't none of her cousin neither," the man with the plate of pigfeet said.

"I done already told you about three times that she's my cousin. I ain't gon tell you no more."

"If she tell me, I believe her. I ain't gon believe you. You his cousin?"

I said, "Yeah."

Alfonso said, "Shit."

"Well, you ain't none of my cousin," the man said. He sucked on another piece of meat.

When they found the queen bee, it went all around the neighborhood. The cops didn't know why she did it, but the people in the neighborhood did.

"It's that man's fault," Cora Monday was telling Mama one day.

We met her in the grocery store.

"If he hadn't been so persistent, and left her alone. I think she really loved the nigger."

"That's what I told Billie Flynn years ago," Mama said. "I told her if that woman met somebody she really loved one of these days, no telling what she might do, the kind of history she's got. Even if he was the man out a hundred that didn't nothing happen to, who'd want to take the chance. It's hard being a woman like that."

"Wonder what marked her like that?" Cora Monday asked.

Mama said she didn't know. Somebody told her she came out trying to bite her own umbilical cord.

Miss Cora said that wasn't nothing but superstition.
"Well, it was three men, wasn't it? I'm just telling you what Billie Flynn told me."

The man she had killed herself on account of left town, and nobody knew where he went.

Davis came in and I turned.
"What are you doing?"

He went over, pulled me toward him, so I could feel him hard.

"I'm still on," I said, kissing him. "I'm still doing it."
He patted my belly, touched my navel.

"Where were you?" I asked.

"I had to go down and tell that bastard I can't pay the rent till Monday."

"I could help you pay the rent."

"Naw." He was angry.

"I'm sorry."

"I thought you'd be through," he said, changing the subject, sitting close beside me on the bed, till I could feel his thigh, firm and muscular through his pants.

"Three days I said."

"Christ could rise in three days," he said, touching his crotch.

"Then let him. I'll be grateful."

He laughed, even in his nostrils. I sat up on the bed and drew up my knees.

"We'll go out and have something to eat later," he said. "No, I'll bring something up."

"Okay." I blew breath on his neck, then looked at my toenails that needed cutting.

"Do you have any scissors?"

"In that drawer over there."

He didn't get them. I got up and got them. He stayed on the edge of the bed. I sat back down bending. When I finished, I scraped the filings into a heap and put them in the sack he used for a trashcan. But it didn't matter though, because the floor was already dirty.

"I could sweep the floor," I said.

"I don't want you to sweep the floor," he said, irritated again.

I frowned. He smiled and put his tongue between my teeth.

"I'll be through tomorrow," I said.

We lay down again. He put his thigh across my belly to feel me, nothing more, then he felt my thighs and my belly. When it was evening, he fed me eggs and sausages and beer.

"Did the eggs get cold?" he asked.

"No, they're fine."

"Mine got cold."

"Here, take mine."

"No," he said hard, then softened. "I have doughnuts."

"They'll give me the cramps."

"I thought you were about through."

"I am."

He ate one doughnut and put the rest away.

V

I SAT ON the floor. My knees hurt. I watched the walls. After a while they came up. I could hear them outside the door talking, whispering. They saw me go up and then they followed me up.

"Yes, she's the one," the landlady said. "I saw her go up. Look at her sitting there. Just look at her. What kind of woman can it be to do something like that?"

One of the cops came over and pulled me up. I didn't even know what he looked like. I just saw red hair growing on the back of his hand.

"She ain't nothing but a whore," the landlady said. "I seen her up in there, but I didn't figure she do nothing like that. If I'da known she was going to do something like that, I'd've had her right out of here. Her and him too."

They put me in the car. The cop with the red hair on his hands sat in the back beside me. The other one was driving.

"They ever find out who it was that called?" the cop driving asked.

"No. The landlady said she didn't call."

"Think the woman called?"

"I don't know."

They sat me in a chair in the Detective Bureau Office. They didn't handcuff me, they just had me sitting there. Then they took me to get my fingerprints and picture taken, then they brought me back to the chair in the office.

He called me Sweet. He said my tongue was like honey in his palm.

"Should I close the window?" he asked.

"No, it's still kind of hot."

"I'll close it a little. It might get cooler. I don't want to keep getting up."

He got up and came back to bed. I kept on my panties, but there was still a little stain in his bed.

"I'm sorry."

"It's all right."

He put his leg between my legs and drew me close so he could feel my breasts against him, so he could feel between my thighs.

"I forgot to put mustard on the sausage. You told me to put mustard on the sausage."

"That's all right. It was good."

He said my hair was a woolen halo. He stroked it back with his hand. He wanted me, but I couldn't. He withdrew his leg and turned his back to me.

The next day he fingered me down between my legs, then he touched my navel. "I ain't never seen a bitch, I mean a grown woman, with a navel that long. Didn't you wear a bellyband when you were a kid?"

"Yes, but it kept slipping down."

"Should I wear a rubber?"

"Do you want to?"

"Naw, I was thinking . . ."

He didn't tell me what he was thinking.

"I thought I'd forget where to put my legs," I said, joking.

But he wouldn't let me joke. "Has it really been that long?"

"I thought you knew."

"No, I was only guessing."

I grinned up at him.

He kissed me, laughing. "I'm not screwed out yet, are you?"

"No."

He came in from the back this time.

The landlady rolled her eyes at me. The landlord wouldn't look at me. They went in the back room to give their statements. The detective with the red hair growing out of his knuckles and the back of his hand sat on the desk watching me. The other detective came in.

"She talked yet?"

"No."

"Look at those eyes. A woman got to be crazy to do something like that."

"Or want you to think she's crazy."

"What do you mean?"

"Do something so people will think she has to be crazy to do it."

"What did they do with it?"

"Freezer."

"Somebody better put a note saying 'This ain't a piece of sausage.'" He laughed.

The detective with the red hair didn't laugh. "When's the captain coming?" he asked.

"I just called him. He said he'd be right in."

The detective with the red hair looked disgusted. He looked at me, then looked away from me. He got down from the desk and stood over by the filing cabinets. The other detective said nothing. He stood with his back to me, his hands clasped behind him. I stared down at my hands. They were dry. The skin around the nails was peeling. The detective was standing up at the cabinets

with his ankles crossed. I looked at him below the waist. I
hadn't meant to look there. I looked away from him. I
picked at the skin around my nails.

"Somebody ought to give her a comb," the detective
with his back to me said.

"I already gave her one. She gave it back to me."

He wouldn't let me comb my hair after we made love.

"What if we go out?" I asked.

"We ain't going out," he said.

He put his leg across me again. Afterwards he sat up in
bed, smoking, making wings of his nostrils. He said he
was a dragon, then he said he was a train.

"Do you like oysters?" I asked.

He nodded.

"At Easter we used to put a hole in eggs and suck them
hollow."

"What does that have to do with oysters?"

I feel like an egg sucked hollow and then filled with
raw oysters, I was thinking.

"Do you like them raw or cooked?" I asked.

"Either way. No, raw better."

"Let's have a party," I said suddenly. "Just the two of
us."

"I'm all fucked out," he said.

I laughed.

He put his arm around my waist. "You've got a little
waist."

"Something I inherited," I said. "My mother had a
little waist. And her mother."

I danced for him, my hair uncombed, my shoulders
careless. I danced and laughed. He sat cross-legged on the
bed and watched.

"You should be all fucked out," he said. He wasn't
joking.

"You got what you wanted, didn't you?" I said. I wasn't joking either.

He kept watching me. I stopped dancing and sat down, sweat in my hands. I was frowning.

"What's wrong?" he asked.

"I'm tired, that's all."

"I said you were all fucked out."

I didn't like that. I wished he would stop saying that, but I didn't tell him. I sat with my thighs close to his. He plucked at my breasts. I laughed. Then I shut my mouth. I have a dark line along one of my teeth.

"What do you really do?" he asked.

"I work in a tobacco factory when I'm not laid off," I said.

"What else have you got to say?"

"Nothing."

"Eva, why won't you talk about yourself?"

I said nothing. He laid me down and sucked on my belly.

I ran till my breath turned brittle. Freddy caught me and put himself up against me.

"Y'all boys get away from here," Miss Billie said. She was laughing. "He's just like a little banny rooster, all stuck out in front."

"What's wrong with you?" my father asked my mother.

"Nothing."

"Sometimes I swear, woman, you . . . ."

He didn't finish what he was going to say.

Elvira raised her dress up. "This damn elastic is cutting me. I swear I wish they issue some bloomers that fit sometime. Shit."

She kept twisting and twisting, her hands under her dress.

"If I had some scissors I'd cut the damn things, but they won't let me have no scissors."

The elastic ripped. "Shit."

A scar on her knee. Knots in her thighs.

The man with no thumb said, "If you married me, I'd go a long way."

"Eva'll tell you where you can go in a minute, buddy, if you don't stop worrin her," Alfonso said.

The man with no thumb laughed. "Naw, she ain't none a your cousin. I caint believe a bastard like you got a cousin like that."

No, sweetmeat, that's what he called me. A sweetmeat like that.

Alfonso kept grinning and watching the man eat pigfeet with his thumbless hand.

"Ask him how he lost his thumb, Eva, he'll say his wife did it. Why don't you go home to your wife?"

"What about *yours*, man . . . Naw, she ain't none of your cousin. A sweetmeat like that."

He pointed at me with his thumbless hand, then he picked up another piece of meat. "I know I be gone somewhere then," he said.

"Aw, cut it out, man," Alfonso said. "She ain't studin you."

"I wont her to take me places," the man with no thumb said.

"Shit," Alfonso said.

I was in the room alone, pretending the floor was the ceiling. He was out doing whatever it was he did when he went out. He'd left the door partly open and a gray cat came in and walked around. It didn't see me at first, but then it saw me and walked around some more and went under the bed and came out again. I didn't touch him. I waited till he went out and then I got up and shut the door.

When Davis came back he said, "There's cat shit in the room."

I didn't tell him how it got there. I said I didn't know either.

"Want a comb?" the detective asked.

I ran my hand through my hair and shook my head. I wanted to sit there and plait it up, but I didn't. I just sat there. He put his comb back in his pocket. He kept looking at me. He was looking like he was thinking of something else. Then he was looking like he was half afraid of me.

The captain came in like he was in a hurry. "She the woman?"

"Yes sir."

"She talked yet?"

"No sir."

The captain picked up a long yellow sheet off the desk. He looked over it so fast he couldn't have been reading it, then he looked at me.

"She got any marks on her?" he asked, still looking at me.

"No, not a mark one. We had one of the policewomen check her over."

"No scratches, or nothing?"

"No sir."

"He didn't beat her or anything?"

"No sir."

"Yeah, I don't know where I'd be if I had you. I'd be in hightime by now."

"Shit," Alfonso said.

. . .

There was a long table in the room. They told me to
sit anywhere I wanted to. I sat in the first chair I came to.
The red-headed detective sat a chair away from me, the
other sat across from me, the captain remained standing.
Before he said anything, there was a knock on the door,
and a policeman came in and handed him a sheet of
paper and then left. The captain looked at the paper,
then said, "Her name is Eva Medina Canada, father John
Canada, mother Marie Canada, born Columbus, Georgia, 1937. When she was five they moved to New York.
She's been in trouble before. When she was seventeen
she stabbed a man. She wouldn't talk then either,
wouldn't say anything to defend herself. She was given a
six-month sentence. She spent the first three months in a
girls' reformatory, and then she was old enough to be
fingerprinted and put in prison for the remaining three
months. She wouldn't even tell why she stabbed him.
The man claimed, 'I wasn't doing nothing but trying to
buy the woman a beer.' She was married. She was married
in 1955 to a man named Hunn. Last job she had was in a
tobacco factory . . . You want to talk, Eva?"
I said nothing.

"I'd be way away from here," the man with no thumb
said.

Alfonso said he was taking me to see Otis and Jean,
but they weren't there. He said why didn't we play cards
till they came. He said he didn't like to play cards at the
table, he liked to play cards on the floor. I had on pants
and I sat with my legs folded. He said he couldn't do
that. He said he was too stiff to do that. When he tried
to sit like that his knees stuck up, he wasn't limber

enough. I cut the cards. I saw where he was looking and changed the way I was sitting. He dealt.

"I thought you said they were coming," I said after we'd played awhile.

"They be here," he said.

He was sitting with his knees stuck up. I didn't like where I was looking now. He saw where I was looking. He put down his cards and pulled on my arm. "Come on, girl."

"Come on, what? Naw."

He had pulled me over where he was and started kissing on the side of my neck. I stood up and he pulled me down again, this time my leg across him. He had hold of my hand. This time when I felt it, it wasn't inside pants. It felt like a wrist. It was throbbing like a wrist. It felt as big and round as a wrist. I said Naw, and broke away from him and for the door. I thought he would grab hold of me before I got there, but he didn't. I got out. He didn't come after me.

"You scratched me down there."

We were sitting at a table in the Froglegs restaurant.

"I didn't mean to."

"I still got the scar."

He got up and came back and pushed my beer over to me. "It's about time you had some meat and juice too," he said.

I said nothing.

"They ain't there. Why don't you come home with me?"

"Naw."

"Why you out with me again? I thought when I asked you, you'd turn me down flat. I asked you anyway, though. You said Yes. That surprised me, you know that. It honestly did. I thought we had something going, but we ain't . . . What if I asked you to come home with me? Otis out with some vamp and Jean staying with some girlfriend of hers that's been having a bad time with some man."

"Naw."

"I'll tell your mama you let me suck your tiddies."

"Naw you won't."

He laughed, and told me to drink my beer.

"You know where I'd like to take you? I'd like to take you out to Chicago and then to Kansas City and then out to California," he said.

I said nothing.

"You don't believe me. I would. Don't you want to go those places?"

"Not with you."

"You hard on a man."

"I told you to tell people I'm your cousin. You haven't been telling yourself, have you?"

"Shit. You went out with me again. You just wont me to take you out somewhere so you can meet somebody."

"I don't want to meet nobody."

"Shit, I ain't never met no hussy that didn't want to meet nobody." He was mad. "That's all, you just wonted me to flunky for you."

"Naw I didn't."

"Must not be nobody here good enough for you. I ain't seen you looking."

"I'm not looking for nobody."

"Yes you are. You lookin for the meat and gravy, only I ain't the right meat and gravy."

"I didn't say I was looking."

"Shit. Drink your beer, woman. You want another one?"

"Naw."

"Naw, you bed not get drunk," he said. "Tell your mama I had my teeth all in your tiddies."

I said nothing. I looked at my beer.

"Yeah, you *out* with me. Won't do nothing but feel, though."

I said nothing.

"Why don't you come home with me?"

I shook my head and then said, "Naw."

"There was a woman," I told Davis, "called the queen bee. I don't even know what her real name was, but she was a real good-looking woman, too. People used to say she was marked, because she had three men, and each of them died, you know. After the first one died they didn't think nothing about it, but then after the second one, people started whispering, and then after the third one, they were sure. I guess she was sure too, because she met this man she was really in love with, and then she killed herself."

"I'd rather hear about you."

"No. I don't like to talk about myself."

"Why not?"

"I just don't."

"You make a man wonder what's there."

"You see me."

"Naw, there's more to you than what I see." He put his hands inside my thighs. "Yeah, there's more to you than what I see."

"You *out* with me," Alfonso said. "But that's all."

"The queen bee. I don't know if she knew that's what people called her. It must've been hard, though. She must've been sucked hollow. She must've had nothing left."

"Naw, those men kept bringing it to her. She must've sucked them hollow. That's why they died. Cause *they* had nothing left."

"Naw, it was harder on the woman."

"Shit, I don't even think it's a real woman anyway," Davis said. "Somebody you just made up."

"Yes, there was a woman called the queen bee," I said.

VI

"SHE'S EDUCATED, though," the captain said. "She spent two years at Kentucky State, then quit and went to work at P. Lorillard tobacco company in Lexington, then she came up to Connecticut and got in tobacco there. Been on the road all her life, just like a man . . ."

I picked the loose skin from around my nails.

The foreman at the plant sent for me. "I thought maybe you could tell me how most of the niggers feel about the union. Whether or not they in favor of it."

I said I didn't know how anybody else was going to vote. I said I just knew how I was going to vote. He said there was ten percent more black people there since he was foreman, and that he liked people that showed gratitude. I said I didn't know how anybody else was going to vote. He asked me how I was going to vote. I said I knew how I was going to vote. He said he had some money for me if I wanted it. I said I didn't know how anybody else was going to vote. He said never mind that. He said he didn't mean that. He said he had some money for me. I said by the time the voting was over, it would be time for me to be back on the road again. He said I didn't seem like I belonged around there anyway. He said I could be on the road before the voting was over. He sent me out and called somebody else in. He said he didn't like people who didn't know how to be grateful.

. . .

I picked the loose skin from around my nails. I sat on the bed. Davis scooted his chair up to me. He sat backwards, straddling the chair, his arms up over the back.

"You had that look in your eyes again," he said.

"What look?"

"Sometimes when I look at you and you don't know I'm looking at you, you set your jaw a certain way, and then you get this look in your eyes."

"What kind of look?"

"I don't know what kind of look. It's just there . . . You hard to get into, you know that."

"I didn't think I was so hard."

"I don't mean that way," he said.

I grinned at him. He grinned back at me, then frowned.

When the psychiatrist told me his name was David Smoot, I laughed. He asked me what was wrong. I said nothing. He had a mustache and goatee and reminded me of the musician.

"Why did you kill the man, Eva?"

I didn't answer.

"Did Davis know why you killed him?"

I still didn't answer.

He leaned toward me. He said he didn't just want to know about the killing, he said he wanted to know about what happened after the killing. Did it come in my mind when I saw him lying there dead or had I planned it all along. His voice was soft. It was like cotton candy. He said he wanted to know how it felt, what I did, how did it make me feel. I didn't want him looking at me. I had my hands on my knees. My knees were open. I closed my knees.

"I want to help you, Eva."

I said nothing.

"Talk to me."

I wouldn't.

"You're going to have to open up sometime, woman, to somebody. I want to help you."

I looked at him, still saying nothing. He sat watching me for a long time and then he said, "I'll see you, Eva."

He got up and left. I listened to his footsteps down the hall. I kept my knees squeezed tight together. I heard a woman a few cells down from me laugh, twice, then she was silent.

"I guess what you done excites people," Elvira said.

"How did it feel, Eva?" the psychiatrist asked.

My mother got an obscene telephone call one day. A man wanted to know how did it feel when my daddy fucked her.

"How did it feel?" Elvira asked.

"They told me you wouldn't talk. They said I wouldn't get one word out of you," the psychiatrist said. "Did you feel you had any cause to mutilate him afterwards? Why did you feel killing him wasn't enough?"

"How did it feel?" Elvira asked.

"How did you feel?" the psychiatrist asked.

"How did it feel?" Elvira asked.

"How do it feel, Mizz Canada?" the man asked my mama. She slammed the telephone down.

"Eva. Eva. Eva," Davis said.

"My hair looks like snakes, doesn't it?" I asked.

I don't want to tell my story. Can I have a cigarette? Thanks. Why don't you go away. Can I have another cigarette before you go away? You know, I used to make these things.

. . .

The gypsy Medina's hair was as thick as a black woman's. In a picture my grandmother's hair was heavy against her face. My Grandmother Medina was married three times. She had fourteen children. About eight of them were born living. One of them was born choked by her own umbilical cord, another was born with the fever, another they couldn't explain, another . . . Her hair was as heavy as a black woman's.

"How much would you take for it?"
"I wouldn't take nothing."
"Five, ten, fifteen . . ."
"I said I wouldn't take nothing."
He sent me away, and called somebody else in. "I just spoke with one nigra, but she . . ."

"Alfonso—that's my cousin—he used to beat his wife outside this hotel. He wouldn't beat her inside, he had to always take her outside and beat her. And they used to always have to go get his brother to make him stop, because that was the only one he would listen to."

Alfonso, sitting in the Froglegs restaurant, brought me a beer.
"I'll tell your mama you let me suck your tiddies."
"Naw you won't."
"I'd have you in Chicago right now if things was the way I wanted them. Have you right in Chicago. And then I wouldn't just be wonting no conversation neither. A man wonts more than conversation. I ain't the kind of man to just wont conversation . . . You see that bitch over there?"
"Yeah."
"That ain't really no bitch, that's a bastard. Dress up like a woman and then come in here. Shit. He don't

bother the men that knows him. Most of us know what
he is. He just pick up on the men that don't. Most of the
ones that hang around here don't fool around with him.
Sometimes she makes pickups, drunks or strangers. They
find out right quick, though. They start messing around
her. Naw, I don't even git drunk when I come in here,
cause I know how I do when I'm drunk. I wouldn't get
mixed up with that bastard for nothing. Wake up the
next morning and find *his* wig in my face. Shit . . . Yeah,
I have you in Chicago right now."

"Yeah, I could go places if I had you," the man with
no thumb said. "I could go high places."

"Yeah, I been places," Alfonso said. "I bet I been
places and done things you ain't never even heard of.
Like I been to parties where everybody's naked, for
instance. I bet you ain't never even heard of that."
"Yes I have."
"Naw you haven't."
I said yes I had.
"I bet you haven't."
I said nothing.
"Yeah, I been like you too," he said. "Just like I was
new in the world. I remember the first time I went up
North, went up to Cincinnati, and I was sitting in this
restaurant and there was this white woman at this
restaurant, and she kept looking at me for me to dance
with her, you know. You know I wasn't going to dance
with no white woman. The others was dancing, though
. . . Yeah, I been a lots of different places. Places that
make you old before your time. I'm old in the world now.
Won't even let me suck on your damn tiddies. To some
women that ain't like nothing but shaking hands. To
some of em fucking ain't nothing but shaking hands.

Shaking hands and dancing. Meat and the gravy too. Ain't even as old as you, some of them."

I told him Mama was going to take me to North Carolina for a coming-out present.

"Coming-out?"

"For graduation."

"Aw. North Carolina? North Carolina ain't shit. I'd take you up to Canada. What's in North Carolina?"

"We got a friend that lives there, we ain't seen in about ten years or something. I think Mama wants to go more for her than for me. I said I'd like to go, though. But I think she feels she needs to get away for a while. And then, she hasn't really had any close friends since Miss Billie left. No woman she can really talk to, you know. I think she wants to get away for herself . . . I don't mind, though."

"Shit, I'd have you up in Canada somewhere. When y'all leavin?"

"Day after tomorrow."

"Shit, well when you come back you ain't been nowhere. If you was with me you would've been somewhere, come back and know you been somewhere."

I shook my head and started laughing.

"What?"

"Nothing."

"You laughing at me, ain't you?"

"Naw, I wasn't laughing at you."

"Yes you was . . . You know you frustrate a man."

I asked him how.

"You already got me beating my meat over you."

I said I didn't know what he meant.

He said shit, then he told me what he meant, then he said, "Coming-out present, I wish I could give you a going-in present . . . I want to see you when you get back."

"I won't be any different."

"I don't care. I still want to see you, you hear?"

I said I heard.

"Way it is now," Alfonso said, "when you get back, you have to say 'I ain't been nowhere.' "

"You know what I think," the psychiatrist said. "I think he came to represent all the men you'd known in your life."

"Who?"

"I got *something* out of you," he said. He was proud of himself.

Davis returned, bringing whiskey.

"I thought you might sleep," he said.

"No, I haven't been sleepy," I said. "Did you take the comb? I couldn't find it."

"Yeah, it's in my pocket. You don't need it."

He poured himself a glass and me a glass.

"Thanks, I can't drink a lot, I think my kidneys got infected."

"How?"

"I don't know."

"One or both?"

"I feel it along here." I touched the V along my pelvis.

He glanced at me and opened the window. "Not enough air." He watched me touching myself. "An excuse for not drinking," he said.

"No, it doesn't hurt then. I've been going to the bathroom too much, that's all."

"I'm sorry I don't have any ice."

"I don't like it with ice in it."

He stood watching me, then he came over and touched where my hands had been. "Women's problems," he said. "It'll go away."

. . .

"Hers was a crime of passion, and his was a crime of coldness," somebody said.

We were at another long table. I only stared at them.

"Why won't she talk?"

"My mother told me once that they buried my grandmother in sand and then went away and forgot about her, and then they remembered, and when they came back she was sucking sand. I don't know how long she'd been there. But Mama said that's why in later years she couldn't see or hear well . . . Fourteen children."

"That's because they didn't practice birth control in them days" was what Davis said.

"When they came back she was sucking sand."

I stopped working out there then, and then I went up to Connecticut and found work in tobacco there.

VII

I HAD A feeling my mother wanted to get away more for herself than for me. After the musician, things weren't really the way they were before. After Daddy first lost his temper, things seemed like they'd gotten back the way they were. She didn't take on any other man. I never saw her let another man get close to her even in friendly talking. She'd always stand kind of at a distance when she even talked to Floyd Coleman, and I know nobody would think she was studying him. She never did even make any real close women friends after Miss Billie left, and the women she'd gone to the nightclub with, she'd stopped going around with them. That's why I thought going to North Carolina and seeing Miss Billie again might be good for her. She'd have somebody she could talk things out with, because I knew she didn't feel she could talk things out with me.

Miss Billie was fatter. She still had the two gold earrings and the wooden bracelets. She hugged Mama, calling her "girl," and then she hugged me. She had a little front room. When they first came there she wrote and said they lived up above a store, but about five years ago they moved into a house. The front room had a fireplace and a mantelpiece, a couch and coffee table and a couple of armchairs and an upright piano.

Miss Billie was still hugging me, and then stood back, with her hands on my shoulders.

"This caint be that little girl?"

"Yeah, that's Eva."

"Naw, this ain't that little girl. How long has it been? About twelve years, ain't it? Honey, I wouldn't know you, you growed so . . . Y'all have something to eat?"

"Maybe a little later," Mama said. "We had some sandwiches on the bus. It's still with me. Maybe Eva might want something."

"No, thank you," I said.

"Y'all sit down . . . Honey, I just don't believe that's you. Marie, you ain't aged none. Still looking pretty."

"Yes I have aged too," Mama said, laughing.

"Well, it ain't the kind you can tell. Maybe little round the eyes. You still thin. Me, I done got all fat. Don't even eat that much and look like a cow."

"Naw you don't. What you got looks good on you."

Miss Billie sat down in a chair. She was sticking out around the waist like older women do, but her legs were still thin.

"I finally got my piano," she said.

"Yeah, I see you have," Mama said. "It's real nice."

"You know I always did want a piano."

Mama said, "Yeah."

"You know, if y'all tired, you can go on back in the house and lay down. Sweet Man ain't home yet." She laughed. "Aw, I call my man Sweet Man."

Mama laughed.

"That's his picture up there on the mantelpiece. He's good-lookin for a old man, ain't he?"

Mama said yeah he was good-looking.

"Yeah, he's out working and Charlotte's out working too. She work as a seamstress."

"How is Charlotte?"

Miss Billie shook her head. "I don't know. She twenty-seven, but she don't act twenty-seven. Ain't got a man or nothing. Ain't got a man one . . . I tell you about it."

Mama said nothing.

"Yeah. Sweet Man works out there for James Beam, you know. Jim Beam we call him, like that whiskey. Works in tobacco. He be home around suppertime. Charlotte too . . . Yeah, that girl's something else. I tell you about it. Y'all don't wont to lay down?"

Mama said maybe a little bit before supper, but she was enjoying talking to her now.

"Eva, you tired?" Mama asked me.

"No ma'am."

"Eva, where's your bracelet?" Miss Billie asked.

"She lost it when she was playing around the playground. Not more than a couple of weeks after you gave it to her."

Miss Billie frowned. "I should've told your mama to keep it for you. It was too big for you anyway."

She sounded like she was angry, but then she looked at me. "Eva lookin all hurt. I ain't mad at you, baby," she said. She reached over and touched my arm. "That a girl. You sho have growed. You know, I see y'all coming up the walk. I recognized you, Marie, but I said Naw, that ain't that little girl that used to sit up in my lap. Taller than me now."

"Taller than me too," Mama said.

"Well, Charlotte ain't gon get her bracelet till she get married," Miss Billie said, sitting back.

"She doesn't have a boyfriend?" Mama asked.

"Naw, she ain't got no boyfriend."

"Eva doesn't have a boyfriend."

"Yeah, but Eva ain't no twenty-seven neither."

"That's true," Mama said.

"I know it's true," Miss Billie said. "You got to be true

to your ancestors and you got to be true to those that come after you. How can you be true to those that come after you if there ain't none coming after you."

I remembered just before we left, Daddy said he was glad he wasn't going because that woman would drive him crazy in two days with her crazy talk.

"But that's the times for you," Miss Billie said. "They ain't like they used to be."

"Naw, times change," Mama said.

"They sho do. My mama had ten children. And I ain't had but one. But a lot of that's on account of Sweet Man and me getting split up the way we did, and then when we did get back together, I felt like I was too old to start bringing children into the world again. And Sweet Man said he didn't wont to be no old man raising no babies. But then if I had've had another child, I'd have somebody else to count on, cause Charlotte ain't gon do nothing."

Mama said nothing.

"I'll tell you about it," Miss Billie said again. She reached over and touched Mama's knee. "It's good to see you."

Mama said it was good to see her too.

"It's good to see both of y'all," Miss Billie said.

After supper me and Charlotte went for a walk in the woods. It was June and didn't get dark early. Sweet Man had stayed talking to Mama for a little while—he hadn't met her before—and then he excused himself and said he was going to take a bath and a nap.

"Jim Beam wont him down there at five tomorrow," Miss Billie had said. "He's kind of shy, though, that's his real reason. You know, he talk a little bit to peoples and then he kind of shies off. Always been that way. I mean he likes peoples, but he always after a while, shies off, you know. He wanted to meet you and Eva, though, I talk about y'all so much. Y'all my family."

"Your father's nice," I told Charlotte.

"Yeah."

I didn't know what to say to her. She didn't know what to say to me, or just wasn't talking, then when we got further into the woods, she started talking.

"When we first came here I was afraid to walk in the woods by myself, then I got so I wasn't afraid," she said. "*They* don't like me to go, though. Not unless I've got somebody with me. Once or twice I'll sneak off and go. I'm twenty-seven. I ought to be able to go without sneaking off, though, don't you think?"

I said, "Yes."

"But I figure when you live with your parents, you owe them a certain courtesy, don't you think?"

I said, "Yes."

"I think so too . . . I wouldn't be afraid to bring a man home, though. I mean, if I wanted a man."

I looked over at her, but said nothing. She was twenty-seven, but didn't look twenty-seven. She didn't really act twenty-seven. She started jumping to catch the leaves from the branches that were low enough. When she got a leaf she would smell it, and then hand it to me to smell. One of them smelled like mint.

"This smells like pepper grass," she said.

"What does pepper grass smell like?"

"Like pepper," she said. She jumped for some more leaves. "This reminds me of jumping for leaves to feed the goats."

"Did you have goats?"

"Yes, we had two of them. A male and a female. They used to chase after me all the time and I was scared to go out in the yard, so they got rid of them. The doctor put Mama on a diet of goat's milk for a while. I don't know why, though. Sweet milk would turn sour on her stomach. Now she drinks sweet milk."

I said nothing.

"I guess we ought to turn back," she said.

I said, "Okay."

She didn't jump for leaves as we went back. She held the ones she had and then would occasionally let one or two drop to the ground.

"No, not there. Over here."

I had started for the house, but she pointed to the garage. It was a big wooden building that looked as much like a barn as a garage. There was a small pickup truck, beside not inside the garage. She opened the door. Inside, hanging from the garage ceiling, were rows of tobacco leaves. She shut the door. Some light came in through little cracks. She went and sat down against the wall. I followed her, and sat down.

"It's nice in here," she said.

I said nothing.

"Daddy's curing tobacco for the man he works for. They didn't have enough room at his place, so they brought some back here. I know all about tobacco. I know as much about tobacco as a man."

"You don't work in it, though. Your mother said you a seamstress."

"Yeah, I work for this ole white woman got a shop. In a couple of years, though, I'ma get my own shop."

"My great-grandfather used to work in tobacco. My grandfather too."

"I know how to twist tobacco. That's the way they used to do it in the old days. Twist it by hand, you know."

She grabbed a piece of tobacco down from the ceiling and started smelling it, and gave it to me to smell.

"Have you ever done it?" she asked.

"Done what? Twist tobacco."

"Naw. Done it. You know, with a man."

It was cool in there, laying back against the wall. I didn't answer.

"I asked you have you ever been with a man."

"No. Have you?"

"No."

She closed her eyes, her mouth was hanging open a little, then she made a sucking sound.

"Mama keeps asking me when am I going to get a man," she said. "I don't want a man."

"That's all right."

"Not for her it's not."

"You not her."

"That's what I told her. But you know how parents wont grandchildren. They wont there to be a lot of generations."

"That's good too."

"Whose way you looking at it?" she asked, angry. "Hers or mine?"

I said both ways.

"That ain't no help."

She said nothing for a while then she took hold of my hand like she was studying my palm, and started tracing her finger along my hand, but barely touching the lines.

"It tickles, don't it?" she asked.

I said, "Yeah."

She let my hand drop.

"He said he could tickle me somewhere else better."

"Who?"

"Never mind who."

She got up real quick. "Your mother doesn't worry you about it, does she?" she asked.

"About what?"

"Having a man."

"Naw."

"I guess you too young, though. Wait till you my age."

I stood up because I thought she was going, but she didn't go. She touched my waist and said that I had a little waist. She kept her hand on my waist and then she walked out of the garage. I followed her. Before she got to the house, she turned. "I don't wont to go in yet. Let's go back." We went back to the garage.

She pulled a mat from the corner and lay down on it. "There's room for two people," she said.

"No, there's not."

I stooped down, watching her. She frowned and closed her eyes.

"What did he do?" I asked.

She opened her eyes and looked at me hard. "Who?"

"That boy," I said.

She said nothing, then she said, "He showed me what a man could do for himself. I mean, if I couldn't do it . . ."

"You mean he . . . beat his meat?"

"Where'd you hear that?"

"I don't know."

"Naw, he didn't beat it, he did something else."

"What?"

She wouldn't tell me. She kept staring up at the tobacco leaves. I picked up a buckeye and started playing with it. She took the buckeye away from me and threw it to the other end of the garage. She told me about how when they first came there, there had been this little girl who'd been playing with a buckeye. At first she was just playing with it, and then she picked it up and started sucking on it, and then she ate it. Nobody had seen her do it. When she started getting sick, they rushed her to the hospital, but she died. She said ever since then she couldn't stand those things. She said the little girl must've thought it was a nut.

"This is how they used to do when they cured tobacco," she said, twisting a tobacco leaf. "She thought it was a nut, so she ate it."

We only stayed there from that Friday till Monday because Mama couldn't get longer than that off from work. I'd spent most of my time with Charlotte. She'd kept wanting to go in the woods. She never did talk about the boy again or what he'd done, but she would keep talking about her mother wanting her to marry. I stayed with her because I wanted Mama to get to talk to Miss Billie. When we were coming back on the bus, I couldn't tell if she had. She had that same look of strain around her eyes that she was beginning to have now. She lay back on the seat and kept her eyes closed most of the time.

"Did you like Charlotte?" she asked once.

"Yes."

"What did you talk about?"

"I don't know. Just talk. She likes to walk in the woods a lot."

"She seems more settled down than she used to be," Mama said. "I know she gets hell, though."

I said nothing. I looked over at her, and then leaned back against my seat and closed my eyes.

"I told Mama if she had another child I'd raise it, but I said I wasn't going to have one myself. That made her real mad," Charlotte said.

VIII

"IT AIN'T ALFONSO, it's Jean," Otis said. He'd come to see us again, this time it was about eleven o'clock at night and Daddy was home too.

The way he was looking when he first came in, nobody was saying anything, just followed him back to the living room and waited for him to start talking. He threw his arm over the couch again.

"We had to pass this hotel, and then she said—said it real quiet, I almost didn't hear it. 'I had to think he was you before I could do anything,' she said. I just looked at her, you know.

"'Then why in the hell did you let him fuck you then? I don't wont nobody fuckin you.'

"'I didn't let him fuck me.'

"'I said I don't wont nobody fuckin you.'

"'I didn't let him fuck me.'

"Then there wasn't no words, just him hitting her. I guess I was kind of hypnotized, you know. Just standing there. He got in two hits before I took his arm. 'All right, man, it's all right now.' *She* starts it, Marie. Not him. She starts it and then he finishes it. She's the one wonts it, though, Marie. I'm living in a crazy house."

Mama said nothing. Daddy got up and went in the kitchen. I didn't think he was coming back, but he did. Otis was already talking again when he got back.

"It was like I didn't wont to cut in, you know. Like I

wanted to just keep watching. Like they were working all that blues out of them, or something. I didn't even wont to put my hand in, but then I knew I couldn't just stand by watching like that."

"Naw," Mama said finally.

Daddy said nothing.

Otis just sat there, and then Daddy told him he had some Old Crow back there in the kitchen, and Otis said he'd better just have a sip and go.

"It's like they my mission in life, you know what I mean, man?"

Daddy said he knew what he meant.

When I looked at Mama, she said she was going to bed.

She shut the door, and I got the sheet and blanket out of the cedar chest and made up my couch-bed.

"He's got his hands full," I heard Daddy tell Mama. "He feels that if he just up and leaves them, whatever happens to them will be his responsibility."

Mama said nothing.

"That's a hell of a situation to be in."

Mama said, "Yes."

I sucked in my stomach.

Alfonso reached over and took my hand. I pulled it away and put it under the table.

"Don't nobody believe you my cousin now."

I said nothing. I touched the foam on the top of my beer.

Alfonso frowned. "You wouldn't do anything for me, would you?" he asked.

"I wouldn't do that," I said.

I wanted to tell him it wasn't me he was worrying about, but I didn't know what that would make him say.

We sat there, saying nothing.

"You see that woman over there," he said after a moment.

I looked at the woman. "Yes."

"She'd do anything for me. If I asked for five dollars right now, she'd give it to me. You don't believe me?"

"I believe you."

"Yeah, she'd do anything for me. She likes me. She's been trying to get me ever since I started coming here. You didn't see the evil eye she give you, did you? Naw, but I seen it. Yessir, if I went up to her right this minute and asked her for five bucks, she'd give it to me. Give it to me and wouldn't ask for nothing in return. I wouldn't do that, though. I wouldn't go up to her and ask, because I'm not that kind of a man. I mean a man that know a woman wonts him and then take advantage of it. But that's the way some men do, though. I ain't that kind of a man, though."

He had gin this time. He drank.

When he took me home, he took me home through this back alley. When he stopped, I stopped. He put his hand down in my blouse. It surprised me at first, and I just stood there, but then when he started to bend his head down—

"Naw."

"I just wont to suck your damn tiddies."

"I said Naw."

"What's that? Where'd you get that?"

He stood away from me. I put the little knife back in my pocket. He stood there saying nothing for a long time, and then he started laughing.

"Shit, a tiddy ain't shit," he said when we were walking back.

He drew tiddies on the wall and the landlord came in and bawled him out, told him to be sure he *did* pay the rent Monday. I was afraid to ask him again to let me help him. When the landlord left, Davis started laughing, and then he pulled up my skirt. He said my knees were like globes. He caressed them with his palms.

"It's like you were a husband," I said.

He looked at me hard. He was frowning.

"I mean you slept with me while I was bleeding, like a husband would, and didn't try to arouse me till I was ready."

"What's a man for?"

I didn't answer. He parted my thighs.

"Why you want me?" I asked.

"Only to ride you."

"You said you used to work with horses."

"Yeah, that's how I got away from my . . . wife. Brought some horses up this way, and stayed."

"You didn't tell me you were married."

"I thought I told you."

"No, you didn't tell me."

Big rusty nails sticking out of my palms. But I let him fuck me again. And when he finished he lay down with his head on the pillow, I wanted him to stay closer longer, to stay inside me longer, but he didn't, and I didn't ask him to. I leaned over and put my tongue in his mouth.

"Where you going?" Daddy asked.

I was going out as he was coming in from work. I told him Alfonso was taking me over to the Froglegs restaurant.

"Jean going?"

"Naw. She doesn't like to go out."

"You used to didn't like to go out."

I said nothing.

"She used to stay up in the house *too* much," Mama said from the kitchen.

"If she need to go out, she ought to find somebody else to go out with," Daddy said. Then to me, "If I was you, I be scared of him, the way he treat Jean."

"He's not a bad man," Mama said.

Daddy told me to go on if I was going. I went out.

Davis said the landlady would always bring him the Sunday's paper. She'd bring it to him on Monday, after they got through with it, but she never failed to bring it to him.

"Yeah, she's got her eyes all out for me. If I was a certain kind of man, I bet I could get out of my rent too, but I ain't that kind of a man. Got her eyes and her ass all out for me. What you frowning at?"

"Nothing."

"I ain't studying her, though. I'm studying you."

He plucked at my nipples and asked me to give him a smile. I showed the dark line along one of my teeth.

"You keep going out with me," Alfonso said.

The man with no thumb passed by our table but didn't sit down.

"How you doing, buddy?" he asked Alfonso. He didn't say anything to me.

"Aw, I'm doing everything," Alfonso said.

"Go high places" I heard the man say as he kept walking.

"He don't believe we cousins now," Alfonso said.

"We are, though," I said.

"He's talking about you taking him high places, I could take you high places. Take you so high you'd start talking to Jesus."

I said nothing.

"Shit. You frustrate a man. Shit."

The man with no thumb passed by our table again. "She make you feel like a king, don't she, buddy?"

"Naw, she don't make me feel like no king, shit."

He got up from the table. He looked at me hard, and then he left me in the restaurant. I thought he was coming back but he didn't. At first I thought he was standing around outside to get some air or smoke, but when I went outside to look for him, he wasn't there. I came back in the restaurant and sat down.

A man sat down across from me. He didn't look old enough to be my father, he looked old enough to be my grandfather.

"My name's Moses Tripp," he said.

I didn't give a shit what his name was, I was thinking in the kind of language Alfonso would use. I didn't want him sitting there and I was wishing Alfonso would come back.

"Alonso coming back?"

I told him my cousin's name was Alfonso.

"Shit, that nigger ain't none of your cousin. He coming back, or are you free?"

I said he was coming back.

"Well, I just take up some of your time till he come back."

I sat there. I didn't know whether to get up and try to go home alone, or wait for Alfonso.

"If I had the money, baby, I'd buy you a beer, but I ain't got the money. I just got enough to, uh . . ." He cleared his throat, but didn't say anything.

I just looked at him.

"You look so sweet," he said. "You look choice. That's how you look. Choice . . . I got, uh, five dollars. You think that'll do?" He slid it across the table at me.

I got up and went out. He followed me out. I was thinking I should've known he'd follow me out.

"Do it for me, huh? Come on, honey. This is my last five."

"Leave me alone."

"Least feel on it for me. That ain't fair. Five dollars for a feel, that ain't . . . Alonso ain't got nothing I . . . Let me." He reached for me down between my legs, then he screamed and pulled his hand back. He called me "bitch."

I could feel him filling the whole crease in my behind. He put his arms around my waist and fingered the front of me. Charlotte said the girl put it in her mouth, because she didn't know it was poison, she thought it was a nut. When the cops came, Moses Tripp said he wasn't trying to do nothing but buy me a beer.

I told Elvira, "He claimed he wasn't trying to do nothing but buy me a beer, but that wasn't all he was trying to buy."

She told me not to tell it to her, there wasn't nothing she could *do* for me. She told me to tell it to them.

"I didn't tell anybody," I said. "I just let the man tell his side."

"How you doing?"

"Awright."

"That's more than me," the man with no thumb said. "I ain't even doing."

Where'd you get the knife from anyway? Daddy asked.

I told him that that was the little knife that Freddy gave me.

I thought that was a play knife, Mama said.

Naw, it was a real one.

Where was Alfonso during all this? Daddy asked.

I didn't answer.

I thought you said you went out with Alfonso.

I did.

I thought it was a rubber knife, said Mama.

Then where was he? Daddy asked.

I said nothing.

You won't talk to them, but you could talk to us, my father said. It's not even like you. Stabbing a man.

I thought it was a toy knife, Mama said.

When my father asked Alfonso where he'd been, he said he'd gone down to the liquor store because it was cheaper there, and he was going to sneak it in. He told me to wait for him, he said. He didn't count on Moses or anybody bothering me. When he got back, they already had me down to the police station. He didn't know where I was till somebody told him.

Daddy said it all didn't sound like Eva.

Mama said I wasn't a bad girl. She said she didn't know it was a real knife Freddy gave me—if she'd known it was a real knife she would have taken it away from me.

Nobody knew why I knifed him because I didn't say. Alfonso said Moses must've done something to me, but they gave me this test, and couldn't find that he'd done anything. They took him down to the medical center and bandaged him up and then sent him home. They said I shouldn't have been carrying a concealed deadly weapon, and Moses Tripp told them that if he hadn't put his hand in the way, I would have gone straight for his heart.

Charlotte took my finger and put it in her mouth. She said she was showing me what the little girl did. I pulled my finger out.

Elvira put up her finger. She said she wanted me to show her how I did it.

I told her that wasn't what she wanted.

"He grabbed at me down between my legs."

IX

My BREATH IN spite of the sausage and cabbage and beer
had a good taste, he said.

I belched. "Excuse me."

"That's all right."

"You're like a lost woman," he said. "Who were you
lost from?"

I didn't tell him.

"Were you ever married, Eva?"

"No." I wouldn't tell him that.

"Who gave you your first fucking?"

I still didn't answer.

"You keep all your secrets, don't you?"

I made a fist, squeezing my fingers in my palms. He
took my fist apart.

"Why won't you talk to me, Eva?"

"There's nothing to say."

"Well, since you won't talk to me, I'll talk to you.
Let's see . . . No, it makes me feel crazy."

"Tell me about the horses."

"Most people don't like the way they smell. My wife
didn't like the way I smelled when I came back from the
horses."

"Is your wife the one you wanted to send the money
to?"

"What money?"

"You said when you sent money home you didn't like
to send just a little bit."

"Naw, I meant my mama."

"Aw."

He held me around the waist, but I kept my back to him. I could feel his breath on my neck. Hot and dark and close.

"You know, the horse business is a funny business," he was saying. "There's a lot of money in it, but the only people that makes the money is those that owns the horses and the big bookies, not the little ones, the *big* ones. The rest of us, we don't get nothing. We train them, we rub them down, we stay with them when they sick, but we don't get nothing. You know, I saw this movie star down to the farm once, what's his name, Dale Robertson. You know, the one plays in *The Tales of Wells Fargo?*"

I nodded.

"He had this beautiful woman with him. Yeah, a lot of movie stars go in the horse business. They like to come see the races, and then they buy theyselves a couple of race horses, you know. You be down to Keeneland or down to the Derby you see a lots of movie stars. Yeah, it's the big men that gets all the money. The rest of us we don't get a thing. You know what I mean?"

I nodded again.

"Say something."

"Yes, I understand."

He turned me toward him, and went in me.

X

I DIDN'T TALK about my husband. He was the part of my life I didn't talk about. James Hunn was fifty-two when I married him. I was eighteen. I married him out of tenderness. Not in a moment of tenderness, not like when you let a man sleep with you in a moment of tenderness. It was like a whole series of tendernesses. He kept coming to see me when I was in the reformatory, and then those three months when I was in jail. He was the only one I would talk to in all that time. Him and the girl they put in the cell with me. I would talk to her. My parents would come to see me, but everything was strained, and near the end they didn't come to see me so much as in the beginning, because we would just sit there most of the time and not say nothing. They told me that Alfonso and Jean were still going at it, and that Otis couldn't be talked into making his own life, because he still felt that they were his "mission." Daddy said Otis was just as crazy as them and that the three of them belonged together. Mama said she was glad they were out of Kansas City anyway so they wouldn't drive Miss Calley mad. And then when they got ready to leave, Mama kissed me and Daddy just looked at me hard.

The first time I saw James Hunn was after the cops arrested me—the first time, I mean, for what I did to Moses Tripp. I was sitting in the Detective Bureau Office. When they found out how old I was they sent me down to Juvenile, but at first they had me sitting down there. When he came in his hair wasn't combed, he was dirty and had a white patch over his left eye. He sat down beside me and said "How do."

I didn't say anything. The secretary asked if she could help him. He got up and went to the desk.

"Yeah, they sent me down here to give my statement. I was in a automobile accident."

"What's your name?"

"Hunn. James Hunn. They call me Hawk."

She told him to have a seat. He sat back down next to me.

"This girl's over here scared of me," he said.

The secretary said nothing.

"I seen her jump when I come in. You didn't jump, but she did."

"I'm used to seeing people all patched up and things," she said. "The reason I can't take your statement now is they got the door closed." She pointed to the door of the back room. She told him that whenever that door was closed she didn't bother them. She told him that when she first started working there once the door was closed and she just opened it and started on in there without knocking or nothing, and there was a man in there with his pants down. "Yeah, I'm used to seeing things worse than that patch over your eye. I mean, people bleeding and things."

The two detectives who had brought me in came out of the back room, and the secretary took Mr. Hunn in there to take his statement. One of the detectives sat at the desk, watching me, and the other one leaned against the filing cabinets. They looked like they were waiting for something.

When James Hunn came out of the back room, he looked at the detectives, and then he looked at me.

"What you do?" he asked when he got near me.

I said nothing.

"I don't blame you for being scared of me. I know I look like the devil."

"You better be careful who you messing with, Hawk," one of the detectives said, laughing.

"What she do?"

"Stabbed a man who was messing with her."

James Hunn looked at me again. "Well, she's still scared of me, though."

"Yeah, Hawk, we know you tough," the detective said, laughing.

The other detective just stood by looking disgusted.

I didn't look at Hawk—after we were married I always called him James. I could feel him looking at me.

"Hawk, we know you tough," the detective repeated.

"You hurt somebody or somebody hurt you?" Hawk asked.

"I just told you she stabbed a man."

"I know what you told me," Hawk said. "I want to hear what she tell me." He was still looking at me. "You scared of me, ain't you, honey?"

The detective who was looking disgusted said, "Shit."

"Hawk, you through, ain't you?" the other detective asked.

"Yeah, I'm going. Y'all take it easy." He looked at me. "You take it easy, you hear?"

I nodded but said nothing.

"Yeah, you get over being scared of James Hunn," he said.

He went out. The detective who was looking disgusted said, "Shit."

A woman came in with a little girl. The little girl was tall for her age and she stood beside the woman calmly. The little girl looked at me questioningly. The woman was angry and nervous and she told the detective that they had her other children down at the Davis Home and that she wanted her other children. The detective told her that she had to go down to Juvenile, straight down the hall.

When they found out I was only seventeen, they sent me down to Juvenile, and then out to the girls' reformatory.

"What's St. Vitus dance?"

The girl had short brownish-red hair, and her complexion was kind of brownish-red too.

"I don't know," I said.

"The girl next door told me she had St. Vitus dance. I asked her what in the hell was that. She don't even know. They give you a pregnancy test?"

I nodded.

"You wasn't, though, was you? Naw. Everybody that come in here, they give them a pregnancy test. You don't have to tell me what you did because I know already. You was easy on him, though. If that old tetter-head nigger had come after me, he wouldn't have no ass or no dick left."

"I didn't say he came after me."

"Well, I can tell by looking at you, sweetheart, you didn't go after him."

I said nothing. She started laughing. She told me her name was Joanne Riley. "You be all right," she said.

We became friends. We were friends until two girls got in a fight over her, and the superintendent moved her to another section.

When James Hunn first came to see me, he had his hair combed, and was cleaned up and the patch was off his eye. He looked handsome. He said he thought he was going to lose it. But there wasn't nothing but a little scar on it.

"You still scared of me, ain't you?"

I said I wasn't scared.

"Yes you are."

We said nothing.

"You surprised to see me, ain't you?"

I said, "Yes."

"They didn't wont to let me in here to see you, since I'm not kin to you or nothing. But I got a woman I used to go with that works here, that spoke up for me. They was looking at me like they thought I was some kind of creature, or something."

I laughed.

"Well, they was."

"You look nice."

He said, "Thank you." Then he said, "You look pretty when you open up. You look just like a flower."

I said nothing. I hadn't even combed my hair that morning. I got into those moods and I wouldn't comb my hair.

We sat there saying nothing for I don't know how long. We'd look at each other and smile sometime, and then he got up and told me to take it easy, and he said, "Don't think I'm not coming back, I be back."

I nodded but said nothing. When I got back to my cell, I took my shoes off and lay down on the bed.

He came to see me the three months I was in the reformatory and the three months I was in jail. He would talk about all kinds of things. He would mostly tell me stories about people. He told me about this man who owned this store and these people wanted to take the store so they could tear it down and make a branch of the

State Mental Hospital there, but in order to get it they had to prove the man was insane. They ended up proving the man was insane, but in a few years ended up moving him back out there on the same ground where his store had been. He said that was a true story. Then he told me where when he was in the army these whores in France would come over to you and tell you right out loud where everybody could hear what it was they could do for you. Like come over to you and ask you right out loud if you wanted a suck job. He said the first time one asked him he was so embarrassed he just turned around and walked right out of the place. Then he excused himself— he said he had a lot of other army stories, but he was forgetting who he was talking to. I told him to tell me another one. He said okay he'd just tell me one more. He said the first time he heard about sodomy was when these men got together and put this mule in this tent and then lined up. I started laughing. He looked surprised that I thought it was funny and then he started laughing.

We'd sit in this little room with a table and both sit up to the table. He'd be leaning across the table, and our knees would sometimes touch.

The strangest thing he told me was a story he started telling me but it wasn't really a story. It wasn't an off-color story or anything. He just started saying, "There was a woman who couldn't love any man and she didn't even like sex or anything that had anything to do with lovemaking." That was all he said and then he stopped, and we just sat there.

"What's St. Vitus dance?"

"What?"

"St. Vitus dance."

He said he didn't know. He told me to take it easy. He left.

Joanne said she wouldn't want to have a baby. She said somebody asked her wouldn't she like to nurse a baby. She said Naw, and then she said she told her the only reason she'd consider having a baby was so she would have milk in her tiddies so when her man sucked on her tiddies, she'd have milk coming out. A man sucking milk from his woman. I asked her what did the girl say.

"She didn't say nothing at first. She just looked at me disgusted. Then she said it sounded gruesome."

James put his hand in my blouse, then he opened my blouse, and sucked my breasts.

The man called up my mother and asked her how did it feel.

"She's my woman," the girl said. "I don't wont you messing with her, cause she's my woman."
They moved Joanne into another section.

Alfonso came to see me. I said nothing to him. He said he heard that I'd gotten to be friends with James Hunn. No, he didn't put it like that. He said he'd heard I'd gotten close to a man they called Hawk. I said we were friends.
"You remember that man I told you about, the one that killed this man over a woman."
"Yes."
"He's the same man."
He tells the story again, of how they got in a fight in a restaurant over this woman. She wasn't even a good-lookin woman, just a woman. They got in a fight and Hawk lost his temper and killed this man. The woman

was gone. They didn't know where the woman went, but Hawk was put in jail for seven years. They say he still carries the gun he shot the man with.

I said James Hunn was a good man.

"I never said he wasn't. He's just got a bad temper. He's a good man with a bad temper. He don't hurt people he likes, though. He wouldn't hurt you . . . But he's not a man to get close to."

I said I hadn't seen him with a bad temper. Alfonso said again that he wasn't the kind of man a woman should get close to.

I got close enough to him to marry him when I got out. The trouble didn't start until we moved down to Frankfort, Kentucky. He said he wanted to put me through school, so I enrolled in Kentucky State. I didn't see his temper. I didn't know that anything was wrong with him until we moved in this house and there was a telephone there and he said he was going to take the telephone out. I said I wanted a telephone. But he said Naw, I couldn't have one. I asked him why and he said he didn't want my lovers calling me. I thought he was joking at first and then I looked at him, and he wasn't joking. I told him I didn't have any lovers. He said every woman had lovers. He said he wasn't going to have a telephone in the house so that my lovers could be calling me up and then meeting me some place. I stayed with him for two years. I can't explain it. It was like the tenderness was still there, but he didn't trust any move I made. And then he would come down to the school and pick me up after classes. I didn't even think of him as an old man until I was at college. He was good to me, though. He would do anything in the world for me. No one believed that he was my husband because he was older than a lot of the teachers there.

. . .

He called the telephone company and told them to take the phone back because he said he didn't want my lovers calling me up at all hours of the day and night.

The house we lived in had four rooms and a bathroom. He said he was too old to have children. He said he didn't want to be an old man raising children. We would sit in the front room evenings and he would tell me stories, or we would listen to the radio. He was a watchmaker. No, I mean he fixed watches. He could fix any kind of clocks and watches. He said he learned how to fix watches when he was in the army.

I don't like to talk about my husband, though. He was fifty-two years old when I knew him. I was eighteen. No, he never once showed me his temper. It was just the thing about the telephone. No, Alfonso said he wouldn't hurt me because he didn't hurt the people he liked. Alfonso said he liked me. I spent two years at Kentucky State, and then I went to P. Lorillard to work. I thought he would come after me, but he didn't. Since then I've been going from one tobacco factory to another. You get tired of one place and then you try another. In the summer, though, most of the times you get laid off anyway.

James put his head inside my blouse, and kissed me between my breasts.

part
TWO

I

"WE NEED BREAD," he said.

"Let me go get it this time."

"No."

"What's there about keeping me here?"

"Where I can find you."

"Did you lose *her?*"

He didn't answer. He looked at me hard. I didn't ask again.

"What else do you want from the store?" he demanded.

I just stood looking at him.

"What's the matter, baby, won't talk?" he asked, smiling.

"Nothing," I said.

He stopped smiling, turned away and went out.

James asked me if I liked the house. I said yes. I said it was good to come in the front door and see the front room instead of the kitchen. He said he'd never seen a house where you saw the kitchen first. I said that was where I spent most of my life.

He said about the telephone, "We won't need this."

I said I'd like to have a telephone, I'd never had a telephone before, why couldn't he keep it in.

"No, I'll have them take it out tomorrow," he said.

"Why?"

"I don't wont your lovers calling you."
He didn't say it like a joke.

Davis brought home bread and bacon.
"We'll have scrambled eggs," he said coldly. "Here's a hot plate. Here, you make them."
I stirred them, saying nothing, watched them harden.
"Eva, why won't you talk?"
I turned with a smile and handed him his plate. "You meant to tell me, didn't you?" I asked.
"Yes, I meant to tell you." He watched me fix my own plate. He was watching me when I sat down beside him on the bed, the plate hot in my hands.
"I like to feel the heat against my lap," I said. I put the fork in my eggs.
"My mama used to say, 'Davy, there's mens that ain't got no ambition except chasing womens. You got to do more than chase womens.' You don't think I'm like that, do you?"
"Naw, I don't think that."
"I thought you were the kind of woman who'd understand."
"I understand."
"I thought I could turn to you for something I needed. Not romance," he said.
I closed my eyes. I said nothing. The eggs were hot in my mouth. Then I opened my eyes and swallowed the eggs, my tongue still feeling them.
"Yes, I know how you feel," I said.
"Where are you from?" he asked again. He probably thought I would answer this time.
"Here and thereabouts."
"You still won't answer?"
"No."
"Eva, Eva, Eva." He grinned. His hand went to my

shoulder. When we finished eating, I undressed again. I turned back the sheets.

He asked me if I'd been hurt in life. He said I looked like a woman who'd been hurt in life. I didn't answer. He said I didn't have to answer. He leaned back in his seat. I was on a bus on my way to Wheeling, West Virginia. He was going to Denver.

"My father used to carry a jackknife around in his pocket all the time. Guess what it had printed on it?" he asked.

"What?"

"In big gold letters," the man said. " 'Trust in God.' "

I asked him why he was going to Denver. He said he was thirty-five years old and liked to run with people who were twenty, twenty-five, but he said, when you're thirty-five people who are twenty, twenty-five don't trust you. "I mean they look at you like you don't belong with them . . . I used to teach school around when I was twenty-six. Taught in a college. I'm thirty-five and ain't never been married. I can't see staying with the same woman." I didn't ask him what anything had to do with anything. He said, "I mean I'ma go to Denver and when I get through there, I'm goin' out to California, and when I get through there I think I'm going to go down to Mexico."

"My father used to carry a jackknife around in his pocket all the time," I told Davis. "Guess what it had printed on it?" I asked.

He had to change buses before I did. Before he got off the bus, he gave me a good look. I gave him back the look.

"You know, sometimes when I meet a woman like you, you know, one I know I'm not going to see again, I wonder if you could've been the one."

I said nothing. He got his bags down. He was a little, attractive man, dressed younger than his age. He had lines all around his eyes.

"No, what?" Davis asked.

"In big gold letters, 'Trust in God,' " I said. I waited for him to laugh. He didn't laugh at first, then he laughed loud and grabbed me around my waist. I could feel him hard against my ass. He took me before we got into bed.

When he came out of me he was sweating, but I wasn't.

"Don't you ever sweat?"

"No." I smiled.

"You made me tired," he said. I was watching the ceiling. We were in bed now, and sweat had dropped from his forehead into my eyes.

"You're too serene," he said.

I said nothing.

"How do you feel about it, Eva?"

"It doesn't matter."

I thought he'd been looking at me, but he hadn't. He was watching my belly, stroking it again. I smoothed his cheek with my hand. I kissed his neck. He lay down. I put my forehead under his chin inside his neck. He grinned, staring at the ceiling. He put my hand on his dick, swelling.

"You did this. Look what you've done. It's your fault," he said.

"It's not my fault," I said. "But I'm not sorry."

"Want to play again?" he said.

"Yes."

II

"YOU SEE THAT woman over there," Alfonso said. "She'd do anything for me. If I asked her to give me five dollars, she'd give it to me."

Elvira pulled a scab off her knee.
"How'd you do that?"
"I don't know. I must've scraped my leg up against something and didn't know it."
"You shouldn't pick at it," I said.
"You care all a sudden?"

"Yeah, that's Sweet Man up over the mantelpiece," Miss Billie said. "Good-looking, ain't he? For a old man. He don't look as old as he is, though. It's a shame the way men keep up, ain't it? And there I be walking down the street and look like my knees give out. Tha's why I got all these scars and bruises on my legs. My knees give out, and people think I'm drunk. They don't believe me when I tell em it's my knees."

"Yeah, when *you* start carrin," Elvira said.

"French woman come up to me and ask if I wont a suck job. Ask me right out loud if I wont a suck job. Ask me right out loud where everybody can hear if I wont a suck job. She come up to me and ask me, she didn't whisper, she ask me right out where everybody could hear, she ask me if I wont a blow job. They use to things like that, though. They don't act like they do around here. Got theyselves a mule and put the mule in a tent, and then lined up."

"You was a little bitta thing, the last time I seen you," Miss Billie said.

Freddy Smoot grabbed my arm hard enough to bruise my arm and pulled me up under the stairs. He got real close to me.

"I'ma put it in you like Mama's men put it in her."

I didn't try to run. I just stayed with him. He still had my arm. He held my arm and unzipped his pants and took his thing out. Then he kept looking from my eyes to his thing. And then all of a sudden he pushed me away from him, and turned and zipped his pants back up, and went upstairs. I didn't know what he'd seen in my eyes, because I didn't know what was there.

Tyrone said, I put your hand on it because I thought you needed it.

The scab was still ripe. Blood ran down her legs. She wiped it on the hem of her dress.

Davis came back into the room. I was sitting in the dark. I must have scared him. He jumped, then got angry. He cut the light on.

"What the hell you doin sittin up in the damn dark. It ain't natural. You ain't natural."

I had my hands in my hair. "I'm natural," I said. My voice was real quiet.

He laughed a little. "Shit, if you was natural, you

wouldn't even be here, woman. You wouldn't even a let Davis Carter lay a hand on you. Not for free."

"What you mean?"

"Anything you decide I mean, baby."

"You don't know."

"I know you can't leave me alone."

I shook my head. "Naw. It's *you*."

He looked at me for a moment, almost frowning, then he went out. Before the door closed, I heard him laugh. Hard.

"Say something, Eva."

"There's nothing."

"What can I do?"

"Try."

"What do you want me to do, Davis?"

"I said try, woman."

I looked at him, but he wasn't looking at me. Then he was looking, but he wasn't. I passed my hand through my hair.

"You might as well do it," he said.

I didn't ask what he meant.

III

"I'M GOING OUT," he said.

"Bring home some brandy. I feel like that instead of beer."

I hadn't meant to call the place home. He must have noticed it, because he laughed and said he would.

"I won't forget the mustard this time," he said.

I nodded. He went out. The door closed hard.

I went into the janitor's closet and got the rat poison. I tore a piece of sack and made an envelope and shook some powder in and put it in the pocket of my skirt, then I went back and sat on the bed. Then I sat on the floor, with my back against the bed, my knees drawn up. I felt tense. My thighs felt like they do after a good lay, or going to the doctor and having him jam that cotton stick up your pussy. I held my arms tight around my knees, then I pushed them up between my thighs. I punched my belly, swollen with too much eating in, and being constipated. I'd get nervous with him there, and nothing would come out.

"What are you doing?" I asked.
"Traveling."
He asked me what I was doing.
"Traveling."

Alfonso asked me if I smoked. I said No. He said I didn't know what kind of smoke he meant. He said they put it in that kind of package to protect themselves. He passed me a Chesterfield King.

The man without a thumb nodded and smiled at us from the other side of the room.

Alfonso had a bottle of Bali Hai in a brown paper bag. He said it was cheaper down at the liquor store. He kept it under the table.

"Bearcat Brown's got a steel plate in his head," I heard somebody say.

I told Alfonso how Medina got kicked by a horse, and the doctor put a steel plate in her head and a dime in her jaw. He said only that she was his grandmother too. He poured some wine in my glass.

"You just keep coming, don't you?"

Finally he took the wine out of the bag and put it up on the table.

"Yeah, that's why can't nobody down him. He's got that steel plate in his head. They call him the cat. Sometimes they call him the bear."

He put his hand in my blouse.
"I didn't know your breasts were so big."
He bent his head down.
"Naw."

"A man talks to himself when he's lonely," James said. "I go out to restaurants sometimes, but I sit way over in the corner by myself. People see me and think I'm crazy because I just be sitting over there laughing and talking to myself. Or either somebody ask, 'What's that nigger talking about?' and somebody answer, 'Probably talking some shit.' A man's lonely and he laughs and talks to himself. He ain't crazy, he's lonely."

IV

WHAT WOULD TYRONE have done if I'd gone with him under the stairs? I dream. There's no hoot. He pulls me hard. He takes his stick out. There's a bubble at the end of it.

"It's to measure you," he says. "It will let me know when you're level."

He slides his back down the wall, and pulls my dress up. He keeps telling me it won't hurt. "Eva, it won't hurt." Pulls my pants down. He tells me it's no different from a popsicle.

"*Ain't no man I wont but you. Ain't no penis I wont but yours,*" Mama says. Where is she?

I'm on the floor. Tyrone and me. He says I make him feel like kindling.

"Sleep with me, Eva."

"No."

"You know you don't wont it like this."

"No."

"You know you don't wont it like this."

"No."

"When you going to let me make love to you again?"

"Never."

"When you going to love me, Eva?"

I don't answer.

"When you going to let me feel you?"

I don't answer.

"When you going to feel me again?"

No answer.

"How long has it been, honey?"

"It's been a long long time."

Mr. Logan is an old owl perched on the stairs.

Mama says, "Ain't no man I wont but you."

Daddy says, "Why'd you take him on then?"

Tyrone puts my hand on his thing. Then he jams himself up inside me.

I got back on the bed, my knees parted. He came in.

"Eva, what are you doing?"

"Nothing, I was waiting for you."

"I think I forgot the mustard." He peeked in the sack. "No, I didn't forget it."

"What about the bourbon?"

"I thought you said brandy."

"Yes, I did. I'm sorry."

"Is this kind all right?"

"Yes."

He sat the things down on the table. Cabbage and sausage. What I had the first night. A big loaf of bread and some cheese. Beer for himself.

"Aren't you going to have any brandy?" I asked.

"Yeah, I'll have a little brandy. I'll wash it down with this."

"I'll rinse out the glasses," I said, getting up. "Do you want the brandy before or after dinner?"

"I'll have mine after dinner."

"I'll wait too."

We sat down at the table, opposite each other. I kept my eyes on my plate. I spread the mustard on my sausage.

"Do you want any?"

"Naw, I told you what it looks like. Baby's doodoo."

"The horseradish kind looks more like that," I said.

"I thought it would bother you."

"No, it didn't bother me."

I tried to think of what he was talking about. I watched his mouth, but not his eyes.

"I think they burnt the cabbage," he said.

"It still tastes good."

"Yeah, it does."

I felt it good against my tongue and in the hollows of my mouth. I thought of him rubbing my back and thighs.

"You eat food as if you're making love to it," he said.

"I'm sorry."

"No, I like it. I like to watch."

I found it hard to go on eating, hard to find my mouth. I looked up, but he wasn't watching any longer. I went on eating, my shoulders bent.

"What are you thinking? You're not talking."

"Nothing."

"Why aren't you speaking?"

"I don't have anything to say right now."

"Did what I say bother you? You said it didn't bother you."

"No, it didn't bother me."

"I don't mean about the mustard."

"No, it didn't bother me."

He looked at me hard. He got up and came over and walked behind me and put his hand on my shoulders. He belched, said excuse me. I could feel my muscles tighten, my skin withdraw, but he didn't act like he could feel it. I held my own belch in, till it made me feel sick. All that gas inside. I said nothing. He took his hand away. His plate was already clear. I soon cleared mine. They were paper ones, so I threw them away. He got out of his shoes and socks and sat up in bed.

"I'm too full now."

"I ate too much too," I said. "Do you want the brandy now?"

"Yeah, I'll have a little. You?"

"Yes."

He leaned back and closed his eyes. I went over to the table, filled the glasses, my back to him, then brought him his. He smiled and took the glass. I got my glass and sat down on the bed beside him.

"Come, sit closer," he said.

I sat closer. He held me around the belly with his left hand, drinking from the glass with his right. I drank.

"You had some earlier, didn't you?" I asked.

"I didn't think you could tell."

"Yes, I could tell."

He rubbed my belly, patted my belly, thumped my belly, drank. I drank.

"I should have a duplicate key made for you," he said.

"I didn't think you'd planned to be here long," I said. "Or have me here."

"Still, you should have one. Where were you living?"

"I was between places."

"It's good to be between places."

"Is it?"

"But you might wont to go on living here."

I didn't answer. Then I said, "Yes, I might." Then I asked, "When will you be leaving?"

"I don't know. It's better not to know."

"Maybe."

"I'll have one made anyway," he said. Then he gripped my waist. I had my back to him and didn't watch. But he gripped my waist hard enough to break my ribs. "Bitch." I belched.

He didn't see me at first and then he saw me and came back where I was. I was leaning against the seat with my

eyes open. He asked if anybody was sitting there. I said
"Naw." He put his bag up and sat down. He said he was
on his way to Denver, Colorado. I said I was on my way
to Wheeling, West Virginia. He'd looked young until he
got up close, and then I could see the lines around his
eyes.

I put my hand on his hand. I kissed his hand, his neck.
I put my fingers in the space above his eyes, but didn't
close them. They'd come and put copper coins over
them. That's why they told you not to suck pennies. I put
my forehead under his chin. He was warm. The glass had
spilled from his hand. I put my tongue between his
parted lips. I kissed his teeth.

*"That kiss was full of teeth," James said. He stood
back and laughed and then kissed me again.*

I opened his trousers and played with his penis. My
mouth, my teeth, my tongue went inside his trousers. I
raised blood, slime from cabbage, blood sausage. Blood
from an apple. I slid my hands around his back and dug
my fingers up his ass, then I knelt down on the wooden
floor, bruising my knees. I got back on the bed and
squeezed his dick in my teeth. I bit down hard. My teeth
in an apple. A swollen plum in my mouth.

"How did it feel?"

A red swollen plum in my mouth. A milkweed full of
blood. A soft milkweed full of blood. What would you
do if you bit down and your teeth raised blood from an
apple? Flesh from an apple? What would you do? Flesh
and blood from an apple. What would you do with the
apple? How would you feel?

*"All women need the fork in their road," Alfonso said,
laughing.*

"Come home with me."

"I'm not good tonight. I'm bleeding."

"Then we'll wait."

Blood on my hands and his trousers. Blood in my teeth.

"A woman like you. What do you do to yourself?"

I got the silk handkerchief he used to wipe me after we made love, and wrapped his penis in it. I laid it back inside his trousers, zipped him up. I kissed his cheeks, his lips, his neck. I got naked and sat on the bed again. I spread my legs across his thighs and put his hand on my crotch, stuffed his fingers up in me. I put my whole body over him. I farted.

"You didn't tell me."

"I thought I told you."

"No."

The blood still came through.

"Bastard."

I reached in his pants, got my comb, took the key he'd promised, washed my hands, finished my brandy, wiped his mouth, and left.

I no longer smelled of perfume and menstruation, I smelled of brandy and sausage. People were watching me. I remembered I hadn't combed my hair. I stood back inside a doorway and picked it out. They passed and glanced at me and walked on.

I went into a liquor store.

"Do you have a telephone?"

"Yes, over there."

I went toward where he pointed, but didn't see it. I looked back at him.

"No, around the corner."

I found it, and called, and told them about the man in the hotel room.

"What's your name, lady?"

I wouldn't tell them. I hung up. I walked out. I went to
the toilet of a filling station, picked out my hair again.
I'm Medusa, I was thinking. Men look at me and get
hard-ons. I turn their dicks to stone. I laughed. I'm a lion
woman. No, it's the men lions that have all that hair. I
got close to the mirror and fingered the streets under my
eyes. The mirror needed cleaning. I peed. I went out.

I went back to the bar where they sold the good
cabbage and the well-done greasy sausage, where they
cooked the cabbage with smoked bacon.

"Yes ma'am?"

"Cabbage and sausage, please. And put a lot of
mustard on the sausage. A can of beer."

I ate, drank beer. I ate plenty. I was already full from
the cabbage and sausage he'd fed me, but it was good to
eat again, to think about being naked and being taken.
No, fucked. To think of my legs wide open, and my
fingers up his ass.

"You eat food like you're making love to it."

I laughed and went on eating. I closed my eyes,
swallowing. I had to pee again. Beer always made me
have to pee. I got up and went to the toilet, came back
and sat down again. I drank the rest of the beer.

"Is there anything else, ma'am?"

"No, thank you."

I paid and left. I wanted to be fucked. I wanted him to
fuck me up my ass.

I went back, but he wasn't there. The sheets and
bedspread were gone. There was only the mattress,
stained with the blood and whiskey. The glasses and
whiskey were gone. They'd taken him. I sat on the floor.
My knees hurt. I watched the walls.

They saw me go up and then they followed me up, and
they were speaking in whispers, and then they came in.

"Yes, she's the one. I saw her go up. Look at her sitting

there. Just look at her. What kind of woman can it be to do something like that?"

Otis said it was like they were working some kind of blues ritual. He said he couldn't stop watching.

A man sucking the milk from her breasts. He is sucking blood.

James said he wanted to tell me something. He asked me if I remembered that time in the reformatory I'd said, "You look like a man who's worried about something." He said I'd just said it in passing and probably didn't remember it, but he said he said he remembered it because he was a man worried about something. And then he told me that twenty years ago he'd killed a man. It had been twenty years and they still hadn't forgot. The man who owned the restaurant still wouldn't let him come in the place. I don't like to talk about the particulars, he said, but it was over a woman.
I didn't tell him that I already knew.
"Yeah, I'm a man that's worried, because I haven't forgot it either," he said.

The queen bee. Men had to die for loving her.

James said he was dying to kiss me. He said he was dying to kiss me. He leaned over. He said my kiss was full of teeth.

V

"LET'S PLAY," he asks.
The sweet milk in the queen bee's breasts has turned
to blood.

part
THREE

I

NOTHING YOU wouldn't know about. Nothing you wouldn't know about. Nothing you wouldn't know about.

The man in his office lays me on top of his desk. He pulls my dress up, takes his pants down. I won't. I won't take anything. How much will you take? I won't take anything. You frustrate a man. He gets up and goes to the bathroom. After that he keeps watching me.

The young boys whistle at me. They are walking behind me. They have taps on their shoes, they keep whistling until they pass me, and turn around and look at me.

"I thought she was a chick."

"Hello, Mama."

"She's a good-lookin mama, for a old woman, though," one of them says. He whistles again.

"She looked young from the back."

"Yeah."

He's got taps on his shoes. He's chewing bubble gum. The foreman keeps watching me.

"I been watching you work," he says. "I been watching how you work. I been watching you."

I rubbed his back and thighs. I thought of what he said about the mustard, and wiped him with toilet paper between his ass. Something I'd never done with a lover. Something I'd never thought of doing. He was on my breasts, sucking blood. He kept laughing. "The blood ducks. The blood ducks." I spread my legs.

"What about once you close them?" Elvira asks.

"They stay closed," I want to answer, but I don't answer.

"How could you tell?" he asks.

"I saw it in your eyes."

I tell him it's nothing he wouldn't know about. Nothing he wouldn't know about. James is on the floor with me. He tells me he is dying to kiss me. He leans over and puts his tongue on me. I don't open my mouth.

"Open your mouth."

I tell him I didn't know I was supposed to open my mouth.

"They stay closed," I tell her.

James, his hair combed, asked me to marry him. He came to get me when it was time to leave. We walked to his car. When he started driving, I thought he was taking me home.

"She good-lookin for a old woman, ain't she?"

I didn't know where we were going. I asked him.

"You look like a flower," he said.

"That don't answer where we going."

"You can get out of the car anytime."

"I don't want to get out of the car."

"Then wait and see. And when we get there, you can say turn back, and I'll turn back."

The car stopped in front of the justice of the peace. I didn't tell him to turn back.

"Do you want me to turn back?"

"No."

He said he was dying to kiss me. He said he was dying to . . . We were married.

I went and told my parents, without him. They just sat looking at me.

"You're married?" Daddy asked finally.

Mama stayed saying nothing.

"Yes."

Mama didn't say anything.

"Mama, aren't you going to say anything?"

"What do you want me to say, honey?"

"It's just that we never dreamed . . ." Daddy said.

Then he said they were happy for me, then he kissed me. Mama looked at me hard, then she leaned forward and gave me her cheek to kiss. I told them I hadn't dreamed either.

I keep watching the man with no thumb until he sees me.

"I could tell you wanted me. I could tell."

"Naw, I didn't want you neither."

"I could tell you wanted me. I was the first one that aroused you. I could tell."

"Naw."

"Have you ever been kissed down there before?"

"Naw, and I . . ."

He said he was from New Mexico.

"What are you doing all the way over here?" I asked.

"Traveling," he said.

He asked me what I was doing all the way over here. I said I was traveling too.

He takes me up to an old room.

It is a dream.

"My name is Moses Tripp. I came to take you on a trip."

He sits snapping his fingers. "Every trip. Every trip. Every trip."

"How high do you want me to take you, honey baby?"

James says he wants to get real high up in me.

"I been dying to."

II

When I asked Otis what did Uncle Nutey do, he said he was sitting on the church steps naked. He just took off all his clothes and went and sat naked on the church steps. The cops came by and picked him up and put him in the asylum.

My breasts are rocks that turn to bread and then to milk. Blood is inside my breasts.

What would you do if you broke bread and blood came out?

The gypsy Medina tells me: Toss his blood into the wind, and it will dry.

God is God, she says, because he can turn milk and sweat into blood.

The owl corners me, lays me on the floor, begins to dig and peck.

"Don't let your man know."

"I won't tell him. If you don't tell your woman."

There is a dead eel between his legs.

I am sitting in a restaurant. The men who work with my father ask, "What are you doing here, sweetheart?"

"That's John Canada's daughter."

"I don't care who she is. She's sweet."

"Naw, she's nothing but a little bitch just like all the rest of em. Think they wont your love, and they wont your money."

"Better not let John hear you saying that."

"What? That she's a bitch or she's sweet?"

"Or that she's a sweet bitch . . . Man I ain't got no more ambition in life than chasin womens."

"Making love and making money."

They come over to me and look me over.

"Naw, you can't tell them nothing," Miss Billie says. "They got to learn for themselves. Got to get stung by the bee before they can see."

"Mama, where does the bee sting?"

"Your heart," Mama says.

"Down in your draws," says Miss Billie.

Is your heart in your draws?

III

JOANNE SAID every time her father fucked her mother, her mother would say, Praise God Praise God. What would your mother say?

Nothing. She would just make little noises, and my father would make noises like he was soothing pain away.

Did you take my rubbers?
No.

She was under sand. And he came and put a hole—not for air—but so he could stick his thing in.

Why do you care for him so much?

He told me to look at his hand. He told me what his hand had done to women.

Suppose he had told you he would stay?

He puts himself in me.

IV

"Is THIS THE savage woman?"
"Yes, here she is."
They stare me in my eyes.

Did you have a bad night?
I dreamed an old man came with a canoe and he had a
troubled expression, till he saw me, then he started
smiling. He handed me one oar and he took the other
one. I thought we were going to plunge both oars in the
stream, but he lay me on my back in the canoe. Water
seeping in my skin. He put one nervous hand on my
belly, the other over my eyes.
When I woke up, he said, "I didn't do it." He kept
saying, "I didn't do it."
Then he scooted down along my body until his head
was at my waist.
"Did you take my rubbers?" he asked.
"No."
"Where's your man?"
"I don't have one."
He said, "Things like this happen in hell."
He put his tongue on me.

The queen bee's men had dice. They were asked what
they were gambling. They said they were gambling their
lives.

She kept telling one man to go. She kept telling him to go.

When he left, she got up on the table and spread her legs open like a book. The men tossed dice.

"Man, she told you to go. Man, you ain't got what she need."

"Whore," he called her, then he took off his shirt and threw it between her legs. Then he left.

The men won the shirt first, and then the meat.

She was a river. There were fins. She's a river. They keep coming back to her until she swallows them up.

Davis put his tongue on my navel.

"I don't go any further than this. I hope you don't mind."

"No, I don't mind."

"I'd only do that with a woman I'd lived with for years. I'd only do that with my wife."

Semen in his drawers.

"A woman like you, what do you do to yourself?"

"Nothing you wouldn't know about."

What did Uncle Nutey do?

If he had told you he would stay?

"Once you close your legs, you keep them closed."

V

KISS ME, the man says. Give me a kiss.

The woman does not.

The man says, Loneliness, you feel loneliness when there's no one you can go to, for anything—no one woman you can go to—I couldn't find one woman.

He's naked, on the church steps. The woman takes her clothes off too and holds her hand out to him. She tells him she has time in her hand, that time is a toy, something they can play with.

The man sits smoking wind. He tells her he is a son of flesh and thunder.

If I had you, I'd do more than eat and live, he says. I'd be able to love again.

He has no thumb on one hand, and the other hand is slashed red. It drips between his legs.

Your breasts are loaves of bread, he tells her. You look like a woman who's been hurt by love.

Yes, I was hurt by love. My soul was broken. My soul was broken.

He puts his hand out to caress her throat, not the bloody one, but the one with the thumb gone. She can't feel the thumb gone.

She kisses him. He has an iguana's tongue. Her body shivers with love, by the fistfuls. When he leaves her, her memory turns into blood.

What is my body made of, she asks, that there is no sweat inside.

She stands naked on the street. She asks each man she sees to pay her her debt. But they say they owe her nothing.

The owl is perched on the stairs.

"I've come to protect this woman," he says.

But he turns into a cock, and descends. A lemon between his legs. She has made the juice run.

I caress his throat. I kiss him.

part
FOUR

I

I LAY ON my back watching a female cockroach climbing
the wall. An eggsack was hanging from its ass. Some
people like to squash that kind. I didn't like to squash
any of them, because of that white stuff coming out.
Sometimes I'd think of pulling the eggsack out before it
was time to come out. Not with my hands, but with
tweezers. I liked to watch them copulate, the male
coming in through the ass, hanging onto the female's
back. I'd think of how small their genitals must be.

The cell had a basin for washing up, but I had to go
out to go to the toilet. I thought of cockroach piss, then I
thought of him. An erection. He took my hand and put it
on his thing. "It's your fault," he said. "You did it." "I'm
not sorry," I answered. He asked if I wanted to play. I
said yes. But then we were turning forward rolls and
backward rolls like I used to do on those long mattresses
in gym class. And then we were using ropes for swings,
and we were naked, and the ropes cut into our asses. I
could see a red cut along his ass. I couldn't see my own,
but I felt it burning, stinging, blood on the tips of my
fingers. I touched his. He was bleeding too, but he was
laughing. I didn't want to, but I started laughing too. He
raised his arms and I kissed him inside his armpits. He
asked, "What next?" I smiled but didn't answer. Then I
said, "You never know." He watched me in silence, then
he said, "Let's play again." I scratched his behind.

"Have you started yet?" he asked.

"No, I haven't started yet."

"We could rub asses and become blood what-ya-ma-call-its," he said, laughing.

I hugged myself, my hands inside my armpits. I was bleeding again.

"I don't like a woman bleeding, it's nasty," he said.

"Get up close to me, honey, it helps the cramps." But he wouldn't. He turned away instead.

He did it while I was sleeping. I was bleeding but he went ahead and did it. His eyes were blood-colored like the eyes of those men who work in metal factories drilling holes in things with their visors on to help protect their eyes. Then I woke up and told him to hurry up and do it, but he took his time. He went in slow and came out slow. But still it was so good. Then he got dressed and went out for some reason he wouldn't tell me and I just stayed laying there, with the towel under me to catch the blood, still feeling him, and then he came back. He told me to get dressed.

"I knew you'd be coming back," I said.

"Get dressed anyway, I don't like to see a woman always naked."

"Honey, you in a trance or something?"

"What?"

The woman in the next cell was watching me. She had her hands on the bars and was peeking in at me. She was wearing the same kind of gray dress I was wearing.

"I said you sitting there like you in a trance. Like one of them demon women or something. I can understand it, though. All em Dr. Frauds coming in and out all the time enough to drive anybody crazy, if they ain't already. You seen yours yet?"

"What?"

"I call em all Dr. Frauds. You know. But that's all they do. Nothing. And get ten, twenty dollars a hour for it too. Except the state pays em. If I had to pay em, I wouldn't pay em. I just stay crazy. Why they put you in here? What you do?"

"I killed a man."

"Aw, that's bad. I bet it was all in the papers, wasn't it? They put me all in the papers. What's your name? Maybe I read about you."

"Medina."

"Naw, I ain't read about you, but seem I heard about it. Was he your nigger or somebody else's?"

I didn't answer.

"I bet I know how it happen. Your man messing around with some other woman I bet."

"Yeah."

"Yeah, I knew it was. I coulda told you that. My name's Elvira Moody. You ever read about me?"

"Naw."

She frowned.

"What did you do?" I asked.

She smiled. Her teeth were crooked and rotten, but she didn't look more than forty-five. "I sold some men some bad whiskey. It didn't do nothing but make them sick. But the bastards called the law on me, and they put me in here. They put you in here for anything. You just look at them funny, they put you in here."

"Aw."

"You be awright, though. They didn't execute you, did they? What I say is as long as you alive and fucking, you awright. You know, I heard on the radio where they talking about letting the men have women visitors, you know, sex visits. I don't know if they mean crazy mens too, but they in prison too and need it too, don't they. It's all controversial now though and all these citizens

621

callin in on the radio bitching about it and talking about
how the good Lord didn't mean for it to happen and it
go against the Bible and how they outraged about it. You
know how they do? But what I say is they ought to do the
same thing for women that they do for men. If the men
can have sex visits, the women ought to be able to have it
too. Don't you think that's right?"

"Yeah."

"You ain't much of a talker, are you?"

"Naw."

"Well, you keep that up. I knew what it was, though.
The minute I seen you, I said that woman done got
herself mixed up with *some* nigger. I didn't know whether
he was yours or somebody else's, though. But tha's just
what I thought. They ain't nothing but bastards. All I do
is sell em whiskey and get what I can get out of em. You
know what I mean? But I bet you loved him, didn't you?
Well, you don't have to tell me. You know it's going to
trouble you, though. I know womens that's killed mens.
It troubles them. It just seems like it just stays with em.
They get back out on the street again, and some new
man gets them mad and they be saying, 'I done killed you
once, I don't wont to have to kill you again. Don't make
me kill you again.' It just stay with em like that, and puts
them out of their minds. I ain't never raised my hand
against a man myself, cause if you don't get them, they
get you, and if you do get them, the law get you. Tell me
how it happened, honey. Naw, I know if you wouldn't
tell them, you wouldn't tell me . . ."

*I submit the insanity of Eva Medina Canada, a
woman who loved a man who did not return that love.
Crumbled sheets and blood and whiskey and spit. You
born fucking and you. Your honor the court recom-
mends that . . .*

"All they think about is where they going to get their next piece."

On the toilet throne, I'm a queen bee. He stings me between my breasts, the buds on my breasts, the bud between my legs. My flower. Come on and take me higher. He strokes me way up in the crease in my ass. He strokes my back. I can't feel the place where the thumb's gone. It's like he's stroking me with all five fingers. I can't feel the place where the thumb's gone.

"After you've done it the first time," Mama said.

Come on and take me higher.

James, with a popsicle, felt me down between my legs.

"How did all that blood happen, Eva?"

"I don't know."

"How did all that blood happen?"

"It looks just like a rose. You look just like a flower, Eva."

He thought I had never had. No I didn't know what he was doing. A boy with a dirty popsicle stick. I didn't even know what he was doing. I didn't know what. He stung me between my legs.

"Take you that long to pee?"

He wouldn't let me have a telephone because he thought some man might call me.

"What man, what man would be calling me?"

"One of your lovers."

"I don't have any lovers. I don't know what you mean, James."

"After you've done it the first time."

"There was no first time."

"You know the first time," Joanne said, "they discovered me in a truck with an old man. He had asked me to get up in the truck with him and said he would give me money. He didn't do nothing but 'handle me.' That's what the court said, 'handled her and gave her some money.' I wasn't nothing but four years old. I didn't even know what he was doing. They said when I was a little girl, I used to have a face like a woman."

She said Miss Floyd, the superintendent, when she bent down, wiped her hand across her ass. That was why she moved her, so she wouldn't have to get in the fight too.

"She dropped something and I stooped down to pick it up. That was when I felt her hand across my ass. When I turned around, though, she was smiling, looking like she hadn't done anything."

"You lying."

"Naw, I ain't lying neither. That's why she wants me in there, where she won't have any competition. I see the way she looks at you too, only she's scared of you."

"Why's she scared of me?"

"I don't know. She just is."

"I don't want your lovers calling you," James said.

When he got between my knees, he said, "I always wanted to meet a woman like you, always wanted a woman like you, always wanted, always wanted a . . ."

The queen bee, sitting on the toilet throne, wipes between her legs. Her nipples are full of blood.

"They told me her father abused her mother when she was pregnant, and she came out gumming her own umbilical cord—she couldn't gnaw because she didn't have no teeth—so she came out gumming."

"Do you know what this is?" James asked.

"No."

"A rubber."

He wanted me to watch him put it on.

"She wiped her hand across my ass," Joanne said. "She won't bother you, because she's afraid of you. You're a queen bee."

"What do you mean?"

She wouldn't tell me. Sour cabbage and spoiled sausage spread with turd mustard.

"Your honor, this woman's already got a record. Stabbed a man in the hand twenty years ago. Was in jail for six months."

"What was the motive?"

"A motive was never given. She never said anything. She just took the sentence."

"What motive did the man give?"

"He called her a bitch. Said all he was trying to do was buy her some beer."

Buy some pussy. Spread my legs so I'll be fucked in the ass again. Go fuck yourself, I told him. I don't want to fuck myself, I want to fuck you. I was seventeen when he tried to. Damn bitch. But he couldn't do a thing. I bet you were born fucking and will die fucking, you fucking bastard. That bitch stuck me. I wasn't trying to do nothing but buy her some beer. What do you have to say? Nothing.

We were in this place. Well, yeah, he wanted to buy me some beer all right. He said Baby, if I had the money I'd buy you a beer. I said that was all right because I didn't want a beer. Then when I got up to go he followed me outside. I told him to get lost.

"Bitch, if you don't wont a man to speak to you, you ought to stay in the house."

I told him to get lost again but he wouldn't so then I knifed him.

"What's been happening here?"

"Shit."

Somebody wrapped a rag around his hand till the cops came. He was holding it, saying "Shit." They were holding him to keep him from getting at me. But I said he wasn't getting at me cause I still had the knife.

"I wasn't doing nothing but trying to kiss her."

"My ass."

"He told me to get up in the truck and he'd give me some money. An old man with hair in his ears and a skullcap on. He slid his hand up between my thighs and told me how nice and soft I was. He didn't have any teeth. A woman saw me get in the truck and called the police. They got him for 'handling me.' He said he hadn't done anything. They asked me what did he do. I was four years old. I said he showed me his stick."

"No matter how old they get," this woman said. "They hands always find the crotch."

"I heard you breathing hard in there last night like you was into something in there," Elvira said.

I said nothing. I watched the eggsack like a turd hanging out. I wanted to be fucked again.

"Still I say they make it simpler if they do something for women. Let us bring men in."

Breath and sweat and desire riding my back. I closed my eyes. I wanted her to be quiet.

"If they let you, would you have one?"

"I don't know."

"You ain't the other kind, are you?"

"Naw."

"We got some in here, you know, that's that kind. Cause if you wont someone to stroke it for you, there's them that will. Stroke anything that need to be stroked."

"I'm not that kind."

"I wasn't saying you was."

"I'm not."

"Don't get huffy. I'll drop it. You know, I bet that nigger wasn't worth it, was he?"

"What?"

"What you did."

I said nothing.

"You know, I ain't seen you laugh, I ain't seen you cry, I ain't seen you do nothing, cept breathe hard last night. You too serene. When a woman done something like you done and serene like that, no wonder they think you crazy."

Stuff a sausage up her ass.

"My head hurts."

"I'll get em to bring you an aspirin."

"I don't want one."

Finger up her raw ass.

"Awright, suit yourself. But listen, I'ma tell you something. If you let them get to you, they break you. But if you don't let them get to you, they can do all the hammering they wont to but they ain't going to break you. What I say is take it easy. The only things that ought to be taken hard is dicks. He."

I said nothing.

"Well, suit yourself."

I lay on the cot, breathing.

"What's wrong?" she asked softly.

I didn't answer. I wanted to make music, hard, deep, with my breath, my tongue inside his mouth. I thought of undoing his trousers, making gestures with my tongue, gestures he'd understand, and then his hands would go into my panties, between my legs and ass.

"Want me to do it for you?"

No answer.

"I'll do it for you if you want me to, honey," she whispered. Her voice wasn't soft now, it was husky even in the whisper. It was harsh. "You won't help yourself, that's why can't nobody else help you, cause you won't help yourself."

I was breathing. I couldn't tell how hard or loud I was breathing. He was there. He wasn't laughing. He just watched me. Then he got on my back. He hung onto my back. We were naked. He went in from the ass like a cockroach. We were fucking. "What am I doing to you?" "You fucking me." Both his hands fingered my clit. He made me. "Oh, Jesus. It's your pussy, Davis. It's your pussy." After I came he kept touching my clit and it hurt. "Please don't."

He parted my hair with a comb, scratching my scalp till it bled.

"I'll do it for you," she said.

"No."

"Did you like it? Was he good?"

"Yes. He was good."

"Bouncing up and down in that hole. I know he was good, wasn't he?"

"Yes."

"I would've did it for you."

"No."

"Did you and him use to undress each other?"

"No."

"Makes you feel closer, or something."

"I don't know."

"You could've shared it with me. Your long fuzzy public hair. I call it public hair."

"Naw."

"I bet you can still feel him going in there between your legs, going in you."

"No."

My teeth bit shadows. I put my legs around his neck.

"What's wrong?"

"Nothing."

"Are you all right?"

"Yes, I'm all right."

"Remember how I told you it just stay with you. It's a sin and a shame, but it do."

I was laying on the bed in his room. My muscles were tense. I was staring out the window. Light came in through the window from the signs over bars. They made patterns on my belly. I was naked. The muscles in my legs were hurting. She was waiting for me to say something. I wanted to reach down and rub my legs, but I didn't move.

"I heard you wrapped it in a *silk* handkerchief when you finished. Honey, you got imagination."

I laid with him as soon as we got there. It was evening but we didn't sleep. He stroked my forehead. I never liked anyone to touch my forehead, but I let him touch it.

"You know. I used to read about things like that in the *Police Gazette* before I started meeting people who did them. You know, you a celebrity in here, you know that? Yeah you are." She sang, "I heard it through the grapevine, how much longer will you . . ."

I licked the palms of my hands. I bit shadows. I put my legs around his neck. He wrapped me in elbows.

"Shit, there's those that won't ask you if they can do it for you, just do it. Especially right in here, they got some crazy people, crazier than I am. They just be thinking they be doing something you wont done. They won't know no different."

Smell in my bloomers. Fuck and urine.

"He was good, wasn't he? I bet he was good."

He said I was good too. He asked me what he was doing to me. I said he was fucking me. He said I was doing hell to him. He called it my stringray. He was on my ass, coming in through that way. I wanted to tell him how I was feeling. But I never would tell him.

"Let me make it feel sweet for you, honey."

"You haven't had it in a long time, have you?"

"You hard, why you have to be so hard?" She sounded like she wanted to cry, but then she got evil. "Knifed a man when you was seventeen. Killed a man when you . . . Couldn't be much younger than I am, are you?"

I said nothing.

"How did it feel?"

He'd undressed me and he was sweating. And then he held onto my shoulders and drew me toward him and I was naked and sweating, not with my own sweat, but with his sweat. He had no tenderness, no none, and then he laid me on my back on the bed. He didn't play first. No, he went in before I was ready. He made sounds in his throat like when you got to go doodoo.

"Felt good, didn't it?"

"Yes."

"I bet it felt good."

"Yes."

"You could've shared it with me."

"No."

"What did he promise you to make you kill him?"

"Nothing."

"What did you promise him?"

"That I'd stay with him. That I'd always be there. In that room."

"Why?"

I didn't answer.

"Did you tell him?"

"No."

He liked my hair that way. He'd never let me comb it. No, he'd never. He'd be doing it and make my pelvis rise up and my ass shake and he kept kissing me and asked, "What am I doing?" I kept wanting him. He kept saying Oh, oh, oh, oh. And I kept wanting him. I just kept wanting him.

"What am I doing?"

"You fucking me."

"What am I doing?"

"You fucking me."

Every Saturday morning and Sunday afternoon James said he had to go down to the train depot. He said he had this friend who had a wife that they let out of the Narcotics Hospital every weekend so she could be with her husband, and every weekend she would make him buy her a bottle—not any narcotics—just a bottle. He said the man was scared of her, because every Sunday evening when he took them back to the depot, the man would have a new scar on him. He said that the man was scared that one of those weekends she would kill him, but he still went and got her.

"What your doctors been telling you?" Elvira asked.

"What?"

"About what you did?"

"They think I was trying to fuck him when he couldn't fuck back."

"What you think?"

"I think I was trying to *get* fucked."

"Eva?"

"What?"

"Don't you want to?"

"No."

"What did you like him to do?"

I liked him to get up against my ass and come in that way. I never told him what I liked, so he didn't do it a lot. I don't know if he liked it or didn't think I liked it. I liked it when we'd go to sleep, lying ass to ass. He said when I stroked his ass it made him come faster. But that meant he didn't want me to.

"Eva."

"Leave me alone."

"Fuck you then."

I'd hug him and afterwards I could smell his smell on me. Cologne and aftershave and blood. I smell his smell on me.

The letter said: "I hope you and your old man is living together pretty. I thought you didn't like old mens. Well, anyway, that ain't why I'm writing you. I'm writing you because I know your nigger from way back. Me and him used to be friends. I just wonted to ask you if James find the town depot yet, because he still looking for that woman to come back."

James said, "That from one of your lovers?"

I didn't show it to him. I put it in my pocket.

"It's from my mother," I said. "She told me to tell you hello."

"It's sweet, ain't it, honey?"

I said yes, it was sweet.

. . .

"I know everything about you, you know," Elvira said finally. "He wasn't *your* man neither. You probably thought you were the only one. He just had to have a woman, not you, just any woman. It didn't matter who. He woulda had me, if I'da had him."

"He waited three days."

"Just to make it better. You know how a woman gets after that, and a man when he's been waiting for some. You thought you were the only one. But you weren't. And you just didn't wont to think about who'd be next, that's all."

I told her to go to hell.

"I'll do it for you."

"Leave me alone."

"Afraid I won't go deep enough?"

II

ONE DAY THIS boy from school showed up at the house. James wasn't at home and we were just sitting there talking. I don't even remember what we were talking about. He knew I was married, so he wasn't trying to start anything. But when James came back, he looked at me and then looked at the boy. It was one of them kinds of looks you can't describe, but it was like his whole body got harder.

"I killed you once, I don't want to have to kill you again."

"Look, I . . ."

He told the boy to get out. The boy looked at me and then looked back at James and then left.

"We weren't doing anything."

James just looked at me.

"We weren't doing anything, James." The way he was looking made me feel like I had to keep saying that. He told me to shut up. He was looking at me, just looking. Then he sat down, not beside me on the couch, but in the chair. He had his hands on his knees.

"She didn't enjoy being with a man or nothing," he said. "She just did it, you know. She didn't care one way or another. She never loved no man. Never did. Not one single day in her life. A woman that'll just fuck because it's there—cause he's got something down between his legs—a woman like that can't love a man."

He didn't say anything else. He was just sitting there,

real hard, and then he just reached over and grabbed my shoulder, got up and started slapping me.

"You think you a whore, I'll treat you like a whore. You think you a whore, I'll treat you like a whore."

Naw, he didn't slap me, he pulled my dress up and got between my legs.

"Think I can't do nothing. Fuck you like a damn whore."

Naw, I'm not lying. He said, "Act like a whore, I'll fuck you like a whore." *Naw, I'm not lying.*

I squeezed my legs around his neck.

"You look like a woman who's been hurt in life," he said. He was dressed younger than his age. The lines around his eyes looked like worry lines.

"Naw," I said.

When he got off the bus, he came back with apples and candy.

"I thought you had to change here," I said.

"I do."

He sat back down beside me.

"I've got fifteen minutes," he said.

He gave me the apples and candy. I gave them back to him. He said, "Please." I took them.

"Denver," he said. "And then California, and then maybe down to Mexico."

There weren't any people sitting in the seats near us, they were out getting snacks and coffee.

"You know why I came back here," he said.

I said nothing. He said when he first saw those eyes of mine, he knew I could love a man. He said when he first saw my eyes, he knew I could love a man.

"Aren't you going to say something?"

"No."

"Sometimes a man and a woman get off the bus."

"No."

"I didn't mean to offend you," he said. "That was the last thing I was trying to do."

I said nothing.

"All right," he said. He got up. He looked down at me while he was standing, but when he got off the bus, he didn't look back.

When James first laid me down in the bed, he kept saying over and over again that things was all right. I couldn't tell whether he was telling himself or me.

I screamed up at him, "Why didn't you kill *her* then!"

Before I left school and went off to work at the tobacco company, I went back to New York—there was somebody there I wanted to see.

He was sitting in the Froglegs restaurant. I was over by his table before he looked up and saw me. He looked at me hard. Then he said, "Damn."

I asked him if I could sit down.

"I reckon you can. I think I glimpsed a ass back there. If I didn't, I got stuck for nothing."

"I got your letter."

Moses laughed. "What makes you think I'd write to you? You ain't promised me nothing."

"I figured the only nigger that could know my nigger 'from way back' was you."

"Alfonso know him."

"I mean twenty years way back. Alfonso probably got the story from you. He didn't know him back twenty years."

"And I did?"

"Yeah."

"You don't want a beer, do you?"

"Naw, thanks."

"What you want?" He grinned. "I guess you don't want the five?"

"Naw."

He looked angry again. "You know, I can't even hold a damn cigarette in this hand. When it burns down I can't even feel it."

He had a couple of burnt places on his fingers.

I started to say I was sorry, but didn't.

"What do you want, Lady?"

"Why do you call me that?"

"Any woman that treat a man like a gentleman have got to be a lady."

I frowned.

"Naw, you don't treat a man like a gentleman, you treat him like a . . . cockroach. I started to say bedbug. But you don't even treat a man like a bedbug. When I found out who you done married, I said Shit. I kept telling myself, Shit. The onliest reason you married the nigger was because he was safe."

"How could he be safe if he killed a man?" I asked.

"You wouldn't've married me, and I'm as old as him, but I ain't safe . . . Y'all still together?"

"No."

"You leave or he send you away?"

I said nothing. Moses looked at me hard.

"Once upon a time," he said, "there was a man who used to hang out at the train depot, because he was waiting for this woman to return to him, you know, but he hung out down there so much he forgot why he was there. You seen these old men hanging around down at the train depot, they don't even know why they there any more. I hang around down there at the train depot myself, except I know why I'm there, cause I work there. You know, if you ever down there between eight and five, look me up."

"I don't travel by train," I said, getting up.

Moses started laughing, then he stopped, he shouted, "One of these days you going to just meet a man, and go somewhere and sleep with him. I know a woman like you. One of these days you . . ."

Elvira and me ended up in the same cell, because they moved us to make room for the new people.

"You know why they put us in here together, don't you?" she asked as soon as we got there and the attendants had left. She sat down on one cot and I lay down on the other one.

"Naw."

"Cause we got the same problem and they think maybe we can help each other out."

"I don't give your kind of help."

"Don't get evil. That ain't what I mean." She sounded as if she was going to cry, but when I looked up at her, she wasn't. She was showing her bad teeth again. "You know what I told you when I give those men that bad whiskey and they got sick. I lied to you. It killed about three of them."

I said nothing. I lay on the cot, watching the ceiling. I finally looked across at her again. She had hiked up her dress. I watched her legs, her bare feet. I didn't look at her face.

"You hear me?" she asked.

"Yeah, I heard you."

"They made us roommates cause they know how well we get along with each other," she said sarcastically.

"Don't fuck with me," I said, looking back at the ceiling.

"That's what my last roommate told me. She said, 'Don't come fucking with me, cause I got my nigger on the outside. All I'm doing is waiting to get out of here.'

But I *know* you ain't got yours on the outside, and you
prob'ly be in here longer than I will."

Eva? Are you afraid to talk to me?
No.
Why did you kill him?
I was lonely.
That doesn't make sense, does it, Eva?
Yes.
What happened before you killed him?
Nothing.
Then why would you kill him? Were you afraid of
him? Did he do something to make you afraid of him?
No.
How much of your story is true?
Everything.
Not all of it sounds true.
Everything.
Did he do something to frighten you? He humiliated
and frightened you, didn't he?
She's crazy. She's crazy.
Hush.
What did he do?
Nothing.
Did he say something to hurt you?
He was on the bed looking at me.
Have you had any hallucinations since I gave you
these?
No.
Why did you think you bit it all off?
I did.
The police report says you didn't.
I did . . . I wanted to.
You want me to leave now?
No . . . He was on the bed looking at me. I wanted to

get out of there. He didn't have no right to keep me in there.

You said you wanted to stay.

A woman doesn't belong in the street.

You had a place to go, you didn't have to stay there.

No.

All right, Eva, I'll give you the medicine again and we'll let you go out with the other women. Would you like that?

A woman doesn't belong out in the street. He thought I was that kind of woman but I wasn't. I used to see them jumping out in front of cars to get men. Do as you please. He wouldn't let me out of there. He thought I belonged in the street.

What did you want him to think?

I came over because I thought I could talk to you. I want to fuck you. Can I fuck you?

Eva.

Don't look at me. Don't make people look at me.

I'm not making anybody look at you . . . What?

He was sitting there looking at me. I didn't even talk to him . . . I don't want to go out there.

You just said you wanted to be with the others . . . Eva, what did he do to you? Why did you think you bit his whole penis off?

He used the room.

He used you?

I wouldn't talk to him. I didn't talk to no man for a long time.

Did he frighten you?

He was sitting on the bed looking at me.

What did he do to you, Eva?

I wasn't like that. I was just sitting over there. And then he came and sat down and then we went back to his room, but I wasn't like that. And he was looking at me.

He wouldn't let me comb my hair or nothing. I was just sitting there. I saw him before he saw me. I knew why he came over. I knew he would come over. I hadn't been with a man for a long time.

What did he do? What else did he do, Eva?

I wouldn't look at him.

You were afraid of him?

No.

I'm wondering if you even liked the man.

What?

Why did you pick him? I'm wondering if you liked him.

I went with him.

Why were you afraid of him?

He was just sitting there watching me. I was in the room. He made me stay there.

Why did you go there in the first place? You had somewhere else to go.

I've been everywhere. I could go anywhere. I . . .

What?

Nothing.

What else were you going to say?

Nothing.

What do you think is the matter with you?

Loneliness. I filled in the spaces. I filled in the spaces and feelings.

Why did you kill him?

I filled in the feelings.

Are you trying to put me on again?

I did it.

Did you think Davis was Alfonso?

No . . . I covered him back up. I saw the blood and covered him back up.

Did you love him?

. . .

Did you think he was Moses Tripp?

No.

You were a lonely woman, weren't you?

No.

You must have been a very lonely woman. You were with him next to no time. And then you did what you did . . . I thought you said you were lonely.

I don't know. I don't remember. I didn't think I would see him again and I keep seeing him again. Over and over.

Did he tell you he loved you?

No.

Did you tell him?

No.

Tell me what happened.

I did.

What did he say or do to you?

Nothing.

You can't keep it in you forever.

Yes.

It's like a bad dream, isn't it?

I can smell it.

He's not here.

No.

How long was it, Eva? How long has it been?

Don't.

How long has it been?

Don't.

He went out and then he came back. What happened? Something must have happened before, I mean after he told you about his wife. What else happened?

He thought I was that kind of woman. I could see it in his eyes. Like that other man. In the car. He opened the car door. He thought I was that kind of woman. He expected me to get in, but I didn't. He slammed the door and drove on.

You think you're the only woman that's happened to?

He thought I would get in. I went up there with him. Moses said I would go somewhere with a man. It wasn't a dream. He kept me there. He kept his hands on me.

It was just because he kept you up in that room and kept his hands on you that you killed him?

He kept thinking I was that kind of a woman. Always. They would, wouldn't they. Always. No matter what I. Just because the places I went, the way I talked or how I wore my hair. Any woman's talk. You know. So he came and sat down. I wasn't going to nobody else. But he thought I would. After he left me or I left him. He thought I was. The way he was looking at me. James wouldn't let me have no telephone. When he was sitting on that bed, the way he was looking at me. He came in the house. I was sitting there in the dark. I scared him. He didn't have to be scared. He could have said anything to me anytime. Every man could look at me the way he was looking. They all would. Even when I. He thought I was his.

Who?

He wouldn't let me comb my hair. I could go anywhere I wanted to. I left him and went to work at Southwestern Tobacco Company, P. Lorillard. I forget. I rode the bus over there. It was a long time ago. Then I wasn't no man's woman. They took me right on. I knew he would come over and I'd get up and go with him.

He didn't seem to be the kind of man a woman could . . . care about.

I did.

Did you really?

Yes.

Why?

I don't know.

He wasn't a very attractive man.

Yes he was.

Not the way you described him to me.

Yes he was.

You're an attractive woman, but he wasn't a very attractive man.

He was. I told you how it was. He wasn't just . . . fucking me. I told you.

No, Eva. The way you told it that was all he was doing.

No . . . He told me things. He told me things too. I learned from him.

What?

I can't remember. Things he said.

Where are you now?

Here.

I mean in your mind.

Here.

With me?

Yes.

You don't remember everything that happened.

Yes I do.

You said you didn't remember.

No.

You don't remember the thing that happened that made you kill him.

It was his whole way.

Describe it.

I did.

Tell me again.

I'm tired.

Take your head out of your hands.

I bit down till the blood came.

Did you want to?

No.
Did you want to do anything you did?
Yes, I.
What kind of man was he?
I told you.
Tell me again.
He drank it and then he called me a bitch.
You called him a bastard.
I have something I want to write down on that paper
you gave me. Leave me alone.
Tell me.
It was his whole way. Can't you understand that? Can't
you?
All right.
Let me go out there with you.
You said you didn't want to go.
He saw me the same way. I knew what he was doing.
Here, take this.
Did you hear what I said? I knew. I knew.
And you took everything. And . . .
Don't explain me. Don't you explain me. Don't you
explain me.

Don't look at me that way.
You don't talk much.
Davis, don't look at me that way.
Why, what way am I looking?
Naw.
Come over here.
What?
I like you.
. . .
Talk to me. I never seen a woman look at me like that.
The way you were looking when you were telling me not
to look at you.

How?
Like you could kill me. Like you could just kill me,
baby.
Kill you this way.
I like you a lot, Eva. I like you a whole lot.
You've got your heart in your knees.
What? Come closer.
Yes.

What did he do to you, Eva?
I don't know. How should I know. I don't know. I
don't know. That was all I could do.
What was all you could do?
But I won't hurt you.
Eva?
I said I won't hurt you.

Eva?
What?
You seem like a lonely woman.
No.
All that blood you raised. Come over here.
No.
What's your name?
Eva. I been a lot of places. I been in New Orleans. I
been out in New Mexico.
You lying.
No I'm not. I been just about everywhere.
You seem like a lonely woman.

You thought you were a bad woman, so you went out
and got you a bad man.
Don't explain me.
And then you . . . Matron? Matron! Hold her! Hold
her!

I hold up my arms.

"You have blood on you," I say.

"You'd do anything for me, wouldn't you, woman?" he says.

"You have blood on you."

I open my fingers. I see a slop jar in the corner of the room. Two glasses of water.

"Whereabouts you from, lady?"

"Whereabouts."

"Swallow me. Swallow me up. I know what kind of woman you are."

"Naw you don't."

"I do."

I kiss his neck and mouth.

"I like the way you wear your hair, but I forgot your name."

"Eva."

"Are your breasts sore?"

"Naw."

"Sometimes women's breasts gets sore around this time."

"Mine don't."

"Put your head in my lap."

"I'm not tired."

He laughs. He hands me money.

"You know you the woman. Kill him, but don't make him bleed." He holds my shoulders. "I said kill him, but don't make him bleed. How long has it been?"

"Two years."

"How long?"

"Five years."

"I like you, Eva. I like you a lot."

"Do you care about me?"

"Yes."

I open my fingers.

"I can't do it, Davis."

"Come on, woman."

He laughs. He holds my shoulders again.

"Do you care about me? . . . You not talking? How long has it been, woman?"

I look at him. I kiss him. "A long time."

"What did I do for you, Eva? What did you feel?"

"Everything."

He pushes my face into his lap. He combs my hair with his long fingers. I am afraid.

We are in the river now. We are in the river now. The sand is on my tongue. Blood under my nails. I'm bleeding under my nails. We are in the river. Between my legs. They are busy with this woman. They are busy with this woman now. They are busy with this woman . . .

"What do you want, Eva?"

"What?"

"What do you want?"

"Nothing you can give."

An owl sucks my blood. I am bleeding underneath my nails. An old owl sucks my blood. He gives me fruit in my palms. We enter the river again . . . together.

They are doing with this woman. See. They are doing with this woman. See what they are doing with this woman.

Last night she got in the bed with me, Davis. I knocked her out, but I don't know how long I'm going to keep knocking her out . . .

. . .

"Tell me when it feels sweet, Eva. Tell me when it feels sweet, honey."

I leaned back, squeezing her face between my legs, and told her, "Now."